Praise for
John Gwynne and The Bloodsworn Trilogy

"A satisfying and riveting read. The well-realized characters move against the backdrop of a world stunning in its immensity. It's everything I've come to expect from a John Gwynne book."

—Robin Hobb

"A masterfully crafted, brutally compelling Norse-inspired epic."

—Anthony Ryan, author of *The Pariah*

"The world is wonderfully rendered with attention paid to what makes the Norse sagas entertaining.…The many layers provide a lavish feast for any reader. A great companion to Neil Gaiman's *Norse Mythology*."

—*Booklist* (starred review)

"There is not a dull chapter in this fantasy epic. As tension mounts with each passing page, Gwynne delivers exhilarating fights and gruesome battles with such vivid prose the choreography jumps off the page."

—*Vulture* (Best of the Year)

"Gwynne, a Viking reenactor, puts in the work, with fine historical details…that make the story come to life.…Fans of the era will be delighted with the accuracy. This is a duly exciting start to the series."

—*Publishers Weekly*

"Visceral, heartbreaking, and unputdownable."

—Jay Kristoff

"*The Shadow of the Gods* is truly an epic in every fashion....[Gwynne] should be in the conversation with the best the genre has to offer today."

—Daniel Greene

"A masterclass in storytelling....Epic, gritty fantasy with an uncompromising amount of heart."

—*FanFiAddict*

"*The Shadow of the Gods* is absolutely stunning, one hell of an epic series opener and a spectacular dose of Viking-flavoured fantasy."

—*Tattooed Book Geek*

THE FURY OF THE GODS

By John Gwynne

The Faithful and the Fallen

Malice
Valor
Ruin
Wrath

Of Blood and Bone

A Time of Dread
A Time of Blood
A Time of Courage

The Bloodsworn Trilogy

The Shadow of the Gods
The Hunger of the Gods
The Fury of the Gods

THE FURY OF THE GODS

BOOK THREE OF
THE BLOODSWORN TRILOGY

JOHN GWYNNE

orbitbooks.net

This book is a work of fiction. Names, characters, places, and incidents are the product of the author's imagination or are used fictitiously. Any resemblance to actual events, locales, or persons, living or dead, is coincidental.

Cover design by Bekki Guyatt
Cover illustration by Marcus Whinney
Map by Tim Paul
Author photograph by Caroline Gwynne

Orbit
Hachette Book Group
1290 Avenue of the Americas
New York, NY 10104
orbitbooks.net

First Edition: October 2024
Simultaneously published in Great Britain by Orbit

Orbit is an imprint of Hachette Book Group.
The Orbit name and logo are registered trademarks of Little, Brown Book Group Limited.

Library of Congress Control Number: 2024940615

ISBNs: 9780316539951 (trade paperback), 9780316539975 (ebook)

Printed in the United States of America

LSC-C

Printing 7, 2026

For my family.
For Harriett, loved beyond words,
For Caroline, the air I breathe,
For James, Ed and Will, my beating heart.
We have been through hell together,
the bonds of love and family holding us up.

Map by Tim Paul 2021

PRONUNCIATION GUIDE

ð: sounds like "th" in "they"; Guðvarr is pronounced "Guthvarr"

j: sound like "y" in "yellow"; Brynja is pronounced "Brynya"

ø: sounds like "ir" in "bird"; Røkia is pronounced "Rirkia"

CAST OF CHARACTERS

The Battle-Grim

Agnar Broksson – chief of the Battle-Grim, slain in an act of betrayal by Biórr on the ash-plain of Oskutreð

Elvar Fire-Fist – daughter of Jarl Störr. She has sworn the blood oath to find Bjarn, son of Uspa the Seiðr-witch, to rescue him from Ilska the Cruel and her Raven-Feeders, in return for Uspa guiding the Battle-Grim to fabled Oskutreð, the heart of where the gods fought and died

Grend – companion and guardian of Elvar. Has also sworn the blood oath to find Bjarn

Huld – youngest of the Battle-Grim after Elvar. She grew up on the hard streets of Svelgarth

Sighvat the Fat – second to Agnar, a fierce warrior, though more interested in food than making decisions. Swore the blood oath to rescue Bjarn from Ilska's Raven-Feeders

Sólín Spittle – one of the longest-serving of the Battle-Grim, she lost some teeth during a fight with a swarm of tennúr

Urt the Unwashed – warrior of the Battle-Grim, bynamed because of his aversion to cleanliness

Orv the Sneak – the only archer in the Battle Grim, a scout and hunter. Bynamed because of his stealth

Uspa – a Seiðr-witch. Captured by the Battle-Grim on Iskalt Island (along with her husband, Berak, and child, Bjarn) where she was destroying the Galdrabok, the *Graskinna.* She swears a pact with Agnar and Elvar, where she will lead the Battle-Grim to Oskutreð if they swear to do all they can to rescue her son, Bjarn, from the clutches of Ilska the Cruel. The blood oath seals their pact

The Bloodsworn

Æsa – a member of the Bloodsworn with a worrying disregard for pain or life. The blood of Fjalla the mountain goat is in her vein

Edel – chief scout and huntswoman of the Bloodsworn. The blood of Hundur the hound is in her veins. Old, shrewd, guarded. Two hounds are her companions

Einar Half-Troll – big as a tree, strongest of the Bloodsworn. A lover of food and well-told tales. Also a *Berserkir*

Glornir Shield-Breaker – chief of the Bloodsworn. A *Berserkir*, with the bear-god's blood in his veins. Husband of Vol and older brother of Thorkel

Gunnar Prow – so-named on account of his nose, which fills most of his face and is curved like a prow-beast on a *drakkar.* The blood of Gröfu the badger is in his veins

Halja Flat-Nose – the blood of Orna the eagle-god is in her veins. Sister of Vali Horse-Breath, who was slain by a troll during the battle at Rota's chamber

Revna Hare-Legs – named Hare-Legs because of her speed in battle, she has the blood of Státa the stoat in her veins

Ingmar Ice – a *Berserkir*

Jökul Hammer-Hand – blacksmith and warrior. Has the blood of Gröfu the badger in his veins

Røkia – *Úlfhéðnar*, the blood of Ulfrir the wolf in her veins. Given the task of training Varg in weapons craft

Svik Tangle-Hair – the blood of Refur the fox is in his veins. Chief skáld/storyteller of the Bloodsworn. He has a particular fondness for cheese

Varg No-Sense – once a thrall of Kolskegg, a wealthy farmer and landowner. Killed Kolskegg when he was betrayed by him, and fled, searching for the killers of his sister, Frøya. Joined the Bloodsworn to gain access to their Seiðr-witch, Vol, in order for her to perform an akáll, a magical invocation that will allow Varg to see the last moments of his sister's life, and so reveal how she died. Since joining the Bloodsworn he has discovered that he is Tainted, an *Úlfhéðnar* with the blood of Ulfrir in his veins

Vol – a Seiðr-witch, wife of Glornir

The Raven-Feeders and their companions

Lik-Rifa – dragon-god, caged for hundreds of years in a chamber among the roots of Oskutreð, the Ash Tree. She has now been freed by a magical ceremony performed by her Tainted offspring, the dragon-born

Rotta – the rat-god. Imprisoned and tortured by Ulfrir and Orna for his part in the slaying of their daughter

Biórr – Tainted, with the blood of Rotta the rat in his veins. He infiltrated the Battle-Grim, slew Agnar Battle-Grim and led Ilska to Oskutreð, so instrumental in the release of Lik-Rifa from her chamber beneath Oskutreð. He is now back with the Raven-Feeders

Brák Trolls-Bane – Tainted, with the blood of Státa the Stoat god in his veins, one of Drekr's crew, a huntsman and trapper

Drekr – Tainted, a dragon-born, brother of Ilska and Myrk. Abducted Breca and slew Thorkel

Ilmur – Tainted, the hound-god Hundur is in his blood. Once a thrall of the Battle-Grim, freed by Biórr and now a member of the Raven-Feeders

Ilska the Cruel – chief of the Raven-Feeders, a dragon-born with Lik-Rifa's blood in her veins. Older sister of Drekr and Myrk

Kalv – Tainted, with the blood of Svin the boar in his veins. Son of Red Fain and brother of Storolf Wartooth

Kráka – Seiðr-witch, once a thrall of the Battle-Grim, but freed by Biórr and now part of the Raven-Feeders

Myrk Sharp-Claw – Tainted, dragon-born with Lik-Rifa's blood in her veins. Younger sister of Ilska and Drekr

Red Fain – Tainted, with Svin the boar's blood in his veins. Father of Kalv and Storolf Wartooth

Storolf Wartooth – Tainted, with the blood of Svin the boar in his veins, son of Red Fain and brother of Kalv. Named Wartooth because he left some teeth in an enemy's shield when he bit into it and tore it from his opponent's grip

Oleif Gap-Tooth – Tainted, the blood of Hraeg the vulture in his veins. One of Drekr's crew, and now part of the Raven-Feeders

Bjarn Beraksson – Tainted, son of Uspa and Berak. Abducted by Ilska and the Raven-Feeders

Breca Thorkelsson – Tainted, son of Orka and Thorkel. Abducted by Drekr

Harek Asgrimsson – Tainted, son of Asgrim and Idrun, who were slain by Drekr and his crew

Others

Orka Skullsplitter – wife of Thorkel and mother of Breca. Once chief of the Bloodsworn and known as Skullsplitter. Thorkel has been slain and her son abducted, and she has followed his trail north, leading her to the Grimholt, where she was captured by *drengrs* and Skalk the Galdurman. She escaped in a bloody battle

Lif Virksson – a fisherman of Fellur village. Son of Virk, and brother of Mord. Orka rescued him from execution, and he travelled north with her. His brother Mord was slain while in chains by Guðvarr the *drengr*

Sæunn – a Tainted thrall with the blood of Hundur the hound in her veins

Gudleif Arnesson – has built a steading with his family north of the Boneback Mountains

Queen Helka – ruler of Darl and the surrounding regions. An ambitious, ruthless woman with a view to ruling all of Vigrið. She has one son, Hakon, and one daughter, Estrid

Prince Hakon Helkasson – son and eldest child of Queen Helka

Princess Estrid Helkasdottir – daughter of Queen Helka

Frek the Úlfhéðnar – Tainted, with the blood of Ulfrir the wolf-god in his veins. Thralled to Queen Helka and one of her honour-guard

Skalk the Galdurman – Galdurman of Darl, in the service of Queen Helka. Sent by Helka with the Bloodsworn to discover what is happening on the northern borders of her realm. He steals Orna's talon and abducts Vol the Seiðr-witch

Sturla – Skalk's Galdur-apprentice

Guðvarr – a *drengr* of Fellur village and nephew to Jarl Störr. He is tasked with leading the band sent after Orka, Lif and Mord

Vilja – a whore of Darl, resident of *The Dead Drengr*

Jarl Sigrún – Jarl of Fellur village and the surrounding district. Embroiled in the political expansion of Queen Helka. Her lover slain and her face scarred by Orka, she sends her nephew Guðvarr after Orka

Yrsa – a *drengr* of Darl in the service of Skalk the Galdurman

Arild – a *drengr* of Fellur village

Skapti – a *drengr*, captain of the Grimholt. In the employ of Prince Hakon and involved in the plans of Drekr and his movement of abducted children

Hrolf – a *drengr* of the Grimholt

Jarl Glunn Iron-Grip – a petty jarl allied to Queen Helka

Jarl Svard the Scratcher – a petty jarl allied to Queen Helka

Jarl Logur of Liga – ruler of the port town of Liga. Friend to the Bloodsworn

Jarl Orlyg of Svelgarth – ruler of the town of Svelgarth and the surrounding region. Old and grizzled, a veteran of war, an enemy of Queen Helka

Prince Jaromir of Iskidan – a prince of Iskidan, one of the many sons of Kirill the Magnificent, lord of Iskidan

Ilia – a *druzhina* of Iskidan

Taras the Bull – a bruised man, Tainted with the blood of Naut the bull in his veins. Thralled into the service of Prince Jaromir of Iskidan

Iva – a Seiðr-witch and Prince Jaromir's thrall

Jarl Störr – lord of Snakavik and most of the western districts of Vigrið. Father of Thorun, Elvar and Broðir. Famed for his *Berserkir*-guard

Silrið – Jarl Störr's Galdurwoman

Thorun Störrsson – eldest child of Jarl Störr

Broðir Störrsson – youngest child of Jarl Störr

Berak Bjornasson – Tainted, a *Berserkir* with the blood of Berser the bear-god in his veins. Husband of Uspa the Seiðr-witch and father of Bjarn. Captured by Agnar and the Battle-Grim and sold as a thrall to Jarl Störr, to become one of the famed *Berserkir*-guard

Gytha – a *drengr* and champion of Jarl Störr

Syr – a *drengr* of Jarl Störr, guard of Snakavik's gate

Hjalmar Peacemaker – leader of the Fell-Hearted mercenary warband

Hrung – a giant's head, magically animated by the power of dying Snaka

Njal Olafsson – jarl of a small fishing village on the banks of the River Drammur

Terna – a thrall of Njal Olafsson, originally a thrall from Kolskegg's farm

Brimil – a slaver based in Darl

Rog – bartender of *The Dead Drengr*

Frøya – sister of Varg

Leif Kolskeggson – son of Kolskegg, he hunted Varg for his father's murder, but upon catching Varg, Glornir and the Bloodsworn took Varg into their care and saved him from Leif's vengeance

Sterkur death-in-the-eye – a warrior and chief of a mercenary band for hire, the Red-Hands

Creatures

Grok – a giant raven

Kló – a giant raven

Spert – a spertus, vaesen, and bound to Orka and her household

Vesli – a tennúr, wounded and found by Breca, she swears an oath to Breca and Spert

NORSE TITLES, TERMS AND ITEMS

Akáll – an invocation, a magic ceremony to reveal the last moments of the dead
Althing – meeting, an assembly of free people
Berserkir – person descended from Berser the bear-god. Capable of great strength and savagery
blóð svarið – a magical blood oath
Brynja – a coat of ring mail
Byrding – coastal boat
Drakkar – a longship
Drengr – an oathsworn warrior, trained to a high level
Druzhina – elite horse-mounted warrior
Galdrabok – book of magic
Galdurman – magician, specifically rune-magic
Graskinna – grey-skin, a book of magic scribed on flayed skin
Guðfalla – the gods-fall
Guðljós – god-lights
Hangerock – a type of dress
Hird – warriors belonging to a lord's household
Heya – agreed
Holmganga – a duel recognised by law, a way of settling disputes
Jarl – lord or earl
Knarr – a merchant/trade ship
Maður-boy – a human child
Niðing – nothing, nobody, an insult, meaning without honour

Nålbinding – to bind or weave. An early form of knitting used to make clothing

Raudskinna – red-skin, a book of magic, made from the flayed skin of a dead god

Seax – single-edged knife, often with a broken back, of varying sizes. A multi-purpose tool, from cooking/shaving to combat

Seiðr – a type of magical power, inherited from Snaka, the father of the gods

Seiðr-witch – a woman who wields magical power

Skáld – a poet, teller of tales, often employed by a jarl or chief to sing of their heroic deeds

Skál – good health

Snekke – a smaller version of a longship

Tafl – a game of strategy played upon a board with carved figures

Thrall – a slave

Úlfhéðnar – person descended from Ulfrir the wolf-god

Vaesen – creatures created by Lik-Rifa the dragon-god

Weregild – a blood-debt

Winnigas – cloth covering for the legs, from ankle to just below the knee

Whale-road – the open sea

WHAT HAS GONE BEFORE

Orka: Orka's husband Thorkel has been murdered and her son Breca abducted. With her companions Lif and Mord she has tracked her son Breca to the Grimholt, a fortress in the north of Vigrið. Once there Orka is captured by the Galdurman Skalk, but with the help of the vaesen Spert and Vesli she breaks free, letting the wolf in her blood loose to rip and tear and rend.

Orka discovers that Breca is not there, although she finds a number of other Tainted children held captive. At the Grimholt she is reunited with the Bloodsworn, a mercenary band that she used to lead, her by-name Orka Skullsplitter. The new chief of the Bloodsworn, Glornir Shieldbreaker, is the brother of Orka's murdered husband.

While at the Grimholt, Orka and the Bloodsworn learn that Lik-Rifa the dragon-god has been set free from her imprisonment beneath the roots of the ancient ash tree, Oskutreð.

Glornir is in pursuit of Skalk, a Galdurman of Darl, because he has abducted Glornir's wife, Vol the Seiðr-witch. He asks Orka to come with him, but she declines, hearing that Glornir and the Bloodsworn have fought a dragon-born at the recently discovered chamber of Rotta the rat-god. Orka hopes to find clues of her son's whereabouts at this place. Glornir sends a handful of the Bloodsworn to show her the way to Rotta's chamber and then they part ways on their separate quests.

At Rotta's chamber Orka and her companions find evidence that children were recently held captive here.

While at the chambers Myrk of the Raven-Feeder arrives. She is a dragon-born, sister to Ilska the Cruel and brother to Drekr, who murdered Orka's husband and abducted Breca, and she is leading a small group of the Raven-Feeders. Myrk discovers the body of her father, who had been slain by Varg No-Sense of the Bloodsworn. Both Orka and Myrk want answers. A fight ensues, the handful of Bloodsworn with Orka coming to her aid. Together they defeat the Raven-Feeders and Myrk is taken captive.

Myrk agrees to lead Orka and her companions to Breca in return for information on who killed her father. They travel to Starl, a trading town on Lake Horndal, where Orka meets Elvar and the Battle-Grim, and Ulfrir the thralled wolf-god. She discovers that Myrk is leading her on a false trail, and she makes a deal with Elvar and the Battle-Grim. They help stage an escape for Myrk in return for Orka sending word to Glornir and the Bloodsworn from Elvar, saying that Elvar wants to hire them in her fight against Lik-Rifa the dragon-god.

Myrk escapes and Orka tracks her, following her to Nastrandir, the halls of Lik-Rifa, and then on to Svelgarth, where a warband of warriors and vaesen under the command of the rat-god Rotta are assaulting the fortress town.

Orka infiltrates the camp while the attack is underway, finds Breca and escapes with him. She is pursued and caught by frost-spiders and tragically bitten, poison seeping through her. With her last strength she throws Breca into the river in the hope that the current will take him to the meeting point with her companions.

Varg: Varg is a slave who has killed the man who owned him, Kolskegg, and escaped the farm he has worked on all his life. He knows that his sister Frøya has died, he felt her die, but he does not know how. With a lock of his sister's hair he has sought a Seiðr-witch to perform an akáll, a spell that shows the last moments of someone's life, and that is how he became involved with the mercenary band the Bloodsworn. They took him on as an apprentice, and he has recently discovered that he is tainted, the wolf-god Ulfrir in his blood, and that the Bloodsworn are all tainted, too, their secret closely guarded.

He is at the Grimholt when the Bloodsworn are reunited with Orka, and he travels south with the Bloodsworn in pursuit of Skalk the Galdurman. They take with them the Tainted children they found as captives in the Grimholt.

During the journey to Darl, Varg meets a thrall he used to know at Kolskegg's farm, and she tells him the name of the slaver in Darl who purchased Varg's sister from Kolskegg. Brimil.

Once at Darl the Bloodsworn assault Skalk's Galdur tower, only to discover that it is already under attack by Prince Jaromir of Iskidan. They fail to find Vol or Skalk in the tower and so continue into the main hall of Darl, attacking Queen Helka and taking her son Prince Hakon captive.

Glornir negotiates with Queen Helka, and Helka agrees to loan the Bloodsworn a longship and hire them to hunt Prince Jaromir in return for the safe return of her son, Hakon.

While in Darl, Varg tracks down the slaver, Brimil, with the help of Svik, Einar and Røkia. They discover that Brimil sold Frøya to Brák Trolls-Bane, a huntsman in the employ of Drekr.

The Bloodsworn sail to Liga and find out that Prince Jaromir has already set sail for Iskidan. They set out in pursuit. During their voyage they are attacked at sea by two crews of tongue-eaters, an abomination of a parasite creature that slowly eats the tongue of its host and takes over their mind. The Bloodsworn defeat them, wipe out one crew and give chase to the second ship as it flees. They follow the tongue-eaters to an island, where they destroy them and their queen. While on the island they discover *druzhina* warriors of Prince Jaromir who have been captured and had the parasites laid inside them. Glornir offers them a quick, honourable death in return for knowledge of where Jaromir is taking Vol.

Varg and the Bloodsworn sail to Iskidan, past the port of Ulaz and up a river, eventually leaving the *Sea-Wolf* to travel across country and catch up with Jaromir as he reaches his fortress of Valdai. A battle ensues, where Vol is set free, Jaromir is killed and dungeons are found full of Tainted thralls, all of them the Tainted children of Kirill, the Khagan of Iskidan. They also find maps and plans in Valdai that suggest Jaromir was plotting an invasion of Vigrið.

Elvar: Elvar has travelled to Oskutreð with the mercenary band the Battle-Grim. Their prisoner Uspa the Seiðr-witch has made a bargain with them, offering to lead them to this fabled place of untold treasure in return for the Battle-Grim hunting down and rescuing her abducted son Bjarn from Ilska the Cruel and her Raven-Feeders. Uspa and a handful of the Battle-Grim – Agnar, Sighvat, Elvar, Grend and Agnar's Seiðr-witch, Kráka – all bind themselves to each other, swearing the magical *blóð svarið*, the blood oath.

Once at Oskutreð they were attacked by the Raven-Feeders, Ilska and her dragon-born kin conducting a Seiðr-ceremony involving many abducted Tainted children, and they set the dragon-god Lik-Rifa free. Agnar chief of the Battle-Grim was deceitfully slain by Biórr, a young man who had become Elvar's lover, but was secretly Tainted and one of the Raven-Feeders. It was Biórr who orchestrated the abduction of Bjarn.

Lik-Rifa bursts from the bowels of Oskutreð, slays two of the three winged women who have stood guard over her for three centuries, and the Battle-Grim can only stand and watch as the dragon and Raven-Feeders leave Oskutreð.

The survivors of the Battle-Grim set about gathering as much treasure as they can, while Elvar and those who swore the blood oath struggle over how they are going to complete their task of rescuing Bjarn, now that he is in the company of a dragon-god.

While searching the battle plain for treasure the winged warrior Skuld regains consciousness. There is a brief struggle and Elvar manages to bind her with the thrall-collar taken from one of the tainted. Skuld agrees to guide them deep underground into the tunnels beneath the great tree, where she says greater treasure is to be found.

Once underground they discover the remains of Lik-Rifa's

chamber and find a Galdrabok of Seiðr-spells that she has written. Within this book Uspa comes across a spell that can raise a dead god. They construct a Seiðr-spelled thrall-collar in a forge beneath Oskutreð and resurrect the wolf-god, Ulfrir, but he is weak from his ancient injuries.

Elvar and the Battle-Grim travel south. A meeting is held to decide who the next chief will be, and Elvar and Huld fight a *holmganga* duel to decide the new chief. Elvar wins, slaying Huld.

Elvar decides to travel south to Snakavik. On the way the Battle-Grim stop at the lakeside trading town of Starl to restock their supplies. While here they meet Orka and agree to help her in return for Orka getting a message to Glornir and the Bloodsworn: that Elvar wishes to hire them in her efforts to defeat Lik-Rifa.

Elvar continues her journey south to Snakavik to see her father, Jarl Störr. She asks to hire his *Berserkir* guards, but he refuses. Instead, he attempts to take her captive and steal the treasure that the Battle-Grim have taken from Oskutreð.

Ulfrir assumes his wolf-form and eats Jarl Störr, a battle ensuing, during which Elvar slays her older brother, Thorun, and as her father's oldest heir she becomes the Seiðr-lord of her father's *Berserkirs*.

Biórr: Biórr is a Tainted rat-blood who has infiltrated the Battle-Grim. He orchestrated the abduction of Bjarn and left clues for the Raven-Feeders to track the Battle-Grim to Oskutreð.

He slays Agnar, chief of the Battle-Grim, and sets their Tainted thralls free – Kráka the Seiðr-witch and Ilmur the *Hundur*-thrall. Then he leaves Oskutreð with Lik-Rifa and the Raven-Feeders.

Biórr is reunited with his old comrades in the Raven-Feeders, Storolf Wartooth, Red Fain and his old lover, Myrk, sister of Ilska and Drekr. The Raven-Feeders travel east as Lik-Rifa leads them to her ancient hall of Nastrandir. She feels weak after three hundred years of captivity and has sustained injuries from her fight with her three-winged gaolers, and so wishes to recover in the safety of her halls. During the journey the Tainted children abducted for the ceremony to release Lik-Rifa are taught about their heritage, their tainted bloodlines and weapons craft.

Once they reach Nastrandir they discover that it is not empty, the rat-god Rotta is there waiting for them.

Lik-Rifa summons the vaesen to her, as they are her creations.

While Lik-Rifa is recovering, many gather to them, and Myrk arrives, vowing vengeance against Orka.

Guðvarr, a servant of Skalk the Galdurman and Queen Helka, arrives. He tells Lik-Rifa of Skalk and Helka's plan to resurrect the eagle-god, Orna, and thrall her.

Biórr travels south. The warband splits, Lik-Rifa leading half to Darl, and Rotta leading the rest to Svelgarth, a fortress town ruled by Jarl Orlyg. They assault Svelgarth, and during this attack Biórr sees Orka and a handful of the Bloodsworn infiltrate the camp in search of Breca. There is a bloody fight and Biórr's friend Storolf Wartooth is slain. Biórr kills one of the Bloodsworn, Revna Hare-Legs, but Orka manages to escape with her son.

Guðvarr: Guðvarr is a *drengr* of Fellur village, nephew to the village's Jarl Sigrún. He had been pursuing Orka, Lif and Mord, and when he arrived at the Grimholt he found them as prisoners and slew Mord while he was spider-poisoned and chained to a wall. He fled when Orka unleashed the wolf in her blood and ended up on a boat with Skalk and the Grimholt survivors, rowing south for Darl.

Guðvarr is ambitious and in Skalk he sees opportunity for advancement, so makes himself useful to the Galdurman. He becomes embroiled in the plans of Skalk and Queen Helka of Darl, but in an unpleasant turn of events he is strapped to a table in Skalk's Galdur tower and the Galdurman used his power to command a hyrndur – a type of large, aggressive hornet – to eat its way into Guðvarr's veins, settling close to his heart. Skalk orders Guðvarr to befriend Prince Hakon, Queen Helka's son, because he suspects Hakon is involved in some kind of plot against his mother, Queen Helka. Guðvarr is still strapped to the table when Prince Jaromir of Iskidan attacks the Galdur tower, defeats Skalk and takes Vol for his own prisoner. Shortly after the Bloodsworn attack and Guðvarr escapes during the chaos.

Guðvarr applies himself to becoming part of Hakon's inner circle, and in time uncovers that Hakon is plotting with the dragon-born Drekr, the killer of Thorkel and brother of Ilska the Cruel. Hakon has been helping in the abduction and movement of Tainted children through Helka's realm.

In an attempt to remain useful and avoid death from Skalk and Helka, Guðvarr volunteers to carry a message north to Drekr and Lik-Rifa. He meets the dragon-god and confesses all, telling her that Skalk and Lik-Rifa are planning to resurrect and thrall Orna the eagle-god, to use her in battle against Lik-Rifa.

In an act of betrayal against Skalk and Helka, Guðvarr helps to orchestrate Lik-Rifa's attack against Darl. His aunt, Jarl Sigrún, slays Queen Helka and Guðvarr slays Prince Hakon while Lik-Rifa descends upon the recently resurrected Orna and rips her to shreds.

Hard it is on earth,
Axe time, sword time, shields are sundered,
Wind time, wolf time,
Ere the world falls

The Voluspa

CHAPTER ONE

VARG

"Ach," Varg hissed as Røkia pierced a flap of skin hanging from his cheek with a fishhook, then stabbed into the flesh of his face and drew a line of thread through it. He felt fresh blood trickle down into his beard. "Ach," he grunted again.

"Stop complaining," Røkia muttered as she began stitching his cheek back together.

"I'm not, but it hurts," Varg said.

"Pain is an enemy. Defeat it," Røkia muttered.

Varg sighed.

A face loomed in front of him: Svik, handsome, braided beard and oiled red hair. Not looking at all like he had fought a vicious battle the day before. Svik frowned at him.

"First your ear, now your cheek. If you keep allowing people to carve pieces from your body soon there will be nothing left of you," he said.

"I didn't *allow* it," Varg scowled, causing Røkia's stitching to pull. He winced. *She is better at stabbing than stitching.*

Røkia sat back and threw her hands in the air. "This is ridiculous," she said.

"First Røkia saves your life, and now she stitches you back together. What would you do without her?" Svik continued, ignoring Røkia.

"I am in her debt," Varg agreed. *Although I gained this wound because I climbed the fortress wall and leaped into a score of enemies to save Røkia. But it turned out that it was she who saved me.*

"Your mail needs cleaning," Svik observed, pointing at bloodstains. "The blood will rust it."

Varg looked down at it, saw dark patches where blood had crusted. Even his silver arm ring given to him by Glornir was caked with blood.

"I've told him that," Røkia said.

"You should listen to Røkia," Svik said with a smile.

"I do." Varg said. "I will. Clean the mail, I mean."

"Do you want me to continue stitching your face back together, or is the pain too great for you?" Røkia asked mockingly.

Svik laughed.

Varg sucked in a deep breath. "Please, continue," he said.

Røkia grunted and went back to her stitching.

They were seated on a bench in the courtyard of Valdai, Prince Jaromir's fortress in Iskidan, a cloudless sky and searing sun overhead, carrion birds circling. The courtyard was stained with patches of blood, corpses piled in a heap to one side of the shattered gates. A tangle of arms, legs, faces, pale in death. Black crusted wounds like open mouths. Jaromir's *druzhina*, all stripped of their weapons and mail, boots and breeks, anything worth taking. Buzzards perched on limbs, their beaks red. Beyond the mound of the dead lay a line of freshly piled stone barrows running along one wall, fifteen of the Bloodsworn fallen in battle yesterday. Varg had helped dig those graves, had shed tears as stones had been piled over his comrades-in-arms. Edel still stood there, looking down at the graves. She had buried one of her hounds with the fallen, her surviving hound lying across the stones. The old huntress was weeping. Varg looked away, his gaze coming to rest upon the largest of the barrows, where Ingmar Ice had been laid. Killed by the blade of Jaromir.

"I only knew him a short while," Varg murmured to himself. "It feels . . . longer." *Like family. Until now the only family I've ever known is my sister.* His hand strayed to the pouch at his belt, where he kept a lock of Frøya's hair.

"When you stand in the shield wall together the bonds of kinship grow strong," Svik said, resting a hand on Varg's shoulder.

"The more you talk, the worse your scar will be," Røkia murmured, focused on her handiwork.

"Scars make you handsome," Svik said. "And irresistible to women."

Røkia snorted her contempt, making Svik grin.

Members of the Bloodsworn were sitting around the courtyard, most of them tending to wounds or to damaged kit, either repairing rents in their flesh or rents in their coats of mail, sewing, stitching, darning, greasing. Some stood on the walls and towers, standing watch.

Glornir and Vol stepped out of the doors of the feast hall, Glornir's long-axe balanced across one shoulder, his other hand protectively on the Seiðr-witch's arm, supporting her as she walked. Though, after having seen what she'd done to Jaromir with her powers, Varg suspected she was fully able to look after herself.

Sulich walked with them, head freshly shaved, dressed in the coat of lamellar plate that Varg had given to him, a bow case and quiver hanging from his belt. Behind him followed more than a score of people, men and women, a mixture of pale and dark-skinned. The prisoners that had been discovered in the rooms behind the feast hall.

"Are they really all Tainted children of the Great Khagan?" Varg asked.

"That is what Sulich said, and he would know, as he is one of them," Svik said.

Vol looked around the courtyard and saw Varg sitting with Røkia and Svik. She said something to Glornir, and they made their way towards them.

"Finished," Røkia said, sitting back and examining her handiwork with narrowed eyes. She tied off the gut thread and cut it with her seax. Varg gently touched the wound, the skin feeling swollen and lumpy.

"My thanks," he said.

"Huh," Røkia grunted.

Glornir nodded a greeting, his bulk casting Varg in shade.

"Chief," the three of them said.

"Vol," Svik said, "it is good to have you back."

Vol was thin, her face bruised, the Seiðr-tattoos on her neck blending and almost hidden by the bruising. There were red pinprick-wounds around her mouth where her lips had been stitched together. But strength emanated from her dark eyes.

"It is good to be back, Svik, good to see you, and all my brothers and sisters," she said through swollen lips, then looked to Varg. "Glornir tells me you have grown. That you are truly one of us now. I have not forgotten that I made you a promise, back in the caves of Rotta's chamber. I owe you an akáll."

"Are you strong enough?" Glornir asked.

"Tsk, I managed to eviscerate Jaromir, did I not?" Vol said.

"Aye, you did," Glornir said, a hint of pride in his voice, a rare smile twitching his lips.

Vol reached out and touched Varg's shoulder. "Is it still something you wish for? To view an akáll is no small thing. It may reveal things that are best left . . . unseen."

Varg's breath caught in his chest. To find out how his sister had died. It had been all that had driven him for so long. *I will see Frøya's last moments.* He had longed for this, but as he thought on it he felt a seed of dread bloom in his stomach. It was one thing to know someone was dead, another thing entirely to watch it happen, even if it was a glimpse of the past.

She is my sister. The only person I ever loved, or who ever loved me. I owe it to her.

"I must know," he said. "But only when you are healed."

Vol nodded, smiled. "I am well enough. Tonight, then."

"Tonight," Varg echoed.

"Your mail needs scouring," Glornir grunted at Varg, frowning at the bloodstained patches. "Else it will rust."

"We've told him," Sulich said.

"I will do it soon," Varg promised.

Vol reached down and put her hand to a blackened iron ring hanging at her belt, two keys hanging from it.

"Where are they?"

"In the tower," Glornir said, waving a hand to one of the gate towers. Two of the Bloodsworn stood before the tower door.

Vol began walking to the tower, Glornir a step behind her.

"Come on," Svik said as he set off after them. Røkia shared a look with Varg, shrugged and they both followed them.

"Chief," the guards said, Glornir nodding, and they opened the door for him. He paused a moment, looking back at Vol.

"You are sure about this?" Glornir said to her.

"Yes," Vol said. "They were thralled to Jaromir, compelled by him. I travelled with them; they were not his willing servants, they are not our enemy." She stroked his cheek. "Trust me."

Glornir entered the tower, Vol behind, and Svik a few paces behind her. Varg quickened his pace to slip in through the door before other Bloodsworn crowded it.

A shaft of daylight from a high window pierced the room, and Varg blinked, allowed the wolf in his blood to filter through him, sight and senses abruptly sharper. The air reeked of blood and sweat.

They were in a square chamber, a staircase at one end leading up to the walkway on the wall. More Bloodsworn sat on chairs, playing a game of knucklebone. Two figures sat inside a pen in the middle of the room, a shaven-haired woman lying on a bed of straw, and a black-skinned, hulking man sitting close to her, frowning at Vol and Glornir. Both were bound with rope, thrall-collars about their necks.

"Leave Iva alone," the bull-man said, his voice a rumble like distant thunder. Blood-caked bandages wrapped his neck and head, from where Ingmar Ice had stabbed and clubbed him with a broken spear shaft. It had taken the combined effort of Ingmar, Røkia, Svik and him to knock the Tainted thrall out. Varg had never seen a strength like it.

"Taras," Vol said gently, stepping forwards, "I have come to help Iva." She paused. "And you, too, if you will allow me."

"Help?" Taras frowned. "Help Iva, not hurt her?" He looked worriedly at the woman lying on the straw. Her head was shaved to stubble, her tunic removed, bandages wrapped around her back and chest. Tattoos curled and writhed across her arms, her torso and up her neck, along her jawline. She was pale, a sheen of sweat covering her, red blooms on the bandages where she had been pierced by Sulich's arrows. Taras laid a thick-muscled arm protectively across her and squeezed her hand.

"What?" Iva muttered, her eyes opening. She lifted her head, looked up at Vol and Glornir.

"What happened?" she asked, her voice a rattling whisper.

"A fight," Taras said.

"I have worked that out for myself," Iva grimaced. She tried to sit up and winced.

"We lost," Taras said morosely.

"I have guessed that, as well."

"Jaromir is dead, with all his *druzhina*," Vol said. "Valdai is ours now."

"Jaromir dead?" Taras rumbled. Slowly a smile spread across his face.

"You should leave," Iva said. "Before Rurik arrives."

"Rurik?" Varg whispered to Svik.

"Jaromir's brother. By all accounts another arseling," Svik whispered back.

"I found these on Jaromir's corpse," Vol said, and held up the iron ring with two keys. "The keys to your collars." She crouched down and put one of them into the lock of Iva's thrall-collar, turned it and pulled the collar away. Then she did the same for Taras. She nodded to the ropes binding them and Glornir drew his seax and gave it to Vol. Taras tensed.

"Trust me," Vol said.

"That is no easy task," Iva breathed, but she laid a hand on Taras' arm, and he nodded.

Vol leaned over and sliced their bonds, then stood.

"You are both free now."

"Free?" Taras said slowly, the word rolling from his tongue as if he was tasting unknown food. He frowned. "What do we do, Iva?" he asked the Seiðr-witch.

"I . . . don't know," Iva said. "I have never been free, before."

"You should stay here and recover, until you are able to travel," Vol said. "There is food and water. Once you are well, go where you wish. I only ask one thing: that you never stand against us again."

"You have my word on that," Iva said, a hand going to her wounds.

"No more fight you. Taras promise," the bull-man said.

"Good," Vol said.

"We will bring you food and drink. But Iva, Taras, know that you do not have to stay in here. You are not our prisoners."

"Taras stay with Iva," Taras said.

"I would like to see the sun and feel the air," Iva said.

Taras effortlessly scooped Iva up in his arms as Vol turned and left the tower, Glornir and the other Bloodsworn following her.

They stepped out into the sun, Taras following with Iva in his arms. She squinted up at the sky and smiled.

"Free," she breathed. Then she focused on something high above them, a frown creasing her face.

"Ware the skies," one of the guards on the wall called out and they all looked up.

Varg saw two shapes in the sky, circling high above and growing larger as they descended. From this distance they seemed small, but then Varg saw the silhouettes of the circling buzzards in the sky and realised that something was wrong. These birds were bigger. Much bigger.

Sulich pulled his bow from his bow case and deftly strung it, nocked an arrow and drew.

"Hold," Glornir growled.

The two birds swept lower, the closer they came the more apparent it was that they were far from normal birds. Varg realised they were two giant ravens, squawking loudly. Dust stirred from the turbulence of their wings.

Varg became aware that there were recognisable words amidst their squawking.

"Bloodsworn," the crows squawked. "We seek the Bloodsworn."

Glornir cupped his hands to his mouth.

"We are the Bloodsworn," he called out.

The two giant ravens swept lower, clouds of dust swirling, Varg and the others stepping hurriedly out of the way, and then the birds were alighting in the courtyard. One squawked and began preening its feathers.

"Glornir," the other raven croaked.

Glornir stepped forwards.

"I am Glornir," he said.

A tennúr jumped from the back of the raven, its wings snapping open to break its fall, alighting weightlessly on the ground. A bag hung from a belt at its waist and Varg recognised the creature. From the Grimholt, Orka's companion.

"I am Vesli," the creature said. "I have travelled long time to find you. I bring a message from mistress Orka."

Glornir waited and a silence fell. "We have searched very far for you. Vesli is cold, tired and . . ." The tennúr seemed distracted by the pile of corpses. She licked her lips. ". . . hungry."

Varg winced.

"Well, what is Orka's message?" Glornir said into the silence.

"Oh, ah, yes," the tennúr said tearing her eyes away from the bodies. "Mistress Orka says Elvar Fire-Fist of the Battle-Grim wishes to hire the Bloodsworn."

"What for?" Svik called out.

The tennúr gave a sharp-toothed grin.

"To slay a dragon."

CHAPTER TWO

GUÐVARR

Guðvarr woke with a sharp hiss, half sitting up from his bedroll on the ground. He had been dreaming, of battling dragons and eagles, of the gaping jaws of an *Úlfhéðnar* snapping at his throat and of creatures burrowing into his flesh. He dragged up the sleeve of the ringmail coat he had slept in and the woollen tunic beneath it and saw the scabbed scar on his arm, where the hyrndur had burrowed into his flesh upon the word of Skalk, Queen Helka's Galdurman, and where it had burrowed back out, commanded by the will of a god. The scab was starting to peel off, and there was no pain other than the horror that the memory stirred in his chest.

I'm safe now, he reassured himself, taking a few breaths to calm his racing heart, *I have the protection of Lik-Rifa and not even the Gods themselves can challenge her successfully.* He remembered Skalk giving life to the eagle bones of Orna and the frenzied battle above the skies when the two Gods had met in battle. It had been a day of betrayal and battle, of blood and ash. Of gods and monsters. Orna was nothing but bones again now. Skalk was gone, Helka dead and a dragon-god owned his fealty.

He was in the longhouse his aunt, Jarl Sigrún, had been given upon her arrival in Darl. The fire pit in the centre of the hall was being lit by thralls, light and shadow rippling across the room. Daylight seeped in from an open doorway, the silhouette and shadow of a *drengr* standing guard before it. All around him *drengrs* were rising.

For a moment it felt like he was back in Fellur village, his home, where all was simple, and safe.

I wish I were back there.

With a deep sigh he reached for his weapons belt and rose sluggishly, body aching and stiff, and buckled his belt over his *brynja*.

A door creaked and Jarl Sigrún emerged from her chamber, set apart at the far end of the longhouse. She saw Guðvarr and beckoned him over to her.

"We are on a knife-edge," she said as he reached her. "We have been useful; you did much to aid Lik-Rifa yesterday. We must remind her of that."

"But carefully," Guðvarr said, wiping a bead of snot from the tip of his nose. "She is proud and unpredictable, prone to . . . violent outbursts."

"Yes, carefully," Sigrún agreed. "But it is vital that we continue to be useful, you know her better – what will convince her?"

I am becoming a master of being useful, Guðvarr thought. *First, I had to remain useful to Skalk the Galdurman to stay alive, now I must do the same to a dragon-god.*

"She likes flattery," Guðvarr said, remembering how he had grovelled and pleaded for his life, and how he had seen her pleasure in the compliments he vomited from his mouth in an attempt to live a few moments more.

"*Drengrs* of Fellur village," Jarl Sigrún said, raising her voice for all in the hall to hear her, little more than thirty warriors left after yesterday's battle. "The world has changed. Gods walk the land and soar in the skies, and we must adapt if we are going to survive. You have sworn your oaths to me, trusted me. Trust in me now, and I shall lead you through this." She gave a rueful smile, the scar in her face twisting it into something less wholesome. "Perhaps we shall even come out of this better placed than if we fought for Helka against Jarl Störr. Time will be the judge."

The *drengr* on guard duty at the longhouse door, a young warrior named Járn, stepped into the hall.

"People approach," he called out nervously. "And . . . other things . . ."

"Make ready," Jarl Sigrún said to Guðvarr and her *drengrs* and they buckled on weapons and drew closer around her.

The *drengr* at the door stepped away and figures crowded through, a shadow blocking out the daylight.

As they stepped into the firelight Guðvarr saw there was a man and woman leading, both dark-haired and clothed in good *brynjas* with swords and seaxes at their belts, the man carrying a spear. Behind them loped a handful of skraeling, their limbs too long for their grey-skinned bodies, muscles knotted like rope, crude weapons of iron in their fists or hanging from belts. A handful of tennúr flitted in the air behind them. One of them flew over to Guðvarr and hovered in front of him. It smiled, revealing two rows of grindstone teeth.

Filthy little vermin, Guðvarr thought as he looked at its rat-like body and too large mouth.

"Well met," Sigrún said, stepping forward. "I am Jarl Sigrún."

"I know who you are," the woman in black said. One of her eyes was blue, the other pale as clouded milk. She looked Sigrún up and down.

"And you are?"

"I am called Blóta," she said. "I am dragon-born. You are to come to the courtyard."

"What is happening in the courtyard?" Sigrún asked.

"Lik-Rifa has summoned all who fought yesterday. What she wants to do . . ." Blóta shrugged. "Who knows the mind of a god." She turned and walked away.

His aunt exchanged a look with Guðvarr and he shrugged. Who knew what Lik-Rifa intended – she was as likely to eat them as reward them.

"With me," Jarl Sigrún said, striding after the warrior and her *drengrs* fell in behind her, Guðvarr hurrying to remain at her side.

They left the longhouse, Guðvarr pausing a moment when he saw the troll standing outside, waiting for the dragon-born. He was huge, gnarled and thick-skinned like an old oak, a wooden club studded with nails in his sledge-hammer hands. With a scowl and a grunt he turned and followed the two dragon-born warriors.

They walked down a street of hard-packed earth that led between rows of longhouses and smithies, joining a procession of people flowing towards the hall of the former Queen Helka: a building once crowned by Orna's bones had dominated this hill that the fortress was built upon. The road spilled into the courtyard and Guðvarr looked around the ruin of the courtyard and remains of the hall as he walked through it. Bodies and debris had been cleared, but the ground was still torn and rent from the destruction that Lik-Rifa and Orna had caused during their savage contest. Feathers and unrecognisable heaps of flesh and bone were scattered across the ground, here and there dark patches of dried blood.

At the far end of the courtyard, before the steps to the feast hall, men and women were kneeling in a long row, fifty or sixty of them, wrists bound behind their backs, all of them *drengrs*, many of them bloodied, bearing wounds from yesterday's battle. Dragon-born and trolls stood over them.

Helka's drengrs, Guðvarr realised, recognising some of them.

Lik-Rifa stood in her female form at the top of the steps to the feast hall, dark-haired, tall and regal, dressed in an ash-grey tunic trimmed with red. Fresh wounds scarred her face and arms, though, and one eye was swollen almost shut, mottled with bruises.

Interesting . . . she's not infallible then, Guðvarr mused, then hurriedly shut down his thoughts in case she could read his mind. Two wooden pillars stood either side of her, the doors to the hall behind her ripped from the wall, one hanging, the other smashed to kindling. Half a wall reared skyward, thick timbers splintered, the roof completely gone. Warriors stood around her, all dark-haired and clothed in fine *brynjas* and war gear. Beside Lik-Rifa, Guðvarr saw the hulking form of Drekr, though she stood taller than him, and beside Drekr his sister, Ilska the Cruel, chief of the Raven-Feeders.

No longer mercenaries for hire, they are honour-guard to a god now.

Vaesen were there, too, skraelings and trolls, tennúr and other things that Guðvarr was unsure of. Just looking at them made him uncomfortable. More warriors lined the courtyard, many of them men and women, the dragon-worshippers that had always lurked in the shadows, now made bold by the coming of their queen.

Jarl Sigrún walked confidently behind the two dragon-born warriors, marching right up to the steps of the hall, where she stopped, Guðvarr beside her, her *drengrs* behind. Sigrún looked up at Lik-Rifa, who stared back at her, and Jarl Sigrún bowed. Lik-Rifa stared unblinkingly, then her eyes moved on to Guðvarr and held his gaze. He gulped and bowed to her, as his aunt had done, and a smile twitched at the edges of Lik-Rifa's lips, and she dipped her head, acknowledging them before her eyes moved on.

Many others were filling the courtyard, warriors and townsfolk, some coming at Lik-Rifa's summons, some out of awe and wonder, others herded by Lik-Rifa's followers. Guðvarr saw jarl Glunn Iron-Grip, fair-haired, broad and squat, and jarl Svard the Scratcher, older, slimmer and taller, with a few score of their *drengrs* behind them being escorted into the courtyard by a ring of dragon-born, skraeling and dragon-worshippers. A handful of trolls strode before them, clearing a way through the gathering crowd none too gently. The prisoners were bought to stand close to Guðvarr, Sigrún and her *drengrs*.

Lik-Rifa took a step forward and a hush fell over the courtyard.

"People of Darl, a new age has dawned, and you are privileged to behold it." She held her arms out wide. "You have a new queen. Not just of Darl, but of all Vigrið. Not some petty usurper, but a GOD." She roared the last word, her mouth growing broader and longer, the flash of a red maw and rows of razored teeth, spittle spraying. Then her face returned to normal, human proportions, a twitch and shudder running through her jawline and cheek.

"Many of you fought against me yesterday," she hissed, casting her baleful gaze across Glunn and Svard and their retinues of *drengrs*, and then to the warriors kneeling at the foot of the steps. "These are the *drengrs* of Helka, oathsworn to her. She is dead now, but these people are still sworn to her, or her bloodline." She sniffed. "Helka was slain by my loyal allies," she gestured to Guðvarr and Sigrún.

"And her son, Hakon," Guðvarr squeaked. "I slew him," he added.

"But one of Helka's brood lives on, I am told," Lik-Rifa said bitterly. She looked over her shoulder and Drekr stepped forward, leaned close to her.

"Estrid, Helka's daughter," Guðvarr heard Drekr say.

"Yes, Helka's daughter. So, these warriors at my feet are still bound by their oaths of fealty." She sighed and shook her head. "Kill them," she said.

There were shouts and screams for mercy from the *drengrs*, as trolls raised their clubs and brought them smashing down, blood spraying, bones cracking, flesh pulverised. The dragon-born stabbed, slashed and chopped with spears, swords, axes, a cacophony of screams and wails cut short and in a dozen heartbeats the *drengrs* were all dead, blood pooling into the hard-packed earth.

Guðvarr took a step backwards and with the back of his hand wiped a fine spattering of blood from his cheek. Even Jarl Sigrún looked shocked, but recovered herself quickly.

"Bring them forward," Lik-Rifa gestured to jarls Glunn, Svard and their followers and they were pushed reluctantly towards the dragon-god.

"You two," Lik-Rifa said, pointing a long-nailed finger at Glunn and Svard. "Step closer."

The dragon-born parted and Glunn and Svard walked forwards, stopping close to Guðvarr in front of Helka's executed *drengrs*.

"You are both jarls, I am told, who fought against me yesterday, because you had sworn oaths to Helka. Yes?"

"Aye," Glunn Iron-Grip said, looking up at Lik-Rifa.

"And you?" Lik-Rifa said, when Svard did not answer.

"I did," jarl Svard said. "But Helka is dead, and my oath does not bind me to her children." He looked nervously to the dead at his feet.

"Well, quite," Lik-Rifa said. "That point is exactly what I wished to discuss with you. Will you swear your oaths to me?"

"I will," Svard said quickly.

Glunn Iron-Grip sniffed and spat, looked back at his *drengrs* and then up at Lik-Rifa. "If I swear my oath to you, fight for you, perhaps bleed for you, what will you do for me?"

A muscle twitched in Lik-Rifa's cheek, then she smiled.

"I will make you mighty, and wealthy, and made famous by skálds for a thousand years. That is all you wish for, is it not?"

Glunn nodded. "Then I will swear my oath to you," he said.

"Good," Lik-Rifa said. Then she frowned. "But I do not think you are *both* worthy to serve me. Though perhaps one of you is . . ." She raised a hand. "Drekr, give them each a blade."

Drekr stepped forwards and drew his seax and short-axe from his belt, threw them down the stairs to land at the feet of Glunn and Svard.

They both stared at the weapons.

"Well, what are you waiting for? Show me who is worthy," Lik-Rifa said.

Glunn burst into motion, Svard a heartbeat later. Glunn swept up the seax as Svard reached for the axe and buried it to the hilt in Svard's belly. A grunt and Svard sagged, knees weak and Glunn ripped the seax free. Svard collapsed, twitched for a few moments, mouth moving, and then he was still.

Glunn leaned down and wiped the blade clean on Svard's tunic.

"It seems you are the worthy one," Lik-Rifa said. "Will that man's warriors follow you?"

Glunn looked back to his and Svard's *drengrs*. "They will. I have just fought a *holmganga* with their jarl and won. By the laws of *holmganga* they can seek no vengeance, no reprisal. All that was Svard's is now mine. So, yes, they will serve me. Won't you," he said to Svard's *drengrs*.

A ripple of "ayes" rang out.

"Good," Lik-Rifa said. "Now all this excitement has given me an appetite. You will come and eat with me. As will you," Lik-Rifa said, pointing at Sigrún. "And you, Guthlaf," she said, pointing at Guðvarr.

It's Guðvarr, you idiot, he corrected Lik-Rifa in his head, then felt a moment of fear. *Can she read my thoughts? She is a god, after all.*

But Lik-Rifa said nothing, just turned and walked through the ruined doors of Helka's Hall.

"Stay close," Sigrún whispered to him as she climbed the hall's steps.

With a sigh Guðvarr followed her.

Into the dragon's den.

CHAPTER THREE

ELVAR

Elvar sat back in her father's throne with a sigh. The seat from which he had ruled Snakavik and all the land as far as the eye could see from this mountaintop fortress.

"My father's seat. My father's hall. *My* seat, now, *my* hall, now," she whispered to herself.

"What's that?" a rumbling voice said behind her, and she twisted to look over her shoulder. Hrung stared unsettlingly back at her with his opaque eyes, his giant severed head upon a pedestal of stone.

"Just thinking on life, ancient Hrung," she said. "And how it is so . . . changeable." *Not so long ago I was a warrior among many, fighting in a shield wall, defeated by dragon-born. And now . . .*

She regarded the ruin of her father's hall.

Close to her feet two chests had been placed, both filled with treasure from the god's battleground, the plains of Oskutreð. Around them blood still stained the ground, visible here and there as dark patches among the snow that fell gently around her, settling on the dais and hard-packed earth of the hall floor and she pulled her bearskin cloak tighter about her neck. Broken timbers reared like the shattered bones of a great whale where the wolf-god Ulfrir had smashed the hall to kindling and above her a pewter sky sat heavy and bloated with fresh snow. *Drengrs* had been working to clear the destruction for some time, lifting timbers and rubble to uncover the wounded and remove the dead, *drengrs* who until yesterday had been oathsworn to her father, Jarl Störr.

Oathsworn to him no longer, as he is meat in Ulfrir's belly, and I put a sword in his heir, my brother Thorun.

Elvar saw members of the Battle-Grim spread around the hall, Orv the Sneak with his bow in hand, an arrow loosely nocked, Sólín Spittle leaning against a timber column, one hand on the hilt of her sheathed sword, Urt the Unwashed standing close to the entrance, others lurking in the shadows.

They are guarding me, my Battle-Grim. Not that I need guarding now. She glanced at the warriors spread around her like a cupped hand, all of them tall and broad, braided beards and mail-clad, axes and knives hanging from their weapons belts. Over a score of *Berserkir*.

My Berserkir.

By some strange Galdur-magic, with the death of her father and elder brother the power of control had shifted to Elvar, the next in line to the kingdom, which is what she had wanted, what she had come here for. What she had hoped for.

Be careful what you wish for.

One of the *Berserkir* stood apart from the others: Berak, dark and hulking. Elvar remembered tracking him to Iskalt Island, hunting him down and finding him in battle with a young bull troll. Her hand went to the troll tusk hanging at her neck. That seemed a lifetime ago. Berak was stooped, talking quietly with Uspa, his wife, and Elvar's Seiðr-witch. Uspa with her tattooed arms and lower jaw, a seax taken from the plain of Oskutreð hanging at her belt. It had been Uspa who had set this new path in motion, Uspa who had told them she knew the way to Oskutreð, Uspa who had sworn them all to help find her kidnapped son with the *blóð svarið*, her Seiðr-spell.

Uspa who planted this curse in my blood.

"Ahh, that is one of the marvels of life," Hrung said behind her, "how it can change on a knife-edge. It keeps things interesting."

"I doubt my father would agree with you," Elvar said darkly. "Or my brother."

She had killed her brother, cut his throat with her blade after he'd tried to have her slaughtered. Thorun's corpse had been removed from the hall along with the other bodies. There was little left of her father to take away. He had been eaten by Ulfrir.

My father is dead. Long had she dreamed of killing her father. She had hated him, yet at the same time craved his respect. In her imaginings she would always say cutting words to him, see him crumble with grief over his treatment of her, listen to his pleading attempts at a reconciliation. Occasionally she would even allow him to live.

But none of that had happened. Instead, he had been swept up by Skuld and cast into the jaws of a giant wolf, torn to shreds in a heartbeat.

Elvar thought she would have felt elated, victorious, full of a grim satisfaction at the vengeance she owed her father.

All she felt was numb.

"You are right there," Hrung chuckled, Elvar feeling it vibrate through her body. "Life can be fickle."

"Heya," Ulfrir agreed from the shadows, fingering the collar around his neck.

"Ahh, Ulfrir, my friend," Hrung rumbled, "you are a thrall now, which I must admit is not the best life to live, but things could be worse."

"Could they?" Skuld sniffed, scowling at Elvar, who had put the iron collar around hers and her father's necks.

"Aye. You could be just a head, and that is not a life I'd recommend."

Ulfrir tipped his head in acknowledgement.

"Uspa, Berak," Elvar called out, and the Seiðr-witch and *Berserkir* approached her.

"Jarl Elvar," they both said.

"Our treasure," Elvar said, gesturing to the two chests at her feet, "they must be moved to my father's treasury." She nodded to a door towards the rear of the shattered hall. "Uspa, protect them with your Seiðr-words."

Uspa nodded and Berak moved to pick one up.

"Not yet," Elvar said. "I have need of them, first."

On a bench before the dais, close to Elvar, sat her younger brother, Broðir. His eyes kept flickering to ruins of the hall and back, nervously, to Elvar and the living gods who now sat among them.

Should I have killed Broðir, too? Her father would have advised her to. Broðir was the last of her bloodline, the only one who would benefit from her death. *Killing me would give him power over the* Berserkirs*, and that is a great deal of power.* But he had surrendered to her, and she had not been able to plunge her sword into him as she had done to the detestable Thorun. She had always liked Broðir.

And I am not my father's daughter. Not in the ways that matter. I refuse to be.

Beside her brother sat her father's Galdurwoman, Silrið. Tall, fair-haired, her face all hard lines, a necklace of bones around her neck. Elvar trusted her less than a viper in her boots, but in the heat of battle Silrið had changed sides and gifted Thorun to her, so for now Elvar would keep the Galdurwoman close, until she had decided what to do with her.

A gust of wind and snow wailed into the room through one of the walls that had been smashed to splintered pulp and Elvar could see crowds gathering in the street beyond to stare in at the carnage.

Not come to see me, I think. She glanced to her left, where Ulfrir stood, changed from his wolf-form back to a man now, wrapped in his wolf-pelt cloak, his grey-black hair framing a sharp-lined and deep-shadowed face, amber eyes burning like coals. His daughter, Skuld, stood beside him, her red hair a smear of colour in the pale hall. Her wings were folded across her back, no longer hidden beneath her cloak. People in the street gawped and pointed. Skuld sneered at them and looked away.

Scuffed footsteps and Sighvat the Fat lumbered into the ruined hall, a sealskin cloak pulled tight around him, a steaming bowl of porridge in his big hand. He approached Elvar on the dais, reached the *Berserkir* and growled something at them, but they stayed where they were, blocking his way.

"Let him through," Elvar called down to them and they parted, Sighvat stomping through them with a glower.

". . . trying to stop me getting to my chief, the arselings," he was muttering as he reached Elvar. "Here, chief," he said, holding out the bowl of porridge. "It's good, I put honey in it myself."

"I'm not hungry," Elvar muttered.

"'Course you are," Sighvat said, "you just don't realise it. Sometimes the killing can rob your appetite, but, trust me, you're hungry. And being hungry steals your wits from you, and right now we need our deep-cunning chief with *all* her wits about her. So, please, eat." He offered the bowl of porridge again and to Elvar's surprise her stomach growled. This time she took it.

Sighvat smiled, nodding, then looked around at the devastation in the hall, at the heaps of the dead, where they had been piled, at carpenters and builders working at the clearing and repairing of the hall, at people gathering in the street, and he puffed his cheeks and blew out a long breath.

"I've a feeling your plan worked out well, but . . ." he looked around and leaned closer. "What do we do now?" he whispered.

Good question.

"We have a task to do," she said to Sighvat, one hand going to the knotwork scar hidden beneath her sleeve of mail. The scar that was the seal and reminder of her blood oath. "Best we get on and do it."

"Aye," Sighvat muttered glumly. Absently he put the back of his hand to his mouth and bit down, pulled out a long splinter and spat it on the ground.

Figures entered the hall, approaching through the snow and debris. Grend led them, his weathered crag of a face stern, a woollen cloak wrapped around him. One hand rested on the head of his axe hanging at his belt. Beside him walked Gytha, champion of Jarl Störr, dark hair braided tight, an old scar running from her cheek into her top lip.

Yesterday she fought against me. What will today bring, I wonder?

Behind them more than two score men and women followed, all warriors wrapped in fur and mail, weapon-clad.

Grend reached the foot of the dais where the *Berserkir* stood guard and paused.

"Move," Elvar said with a flick of her hand and the *Berserkir* parted.

"I have brought them, as you asked," Grend said as he came to stand beside Elvar, shuffling close to her right side and turning to stare balefully out at the crowd gathered before them. "Your father's petty jarls, Snakavik's captains, and the chiefs of all the mercenary bands who answered your father's call."

Elvar sat and looked at them, met their eyes. She saw questions there, fear, wonder, resentment. Greed. Many eyes flickered between Ulfrir, Skuld and the chests at Elvar's feet.

She sucked in a deep breath and stood. She still wore her blood-stained *brynja* from the battle, her sword hanging at her hip and a gold ring wrapped about her arm. Agnar's black bearskin cloak hung about her shoulders. She focused first on Gytha and her father's *drengrs*.

"I have slain the man you were sworn to," Elvar said, relieved that her voice did not betray the depths of her worry. "Gytha, what will you do now?"

Gytha took a step forward and a handful of *Berserkir* growled.

"We fought you and lost," Gytha said with a shrug, ignoring the *Berserkirs*. "To my thinking, Jarl Störr is dead, and you are his eldest still breathing. You are our jarl now, by birthright and by battle claim. I would swear my oath to you, to serve you as I served your father."

Jarl. She felt a flutter in her belly at that. Dread and excitement mingled.

Elvar nodded, trying not to let the relief she felt etch itself across her face. "And my father's *drengrs*?" she asked, letting her eyes move slowly across the mail-clad warriors gathered behind Gytha.

"They feel the same as I," Gytha said.

"I would hear it from them."

"We are ready to swear you our oaths," a man said, tall and wiry, a red-haired beard.

"Aye," another *drengr* said, and one by one each captain stepped forward and added their voice.

"Good," Elvar nodded. Her eyes moved to a handful of men and women, all mail-clad, with rings of silver or gold about their arms. Her father's petty jarls.

"And you all?" Elvar said. "You served my father well. Will you serve me?"

A woman stepped forwards, mouse-haired, broad and squat and clothed in a fine *brynja*, two bearded axes thrust through her weapons belt.

"Runa Red-Axe," Elvar said.

"We swore our oaths to your father, and you have bested him. You rule here now. We will swear our oaths to you," Runa said.

Elvar nodded. "I will hear your oaths, but save them until you know where it will take you." She shifted her gaze to look at the other group of warriors gathered behind the jarls and *drengrs*. "And what of you chieftains and your mercenary bands?"

"We were sworn to Jarl Störr's war against Queen Helka," a man said. A tangle of black hair, his beard covering most of his face, a shield with two ravens hanging loosely in his grip. "We will happily take your silver for the same job." His eyes flickered to the treasure chests at Elvar's feet.

"You were sworn to my father's war, Hjalmar Peacemaker, chief of the Fell-Hearted," Elvar said. "But that is not *my* war. I have a different battle to fight."

Uspa moved away from Berak and came to stand at Elvar's left hand. Elvar noticed the *Berserkir* did not try to stop her.

"My battle is against Lik-Rifa, the dragon-god. Against her dragon-born children, against her dragon-cult followers, and against the vaesen that have flocked to her."

A silence filled the hall, gusts of wind and snow swirling.

"Fighting a god, now that is different from fighting a jarl. More expensive than fighting a jarl, I would say," a fair-haired woman called out, a silver-gilt sword at her hip. "Two things are needed for us to side with you. More silver than your father promised, and the knowledge that we will have a chance to live and spend it. Fighting a dragon is no small thing."

"Fair points, Ingvild Wave-Roamer," Elvar said. "I have been to Oskutreð, I have seen the battleground of the gods, I have seen the dragon set free, and she is fearsome. But she is just one dragon, and I have Ulfrir the wolf-god and his winged daughter, Skuld, and they are fearsome, too. I have my father's *Berserkir*, I have the jarls and *drengrs* of Jarl Störr, and I have the feared Battle-Grim. And I have a river of gold and silver to pay you all." She stood and kicked one of the chests, its lid bursting open to reveal a heap of gold and silver coins, cups, jewellery, and gems spilling out. "And I have enough left over to pay a thousand more warbands like you. If you follow me, I cannot promise you will all survive, but those who do, you will be rich beyond your wildest imaginings."

Another silence, Sighvat leaning close to whisper. "You speak well, you almost make me want to go and fight a dragon. Almost."

And then Hjalmar Peacemaker punched his arm into the air.

"Jarl Elvar," he bellowed, his eyes never leaving the open chest of treasure. "Jarl Elvar, Jarl Elvar."

Every warrior in the room raised their arm and took up the cry.

CHAPTER FOUR

ORKA

"I am going to kill you," Orka spat through a mouthful of blood.

"You can try," Rotta snarled as he slammed his fist into Orka's nose, "others have and yet, look, here I am still . . ."

The last time Orka had seen Rotta he had been transforming into his rat form, screaming in agony after Spert had vomited his black-breath pestilence upon the god. Rotta had returned to his human form now, his face a mass of weeping sores and red weals from Spert's venom. A red stain on the rat-god's tunic was the only evidence that he had been skewered through the chest by a spear cast by Halja Flat-Nose as well, but the spear was gone now, and Rotta seemed remarkably alive and healthy. Although his ruined face twitched and juddered, raw holes weeping blood and pus, pain and rage shuddering through him. "Where is my *brother*?" he snarled through gritted teeth.

Orka just gave him her wolf-grin, showing bloodied teeth through her blue-tinged, shivering lips and Rotta drew his fist back.

A pale sun glinted on ice-crusted snow, Orka lying on the charred ground before the broken gates and walls of Svelgarth, clouds of smoke swirling sluggishly as the town burned. She was dimly aware of a crowd gathered around her, trolls looming, tennúr hovering in the air, spertus and frost-spiders scuttling. But everything was blurred and ice-tinged, the frost-spider venom still coursing through her veins, her limbs numb, the wolf in her blood distant, confused and cowed by the ice that had flooded her.

Rotta's fist slammed into her face again, snapping her head back onto the ground, the sound of cartilage cracking. She rolled her head, a burning sensation in her neck as muscles slowly began to return to her control.

When my body returns to me I will show you why the rat fears the wolf.

"Strange, the power of emotion," Rotta grunted as he pounded Orka with another blow. "My intellect tells me that this is *not* the way to get you to talk, I am aware that violence is unlikely to give me the answers that I want." He paused, wiped sweat and dribbling blood from his face, "And yet, I cannot stop. It feels so satisfying."

Voices drifted through the smoke and Rotta turned to look over his shoulder, a red-knuckled fist raised high. Figures emerged from clouds of smoke and ash, the first one a dark-haired woman dressed in oil-black mail, a raven's feather braided with silver wire into her hair. One of her eye sockets was a puckered, scarred hole. She gripped a rope in her fist, dragging a handful of bound captives behind her, a man, a woman and a child.

Myrk. Orka spat a glob of blue-tinged blood.

"Jarl Orlyg's brats," Myrk called out as she strode towards Rotta, hauling her stumbling prisoners, and then she saw Orka. Her face shifted, red flecks sparking to life in her one eye, and she threw the rope in her fist to a warrior behind her, hands reaching for sword and seax at her belt as she broke into a run.

"No," Rotta said, taking a step to stand between Myrk and Orka. Myrk twisted to run around him, and Rotta moved again, faster than Orka thought possible, and then Myrk was bouncing off him, falling onto the ground and rolling to one knee.

"No," Rotta said again.

"This bitch took my eye," Myrk snarled, "I have sworn to kill her."

"Perhaps you will kill her, perhaps you won't, but you will definitely not kill her *now*," Rotta said. "She's one of my brother's ilk, has spoken to him, may know where he is lurking. And, besides, you are not the only one who owes this she-wolf a red death." He gestured to the ruin of his face, then to bodies laid out upon the snow. A hulking, red-haired warrior, his face purple and swollen, a lattice of black veins and unseeing eyes. A dozen dead skraeling. A white-haired warrior mumbling and twitching, blood frothing through his torn cheek and jaw. He looked like he would soon be joining the dead. Other corpses were being carried over and laid beside the fallen.

"Look at the results of your visit," Rotta said to Orka with a sweep of his hand. "Ill-mannered, I call it," he tutted.

Orka looked at the dead and wounded. "They stood in my way," she grunted. *They tried to keep my son from me.*

Breca, where are you? She knew the river she had thrown him into would have carried him to the lake and meeting point, where Gunnar Prow, Halja and the others would surely be. *They will get him away from here.* But she remembered the frost-spiders that had hunted her down, felt a stab of fear at the thought of them catching Breca before he reached the lake. Some life was returning to her fingers, a tingling burn in her joints and knuckles and she clenched her fists, but her wrists were bound with frost-spider web. She looked at the sky, saw it was past midday. *No, if they had caught him, they would have brought him back by now. He is away with the others.* That thought seeped through her. She had been chasing after Breca for so long, trying to find him, trying to save him from these *niðing* dragon-born, that it snatched her breath away to realise she had accomplished that goal. *He is free, my Breca. I have done what I came to do.* She blew out a long breath, feeling the truth of that settle in her heart, and looked up at Rotta and Myrk. *There are more I would like to kill, though. These two, for a start. And Drekr, who slew my Thorkel. And Lik-Rifa is behind it all – so I owe her a blood debt.*

"You have beaten her half to death," Myrk growled sullenly as she stood, reluctantly sheathing her sword and seax.

"Yes, *half* to death, not to full death," Rotta said as he regarded his blood-spattered, mangled knuckles. "Unfortunately, she must live, for now."

"She will not talk, she is a stubborn bitch," Myrk said, stepping closer to Orka.

"There is always a path to making someone talk," Rotta said. "Pain is usually the fastest road, but not with her. Not her own pain, anyway." He looked at Myrk. "Feel free to try, as long as you promise to act with . . . restraint."

Myrk grinned and kicked Orka in the belly.

Feeling was returning to Orka, the ice in her veins thinning, retreating, and she felt the power of Myrk's kick shudder through her gut. She rolled onto her side, retching, and spitting out blue-tinged bile.

"Where is Ulfrir?" Rotta asked her.

Orka spat blood at his feet, felt the wolf returning to her and she glowered up at him with amber-flecked eyes.

"See," Rotta shrugged to Myrk.

Myrk screeched and kicked Orka again.

"Good girl," Rotta clapped. "Whatever you do, do it with all your heart."

Myrk drew back for another kick and paused, staring at Orka. "I will take these back," she snarled, seeing what hung from Orka's weapons belt. She ripped the buckle undone and dragged the belt from Orka's waist. "My brother will be glad at the return of these," she said, dangling two finely wrought seaxes in leather-tooled scabbards before Orka. "I believe he left them in your dead *niðing* husband."

My Thorkel.

Without thought Orka struggled against her bonds, veins bulging, the wolf in her heart howling. Thorkel's blood-streaked face filled her thought-cage, her oath to avenge him a storm in her blood.

Myrk laughed.

"You see, she feels more for others than herself," Rotta said thoughtfully. "Even when they're dead. The road to loosening her lips about my brother lies with her son."

"Well, where is the little shite?" Myrk asked, still smiling down at Orka.

"Escaped," Rotta said, "but we shall find him. And then . . . then she shall tell us whatever we need to know."

Screams and whimpers drew their attention and they all looked to see a fur-clad man step from the wooded slopes, a line of bound children stumbling behind him.

A cold fist clenched around Orka's heart.

CHAPTER FIVE

BIÓRR

Biórr grunted as he lifted Ilmur's corpse under the shoulders, a long-armed skraeling named Skaga hefting Ilmur's ankles. They strode through the carnage of last night, bodies strewn on the ground, burned-out tents and wagons smashed to kindling in Rotta's agony and rage, and made their way to the pile of the dead, close to where Rotta had been venting his pain and fury on a bound and frost-spider-poisoned Orka.

I hate that woman, Biórr thought, eyes on Orka as he laid Ilmur's corpse beside Storolf. He looked down at his dead friends, felt the weight of grief in his chest, a constriction in his throat, a burning in his eyes. Felt a measure of responsibility and guilt, as well. *I almost let Breca go, almost let Orka and the boy leave. Perhaps I should have. Ilmur and Storolf would still be alive.* It was self-preservation, that strongest of instincts that he had inherited from his rat-god blood that had guided him, made him shout out a warning and draw his weapon. Made him attack Orka and her Bloodsworn companions. He had been tasked with guarding the Tainted children and knew that there were already those within the warband who viewed him with suspicion after Kráka the Seiðr-witch's attempted escape with Bjarn.

I had no choice.

He heard Myrk's sharp voice and saw her standing over Orka, holding a weapons belt with two sheathed seaxes upon it. Then her head turned to look to the wooded slopes of the valley.

Brák Trolls-Bane was emerging from the trees, draped in a wolf pelt, a whip in one hand, his troll-tusk necklace glinting in the pale sun. He led a handful of children, all bound at the wrist, a dozen of Brák's hunters spread around them, Tainted humans, skraeling, a few tennúr whirring in the air above.

"Get on," Brák snarled as he cracked his whip. Children whimpered.

Brák led them to stand before Rotta. He looked down at Orka, hawked and spat on her.

"Found some of the little runts," Brák grunted at Rotta.

"Breca?" Rotta asked, eyes scouring the line of children.

"No," Brák said. "There's no trace of that goat turd. No tracks, no scent past where she was caught," he said, nudging Orka with his toe.

Biórr saw the relief flicker across Orka's face.

"Think he must have jumped into the river." Brák shrugged. "Most likely drowned, or frozen."

"I want his body, dead or alive," Rotta said. "Find him."

Brák nodded. "What about these," he said, gesturing to the captured children behind him. "I could nail them to a tree, make an example of them to any others thinking about making a run for it. I've a bag of nails I made just for the job." He patted a pouch at his belt.

"No," Rotta frowned. "They have god-blood in their veins. They are best living and fighting for us."

"Aye," Brák said, the twist of his face suggesting he didn't agree.

"Put them in a wagon and leave them bound, for now," Rotta said. "Biórr will guard them, won't you, Biórr?"

"Yes, lord," Biórr called out. "Skaga," he said to the skraeling, "take them."

"Aye," Skaga grunted and loped over to Brák.

Biórr squatted down beside Red Fain. The white-haired warrior was sitting propped up against the shattered wheel of a wagon. One side of his face was bound with cloth, where Orka had bitten him. She had torn and ripped his cheek and jaw to bloodied strips. Fresh blood was seeping through the bandage and Fain was shivering with the first touches of a fever.

"My Storolf," Fain wheezed as he reached out and took his dead son's hand. He looked at Biórr. "The cost of this war," he said through his tears, "I fear it is more than I can bear. Fear I cannot go on."

"We must bear it," Biórr said, "or else the world stays as it is, our kind thralled, beaten, killed. We are the hard edge that will change the world." He sighed, puffed his cheeks, looking at Storolf and Ilmur, a fresh wave of emotion building in his chest. "To stop now, to walk away now, would mean they died in vain. Their deaths, their sacrifice, it must *count*. It must mean *something*." Biórr reached out and laid his hand upon Fain's and Storolf's, squeezed them as he held Fain's gaze. "Heal, old man, and then we will change the world." He glanced at Orka on the ground before Rotta. "And we will have our vengeance."

Fain's face twitched, blood and froth seeping through the bandage of his torn cheek, emotions at war within him. Eventually he nodded.

"Biórr," Rotta called out, gesturing and Biórr stood and strode over to the god.

"I'm going to go and find your wolf cub," Brák was saying to Orka. "This is what I do to wolves," he added, spreading his wolf pelt wide. "Perhaps there'll be enough skin on your Breca to make a decent belt."

Orka pulled her lips back, snarling.

Brák walked away chuckling. "With me," he called out and his hunting crew drew in about him, all of them disappearing into the treeline.

"Biórr, I want you to guard our new guests," Rotta said, nodding down at Orka, then gesturing to the bound prisoners Myrk had led out of Svelgarth.

"Yes, lord," Biórr said, nodding a greeting to Myrk.

"Lover," she said to him, a smile twitching her lips.

He blushed. Myrk always made him blush.

I don't want to guard Orka, I want to kill her, he thought, trying to keep his emotions from his face, though his eyes were drawn to Orka. Bloodied and bound as she was, violence still radiated from her like a heat haze. *And why am I always the one guarding children and prisoners. This age will be sung of by skálds, and when will I be mentioned?*

"This is no small task," Rotta said, seeming to read his mind. "It is important. Orka has spoken with my arseling, bite-first-and-talk-later brother; she could help us end this war if we find him before he has time to consolidate his power. And the Tainted children, they must be won over to us, else they will end up fighting against us. I am trusting you with this task as I need someone with a clear head. A thinker," he tapped his head and glanced at Myrk.

Yes, well Myrk tends to act first and think . . . not much at all.

"Yes, lord," he repeated.

"Good man," Rotta said, clapping a huge hand on Biórr's shoulder. "Make ready to leave," he bellowed, his god-voice filling the valley and shaking the tree-shrouded slopes.

The camp burst into motion, people, trolls, skraeling, frost-spiders, spertus all moving, tennúr taking to the air in a flurry of wings.

"Where are we going, lord?" Biórr asked Rotta.

"South-west, to Darl," Rotta said. "To rally with my sister." He looked at Orka and smirked. "She's going to *love* meeting you."

CHAPTER SIX

VARG

Varg sat on a bench in the hall of Valdai, eating pork and onions, hard cheese and warm flatbread.

Most of the Bloodsworn were there, eating their evening meal, the carcass of a wild boar turning on a spit over a fire pit. Glornir sat with Vol and Edel, leaning close in deep conversation.

Svik sat down beside Varg with a wooden plate full of food in one hand and a cup of mead in the other.

"What do you think?" Varg asked him.

"About what?" Svik said, filling his mouth with cheese and thinly sliced onion.

"About the dragon. About what we are going to do!" Varg said, stunned that Svik had to ask. He had been able to think of little else since Vesli and the two giant ravens had arrived.

"Glornir's the chief, it's his decision to gnaw at," Svik shrugged. "Fight the dragon, fight someone else. Fighting is what we do, but it is Glornir who decides who we fight. Or what." He shrugged again.

Røkia joined them, pausing to examine the stitches in Varg's cheek. She brushed them gently with her fingertips and Varg felt his neck flush with heat.

Svik smirked.

"What?" Røkia said.

Svik just shook his head.

"What do you think, about the dragon?" Varg asked Røkia.

"It will be the fight to end all fights. Obviously we must be there," Røkia said with enthusiasm. "Imagine the songs that will be sung about us."

"Not much use if we're all too dead to hear them," Varg muttered. "This is the attitude I'm worried about."

Røkia rolled her eyes.

The hall doors opened and Sulich entered with a handful of his kin behind him. The sound of bones cracking and flesh tearing filtered in from the courtyard beyond. Varg pulled a face.

"How can those ravens *still* be eating," he asked.

"Look at it this way," Svik told him cheerfully, "the more they eat, the less there is to stink up the place when the bodies start rotting."

Once Vesli had delivered her message from Orka she had asked politely if she could rip the teeth from the gums of the dead that lay piled in the courtyard. Glornir had told her she could help herself to any part of Jaromir's *druzhina* that she wished to eat, at which point the ravens had started hopping from foot to foot and croaking about how hungry they were, having flown hundreds of leagues out of the kindness of their hearts, just as a favour to a friend. Glornir had told them they could feast on the dead, as long as they did not dig up the Bloodsworn who had been buried, and the ravens had wasted no time in getting started. Varg had left the courtyard soon after, the sound of their meal turning his stomach.

"Everyone has to eat," Røkia shrugged.

"I know, but . . ." Varg wished he could block his ears. Even with one of them missing he still managed to hear the sounds drifting in from the courtyard perfectly well. Too well.

Perhaps it is the wolf in my blood, he mused.

Sulich and his kin sat at the bench opposite Varg. Some were dark-skinned like Taras the Bull, others pale as Røkia, and others every hue in between. Some had shaven heads and braids, like Sulich, others were shaved to stubble, as Varg had been when he was a thrall. Many of them had a wariness about them, twitching at every sound or creak of the doors. Some had red weals around their necks where thrall-collars had rubbed them raw and Varg felt his own hand twitch, moving to the scars about his own neck.

"You are free now," he said without thinking.

"Aye, brother," Sulich said to him, "they are. They know it, up here." He put two fingers to his temple, "But some do not know it here, yet." The same hand moved to his heart.

"It takes time," Varg said, adjusting the neckline of his mail and tunic to show them his own scars.

A black-skinned woman nodded her thanks to him.

"Why were you locked in Jaromir's cellars?" Svik asked them.

"Jaromir and Rurik are planning a war," the black-skinned woman said. "We are Tainted," she gestured with her hand to the others around her. "They were going to use us, as weapons."

"Jaromir isn't planning anything now," Svik grinned.

"No," agreed Sulich. "He cannot hurt you now, Kesha."

"Jaromir cannot," Kesha agreed. "But Rurik can." She glanced at the doors. "We should leave."

"We will leave with the sun," Sulich said. "You are safe here tonight."

Kesha did not answer, but did not look as if she agreed.

"What war?" Røkia asked.

"To invade Vigrið," Kesha said. "To impress their father. Our father."

"Kirill, the Khagan of Iskidan?" Varg asked.

"Yes," Kesha nodded.

Svik whistled. "Those two had big stones, I'll give them that," Svik said.

There was a whirring of wings and Vesli the tennúr swept into the hall. She was labouring through the air, her wings working hard, and then Varg saw why and grimaced. The bag at her belt was huge, bulging, almost splitting.

She has filled it with the teeth of the dead druzhina.

Vesli alighted on the bench in front of Glornir and Vol.

Glornir nodded to her and stood, his bench scraping. "Bloodsworn," he said. "We have a decision to make." He looked around as a hush fell over the hall. "Orka Skullsplitter has sent us a message. We have been offered a job by Elvar of the Battle-Grim. Do you wish to fight this dragon?"

"It's your decision, chief," Svik called out. "We'll go where you point us."

"I know," Glornir said. "But it is no small thing, to make war against a god. I would know your hearts on this."

"We should fight her," Svik said. "From my understanding, the gold being offered will make us rich beyond our wildest dreams." Svik considered. "And I can dream a lot." The warriors around him laughed. "But we'll need to go and get Einar Half-Troll and Æsa first from that gods-cursed tongue-eaters' island."

Einar's cracked skull from the battle with the parasitic creature on the island off the coast of Iskidan had meant he'd been unable to travel and Æsa had volunteered to stay with him – and the children they had rescued – to heal him. Varg only hoped they were all still alive.

Glornir nodded. "Whatever we do, Einar and Æsa will be with us," Glornir said.

"*Obviously* Æsa will want to fight the dragon," Svik said to chuckles around the hall. "And Einar will most likely enjoy the challenge of fighting something bigger than himself for a change."

Others laughed and Glornir grunted. He looked around the hall, eyes settling on Edel.

"We should fight," she said, tugging on the ear of the hound sitting at her feet. "I do not think this is a problem that will go away. Best to end it now, before it grows. And I've seen these dragon-born." She pulled a sour face. "I did not like them much."

Glornir went around the room, asking each of them, leaving no one out. Eventually he reached Varg.

"Well, No-Sense?" Glornir asked him.

"I do not like the thought of fighting a dragon," Varg said.

"Only Æsa is mad enough to *like* that thought," Svik said, laughter rippling around the hall.

"But," Varg continued, "I think Edel is right. A dragon-god is not going to just go away, and if only half of the tales are true, having her loose in Vigrið is no good thing for anybody."

There were nods and heyas of agreement around the hall.

"Wise words from No-Sense," Svik said, feigning shock. "The world is indeed changing."

"And you, Glornir," Vol asked, "what do you think about going back to Vigrið to fight this dragon?"

"Her followers killed my brother," he growled. "And they have stolen my nephew. That is all I need to know."

Vesli hissed and Glornir looked at her. "Not just Breca stolen." Vesli told him. "In Vesli's hunger, she forgot part of mistress Orka's message." Her belly was swollen, and she picked a sliver of flesh from between her teeth, examined it and flicked it away. Belched.

"What did you forget?" Glornir prompted her.

Vesli concentrated. "Mistress Orka said to tell you that Uspa the Seiðr-witch is with Elvar and the Battle-Grim."

"Uspa is with them!" Vol said, rising from her chair.

"Who's Uspa?" Varg whispered.

"Vol's sister," Røkia answered.

"There's more," Vesli squeaked. "Mistress Orka said to tell you that the dragon-born have taken Uspa's son, Bjarn."

"Taken Bjarn!" Vol snarled. A dark fire kindled in her eyes.

Glornir reached out and wrapped a big hand around hers. He looked around the hall.

"It is decided, then. The Bloodsworn will fight this dragon. We leave at dawn for the *Sea-Wolf*."

Varg sat on his bed roll, leaning against the wall of the hall. The fire pit had burned down to embers, casting the hall in red-gilded shadow. Svik snored one side of him, and Røkia lay with her back to him on the other. She was twitching, her lips moving, muttering incoherent words.

Dreaming.

Varg had been having strange dreams of late, too. Of a black wolf calling to him. Of a green-eyed man staring at him from the shadows. But that was not the reason he had not lain down to sleep.

Soft footfalls and Vol stood over him.

"Are you ready?" she asked him.

Varg sucked in a breath. "Aye," he breathed.

"Follow," Vol said, turned and walked away.

Varg rose quietly and stepped over Røkia's sleeping form. Her hand reached out and touched his leg.

"I will come with you, if you wish," she said, looking up at him.

He paused a moment, then nodded. She rose soundlessly and together they passed through the hall, following Vol as she climbed onto the dais and walked through the shattered door at the back of the hall. Varg and Røkia hurried after her, seeing her disappear down a stairwell. The fire glow from the hall lit the first few steps but they were in darkness by the time they reached the corridor at the stairwell's end.

Varg whispered to the wolf in his blood and his vision grew sharper, Vol separating from the shadows ahead of him, striding down the corridor.

"*Logi*," Vol growled and iron sconces on the walls crackled into flame as she passed them. She took a torch from the wall and turned into a room, Varg and Røkia following close behind.

Jaromir's corpse still lay slumped against the bars of the hidden room, his body pierced by a thousand splinters of wood. Vol ignored him, walked to the desk in the middle of the room and rested the torch upon it. She drew a small seax from her belt and sliced a red line across her palm, clenched her fist until blood welled at her fingertips, then traced sharp lines with her blood across the desk. Sixteen lines radiating out from the torch, joined like a spiderweb. She inscribed runes at the end of each line.

"Give me your sister's lock of hair," Vol said, opening her bloodied palm.

Varg fumbled with the pouch at his belt, his heart abruptly hammering in his chest. Pulled out the lock of hair and put it in Vol's open hand.

"Your sister's name?" Vol asked.

"Frøya," Varg said.

Vol closed her eyes and clenched her fist around the hair.

"*Andi Frøya, ég kalla þig. Síðasta sýn Frøya, ég kalla þig, síðasti andardráttur Freyja, ég kalla þig, kallaður af blóði, af holdi, af hári, af beinum, kallaður af krafti Snaka,*" Vol intoned, then opened her palm and dropped the bloodied hair into the torch's flames.

Varg gasped and involuntarily snatched at the hair, and Røkia gripped his wrist. It was all that he had left of his sister.

The flames hissed and crackled, climbing higher, spreading within the boundaries of Vol's blood-stave.

The air grew colder, the room darker, only the flames visible. Varg shivered, blew out misted breath. The flames grew higher, and an image appeared within them. Seeing through someone else's eyes. They were running through woodland, trees rearing, boughs heavy with snow. The sound of laboured breathing, the crunch of footfalls through snow, running, stumbling. Varg felt an overwhelming weight of exhaustion fill him, his limbs heavy, his lungs burning.

"What is happening?" Varg hissed.

"You are seeing through Frøya's eyes," Vol said gently. "Seeing what she saw, hearing what she heard, feeling what she felt."

Voices shouting, a spike of fear in Frøya that echoed through Varg and she increased her pace, tripped over a branch hidden by snow, stumbled, righted herself, ran on. An impact that Varg felt on his back and Frøya cried out, fell to the ground, snow in her face, pain lancing through her shoulder blades. Varg felt it all, the pain, the cold, the fear.

Frøya tried to rise, got to her hands and knees, voices loud behind her, another crack to her back and she collapsed, a weight pinning her to the ground.

"Didn't think you could escape me, did you, you *niðing* little bitch?" a voice in her ear. A hand on the back of her head, grinding her face into the snow. In her eyes, her mouth, filling her nostrils, tasted pine needles and damp earth. She tried to breathe, panicking, thrashed in her captor's grip.

"Get her up," a deep voice called out, dull and muted by the snow, and she was heaved from the ground, coughing snow, pine needles, dirt and sucking in deep breaths. Spun around and slammed into a tree, her breath crushed from her body. A man's smiling face filled the flames, weathered and lined like the bark of an old tree, a raven's feather bound in his hair, a necklace of teeth or tusks hanging around his neck. Behind him other figures approaching, one taller and broader than the rest, long black hair tied at the nape and a braided black beard. He wore two seaxes in fine-wrought scabbards at his belt. Varg memorised the faces, burned them into his thought-cage.

"Three times," the black beard growled as he reached her. "Three times you've led my crew a dance. I told you no more. I've offered you wealth, a new life. Freedom."

"What you've offered is not freedom," Frøya snarled at him, thrashing and kicking at her captor, trying to bite him, her teeth clacking. A knee in her belly, driving the breath from her and she slumped, her head drooping. "I just want to go back to my *brother*," she wheezed.

Varg's heart stuttered.

The dark-haired man leaned down to stare in Frøya's eyes, and Varg saw the sparking of red flames in his pupils.

"Ungrateful, stupid," he said.

"Murderer," Frøya spat back at him.

"What shall I do with her, chief?" the weathered face said. "Reckon she should be made an example of. I can do that."

A silence, dark hair staring at Frøya.

"Do it, Brák," he said, turning his back and walking away.

A name. Varg thought. *A face I will never forget, and a name.* Other figures followed him, and Brák smiled. He struck Frøya across the mouth, Varg tasting blood, and Frøya dropped to her knees, looked up to see him opening a pouch at his belt, pulling out a long nail.

A rush of fear, and anger, new strength stirring in her blood and Varg recognised the touch of the wolf. She launched herself from the ground at the man, biting and clawing, and he cried out, fell stumbling back.

Unseen hands grabbed her arms, dragged her off Brák and he punched her in the gut, struck her on the side of the head with the butt end of the nail. All the strength emptied from her, her knees weak and she slumped in the grip of her captors.

"Hold her," Brák snarled as he cuffed blood from scratches across his cheek and she was dragged back to a tree. He grabbed her wrists and wrenched them up high, slammed the nail through her palms and into the trunk.

Varg felt himself sobbing and didn't know if it was from her shared terror or the horror he felt at her suffering. Røkia squeezed his hand.

Frøya's screams filled the room, the flames writhing and twisting.

Brák pulled a seax from his belt and hammered the nail into the tree trunk with the seax's butt end, each blow sending pain pulsing through Varg. When Brák was finished he stepped back and smiled up at her.

"Your pointless life will have a meaning now," he said. "A lesson to others, to behave."

"I pity you," she snarled at him.

He stepped closer, pulled his arm back and stabbed his seax into her belly. It felt like a punch, numb at first. Then he began to drag the blade across her stomach, slicing her open. Pain like Varg had never felt before. He staggered, Røkia reaching out and steadying him. He felt Frøya's strength leaving, her life emptying from her like a pierced sack of wine.

She sucked in one last breath.

"Varg," she whispered as her head slumped and the image in the flames faded and disappeared.

Varg fell to his knees and howled.

CHAPTER SEVEN

ORKA

A distant scream echoed through the vale and Orka looked to the treeline, allowing the wolf in her blood to sharpen her senses. She heard another scream faint on the wind, followed by the sweet scent of blood, a long pause, and then footsteps crashing through undergrowth, shouting.

She was bound with chains at the wrists, walking among four or five score prisoners taken from Svelgarth. They were far back in a long column that wound its way through a frozen vale, steep-sided slopes cloaked with pine rearing to either side. The sky was the colour of lead, bloated clouds gilt with silver.

She glanced around, saw that others were looking into the trees, too. With her wolf-eyes she could make out the angular forms and movement of frost-spiders in the tree boughs, and the shadow-smooth gliding of night-hags among the pines, both vaesen that disliked the daylight and so were clinging to the gloom. But they were all just within the treeline. The screams Orka heard had been further away, higher up the slopes and deeper into the woodland.

"You heard it, too," a voice said beside her. Biórr, her almost constant guard.

Orka said nothing, just continued to stare into the distance, but her wolf sense could see nor hear anything else. Whatever it was, whatever had happened, it was over.

"You should not be breathing," Biórr muttered beside her. "You do not deserve to be breathing."

Deserve has nothing to do with it, she thought. *And believe me, I feel the same way about you.*

"You should answer, when you are spoken to," Biórr said, and she could taste the hate and rage pulsing from him. She gave him only her silence. He wasn't worth anything else.

"I do not understand you," Biórr said and poked her in the arm with a finger.

Orka just looked at him, then looked away.

"You are Tainted, and yet you fight against us," Biórr continued. "We fight against the slavery of our kind, against those who have enslaved and tortured us for countless years. Centuries. We are fighting for our freedom. For *your* freedom. You should have joined us, not fought against us."

Orka turned her head to look back at Biórr, and gave him a cold, flat stare.

"What?" he said.

"I care nothing for the whims and wars of gods," she growled. "And you are an idiot if you believe they care anything for you."

"What do you care for?" Biórr prodded.

Orka wished this young zealot would close his flapping lips. She wanted to *make* him close his lips.

"What do you care for, then?" he repeated.

Images of Thorkel and Breca flashed through her thought-cage, memories that stirred a pain in her chest and a fire in her veins.

"I cared for my husband," she growled at him, "and *our kind* murdered him. I care for my son, and *our kind* stole him from me. You claim to be working to free the Tainted from enslavement and torture? Tell *them* that." She snorted, looking pointedly back to the group of children and prisoners.

Biórr frowned, seemed to think about that. He was young, slim and handsome, perhaps a little older than Lif, but despite the rage that leaked from his gaze his eyes made him seem older, as if he had seen and suffered much.

"That is unfortunate, I admit," Biórr said.

Unfortunate, she felt her wolf stir to anger, surging in her veins, her own rage bubbling, boiling.

"But these are hard times, and hard deeds are needed if we are going to change this world."

Orka curled her lip. "Nothing will change," she said, her voice cold, emotionless. "Perhaps you will remove a dozen tyrants and replace them with one."

"No, it will be different, we are not slavers, we will make a new world, a fair world. Lik-Rifa and Rotta will set us free," Biórr said. "That is what I am trying to explain to you. How can you not understand that?"

"You are a misguided fool to believe them," Orka sighed. "The sheep follows the farmer blindly and with trust. That does not mean it won't get eaten. Do *not* trust the promises of gods. They broke the world, remember. They did not care for the lives of anyone then, Tainted or not, they used them for their own ends and will do the same again now."

Biórr was silent as they walked on, her words silencing him for a while. She hoped that was the end of it and looked back to the treeline, wondering where Breca was, if he was safe with Gunnar and the others. Hoped that they were all together and far from here. Hoped that Gunnar would take Breca to the Bloodsworn, to Glornir.

"Perhaps you are right," Biórr said eventually, "but I do not think so. And at least we must try, or we will never know." He looked at her, the rage in his eyes dimmed now. "We did take your son, but he was not harmed. I swear. I taught him to play tafl. We treated him well."

Treated him well.

"You *murdered* his father in front of him," Orka snarled. "You took him from his home, took him from *me*."

Biórr nodded, some guilt showing. "Not me, but yes . . . Drekr is a hard man. This world has made him hard." He looked up at the sky. "Things are complicated, I admit," he said. "I just wish that us Tainted could stand together, not fight each other, that is all. Not that there is that option for you now." She saw the fire of his anger kindle and flare again. "You have killed my friends and I hate you for it," he spat. "They were good men. You have taken Myrk's eye. You have hurt and scarred Rotta. You have slain countless others. You have made *no* friends here."

Orka rolled her eyes and snorted. *I do not want them.*

They walked on in silence.

The sun was sinking behind the mountains, a soft pewter glow through the clouds, and shadows were thick in the vale when horns blew and slowly the marching column staggered to a rippling, segmented halt. Sacks and barrels of food were unloaded from wagons, fire pits scratched out in the snow, tents raised and fire kindled. Biórr set about separating the prisoners into groups of ten or twelve and food was handed out, hard bread, cold strips of beef and pork, seal and whale meat in brine.

Orka sat facing the fire, a *drengr* from Svelgarth one side of her, a woman with a child the other. She looked into the flames, slowly, gently tested the chain between her wrists, allowed the wolf to trickle through her blood, giving her new strength. She strained, muscles taut, gritted her teeth, felt a vein throb in her temple, looked for the slightest movement in the links, but the chain did not give.

The sound of hooves and riders cantering back down the column, Myrk at the head of a half-dozen dragon-born. They rode past warriors and skraeling, past a long line of wagons, most of them full with supplies taken from the sack of Svelgarth. Sitting upon the driver's bench of one of them Orka saw the white-haired man she had mauled, a child sitting beside him. She realised it was Harek, the lad who had been her Breca's friend, back in Fellur village. That felt like another life, before Thorkel was killed and Breca taken. Behind them, in the wagon bed she saw rows of children sitting, more of the Tainted who had been stolen. She recognised one of them, dark-haired, heavy-browed. Bjarn, Uspa's son.

He did not escape, then, during the chaos of our raid.

The drum of hooves grew louder, Myrk and her riders closer

and Orka blew out a long, soft breath, let her chains fall slack. She chewed on a piece of hard bread.

"I am going to kill you," Myrk said cheerfully when she saw Orka, then gave Biórr a smile, who was stirring a pot over the fire pit. "Take the stragglers from the back," she called out as she slid from her horse and took Biórr in an embrace, kissing him hard. The riders with her rode on, past the bulk of the prisoners and circling seven or eight of the stragglers from the rear of the column who had fallen behind and were being harried by skraeling with spears and whips. Most of them were injured and limping, a few children among them. They started to scream as they saw Myrk's riders, tried to run, but they were herded out and away from the column, towards the treeline.

It was almost full dark now, the glow of the fresh-lit fire pits making the shadows deeper and darker, but the wolf in Orka's blood showed her what was happening.

Shapes emerged from the treeline, frost-spiders scuttling, night-hags flowing like mist, moving swiftly towards the prisoners. Myrk's riders and the skraeling stabbed with spears at the prisoners to stop them fleeing back towards the warband, their screams rising, laced with panic. Then the first of the frost-spiders was on them, leaping, legs wrapping around a woman, both of them crashing to the ground. A gurgled scream which dwindled to a bubbling groan. Others in the group beat at the frost-spider but then more of the vaesen were on them, leaping, biting, and the night-hags swept into the group. A child broke from the circle and ran wailing back towards the column, a frost-spider speeding after her, leaping and fangs biting as the two of them fell to the ground. The child screamed.

The *drengr* beside Orka surged to his feet and took a step towards the prisoners, but Myrk kicked at his ankle and he stumbled, a hiss of steel and her seax was at his throat.

"One more step and you will join them," she hissed at the *drengr*. Orka could see the knife-edge of indecision war within the warrior.

"Sit, Hagal," a voice said: Dagrun, Jarl Orlyg's son, who was sitting on the far side of the fire pit, glowering at Myrk.

"Listen to your chained chief," Myrk said with a smile, "or don't," she shrugged. "The frost-spiders are hungry."

With a ripple through his body the *drengr* stepped back and sat down by the fire.

The screaming was over now, a few whimpers drifting on the wind, all the prisoners were down, wrapped in web, and the frost-spiders began to drag them across the snow, back towards the treeline.

Orka looked to Biórr and caught his gaze.

"A fair world and *freedom*," she said to him and spat on the ground.

Biórr looked away.

"We are at war, and they are our enemy," Myrk said with a shrug, looking at him. "They have fought against us, have enslaved us. They have done far worse to us."

"Those children?" Orka said.

"They would come to, when they were grown," Myrk said, brows knitting into a scowl. "Besides, we need to move fast. They would slow us down, and feeding them to the vaesen is easier and faster than foraging." She looked at the *drengr* who had stood. "At least they are being put to good use, rather than dropping and freezing where they lie. Even their teeth will be eaten by the tennúr."

"You think that is a comfort to us?" Dagrun said.

"I hope not," Myrk smiled.

Orka's wolf-ears heard new sound from the woodland, and she turned to look, saw a line of figures emerge into the vale. She recognised Brák leading his crew of hunters and saw they were carrying something. Her heart lurched in her chest.

Do they have Breca?

Myrk hailed them as they crossed the vale, ice-reamed snow crunching under their feet, and they changed their course, heading towards her. Orka saw there were about a dozen with Brák, a mixture of skraeling and humans. There were no bound captives being led. Two of the skraeling had bodies slung across their shoulders.

The thud of hooves and Rotta came riding down the line on a big bay gelding. He reined in but stayed mounted.

"What news, Brák?" Rotta asked the hunter as he drew near. "Have you caught more runaways?" He nodded at the bodies the skraeling were carrying.

"No," Brák grunted. "Show them," he said to the skraeling, and they dropped the bodies on the ground.

A man and a woman, both dead. The man's throat had been cut, a neat slice made by sharp iron, crusted blood black in the moonlight. The woman's face was latticed with black veins, like a cobweb of ink beneath her skin, the eyes bulging in pain and mouth open, tongue black and swollen. Orka felt her heartbeat rise. She recognised that handiwork.

Spert.

She looked to Rotta and saw that he realised it, too, a hand involuntarily rising to his own face, where Spert's venom had wreaked such pain.

"No sound or sign of who did this, the sneaky *niðing* troll-humpers," Brák growled. "First I knew of them was Svea's screams."

The hunters have become the hunted.

Orka felt a smile twitch her lips at that, felt a flush of pride that Spert and whoever had slain the other warrior had outwitted these hunters. But she felt a flicker of fear in her belly, too.

Is Breca with them? They should have been far from here by now.

She looked to the mountain slopes, black as night, and knew that her crew were out there somewhere, and a glance at Rotta showed that he knew that, too.

CHAPTER EIGHT

GUÐVARR

I wish I was back in Fellur Village, Guðvarr thought again as he followed Jarl Sigrún out of their longhouse, summoned for the second time this day by Lik-Rifa. This time a tennúr had come to give them the dragon-god's summons, and it was whirring in the air before them now, flying forward, then sweeping high and swooping back to them, urging them on, into the courtyard and up the steps, into the ruined feast hall. They stepped up onto the dais where Helka had once sat, walked into a corridor and past Helka's chambers, the stars bright above where the roof had been torn away, and then they were descending steps into a passageway lit with flickering torches that Guðvarr remembered none to happily. It had been the secret passage to Skalk's Galdur tower, a place of nightmares that had brought Guðvarr much pain. But now Skalk was gone, and Lik-Rifa had settled there.

The tennúr disappeared as the corridor reached a set of steps, and then Sigrún and Guðvarr were stepping into the entrance chamber of the tower, torches in sconces flickering around the vast room. Guðvarr remembered there had been some Galdur-spell over the entrance, that had frozen him, held him fast until Skalk had uttered the Galdur-spell that released him.

It is easier to gain entrance now.

Guðvarr walked into Sigrún's back, as she had abruptly stopped.

"What—" Guðvarr said, then he saw why.

Serpents were writhing across the ground. Hundreds of them. Some huge, their bodies thick as tree trunks, heads and jaws broad and powerful. They moved slow and sluggish across the floor, the hiss of scales on stone. Others were small and fast, heads weaving. The whole floor moved with them, as if the ground were formed by the intertwined bodies of serpents. They climbed stone columns like ivy, even the staircase that wound upwards in a circle around the tower. As he looked higher, he saw something glinting. Glittering ropes criss-crossed the shadowed eaves. Then he saw the movement of limbs, saw the reflection of fire light in clustered eyes.

Frost-spiders. He resisted the urge to turn and run. *I take it back. This is a far greater protection than some snivelling Galdur-spell,* Guðvarr thought with a shiver.

The only space clear of the snakes was the centre of the chamber, where Lik-Rifa sat, reclining in a high-backed chair sipping mead from a fine-tooled cup. A table in front of her was filled with food and drink. Ilska and Drekr were there, as was Glunn Iron-Grip. A skraeling, grey-skinned and thick-muscled, also sat at the table. Guðvarr thought it was a female, but he was not sure. A handful of guards were spread around the great gates at the far side of the chamber.

"*Slepptu Þeim,*" Lik-Rifa said with a wave of her hand and the serpents hissed and writhed before Sigrún and Guðvarr, parting so that a path appeared before them. Sigrún stepped confidently along it and Guðvarr followed cautiously.

The tennúr that had led them here whirred and hovered over Lik-Rifa, alighting on her shoulder. The dragon-god smiled and stroked its rat-like head, then reached into a bowl on the table and threw something into the air. The tennúr's wings snapped out and it leaped into the air, snatching whatever it was and popping it into its mouth. Guðvarr heard crunching and grinding.

"Sit, eat," Lik-Rifa said as Sigrún and Guðvarr reached the table.

As he sat Guðvarr looked into the bowl that the tennúr had eaten from, and saw that it was full of teeth, many of them still bloody, slivers of flesh hanging from them. He tried hard to keep the horror from his face.

"You honour us," Sigrún said, and Lik-Rifa smiled. "And fine company you keep," Sigrún added, gesturing to the serpents all around.

"They feel my presence, cannot help but come to me, the sweet things," Lik-Rifa said, almost a purr.

Guðvarr remembered the horror he had felt when he had walked into Skalk's chamber, where all manner of vaesen had been imprisoned; faunir, a Näcken, hyrndur, other creatures.

This is far worse. He glanced at the serpents and shuddered, tried to keep the grimace from his face and filled a plate with food, oat-wrapped cod and pickled herring, spit-roasted lambs' hearts stuffed with walnuts and spinach, buttered turnips and soft cheese, then poured himself a cup of ale from a jug and sat back in his chair, looking around the table at his companions.

Jarls, dragon-born, and a god, I am in fine company, he thought. *Things seem to have turned out far better than expected. It was not so long ago that my greatest hope was to live another day, and avoid a hyrndur eating its way through my chest. And the odd thing is, I feel at home here, feel like I was born for this. Born for great deeds, for high honour and battle-fame.*

The skraeling filled a plate and put its face into it, snuffling and snorting, eating like a hog.

You do not deserve to sit here, among us heroes and great people, Guðvarr thought.

"I like it here," Lik-Rifa said, looking around the chamber.

I'd like it more without the moving floor of serpents, or the spiders that would like nothing better than to drain me of my blood, Guðvarr thought. *But apart from them, this is quite fine.* He wiped his nose with the back of his hand.

"I am pleased with the taking of Darl," Lik-Rifa said. "And more than pleased that I have destroyed my sister." Her face twisted in a savage, gleeful snarl. "Let me tell you, that has been a few hundred years coming, and something that I have thought on often during my imprisonment." She smiled, the fresh cuts on her face twisting. A scab opened and leaked a thin trail of blood down one cheek. "And I thank you for your part in that, Sigrún and Guthlaf."

"Guðvarr," Guðvarr corrected absently.

"What?"

He flushed, as his aunt dug him in the ribs with her elbow, and added quietly, "Apologies, my queen, my name, it is Guðvarr, not Guthlaf."

Lik-Rifa scowled, her brows knitting, and there was a ripple through her face, her jaws jutting, a hint of teeth growing, and Guðvarr felt a moment of total, all-encompassing terror.

She is going to eat me.

But then her expression shifted back into a thin smile.

"Guðvarr, *of course*. We cannot have the wrong name remembered in the saga that the skálds will sing, can we?"

Guðvarr breathed a sigh of relief. *Skálds, sagas, my name is going to live on forever.* He could not stop a smile spreading across his face.

"Ilska and Drekr have suggested to me that I invite you all here to discuss the way forward," Lik-Rifa said.

"The way forward?" Sigrún said. "Whatever you wish of us, we shall do. We are honoured to serve you, Queen of all Vigrið."

Lik-Rifa dipped her head.

"But what is the way forward?" Guðvarr asked.

"Slaying my brother, Ulfrir the wolf," Lik-Rifa said with a smile. "We must find him and kill him."

"There are other things that need to be done, my queen," Ilska said. "Stepping stones towards the goal of finding your brother. Towards your final victory. We should consolidate your power, move against those who would stand against you."

"So you keep saying," Lik-Rifa said and gave a disinterested sigh. "Orna is dead. The upstart Helka is dead," she said, sipping from her cup.

"It was my honour to slay her for you, Lik-Rifa the magnificent," Sigrún said.

Lik-Rifa smiled, a twitch of pleasure touching her lips and eyes.

"And I am told that Helka's eldest son and heir is dead," Lik-Rifa added. She frowned. "What was his name?" she asked Ilska and Drekr.

"Hakon, my queen," Drekr rumbled. "He is dead, I saw his body."

"I . . . I slew him," Guðvarr said.

"Yes," Lik-Rifa said. "You did well . . . Guðvarr," she said, humour in her eyes. "I must confess, I was not sure about you when first we met. You seemed weak, a coward, a tool to be used and discarded." She smiled at him with a sharp-toothed grin. "But you have done exceedingly well."

"My thanks, my queen," Guðvarr said, bowing his head. "I only wish to serve you." *As long as there is no pain involved. And, to be brutally honest, only if it serves me.*

"But not all of your enemies in Darl died yesterday, my queen," Ilska said. "Helka's daughter Estrid still lives," Ilska said matter-of-factly. "She fled and took with her the remainder of Helka's *Ulfhéðnar* thralls, and some of Darl's *drengrs*. With Helka and Hakon dead, Estrid will now think of herself as the rightful Queen of Darl and may well seek to rally those who oppose you."

"She is queen of NOTHING," Lik-Rifa roared, dragon-jaws shimmering, and Guðvarr fought the urge to stand and run from the room.

"No, my queen, Estrid is no queen. But she can still pose a threat. Can be a thorn in your foot."

"Then she should die," Lik-Rifa said.

"Yes," Ilska said.

"And Jarl Orlyg escaped, with his Tainted thralls and two ships crews of *drengrs*," Drekr said. "His longships were seen leaving Darl's docks."

"He will most likely go home, to Svelgarth," Ilska added.

"Where my brother, Rotta, will give him a warm welcome," Lik-Rifa sniffed.

"Skalk the Galdurman fled, too," Guðvarr said. "I had him under my sword, but then Orna fell . . ." he shrugged. The truth was that Yrsa, Skalk's oathsworn *drengr*, had Guðvarr at the point of her blade when Orna fell, but that would not sound anywhere near as heroic in a skáld's saga-song.

"Perhaps Skalk is with Estrid?" Glunn Iron-Grip said. "I saw them in the courtyard together, after Orna fell." Guðvarr was pleased to see that Iron-Grip looked almost as uncomfortable as Guðvarr felt, his eyes continuously flickering from the serpents slithering close to his feet to the still and unnerving stares of the frost-spiders above them.

"That would be his most likely course of action," Ilska said. "Fleeing rats tend to stick together."

"Well, if you think they are so important, can someone find this Estrid and Skalk and kill them for me?" Lik-Rifa said.

"Yes, my queen, of course," Ilska said. "But first we must find them."

"Then find them," Lik-Rifa said with a wave of her hand.

"We would help you with that," Sigrún said. "My nephew and I."

Would we? Guðvarr thought, shifting in his seat.

"It will be hard to track them, many fled Darl, in all directions," Ilska said.

"If Brák were here, he could track them easily, but he is with Rotta," Drekr said.

"Heya," Ilska agreed. "We must use our wits, think like them. At first they would have just fled, and fast. Death was in the air, and they would have wanted to get as far from here as possible, as quickly as they could." Ilska tapped the arm of her chair with long fingers. "But once they felt they had some distance and safety," she shrugged. "Perhaps they would travel south, to Liga, or west, to Snakavik. Helka was on the verge of war with Jarl Störr at Snakavik, but in the past there was talk of a marriage between Estrid and Störr's son, Thorun."

Ilska took a bite from a piece of pickled herring on her plate, then drank from her cup. Every movement was sharp and efficient. "It would all depend on whether she will decide to run or fight. If she decides to run then Liga would make more sense, it is a port, and she could leave Vigrið and disappear into Iskidan. But if she decides to fight, well, after Helka Jarl Störr is the greatest power in Vigrið, so it would make sense for her to unite with him."

"She would *dare* to fight against me, after she has seen my power?" Lik-Rifa said.

"She would," Guðvarr said, remembering Estrid drawing her

blade on him yesterday. She had almost bested him. It had been an unpleasant and unexpected shock.

"Good," Drekr said. "Better that they turn and fight now, rather than hide under a rock, where they can grow stronger."

"I need her found," Lik-Rifa said, "and this upstart Galdurman, who thinks he can enslave a god, thrall the Tainted and work powerful magic." She snorted.

"Would you hunt them from the skies, my queen?" Ilska asked.

Lik-Rifa frowned at that.

"Ulfrir is out there, somewhere. I have been tricked by him before, my brother is sly and wolf-cunning, you know." She drummed a finger on her cup. "No, I will rest here a while and recover from my contest with my sister, perhaps wait for Rotta to join me. Before I travel alone I must discover where Ulfrir is hiding." She looked around, scanning the shadows as if he may even now be creeping up on her. "He will be scheming and plotting, not sitting idle, of that I have *no* doubt."

Guðvarr did not like the thought of a giant wolf plotting war against them.

"I would be honoured to hunt Estrid and Skalk for you, my queen," Glunn said.

"No," Drekr said. "Yesterday you fought against us. We will not send you after those who were your allies just one day gone."

"I have sworn Lik-Rifa my oath, I would *not* betray you," Glunn said, a twist of anger in his lips at the insult.

"Oaths are easy to say, harder to keep," Drekr growled, fixing Glunn with a red-eyed stare that sent a shiver down Guðvarr's back. "You will stay close, prove yourself to us here. I am sure there are more of Helka's supporters lurking here in Darl. You shall root them out."

"As you wish," Glunn muttered, eyes flickering to Lik-Rifa. Guðvarr thought he looked none too pleased with the prospect of staying close to the dragon.

"Let me hunt these *niðings* for you, Mother-Maker," the skraeling grunted through a mouthful of food.

"If Ilska thinks you are needed to capture these pathetic humans," Lik-Rifa said.

"I do, my queen," Ilska said. "Krúsa, go with Sigrún and Guðvarr. Hunt this Estrid and Skalk together. Sigrún, take your *drengrs*."

Me! Us! Guðvarr was not sure if he was pleased or upset. Pleased to get away from this nest of vipers, yes, but heading back into danger, most definitely upset. After yesterday he was hoping for some time to recuperate from the stress of betrayal and battle. It was an exhausting business. In truth he'd spent much of the afternoon thinking about paying the whore Vilja a visit, down at *The Dead Drengr.*

If she wasn't stabbed, eaten, crushed, eviscerated or killed in some other equally unpleasant manner yesterday.

Krúsa grunted and shrugged, as if she did not care if Sigrún and he came or not, then she went back to eating like a hog from a trough.

"My queen," Sigrún said, "it shall be our honour."

"Krúsa, take your clan with you," Ilska said, "and whoever or whatever you think you will need." She gestured to the vaesen around her, tennúr, trolls and frost-spiders. "Any of our queen's children will be happy to go with you."

"Yes, do as Ilska says," Lik-Rifa said.

"Yes, Mother-Maker," the skraeling grunted, hardly pausing from her eating. She lifted her head and grinned at Sigrún and Guðvarr, showing a mouthful of fangs and half-chewed food.

Just perfect, Guðvarr thought with an internal sigh. *We get to take the monsters with us.*

CHAPTER NINE

ELVAR

Elvar lowered her sword and let her shield hang loose at her side. Steam rose from her in a cloud amid the ice-crusted cold, sweat prickling on her skin. She was in the weapons court of Snakavik, training with Grend and, for a few brief moments, she had forgotten all about gods, oaths, responsibilities and the thousand tasks she had to get through before the evening meal. Winding steps carved into the bone of Snaka's skull led down to the plateau where the weapons court stood, a steep-sided cliff dropping away from it to the fjord far below. Distant lights glimmered within the eye sockets of the serpent, the town of Snakavik existing in its perpetual gloom. Beyond the rim of the fjord cliffs the sun was a pale, diffuse glow on the horizon as it sank into the sea, making the fjord of Snakavik glow as if it was threaded with molten silver. Snowflakes fell gently about her, tingling on her skin.

"Good," Grend grunted, lowering his own axe and shield. He was wearing a sea-blue nålbinding cap on his head and mittens on his hands and wore his coat of mail over a thick woollen tunic. Stepping forward, he leaned his shield against a low wall.

Elvar took her cap off, wool with a thick band of otter fur, and ran a hand through her sweat-drenched hair.

"It is strange, being back here," Elvar said. "So many memories, even just here, upon this small square of earth and bone." She tapped the ground of the weapons court with her heel.

"Heya," Grend agreed. "The memories of this place are good." He looked around the weapons court, a faint smile twitching his lips. "Of me training a savage war-hound." He looked up the steps that wound back up to the fortress, saw the silhouette of walls and the jagged remains of Jarl Störr's feast hall. "The memories up there, though . . ." He shook his head, looked at her with bright shining eyes. "Being there, it brings back your mother's pain, how he treated her." His face twisted, part grimace, part snarl. "I do not like being up there. In that hall, those chambers."

"He is dead," Elvar said, a fierceness that she did not realise was there spilling from her lips.

"Aye," Grend nodded, "and that is good. But it does not take away the pain, does it?"

"No," Elvar said, tugging on the troll tusk that hung about her neck. She had been surprised at that, had expected to feel euphoria at her father's death. To feel the satisfaction of justice, of vengeance. But that had not happened. If anything, there was a regret. At the words unsaid between them, that could never be said now.

"No point dwelling on it," Grend murmured. "There is nothing we can do to change it now." He looked up at her, sat straighter.

"Here, I have something for you," Grend said, and reached round to his back, pulling an axe from his belt. He held it out for her.

"I fight with sword and shield," she said, with a frown.

"Aye, you do, but you can never have too many sharp edges on you. And perhaps you will find yourself in a situation where your shield has been splintered, or you only have your weapons belt to hand. You should learn to fight with sword *and* axe."

"I am clumsy with an axe."

"Aye, but there's something you can do about that. It's called practice. And," he smiled lovingly, as a parent over their child, "this is no ordinary axe."

Elvar looked more closely at it. The shaft was longer than usual for a hand-axe, and thinner, and the head was smaller, with an iron hammer as a counterweight to the blade. The lower half of the haft was wound with a leather grip, a thread of silver wire running through it. Elvar took it from Grend and gasped at the lightness of it. The wire seemed to tingle in her palm. She chopped at the air, felt how easy and flowing it was to use.

"It is perfectly balanced," she said, taking a slice at the bough of a tree that hung over the wall. It carved through the bough as easily as a knife would cut through skyr. "Where did you get it?"

Grend's smile broadened. "I found it among the treasure we have brought from Oskutreð. It is . . . remarkable."

Elvar ran a thumb across it and whistled; it had shaved a neat slice of her skin.

"You don't think it is the Fate-Maker?" she whispered.

"Berser's axe? No," Grend shook his head, though he frowned for a moment. "No," he repeated. "That was a long-axe, and it is said to hold the souls of twelve of his *Berserkir* children." He looked suspiciously at the axe in Elvar's hands. "Can you hear them whispering to you?"

Elvar dipped an ear closer to the axe blade, but all she could hear was the raucous calling of gulls and distant waves lapping in the fjord far below. She laughed and shook her head.

"No, not the Fate-Maker, then," Grend said, "but this one could be its little brother or sister. One thing for sure, it is as sharp as sickness."

Elvar smiled. "Teach me how to use this axe, then."

Grend smiled back at her.

Elvar woke with her heart hammering, the echo of a booming voice ringing in her ears, so loud she felt it reverberating in her chest. For a moment she did not know where she was as she struggled to her feet, then memory returned in a flood.

My father's chamber. She reached for her weapons belt slung over a chair and strapped it over her *brynja*, which she had grown accustomed to sleeping in. She had taken it from the battle plain about Oskutreð and it weighed less than her linen under-tunic. Her fingertips brushed over the axe Grend had given her, and hefted her war shield from where it leaned against a wall, slinging it over her back.

"THIEVES," a booming voice bellowed, timbers shaking, dust

falling, and Elvar ran, crashing through a door into a corridor as she drew her sword. Orv the Sneak was there, standing guard over her chamber with a spear in his fist, alongside a *Berserkir* named Thorguna. She was standing with twin axes in her fists, growling. Grend emerged from another door, pulling his axe from his belt, Gytha behind him leaping up from a cot and slithering into her ring mail. Another door to a chamber was pulled open and Ulfrir appeared, Skuld filling the doorway behind him.

They all fell in behind Elvar as she ran down the corridor, threw her shoulder into another door and burst into the ruin of her father's feast hall, the first thing to hit Elvar's senses the sweet stink of charred flesh.

Hrung was there, on his pedestal of stone.

"*THIEVES*," he bellowed again, mouth as wide as a shield.

She scanned the room, saw a charred body lying on the ground before the doors to her treasury, flesh blackened and steaming in the cold, one arm draped over a wooden chest. Soft falling snow-flakes hissed into steam as they settled upon it.

My treasure, Elvar realised, looking at the chest.

She ran to the treasury, the doors smashed open, one hanging from its hinges, and peered inside.

It was empty. The other chest filled with her gold and silver from Oskutreð was gone, along with the bags of silver and jewels her father had collected. There was another scorched body lying where the chest had been.

"They took your gold," Hrung said to Elvar as she ran to the fallen bodies. She kicked one over, flesh falling away in clumps from the blackened corpse.

Uspa's Seiðr-spell.

Other figures swarmed into the hall from different directions and ran to Elvar. Uspa with Berak, Sighvat and Sólín, more of the Battle-Grim, a score of Jarl Störr's *drengrs*, now sworn to her.

"Where are Hrut and Siða? And my *drengrs*?" Elvar said, referring to the two *Berserkir* and the warriors she had left guarding the treasury.

"There," Hrung said, looking in the direction of the shadowed mound. Sighvat went to it, pulled on an arm to reveal a man with his throat cut.

"Hrut," Berak said, stalking over to his fallen comrade. He knelt beside him. "His weapons are still in his belt." He looked at the other dead, all piled in a mound. "None of them drew a weapon." He looked up at Uspa. "How?"

"Seiðr," Uspa said, sniffing the air like a hound. "It is all around us, like a malignant fume."

"Yes," Hrung said, "but they did not realise you have some Seiðr of your own." He chuckled. "Uspa's Seiðr-spell on the chests cooked some of them," he continued. "I reckon it taught them to think twice before they try to steal your hard-won gold. Though they still managed to take one chest, used that man's body to push the chest into a sack. Resourceful, and persistent, even if they are thieves. And then they ran for it."

"How many?" Grend asked Hrung.

"Oh, *now* the silent one speaks to me," Hrung said.

"How many?" Grend snarled.

"No less than thirty, no more than forty," Hrung said with a sniff.

More *Berserkir* arrived, ten or twelve of them, a snarling mass of iron, fur and braids.

"Who are they?" Elvar said, leaning as close as she could to study the fallen bodies. Silver armbands and leather had melted into the flesh and bone.

"The Wave-Roamers," Orv said, kicking over a scorched shield, the sigil of a ship's sail partially visible.

"Ingvild," Elvar snarled.

Gytha tied her hair back.

"After them," Elvar said and strode through the shattered wall of the feast hall and out into the shadow-dark street.

Sighvat caught up to her as Elvar broke into a run.

"Where are we going? Shouldn't we be tracking their trail first?" he grunted.

"I know where they're going," Elvar said.

"Where?" Sighvat huffed.

"The docks and their *drakkar*," Elvar grunted. "That's what I'd be doing."

Sighvat smiled and grunted admiringly.

"Gytha," Elvar called over her shoulder and the warrior caught up with her. "Close the gates."

Gytha reached for a horn banded with silver hanging at her belt and blew, Elvar hearing it answered somewhere ahead of them a few heartbeats later, fluttering through the snow-dark, but along with it she heard the clash of steel and fractured screams.

Elvar shrugged her shield from her back and, hefting it, ran on.

She turned a corner in the street and the fortress gates came into view, light and shadow flickering across them from flame-filled iron braziers. The gates were open, bodies on the ground, *drengrs* rushing from the ramparts. Elvar reached them and slowed, her *Berserkirs* flowing around her. She looked about her. The ground was littered with bodies, most of them *drengrs* with Snakavik's serpent-scribed shields.

They were caught unawares. No one expects enemies to attack from within the gates.

Grend crouched and lifted a shield from a body, blue, a *drakkar*'s sail scribed upon it. He looked at Elvar.

"Hrung was right," Elvar said. "Ingvild's Wave-Roamers."

They ran on, breath misting in great clouds, more *drengrs* joining them. Snow crunched as they thundered along the wooden walkway that led from the fortress across a plateau to the stairwell that led down through Snaka's serpent skull into the town of Snakavik. They passed mercenary camps on either side lit with flickering fire, Elvar noticing there were fewer than when she had arrived at Snakavik.

Dragon-hunting is not for some of them, then. She had expected some to leave, but was pleased by the numbers that had remained. She saw flashes of staring faces, heard shouted calls from either side as she ran, heard the thud of feet as more warriors joined them from various camps, caught a glimpse of Hjalmar Peacemaker with a handful of his crew running to join her, and then she saw the entrance to the skull-steps, the stairway that led down through

Snaka's skull into the town of Snakavik. Torchlight revealed more bodies on the ground, more of her *drengrs* overwhelmed by the rush of Ingvild and her Wave-Roamers. She slowed and glanced at the corpses, ran on.

They are my warriors, mine to avenge.

Still she ran on, saw Grend on one side of her, Ulfrir on the other. His face was grim, amber eyes blazing with reflected torchlight as they descended into the tunnel. Smoke from torches and whale-oil braziers was thick in the passage, stinging her eyes, and ahead Elvar heard weapons clashing, screams echoing. They passed more dead, a few of Ingvild's among them, and then Elvar was bursting out from the tunnel into the town of Snakavik. The orange glow of torch and hearth light spread beneath her, leading down to the fjord, where black water lapped at a hundred longships. The pathway down through Snakavik to the docks was marked by torchlight, a winding, serpent-like constellation of stars. Elvar glimpsed a huddle of figures flitting through the glow and disappearing around a bend in the street, saw a pale face look back at her, black braids flying, her lower jaw a mass of swirling tattoos.

Elvar snarled and sprinted on, leaping down steps three at a time, slipping on timber walkways, her breath heaving in her chest. She skidded and slammed into a wall, Ulfrir reaching out to steady her, and then the ground was levelling, the stink of fish and salt growing as they approached the docks, turned a corner and saw Ingvild's crew hurtling down a pier, a *drakkar* at the end of it heaving with people readying the ship to sail, the oar mast being raised and slotted into the mast hole, sail still furled, oars heaved from the central racks.

Elvar saw a fair-haired woman with sword and shield turn and look back. She said something to the woman next to her, the dark-haired, tattooed woman Elvar had glimpsed earlier.

Ingvild, the traitorous bitch, and her Seiðr-witch.

A handful of words was exchanged and the Seiðr-witch was turning, one arm gesturing in the air, shouting words that Elvar did not understand.

Movement on the dock caught Elvar's eye, something slithering across the timber, and she slowed, stumbled to a halt, her crew rippling to a standstill around her. A serpent, black-skinned and long as a man. It moved across the dock, raised its head and looked at Elvar, hissed at her, venom dripping from its fangs. More movement, the shadows churning, and more serpents slithered onto the dock, ten, twenty, more and more of them, filling the space between Elvar and Ingvild's crew until the whole of the dock was seething.

Ulfrir stepped forwards.

"Pathetic," he muttered. "*Farnar, aumkunarverðir vinir*," he snarled with a dismissive gesture and the serpents were suddenly evaporating, hissing into so much mist and smoke.

Elvar blinked.

"What?" she muttered.

"They were a Seiðr-spell," Uspa said beside her. "A glamour, an illusion."

With a shriek Skuld's wings snapped open and she was leaping into the air, wings beating as she drew the sword at her waist, and she swept higher as Ingvild's Seiðr-witch raised her hands. Runes sparked to life as she traced them in the air with a black-nailed finger. Beside Elvar, Uspa stepped forwards, snarling and spitting out her own Seiðr-words.

"*Binddu varir hennar*," Uspa cried out and at the feet of Ingvild's Seiðr-witch tendrils of mist rose up from between the timber planks, coiling about her like vine on a tree and wrapping around her mouth, solidifying and pulling tight. The Seiðr-witch mumbled, staggered backwards, clawing at her mouth, but the mist just parted for her fingers and reformed. A shriek from above and Skuld came hurtling down, a glitter of ice as her sword swung and the Seiðr-witch fell backwards, crashed to the docks, blood erupting.

Elvar strode forwards, Grend and her crew moving with her.

Ingvild was shouting orders at her crew, a dozen on the ship, more on the docks. Two warriors carrying a hemp sack between them were clambering into the *drakkar*. Ingvild turned and saw the Seiðr-serpents evaporate and her Seiðr-witch fall. She stood there a moment, looked at Elvar and her warriors.

"Shield wall," Ingvild bellowed.

The warriors on the dock turned, shields clattering and slamming together, forming up into three lines. Iron glinted as axes and spears were hefted.

"Kill them," Elvar snarled, breaking into a jog and around her the *Berserkir* roared, thundering forwards. They overtook her and as they ran Elvar saw them change, muscles swelling on backs and shoulders, hunching, eyes blazing. They growled and frothed, axes rising, and swept forwards like a wave of muscle, claw and iron. She saw Ingvild's shield wall brace before impact, then there was a crash that shook the timber beneath Elvar's feet, making her stumble. As she righted herself, she saw that the shield wall was gone, bodies spinning through the air, bodies on the ground, *Berserkir* hacking about them with a savage fury. Here and there pockets of combat raged, some of Ingvild's shield wall regrouping, more warriors leaping from the *drakkar* back onto the dock, joining the battle. Elvar saw three of them skewer a *Berserkir* with their spears, but he only snarled and hacked at the spear shafts with his axe, splintering two of them.

Elvar hefted her sword and shield and ran into the carnage, bodies strewn about her, blood slick on the timber boards. She saw a knot of Ingvild's Wave-Roamers and ran at them, skidded and leaned back to avoid a stabbing spear that hissed over her shoulder, stumbled and fell crashing into the spear-holder. Her momentum knocked his legs out from beneath him and they fell in a tangle, rolled, spear and shields snaring, Elvar trying to stab with her sword but getting no power behind it. They snarled and spat, a wash of fetid breath as the man tried to bite her and Elvar smashed her head into his nose, came to a halt and she scrambled free, rose to one knee and saw Grend and Berak descend upon the spearman. Axes chopped and blood sprayed, a short scream ended with another hack of Grend's axe.

Elvar stood, caught a blur of movement to her right and turned, sword swinging, a warrior leaping at her, a woman chopping with a bearded axe. Grend bellowed and leaped, slammed his shoulder into her and they fell together and rolled. Elvar followed them, her sword stabbing down and the woman screamed, arched her back.

Elvar ripped her blade free and raised it for another strike, but the woman was flopping, Grend climbing to his feet. Blood sheeted his face from a cut across his forehead.

"You're hurt," Elvar said and he touched the wound.

"A scratch," he grunted.

"Good scrap, this," Sighvat grinned as he joined them, his axe red and dripping, shield as big as a table.

The three of them strode on together, combat raging around them, Elvar stabbing with her sword, punching with her shield, Grend hacking with his gods-touched axe, cleaving through mail, flesh, bone, Sighvat sending people crashing to the ground with blows that would fell trees. Elvar glimpsed Ulfrir, still in his human form, though he was growling and slashing about him with long-taloned hands. A handful of warriors were gathered around him, amber-eyed men and women snarling, protecting his flanks and carving into any who dared attack him. Sólín Spittle fought alongside a group of the Battle-Grim, her Oskutreð spear-head glowing silver as it carved through a warrior. Hjalmar Peacemaker was bellowing in rage through his spittle-flecked beard, his Fell-Hearted warriors bunched behind him. Some were sheathing their weapons to drop to their knees and strip the dead.

And then Elvar saw Ingvild. She was stood over the body of one of Elvar's *drengrs*, a shield in one fist, bearded axe in the other. Fair-haired with a fine nasal helm, a coat of blood-spattered mail and silver rings upon her arm.

"She's *mine*," Elvar snarled at Grend and Sighvat, stepping forwards, shield held in front, sword tip balanced on the top rim. Ingvild grinned at her and took a step to her right, away from Elvar's sword arm. Then Ingvild was darting in fast and chopping high, Elvar moving to block, realising it was a feint as Ingvild's wrist twisted and the blow slipped low, around her shield and scoring a line across Elvar's ribs, the rings on her *brynja* holding. Elvar stepped back, annoyed with herself, felt her ribs throbbing from the blow, growled and moved in, sword hidden behind her shield, stabbing at Ingvild's axe-arm. The woman stepped back, knocked Elvar's sword away with her shield, began to smile, but then Elvar's shield rim was punched into her jaw and she stumbled back, spitting blood. Elvar followed fast, movement from her left and she twisted, saw a spear-wielding warrior lunging at her. Sighvat stepped in and hammered the man to the ground.

"You weren't invited," he rumbled as he swung his axe down.

Elvar stepped after Ingvild, who was setting her feet and raising her shield, blood on her lips. Elvar swung high and low, both blows blocked by Ingvild's shield, wood splintering, then Ingvild was stepping close, hooking the beard of her axe over Elvar's shield and stepping away, pulling and twisting. A sharp pain in Elvar's wrist and she hissed, her grip loosening, and her shield was ripped from her grip.

Elvar stepped back, glimpsed a crowd around them, formed in a half-circle, Skuld, Ulfrir, many of the Battle-Grim, her *Berserkir* all snarling and prowling. The battle was done. But if she backed away now, didn't prove herself the better warrior – how would they ever believe her fit to lead them against a dragon-god. Berak stepped forwards.

"No," Elvar barked at him. "She's mine."

"That will be your last mistake," Ingvild said through bloodied lips.

Elvar's left hand reached for the axe Grend had given her. It slipped from her belt into her fist and she set her feet, spun her sword in her fist.

"Come then, thief," she growled at Ingvild.

Ingvild grinned and shuffled forwards, shield in front of her, axe raised high.

Elvar turned, side on, left side facing Ingvild, her small axe raised to head height, sword held low. As Ingvild stepped closer Elvar pivoted on her heel, chopped with her sword and Ingvild blocked it, struck with her axe, but Elvar's own axe snaked out and met Ingvild's blade. A twist of Elvar's wrist and her axe head hooked around Ingvild's weapon, locking them together, a rotation of Elvar's arm and wrist and she was dragging Ingvild's axe head low, pulling her enemy off balance as she twisted her arm, steering Ingvild's axe beneath the lower rim of her shield and at the same time swinging her sword high in a looping chop, coming down between Ingvild's neck and shoulder. Shattered links of mail and blood sprayed as Elvar ripped her sword free, Ingvild falling to her knees. The sword swung again, clanging off Ingvild's helm, denting it and sending her crashing onto her back. She tried to roll away but Elvar's blows were too fast now, the small axe chopping down into Ingvild's face, a scream, the axe rising and falling, blood and teeth spraying, rose and fell again, and again, rage flooding Elvar.

Eventually she paused, her chest heaving, breath loud in her ears and she blinked sweat out of her eyes, looked around.

All were staring at her.

"She stole my treasure," Elvar said, spitting blood onto the floor.

"Remind me never to take anything from you without asking first," Sighvat boomed.

CHAPTER TEN

VARG

Varg ran, sweat dripping into his eyes as he splashed across a shallow stream. A sandy road wound ahead of him, mountains rearing either side, dotted with scrub and twisted hawthorn. The sky above was blue and cloudless, the sun a hammer beating down upon him, his coat of mail heavy upon his shoulders. He did not care, was hardly even aware. In his head he was in a cold land, snow all about him, watching as his sister was nailed to a tree. He saw her killer's face, weathered and sharp-featured, grinning as he hammered the nails in, grinning as he gutted her.

I will kill you, Brák, he thought, his teeth grinding and lips pulling back in a snarl.

"Slower, brother," a voice said behind him.

"Huh?" Varg grunted and looked around. Svik was riding upon a fine roan mare.

"Slow down," Svik said, "the horses cannot keep up."

A shout behind them and Varg saw Sulich raise an arm, pulling his horse from a trot to a walk, and then stopping. A line of riders slowed behind him, all of them gathering along the stream that Varg had just crossed.

"Thank the dead gods, I'm starving," Svik said, clicking his tongue and guiding his horse around, riding back towards the stream. "Come on, brother," he said, looking back at Varg, who had slowed and paused. "Let's go fill our water bottles and eat some cheese."

"Røkia?" Varg said, looking ahead again, to where the road twisted around an outcrop of rock and disappeared.

"She'll be back soon," Svik said. "Come on."

Varg grunted and broke into a slow jog back towards Sulich and the stream, where riders were dismounting, letting their mounts drink and squatting to splash water into their faces and refill water bottles tied to belts and saddle horns.

Varg reached the stream and untied his own water bottle, unstoppered it and raised it to his lips. Realised it was empty.

When did that happen?

Svik dismounted and led his horse to the stream, letting it drink while he rummaged in a saddle bag, pulling out a wedge of cheese wrapped in linen. He grinned at Varg.

They sat in silence beside the stream, Varg filling his water bottle and sipping at it, Svik contentedly slicing slivers of cheese and chewing. He offered some to Varg but he shook his head.

"Starving yourself to death is not going to help you put Brák Trolls-Turd in the ground," Svik said with a frown, shaking a slice of cheese at Varg. He scowled but took the cheese and chewed. His stomach growled. He had not realised how hungry he was.

Footsteps and Sulich joined them, squatting in his lamellar plate and drinking deeply from his water bottle.

"We should reach Ulaz soon," Sulich said.

"Aye," Svik agreed. He looked at the people milling at the stream, all of Sulich's Tainted kin that they had found in Jaromir's prison. They were clothed in kit taken from Jaromir's *druzhina*, lamellar plate, horse-hair plumed helms, curved swords and bows in cases at their hips. "Are you sure about this? Are *they* sure about this?"

"There is nothing for them here," Sulich shrugged. "Nothing good, anyway. If they stayed, they would be hunted down, put to the question about Jaromir's death, then killed or returned to the life of a thrall. This way they have a chance, at freedom, at life."

"Fighting a dragon?" Svik said with a raised eyebrow.

"A chance, I said," Sulich muttered. "And dying free is better than a lifetime on your knees." He scrubbed a hand across his shaved head and tugged on his long braid. "Besides, it is their choice, and that is worth more than gold to them."

"Aye," Varg grunted. He had been a thrall all his life. It was less than a year since he had slain his owner, Kolskegg the farmer, and fled his farm, and yet the memories were dimming, superseded by the bright light of the Bloodsworn. Life with them had changed everything. If only Frøya had been given the same chance.

"Can they fight?" Svik asked Sulich.

"Of course they can fight," Sulich said. "We are all children of Kirill, Tainted or not. Riding and bow-work began for us before we could walk."

Svik nodded. "And they will fight for Glornir? For us Bloodsworn?"

"We have just given them the gift of freedom, as Glornir gave to me," Sulich said. "They will be loyal unto death, as will I."

Svik reached out and took Sulich's wrist.

"I do not doubt it, brother."

Varg heard footsteps and looked up, realised that Svik and Sulich had not heard anything. It was his wolf-ears. He stared back up the pass and saw Røkia appear around a curve in the road. She covered the ground quickly and splashed across the stream. She was not breathing heavily, just a trickle of sweat running down her forehead and cheek giving any indication that she had been running since dawn.

"Ulaz is close," she said.

Varg ran to Røkia's left. They were well ahead of Svik and Sulich's column of Tainted riders. Varg could hear the rhythmic thud of their hooves but the sounds and scents of the seaport of Ulaz were filling his senses and overwhelming everything else. Brine, fish, rotting food, spices, the screeching of gulls and lapping of waves, and behind it all the thrum and stench of human habitation swept over him like a great wave on the whale road. And then they were turning a corner and Ulaz spread before them, Varg stuttering to a halt. They were higher than the port, the road they were on winding down through foothills to the port. Varg blinked at sunshine reflecting from countless whitewashed houses and red-tiled roofs built upon the east and west banks of a brown, sluggish river that spilled out into the sea, masts and sails bobbing on the swell and ebb of the bay. Here and there groves of green trees and pools sparkled, punctuating the endless lime-washed houses.

Røkia shifted her course and came to stand alongside him. They stood in silence awhile, Varg just staring at the immensity of Ulaz, almost overwhelmed by it. Despite the storm of sensations, though, Frøya returned to his head, her screams ringing through him as she was nailed to the tree.

"Grief," Røkia said, not meeting his eyes. "It gnaws at the soul."

Varg swallowed.

She turned to face him. "But it can be a weapon, too."

Varg looked at her. "You speak as if . . . you know?"

"Aye," Røkia nodded, her face like carved stone. "My mother, murdered before my eyes by my village, because she was Tainted." A muscle twitched in her jaw. "I ran. I can still hear her screams as I fled from them. From her."

"How old were you?" Varg asked her.

"Nine, perhaps? Maybe ten?" Røkia shrugged.

Varg reached out and touched her hand. She did not pull away.

"I used my grief, felt it turn into a white-hot rage in the forge of my soul. I hunted them all down eventually, some in groups, some one by one. Five years it took me." She sighed, her lips a thin line. "Killing them did not bring my mother back, nor did it ease the pain of her loss. But . . ." she leaned her head left, then right, her neck clicking. "It felt good." She looked at him. "Do you understand what I am saying to you?"

"Aye," Varg nodded. "Revenge may not bring Frøya back – but seeing those *niðings* in the ground . . . that may bring me some peace."

Varg walked through the streets of Ulaz, the wolf in him overwhelmed by every sense. All around him was noise, street vendors shouting to sell their wares, people haggling, moneylenders sitting with their birch-bark tally sticks and strongmen behind them with clubs and dour faces. Everything that could be sold was here, and more besides. Pots of honey and mead, seal skins, walrus ivory, deer hides, beaver and fox pelts, salt in sacks, shark meat in barrels, troll tusks, trestle tables filled with jewellery carved from amber, jet and ivory, enamel pins, silver pendants, iron brooches. Weapons and armour of all description. All around him fires were burning in braziers, meat turning on iron spits, fat dripping and sizzling. And it was not just the goods for sale, it was the variations among the people. Here and there Varg saw others like him, clearly from Vigrið, looking familiar with their beards and braided hair, woollen tunics and breeches. One man with different coloured eyes and a shield slung over his back looked at Varg and looked away. But there were many others around him with shaven heads, thick braids and drooping moustaches, like Sulich, dressed in kaftans and baggy breeches, and others with clean-shaven faces, giving them the appearance of children, and others with oiled and gleaming hair and silver rings hanging from their beards, their clothes bright and dazzling. All shades of skin were swarming around him, from milk-pale to teak-dark.

They moved on, Sulich and his riders dismounting and leading their horses by the reins. The streets narrowed, the sound ebbing, the noise and scents rising to a new level as they stepped into another courtyard.

Blood. The wolf inside him growled.

People were gathered around huge pits carved into the ground, waving arms and shouting and screaming as if their village were being burned down. Varg changed his direction and elbowed through the crowd, coming to stand on the rim of one of the pits.

Two bull trolls were fighting within it, gripping each other with heads down, trying to gore one another with their tusks. They were standing almost entirely still, muscles bunched like cord, veins bulging and squirming. They were both naked apart from a woven rope tied around each one's waist, one red, one yellow.

One of the trolls managed to hook a tusk below the jawline of the other, gave a savage wrench of his neck and there was an explosion of blood, the other troll stumbling back and crashing into the pit's curved wall. The first troll raised its head and let out a deafening bellow, then ran at his injured foe.

"Stop gawping like a hooked fish," Svik said, grabbing Varg's arm, "we need to find Glornir."

They had descended quickly from the foothills beyond Ulaz and were now marching as straight a path as was possible through the maze of wide streets and open courtyards towards the docks, where they were to meet Glornir and the rest of the Bloodsworn upon the *Sea-Wolf*. The plan had been for Glornir to sail ahead of Sulich and his riders to have time to purchase a boat at Ulaz capable of taking horses across the whale road to Vigrið. In Jaromir's chambers at Valdai Svik had found three chests full of silver and gold, which Glornir said should be given to Sulich's Tainted kin, as some recompense for Jaromir's treatment of them. They had spoken among themselves, then found Glornir and told him they wished to travel with the Bloodsworn, if he would take their oath, to fight this dragon. They had tried to give the chests back, but Glornir had said he would use it to buy them a ship, which had made them stand taller with pride.

Svik steered Varg away from the pits and their crowds and they continued through the streets of Ulaz, the smell of brine and fish growing as they drew nearer the docks. Røkia led them to a street that followed the river and they passed a wide bridge that crossed over to the east bank. *Druzhina* stood guarding the bridge before a wooden gateway, allowing a heavily laden cart to cross over. Svik slowed and stared, frowning.

"What's wrong?" Varg asked him.

"There have never been gates and guards to the east bank before," Svik said quietly. "And look," he pointed at the docks on the east bank. They were bristling with hundreds of sleek-lined longships and wider-bellied transport ships.

Røkia and Sulich came to stand beside them.

"Well, they are not here for the food and good gambling at the fighting pits," Røkia said.

There was the clatter of hooves behind them and they turned to see a double column of *druzhina* riding down the street. A man rode at their head in gleaming lamellar plate, head shaved with a thick blond braid looped across his shoulder and a dangling blond moustache, his helm and sword hanging from his saddle.

"It is Rurik, Jaromir's brother," Sulich hissed.

"Go," Svik said, "keep your head down and get your Tainted to the docks."

"What are we going to do?" Varg asked as Sulich hurried away.

"Just watch," Svik said.

Rurik rode to the gates, and Varg saw a man riding at his side. Lean as a half-starved wolf, his head shaved, beardless, dark tattoos mapping his lower jaw, his eyes sunken in shadow. A thick iron collar bound his neck.

"Who is that?" Varg whispered.

"Rurik's rune-wielder," Svik answered. "As Jaromir had Iva. They wield Seiðr much like Vol." Svik nodded at the longships on the east bank. "Every longship will have its own rune-wielder, to protect them from Sjávarorm serpents and other dangers while they sail the whale road."

Varg nodded, looking back to Rurik. *Druzhina* rode behind him, gleaming in their coats of lamellar, curved swords and bows at their hips, spears held upright in saddle cups, the iron tips glinting like stars and the crowds in the street parted before them. Guards on the bridge shouted orders and the gates opened, Rurik and his *druzhina* riding onto the bridge and crossing over in a thunder of hooves.

Svik stood watching for a while as they crossed the bridge, waited until Rurik reached the far side and then he led his men north, along the bank of the river towards the eastern docks.

"Come on," Svik said eventually, and led Varg and Røkia back towards the street.

"What's going on?" Varg asked as they slipped into the crowds.

"The invasion of Vigrið seems to be much more advanced than Glornir thought," Svik said. "That fleet looks almost ready to sail."

"What shall we do?" Varg asked.

"Tell Glornir and let him worry about it," Svik answered with a smile, although it did not reach his eyes.

A man stepped through the crowd, a shield slung across his shoulder, Varg realising it was the man he had seen earlier, with the different coloured eyes. He stopped and looked at Varg and smiled, as if they were old friends.

"I've been looking for you," the man said.

Others stepped into view, drawing axes, levelling spears, some with shields in their fists, painted with a golden eye.

As the crowd in the street scattered Røkia and Svik took a step away from Varg, half turning and reaching for their weapons, then hands were grabbing Varg from behind, a bag dragged over his head. The wolf inside him howled and he felt its strength, began to struggle, ripping free from someone's grip. He heard Røkia snarl, heard a man scream.

A crunch and white lights exploded in his head, his knees buckled and he was falling.

CHAPTER ELEVEN

BIÓRR

Biórr looked up at Myrk where she sat astride him, her breeches bunched around her ankles, her coat of mail glistening with dew, the flesh of her thighs pale as milk. She blew out a cloud of misted breath and sighed. Her eyes were closed and, for a moment, the lines in her face were softer, carefree, even the puckered scars around her ruined eye did not look so deep. She sucked in a long breath and made a contented sound, then opened her eyes and smiled at him.

"Ahh, I *needed* that," she breathed. "You have always been a good hump," she said, a grin stretching across her lips and, even though she smiled, the hardness returned to her features. She wriggled off his hips and rolled onto the ground, pulling up her breeches.

"Well, I'm glad to have been of service," Biórr said, reaching to drag his own breeches back up and tie them off as the cold began to bite at his goose-prickling flesh.

"Oh, you have, I would recommend you to my friends, if I had any left alive," she said.

"Are we not friends?" Biórr asked her.

Myrk leaned over on one elbow and looked at him, her bold smile fading, and she stroked one finger down his cheek to his stubbled jaw.

"We are," she whispered, "and more", then bent and kissed him on the lips. It was different from her normal kiss, soft where it was usually hard, tender where it was usually passion and fire. Then she was standing and buckling on her weapons belt over her coat of mail, her brother Drekr's two seaxes that she had retrieved from Orka hanging from it, one across the front of her hips, one across her buttocks. She stood over Biórr and offered him a hand.

He took it and she heaved him upright. He adjusted his coat of mail and cinched his weapons belt tight, bent to retrieve his cloak and threw it across his shoulders, tying it. They were standing among tall reeds beside the bank of a river, mist swirling off the water and around their ankles. The Bonebacks reared to the north, the rising sun gleaming pink and gold on the snow-capped peaks, forests of pine draping the mountain slopes like a shadowed cloak of black feathers. In a valley between the river and mountains Rotta's warband was stirring. Smoke was rising as fires were kindled, pots of water bubbling, porridge being stirred. Behind Biórr there was a soft splash and he looked over his shoulder, saw two spertus crawl from the water onto the riverbank and disappear among the mist and thick reeds. He shuddered, remembering the same species had stabbed Storolf with its poisonous sting, and then vomited a black pestilence into Rotta's face.

"Come on," he said to Myrk and made his way through the foliage along the riverbank, being careful to move away from where the reeds rustled as the spertus scuttled through them. He did not want to get stung by mistakenly treading on one of the nasty little creatures.

The snow was only a thin crust underfoot now, as they had travelled further south and turned west to follow the curl of the Bonebacks towards Darl, though the ground beneath the snow was hard and cold as iron. As they approached the rear of the column a handful of infant trolls ran laughing and squealing from the camp and leaped into the river, crashing like boulders, spumes of water exploding about them. Biórr smiled at the sight of it, then he saw Red Fain leaning on a long-axe.

"I'll see you after," Biórr said to Myrk and she nodded distractedly, no doubt thinking on the tasks at hand, before she marched off towards the head of the column.

"You need to be careful, sneaking off beyond the guard-line," Fain said, frowning up at the mist-shrouded trees.

"I'm always careful," Biórr said.

"I'm sure Brák's lads thought the same, right up to the moment when they got their throats slit or faces stabbed by that poisonous little monster. And those skraeling that were our rearguard probably thought the same, until they were butchered as they walked." That was fresh in Biórr's mind because he had found them. It had been the end of yesterday's march, when the daily ritual of the trailing prisoners being given to the frost-spiders and night-hags was supposed to happen. Myrk had ridden down the column with a handful of her dragon-born kin, ready to herd the stragglers towards the treeline. But there had been no sign of any stragglers, or the skraeling rearguard. Biórr had mounted a horse and ridden back along their route, and found the bodies of a half-dozen skraeling, some slain with weapons, others bearing the black marks of the spertus' poison, and the stragglers were nowhere to be seen. Myrk had been enraged.

"I was with Myrk, she's fiercer than any vaesen, and she has sharp ears," Biórr said.

"I'm sure she has, when she's not . . . distracted." Fain reached out a big hand and squeezed Biórr's shoulder. "I just don't want to lose you the way I lost Storolf," he growled, taking his eyes from the trees to hold Biórr's gaze.

Biórr nodded and patted Fain's hand on his shoulder.

"I'll be careful, old man." He rubbed his hands together in the cold and blew misted breath into them. "Anything to report?" he asked.

"A quiet night, apart from Harek's snoring," Fain said, his words slurring as he spoke through the swelling of his cheek. The cuts were healing where Orka had ripped at his face with her wolf-teeth, now mostly scabs and red-swollen skin. "I had to kick him to make him stop." He nodded his white-bearded jaw at the young lad, who was now busy stirring porridge in a bubbling pot.

"He's a good lad," Biórr said. "Took some stones to stand there and let us know Orka and her Bloodsworn were in the camp."

"Aye, it did," Fain grunted, shifting his weight on the long-axe he was leaning upon, "doesn't change the fact he snores like a sow."

Biórr grinned. "Orka?" he asked, his smile fading.

"She's not moved all night, woke up in the position she went to sleep in," Fain said with a grunt.

"You might be taking this guarding prisoners' job too seriously," Biórr smiled.

"She killed my son, nearly did for me. I'm not going to wake up to find she's slaughtered half our troops and walked out of here," Fain said.

"No chance of that," Biórr muttered as he looked around the camp, saw guards spread around them, skraeling in small clumps along the riverbank, dragon-worshippers in a loose line between the camp and the treeline, saw bull trolls standing still as boulders, the whirr of tennúr-wings above them and the odd movement of frost-spiders among the boughs of trees. "Nothing's getting in or out of this camp." He shifted his gaze to look over the small knots of prisoners huddled around fires, saw Orka sitting a little apart from Dagrun, Jarl Orlyg's son. She sat with her legs pulled up, flecks of amber in her eyes as she stared at the flames in the fire pit before her, her bound hands resting upon her knees.

Horns blew from the head of the column along the vale, signalling the time to break camp was close.

"Best get some porridge into you and some heat into your bones," Fain said and led Biórr towards Harek and the pot he was stirring.

Biórr gave a small bow to Rotta as he strode back along the column and fell in beside him. They had just begun marching again after stopping for a brief noonday meal. Rotta looked at the wagons with the Tainted children sat upon them, and to the rows of prisoners taken from Svelgarth. There were fewer of them now. More than a hundred had set out from Svelgarth, but there were no more than fifty of them left now. The frost-spiders and night-hags were eating well most nights.

"The children who fled, they are no longer bound," Rotta remarked.

"No, lord," Biórr said. "I do not think they will try to flee again, so I removed their bonds."

"And how have you managed that?" Rotta asked him.

"A little kindness," Biórr shrugged, looking at Bjarn, who sat beside Harek on a wagon. "The odd game of tafl, and three meals a day." After Orka's raid during the sack of Svelgarth many of the children had fled. Biórr had found Bjarn unconscious and half-buried beneath the wheel of a wagon that had been smashed to kindling by Rotta as he had changed into his rat form, thrashing in pain from the poison of the spertus.

"I have always tried to make my sister understand that there are other ways to achieve your goals besides stabbing, beating or eating people," Rotta said. "Unsuccessfully, so far, I must say. But you are doing well."

Biórr felt a flush of pride and walked a little taller.

Something drew Biórr's attention towards the treeline, his rat-sense tingling, which usually meant danger. He slowed his pace and stared, saw that Rotta was looking, too. Snow had begun to fall gently, following them out of the north.

Biórr narrowed his eyes and focused his sight through the soft-falling snow, strained his hearing, could not see or hear anything, no sign of movement, but he felt it. A prickling of his hairs, as if he were being watched.

Rotta called to a tennúr and sent them to investigate. A blur of wings and they were speeding over to the trees, flitting among the boughs.

"What is it?" Biórr murmured.

"I'm not sure," Rotta answered with a frown. "But something is out there, watching us."

The tennúr broke from the canopy, in a puff of snow and flew back towards them.

"Nothing there," it squeaked.

Rotta scowled at the treeline, but Biórr knew the tennúr was right, his rat-sense had calmed.

"Her crew?" Biórr asked, nodding to Orka.

"Most likely," Rotta said, tearing his eyes from the treeline to look at Orka. "And how is the wolf spawn?" he said, glaring towards Orka where she walked slightly apart from the other prisoners. She wore a woollen tunic and an under-tunic, had refused the cloak Biórr had offered her when he had taken her coat of mail from her.

"She is stone," Biórr muttered, remembering his conversation with her a few days gone. "There is no give in her."

"Is there not? Well, she has information that I need. I must find out where my brother is lurking." He frowned, looking at the treeline. "But Brák has not delivered the tool I need to bargain with her, despite them being so close I can almost smell them." He scowled at the shrouded slopes and tugged on his neatly groomed beard. "Perhaps I should learn from you and try your tactic."

Biórr raised an eyebrow at him.

"Kindness," Rotta smiled sharply, and walked towards Orka. Biórr followed.

"Things do not have to be like this," Rotta said to Orka as he fell in beside her. She just looked straight ahead, as if he had not spoken. "My father created a beautiful land for us to live upon, just look at it," Rotta continued in his finest honeyed tones. "Snow-capped mountains, rich forests, flowing rivers, all of it crafted for us. It does not need to be a battleground. It could be a garden." He looked at Orka and received more silence. A scowl twitched his lips, but then he was smiling again. "I could take those chains from you. I want to take those chains from you. You are descended from a god, descended from my brother." He sucked in a long breath. "Granted, he is not my *favourite* family member, but that does not mean that you and I must be enemies. This world calls you "'Tainted'. You are not 'Tainted', you are blessed. And I am fighting now so that you and all like you are given your freedom."

Orka looked at him then, her eyes flickering amber, and then she looked away.

Biórr remembered his conversation with Orka, and how he had said something similar to her.

"*Do not trust the promises of gods,*" she had said to him. "*They broke the world, remember. They did not care for the lives of anyone then, Tainted or not, they used them for their own ends and will do the same again now.*" Those words had crawled around inside Biórr's head, refusing to stay silent.

"You could *join* us," Rotta continued. "I could take those chains from you, give you back your weapons, and you could join our fight against the oppressors of your kind, of our kind. Or you could just leave, go, and find your son and walk away from us in peace, as friends, knowing that if you ever needed me, that I would be here for you, my friendship gladly given."

Orka looked up at the tree slopes, then at Rotta, though Biórr saw her eyes flicker to Red Fain and the long-axe he carried.

Rotta held out his open hand to her. "Take the hand of friendship, end this pain, live in peace with me. And see your son again. All you have to do is tell me what you know about my brother. Tell me where he is he and your life can change immediately, and for the better. What say you?"

Orka stopped and turned to face Rotta, looked him in the eye a long moment.

"No," she said, then turned and began to walk on again.

A muscle twitched on Rotta's face.

No! Biórr heard Rotta's voice inside his head. *You say no to me! A god!* But outwardly Rotta's face appeared calm, unfazed.

"Friendship is a rare gift, and seldom offered twice," Rotta said to Orka.

She ignored him.

A chuckle from one of the prisoners walking nearby, Dagrun, Jarl Orlyg's son. Red Fain cuffed him with the butt end of his long-axe and the man stumbled, other prisoners around them shifting and growling, battered *drengrs* whose oaths still steered them.

"Easy," Biórr said, stepping close to the prisoners with his spear in his fist and they shifted.

"Do nothing," Dagrun said and the *drengrs* calmed.

A voice shouting from the treeline drew all their attention.

Brák emerged from the shadows into the snow, a handful of his crew following him, frost-spiders scuttling around them. Biórr counted four of Brák's crew where there had been twelve. All of them were bloodied, two of them limping. Brák and another carried a sack tied to a spear shaft between them. Something inside was bucking and writhing.

Rotta smiled and looked at Orka.

"Well, now," he grinned. "What have we here?"

CHAPTER TWELVE

VARG

Varg became aware of sensations, sounds, the smell of old onions and his breathing loud and magnified inside the sack tied over his head, his feet scuffing the ground, firm hands under his arms, half carrying him, half dragging him. A rhythmic, thumping pain in his head. He opened his eyes, but it was just darkness and for a moment he panicked, thought he was blind, but then realised it was the sack.

"This way," a muffled voice said and Varg was changing direction, heard hinges of a door grate and then the sound changed again, footsteps thudding on wooden floorboards. The hands holding him disappeared and he fell to his knees, heard grunts and thuds around him and the sack was being pulled from his head.

He was inside a wooden building, daylight leaking through gaps in the timber, the sound of lapping waves suggesting they were in a warehouse close to the docks. The man he had seen in the streets sat on a bench before him, a warrior draped in mail with a shield slung over his back, axe and seax at his belt, greasy fair hair tied at his nape, his beard thin. He stared at Varg with pale eyes, and Varg noted that he was not smiling now. A dozen or so warriors milled behind him, more behind Varg, others coming in the door. Someone threw a bundle of belts and weapons onto the table, Varg realising they were his, Røkia's and Svik's.

There were footsteps behind him and Svik and Røkia were

dragged in and thrown to the ground beside Varg. Both their hands were bound. Svik was unconscious. Røkia snarled at everyone in the room, blood on her lips and chin.

"She's a wild one," a voice said, a warrior stepping around into Varg's sight. He was supporting a man with half his face torn and shredded. "Look what she did to Unlaf."

Unlaf groaned and he was helped to a chair.

"At least Unlaf's still breathing, that little shite there has spilled Idrun's guts all over the street," another warrior said, pausing to give Svik a kick in the ribs.

"Enough," the man sitting in front of Varg said. "You all knew the job, knew who Varg travelled with. That's why you're getting paid so well."

"Who . . . who are you?" Varg mumbled, his mouth feeling slow, unresponsive.

"Name's Sterkur," the man said. "You don't know me. But you do know *him*." He pointed to a shadowed corner of the room. Varg allowed the wolf loose in his blood and his vision sharpened, the shadows shrinking, and he saw a man leaning against the timber wall. Tall and broad, a thick snarl of black beard on a weathered face, a scar down one cheek and carving through his lips. He wore a fur-trimmed hat and embroidered wool tunic, a seax hanging at his belt. He stepped out of the shadows into the half-light, his lips twisting into what passed for a smile.

"Leif Kolskeggson," Varg mumbled.

"Did you think that I would not find you? That I would allow you to live your life after you have murdered my father?" Leif said. His voice shook with barely contained fury.

"I did not murder him," Varg said. "He cheated me, lied to me."

"You are a thrall," Leif spat, leaning forwards, spittle spraying. "My father's property, my property. We could lie to you, beat you, kill you, and we are within the law to do so."

"Varg is no thrall," Røkia said, and spat a mouthful of someone else's blood on the floor.

Leif took another step closer and Sterkur put a hand out to stop him.

"Not so close," Sterkur said. "They are bound, but . . ."

Røkia smiled at them.

"You are all dead men walking," she said.

Svik groaned and moved, his eyes opening. He rolled onto his knees, put his bound hands up to his head and realised his hair had been torn loose from its braiding.

"You *niðings* are going to pay for messing my hair up," he snarled, looking the angriest Varg had ever seen him.

"See," Røkia laughed. It was unsettling, even to Varg.

"Did you think your new friends would protect you from me?" Leif said, looming over Varg. "They offer hard words, but they are on their knees, beaten and bound."

"Bound, yes," Svik said. "Beaten?" He smiled and shook his head.

Varg looked up at Leif and remembered the years of beatings, the mocking, the starvation, and how Leif had looked at his sister. The wolf in his blood gave a low-rumbling growl.

"I have long hoped we would meet again," Varg said, cold as winter.

Leif blinked at that. His mouth twisted in a sneer and he put his hand to the seax at his belt.

"You have come a long way, waited a long time for this moment," Svik said, looking Leif up and down.

"I have," Leif grunted.

"You should have combed and braided your beard, at least," Svik said, shaking his head and tutting. "A shame to die not looking your best."

"It is you who will be doing the dying," Leif said.

Voices passed by outside the warehouse and Sterkur stood, put a hand to the axe at his belt. All in the room were still, violence hanging in the air.

The voices passed by.

"It is not the voices you hear that should worry you," Svik said. "You will not hear Glornir when he comes for you, until it is too late. You have all sealed your fate." He looked around at the roomful of warriors and frowned. "Drunk, or insane?" he said.

"What are you talking about?" one of the warriors growled.

"Were you all drunk when you agreed to come after the Bloodsworn, or are you all insane?" Svik said. He looked closer at Sterkur.

"How much mead had you put down your throat when Leif rattled his purse of silver under your nose?"

"Just making a living," Sterkur said.

"Dying is not much of a living," Svik shrugged.

"Enough of this," Leif said, looking over his shoulder at the sound of people walking past the warehouse. "We should take them to your longship, Sterkur, and kill them there."

"Best to kill the other two now," Sterkur said. "Carrying one to the ship is less conspicuous than three." He drew the axe at his belt. "Hold her," he barked, and hands were grabbing Røkia, hauling her towards Sterkur. Varg launched himself forwards and bit into a woman's leg, a scream and others rushed to drag him off, blows raining down on him.

He was thrown to the floor, pinned down, cheek pressed tight to the timber. A shadow loomed over him and he saw a boot and the blade and shaft of a long-axe.

"Which one first, chief?" a voice said.

"Kill the bitch," Unlaf said from where he was still sitting, blood leaking through rents in his face.

"No, kill the little shite who slew Idrun," another voice said.

"You should kill me," Svik said. "Because if you do not I shall hunt you all down and kill each and every one of you arselings." He smiled pleasantly at them. "And I shall finish with you, you pale-eyed, goat-humping turd," he ended, smiling up at Sterkur.

"Easy choice, then," Sterkur said. "Kill him first."

Svik was dragged from the ground and hauled over to the table, his head slammed down onto the wooden boards, arms and shoulders held tight. The woman with the long-axe stepped close and raised the axe high.

"Wait," Svik shouted, and the axe hovered.

"If I am walking the soul road this day, at least let me go with all my fine hair intact. Hold it away from my neck, where this bitch will be cutting."

A chuckle from some of the warriors.

Svik looked at Sterkur. "We are all warriors here. Do not shame me."

"Do it, Norv," Sterkur said and a dark-haired warrior with a drooping moustache stepped in front of Svik and took hold of his loose hair, pulling it up over his head to reveal the flesh of his neck. Norv gave a yank on the hair, slamming Svik's head down onto the table.

The axe rose again.

"No!" Varg shouted but it was too late, the axe head was falling.

Svik's muscles bunched and he gave a savage wrench backwards. Norv was not expecting it and was dragged forwards, the axe slicing down, chopping into Norv's wrists, severing his hands and burying the blade deep into the table top. Norv screamed, holding up his severed wrists, staring at them, blood jetting. Svik twisted in the grip of those who held his arms, both of them loosening their hold for a moment and Svik kicked the legs out from beneath one of them, dragging them both tumbling to the floor.

There was a moment of stunned silence, then Sterkur was bellowing and warriors were descending upon Svik.

Røkia nudged Varg, jutted her chin at the far wall.

Varg's wolf-ears heard a snuffling sound and then a growl.

He smiled.

CHAPTER THIRTEEN

ORKA

Orka stared at the sack carried between Brák and one of his crew. Brák limped towards them, frost-spiders scuttling either side, skraeling and dragon-cultists falling in around them, escorting them towards Rotta. For Orka the world faded, everything blurred and muted apart from the sack, which heaved and bunched.

She refused to name him, or even think the name, refused to give voice to her greatest fear. Despite the venom of the frost-spiders having cleared her body days ago – she felt ice in her veins.

Rotta used his god-voice to bellow for the warband to halt and it came to a stuttering stop. Riders cantered back from the head of the column, snow falling more heavily now, Myrk leading a handful of her dragon-born kin.

"What is it?" she said as she dismounted.

"Brák returns to us," Rotta said, his grin still wide, "and it appears he is bringing us a gift."

He looked at Orka with smug satisfaction.

Warriors and vaesen parted to let Brák through. He came limping towards Rotta, blood-stained bandages wrapped around his head and one thigh. His remaining crew members looked like they had fared worse.

Brák turned the spear and stabbed it into the ground before Rotta, drew a seax from his belt and sliced the sack open, spilling its contents onto the ground.

It was Spert.

Warriors and vaesen ringed the spertus.

"Mistress Orka," the vaesen said, looking up at Orka. His face was bleeding black blood, and there were wounds in his dark carapace that leaked ichor-like fluid.

"Spert," Orka breathed, both relieved that it was not Breca in the sack and horrified that it was Spert.

"Ah, the traitor," Rotta said.

"Spert no traitor," Spert hissed, looking up at Rotta with his battered, melted-candle face. "Spert loyal." His sting twitched and Rotta took a step back. Spears, axes and swords were levelled at the vaesen.

"You are a traitor," Rotta said. "Your Mother-Maker called you, and you did not come. Worse, you fought against her. Fought against all of us." Rotta gestured, taking in the multitude of vaesen all around.

"Spert make promise, Spert keep promise," Spert rasped.

"What promise?" Rotta asked.

"To mistress Orka. To protect master Breca."

"Well, Breca is gone, only Orka here now, so why are you still fighting for her?" Rotta said, frowning.

"You would not understand," Spert wheezed, coughed up a glob of black blood.

"I am a god," Rotta sneered. "My understanding of all things is far greater than your pathetic comprehension, you miserable slug with legs, so please indulge me. Tell me."

Spert looked from Rotta to Orka, met her gaze.

"Friendship," Spert said quietly. "Mistress Orka been good to Spert."

Rotta frowned, a ripple passing through his face, then laughed. "Ha, well, let us hope that the feeling is mutual." He gripped the spear Brák had stabbed into the ground and pulled it free, held it over Spert's body, then looked slowly to Orka.

"So, friend of vaesen, tell me where my brother is."

Orka looked from the spear to Rotta to Spert.

Fractured memories of life before Thorkel was slain, before Breca was taken. Of life at their steading. She had always thought of it as just the three of them, but really it had been four. Spert had been part of their life. Always there. Always protecting them. Like family.

"Tell nasty rat nothing," Spert said viciously.

Rotta raised the spear higher.

"Last chance," he said.

Orka felt her lips pull back in a snarl, the wolf within her straining to be set free, to rend and tear and kill.

The spear fell.

"Snakavik," Orka shouted, and the spear stopped. The gods were nothing to her. Ulfrir, Rotta, they could fight each other to the death, and she did not care. But Spert. He was family.

"Snakavik?" Rotta said, holding the spear quivering above Spert's body. "Where this Jarl Störr rules?"

"Yes, lord," Biórr said.

"And why is my brother in Snakavik?" Rotta asked.

"I do not know," Orka shrugged.

"Tell me what you do know, or this nasty little vaesen dies."

Orka sucked in a long breath, aware that her knowledge had been keeping her alive, had given her time. And now that time had run out. She looked at Spert.

But now my knowledge is keeping him alive.

"Ulfrir travels with the Battle-Grim and their chief, Elvar Troll-Slayer," Orka said. "It was her wish to go to Snakavik, I do not know why."

A sharp inhaled breath close to her and Orka saw Biórr frowning.

"Elvar is chief!" he said.

Myrk looked at him, her eyes narrowing.

"Elvar is daughter to Jarl Störr," Myrk said slowly, her eyes still on Biórr, "perhaps she wished to enlist her father's aid in the fight against us. Jarl Störr is powerful and has many *Berserkir* thralls."

"Hmm," Rotta breathed. "And where exactly is this Snakavik?"

"West, lord," Biórr said. "It is a fortress and town built within and upon the skull of your dead father."

"A dark lair for my wolf-brother to hide within, I imagine he thinks," Rotta murmured. He blinked and looked back at Orka.

"Is there anything else?" he asked her.

"No," Orka said. She tensed, waiting for the spear thrust that would inevitably come towards her.

"Good, well, my thanks," Rotta said. He wiped a snowflake from his cheek, then stabbed the spear down, into Spert's back, punctured his carapace, on through his body, the spear blade plunging deep into the cold earth, pinning Spert. The vaesen screamed and spasmed, head and tail arching, sting stabbing at the spear shaft, legs scratching at the ground. Rotta twisted the blade and left the shaft quivering and with a long, stuttering breath Spert sagged and was still.

"No," Orka screamed and launched herself at Rotta. She reached him so fast that even Rotta was taken by surprise. He stumbled back as Orka tore at him, the wolf in her blood surging through her, claws and teeth ripping and tearing. He screamed, blood spraying as she gouged his face and bit into his arm, crushing mail links and piercing flesh. A blow across her shoulders that she distantly felt but ignored, another across her lower back, more raining down upon her as Rotta fell and she rolled on top of him, then hands were grabbing her and heaving her from him, pulling her snarling away. She spun in their grip, ripped her arms free and raked a face with her claws, smashed the chain between her wrists into a nose and a woman was falling away, screaming. A crunch on the back of her head, stars bursting, and she was falling to her hands and knees in the snow, tried to roll but a boot caught her in the belly and she was sagging and coughing bile, the wind knocked from her. Hands grabbed her and heaved her upright, spears and axes levelled at her.

Rotta stood and brushed himself down, wiped a trickle of blood from his cheek.

"Well, perhaps friendship does count for something," he said, breathing hard. "Not that it did him much good," he added looking at Spert's corpse. "And now you have outlived your usefulness." He took a step towards Orka.

"Let me kill her," Myrk pleaded, stepping between Rotta and

Orka. "I *owe* her." She put a finger to her cheek, pointing at the ruined scar where her eye had been.

Rotta sucked in a long, quivering breath.

"Very well," he said. "But make it painful."

"I intend to," Myrk smiled. "Stand aside," she said to the warriors and vaesen circling Orka and they moved back, forming a wider ring. Myrk stepped within it, drawing the two seaxes hanging from her weapons belt.

"Only fitting that I kill you with the blades that slew your husband," Myrk said with a smirk.

Orka crouched and snarled, raising her bound hands, the chain dangling between them.

"Come and meet your death," she growled.

Myrk smiled, shifted her weight and moved forwards, one seax held high, the other low. A red glow kindled in her eyes and her teeth grew to razored points, setting the hairs on Orka's neck standing on end, like the hackles on a wolf.

Orka moved left, Myrk stepping to her right, inching closer, then she was lunging forwards in a burst of speed almost too fast to follow. Orka raised her hands, caught one seax on her chain as it chopped down at her, twisted her hips and the other seax stabbed through empty air. Sparks flew as the first seax grated against Orka's chain and she twisted her wrists, wrapped the chain around the seax blade and wrenched as she pivoted away, heard Myrk gasp with pain as the blade was ripped from her grip, at the same time felt a hot line across her ribs. Orka caught the falling seax by the hilt as it spun through the air, crouched and gave Myrk her wolf-grin.

Myrk nodded to Orka's ribs and Orka put a hand there, finger-tips coming away red where Myrk's other seax had sliced her as she had spun away.

Myrk smiled.

"The wolf is blooded," she said.

"Hold," Rotta barked, stepping between them, and Orka became aware of those around her staring towards the treeline. She took a few steps away from Myrk and followed their gaze. The sun was sinking into the mountains, a pale, diffuse glow behind bloated clouds, snow falling in swirling gusts. The wooded slopes of the valley were a dense, impenetrable darkness.

Boughs shook, a hissing scream echoed from them, cut short. A wolf howled. The hint of movement, shadows within shadows.

Orka focused the wolf within her, heard sounds from the edge of the treeline. Growling, but not from one creature, more like many, spread throughout the trees. The shaking of boughs and the hissing screeches she had come to recognise as the screams of frost-spiders rang out. A silence followed, the branches settling. Orka saw movement within the gloom, creatures stalking them. The glitter of eyes.

A high, eerie horn call rang out from the trees, filling the glade, slowly died away, and a roaring and howling rose up, growing in volume, shaking the trees. People around Orka put their hands to their ears.

A cluster of tennúr burst from the trees, speeding towards Rotta.

"WARE THE WOODS," they wailed as they flew overhead.

A lone warrior stepped from the treeline. A woman, dark hair braided, clothed in mail and fur, twin axes gripped in her fists. An iron collar about her neck. She was snorting and growling, stalked a few paces along the treeline. Orka saw the muscles of her neck and shoulders were bunched, thick as knotted rope, and her eyes flickered green.

She glared at Rotta and the warband, opened her mouth and roared, spittle spraying, broke into a lumbering run towards them.

And then figures were bursting from the treeline behind her, hurtling through the snow towards them, men and women clad in mail and fur, sharp iron in their fists, snarls upon their faces, eyes glowing amber and green, iron collars around their necks.

CHAPTER FOURTEEN

VARG

The wall exploded inwards, splinters of timber flung through the air. A warrior fell, a shard of wood in his eye.

Varg stared as Glornir and a handful of the Bloodsworn exploded into the warehouse. Glornir buried his long-axe in someone's chest, hurling them through the air, Edel's hound leaped at another, jaws clamping around their throat as they fell, and arrows flitted through the room, shrieks ringing out as they found their mark. Beside Varg he felt the wolf in Røkia swell and he glanced at her, saw her teeth had grown and she was gnawing at the rope around her wrists.

A good idea, he thought and did the same, felt the rope fall away and then they were both leaping to their feet, running to the tangle of limbs that was Svik and his two guards and dragging them off Svik. The table had been overturned, Norv lying on his side, dead from blood loss, still staring at his severed wrists. Røkia grabbed her weapons belt from the floor and drew her seax, dragging it across the throat of one of the warriors wrestling with Svik, Varg heaving the other one up and head-butting him across the bridge of the nose, sending him crashing back to the floor. Svik rose from the ground snarling and spitting, blood on his lips, his teeth small and sharp. Røkia threw him his weapons belt and he buckled it on. His sword hissed into his fist and he slashed at the hamstring of a warrior close to him who was trading blows with Edel. The man swayed and folded as Edel's spear punched into his throat.

Varg buckled on his weapons belt, drew his hand-axe and cleaver and looked around the room, searching for a face.

"Leif, where are you?" he growled. The room was knots of chaos, men and women screaming, roaring, snarling, the stink of blood and iron thick in the air. Varg caught a glimpse of a fur-trimmed hat and snarl of black beard, Leif with his seax in his fist falling back before Kesha, one of Sulich's kin, Sterkur slamming his shield into her, sending her stumbling into a wall, and Sterkur was grabbing a fistful of Leif's tunic and dragging him through the hole in the warehouse wall.

"No," Varg snarled and ran after them. A body crashed into him, a woman with a long-axe in her fists and he slashed with his cleaver, felt it bite and heard a scream, ripped the blade free and shoved the woman away, moved on. The bulk of Taras was before him, holding a man over his head. He flung the body into a knot of Sterkur's crew, sending them all crashing to the ground and Edel and Svik waded in, stabbing and chopping.

Varg swerved around Taras, stepping through the hole in the warehouse wall, blinked in the bright day and saw Leif and Sterkur running along the dockside, a handful of warriors with them. Horns were blowing, dock-workers shouting and pointing, the harbour officials calling for their guards. Varg made to run after Leif and Sterkur and a hand grabbed his wrist. He pulled his cleaver back for a blow, then saw it was Røkia.

"No," she said to him.

Glornir and Svik stepped out of the warehouse.

"Leave them," Glornir said.

"But—" Varg snarled.

"The docks are seething like a kicked hornets' nest," Svik said. "We need to get to the *Sea-Wolf* before Rurik's *druzhina* come sniffing."

A horn call echoed along the docks, and Varg heard the distant clatter of hooves. He blew out a breath and nodded.

Others emerged from the warehouse, Sulich and Kesha, Taras, Edel and her hound. All that remained of Sterkur's crew were dead or down.

"With me," Glornir said and then they were all jogging along the docks, past all manner of vessels, mostly wide-bellied trading *knarrs* being loaded or unloaded. Sailors and dock-workers stopped in their labour to watch as the Bloodsworn passed by, and the horn calls grew louder. Varg saw a handful of harbour officials with their guards striding towards them and Glornir turned left onto a long pier. They increased their pace, rushing past dozens of moored boats, feet drumming on timber, and Varg saw the *Sea-Wolf* ahead of them, right at the end of the pier, the mast-pole already set in place, the sail upon it still furled. Vol stood in the stern, watching out for them. Before the *Sea-Wolf* another vessel bobbed on the swell of the bay, a wider-bellied transport ship, horses loaded on the central deck, heads down eating at racks of hay. As they drew nearer, Varg saw it was crewed by Sulich's kin, their coats of lamellar plate and weapons stowed in oar-chests now. They were seated ready and waiting with oars upright.

The sound of hooves grew louder behind them, and they increased their pace, reaching the *Sea-Wolf* in a rush, Glornir leaping onto the top-rail and standing there a moment. Sulich and Kesha boarded the other boat, while Varg and the others leaped onto the deck of the *Sea-Wolf*, Taras rocking the boat with his weight. Røkia slowed to untie the mooring rope and followed them all over the top-rail and onto the *Sea-Wolf*'s deck. Oars were thrust at them and Varg hurried to his oar-bench.

Glornir jumped from the top-rail and strode to the steering oar in the stern.

"Away," he shouted and oars were pushing them from the pier. When they were far enough out oars were threaded through the oar-holes, Glornir barking orders and Taras began beating a rhythm with knotted rope on a shield. The oars dipped, slicing into water, and the *Sea-Wolf* picked up speed, pulling away from the docks.

Varg saw Sulich shouting orders on the other craft, his crew rowing behind them, and the two boats carved out into the bay as a score of mounted *druzhina* thundered along the pier and skidded to a halt. A warrior stood in his saddle and shouted for them to stop, to row back, but Glornir ignored them. The warrior shouted more orders and arrows were flitting through the air, fizzing out of the blue sky, thumping into timber. Crew members who were not rowing hefted shields and stood over those who bent their backs at the oars. Arrows punched into shields and Varg heard a hoarse scream, but each pull of the oars moved them further out of range and within heartbeats arrows were sinking into the wake of the *Sea-Wolf* with barely a splash. Cheers rang out as the *Sea-Wolf* and Sulich's ship behind passed out of range and to safety.

Varg was sweating as they passed between the two huge statues that marked the entrance to the Bay of Ulaz, a colossal bull one side and an unknown creature the other side that Svik had told him was a scorpion. He glanced up at it and hoped that he would never meet one. Gulls rested on the statues' limbs as the sun sank low over the western horizon, reflecting red and orange upon the forms, making them seem as if blood pulsed through their veins.

Glornir called for the sail to be unfurled and it billowed, catching the south-westerly wind, and then the *Sea-Wolf* was carving through waves, salt-spume whipping across Varg's back. Oars were raised and shipped, stowed in racks on the deck and Varg stood, stretching his back, and leaned on the top-rail.

"Well, that was a close one," Svik said as he stood next to Varg, braiding his hair. "That Leif Kolskeggson has a lot to answer for, not least making me go through all this without my hair combed and braided."

"Aye," Varg grunted.

"And Sterkur," Røkia said as she joined them. "He has to die."

"I did not like him either," Varg muttered.

"'Like' has nothing to do with it," Røkia said. "My wolf broke loose, ruled me for a moment. He saw it in my eyes. He knows I am Tainted."

Varg and Svik stared at her, the implications of what she had said sinking in.

"We will find the *niðing*, sister," Svik said, "and we will silence him."

"I am sorry," Varg said. "I have brought this trouble upon you. Upon the Bloodsworn." He gripped the top-rail, knuckles white, and looked back towards Ulaz. As he stared he saw shapes appear on the horizon, dark smudges. He let the wolf trickle through his blood and his eyesight sharpened, the blurs coming into focus. Longships, five of them, and as he watched he saw sails drop on masts, the wind filling them. White sails with a black hawk.

"Bollocks," Svik muttered, following Varg's gaze.

"What?" Varg asked him.

"They are Rurik's longships," Svik said, "and my guess is that they are following us."

CHAPTER FIFTEEN

ORKA

Orka stared at the *Berserkir* and *Úlfhéðnar* as they charged from the treeline, roaring and howling as they came, puffs of snow erupting around their feet as they ran. They wore bear and wolf pelts, making them appear more animal than human.

"TO ME, PROTECT YOUR GOD," Rotta bellowed in his god-voice as he ran towards the head of the column and all along the warband warriors jumped into motion, Orka seeing Biórr and Red Fain move on the rat-god's command. Shields were shrugged from shoulders or grabbed from wagons and slammed together, men and women setting their feet and a long row formed, two lines deep, made up of dragon-born, Tainted warriors and dragon-cultists. Those wielding spears and long-axes stood in the back row, seaxes, swords and hand-axes in the front.

Too thin, Orka thought, looking from the shield wall to the onrushing *Berserkirs* and *Úlfhéðnar*.

Skraeling and trolls milled and shuffled in front or behind the line, looking unsure what to do, and overhead tennúr whirred through the snow.

They may have a belief of unity . . . but they have no cohesion in battle.

Horn calls from along the line, shouting, and Orka saw warriors in the column turning, looking towards the river.

Two longships were rowing up the river towards them. One

ploughed through the dense reeds along the riverbank, its hull grating as it shored on earth, warriors in mail and fur leaping over the top-rail and breaking into a run towards the column's rear. Warriors with round shields, knotwork wolves scribed upon a snow-white field.

"Father!" a man hissed close to Orka. Dagrun, and he threw himself at a dragon-cultist, wrapping the rope that bound his wrists around the man's throat. Other prisoners around him leaped at their guards.

There was a deafening crash as the first *Berserkir* hit the shield wall, smashing through it in a frenzy of muscle, teeth and iron. All along the line *Berserkir* and *Úlfhéðnar* hurled themselves against shields, smashing through, warriors spinning through the air, shields splintering, bones breaking, blood spraying. Screams echoed, iron clashed, warriors roared and almost immediately the shield wall was fracturing into smaller knots, holding together here and there.

A huge bull troll roared and lumbered through a gap, swinging his club, hitting as many friends as foe. A *Berserkir* spun through the air and crashed to the ground, rolled and stopped, smashed to bloody pulp. *Úlfhéðnar* leaped at the troll, swarming over him, stabbing, biting, gouging.

Orka looked around, right in front of her two *Berserkir* smashing a hole through the wall. One crashed to the ground, a woman with blood frothing on her lips, warriors spreading around her, stabbing with spears, but the other kept their feet and hacked at anything that moved, a short-axe in each fist. Orka saw the hole in the wall, bodies lying broken and trampled on the ground, through the falling snow saw the treeline beyond, and two figures emerged from the shadows, stood staring at her. A man and a child.

Her heart stopped in her chest.

"Breca," she whispered as her son beckoned frantically to her.

Without realising it, she was moving.

Then something crashed into her side and she was thrown to the ground, rolled and a seax plunged into the earth beside her.

"No, you don't," Myrk said, looming over her and ripping the seax free in a spray of snow and earth. Orka snarled and kicked out, knocked Myrk's legs from under her and she fell, Orka scrambling on the ground, slicing her seax across Myrk's back as she rolled away, sparks flying where the blade grated on Myrk's coat of mail. They both came up together, slicing and stabbing, iron clashing. Myrk stabbed at Orka, blade hissing through empty air, twisted to avoid Orka's blade and punched Orka on the jaw. She staggered, off balance, tried to swing an arm for balance but her bound wrists hampered her, and she stumbled, ducked as Myrk came at her and she sliced her blade across Myrk's thigh. A grunt of pain and Myrk lurched backwards, her eyes flickering red, her lips moving.

"Sársaukarúnir, brenndu hanna," Myrk muttered, one hand moving in the air and red runes sputtered to life before her, flames flickering.

"No," Orka growled and ran at Myrk, head low, and rammed into her, lifting Myrk on her shoulder, both of them flying through the air, crashing to the ground, Myrk grunting, air hissing from her, twisting, Orka clinging to her, wrapping the chain binding her wrists around Myrk's throat, and heaving back.

"Sársaukarúnir, brenndu—" Myrk wheezed, breath laboured, red runes appearing around them as they rolled.

"I said *no*," Orka snarled again and dragged Myrk's head back, bit into her throat with her wolf-jaws. Flesh tore and blood spurted into Orka's throat, a scream, Orka ripping and biting, teeth plunging deeper, blood slick, hot, running down her throat, her chin. Myrk bucked and writhed, arms flailing, stabbing at Orka. If the blade bit into her, Orka did not know, a blood-hazed, frenzied madness surging through her. Slowly she became aware that Myrk was no longer struggling. She released her grip on the woman, pushed herself away and up onto all fours, Myrk flopping lifelessly on the ground, her throat a red ruin torn to bloody strips.

Orka threw her head back and howled.

A shadow over her. A hand touching her shoulder.

"Mama," a voice filtered through to her and she blinked, looked up and saw Breca standing over her, gripping a hand-axe in white knuckles. Figures loomed behind him. Lif with a shield and bloodied spear in his fists, Halja Flat-Nose and Gunnar Prow, both mail-clad and helmeted, and Sæunn, the *Hundur*-tainted thrall who Orka had purchased at Starl, now with her thrall-collar gone, clothed in leather and fur and gripping a spear.

"Come with us," Breca said, grabbing her hand and trying to pull her up.

CHAPTER SIXTEEN

BIÓRR

Biórr took the axe swing of a *Berserkir* on his shield, felt the blow shiver through his wrist and up his arm. He leaned against the man in the shield wall beside him, a fox-tainted warrior of the Raven-Feeders, set his feet and stabbed over the shield rim at the *Berserkir*'s face. She shifted to the left, his blade slicing a red line across her cheek and carving through her ear, but if she felt it she did not show any pain, just roared and threw herself at Biórr's shield, hooking her axe head over the rim and dragging it down, lunging with mad-bulging eyes and red froth on her lips as her teeth snapped at his face, the head of her bear pelt making it seem like the creature itself was lunging at him, not a person.

A long-axe crunched down onto the bear-head of her pelt, a clang revealing that she wore a helm beneath it, but the blow was so hard it caved one side of the helm in. A moment as the *Berserkir* grunted, eyes unfocused, then blood was streaming down her face from beneath her helm and she was swaying, dropping to her knees. Biórr stabbed again, piercing her throat, and ripped the blade back, risked a quick glance over his shoulder to nod his thanks to Red Fain, who stood with his long-axe in the second row of the shield wall.

Biórr was standing with a knot of the Raven-Feeders, twelve or fifteen of them who had held the shield wall against the first rush of the *Berserkir* and *Úlfhéðnar*. Battle raged around them and Biórr had fought every moment to stay alive, heart thumping in his chest. There was a lull now, most of the *Berserkir* and *Úlfhéðnar* spread out among Rotta's warband and fighting like cornered, frenzied animals, no more coming at what remained of the shield wall. His comrades around him took the brief respite to drag deep breaths into their lungs and rest their shield arms. In the gap to his right, Biórr saw Brák and his remaining crew fighting together, a handful of skraeling with them. Despite his injuries, Brák was impossibly fast, his long, thin sword darting out and piercing a *Berserkir.* His crew and the skraeling had it encircled, all of them darting in and stabbing, then stepping away as it spun to face them, like hounds worrying at a bear.

A wolf howl behind and to Biórr's right and he glanced quickly. Saw Orka on her hands and knees in the slush-churned snow, head thrown back, howling, a corpse partially hidden behind her. A handful of warriors ran up to Orka, some mail-clad with black, blood-spattered shields in their fists. A fierce-looking child was with them, wrapped in thick furs. Biórr blinked, realised it was Breca, an axe in one of his fists. He was pulling Orka to her feet, the others spreading around her like a protective hand.

Orka rose slowly, shook herself like a dog emerging from a river, then Biórr saw the body at Orka's feet. Time froze for him, the world fading down to Myrk's pale, lifeless face. Orka bent and unbuckled Myrk's weapons belt, dragged it free and buckled it around her own waist, sheathed the seax in her fist, then leaned over and took the other seax from the ground beside Myrk, wiping the blood on her tunic.

Biórr heard a scream, realised it was him, found himself moving, heard Fain's voice calling behind him, the drum of feet, Fain and others following him. He ran through a field of chaos, snow swirling about him, battle raging all around. The dead or dying scattered like strewn leaves, lifeless eyes staring, gaping mouths fixed in death, blood on the snow, black as ink, the stench of voided bowels and metallic tang of blood hanging like mist in the air. He saw two trolls tip a wagon over, crushing an *Úlfhéðnar* beneath it, heard the roar and clash of new combat as warriors from the longships crashed into the rear of remaining clumps of the shield wall, heard Rotta bellowing in his god-voice, saw the crackle of rune-magic sparking in the air, saw tennúr flit out of the sky to swarm over a *Berserkir*'s head, raking him with their claws, grabbing at his teeth as he opened his mouth to roar. Biórr ran past Skaga and a handful of her skraeling kin. They were hacking at an *Úlfhéðnar* on the ground. Skaga saw him, called something out to him, but he did not hear what she said. She shouted at her kin, and they followed after Biórr, Fain and the others.

One of those around Orka saw Biórr, and the others charging, a tall, fair-haired man with a braided beard, mailed and helmeted, a black blood-spattered shield in one fist, hand-axe in the other. Biórr recognised him, had fought him not so long ago.

I slew his woman.

Biórr saw a green fire kindle in the man's eyes and he hefted his shield, banged his hand-axe upon it.

The rat within Biórr squealed, flight its first instinct.

No, brother, Biórr hissed at it, *find your courage, this is the time to fight.*

He felt the rat shift in his blood, an adjustment from flight to fight, as if he were cornered. Felt a vicious strength flood him.

A red-haired, mail-clad woman beside the fair-haired man drew her arm back and hurled a spear, was drawing her sword from its scabbard before the spear had hissed past Biórr. A scream behind him, a skraeling knocked from his feet and hurled to the ground. He heard Skaga shout a curse, ran on, swerved around three *Úlfhéðnar* as they ripped through a knot of dragon-cultists, heard some of the Raven-Feeders behind him crash into the *Úlfhéðnar*, and then he was almost upon Orka and her small crew.

The two Bloodsworn with their black shields were standing together, shields locked, behind them a man and woman, both with spears held high and ready in underhand grips. He could not see Orka or Breca.

Biórr yelled a battle cry but slowed.

I am no frothing-mad Berserkir *to rush headlong into an impaling.* He swerved to avoid the Bloodsworns' shields, slashed low with his sword at the shins of the green-eyed man, who struck down with his shield and knocked Biórr's blade into the turf, hacked with his hand-axe at Biórr's chest, but Biórr twisted and raised his shield and caught the axe blow. It was so powerful it sent Biórr stumbling and he ran on a few paces, ducked as a spear blade stabbed at his throat and staggered backwards, tripped over something and fell crashing onto his back.

Red Fain and the other Raven-Feeders hit the small shield wall, sent it skidding backwards, but somehow the man and woman held against their weight. Axes chopped, swords stabbed and Biórr saw spears dart out from the back row, each blade coming back blood-dark. An iron boss punched Red Fain in the face, and he stumbled backwards, fell to one knee. Then Skaga and the skraeling hit the wall, sent it reeling back a few more steps, and skraeling were pouring around the side of the two shield warriors, too many of them to be held back. The wall broke apart, each black shield moving, the spear-wielders separating, one staying with each of the Bloodsworn. They left bodies falling in their wake.

Biórr rolled onto his hands, pushed himself up, saw he had tripped over a body. It was Myrk. He stared at her, eyes dark and lifeless, staring into nowhere, could hardly believe that this was the hot-blooded, passionate, fierce woman who had dragged him into the reeds beside the river only a short while ago.

A sound choked out of his throat, part sob, part growl, and he was climbing to his feet, snarling, grabbing his shield and sword, looking for Orka.

Red Fain was back on his feet, leading the small band of Raven-Feeders against one of the black shields, Skaga and the other skraeling trying to surround the other one. Then Orka was there, moving fast and low, a seax in each fist, slicing, stabbing, snarling, arcs of blood in the air marking her passage. A skraeling leaped at her, crashed into her and she staggered, the skraeling clinging to her, trying to saw at her throat with a thick iron blade.

Something small hurtled out from behind a wagon, Breca, making a high-pitched howling, a hand-axe gripped in a white-knuckled fist, his face twisted in a rictus of rage. He leaped into the air and swung the axe overhead in a two-handed grip, the blade crunching down onto the skraeling's skull. It collapsed like a brained cow, legs folding, blood, bone and brain leaking from its head. Breca fell with it, came to his feet chopping and hacking at the dead skraeling until Orka pulled him off, held him in the air by the scruff of his cloak, where he spat and snarled, eyes blazing amber and green, slowly calmed.

Biórr glanced down at Myrk's corpse, and then he was running at Orka.

A figure stepped in front of him, a black shield and green eyes, lips pulled back in a snarl. Biórr dipped his head and ran, smashed into the Bloodsworn, their shields crashing together, sent the Bloodsworn staggering back, his momentum carrying him on past the warrior, a backswing with his sword, heard the Bloodsworn grunt as his blade crunched into the top of the man's back, tearing a rent through his mail coat, rings spraying.

Biórr skidded and turned, saw the Bloodsworn turn and set his feet as Biórr fell upon him in a rush. His sword battered at the Bloodsworn's shield, stabbed at his face, stabbed down, under the shield rim and the Bloodsworn gave ground, chopped at Biórr's head with his axe, but Biórr shifted left and slammed his shield into his enemy's, snarled and spat at him over the shield rims. A pivot of the Bloodsworn's feet and he pushed with his shield, sent Biórr staggering past him, the axe chopping and raking down the back of Biórr's shield arm. Mail rings shattered and blood welled, Biórr feeling a hot line of fire down the back of his arm. Green-eyes came at him hard, shield up, axe blows raining down on him. Splinters of wood sprayed from Biórr's shield, the blows powerful, sending shock waves rolling up his injured arm. He struggled to keep his shield up, swung his sword, but his feet were not planted, the blow too weak and green-eyes swatted it away, smashed his shield into Biórr's and sent him crashing to the ground in a spray of snow, losing his grip on his sword.

Biórr rolled, reached for his sword hilt, but green-eyes stamped down on his wrist, pinning it.

"You killed my Revna," green-eyes spat. "She was worth a *thousand* of you." And he raised his axe.

Something small crunched into green-eyes, sent him stumbling back, and Biórr saw Harek standing over him, feet set wide, fists balled, his eyes glowing yellow and his chin and jawline swollen, small tusks protruding from his lower jaw.

"You leave him alone," Harek shouted.

CHAPTER SEVENTEEN

ORKA

Orka looked at Breca as she held him suspended in the air, could hardly believe it was her son. He was calming from the frenzy that had swept him, and he looked at her now with dark eyes in a pale, blood-spattered face.

"Are you in control?" she asked him calmly, and he nodded. She set him down next to the skraeling he had just killed.

"It was trying to hurt you, Mama," Breca said, looking from the skraeling and up to Orka.

"Aye," Orka grunted.

"We need to get out of here," Breca said and Orka nodded. She looked around, saw Halja Flat-Nose fighting off Raven-Feeders, Lif standing a pace behind her, guarding her flank with his shield and spear. A pile of the dead lay around them.

A thick-antlered troll roared, stumbled out of the snow and passed close to them, three or four *Úlfhéðnar* clinging to its shoulders and limbs, stabbing and clawing at it. Two more trolls came lumbering through the chaos, one swinging a huge club, the other stabbing with a thick-shafted spear. People dived out of the way, and then men and women clad in mail with wolf-painted shields were swarming among them, hacking and stabbing. Orka saw a white-haired, barrel-chested man clad in mail and fur leading them, recognised him – Orlyg – Dagrun's father, shouting orders, chopping about him with a long-axe. A Galdurman stood close to him, dark-haired, animal skulls braided into his hair, a staff in his hands. He was shouting in a strange tongue, tracing red runes in the air with his staff, and a flaming shield appeared before Orlyg just as a skraeling ran at him. The creature crashed into the rune-shield and burst into flames, shrieking and collapsing to the ground.

A figure ran up to Orka, Sæunn, wrapped in thick furs, a spear in her fist.

"We must leave, mistress," Sæunn said.

"Aye," Orka grunted. "Halja, Lif," she shouted, putting her hands to her mouth and they ran to her.

"Where is Gunnar Prow?" Orka asked Sæunn.

"There," Sæunn pointed with her spear and Orka saw Gunnar standing before a child and a man trying to rise from the ground.

"Harek," Breca said, "the betrayer," he snarled, his eyes kindling to amber and green, his body starting to tremble.

"No," Orka said to him, grabbing his wrist and shaking him, even as she calmed the wolf in her own blood.

"Gunnar," she shouted, and he glanced over at her, then back to the man on the ground. Orka saw it was Biórr, remembered that he had slain Revna.

The troll with the *Úlfhéðnar* clinging to it came staggering between Gunnar and Biórr. It let out a roar, swayed and toppled to the ground, its throat cut, the *Úlfhéðnar* on its back and shoulders thrown loose as the troll hit the ground. The earth around its fall trembled, sending Gunnar reeling backwards, and Harek and Biórr tumbling.

Behind them Orka heard Rotta's voice swirling through the battleground. Words she did not understand, that made her hackles stand on end. She looked back, saw him riding out of the snow into the ground between the treeline and the warband, a score or more of the dragon-born around him.

Orka broke into a run, the others following her, and she reached Gunnar in a few heartbeats, heaved him to his feet. He was looking around wildly for Biórr but could not see him, fresh battle sweeping around them.

"Brother, we *must* leave," Halja said to Gunnar.

"Revna," he snarled, eyes searching for Biórr.

"Is gone," Halja said. "You will see that *niðing* again, will have the chance to avenge her then. If we do not leave now, chances are none of us will be leaving." She pointed towards Rotta and the dragon-born. They were shouting unknown words, runes of fire and ice sizzling and crackling into life in the air before them.

Gunnar froze a moment, mouth twisting in a grimace, then he nodded. He swept up his axe from the ground.

"Skullsplitter," he said, and gestured to the chains that still bound her wrists.

She dropped to her knees and spread her wrists on the snow-covered ground, Gunnar hacking down with his axe, sparks flaring. On the third strike a link snapped and twisted, and Orka let the wolf run through her, used its strength to strain, veins bulging, and the chain snapped.

A grunt of thanks to Gunnar and they were all running through the pitched battle, swerving around knots of combat. Orka sheathed her seaxes, bent and swept up a long-axe as she ran, saw that it was Red Fain's, the old man wrestling with a *Berserkir*, corded muscles bulging, his jutting jaw and tusks gouging into the *Berserkir*'s chest. The *Berserkir* plunged a seax into Red Fain's thigh, the old warrior bellowing and he ripped his tusks up into the *Berserkir*'s throat.

A scream to her left and she saw Dagrun and a handful of his *drengrs* being beaten down by skraeling and dragon-cultists. Orka changed direction, the others following her, and she swept through those attacking Dagrun, hacking them down. He was on the ground, a skraeling on top of him, huge hands throttling him. Orka swung her long-axe and Lif stabbed the skraeling through the back with his spear, the creature falling away with a gurgling scream. Gunnar, Halja and Sæunn cut the others down like an ice wind, and then they were running on, leaving Dagrun gasping on the ground.

Orka saw Spert's body, snow settled upon it, the spear still pinning him to the ground; she ran to it, ripped the spear out and cast it away, lifted Spert's body and cradled it in one arm, then ran on. She checked that Breca was close, saw him running hard a pace behind and to her right.

They broke into open ground, Rotta and his dragon-born

between them and the treeline. Dusk was falling, snow swirling in gusts, a pale shadow-light filling the vale, and Orka saw movement from within the treeline, frost-spiders and night-hags emerging from the darkness like a quick-flowing mist.

Rotta saw her and raised his arms, ice-blue runes spiralling in the air, growing and expanding with every heartbeat. The mounted dragon-born behind him raised their voices, red runes crackling to life above them, and the frost-spiders and night-hags flowed past their horses' feet.

Orka skidded to a halt.

"No escape that way," she growled, and they turned, running back towards the battle, filtered through it, chopping and hacking at all in their way. They passed an overturned wagon where a dozen children huddled.

"Bjarn," Breca cried out, slowing. "Bjarn, come with us."

A dark-haired lad looked up at Breca, rose hesitantly and began to follow them.

Screams behind them and Orka glanced back, saw Rotta and the dragon-born close to the battle-lines. They were casting their rune-spells through the air, Orka seeing rings of red flame and blue-burning ice falling upon *Úlfhéðnar* and *Berserkir*, setting them alight like candles or freezing them instantly into pillars of ice. Panic spread through the combat, Orlyg and his wolf-shields halting their advance, beginning to fall back.

Orka ran on, breaking through the combat and out into an open space before the river. Breca, Gunnar and the others were at her heels, and she saw Bjarn following behind them. To her right stood Orlyg's two longships, a half-crew upon each of them, to the left the river wound back the way she had walked from the north, from Svelgarth.

"Where to, chief?" Halja Flat-Nose asked Orka.

Orka hesitated.

People ran past them, some in full flight, others retreating backwards with shields locked. Orka saw Orlyg with a score of his warriors, his Galdurman holding a protective rune-shield above the jarl. Orlyg shouted orders and a woman close to him put a horn to her lips, blew an ululating call as they retreated.

We cannot go north, there is only a cold-freezing death for us there. And the trees to the west are blocked to us.

She looked back, saw Rotta walking his horse through the battleground, red flames and blue ice erupting around him, spreading across the snow-covered ground.

"Wolves behind, a cliff ahead," Halja muttered.

"Aye," Orka grunted.

"Come with me," a voice close by shouted and Orka saw Dagrun beckoning to them. "Come with us," he shouted, running towards the longships with a handful of *drengrs* around him.

Another glance backwards and Orka made her decision. She ran after Dagrun, sprinting towards the longships.

Runes flew over her head, leaving fiery red and blue trails through the sky above, snowflakes hissing. They fell upon the first longship that had grounded upon the riverbank, exploded in bursts of red and blue incandescence. Flames spread, crackling across the hull's strakes, across the timber deck, and in moments the ship was ablaze. Orka veered and changed her course, running past the first ship where flaming figures were leaping, screaming, into the river.

She saw Dagrun reach the second longship. He turned and hoisted a woman up onto the deck, then lifted a child, a girl, and hurled her up, hands catching her. Orlyg leaped and grabbed the top-rail, hands hauling him aboard, his Galdurman leaping nimbly aboard behind him.

Orka crashed through reeds and waded into the river, reached the ship's hull and turned and grabbed Lif, heaved him up so that he flopped over the top-rail. Then she was grabbing Breca and lifting him up, Lif reaching down to grip his wrists and drag him aboard. Halja and Sæunn ran into the water and leaped, grabbing the rail and pulling themselves over, then Gunnar was there and he and Orka leaped together, hands reaching down and gripping them, hauling them aboard.

Orka slithered over the top-rail and fell onto the deck, where Orlyg was yelling commands and warriors were grabbing oars from the central racks, threading them through oar-holes, others pushing off from the bank. Oars began to dip into the water, the longship moving slowly into the river. Shouts and yells from the riverbank.

Feet drummed on the timber deck as warriors ran with shields to protect the rowers. Orka saw Orlyg's Galdurman stand at the top-rail and hurl runes from his staff at vaesen on the riverbank.

She gently laid Spert's body down, stood, and went to the top-rail, watching a handful of *Úlfhéðnar* and *Berserkir* running for the longship, pursued by skraeling and frost-spiders. Orka grabbed a spear from a spear rack and hurled it, saw the spear pierce a frost-spider as it leaped at an *Úlfhéðnar*. Then they were crashing through the reeds and leaping for the longship. Orka leaned over and grabbed a grasping wrist, hauled a *Berserkir* over the top-rail.

Breca appeared beside her, staring out into the confusion.

"Bjarn," he yelled, "Bjarn", looking frantically at the chaos beyond the riverbank. Then a small figure appeared, running between a troll's legs and sprinting towards the ship.

"Come on, Bjarn," Breca yelled, and Orka added her voice to her son's, urging Bjarn on. Another child appeared behind Bjarn, running fast. It leaped and crashed into Bjarn's legs, the two of them rolling and disappearing into the reeds along the riverbank.

"Harek," Breca snarled, made to climb over the top-rail, and Orka grabbed him, pulled him back.

Rotta appeared, riding through the dusk and snow, one hand held high over his head, blue runes crackling to life. He looked at the longship, straight at Orka, and cast the rune at her. It flared through the air, leaving a trail of blue sparks, and Orka grabbed a shield from a warrior close by, held it up and felt the rune-magic crash into the shield, staggering her. Frost crackled, cold seeping through the linen and timber, and speckles of frost appeared on the inside of the shield, rapidly turning to shards of ice, the timber strips of the shield freezing, cracking, splintering, and cold rolled into Orka like a wave, numbing her hand but also burning, spreading up her wrist and with a roar she heaved the shield away, saw it fall into the river, water turning to blue-tinged ice. The ice-rune sputtered, ice cracking, and died.

Oars dipped and pulled, dipped and pulled and the longship gathered speed, carving away from the bank and into the current of the river, started to speed away. Orka saw Rotta standing in his saddle, body twitching and trembling, and then he was disappearing, veiled behind the swirling snow. She heard him yell, a bellow of rage and frustration, and she slumped to the deck, her back against the top-rail, flexing her fist that was still numb from Rotta's rune-spell.

Breca bent over and vomited beside her.

Killing is no easy thing, she thought as she looked at him, saw his trembling hands. "Breca, come here," she said, and Breca looked up, cuffed vomit from his lips and walked over to her.

"You should have been far from here," she said to him. "Should have fled."

"I could not go without you, Mama," Breca said.

"People died to save you, to get you away from here," she said, and he dropped his head.

Lif, Gunnar, Halja and Sæunn gathered around them, squatted or sat.

"You should have taken him like I told you to," Orka said with a scowl, "taken him to Glornir, where he would be safe."

"There is nowhere safe in Vigrið now," Halja said. "The dragon is free."

"Safer than here," Orka grumbled.

"Perhaps, but only for a while," Halja shrugged.

"It was *all* our choice," Sæunn said fiercely, "none of us wished to leave you. Spert was the first to speak of staying. He refused to leave you."

Orka looked at the small shadow that was Spert's corpse, nestled behind an oar-chest, and she knelt beside him, rested a blood- and grime-crusted hand on the vaesen's body.

"Friendship," she whispered, and felt a knot tighten in her chest. *He was loyal, faithful. These gods and their dragon-born have taken much from me, have much to answer for. I shall take it back from them in their blood.* Muscles twitched in her jaw and she blew out a hard breath, looked at Breca. He was trembling, tears in his eyes. She reached out her hands and cupped his cheeks, dragged him close to her and kissed his tears away, squeezed him hard, felt the emotion quivering through his body, and her own.

"My Breca," she breathed and felt his arms wrap around her and hug her with a fierce strength.

CHAPTER EIGHTEEN

GUÐVARR

Guðvarr shifted in his saddle, his arse aching, and lifted himself up, but within a dozen heartbeats he felt the insides of his thighs start to burn. A few more moments were all he could bear, so he returned his backside to the saddle, sighed as the ache returned, then rubbed at his nose, where snot had frozen and left his skin raw and chaffed. He pulled his cloak tighter about him.

I hate *travelling. I wish I was back in Darl*, he thought.

Then he remembered Lik-Rifa and her room full of serpents and frost-spiders and thought again.

They were riding through open woodland, the sun sinking into the west, the last fractured rays of the day filtering through the canopy. His aunt Jarl Sigrún rode beside him, her *drengrs* spread in a double column behind them. That was not so bad, but up ahead of Sigrún there loped about a score of skraeling, and others ran through the woodland on their flanks, led by their ill-mannered matriarch, Krúsa, and up above him he heard scuttling and saw the many-limbed movement of frost-spiders. Tennúr whirled and flitted all around them.

No, not better off here, surrounded by vaesen. I wish I was back in Fellur village, he thought. *Where I was respected. And, more importantly, where I was safe.*

They had left Darl five days ago, set out south, heading towards Liga, but then tennúr-scouts had found tracks of a large group travelling west. They had changed course, found the new tracks and within a day of following them had come upon a homestead, where a disgruntled goat farmer had told them that *Úlfhéðnar* wearing thrall-collars had raided her flock and stolen a dozen goats, and so they knew they were on the right trail. For three days now they had been heading steadily west, and hopefully gaining upon Estrid and her crew.

"How long, do you think?" Guðvarr said to Jarl Sigrún.

"How long until what?" she answered with a frown.

"Until we catch Estrid and Skalk," Guðvarr said.

"Soon, I hope," Sigrún said with a shrug.

Guðvarr thought about that, the realisation that battle would most likely be at the end of this chase settling upon him. And no ordinary battle, against *drengrs*, or preferably farmers, which was what he was accustomed to back in Fellur village and more to his liking. No, this battle would be against a weapon-trained princess, at least one Galdurman, probably more, against trained *drengrs* and maybe a score of half-beast wolf men and women. He gulped, remembering his experience against one *Úlfhéðnar*, Orka at the Grimholt. That was not something he wanted to go riding heedlessly into.

I'd rather be riding away from it.

"I hope it is not soon," Guðvarr muttered.

"If it is not soon, then we will have to cross the River Slågen, which will take us into Jarl Störr's land, where we will have enemies all about us," Sigrún said with a scowl at him. "That will be worse than catching up with Estrid this side of the river."

Guðvarr thought about that.

"You're right," he said. "We should ride faster."

"That is a decision for Krúsa to make."

"I do not like being ordered about by a skraeling," Guðvarr muttered.

"This world is full of things we do not like," Sigrún said back to him. "But I, for one, do not want to put myself on the wrong side of Lik-Rifa. Do you?"

Guðvarr shivered. *Fair point.*

They rode into a glade, the path widening, a single ash tree at its centre. Skraeling were gathered together in a knot, muttering among themselves and pointing, obviously uneasy, causing Guðvarr and Sigrún to rein in, skidding to a halt.

Krúsa was standing before the tree, staring up at it with a frown.

"What is it?" Sigrún said, riding over to the skraeling and dismounting.

"Ash trees," Krúsa grunted. "We do not like them."

"Why not?" Guðvarr asked, riding closer, Sigrún's *drengrs* spilling into the glade behind him. He slipped from his saddle and stood beside Krúsa.

"Because of the Froa," Krúsa said, staring suspiciously up at the tree.

"You don't like other vaesen?" Guðvarr said. "I thought you were all on the same side."

"No," Krúsa said, spitting on the ground. "Skraeling, tennúr, frost-spiders, trolls, night-hags, hyrndur, we are Lik-Rifa's children. We are on same side. But Froa were made by Snaka. We are *not* friends with Froa."

"Oh," said Guðvarr. "Did Snaka make other things?"

"Yes," Krúsa said. "Faunir. Näcken. All the beasts you farm. *You*."

Guðvarr did not like the thought of being created at the whim of a god's mind. A plaything. One creation among many. He felt superior to all of them.

"Are Froa . . . dangerous?" Guðvarr asked.

"Of course," Krúsa said. "Froa powerful."

Guðvarr looked up at the ash tree, its bark gnarled and knotted, the boughs thick and dense, impenetrable leaves. A breeze blew through the glade, shadows shifting and leaves rustling, almost like a voice.

Be gone be gone be gone it seemed to say to him.

"Then shouldn't we be moving along?" Guðvarr said. "Why are we just standing here?"

"Not all ash trees have Froa now. And they only hurt you if they feel threatened."

"Then why are we standing so close?" Guðvarr said, taking a step back. "All the more reason to move along, and quickly."

Krúsa grinned at him, revealing yellowed fangs and tusks. "Be brave, little man."

"Brave! I'll have you know that I am exceptionally brave," Guðvarr spluttered.

The limbs of trees around the glade rustled and creaked and Guðvarr looked up to see frost-spiders moving among them. He saw one pass onto one of the ash tree's boughs and scuttle along it.

"No," Krúsa shouted.

There was a silence in the glade, then branches shook in the ash tree. A hissing screech rang out, leaves drifting gently down. All gazed up at the tree, and the frost-spider fell from above, crashed to the ground on its back, legs curled.

Guðvarr took a step and tentatively leaned over it.

"It's dead," he pronounced.

"Back," Krúsa shouted as something dropped like a stone from the branches above.

Guðvarr stumbled back, reaching for his sword. A rounded form crouched on the ground, as if carved from wood, slowly stood, unfurling into a woman, long flowing hair like new roots twisting down her back, skin grey as ash and rough as bark with a dark grain like veins running through it, her body covered with moss and leaves and patches of yellow lichen.

"You dare set foot in my boughs and my glade, dragon's spawn," the woman hissed, sounding like the wind rustling through leaves.

"A mistake, lady," Krúsa said, hands up and backing away.

"Your last," the Froa snarled and reached her hands out. "*Vínviður systur minnar, snara og kyrkja*," she roared loud as a storm wind, trees around the glade shaking and vines bursting from the ground all about them, lashing out like whips. A skraeling fell screaming, red weals down his face, and more vines were bursting from the ground, snaring him, dragging him into the earth. One of Sigrún's *drengrs* cried out, vines wrapped around one ankle and wrist. He struggled, tried to draw the axe at his belt but more vines were climbing him, binding his arm to his side, swirling higher, threading around his throat and squeezing. Sigrún cried out and ran to him, drawing her sword and slicing at the vines. Some of them burst, but more vines were slithering across the ground, reaching for Sigrún. Guðvarr ran to her, not hard for him to do as he was already moving, and grabbed Sigrún's wrist, dragged her away from the *drengr* even as he collapsed, face purple, eyes bulging. Guðvarr stumbled to their horses, pushed Sigrún to hers and helped her mount, then hurled himself at his own horse, slid into the saddle and was dragging on his reins, kicking wildly and the horse was running.

"Away," Krúsa was crying out, pushing skraeling away from the Froa and her ash tree, running for the path that led out of the glade. Guðvarr steered his horse that way, almost trampled a handful of skraeling, and then he was galloping along a narrow path. He glanced back, saw Sigrún and *drengrs* following, caught a glimpse of Krúsa and more skraeling flitting through the woodland, heard the Froa-spirit cry out, the whole forest seeming to shake and tremble and Guðvarr put his head down and let his horse run.

"I wish I were back in Fellur village, I wish I were back in Fellur village," Guðvarr repeated to himself over and over as he galloped down the path.

CHAPTER NINETEEN

ELVAR

Elvar strode through her shattered feast hall, a cold wind sifting snow about her feet. Uspa walked at her side, Ulfrir and Skuld a pace behind her, and Sighvat, Sólín Spittle and two *Berserkir* a step behind them.

"Ulfrir, walk with me," Elvar said. A whisper of footsteps and Ulfrir was at her side. "I am wondering, when Ingvild stole my treasure," Elvar said to him, "I saw you fighting on the pier, against her crew."

"Aye," Ulfrir said, and raised a hand to the iron collar about his neck. "I am compelled to fight for you."

"You are," Elvar agreed. "But I saw others with you. Fighting with you, fighting to protect you." She looked at him. "I have not seen them since then."

Ulfrir held her gaze, his amber eyes flickering, and Elvar refused to look away.

"Who were they?" she asked into Ulfrir's silence.

"You see much," Ulfrir muttered, then sighed. "My children," he said. "*Úlfhéðnar*. Tainted, you call them," he added with a twist of his lips.

Elvar nodded.

"And where are they now?" she asked. "Why are they not here now?"

Another drawn-out silence from Ulfrir.

"I asked you a question," Elvar said.

"They are . . . close," Ulfrir said, "but they stay hidden."

"Why?"

"Because they are afraid."

"Afraid of what?"

"The iron collar," Ulfrir snarled.

"They cannot stay hidden," Elvar said with a frown. "I do not like it, warriors who have not sworn oaths to me lurking so close in the shadows. Tell them to come out into the light."

"If they come to me, you cannot put a collar about their necks."

"Cannot," Elvar said. "You do not tell me that."

A long sigh from Ulfrir.

"You would not *need* to put a collar on them," he said. "They would fight for me, and I fight for you. The enemy of my enemy is my friend, no?"

"Yes, that is true," Elvar said. "But when the enemy is dead, what then? Would they still be my friend, then? Friendship is fickle. Fear is safer." She paused at that, realised her father had said those words to her, many times.

Fear is safer. Am I becoming my father?

"You do not put collars on these mercenaries that come to you. They are ruled by their greed, have no loyalty, no honour. You should fear them, not my children."

"I agree about the mercenaries," Elvar said, Ulfrir giving voice to thoughts that had been swirling through her thought-cage since she had become jarl. "But greed keeps them loyal. Silver is a tool, just like a collar, and fortunately for me I have a lot of silver."

"Heya," Sighvat murmured from behind her.

"Aye, but do you not think Lik-Rifa will have access to silver, too?" Ulfrir asked. "These vermin will sell themselves to the highest bidder. My *Úlfhéðnar* are safer, more trustworthy."

It was Elvar's turn to be silent a while.

"I will think on it," Elvar said to him. "Bring them to me."

They had left the feast hall now and were passing through long corridors. They strode past Elvar's chambers and approached a wide-arched doorway, more *Berserkir* guarding it. The *Berserkir* dipped their heads to Elvar and opened the thick-timbered doors, iron hinges creaking, and Elvar and her party swept through into the Galdur tower of Snakavik.

They entered a high-vaulted room, circular, a wide, open space with a fire pit at its centre. Hrung was there upon his pedestal. He had complained of the cold in the feast hall, now that it only had half a roof and two walls, so Elvar had moved him here, as she had chosen this room as her new council chamber.

"Jarl Elvar and Ulfrir-wolf," Hrung boomed, seemingly enjoying his change of scenery immensely. Behind him and the fire pit, half-buried in the ground, was a giant link of chain and Elvar heard Ulfrir let out a low, rumbling growl at the sight of it.

"It is a link of the chain that Lik-Rifa forged to tame you," Elvar said, "or so the skálds tell us. Shards of broken links were scattered across all Vigrið in Snaka's fall, many buried, but here and there some were discovered. It was at those sites that Galdurmen learned their rune-magic and used shavings from your chain to forge thrall-collars. Each Galdur tower is built around a link of your chain."

"So, the history of your people is braided with the slavery of mine," Ulfrir said grimly. "You have more in common with Lik-Rifa than you realise."

Elvar did not like that and turned away.

Beyond the link of chain, built into the far wall of the tower, was a forge, though it was cold now, no ember-glow emanating from it.

Chairs and a long table were set around the fire pit, and Elvar saw Gytha was there, dressed in mail, her dark hair pulled back into a tight braid. Silrið the Galdurwoman was standing beside her, a necklace of bones about her neck glinting in the firelight, a drinking horn in her hand. She was talking to Broðir, Elvar's brother. Broðir looked up as Elvar entered the room and gave her a broad smile. It was guileless, that smile, reminding Elvar of happier times, and she smiled back at him.

"Sister," he said, striding over to her, arms wide to embrace her. The *Berserkir* growled and stepped in front of him and his arms drooped.

"Let him through," Elvar said and Broðir smiled like a puppy and hugged her. She was stiff at first, then lifted a hand and patted his back. "Well met," she muttered, then walked on to the centre of the hall.

Elvar went to her father's chair that had been brought here along with Hrung and sat down, Sighvat going to the table and pouring a cup of ale for her, one for Sólín Spittle and a bigger one for himself.

"Gytha," Elvar said, dipping her head to her captain. "Where is Grend?"

"He left my chambers at dawn, I have not seen him since then," Gytha said.

"Well," Hrung boomed, "now that we are all here, what shall we talk about?"

"War," Skuld said.

"Yes, a good topic, full of excitement to the young glory-seekers, I don't doubt, though it often ends unfortunately, as I can attest," Hrung said, trying to look down at the frayed skin of his severed neck.

"We must discuss how we are going to get Bjarn back for Uspa," Elvar said.

"By guile or by force?" Silrið asked.

"Guile sounds good to me," Broðir said. "Less dangerous, perhaps." He looked around at them all, at their stern faces. "Fighting a dragon does sound . . . worrying."

"Not my first choice," Sighvat agreed. "I have seen her, and she does not look that easy to kill. But I will do it if I must," he added quickly, looking suspiciously at his forearm in case the *blóð svarið* set his arm aflame in pain for questioning the vow they'd made.

"Let us discuss guile," Elvar said. "In other words, stealing Bjarn from wherever he is being held. Which would mean we would need to find him first. Where is he?"

"Nastrandir, perhaps?" Uspa said.

"That is where Lik-Rifa would have gone," Ulfrir said, "to recover, to lick her wounds somewhere that she would feel safe, of that I am certain. But is she still there now? I do not know."

"We need spies, scouts," Broðir said. "Perhaps some of the mercenary bands that have sworn you their oaths could be sent out?" He looked at Elvar.

"Perhaps," Elvar said, though Ulfrir's words were still worming through her head. *They are ruled by greed, have no loyalty, no honour.* "But you are right, brother, we need information." She had already thought of this, and the best source of information she had come across in her years in the Battle-Grim had been traders. They travelled all the ports and towns of Vigrið. She had sent some of her Battle-Grim down to the docks at Snakavik, tasked with questioning all new arrivals at the port.

"Even if you managed to find where Lik-Rifa was keeping the boy, and guile worked and you managed to steal him back from Lik-Rifa," Ulfrir said, "you will still have a dragon to contend with. There is no escaping her. She will not just make peace with you and allow you to live your lives free of her. She is proud, and would be enraged if you managed to steal Bjarn from her. There is no reason in her, no reasoning with her."

"Forgive me if I do not trust you fully," Silrið said. "Perhaps you have, how shall I say it, another agenda? Perhaps you wish to use us to accomplish your own desires, perhaps you wish your sister dead, and we are your best means of accomplishing that? Please, do not feel insulted by what I am saying." She shrugged. "I know how families work, that is all. Look at this one." She glanced at Elvar, who could not argue with that.

"I do wish to see Lik-Rifa dead," Ulfrir acknowledged.

"As do I," Skuld snapped.

"But killing her is not just *my* path, it is the only sensible path. With Snaka gone Lik-Rifa believes that Vigrið is hers, along with all in it. She will seek to dominate Vigrið, to rule it. And her rule will not be gentle. And, of course, she is insane." He looked around at them all. "Do not take my word for it. Ask Hrung, he has been your counsellor for many years, I understand."

All eyes turned to the giant head.

"Lik-Rifa cannot be reasoned with," Hrung agreed. "Ulfrir speaks true, she is insane. Or at least she was. And that was before she spent three hundred years locked in a cave deep beneath the earth." He shook his head. "I doubt that has made her any better." He sucked in a breath, puffed his cheeks up, and blew the breath out again, his lips flapping. "So, what about force?" he rumbled.

"Perhaps we should ally ourselves with Queen Helka of Darl?" Broðir said. "I know father wished to make war on her, but Helka is powerful, has her own Tainted, *Úlfhéðnar*, I think. And times have changed, have they not? She will most likely not take too kindly to anyone trying to tell her what to do, or rule her, even if they are a dragon. The enemy of my enemy is my friend, you know . . ." he trailed off.

Elvar glanced at Ulfrir.

"Not a bad idea, brother," Elvar said, which made him smile.

"No matter what action we choose, guile or force, who we are allied with, no matter who stands with us in the shield wall, to defeat Lik-Rifa we must find her first," Sighvat said. "I am no deep-cunning thinker, but even I know that."

"You are right, Sighvat," Elvar said, and he grinned.

"Wherever she is, we should not stay here," Ulfrir said.

"Why not?" Silrið asked him. "We are in a fortress, on an unassailable mountain, a warband thousands strong about us, and sitting within a Galdur tower that harbours ancient power."

"Nowhere is unassailable to a dragon, and she is powerful, too. She will have her own resources, her own warbands. Her dragon-born offspring, and vaesen will serve her," Ulfrir said, looking around at them all, seeing that sink into them. "Your question was guile or force. That was the wrong question. To defeat Lik-Rifa we will need *both*. She must be tricked, made to think she is safe to attack us, made to think we are weak when we are strong."

"I like the sound of that," Sighvat rumbled. His brow furrowed. "But how do we do it?"

Ulfrir smiled for the first time, revealing the tips of sharp teeth.

"Now that is the right question," he said.

Sighvat blinked, then grinned.

A silence settled among them and Elvar stood.

"Much has been said, much to think on," she said. "We shall

prepare to leave, shall be ready, but we will not march or sail until I know where this dragon is." She stood, and then there was a banging at the Galdur-tower door. One of the *Berserkir* guards opened the door.

"Orv the Sneak of the Battle-Grim wishes to speak to you, Jarl Elvar," the *Berserkir* said.

"Let him in," Elvar gestured.

Orv walked into the chamber a little hesitantly, eyes looking everywhere, then focused on Elvar and strode towards her. A woman followed behind him, dressed in a wool tunic with fine embroidery, a sealskin cloak about her shoulders and a fur-trimmed felt hat on her head, thick mittens on her hands.

"This is Svea, chief, I mean Jarl Elvar," Orv said as he drew close. "She is a trader with a hull full of wool and honey."

Svea bowed her head to Elvar, eyes wide as she looked around the room, settling upon Ulfrir.

"Go on, tell her what you told me," Orv said.

"I . . . I sailed from Darl eight days ago, Jarl Elvar," Svea said.

"Go on," Elvar said. "What news from Darl?"

"Queen Helka is dead. The dragon came and slew her. And the eagle-god that Skalk the Galdurman resurrected. Tore them to bits, she did."

A silence, gasps. Then Skuld shrieked and Ulfrir threw back his head and howled.

CHAPTER TWENTY

GUÐVARR

Am I a . . . coward? Guðvarr thought to himself. He was thinking of how he had fled from the Froa-spirit in the glade, of how he had fled from Orka at the Grimholt, of how he had fled from Skapti and Hrolf at *The Dead Drengr*, and a voice in his thought-cage that refused to stay silent was telling him that he was a *niðing* coward.

But think what I have been through. Tricked and used by Skalk the deceiver. I hate that man. Memories of being strapped to a table in Skalk's Galdur tower floated up, of the terror he had felt as the hyrndur alighted upon his forearm, of the pain he had felt as it began to gnaw its way into his flesh. *And because of him I had to go in search of a dragon and seek a way to bargain with her.* He shivered, remembering the cold of the north, of the frost-spiders' venom, of their webs wrapped around him. Of Lik-Rifa bursting through the doors of Nastrandir in all her bowel-churning, terror-inducing glory.

And yet I have survived. I am here, I have faced my enemies and outwitted them. Many are dead now, while I still draw breath. Queen Helka, Prince Hakon the niðing *. . .*

He felt a smile stretch across his face at the thought of Hakon, and the expression on the prince's face when he'd realised that Guðvarr had tricked him, had got the better of him.

No, I am no niðing *coward. On the contrary, I am clever and brave.*

A branch snapped overhead and he jumped and flinched in his

saddle, looked up to see a frost-spider staring down at him with many eyes. He urged his horse on a little faster. Shifted his backside in his saddle, trying to ease the aching in his arse.

I hate travelling, I wish we could just catch up with Estrid and have this over and done with.

They were still travelling through dense woodland, every now and then passing through a clearing and glimpsing the River Slågen growing ever closer. Up ahead Krúsa splashed through a stream that crossed their path. She slowed, stopped, raised a hand and called out something unintelligible, no doubt in her own disgusting tongue. The skraeling slowed and stopped, and Jarl Sigrún looked at Guðvarr.

"Time to make camp," she said.

"Why is she leading this crew," Guðvarr said. "I'm not inclined to take orders from vaesen."

"It's a new world," Sigrún shrugged. "We are here, we are being useful to the future ruler of all Vigrið. There are worse paths we could have walked down."

"True enough," Guðvarr muttered, remembering Skalk and the hyrndur he had set to burrowing into Guðvarr's chest.

They stopped and dismounted, led the horses to the stream and let them drink while they unbuckled girths and removed saddles. Hobbled the horses, scratched out fire pits in the earth, fetched kindling and wood for burning, water for pots. It was dark as pitch pine when Guðvarr sat down around a fire pit with Sigrún and a handful of her *drengrs*.

"Why did Estrid not get on a longship and sail away from Darl?" he asked his aunt. "It would have been much quicker, if they were heading for Snakavik they could have been there in seven or eight days."

"True enough," Sigrún said, nodding thoughtfully. "Perhaps they remembered Lik-Rifa descending upon Darl from the sky. Once you are on a ship there is no cover; you are open to attack from above. The path they have taken, they have travelled through woodland wherever possible, used every patch of cover the land has to offer, that rivers and the sea do not."

Guðvarr nodded at that, liking the way his aunt could answer his questions. He took a slurp from a bowl of beef and turnip stew and Krúsa shambled up, pushed her way between Guðvarr and Sigrún, squatted on her haunches and held her hands up to the fire.

"I like fire," the skraeling grunted.

Guðvarr wasn't sure what to make of that, but he found something unsettling about the way she said it.

"We are close to catching our prey," Krúsa said, rubbing her hands together.

"How do you know?" Guðvarr asked.

"Munni has spotted them."

"Munni?" Sigrún asked.

A whirring of wings and a tennúr alighted upon Krúsa's shoulder.

"Munni," the skraeling said. "Tell them what you told me."

"Munni see group of filthy *Maður*, and wolf-bloods with collars of iron," the tennúr said. "That way." It pointed into the darkness, vaguely west, Guðvarr thought, and the tennúr smiled, its mouth far too large for its face, revealing two rows of teeth, the first small and needle-sharp, the second row wide and flat, like grindstones.

"*Maður?* What are *Maður*?" Sigrún asked.

"Humans, people, like you," Krúsa said.

Guðvarr scowled at that.

This vaesen dares call us filthy! he thought, feeling insulted. He wiped at his nose, his hand coming away wet.

"How far ahead?" Sigrún asked the tennúr.

"A day, maybe less," Munni said. "Should catch them before big river."

"The Slågen," Sigrún said.

"Aye," Krúsa nodded. "Good Munni," she said. She took something from a pouch at her belt that looked suspiciously like a tooth, threw it into the air and Munni caught it and popped it into his mouth. Crunched down hard, the sound of something cracking. Then sat there contentedly grinding and crunching at whatever was between his teeth.

"How many of them?" Guðvarr asked Munni.

The vaesen frowned, then held up both hands, fingers splayed.

Guðvarr saw it had five long fingers and one stunted thumb, all with nasty looking claws for nails. It closed and opened its hands three times.

"Thirty-six, then," Guðvarr said.

Thirty-six! Including Úlfhéðnar, *a Galdurman and* drengrs.

He looked at the company he was in.

And I have to rely on vaesen!

He tried not to let the worry show on his face.

I wish we could just travel forever, and not actually catch up with them. Travelling isn't so bad.

"Maybe," Munni shrugged. "Maybe more, maybe less. Munni not good with numbers."

"Maybe more," Guðvarr echoed.

Wonderful.

"Munni did good," Krúsa said and fished out another tooth, tossed it in the air and Munni caught it with a long-fingered hand. "We will catch them soon, maybe tomorrow," Krúsa said to Sigrún, then stood and walked away, the tennúr still sitting on her shoulder.

Guðvarr was silent a while, listening to Krúsa's footsteps fade. He leaned close to his aunt.

"What's our plan?" he whispered. He doubted that Krúsa could hear him, but he was not sure how good a skraeling's hearing was, so wanted to be careful.

"Catch Estrid and Skalk," Sigrún shrugged. "But, more importantly, stay alive."

"That's the bit I'm worried about," Guðvarr whispered. "These aren't just any old people we are chasing. There is at least one Galdurman, possibly more if Sturla or any of Skalk's apprentices fled with him. Estrid is a nasty bitch who knows how to use a sword, I can tell you." *I can vouch for that; she nearly carved a hole in me.* "And they have quite a few *Úlfhéðnar* with them. I've seen them at work, and one is bad enough." He thought of the carnage Orka had wreaked at the Grimholt, remembered the screams, the piles of the dead. He shook his head.

"It's not pretty," he muttered, trying to suppress a sensation in his chest and throat that felt suspiciously like a sob trying to escape.

"We have my thirty *drengrs*, another forty or so skraeling, and I don't know how many frost-spiders and tennúr," Sigrún said. "We will outnumber them."

"But *we* are not Tainted, do not have the power of gods in our veins. And I do not like relying on vaesen when my life is at stake."

"I agree," Sigrún said, leaning close to Guðvarr.

"But, if Krúsa wants to be in charge, she can be. She can lead us into this, be the first to take the brunt of their Galdur-power and Tainted half-people. If anything goes wrong, then she will be the one that suffers. We can hang back and let her and her kind do the hard work."

"I like it," Guðvarr nodded, a slow smile stretching across his face.

"You should lead us, today," Krúsa said to Jarl Sigrún as Guðvarr tightened and buckled the girth on his saddle.

"What did you say!" he squeaked as he stood straight.

"You lead us today," Krúsa said. "Krúsa know you have much to prove to my Mother-Maker, that you want to return to her with glory." The skraeling shrugged. "Krúsa not care about glory. You lead." She smiled at them, as if she were giving them the greatest gift.

"No," Guðvarr said, desperately. "You have led us to here, you can carry on leading."

"Ah, *Maður*-boy kind," Krúsa said, and patted Guðvarr's cheek. "But no. Krúsa has made decision. You lead," and she turned and walked away, Guðvarr's mouth moving but nothing coming out. He just stared at his aunt. She shrugged.

"We will lead," she said, walking towards her horse. He hurried after her.

"What shall we do?" he asked her.

"Be careful and sharpen our blades."

Guðvarr sat on his horse, his head twitching left and right at every sound. They had passed through the woodland onto open heaths, the land undulating and wind-blasted, but despite the cold wind gnawing at his bones he had been pleased, because there was no sign of Galdurmen or *Úlfhéðnar*, and so no chance of battle and death, and the open heath meant no chance of nasty surprises, like ambushes, or Froa-spirits. But then they had seen the bright smear of the River Slågen in the distance and Guðvarr had remembered his aunt's words, that if Estrid crossed the river then she would be in Jarl Störr's land, and they would have to follow her there, with enemies all around. Before the river stood another thick swathe of woodland, far denser than the open woodland they had passed through earlier. And now they were riding along a narrow path, trees and bushes tight on either side, everything bathed in a half-light. Jarl Sigrún rode ahead of him, the path only wide enough for one horse at a time. Above him he could hear the scuttling legs of frost-spiders, but it did not reassure him.

The perfect place for an ambush, Guðvarr thought.

Crows squawked and he jumped in his saddle.

"Nephew," Jarl Sigrún looked back over her saddle and said to him, frowning.

"Aye, aunt," he muttered.

"You must master your fear. You are spooking the horses."

"Fear? I feel no fear!" he snapped, though his voice came out higher in pitch than he would have liked.

Jarl Sigrún just looked at him, then looked ahead.

Master my fear, master my fear, he repeated to himself. *I am Guðvarr,* drengr, *survivor, cunning and brave.*

Well, I'm alive, which is saying a lot considering what I've been through. And now I am on a task set by a god. I must have some qualities to have brought me this far.

He thought on that a while, and slowly began to feel a little better for it.

We have had to slow down so much to get through this snarl of forest, Estrid, Skalk and their band of murderers must be far from here by now. Confusingly, that thought made him feel both relieved and also worried.

The path ahead opened into a glade, wide enough for three or four horses abreast, and Guðvarr felt a worm of fear squirm in his belly. He looked suspiciously around, searching for an ash tree, and blew out a long sigh of relief when all he saw was a pile of boulders at the glade's far end. He drew abreast with Sigrún as her *drengrs* spilled into the glade behind them.

"I am worried that Estrid and the others are bound to have reached the river by now," he said to her. "Do you think we should speed up."

A figure stepped out from behind the boulders at the far end of the glade. Guðvarr dragged on his reins and reached for his sword, half drew it from its scabbard. Then he frowned, eyes narrowing.

The man who had stepped from behind the boulder was dressed in mail, an axe at his belt and a shield slung across his back. He had thinning hair, a white beard and a scar running through a bulbous nose. And Guðvarr recognised him.

"Skapti," he said with a scowl, urging his horse closer to the man.

"Guðvarr," Skapti nodded amicably. "Still alive, I see."

Sigrún and her *drengrs* spread in a line and approached Skapti, weapons held ready. Sigrún barked an order and warriors moved to the edge of the glade, searching the treeline.

"I'm alone," Skapti said.

Krúsa and her skraeling entered the glade, and frost-spiders crept through the foliage at the glade's edge.

"What are you doing here?" Guðvarr said, riding slowly up to Skapti and levelling his sword at the old warrior.

"I have a proposition for you," Skapti said, "and an offer."

"What could you possibly have that we would want?" Guðvarr said.

"Information," Skapti said and shrugged. "Knowledge is power."

CHAPTER TWENTY-ONE

VARG

Muscles burned in Varg's back as he leaned and pulled, his oar slicing through water, the *Sea-Wolf* carving through waves. They were threading among a knot of islands in an attempt to lose the five *drakkar* that had been following them from Ulaz, and Varg was relieved that he had not seen the tips of their masts on the horizon since early morning. A little behind them Sulich's *knarr* rose and fell on the swell, its fat belly making slower going between the islands.

At the stern Glornir pulled on the steering oar and abruptly the rowing became easier, Varg glancing up to see that they were sailing into a natural harbour, wooded banks skimming by on either side of the *Sea-Wolf*. He put his head down and kept pulling to Taras' regular drumbeat. The big man seemed to be enjoying sitting in the stern and banging rhythmically on an old battered shield with a knot of rope.

"OARS," Glornir bellowed and Varg and thirty other rowers lifted their oars, the *Sea-Wolf* coasting, then pulled the oars in through oar-holes, setting them in the racks on the deck.

The *Sea-Wolf* slowed, hull grating on sand and, at Glornir's command Taras heaved the anchor stone overboard. Glornir tied off the steering oar and then he was leaping over the top-rail and splashing into water, wading through the surf to a sandy beach. Røkia was next over the rail and Varg quickly followed, holding his spear high, the shock of cold water flooding his boots. He looked up the sloping beach to a treeline where there was a tangle of huts. Figures were running out of buildings and staring, children, and behind them appeared a man and woman. The man was huge, broad and tall, a bandage around his head, a fair-haired child sitting on his shoulders, the woman limping, shorter than the man but still wide across the back and shoulders.

"EINAR," a voice shouted and Svik ran past Varg and Røkia, sprinting up the beach.

Einar started laughing and lumbered down the beach, snatched Svik up into an embrace, lifting the man's feet from the ground and squeezing him tightly. The child on his back laughed, and other children swirled around them, laughing and chattering as Glornir, Røkia and Varg reached them.

"Where's my hug?" Æsa asked Svik as Einar put him down.

"You can have a hug, Æsa," Svik said, wrapping his arms around the warrior, "but just do not think that it means I want to hump you."

"Ha, of course you want to hump me," Æsa laughed and squeezed Svik until he stepped away, blushing.

The child slid down from Einar's shoulders and wrapped her arms around Glornir's thick leg, hugging him tight.

"Well met, Refna Strong-Hands," Glornir said.

"I'm glad you're safe," Refna said.

"Safe?" Glornir said, "I would not say that. And right now I am at risk of losing my leg through blood loss," Glornir grunted and Refna let him go. He tousled her fair hair.

"Your leg?" Glornir asked Æsa.

"Healing well, chief," Æsa said, "though I'll not be winning any races for a while."

"Good," Glornir grunted. "And your head?" he asked Einar.

"All good," Einar said, rapping his knuckles on the bandage around his skull.

"That tongue-eater cracked it like a nut," Svik said, "but with you I doubt it will make any difference."

Einar grinned. "It is good to see you, little Svik, good to see all of you," he boomed, holding his arms out and looking at the Bloodsworn on the beach, and the *Sea-Wolf* in the surf. He saw the second ship.

"You've made some friends in Iskidan, then?"

"Aye," Svik said, "Sulich and his kin. You have missed out on some fun, I can tell you."

"No time for that now," Glornir said. "We need to get you all on the *Sea-Wolf* and away from here."

"Trouble?" Einar asked.

"I hope so," Æsa said. "Sounds like I've missed out on enough scraps." She patted the axe at her belt.

"There'll be plenty of that to come," Svik said, "we are going dragon hunting."

"Time for that tale later, as well," Glornir growled. "There are five of Rurik's longships out there hunting for us among these islands. We need to make sure they don't find us."

They all hurried back to the longship and clambered aboard. Varg took an oar from the rack and returned to his bench as Glornir untied the steering oar. Taras heaved on the rope that held the anchor stone, hauling it over the deck, then resumed his position sitting on a barrel close to Glornir.

Einar strode towards his familiar place on the ship, close to Glornir where he would beat time for the rowers, and saw Taras sitting there with a shield resting across his lap and a knotted piece of rope in his fist.

"You're in my spot, big man," Einar said to him.

"This is Taras' spot," Taras said, frowning.

"Who are you? Who is he?" Einar said, looking around.

"A friend," Vol said, hurrying down to them from the prow.

Taras blinked at that.

"Taras has friends now," he grinned.

"Will somebody tell me who he is?" Einar boomed.

"I am Taras the Bull, friend of the Bloodsworn," Taras said proudly.

Einar scratched his head. "Well, that makes you a friend of mine, then, Taras the Bull," Einar said. "Because I am one of the Bloodsworn, too."

"And what is your name, big man of the Bloodsworn?" Taras asked him, standing and looking Einar up and down. They were roughly around the same height. Varg thought the *Sea-Wolf* was dipping lower in the water with them both in the stern.

"I am Einar, who men call Half-Troll."

"Ha," Taras barked a laugh. "A good name. Come, have a drink with Taras and we can share this seat." He lifted a leather bottle from his belt and unstoppered it, offering it to Einar.

Einar took it, sniffed it, took a drink, coughed, then smiled.

"OARS," yelled Glornir.

Varg leaned on the top-rail, lifted a ladle from the water barrel and took a deep drink. He had just finished his shift on the oar-bench and was stretching his back, looking out at the horizon beyond the prow of the *Sea-Wolf*. They were still moving through the islands that clustered the northern coast of Iskidan, but Varg could see the open sea beyond. He stared into the distance, saw only white-tipped waves on the grey-green sea and heavy grey skies, but he knew that Vigrið lay beyond it.

Vigrið, and bloodshed. There is a dragon to slay.

And my sister to avenge, Brák Trolls-Bane to put in the ground.

"I owe your friend Leif Kolskeggson, Sterkur death-in-the-eye and all his crew a painful death," Svik said as he came to stand beside Varg. A bruise still mottled one side of Svik's face where he had been clubbed.

As do I.

"It's a nasty bruise," Varg said.

"Not because of the bruise," Svik said with a sniff, "because of how my hair was pulled from its braids."

"A terrible crime," Varg agreed with a hint of a smile.

Edel walked along the deck with her hound at her side and a roll of what looked like parchment papers tucked under one arm. She nodded to Svik and Varg as she passed them and strode on towards the bow, where Vol was standing with one hand resting on the carved prow beast of the *Sea-Wolf*, staring into the distance.

"Vol," Edel said. "I took these for you, thought that you might be able to understand them, use them, but with all that has happened," she shrugged, "I think they are something that you should see."

"What is it?"

"Copies of rune-magic that were found in Rotta's chamber. Orka and Gunnar Prow found them and gave them to me." She handed the roll of parchments over to Vol, who opened them and stared, then hissed.

"This can only be the *Raudskinna*!" Vol breathed. Fear and excitement leaked from her as she stared intently, reading, then looking at another sheet of parchment, then another, and another. "Or, at least, copied fragments," she muttered. She sheafed through more pages, then looked up at Edel. "There are powerful spells here, spells of cunning and deep malice. It is . . . terrifying." Reaching out she squeezed Edel's wrist. "You have done well to bring me these. Better that we have them than Ilska's dragon-born."

"Aye," Edel nodded.

Vol read some more, appearing lost in the runes. She looked up.

"I need to speak to Iva," she said and strode down the longship's deck to find Iva, who was sitting on a barrel near the mast, wrapped in a cloak.

A gust of wind tugged at Varg's hair, and he looked up to see that the *Sea-Wolf* was leaving the protection of the islands, the waves becoming wilder, the wind keener as they carved into open sea.

"How long until we reach Snakavik?" Varg asked Svik.

"Maybe ten days with the right wind," Svik said, "although maybe longer with Sulich's sow of a ship slowing us down." He looked back at the *knarr* behind them, then swore.

"What is it?" Varg said, and Svik pointed south, into the channel between the islands.

In the distance two longships appeared, moving fast. As they watched two more appeared from the west, and then one more.

"Perhaps it will take us a little longer," Svik muttered. "No outrunning them now. We will have to put those arselings at the bottom of the sea."

CHAPTER TWENTY-TWO

ORKA

"Your shield is dropping," Orka warned Breca, who was standing on the deck of Jarl Orlyg's longship with Gunnar Prow's shield in one fist and a short-hafted axe in the other.

"Sorry," Breca grunted as he hefted the shield back into position. It was too big for him, but he was fighting in an adult's world now, so he should train with an adult's weapons.

"Don't be sorry," Orka said.

"Be better," Lif, Gunnar and Halja finished for her.

Orka frowned at them as they smirked watching the training.

Breca lunged at her, and she stepped away, inwardly pleased that he took his opportunity when he thought she was distracted, though she gave no sign of it on her face. She stepped left then pushed off hard to her right, moving away from Breca's axe-hand, darted in low, stabbing at Breca's shins with a spear she had borrowed from Lif. Instinctively he slammed his shield rim down at the spear head, but Orka had already pulled it back and in a heartbeat the spear-tip was at Breca's exposed chest.

"Do *not* lower your shield," Orka said.

Halja Flat-Nose laughed, and Breca's eyes flickered amber and green.

"No," Orka growled at him. She glanced around but could see no one else watching them. Jarl Orlyg's *drengrs* and Tainted were bending their backs on oar-benches, speeding the longship down the river as it widened, silt flats spreading along either bank as they drew closer to the river's estuary and the sea.

"Come," Orka said, beckoning to Breca and the others as she squatted on the deck. They drew close around her.

"What's the plan, chief?" Halja asked Orka.

"To get to Snakavik," Orka said. "To join Glornir and the Bloodsworn."

"Will they go there? Take up Elvar's offer?" Lif asked.

"They will," Orka grunted. "It is an offer of payment to avenge Thorkel's death. Glornir would be after Lik-Rifa and her dragon-born without payment, so it is the sensible thing for a chief to do."

"Aye, why not get paid for something you plan to do anyway," Halja said.

"If they have managed to get Vol back," Lif said. "If they have not . . ." He looked at Gunnar and Halja.

"If they have not been defeated, or slain," Halja finished for him.

Lif shrugged. "I mean no offence," he said. "This is Vigrið. No one is safe."

"Not even the Bloodsworn," Gunnar murmured.

"They will be at Snakavik," Orka said firmly.

"And how are we to get to Snakavik, mistress?" Sæunn asked.

"We will sail or walk," Orka shrugged.

"Faster to sail," Gunnar said.

"Sailing would be best, aye," Halja said, "but this Orlyg may have other plans than sailing to Snakavik."

"It would be faster, yes," Orka said. "But safer?" She leaned closer to them all. "We are Tainted, and risk being thralled if Orlyg finds out." She looked at Breca. "If we are to stay on this longship, which I agree would be best, if we can convince Orlyg to sail for Snakavik, then you *must* control the beast in your blood. Be the master, not the thrall. Or you could end up like that." She jutted her chin at a Tainted warrior pulling at an oar, an iron collar around his neck.

"Yes, Mama," Breca said seriously.

She looked at him, his dark eyes in his pale, dirty face, his black, scruffy hair. She brushed a strand away from one cheek.

I have him back. I will not lose him again.

"I have something of yours," she said, and reached inside the neckline of her tunic drawing out the wooden pendant of a sword that Breca had carved in their steading near Fellur village. She remembered him carving it the night before he had been taken, remembered finding it in the wreckage of her home. It seemed so long ago now. Another time, almost like a dream. She slipped the leather cord over her head and held it out to him.

"I remember . . ." he said, taking it and holding it, then tears welled in his eyes. "Before they came, before Papa . . ."

Without thought Orka was pulling him close, felt his tears spill onto her cheek.

Footsteps, and she leaned away from Breca, wiped his tears away with her fingertips and looked up to see Jarl Orlyg's Galdurman striding past them with his staff in his fist, Dagrun, the jarl's son, walking with him.

"Come, join us," Dagrun said to Orka.

She hesitated a moment.

Dagrun slowed and stopped. "Please, my father wishes to speak with you," he said.

Orka nodded and stood.

"Lif, teach Breca some more shield work," she said to the young warrior, handing him back his spear.

"Me?" Lif said.

"Aye. You are a warrior now. I saw you." Then she was walking away, following Dagrun and the Galdurman towards the stern of the longship. They passed a row of men and women lying on the deck, all injured from the raid against Rotta. Some had since died and were wrapped and bound in cloaks and linen sheets.

Orlyg was stood at the stern, white-haired and wearing a coat of mail, a patchwork cloak of fox pelts about his shoulders, an axe at his belt. He had a newly stitched cut across one cheek, scabbed and bruised. A *drengr* stood one side of him, a woman, iron-grey hair tied tight at her crown, and a Tainted thrall stood the other side, straw-haired and lean, his face all sharp lines and shadows.

"Who are you?" Orlyg asked Orka as she reached them.

"A farmer," she said with a shrug.

"Dagrun tells me you saved him, that you and your crew cut down skraeling and dragon-born like they were wheat ready for the scythe. *Farmers* do not have that kind of weapons craft."

Orka said nothing.

"And your crew, two of them are Bloodsworn, yet they defer to you." Orlyg smiled. "I recognise their shields." Then his eyes narrowed. "You saved my son, and I owe you a blood-price for that, but do not lie to me, or treat me like a fool. If you do, I shall throw you into the river myself."

Orka looked at him, held his gaze a long moment.

"I was Bloodsworn once," she said.

There were mutters among the *drengrs* around her, the female warrior at Orlyg's side looking her up and down.

"That was many years ago," Orka said. "I am a farmer now, or I was. Until some of the dragon-born swept through my steading, slew my husband and stole my son. Since then, I have been following them, to get him back."

Orlyg looked along the deck to Breca and the others.

"And the two Bloodsworn with you?" he said.

"I met them along the way. They joined me because I was one of them, once, and they hold their oaths dear."

"Huh," Orlyg grunted, nodding. "Go on," he said. "There is more to this tale."

"Not much more," Orka said. "I tracked them to Svelgarth, slipped into Rotta's camp as they attacked your town and got my son out, but I was captured." She gestured towards Dagrun. "The rest your son knows."

Orlyg looked at her a long moment with narrowed eyes, then looked to Dagrun, who nodded.

"Your tale has the ring of truth, to me. And my son speaks for you. So, welcome, and my thanks for saving his scrawny arse." He held out his arm and Orka took his wrist. "You are welcome to travel with us as long as you wish," he said.

"Well, that will depend on where you are going."

"Ha, a straight talker. I like you more with each word," he said. "And that is what I have called Dagrun and Gösta here to discuss.

Where shall we go?" He looked at Dagrun and the Galdurman with him, then glanced back over his shoulder at the river and land they had sailed down. "It looks like we've put some distance between us and that *niðing* rabble of Tainted and vaesen filth," he boomed.

"That *rabble* sacked Svelgarth, Father," Dagrun reminded him. "Trolls ripped the gates down, and Seiðr-witches burned the town to ashes."

"They are not Seiðr-witches, they are dragon-born," Gösta the Galdurman said bitterly. "Servants of Lik-Rifa."

"What's the difference?" Dagrun said.

"A different magic," Gösta sniffed. "Seiðr-witches gain their power from the blood of Snaka. These dragon-born, I presume their power comes from their mother's weaker blood, Lik-Rifa."

"I do not care about the ancestry of rune-magic," Orlyg snapped. "Serpent or dragon blood, it is all foul magic to me, and it has destroyed my home." He tugged on the thick braid of his white beard. "How can this be? The world is upside down," he muttered. "They did almost the same to Darl." He shook his head, lost in thought.

During the last two days while they had rowed downriver Orka had heard mutterings from the crew that Lik-Rifa had fallen upon Darl, that Orna the eagle-god had been resurrected and then slain, and that Helka was dead, and her fortress razed to rubble in the battle.

It seemed there was no limit to Lik-Rifa's ambitions.

"We are approaching the sea, my lord," the Galdurman said, a slim, dark-haired man, tattoos covering his lower jaw, small bones braided into his hair. "Which direction will we sail?"

"My heart tells me to sail to Svelgarth, Gösta," Orlyg said. "To my home, where I was born, the place I have fought for and protected all my years. It is ash and rubble, you say?" He looked to Dagrun.

"It is a ruin, Father," Dagrun said, shaking his head.

"The Galdur tower?" Gösta asked.

"They smashed it to the ground, and burned what was left of it," Dagrun said.

Gösta looked away, face draining of colour. A muscle twitched in his cheek.

"We could rebuild," Orlyg said.

"And if they return?" Gösta said. "They have broken Svelgarth, and they did not even have the dragon with them."

"Just some *niðing* rat," Orlyg muttered.

"Indeed," Gösta said. "We saw what the dragon did to Darl. What would she do to Svelgarth?"

"Aye," Orlyg scowled. "Agreed, it would be foolish to try and rebuild Svelgarth now. So, what do we do?"

"We could join them?" Gösta said.

"No," Orlyg and Dagrun said, both glowering at Gösta.

"I am going through the options, lord," Gösta said quietly. "A list of what we can do, then we must choose one of those options. So, we do not join them. That leaves two other options."

"And what are they?" Dagrun said.

"Fight, or flee," Gösta said.

"How do you fight a dragon?" Dagrun murmured.

"If it were a man I would challenge him to a wrestling match," Orlyg said. "No warbands, no more mass death or destruction, just the two of us testing our strength, one against the other." He flexed his barrel chest and shoulders, looked at those gathered around him. "I would win," he growled, a smile twitching his white moustache and beard.

"If we fled," Gösta said, "I do not think we could hide in Vigrið. We would have to go to Iskidan."

"And bend the knee to that arseling Kirill," Orlyg spat. "Not while I draw breath."

"Then we do not return to Svelgarth, and we do not flee to Iskidan," Gösta said. "You see how we are narrowing down our options. And that leaves only one. We fight."

"Yes," Orlyg said, clenching a fist.

"Aye, but how?" Dagrun said.

"We need allies," Orlyg said.

"Helka is gone," Gösta said. "Which leaves only Jarl Störr as a real power in Vigrið."

Orlyg sniffed. "I like that arrogant, conceited, sneaky arseling less than I liked Helka, and I *hated* that bitch." The *drengr* beside him chuckled, and Orlyg looked at her, then began to laugh, too, a deep rumbling in his belly.

"But you were prepared to make a pact with Helka," Gösta pointed out.

"Aye, she was the enemy of my enemy. I thought we could defeat Störr together, and I could betray her after." He laughed again.

"I would have taken her head for you, lord," the *drengr* close to Orlyg said.

"I know you would, Aila," Orlyg said, patting her arm.

"Well, I imagine Jarl Störr would not take kindly to a dragon taking his realm from him, so that would make him the enemy of our enemy . . ." Gösta continued.

"Aye, but Störr is more devious than Helka. I did not trust her, but I trust Störr less. And I do not like the thought of sailing into Snakavik now. With Svelgarth fallen I have less to offer Störr than I had to offer Helka. I would not make so strong an ally that Störr would think twice about cutting my head from my shoulders."

A silence settled among them.

"There is another reason to sail to Snakavik," Orka said.

Orlyg's eyes fixed on her. "And what is that?"

"Ulfrir the wolf-god is there."

All heads turned to look at her.

"I thought the gods were dead, and yet more seem to appear with every breath I take. A dragon-god, a rat-god, the eagle-god, briefly," Orlyg said. He puffed out his cheeks. "And now you say Ulfrir the wolf-god is roaming Vigrið. This is the first we have heard of this. Surely word would have spread through Vigrið if a giant wolf was prowling around."

"Ulfrir lives," the thrall-guard at Orlyg's shoulder said.

"How do you know, Tjorvi?" Orlyg said, frowning at his guard.

"I have heard his call, in my dreams," the warrior said. "We all have," he gestured a hand to Tainted warriors on the oar-benches. "He calls the *Úlfhéðnar* to him."

"And why have you not spoken to me of this?"

"You have not asked, my lord," Tjorvi said.

Orlyg let out a low rumbling growl, frowning at the *Úlfhéðnar*. Slowly he turned to look back at Orka.

"So, how do you know about this wolf-god," Orlyg asked her, "and why should we seek him out?"

"Ulfrir is thralled to Elvar, chief of the Battle-Grim," Orka said. "I met her in Starl, and she had Ulfrir thralled to her, an iron collar about his neck."

Orlyg whistled. "Elvar, Jarl Störr's Elvar? His runaway daughter?"

"Aye," Orka nodded.

"Little-Elvar," Orlyg whistled. "Ha, I always liked her. I saw her kick her arseling brother Thorun in the stones once, in front of everyone. He dropped like a felled ox." Orlyg laughed at the memory of it. "What is she doing running the Battle-Grim and dragging a wolf-god around with her?"

"She was at Oskutreð when Lik-Rifa broke her bonds," Orka said. "And she has some grudge against Lik-Rifa, which is why she has Ulfrir. To use him as a weapon to slay the dragon."

"That sounds like a dangerous, deep-cunning plan; I like it," Orlyg muttered. "Though, if she succeeds, that would make her a powerful foe. Too powerful."

"Right now, Elvar is the enemy of our enemy," Dagrun pointed out.

"Aye. She is. The dragon and the rat must die, of that there is no question, and what better way than to get a wolf to do the job." Orlyg looked at Orka. "But how by all the dead gods did Little-Elvar manage to thrall a god?"

Orka shrugged. "You will have to ask her that yourself."

"I intend to," Orlyg said. He cupped his hands to his mouth. "We sail for Snakavik," he shouted.

CHAPTER TWENTY-THREE

ELVAR

Elvar sat in the Galdur tower of Snakavik, drumming her fingers on the arm of her chair. Behind her she heard the rhythmic snoring of Sighvat. He was supposed to be her guard in this chamber, but she knew that there were *Berserkir* close, and others guarding the door to the chamber, so Elvar had not scolded him when she had heard his snoring begin. She lifted a drinking horn to her lips and drank a mouthful of mead, felt its honeyed heat roll down her throat and warm her belly. Flames flickered in the fire pit before her and she stared into them, lost in her thoughts.

Darl is fallen, Helka dead. Orna resurrected, then slain by Lik-Rifa. This is real. Now, I am at war with a god, and suddenly Vigrið does not feel so large. There is nowhere to hide from a dragon-god. Where will I face Lik-Rifa and her followers? How will I defeat her and get Bjarn back? What should I do? Her thoughts spiralled, stirring emotions like a storm wind swirling leaves. She felt scared, overwhelmed by the myriad decisions she had to make, frozen by the fear of making the wrong choices. *So many lives depend on my decisions, not least of all my own. I wish Grend were here to advise me. Where is he?*

After Grend had failed to appear for sparring in the weapons court the day after news had arrived of Darl's destruction, Elvar had sent *drengrs* out to search for him. That had been three days ago, and worry was gnawing at her. Even Gytha did not know where he was.

"It is the waiting that hurts, is it not?" a voice said, startling her and making her jump. She sat straighter in her chair and looked at Hrung, his opaque eyes reflecting the flickering firelight.

"The waiting is harder than the doing, I always found. Now, of course, all I can do is wait." He sighed and blinked. "I remember when I decided to try and kill Snaka, I was happy that I made the decision, but then I had to work out how, and then I had to wait for an opportunity." He shook his head. "It was difficult. Time passes so slowly when you are just . . . waiting."

"What?" Elvar said. "You tried to kill Snaka?"

"I did not try, my dear, I *succeeded*," Hrung said, his huge forehead knotting into a frown. "I killed Snaka."

"You killed Snaka!"

"Why are you repeating everything I am saying?" Hrung said. "Yes, I killed him. How do you think my head came to be between his jaws?"

"Uh, I just thought, he ate a lot of his creations, did he not?"

"Aye, he did," rumbled Hrung. "He ate my mother, my father, my brothers and sisters, my uncles and aunts, my nephews . . . my wife, my children." He flapped his lips. "He ate my whole clan, everyone I knew. Everyone I loved." His eyes welled and one fat tear spilled onto his cheek, rolled down to his lip.

I forget that Hrung was more than he is now, lived a life, had a family. And Snaka destroyed all of that on a whim. The gods are a curse.

"How did you do it?" Elvar asked him. "How did you kill Snaka?"

"I poisoned myself," Hrung said with a bitter grin. "Filled my body with poison and hurled myself into his mouth. It was the Guðfalla, the gods were at war, all of Vigrið trembled with it, and Snaka was angry, in a feeding frenzy, eating every living thing he encountered, so it was not hard to get him to eat me."

Elvar was silent, imagining the chaos and bloodshed. The destruction. "So, how are you . . . alive?" she asked him.

"I do not know," Hrung said. "I have had a long time to ponder that question. Snaka was a creator as well as a destroyer, remember, he had powerful magic that flowed within him. When his fangs struck me, severed my head from my body, I think something of his power must have leaked into my flesh and blood. Or perhaps it was as he died, his flesh and blood filling the fjord, leaking around me, into me. The Tainted, as you call them, they get their powers through their bloodline, so perhaps it was Snaka's blood. But, really, who knows? All that is for sure is that I am alive. Well," he looked at Elvar mournfully. "Is this really living? I think, I speak, I taste, but . . ."

Elvar stood and walked over to him, stroked his cheek.

"I for one am glad you still live, ancient Hrung," she said and lifted her mead horn to his lips, emptied it into his mouth.

"Ahh, that tastes good," Hrung said, smacking his lips.

There was a knock at the door.

Behind her Sighvat spluttered and wheezed.

"What, where?" he mumbled, stumbling to his feet.

"Come," Elvar called out and Berak the *Berserkir* opened the Galdur-tower door and stepped into the room.

"Ulfrir, Skuld and Uspa to see you, my lady," Berak said. He looked back over his shoulder. "There are others with Ulfrir."

"How many?" Elvar asked.

"Two score, perhaps more," Berak said.

"Let them in, and Berak, you come, too."

Uspa stepped into the room, Ulfrir and Skuld behind her, and a line of men and women filed in behind the wolf-god. Some were clothed in mail with well-cared-for weapons at their belts, but most just wore tunics and cloaks, perhaps a seax or axe at their belts. They were all lean, wary and hungry looking, their eyes darting around the room nervously, taking in the shadows.

"You asked me to bring them," Ulfrir said as he came to stand opposite Elvar, the fire flickering between them. "My children."

Elvar stood beside Hrung and stared at the *Úlfhéðnar*, heard Sighvat move to stand behind her left shoulder. Berak stood just behind the new arrivals, hulking and glowering in his mail, one hand resting lightly on the shaft of the axe at his belt.

"You are Tainted," Elvar said, and eyes fixed on her. She felt a tension flood the room, a sharpness in the air. "I have two voices in my thought-cage. One says that you are Tainted and should be thralled. That you are dangerous, a risk, and that I cannot trust you unless you have an iron collar about your necks."

Feet shuffled, Elvar seeing hands go to weapons, muscles tensing. Growls came from the shadows around the edges of the tower, hulking figures moving, shadows within shadows as her *Berserkir* shifted, green eyes reflecting the firelight. She saw Ulfrir and those with him saw them.

"And the other voice in my thought-cage tells me that you are brave to come here," Elvar continued, "where you are at such risk, that you have already fought for Ulfrir on the docks against Ingvild and her Wave-Roamers, and so you have already fought for me."

She looked to Ulfrir, could still see the grief etched in his face from the news of Orna's destruction.

"My question is, who are you loyal to?"

"They are loyal to *me*," Ulfrir said.

Elvar looked at the *Úlfhéðnar*. All of them met her gaze.

"And you are loyal to me," Elvar said to Ulfrir.

"I am," he nodded.

"For now." Elvar added. "Of course, you have no choice, which sours things a little, but nevertheless, you are loyal, of that I have no doubt. So . . ." She walked around the fire pit to stand directly in front of Ulfrir and his *Úlfhéðnar*. Sighvat hurried to stand with her, and Berak moved closer, frowning. The *Berserkir* in the shadows stepped out into the light. "I do not wish to put collars around your necks, but I also need to be sure that you will be loyal to me in the coming war, that you will not betray me. How do I do that?"

"We will swear you our oaths," one of the *Úlfhéðnar* said, a man, lean and haggard. "If that is what Ulfrir wishes."

"Is that enough, though, to secure your loyalty?" Elvar mused.

"Let them swear their oaths to you, and let Ulfrir command them to serve you," Uspa said. "That will be enough, that will ensure more loyalty than you will get from any of the mercenary bands gathered here for your coin."

Elvar looked at Ulfrir who returned her gaze, then gave her a curt nod.

"Good, then do it now," Elvar said.

"That was well done," Hrung said as Ulfrir's *Úlfhéðnar* left the chamber.

"Was it?" Elvar said. "If it works, then I have just doubled the number of my Tainted warriors. But I wonder, can I trust them to keep their oaths?"

"More than you can trust most, I would wager," Hrung said.

"Aye, but that is not as much as I can trust my *Berserkir*."

"*Your Berserkir*?" Hrung said. "Like a fine-tooled cup, or a sharp seax?"

"Yes, exactly like that," Elvar snapped.

"They are people, too," Hrung said.

"They are my thralls, to do as I bid."

"That is what your father used to say," Hrung said.

Elvar scowled at him.

The door creaked as Ulfrir pulled it shut behind him.

"Ulfrir," Elvar called, and he paused and looked back, Elvar beckoning him back to her. Skuld came with him and Elvar decided not to point out that she had only summoned Ulfrir.

"Yes, Jarl Elvar," Ulfrir said.

"You said that Snakavik is not safe from Lik-Rifa."

"I did," Ulfrir said. "It is not. She would descend upon it and tear this fortress to ribbons." He paused a moment, studying her. Elvar was still not used to the intensity of Ulfrir's gaze, but she met it unflinchingly.

"And I recall you refused to leave Snakavik until we discovered where Lik-Rifa was," Ulfrir said. "We know, now, that she is in Darl, and yet we are still here, in Snakavik."

"Aye," Elvar nodded. "I admit I do not like the thought of sitting here, waiting for her, and what you said, about finding better ground, about making her think we are weak when we are strong, it has merit."

Ulfrir just looked at her.

"But where would be a stronger place to fight her from?" She sucked in a breath, steeled herself and her pride. "Ulfrir, I do not know where to go. Where do you think we should go?"

Ulfrir smiled, the tips of his sharp teeth glowing in the reflected firelight.

"My den," he said. "The Wolfdales."

"Where is that?" Elvar asked.

"Close to the Jarnvidr, the Iron Wood," Skuld said, her wings twitching.

"I know where that is," Sighvat said.

"Everyone knows where that is," Hrung said. "Even a talking head knows where it is."

Elvar knew of the Iron Wood, a great swathe of forest that snared the south of her father's land, *her* land now, running in a tangle along the southern border marked by the River Slågen.

"And why is it better there?" Elvar asked him.

"It is not open to the skies, like here. The Iron Wood gives cover from eyes in the sky, and there is more of my Wolfdales below ground than above it. To defeat Lik-Rifa you do not walk into a fight of strength, of muscle and magic. She would win. To defeat her you need cunning." He tapped a finger against his temple. "You need ground that will conceal you and confuse her."

"I will think on it," she said.

Ulfrir turned to go, then looked back at her.

"My . . . thanks," he said haltingly, "for your kindness to my children."

"I hope I do not come to regret it," Elvar said.

"You will not," Ulfrir said, looked at her a long moment and then turned and left, Skuld following him in a swirl of red-feathered wings.

Elvar sat with a sigh. As the door closed, she looked up and saw that Uspa remained, Berak with her.

"Yes?" Elvar said.

"You dealt with Ulfrir and his *Úlfhéðnar* well," Uspa said.

"Thank you," Elvar said.

"But you must know this is only the beginning. The more this war gathers pace, the more the Tainted will become a bigger issue," Uspa said. "Most will flock to Lik-Rifa because she fights for their freedom. And they are powerful. Imagine how many there are, lurking in the hidden places of Vigrið."

"She makes a good point," Hrung said.

"This has crossed my mind," Elvar said.

Consumed my mind, more like.

"But there is nothing I can do about that. Grend always says worry about what you can change. I cannot change that."

"You could," Uspa said.

"How?" Elvar asked, filling her mead horn from a jug and taking a sip.

"Set your Tainted free and let all of Vigrið know that you have done it."

"What!" spluttered Elvar, spitting out her mead.

"Set them *free*," Uspa repeated. "You are not a god. You are not an unknown. You are a jarl of Vigrið. If you do what others would not – the Tainted would trust you over some crazed god. Some would come to you because of Ulfrir, it's true. But many, many would come to your side to fight for Vigrið – if they knew that they would have a place in it afterwards. Perhaps it would even *weaken* Lik-Rifa's forces, because she has set herself up as the champion of the Tainted. Currently, she is their only option."

"Are you insane?" Elvar said in disbelief. "If I set my *Berserkir* free they would leave me, perhaps fight for Lik-Rifa, perhaps just walk away from this war. I do not think *any* would stay to fight for me, the person who has enslaved them."

"I would stay," Berak said.

"That is because I am going to war with Lik-Rifa for your *son*," Elvar snarled. "This war is happening because of your son, because of this." She dragged her sleeve up to reveal the white scars of her blood oath, the *blóð svarið*. "And what of Ulfrir, shall I release him, too?"

"Yes," Uspa said.

Elvar opened her mouth, but only strangled words came out. "You have lost your mind," she eventually spluttered. "If I set him free the first thing he would do would be to rip my throat out. I have tamed him, shamed him, humiliated him. Yes, we share a common enemy, but he would fight Lik-Rifa with or without me. If he were free, he would not need me. I need him, I need the *Berserkirs*. Set them free and I lose them. *We* lose them. And then we lose the war, which means we lose Bjarn. Do you want your son back?"

"I do," Uspa said, but she looked to the ground. "But this, it is wrong," she whispered.

"Right, wrong, just words," Elvar said, though she felt uncomfortable even as they left her mouth, because her father had said the exact same words to her. "All that matters is winning. We cannot lose. We must win, and I need Ulfrir and the *Berserkir* if we are to stand the slightest hope of defeating Lik-Rifa and getting your son back."

"But—"

"No," Elvar snapped, "I will hear no more of this madness. We will prepare to march tomorrow for the Jarnvidr." She poured herself another horn of mead and looked up, saw Uspa leaving.

Elvar slumped down in her chair and drank deeply.

"Ruling, it is not all the skálds lead you to believe, eh," Hrung said.

Elvar did not answer him.

Where is Grend? she thought.

CHAPTER TWENTY-FOUR

BIÓRR

Biórr rode into Darl from the east, Rotta leading the warband through streets that followed straight canals and curving rivers that fed into the River Drammur. The streets were unusually clear, pale faces peering from shuttered windows and cracks in doorways while other figures scuttled down gloom-filled side alleys.

"Hardly the triumphant homecoming of the conquering heroes," Rotta said.

"No," Biórr agreed, though it was hardly surprising. He glanced over his shoulder, saw Red Fain sitting on a wagon bench, one leg wrapped with a blood-soaked bandage. Harek sat beside him, a score or more wagons behind them. Dragon-born rode alongside the column, and warriors marched, Brák striding there with his shrunken crew. That was normal enough, but behind them all trolls lumbered through the streets, the bull trolls pausing periodically to urinate on walls or defecate in steaming mounds, marking their territory, and there were clumps of skraeling about them, spertus scuttling on the ground, tennúr flying in swirling knots above them, and behind them all came the frost-spiders and night-hags, a dark river of them flowing through the streets of Darl.

If I saw this marching into my home, I would be hiding, too.

They began to climb a hill, passing through what Biórr remembered as the markets and traders' ring. It should have been filled with a crush of people, the scents of all manner of food cooking, a cacophony of voices shouting and haggling, goods from across all Vigrið for sale, but it was empty.

Looks like a dragon living in your town is not good for trade. But it will get better. It has to.

They passed through the eerily quiet streets, the Galdur tower of Darl looming ahead of them, beyond it an empty space where Helka's fortress had been built around the skeleton of Orna, the eagle-god. Now there were just a few shattered timbers poking up into the sky, like the desiccated bones of a giant's grasping fingers.

"I must be . . . *tactful*, when I tell my sister of the events of our journey," Rotta said to Biórr. "I cannot lie to her, she would disapprove of that most strenuously." He grimaced, which Biórr took to mean that Lik-Rifa would probably eat Rotta. "But she does not like bad news, either, so I must be careful how I phrase the events of our journey. Whatever you do, do *not* mention how many we lost in the raid from that *niðing* Orlyg."

"No, lord. But we must tell her of Myrk, though. She is Ilska and Drekr's sister." Biórr looked back over his shoulder, at Myrk's corpse wrapped in linen and slung across his horse's back.

"Of course," Rotta said. "We should do that as soon as we can, get it out of the way. Just do not mention the numbers we lost." He looked at Biórr. "She will not like it."

You mean, she will eat us.

"Yes, lord, my lips are sealed," Biórr said.

"Good boy," Rotta said with a nervous grin. "It is good to know we understand each other."

Noise drifted down to them, a rhythmic pounding, and Rotta led them into a street that reeked of charcoal and iron. Clouds of steam hissed from open doorways and shadowed figures stood silhouetted by the red glow of forge fires.

"The Blacksmithing district," Biórr said to Rotta.

"The business of war is keeping them at work, no doubt," Rotta said.

They passed through the street, the hill steadily climbing then levelling out and Biórr saw the wall that surrounded Darl's Galdur tower. A huge gate stood closed, warriors in mail guarding it. They saw Rotta and thumped on the gates, others blowing horns, and the oak gates opened.

Hooves clattered on stone and thudded on hard-packed earth as they rode into the tower's courtyard, a wide space ringed with barracks, stables, pens, a dairy and a brewhouse, the Galdur tower rearing over them, black-stoned and looming like a brooding crow. Its doors opened and Lik-Rifa stood there in her human form, tall and regal, flanked by Ilska, Drekr and a handful of skraeling.

"Sister, my dear sister," Rotta cried out as he slipped from his saddle and hurried to Lik-Rifa. He dropped to one knee before her and took her hand, pressing his lips to it.

"I have missed you," he said.

Lik-Rifa stood there, regarding him. Her lips twitched in a smile.

"Stand," she said, gesturing to him.

"I have accomplished the task you gave me. Svelgarth has fallen," Rotta said triumphantly, "as I see Darl has." He looked around. "Though I never doubted you. Two of the supposed powers of Vigrið defeated already. It is almost too easy. This war will be over before it has begun, and Vigrið will be yours, my sister."

"It will not be over until Ulfrir is a corpse at my feet, and until then we are still in danger," Lik-Rifa snarled. She shivered, composing herself. "Come, eat and drink with me, we have much to talk on."

"Of course," Rotta said. He looked over his shoulder and waved for Biórr to follow him. "But, before we do that, I have news for Ilska and Drekr. Unfortunate news, I'm afraid." He gestured to Biórr and the horse that he led by the reins. Biórr stopped and moved back to Myrk's corpse, untied her and lifted her into his arms, carrying her to Ilska and Drekr. He laid her down gently at their feet, knelt and cut the rope that tied the linen sheet, pulled it back to show her face. He took care not to reveal her shredded, wolf-torn wound of a throat.

Ilska looked down at Myrk, her face draining of colour, her body stiff, muscles twitching. Drekr dropped to one knee and swept Myrk up into his arms, squeezed her to him. Biórr was surprised to see tears spilling down his cheeks.

He looked up at Biórr, his face twisted and contorted, the scars on his face white and livid, eyes burning red.

"Who did this?" he snarled.

"Come," Lik-Rifa said, turning and walking into the Galdur tower, ignoring Ilska and Drekr. Rotta looked down at Drekr, then followed his sister.

"Biórr, with me," Rotta said. Biórr hesitated.

"I am sorry," Biórr said, looking down at Myrk, a tightness in his chest, then he started to follow Rotta. Ilska grabbed his wrist, her grip like iron.

"Who?" she hissed.

"Orka," Biórr said.

Ilska frowned.

"The one who tracked Drekr to Darl. The mother of the Tainted child Breca."

Drekr let out a strangled sound, part growl, part sob.

Biórr left them to their grief and walked into the entrance hall of the Galdur tower and saw that it had been turned into a feasting chamber. A fire pit sat at its centre, tables and benches about it, but as he stepped deeper into the room he paused. The ground was . . . moving. Then he saw them, serpents, some still, others slithering and hissing across the stone-flagged floor.

Rotta paused, too.

"Don't be afraid of my beauties," Lik-Rifa said. "You are perfectly safe, as long as you mean me no harm."

"Oh, well, that's a relief," Rotta said, grimacing as he took a hesitant step among the writhing mass. Serpents slithered away from him, clearing a path as he walked. He looked back at Biórr and beckoned him on. The rat in Biórr's blood screamed at him to leave, to flee. Rats are not the friend of serpents. He sucked in a breath and told his beast to be calm. From the beating of his heart his advice did not seem to be working.

Biórr reached a table, filled a cup full of ale, drank it and filled another, then loaded a plate full of carved mutton, cheese, onion and dark bread and sat, took another large gulp of his ale.

Rotta sat with a cup in his hand and took a sip.

"Sister, did all go here as planned?" he asked.

"It did," Lik-Rifa said. "That worm . . . Guthlaf? Guthrum? I cannot remember," she said with a wave of her hand. "Anyway, it was as he said. Helka's Galdurman, the arrogant little maggot, attempted to resurrect Orna. Well, he succeeded. She was alive as I fell on Darl from the sky." Lik-Rifa leaned back in her chair and smiled, her grin unnaturally large, long teeth protruding over her lips. "But not for long. I slew her. Killed our sister, that spiteful, conceited bitch. After all this time, hundreds of years I have imagined meeting her. Hurting her." A ripple of pleasure passed through Lik-Rifa, from head to toes.

"That must have been . . . satisfying," Rotta said. He looked relieved, and Biórr remembered that the skálds told of Rotta having killed Orna's daughter, draining her blood and skinning her, using her blood to write his infamous Galdrabok, the *Raudskinna*, upon her flayed skin.

If Orna had lived that would be one more god with a blood feud against Rotta. Now that Orna is dead it just leaves her husband, Ulfrir.

"And where is her heart?" Rotta asked.

"Ah," Lik-Rifa said. "In the heat of the battle, and my victory, I forgot about our plan." She waved a hand, as if it were of no importance.

For a moment Rotta's face twisted in anger, a spasm through his face, but it passed so quickly that Biórr could not be sure that it had happened.

"That is a . . . great shame," Rotta said slowly. "So, what happened to her heart?"

Lik-Rifa shrugged. "There is nothing left of her. I eviscerated her, destroyed her, turned her to nothing but mist with my jaws and talons." She put a finger to her lips, as if remembering the taste. Then she giggled.

"Nothing left of Orna's heart, not even the smallest part?" Rotta pressed. "You know the power we would both gain from eating it, or even a fragment of it. We needed that power, to tip the scales in our favour when we meet Ulfrir."

"No, nothing left," Lik-Rifa said, "not even a bone. Perhaps a feather or two," she sniffed. "I do not need Orna's power, I slew her, obviously I am the more powerful."

"Yes, of course you are," Rotta said slowly, carefully. "But we still have Ulfrir to think about. Orna's heart would have ensured our victory against Ulfrir. He was always the more dangerous of the two."

"Yes, I know that," Lik-Rifa said. "Which is why I have been waiting for you. We must plan our next move, must strike at him together."

A twist of unease across Rotta's face.

"There is another," Rotta said. "Their heart would give us power beyond imagining." His eyes locked with Lik-Rifa's. "But the risk to us would be great."

"Too great, brother," Lik-Rifa said. A hint of fear shivered across her features. She was silent, thoughtful. "No," she said, shaking her head. "No. Let us concentrate on finding where our mange-ridden brother is lurking. I am sure he is plotting against me."

"Of course he is," Rotta said. "You have killed his wife, twice."

Lik-Rifa grinned, then frowned.

"We must find him," she said. "I have sent out all my tennúr, all my hyrndur, to seek him out, but I have heard nothing," she snarled, a mixture of fear and rage leaking into her voice.

"You need look no longer," Rotta said, leaning back in his chair, a smug look on his face. "I know where Ulfrir is."

"Where?" Lik-Rifa hissed, leaning forwards.

"Snakavik. He is hiding within the skull of our dear departed father," Rotta said.

"How do you know?"

"A captured *Úlfhéðnar*," Rotta said. "Orka, the woman who slew Myrk," he waved a hand towards the tower's entrance, although Ilska and Drekr were no longer there. "I smelled Ulfrir's stink upon her. She had seen him, spoken with him."

Lik-Rifa leaned back, grinning. "Rotta, you have done exceedingly well. I am well pleased with you."

Rotta grinned and raised his cup to her, took a deep drink.

"This wolf-child, did she tell you anything else?" Lik-Rifa asked, leaning forwards.

"Aye, she did," Rotta said. "Ulfrir is in the company of one called Elvar Troll-Slayer and the Battle-Grim. A mercenary band that Bióorr happens to know better than his own kin."

Lik-Rifa fixed her eyes upon Bióorr.

"How . . . useful," she purred. "Tell me about them."

Bióorr gulped.

CHAPTER TWENTY-FIVE

VARG

Varg opened his sea-chest and looked upon his kit. Ring-mail coat, helm, weapons belt and a neatly folded sealskin cloak. He reached in and pulled out the coat of mail, hefted the weight of it high and threaded his arms into it, finding the sleeves and slipping it over his head, wriggling and shaking to help the mail slither down his body. He took his weapons belt and buckled it around his waist, cinching it tight to ease the weight of the *brynja* across his shoulders, brushed the tops of his weapons with his fingertips. Seax, cleaver and bearded hand-axe. Then he took out a nålbinding woollen cap and pulled it onto his head, lifted his helm and placed that over the woollen cap, pulling it tight with the leather straps, buckling it under his chin, careful not to trap his beard in the buckle. Sound became muted and his vision a little restricted because of the eye-socket metalwork of the helm. He adjusted the helm's mail curtain that protected his neck, letting it fall across his upper back, neck and shoulders. Finally, he reached into the chest and took out the silver arm ring that Glornir had given to him so long ago, at Rotta's chamber. Twisted strands of sliver and two growling bear-head terminals. He slipped it around his left bicep and squeezed it tight.

A deep, indrawn breath as he stood tall.

"Ha, you look like a warrior born," Svik said, who stood beside Varg gleaming in his mail, his red beard rope-braided and tied with silver wire. "Who would have thought you would live this long?"

"Not me," Røkia piped from where she was pulling her *winnigas* leg-wraps tight and using an iron brooch to pin them in place, which raised some chuckles among the Bloodsworn around them.

"Let us hope I live through another day," Varg muttered, feeling the tremble of imminent violence in his gut, his eyes fixing upon the *drakkars* that were gaining on them across a white-churning sea. The wolf in his blood gave off a low rumbling growl that he felt vibrate through his body.

"Ha, we live in hope," Svik laughed, then buckled on his own helm.

For a whole day they had laboured across the open sea, the sails of the *Sea-Wolf* and Sulich's slower *knarr* filled with a south-easterly that had driven them hard towards the coast of Vigrið, but Rurik's longships behind them were using the same wind, and Sulich's fat-bellied *knarr* was too slow, so the longships had gained steadily. They would catch them today, so Glornir had made the decision to stand and fight.

Varg turned and looked to the prow and saw the dark line of land on the horizon. Vigrið.

Close, but not close enough.

Glornir had called for the sail to be furled and stowed, for the mast to be stepped, the mast-block pounded into the mast-hole, and it had been hard oar-work for a while. But now it was time to save their strength and so only a quarter crew were manning the oars, rowing close to Sulich's ship before Rurik's *drakkars* reached them.

Varg pulled his shield from the shield-strake and slung it across his back.

"Come," Svik said, nudging Varg's arm and they walked to the spear-racks on the deck, Varg finding his spear and testing its weight.

Voices shouted and Varg looked up to see the *Sea-Wolf* was close to Sulich's ship. Oars were pulled in on the starboard side and a rope thrown over to Sulich, who stood near the *knarr*'s prow. Hands caught the rope and heaved the two ships closer, the hulls thudding together, grating. More ropes were thrown across, all along the top-rail, and warriors moored the two boats together.

"Why are we doing this?" Varg whispered to Svik.

"Those *drakkars* will try to separate us, like wolves would do to the weak and young in a flock of sheep. Easier to overwhelm us if we are apart." Svik grinned. "They are about to find out that we are not sheep. We are the Bloodsworn, and we stand together, fight together. Die together, if needs be."

Varg nodded, liking the cunning of it.

Glornir had a shouted conversation with Sulich and then Iva and Taras were clambering over the heaving rail of the *Sea-Wolf* and boarding Sulich's ship. Taras stood on the top-rail and turned.

"I'll see my Bloodsworn friends after," Taras bellowed to them. He was mailed and helmeted, dressed in battle kit that Einar had gifted to him. Even that was a little tight across Taras' shoulders. He wore a nasal helm, had two bearded axes thrust into his belt, a thick-shafted spear in his fist and a shield slung across his back. Einar strode to him, took his forearm in the warrior grip.

"I'll see you after, friend," Einar said. Taras grinned and leaped onto the *knarr*'s deck.

Horses were tethered in the wide belly, wild-eyed and stamping, Sulich's crew shipping oars and stringing bows. Screens of wicker and willow were raised around the horses.

"To protect them from arrows," Svik said as Varg opened his mouth to ask.

Five of the Bloodsworn stayed at their oar-chests on the port side, while five of Sulich's crew sat with oars at the starboard side. Varg looked at Svik.

"They will hold the oars to keep us prow-facing Rurik's longships," Svik said. "Otherwise, the sea will snatch us and spin us like a wooden toy and we will be facing in the wrong direction when it's time to start scrapping."

"Ah," Varg grunted. "There is much to learn about this ship and sailing business," he muttered.

"Aye," Svik smiled.

"Make ready," Glornir bellowed and the Bloodsworn gathered on the deck of the *Sea-Wolf*.

"Bloodsworn, we face battle once more," Glornir called out, Vol at his shoulder. "These arselings would take our ship, take our lives. We shall show them what happens to our enemies." He shuddered and tremored, muscles hunching, eyes glowing green, and gave them a savage-toothed grin.

The Bloodsworn roared, shaking shields and thumping weapons upon the linden wood.

Einar stepped close to the prow. He was mail-clad and helmeted, a long-axe in his fist, a seax and hand-axe at his belt, a huge shield strapped across his back. He gripped the prow-beast with one hand and put one foot on the top-rail, taking the position of honour, the champion's place on the prow. First to be seen by the enemy, first to take the brunt of the enemy's attack.

"Come and taste our steel, you *niðing* dogs," Einar bellowed, spittle spraying, and he punched his long-axe into the air, shook it at the approaching *drakkars* and let out a deep-bellied roar that was taken up by the Bloodsworn, until the *Sea-Wolf* must have sounded like some angry, feral beast.

One longship was pulling ahead of the others, cutting through waves in a white-spumed trail, oars rising and falling, heading like an arrow for the *Sea-Wolf*. The others began to spread into a wider line behind the first *drakkar*, like a net.

"They will seek to circle us, overwhelm us from all sides," Røkia said to Varg, still taking her role as teacher seriously, even on the brink of battle. "We need to make fast work of that first ship, who is overeager, like a young wolf, blinded by hope of battle fame and tales of glory."

That *drakkar* was close enough for Varg to see faces on the deck, saw warriors in lamellar plate stringing their recurved bows and the backs of rowers heaving. A crowd parted and a figure stepped forwards, a cloak and cowl pulled over their head, but Varg saw the glint of an iron collar around their neck. Beside this figure walked a huge man with a black thicket of a beard. He clambered onto the prow, wearing a helm with a wind-whipped horse-hair plume that snapped like an angry serpent, dressed in a coat of lamellar that hung below his knees, a curtain of mail over his lower face and two short-axes in his fists. He spat unheard curses at the *Sea-Wolf* and Einar.

Vol's voice rose up behind Varg, hissing, Iva's joining hers so that they twisted about each other like the knotwork silver on a jarl's torc, making a song that rose and fell, spreading across the waves.

Varg saw movement in the sea, the swell of something large beneath the waves, saw the crest of something scaled and serpentine approaching them, moving into the space between the *Sea-Wolf* and the approaching *drakkar*. A serpentine head reared up, red-eyed and sharp-fanged.

"Sjávarorm," Varg hissed.

"Aye, but it is ours," Svik said. "Vol and Iva have summoned it."

Varg watched as the sea serpent loomed high over the approaching *drakkar*.

The man in the iron collar climbed up onto the prow and Varg heard another song drift out across the waves. The Sjávarorm hissed and screeched, as if the song caused it pain, and then it crashed back into the sea and disappeared beneath the waves.

"Rurik will have a rune-wielder on each of those *drakkars*," Svik said.

The longship crawled towards them, oars rising and falling, water spuming white as warriors laboured at the benches.

"Let them use their strength on reaching us," Svik called out, "while we are rested and eager for a scrap." He danced on his toes, grinning.

A hissing sound and an arrow whipped between Varg and Svik, thunking into the deck behind them. More arrows fizzed, Einar grabbing the prow with one hand and swinging behind it for cover.

"SHIELDS," Glornir bellowed.

Varg shrugged his shield from his back and raised it, a heartbeat later an arrow thumped into it, a spray of splinters in his face as the tip burst through. Arrows rattled like hail all along the shield-line. A cry of pain behind him, and further away horses neighed wildly. Varg risked a glimpse over his shield rim and saw archers filling the foredeck of the approaching *drakkar*. In front of them the figure with the cloak and cowl threw their hood back, revealing a gaunt-featured man, black hollows for eyes. He dragged a knife across his palm and clenched his fist, raised it high and began to sing. Red runes flickered to life in the air before him, spread wider, circles interlinking and growing, covering the prow of the *drakkar* like a curtain of red rain.

"LOOSE," a voice cried behind Varg, Sulich, and an answering volley of arrows swept into the air, falling upon the approaching *drakkar*. Some of them hissed and sizzled as they passed through the red-glowing runes, turning to ash and blowing away on the wind. Other arrows thumped into timber and flesh, screams ringing out.

Close to Varg another voice rose up, part song, part chant, high and keening, swirling on the wind and salt spray. Vol, standing close to Einar in the prow of the *Sea-Wolf*, and Varg heard a more distant voice join hers. Iva, on the deck of the other ship, her voice a low rumble, snatched away and then brought closer by the wind, weaving around Vol's words like a warp and weft thread on a loom. Varg saw blue lights flare into life above the prow of the *Sea-Wolf* and the prow of Sulich's ship, forming ice-blue rune-circles. Shards of ice stabbed out towards the approaching *drakkar*, one crashing into the prow where ice exploded upwards, sweeping over the top-rail and hissing into the red rune-spell above the prow. Ice and fire warred in the air for a few heartbeats, crackling and hissing, but then the ice began to spread through the red runes like spilled ink seeping through parchment, turning them to ice. The frozen runes cracked and collapsed into the sea.

The other shard of ice that came from Iva's voice crashed into the churning waves between the *Sea-Wolf* and the longship and in moments the waves were thickening, the water glinting, ice forming, waves becoming sluggish as gruel at first but rapidly thickening, until the longship was slowing, ploughing through sheets of ice that splintered, but continued to spread in the water around the *drakkar*. Then ice was crackling up the longship's oars, and where the hull touched the ice-thick sea frost crept up the strakes of the hull. Timber strained and creaked and snapped, the *drakkar* turning blue as frost-bitten fingers. The longship glided slowly towards the *Sea-Wolf*, drew close, and stopped, bobbing as the icy sea rose and fell, blue frost-runes hissing, reaching the top-rail. Varg saw a woman rise from her oar-bench, staring at her hands, which had turned blue, ice climbing her arms, tendrils weaving across her chest and up her neck. She screamed, began to run, slowed, and stopped as the ice consumed her body, frozen. Another figure stumbled into her, and she exploded in a spray of shards. The ice continued to spread and Varg and all the Bloodsworn stood and stared, lowering their shields, many of them open-mouthed.

A crack loud as thunder and a fissure raced across the longship's hull, strakes tearing apart as the timber contracted, the crack widening, water pouring into the *drakkar*, the prow dipping, the stern rising.

A series of cracks, each one louder than the one before and the longship was tearing apart like a ripped loaf of bread in the hands of a hungry man. The sea gushed into the *drakkar*, foaming white and ice-touched, people screaming, running, leaping overboard, or clinging to shattered timbers as the longship began to sink.

Varg stood and stared, horrified and fascinated at the same time as the *drakkar* sank into the sea, the prow last to disappear beneath the slow-churning waves. All that was left to show it had existed were a handful of ice-frozen timbers, bodies floating in the water, some rigging and a few barrels bobbing in the swell.

"Well, I hope that doesn't happen with all of those *niðings* and their *drakkars*," Æsa said next to Varg. "I want a good scrap." She looked at his stunned expression.

"What? I didn't get all dressed up for nothing."

CHAPTER TWENTY-SIX

ORKA

Orka sat on a barrel, swaying with the rise and swell of the sea as Jarl Orlyg's *drakkar* travelled along the coast of Vigrið. Sæunn, Gunnar and Halja were bending their backs at an oar-bench, Orka steaming with drying sweat as she had just finished her shift. She rubbed her calloused hands together and took a sip from a cup of watered ale as she watched Breca and Lif sparring on the deck. Breca stabbed a spear at Lif, his spear-work fast, which pleased her. Lif defended and moved left and right, keeping Breca off balance, which also pleased her, and Orka could see the frustration building in Breca, bubbling and boiling, which did *not* please her. As she watched it spilled over and with a growl Breca threw himself at Lif, taking him by surprise, ramming his shoulder into Lif's shield and sending him stumbling back. Lif righted himself and set his feet as Breca came after him, a pivot on one foot and nudge of the shield and Breca was sent staggering past Lif. A stab of his spear that touched the back of Breca's neck and the contest was done. It took a moment for Breca to realise, but then his shoulders slumped and he lowered his shield and spear. He looked sheepishly at Orka and she beckoned him over to her.

"You have a warrior heart," Orka said, "but it is usually your wits that will win or lose a fight, not the strength in your arms. Or shoulders."

"I know," Breca muttered. "Strategy, like tafl," he said.

"Aye," Orka said, then frowned at Breca. "Who told you that?"

"Biórr, he taught me how to play," Breca said.

"Huh," Orka grunted, not sure she liked the thought of Biórr the rat teaching her son anything.

But it sounds like good advice, although Breca hasn't taken it.

She offered Breca her cup of ale and he took it and drank thirstily. It felt dreamlike, sitting here, talking with him, almost as if he had never been taken from her. She remembered carrying Thorkel from their burning home, remembered the blood on his lips as he told her that Breca had been taken. Just the memory of it felt like a knife was twisting in her belly.

"What are you thinking?" Breca asked her. "You look . . . sad."

"Of your father," Orka said.

Breca's eyes filled with tears.

"I knew you would find me," he said, a tremor in his lips. A tear spilled and rolled down one cheek.

Orka wiped it away.

"No one will ever take you from me again," she breathed, and Breca put his head on her chest, hugged her tight.

After a while he stepped back and looked at the barrel that Orka was sitting upon.

"When will we go home to bury Spert?" he asked her.

Orka had wanted to give Spert a sea burial, but Breca had pleaded and sobbed that they take the vaesen's body back to their steading at Fellur village and bury him there.

Not a sensible idea, Orka had thought, knowing that the tide of war was rising in Vigrið and who knew where it would carry them. Or where it would drown them. She did not think it was likely that she would ever see Fellur again. They had sailed past the fjord inlet that led to Fellur village a day ago, and that was likely the closest they would come to seeing their homestead again. And also, carrying a corpse across Vigrið was not a practical idea. The body would begin to decay and rot soon. But part of her had softened at Breca's tear-stained face, and part of her hoped to go back to their homestead at Fellur, so that she could stand over Thorkel's grave and tell him that he had been avenged. And so, she had agreed, which meant they would have to store and preserve Spert's body. That had meant asking Jarl Orlyg for a barrel and enough salt to pack Spert's corpse with, to stop him from rotting.

"*Ha*," Orlyg had said. "*This will have to go on my tally stick. You are in my debt now, Farmer, salt is not cheap*," he had laughed. That had not pleased Orka, as since being captured by Rotta she had no silver or arm rings to trade with. But she had agreed because she had no choice.

"When this is done and Drekr is dead," Orka said.

"Yes," Breca snarled. He was fiercer than she remembered.

"Or perhaps, when you can survive sparring for longer than a slow count to ten."

She took his shoulder and turned him to face Lif.

"Again," she said and Breca walked back to Lif. They raised their shields and touched spears. Set their feet.

Footsteps, and Orka looked up to see Dagrun walking towards her. He was carrying a hemp sack over one shoulder.

"Slow going today," he said as he reached her. His face was flushed red from the wind, a strand of dark hair whipped out of his braids by sharp gusts.

"Aye. Slow going since the wind changed," she said. When they had left the river and rowed into the sea a north-easterly wind had filled their sail and swept them like a cast spear down the eastern coast of Vigrið, but while they had nestled in the shelter of an inlet overnight the wind had changed and now they were rowing into a south-westerly headwind that had slowed the *drakkar* down to a crawl. The sail had been furled and the oars dipped.

"Hard rowing," Dagrun agreed. Orka had seen him take an oar and sit a shift at the bench, which she liked. She had seen many jarl's sons and daughters think they were too good for the oar-bench.

"I have something for you," Dagrun said. He held up the sack from his shoulder and emptied it, a coat of mail and a nasal helm spilling to the deck at Orka's feet.

"A fine *brynja*," she said, looking down at it. She could see the half-sleeves and hem were edged with brass rings, the sign of a wealthy warrior, and the nasal helm had a curtain of mail to protect the wearer's neck, that too edged with brass rings.

"Aye, and they are yours," Dagrun said. "The *brynja* should fit you. Brynjolf was built like a plough-ox." He looked her up and down.

"It is not mine," Orka said.

"Well, it is if I give it to you," Dagrun said with a smile. "Brynjolf is no longer needing it. He died in the night, and as my oathsworn man it is my *brynja* and helm now. My coat and helm to keep, or to give away, and I do not need them, my ring mail is good enough, and I have a fine helm. And besides, this *brynja* would not fit me, it is too big." He nudged the mail with his toe, then looked at Orka and her sweat-stained tunic. "A fine tunic," he said, "but it will not take care of you in the steel-storm of battle like this will. A good friend, this war gear could be to you."

"True enough," Orka said. "But I have no coin or hacksilver to buy them, and I am already indebted to your father for a barrel of salt." She scowled at him. "I do not like to be in debt."

"But it is me who is indebted to you," Dagrun assured her. "You saved my life, and to my thinking that is worth more than a helm and a coat of mail. Think of this as a down payment."

She looked at the helm and *brynja*, knowing that it was a good offer, knowing that she would need them.

"Your father is already paying me back for saving your life," she said. "Giving me, my son and my . . . friends safe passage."

The word *friends* felt and sounded strange coming out of her mouth.

"Aye, well, that is his payment for a son, as a father is like to give. But I pay my own debts, not just let my father pay them for me." He gave her a quizzical look. "Do you not think you will need it? I do not think you have seen your last days of battle, Farmer," he said, calling her by the by-name Jarl Orlyg had given her.

She looked at the coat again, then stood, unbuckled her weapons belt, upon which hung the two seaxes that she had taken from Myrk's corpse, then bent and lifted the mail up. It was heavy and she grunted as she raised it, slipped her arms in and found the sleeves, then lifted the coat overhead and let gravity help it slip down her arms, over her head. She shook and wriggled to stop it from bunching and then her head was through the opening, the skirt slithering over her hips and hanging above her knees. She adjusted the weight, then buckled the weapons belt back up, moving the seaxes so that one hung across her front and one across her back. Rolled her shoulders. The weight of the *brynja* felt good.

"A fine fit," Dagrun said.

"Heya," Orka said, agreeing as she took up the helm and put it on, buckled it under her chin. It was a little loose, but it needed a wool cap for padding, anyway.

"I have a spare nålbinding cap you can have," Dagrun said. "A gift." He smiled.

"My thanks," Orka said, still uncomfortable.

"You do not have to thank me, it is part of my debt to you paid," he said. "The other part is this . . ." Then he leaned forwards, his lips close to her ear.

"I know what you are," he whispered.

A tremor shivered through her and the world seemed to slow, hairs standing on end like hackles.

Dagrun leaned back, looked her in the eye.

"Your secret is safe with me," he said, and before she could answer him he was turning and walking away.

A horn rang out, signalling the changeover at the oar-benches.

She was still staring after Dagrun when a hand touched her elbow and she spun around, one hand reaching for a seax. It was Gunnar and he stepped back quickly, hands raised in surrender.

"Easy, chief," he said. He was dripping with sweat from the oar-bench, Halja and Sæunn behind him. "Is all well?" He looked her up and down.

"Aye," she grunted, Dagrun's words still echoing through her thought-cage. She shivered, like a horse shaking off flies, and lifted a jug of watered ale to Gunnar. He took it, filled a cup and passed it on to Halja and Sæunn. Halja took her cup and walked away, leaned on the top-rail, the wind whipping her red hair and dragging strands out from her tight braiding. She looked up at the sky where gulls whirled and floated.

"A new *brynja*," Gunnar observed.

"Aye," Orka muttered.

"It fits you well," he said.

The *clack* of spear shafts drew their attention, Orka looking to see Breca launching another furious attack at Lif, who used his shield well, fending off Breca and swivelling around him, stabbing low and high with his spear, forcing Breca to leap backwards.

Well, he is surviving longer, at least, thought Orka.

"Chief," Halja called out and Orka walked to her, enjoying the weight of her new coat of mail. She stood and put one hand on the rail, steadying herself from the heave and roll of the *drakkar* through the waves. Halja was staring up at the grey sky, and her eyes flickered with gold flecks.

"What do you see?" Orka asked her.

"Above us there are two birds high in the sky."

"Aye, what of them," Orka said, looking up and seeing gulls and clouds.

"They are large. Unnaturally large," Halja said, "and they are black, not gulls."

Orka smiled.

"And there is something else, out to sea, that way," Halja said, pointing to the south.

"What?" Orka asked, again, seeing nothing but the horizon.

"Sails," Halja said. "And I think one of them is the *Sea-Wolf*."

CHAPTER TWENTY-SEVEN

VARG

Varg hefted his shield, gritted his teeth and braced himself, the prow of a *drakkar* looming close. It was brimming with snarling faces spitting curses and wrapped in iron, steel in their fists.

"Come to me, you goat-humping *niðings*," Einar bellowed from the prow of the *Sea-Wolf*.

The air was laced with streaks of red and blue, waves of glowing heat and crackling-cold frost ripping through the air above Varg. Vol and Iva were locked in a Seiðr- and rune-battle with the rune-wielders of the four remaining *drakkars* who were attacking in unison. Having seen the fate of the first *drakkar*, they had circled the *Sea-Wolf* and Sulich's *knarr*, attempting to board from four sides and overwhelm their prey. Vol stood close to the mast-hole of the *Sea-Wolf*, and Iva in a similar position on the deck of the *knarr*. Varg could not tell exactly what was going on, but it seemed to him that Vol and Iva were hard-pressed defending the *Sea-Wolf* and Sulich's *knarr* from rune-spells that were flying thicker in the air than the arrows, the stench of scorched iron and a winter's storm swirling around him. The sea churned with ice, but no *drakkars* had been consumed or shattered like the first one, only slowed.

Arrows zipped through the air, Varg keeping his shield up. There was a concussive crash as a longship's prow crunched into the *Sea-Wolf* that shook Varg, nearly threw him from his feet, warriors either side steadying him. Einar bellowed, setting his feet on the top-rail at the prow and swinging his long-axe. It chopped into the raised shield of the other *drakkar*'s prow-champion, splinters flying, and then Einar was ducking and leaning, a sword hissing through the air where his head had been. The clash of iron, a spray of sparks, Einar yelling and swinging, a scream and an explosion of blood, Einar bellowing his victory as the longship's hull grated down the portside of the *Sea-Wolf.*

"SHIELD WALL," Glornir bellowed and Varg was moving, forming a line facing the enemy *drakkar*'s portside hull, his shield raised, overlapping and locking with Æsa's and Edel's, who stood either side of him. He raised his spear high over his shoulder in an underhand grip, ready to stab out between Røkia and Svik, who stood in the front line before him. The attacking longship had fewer oars than the *Sea-Wolf* and sat lower in the water, making it harder for the enemy to board. The twang and hiss of loosed arrows, all in the shield wall raising their shields, a clatter and thud rippling along the line as arrows struck, then grapple hooks and ropes were hurled up, some snaring, and with a crack the two ships were heaved together.

"FORWARDS," Glornir shouted and the shield wall shuffled forwards almost tight to the top-rail. Varg saw Røkia chopping with an axe at a boarding rope and Svik slicing another with his seax. Another volley of arrows, the Bloodsworn ducking back, and faces appeared over the top-rail, steel-helmed and snarling, spears stabbing up. Røkia hacked one in the face, the clang of steel and spray of blood, a scream, the man falling back, his face a red wound. Varg stabbed his spear at a *druzhina* woman in a lamellar coat who was half slithering over the rail, hacking with a curved sabre at Svik. She saw the spear coming and threw herself backwards, slipped and disappeared with a squawk back over the rail. There was a push forwards as the surge of warriors trying to clamber onto the *Sea-Wolf* became stronger, the first line of the Bloodsworn's shield wall chopping, stabbing, hacking, warriors screaming, snarling, dying.

A concussion from the stern of the *Sea-Wolf* that rippled through the shield wall, Varg feeling it through his boots. A snatched glimpse and he saw another *drakkar* drawing alongside the *Sea-Wolf*'s stern, grapple ropes flying over the top-rail.

We are too few to defend all sides, Varg thought. *Should some of us go back there?*

Even as he thought it Glornir was moving towards the stern, calling a handful of warriors with him. Varg made to move with them and then he heard a cry in front of him, looked to see hands grasping Røkia, a blonde woman with a bearded axe hooked over Røkia's shield rim, her other hand gripping Røkia's axe-wrist. Røkia head-butted the woman, their steel helms clashing, Røkia's nasal bar mashing the blonde woman's lip and she fell backwards. Røkia let out a feral snarl, clambered onto the top-rail and leaped after her, disappearing.

The wolf in his blood howled and, without thought, Varg was moving, shouldering his way forwards into the front line, all notions of following Glornir to the portside to form a new shield wall gone from his head. He scrambled onto the top-rail and stood there, blocked a spear thrust with his shield and saw Røkia below him in a tangle of bodies on the *drakkar*'s deck, her shield raised, snarling and lashing out with her bearded axe. A *druzhina* warrior was behind her, raising their sabre high. Varg hefted his spear and threw it, saw it punch into the back of the warrior and hurled him to the ground. With a wolf-growl he leaped, crashing into bodies, all of them falling, Varg hitting the deck, a sharp pain in his ankle but he ignored it, heaved himself up, blocked an axe swing with his shield, felt the blow shiver up his arm and reached for his seax. Felt something grip his shield and drag it down. Instinctively he ducked and air hissed as a sword stabbed at his face. He ripped his seax from its scabbard and slashed over the top rim of his shield, sliced through flesh and heard a scream, saw a warrior reeling away, blood spurting from her cheek, the pressure on his shield abruptly gone. He moved forwards, slammed his shield boss into the head of someone slashing at Røkia's back, saw them stagger and fall, slashed his seax across another's hamstring, their leg giving way and they collapsed, Varg stamping on their throat and then the warriors behind Røkia were gone and he was pushing in next to her, locking his shield with hers. They stood there a moment, Varg heaving breath into his burning lungs, snarling at the warriors before him and Røkia. Thirty, maybe more.

Thuds behind him, Svik stepping up on his left, locking his shield over Varg's, Æsa moving to the other side of Røkia, Edel there, too, and their line was close to filling the *drakkar*'s deck, from oar-chest to oar-chest. More of the Bloodsworn were leaping onto the longship, a pressure of weight behind Varg as they joined the shield wall, forming a second row, and a third.

"Forwards," Røkia snarled, and they were moving, Varg feeling the wolf in his blood straining, snapping and snarling with the need to kill and tear. He allowed it to flood his veins, filling his muscles with strength, his limbs with speed, but kept enough control to not leap from the shield wall in search of blood.

They faced a mixture of warriors, some *druzhina* in their lamellar coats, curved sabres and slim-hafted axes, and others that looked like warriors from Vigrið with *brynjas* and round shields. They came to the front and began to lock shields. Arrows fizzed through the air, one slamming into Røkia's shield from the *druzhina* behind the forming shield wall, another grazing Varg's shoulder.

"DOUBLE TIME," Røkia yelled, and they sped forwards, smashing into the shield wall forming in front of them a few moments before it was ready. Varg ducked his shoulder behind his shield, set his feet and shoved hard, all along the front row with him doing the same, all stabbing high and low above or below their shield rims. Warriors screamed and snarled, a blow struck Varg's shield as the enemy rallied, but the Bloodsworn's weight and momentum were too great, and the enemy shield wall buckled and broke. A man slipped and fell before Varg and Røkia chopped down at him as they trampled over him, a scream cut short, and then they were among the enemy, stabbing, chopping. A *druzhina* woman stood and faced Varg, a shield and sabre in her fists. Varg blocked her overhead swing with his seax and punched his shield into her, rocking her backwards, swept on and stabbed high over her shield rim into her throat. She fell gurgling, blood gouting down her chest. Others were turning, trying to escape from the Bloodsworn's inexorable onslaught. Svik chopped his sword into the back of a man's neck, Æsa laughing as she hacked people down with her hand-axe, Edel moving forward relentlessly, her hound leaping and bringing a fleeing woman down, Edel finishing her with a thrust from her sword. Warriors started leaping over the top-rail into the sea, panic sweeping them, and then Varg was standing still, his chest heaving, dead all around them, blood pooling on the deck.

"Come back and fight, you *niðings*," Æsa was shouting, turning in a slow circle, looking for fresh foes. Varg looked around, the deck of the *drakkar* clear except for the dead or dying. He saw that the rune-wielder of this *drakkar* had boarded the *Sea-Wolf* close to the prow, a cluster of druzhina about him. He was waging a rune-battle with Vol, Einar and a handful of the Bloodsworn locked in combat with the *druzhina*.

Røkia stood with one boot on a fallen warrior's shoulder, wrenching her hand-axe from his chest. Svik was close by, a trickle of blood under one eye. Probably not his. He nodded to Varg.

"Still alive then, No-Sense," he said. "Good."

The sound of Glornir's voice bellowing dragged their eyes back to the *Sea-Wolf*. Without a word they were all running back along the deck, Edel reaching the *Sea-Wolf* first and leaping up and over the top-rail, her hound following in an effortless bound. Varg followed next, slithered over the top-rail and landed between two oar-chests. He looked around, trying to make sense of the carnage. The three longships left were all around the *Sea-Wolf* and *knarr*, looking like most of their crews had boarded, as battle raged wherever Varg looked. The decks of the *Sea-Wolf* and Sulich's *knarr* were a chaotic melee, and Varg could hear Taras' bull-like roaring. Vol and Iva's voices ebbed and flowed in the din, blue and red spells slicing through the air above the battle, but they looked drained. Varg glimpsed figures on the other *drakkars* standing with arms upraised, guttural voices chanting, red runes thick around them. Einar still stood in the prow of the *Sea-Wolf*, trading blows with a thick-muscled woman wielding a sword and hand-axe. As Varg looked she hooked the haft of Einar's long-axe and dragged him off balance, slashed with her sword across Einar's chest. Sparks and ring mail shattered, blood seeping, and Einar roared, staggered back and dropped from the top-rail to the deck, stumbled to one knee. She leaped after him, hacking and stabbing, kicked him in the ribs. Svik was heading to his aid when he slowed. Varg watched as a small, dark figure dropped from the *Sea-Wolf*'s prow onto Einar's attacker. A fair-haired child. She wrapped her hands around the head of the prow-champion and dragged her backwards, then leaned back and Varg saw it was Refna Strong-Hands. She opened her mouth wide, revealing sharp-growing teeth, and bit down into the neck of the prow-champion. Other children appeared from the shadows, leaping onto the warrior, wrapping around her arms and legs, dragging her screaming to the deck.

There was a bellow from the stern of the *Sea-Wolf* and Varg saw Glornir, fighting alone against what seemed to be an entire longship's crew as they boarded the *Sea-Wolf.* Glornir swung his long-axe in great looping arcs, blood spraying in the wake of every stroke. The enemy swarmed around him. His long-axe took a man's arm off at the elbow, two more warriors coming at him from left and right and he swivelled, blocked a sword cut with the haft of his axe, took a blow from a woman with a hand-axe on the shield slung across his back, crunched the butt of his long-axe into the swordsman's chin, sent him crumpling to the floor, spun around to face the warrior behind him and slashed diagonally with his axe-blade, opening up a wound across her chest, sent her stumbling away in a mist of blood. But more were coming, leaping onto Glornir, grabbing him, stabbing at him and he was disappearing from view, smothered by their numbers. Varg ran, heard a wolf-howl scream and realised it was him, was dimly aware that others were following him. His foot slipped in blood that sluiced the deck and he crashed into an oar-chest, righted himself, carried on. He was thirty paces from Glornir, ducked an axe swing and slashed his seax across a throat, shouldered the warrior out of his way, twenty paces away, punched his shield boss into a snarling face that came at him out of nowhere, saw the man reel away, teeth shattered, nose and lips mashed to bloody pulp, ten paces from the heaving mound of bodies where Glornir had stood. It looked like he had been crushed to the ground, smothered by a wave of flesh and iron. Behind Varg he heard Røkia's snarling howl.

There was a deafening roar and bodies were exploding from where Glornir had been, warriors flying through the air in all directions. A woman crashed into Varg, sending him reeling and falling to the deck. He lost his grip on his shield, rolled, grabbed an oar-rack and heaved himself back to his feet, seax in one fist, his other hand reaching for the cleaver at his belt. He came up slashing and snarling, sent a *druzhina* falling away with blood jetting from a red wound in his throat, heard a deep-rumbling roar that vibrated through his chest, stood and stared for a moment, trying to understand.

Glornir stood in the stern of the deck, an empty space around him. His long-axe was gone, his shield, too, but he was grabbing warriors barehanded and ripping them apart, tearing limbs, bones cracking, ripping with long-taloned claws, grabbing and pulling bodies close to tear at them with his teeth, hurling them away when they stopped screaming, became limp.

An arrow punched into Glornir's shoulder, sank deep, though he hardly seemed to feel it, just growled and swatted at it, snapping the shaft.

More *druzhina* had clambered over the stern of the *Sea-Wolf* and they hesitated upon seeing Glornir, forming a loose half-circle around him. Varg saw some of them were reaching for the bows in cases at their hips.

"CHIEF," Edel roared, and she was leaping forwards, shield in her fist, her hound with her. Røkia hurled her hand-axe, was moving before it smacked into a *druzhina*'s face with a sound like wet wood splitting. Varg moved a heartbeat later, and he heard Æsa yelling behind him. They swept around Glornir like the tide around a boulder, Edel's shield raised before Glornir, the rattle-slap of arrows punching into the wood, then Røkia, Æsa and Varg were among the *druzhina*, slashing, stabbing. Varg struck out with his seax and opened a wound just above a *druzhina*'s knee, saw them stumble and collapse as the leg buckled, chopped down into a face with his cleaver, ripped it free in a mist of blood and teeth, ducked and turned, hacked through an upraised bow, wood splintering, on into the chest of another warrior, dented lamellar plates, the sound of ribs cracking, kicked out with one foot and knocked the staggering warrior to the ground. A crunch at the back of his head, stars exploding and Varg was reeling, the world sloughing away, sound abruptly muted, everything merging, and he was turning, trying to raise his weapons. Pain in his knees and he realised he had fallen to the deck, put a hand down to steady himself but it slipped away in a pool of blood. He fell forwards, rolled onto his back, white lights before his eyes, looked up and saw arcs of red and blue tracing lines of fire and ice above him.

A man stood over him, mail-clad and black-bearded, raising the axe that had already dented the back of Varg's helmet. Varg kicked out and caught the man's knee, made him sway, put his other foot straight up into the man's stones. He wheezed and crumpled, falling on top of Varg, the axe hissing past Varg's ear and chopping deep into the deck. Varg wrapped his arms around the man and dragged him close, the wolf in his blood snarling.

Rend, rip, tear, Varg told the wolf, and distantly he heard the man screaming.

He did not know how long he had been there, but slowly he became aware that the warrior upon him was limp and still. The stink of blood was thick in Varg's nostrils, the taste of it cloying and sweet in his throat.

Abruptly the warrior on top of him was moving and Varg scrambled to find his weapons, looked up and saw Røkia standing over him, heaving the dead man away.

"On your feet, No-Sense, this is no time to be resting," she snarled and offered her hand. He took it and heaved himself up, saw his seax and cleaver close by and swept them up. Varg swayed, his head thumping, felt his stomach lurch and vomited bile.

"No time for that," Røkia said, putting a hand to his back and steadying him. There was a lull in the battle around him, Glornir and a handful of the Bloodsworn standing amidst a carpet of the dead. More warriors were still coming from the *drakkar* that was boarding at the *Sea-Wolf*'s stern, but they were slower, more hesitant, and many of them were stringing the bows at their hips and nocking arrows. Varg looked for his shield but could not see it. He glanced to Sulich's ship, saw that the other two *drakkar* were moored to it at prow and stern, and that Sulich and his warriors were being crushed into the centre of the deck from overwhelming numbers. He glimpsed Taras hoist a warrior over his head and hurl him overboard.

"Ready, No-Sense," Røkia said to him, slapping his shoulder, and he saw that the enemy were coming in a new wave over the top-rail, spearmen first, archers behind.

"*Niðing* cowards," Røkia snarled, trying to cover Varg and herself with her shield from the arrows which began to buzz and whip through the air.

Varg raised his weapons and set his feet. Saw something that drew his eye to the sea beyond the enemy *drakkar*, something moving. He blinked blood and sweat, cuffed his eyes to clear them.

Another *drakkar*, rowing hard and coming straight at the *Sea-Wolf*.

Røkia saw it, too.

"We'll make a song for the skálds to sing of us," she snarled.

CHAPTER TWENTY-EIGHT

ORKA

"Stay behind me," Orka breathed to Breca. "And whatever happens, stay close to me."

She was standing with Breca and her crew in the prow close to Orlyg, his handpicked *drengrs* and Tainted about him.

"Yes, Mama," Breca said. He was holding a shield too big for him and wearing an iron nasal helm, also too big for him, that Orka had padded with linen and wool and adjusted the leather strap so that it would not fall over his eyes as soon as he started moving. Both had been taken from warriors who had died of their wounds on Orlyg's longship since the escape from Rotta and his warband. Orka had asked Jarl Orlyg for them and he had added their worth to his tally stick, Orka's debt with him climbing, which had set a hard scowl across her face.

Better more debt than Breca dead, she had told herself through her scowl.

Although Breca was big for his age, she had not been able to find a *brynja* that would come close to fitting him, and so he was wrapped in his woollen tunic and strips of leather and fur, and he gripped a hand-axe in one fist and wore a small seax at his belt, more an eating knife than anything else.

"Breca, fetch us water," Orka said. "Best to drink now. Nothing gives a thirst like battle."

Breca nodded and scurried away.

Orka looked at Gunnar, Halja, Sæunn and Lif, all of them hard-faced.

"Lif, Sæunn, you have two tasks in this battle. To stay alive, and to keep Breca safe."

"Aye," Lif and Sæunn nodded together.

"And us, chief?" Halja said.

"Kill your enemies," Orka snarled.

Halja smiled and Gunnar grunted.

Breca returned with the water and poured cups for them all.

Orlyg's *drakkar* was rowing hard, a seething mass of longships ahead of them. The sea around the *drakkars* was churning with ice, bodies and bloody froth, the sky above them turned to crackling lines of frost and fire by rune-magic. Orka could hear the screams and smell the blood. It had not been hard to convince Orlyg to attack the *drakkars*. As soon as human eyes could see the ships Orka had gone to him and told him that one was the *Sea-Wolf*, the famed longship of the Bloodsworn, and that they were outnumbered.

"Ha, a chance to have the Bloodsworn in my debt. I am liking this voyage more and more," he had boomed.

Orlyg had raised the sail but because of the crosswind they had been forced to tack out to sea, zigzagging their way across to the sea battle, so it had taken much longer than Orka had hoped, and all the while she and her small crew had stood alongside Orlyg and his guards in the prow and stared, Halja carefully letting her eagle filter through her, sharpening her eyesight. She had told them of the four *drakkars* that circled and closed on the *Sea-Wolf* and the trading *knarr* it was moored to, and they had seen for themselves the Seiðr- and rune-magic that was scarring the sky. Now they were closer, and all could see what was happening. Icy rune-spells were being cast and hurled at the *drakkars*, some of them intercepted by runes of fire, exploding in the sky in bursts of frost and flame, while some of the ice-cast spells hit the *drakkars*, frost spreading like vines, but then red runes would envelop the frost, melting it, the flames hissing and sizzling, fire and ice consuming each other.

Orlyg had yelled orders and the sail had been furled on his

drakkar, the oars taken from racks and dipped, and they were cutting through the last few hundred paces to the battle.

"The other ship needs the most help," Orlyg said grimly, "but I want the *Sea-Wolf* in my debt, not some fat sow of a *knarr*."

"The Bloodsworn are fighting with that *knarr*, fighting for that *knarr*," Gunnar pointed out, "so helping the *knarr* will be the same as helping the Bloodsworn."

Orlyg frowned. "Well, you are Bloodsworn, so as long as you remind your chief of those words when I have saved them, I am happy to go where we are needed."

"I will," Gunnar said.

Orlyg cupped his hands to his mouth and yelled an order to the warrior on the steering oar, their direction shifting towards the *drakkar* that was boarding the *knarr*'s stern. They skimmed by a longship boarding the *Sea-Wolf*, Orka glimpsing a line of the Bloodsworn forming against the raiders, Glornir standing with a handful about him. She saw *druzhina* in lamellar plate drawing bows, arrows flying at the Bloodsworn.

Gunnar Prow leaped onto the top-rail of Orlyg's ship, set his feet and hurled his spear. It pierced a *druzhina* who was drawing and aiming at Glornir, hurling the warrior to the ground.

"BLOODSWORN," Gunnar yelled, punching his shield into the air, screaming across the distance to where the *Sea-Wolf* was being attacked. "BLOODSWORN", and Halja leaped up beside him, cast her spear, too, taking a *druzhina* in the chest as many of them turned, confusion and shock sweeping them. Warriors on the *Sea-Wolf* let out an answering roar, "BLOODSWORN, BLOODSWORN". They thumped weapons on shields and broke into a run at the boarding party.

Then Orlyg's ship was sweeping past the *Sea-Wolf* and carving towards the prow of the *drakkar* boarding the *knarr*'s stern. It was almost empty of warriors, most of them having already boarded and attacking the *knarr's* crew. Only a dozen or so remained and they ringed a dark-cloaked woman, shaven-haired, an iron collar about her neck. She had her arms raised, muscles trembling as if she carried a great weight, and runes of red flame flickered in the air before her, leaping in incandescent arcs over the trading *knarr*, where they were met with gouts of blue-frosted runes exploding in bursts of competing elements.

"READY," Orlyg bellowed as he leaped onto the prow's top-rail, his white beard and fox-fur cloak whipped by the wind, salt spray in his face. He laughed. Looked at the rune-wielder in the *drakkar*. "Gösta," he shouted, "some work for you", and the Galdurman drew close to the top-rail, muttering incomprehensibly as flames began to flicker around the tip of his staff.

Orka turned and knelt, cupped Breca's cheeks in her palms and pulled him close.

"I was Bloodsworn, once, and your father, too," she whispered fiercely to him. "We broke our oaths to them, to Gunnar and Halja, to all on the *Sea-Wolf*, so that we could raise you in peace." She paused, felt as if a fist had clenched about her heart as she thought on how that had turned out: Thorkel dead and in the ground, her son now in the midst of battle and nowhere near as prepared as she needed him to be. "But the Bloodsworn are kin to me, still. They are our family, still, and that is why we fight. Not for wealth or fair-fame, but to keep each other alive. Do you understand me?"

"Aye, Mama, they are like our pack." She could see the fear in him, smell it rolling off him in waves. But the battle-lust was there, too, she could see it in the amber flicker in his eyes.

"I've a mind to tell you to stay here, to hide among the barrels and not move until I come and find you, but I do not think you would listen to me."

"I'm fighting," he snarled.

"I know you are," she said. "Stay close, stay behind me, stay alive." She rested her forehead against his, wrapped her arms around him and felt him hug her fiercely. Then she was standing, turning, pulling a grey nålbinding cap from where it was threaded through her belt and slipping it over her head, unbuckling the nasal helm and pulling it on, buckling it tight under her chin. She slapped her head, checking the fit, then lifted the long-axe she had taken during her escape from Rotta's warband. Looked at Lif and Sæunn, Gunnar and Halja, looked into each one's eyes and nodded, liking what she saw.

A crunch as Orlyg's *drakkar* ploughed into the longship that was moored to the *knarr*'s stern, timber grating and creaking as the ships clashed together. Iron hooks were thrown, dragged back, snaring on the top-rail, and the two ships crunched together closer. Jarl Orlyg was leaping before the hooks were thrown, hurling himself onto the *drakkar*, Dagrun and their oathsworn following them, Gösta with them. The sound of steel on steel, the crackle of rune-fire, voices raised chanting, screams.

Orka stepped up onto the top-rail, taking a fistful of Breca's tunic and hauling him up with her, leaped over onto the enemy ship, landed with a thump and bend of her legs, Breca stumbling beside her.

"Remember, stay behind me," Orka snarled at Breca and then she was moving, Gunnar and Halja leaping onto the deck and spreading to either side of Orka, shields raised, Lif and Sæunn behind, flanking Breca.

Orlyg and Dagrun fought on the deck, already trading blows with *druzhina*, Gösta behind them, standing with some of Orlyg's *drengrs* about him, runes kindling in the air before his staff.

"Nett af loga, binda og brenna, brenna og mjúka," Gösta chanted and the runes shifted, flew through the air, turning into a hot-glowing net that fell upon two of the rune-wielders' guards, drawing tight, constricting about them. The stench of metal burning, then wool and flesh hissing, screams rising in pitch as the two warriors collapsed, bucking and writhing. The rune-wielder staggered, glancing at the fallen guards, now little more than two piles of melted metal and scorched, seared flesh. The rune-spells that were spread around her like a shield flickered and faded for a moment and Dagrun cast a spear, the blade punching into the woman's belly and sending her crashing back into the top-rail, tumbling over and disappearing with a scream and a splash.

Close by, Jarl Orlyg was chopping at the last of the guards, a fair-haired warrior in a coat of mail. He fell, an axe raised to fend off Orlyg's blows, but the old jarl stabbed below it, his blade punching through ring mail into the warrior's belly. His *Úlfhéðnar*, Tjorvi, stepped in and finished the man with an axe blow to the head.

Orka and her crew swept past Orlyg, speeding to the top-rail of this *drakkar*, and in heartbeats they were up and over, thumping onto the deck of the *knarr*.

It was blood and chaos, bodies on the deck, draped over sea-chests, blood slick on the timber. Wicker palisades partially covered tethered horses that stamped and reared in a pen along the centre of the wide deck. Some of them were dead, pierced with arrows, others screaming and desperately shying. The battle had passed them, Orka seeing the backs of *druzhina* further along the deck, those at the rear with arrows nocked, loosing over the heads of their comrades, or standing on sea-chests to get clearer shots at the *knarr's* defenders, who were gathered in a knot at the centre of the deck. They were circled around a short-haired woman who stood with her arms raised. She was singing, blue frost-runes flickering above her. Close to her a huge, black-skinned warrior in mail and helm was bellowing, grabbing *druzhina* and hurling them overboard into the sea. He was pierced with many arrows. Orka glimpsed Sulich close to them, dressed in his horse-hair helm and lamellar plate, a sabre and a round, black-painted and blood-spattered shield in his fists. More *druzhina* were boarding from the bow, where another *drakkar* was moored. A glance to her left and Orka saw the *Sea-Wolf* was tied to the *knarr*, the combat on her deck focused on the stern of the ship, apart from Vol, who was standing near the prow, casting her own Seiðr-spells against the rune-wielders of the longships. Einar Half-Troll and a handful of the Bloodsworn were with her, hard pressed by *druzhina* who had boarded from a longship moored at the bow of the *Sea-Wolf*.

"Where to, chief?" Halja asked.

"Sulich first," Orka grunted and they were moving, speeding silently along the deck, past the horses, only the thud of their feet, but the *druzhina* could not hear that over the din of battle. They struck the rear ranks of archers in a storm of steel, cut a dozen down in heartbeats, Orka swinging her long-axe in two-handed blows, Gunnar and Halja stabbing and chopping, Sæunn and Lif cutting into those that turned on their flanks. Orka glanced back and saw Breca trying to push past Sæunn to get at the *druzhina*, but she stepped in front of him, fast as a snake, and stabbed her spear above the rim of a shield, in and out of the warrior's mouth, blade returning red and dripping.

A screaming face lunged at Orka, a woman in a horse-hair helm, curved sword in one fist, slim hand-axe in the other. Orka blocked the sabre's chop with her axe-haft, swayed left and felt the *druzhina*'s axe blade hiss past her cheek, the blade pinging off her helm in a fountain of sparks. She struck diagonally down the *druzhina*'s body with her axe head, a spray of lamellar plates and blood welled, the woman grunting and knocked stumbling back. Orka followed her, swung her axe high, two-handed, and she cut down, hacked through the wrist of the woman as she raised her sword, the axe blade carving on, chopping into the meat between neck and shoulder, sending the woman crashing to the ground. With a heave of her wrists, she wrenched the axe blade free and howled a battle cry.

The snap of bowstrings and Halja stepped in front of Orka, three arrows thumping into her raised shield. Gunnar ran at the archers, barrelled into them, all of them falling, rolling. Orka and Halja rushed to them, Orka hacking, Halja stabbing with her sword. Breca slipped between them and smashed his shield into the face of a *druzhina* trying to rise, chopped his axe through a beard into mouth and chin, ripped it free, and Halja's sword finished off the *druzhina*.

The remaining *druzhina* realised they had enemies ahead and behind and Orka could feel the panic spread through them like sickness. Many of them were turning, trying to form a shield wall against this new threat, and then Orlyg and his crew were scrambling onto the *knarr*, running and howling towards them with their white-painted wolf-shields, Tainted warriors snarling, growling, howling as they ran, and the *druzhina* broke. Orka and her pack fell upon them like slaughter-wolves, cutting, hacking, chopping, blood flying, death screams ringing out. Orlyg and his crew followed, driving a wedge through their enemies, and in heartbeats they were dead, dying or running, though they had nowhere to go.

A dark-haired *druzhina* came at Orka in a blur, a glimpse of long moustaches tied with silver wire, a mouth drawn in a snarl, sabre darting over the top-rim of a black shield.

Orka swept the first blow away with her axe, stepped back a pace, defending against adder-hissing blows. Then Gunnar was leaping between them.

"Sulich," he cried, "stop, stop."

Sulich froze, looked at Gunnar, then at Orka. He lowered his sabre.

Halja was there then, gripping Sulich's wrist and grinning.

"Well met," Sulich said, "well met." He sucked in a breath, smiled. "Your timing," he drew in another ragged breath, "is very good."

"This is Jarl Orlyg," Orka said, gesturing to the white-haired jarl as he drew near to them. His face was blood-spattered. "Orlyg, this is Sulich of the Bloodsworn."

"Well met, Sulich of the Bloodsworn," Orlyg said. "I am glad to help you."

"We have more enemies to kill yet," Sulich said, and pointed. His warriors had been pushed into a central knot by the crews of two *drakkars*. Orka and Orlyg had cleared one crew, but the other remained, battle raging only a dozen or so paces away.

"Well, what are we waiting for," Orlyg said with a grin.

CHAPTER TWENTY-NINE

VARG

Varg sidestepped a spear thrust, hooked the shaft with his bearded axe and dragged his opponent off balance, swung his cleaver and it chopped into their shoulder, carving through ring mail and deep into flesh and bone. A scream as he wrenched the cleaver free, slashed at the warrior's face with his axe and sent the woman falling away, her face a red ruin, one arm hanging limp, muscle and tendon severed. She stumbled into a sea-chest and fell into Æsa, who spun around and buried her axe in the woman's neck.

Varg glanced around. He was stood in the prow of the *drakkar* at the *Sea-Wolf*'s stern. Most of the *druzhina* had been slain. The hurled spears and sight of Gunnar Prow and Halja Flat-Nose sailing by on the top-rail of another *drakkar* had distracted the *druzhina* for a few moments and the Bloodsworn had taken full advantage of that, Glornir leading their shield wall forwards in a rush that had stormed over the first line of archers and pushed through so that the Bloodsworn had spilled onto the enemy *drakkar*'s deck. There had been a savage melee where Varg's wolf had consumed him in a frenzied madness, and now he stood breathless and exhausted, chest heaving, leaning with one hand on an oar-chest.

Røkia was close by, Edel and Æsa, too, Glornir a little further down the deck, a handful of Bloodsworn with him. He stood facing a dozen *druzhina*, their rune-caster behind them, surrounded by a dome of red-glowing runes. One of the Bloodsworn with Glornir hurled their spear and it hit the runes in a flare of sparks and flame, instantly incinerated, a cloud of ash blown away on the breeze.

The rune-wielder had his arms raised, was shouting guttural words that Varg did not understand, red runes flaring to life and crackling through the sky, meeting Vol's and Iva's spells in explosions and fountains of flame and frost cascaded down from above the *Sea-Wolf*. Slowly the rune-wielder turned to look at Glornir and the Bloodsworn. Varg saw tendons bulging in his neck, mouth twisted in a grimace.

A scream from the *Sea-Wolf*, rage and pain mingled.

"Vol," Glornir growled, and was turning, lumbering back along the *drakkar*'s deck, leaping at the *Sea-Wolf*'s top-rail, using the blade of his long-axe to heave himself up and over, back to the deck of the *Sea-Wolf*. Varg and the others followed, hauling themselves up and slithering over the top-rail, Varg thudding down onto timber decking.

Ahead of him Einar and Svik were close to Vol, who stood in the middle of a red and blue conflagration, flames hissing, quenched by frost, fresh flames melting the ice, great billowing clouds of steam, and before her stood another rune-wielder, striding down the deck of the *Sea-Wolf* towards her, red runes crackling and curved around him like a protective hand. Each step he took was slow and laboured, as he ploughed through Vol's ice-storm. A score of *druzhina* came with him. Einar Half-Troll howled and ran at them, Svik, Refna and a knot of children a pace behind him.

Glornir bellowed and charged towards Vol's attackers, Varg and the others following. Vol stood with a snarl on her face, veins bulging, sweat-drenched, shifting her rune-spells to focus on this man. Blue, frost-touched runes blazed to life in the air before her and she hurled them at the approaching man, Varg seeing them explode in bursts of incandescent sparks against his rune-shield. His mouth was moving, red runes flaming to life, and he hurled them at Vol. She staggered back a step, her shield bowing, ice-blue runes hissing and crackling, but it rippled and held.

There was a clash of steel as Einar fell upon the *druzhina* guard, his axe splintering a shield and breaking the warrior's arm, Svik blocking a blow aimed at Einar's back, his sword snaking out, stabbing into a throat as he danced away. Refna and the children swarmed over another *druzhina*, clawing and biting, the warrior dragged to the ground. The *druzhina* circled them, penning Einar and Svik, spears jabbing at them. A blade punched into Svik's hip and he cried out, stumbled. Another *druzhina* stepped in, sabre raised high over Svik's head.

Varg screamed, a surge of fear in his belly, heard Røkia yelling, Glornir bellowing, Edel and Æsa howling, but they were all too far away.

The sabre sliced down at Svik's neck, and then a body was crashing into the *druzhina*, a woman with blonde-braided hair, laced with grey, the two of them hitting the ground, rolling apart. The woman came up in a snarling crouch, lips drawn back, teeth sharp, eyes blazing amber. She wore a coat of mail and helm, gripped a long-axe in her fists. A sweeping blow, low to high, axe head slicing up from hip to jaw, and the *druzhina* was hurled backwards in an eruption of steel and blood. The fair-haired woman rose, turned, still snarling, swung her long-axe and chopped into the neck of another *druzhina*, almost severing his head, the man collapsing in a fountain of blood. Then other warriors were there, carving into the *druzhina* about Einar and Svik, a woman dressed in leather and fur like a tracker-hunter with short hair and a slim-shafted spear, another warrior in mail with shield and spear, a child between them with a shield almost bigger than his body, hacking out with a hand-axe, and two more, a man and woman with black shields in their fists.

Gunnar and Halja, Varg realised. And, of course, he had seen the blonde-haired woman before, too. At the Grimholt, a pile of corpses about her.

Orka Skullsplitter.

In moments they cut through the *druzhina* in arcs of blood, a few heartbeats later Glornir reaching them and roaring as he ploughed into the last *druzhina* with his shoulder, slamming them to the ground and stamping on their head. Then Varg and the others were there, but their enemy were fallen. They stood there a handful of moments, breathing hard, looking for someone to fight. Glornir grabbed Orka and pulled her to him in a bear-crushing hug.

"WARE," a voice screamed, and Einar was shoving Orka and Glornir away as the rune-wielder drew nearer, his shield of flaming runes sizzling and blackening the deck as he approached. The child with Orka ran at the rune-wielder with his axe raised high, his face twisted and growling like a young wolf cub, but Orka grabbed his tunic and hauled him back, throwing herself and the child out of the rune-wielder's way. He walked through them, the Bloodsworn scattering around him, heat rolling from him in waves as he set his eyes upon Vol and began a new song, high and discordant, Varg hearing it in his head like the wind stirring scratching thorns.

Then another voice cried out, Varg turning to see the rune-wielder from the *drakkar* moored to the *Sea-Wolf*'s stern step from the top-rail onto the *Sea-Wolf*'s deck, his *druzhina* still about him. He was chanting and casting runes as he came forwards, spells rippling to life and spinning in the air before his shield of runes.

New rune-spells began to form in the air before both of the rune-wielders, round as shields, turning slowly, growing brighter, shifting from red flames to amber, then to white incandescence and the rune-wielders were shrieking and casting the flames at Vol. She snarled, sung out her own song, high and keening, as the white heat of the runes hit her ice-shield. An explosion of sparks, engulfing Vol, a cloud hissing into instant life, heat and boiling steam bursting across the *Sea-Wolf* like a thunderclap, hurling Varg and the Bloodsworn to the ground.

CHAPTER THIRTY

ORKA

Orka groaned, pushed herself up from the deck of the *Sea-Wolf*, searching for Breca. He was close beside her, face down on the deck.

"Breca," she wheezed, the air hot in her lungs.

"Mama," Breca groaned.

Orka rose to one knee, saw that where Vol had stood flames still crackled amidst the steam, glimmers of red and gold, blue and white, and slowly the wind tore at the steam, shredding it to tatters and sweeping it away. Vol was standing there, her rune-shield buckled, cracked in places, but intact, her feet set, arms at her side, head hanging. She looked up, a white-blue balefire lit in her eyes.

"Hamar af ís, brjóttu hann, reipi af ís, mylja hann," she cried out, and two ice-glowing rune-shields appeared, one shifting into the shape of a hammer, rising up and crashing into the first rune-wielder's red-shields. They rippled and buckled, the man stopping, words pouring from his mouth in a gasped chant. His shield flickered, red runes dim and guttering, then flared bright again. The second ice-rune sped towards the second rune-wielder, becoming tendrils of ice that whipped at the *druzhina* guarding him, sent them leaping away, wrapped around one, frost spreading across his body, crystallising, tightening, crushing, and he burst apart in an explosion of ice-shards. The other tendrils hit the rune-wielder's red shield, steam hissing as the strands curled and coiled around

the dome of runes like vines around an ancient wall. The red runes began to crumble, cracks and fissures opening as frost spread through them and the rune-wielder cried out a new spell, panic lacing his voice.

Orka saw the cracks and holes appear in the rune-wielder's shield, snatched up a spear on the decking and hurled it, saw it fly through a gap made by the coils of ice in the rune-shield. It struck the rune-wielder in the shoulder, spinning him. His rune-shield flickered, wavered, disappeared for a moment as he crashed back into an oar-chest. With a scream he ripped the spear from his shoulder, began chanting, even as Vol began a new song.

Before either of them could finish their spells, a shadow fell across the deck of the *Sea-Wolf*. There was a squawking from up above, a great wind beating Orka back to the ground, and she looked up, saw two giant ravens swooping from the sky, talons extended. One of them grabbed the rune-wielder and in a turbulence of wings dragged him screaming into the air. Orka heard his voice chanting, saw runes crackle into existence around him as the first raven climbed higher in looping spirals above the *Sea-Wolf*. The second raven swept in with its talons extended, grabbing his limbs and then the two ravens were flying apart, a wet ripping sound and the crackle of bones breaking. Screams filtered down to them, rising higher in pitch and abruptly ending. Blood spattered onto the deck of the *Sea-Wolf*. A thud as a severed arm hit the timber.

Vol turned and looked to the first rune-wielder, who was frantically repairing the cracks in his shield from the ice-hammer and was chanting, deep and low, more flaming runes flickering before him.

Vol began to walk towards him, singing her keening song as she went.

"Sjóvindur blása, sjóstormur og úði sópa þessum logum í burtu," Vol growled, and with a wave of her hands a great wind hissed across the deck of the *Sea-Wolf*, tearing at the new runes. A wave rose up over the deck and crashed down upon the rune-wielder, his rune-shield of flames hissing, fissures rippling through it, the man within staggering back, crying out as his rune-shield was swept away. He

stood there a startled moment, then raised his hands, incomprehensible words pouring from his mouth in a panicked gush.

"Binddu munninn, bindðu ökkla hans," another voice called out, Orka looking to see the short-haired woman who had been casting her Seiðr-spells on the *knarr* climbing onto the *Sea-Wolf*, blue-ice glimmering around her fists. The bull-like black warrior loomed at her shoulder, Sulich, Orlyg and a knot of warriors following them. Orka heard the clatter of oars, looked beyond Sulich and his crew, and saw the last *drakkar* limping away from the *knarr*, heading south.

"Binddu munninn, bindðu ökkla hans," the short-haired woman said again, and a clustered weave of frost-vines snaked out from her blue-glowing hands, slithering across the deck and wrapping around the rune-wielder's ankles, hoisting him into the air, other vines snaking down binding his arms to his torso, spiralling onto his neck, wrapping around his throat and mouth and gently squeezing. He squawked and gasped, words muffled, then he was silent. The runes that had been sparking to life guttered and died like a snuffed candle.

Vol looked to the short-haired woman.

"Iva," she said, gave her a nod of thanks and walked towards the captured man, her rune-shield crackling and melting away. She sang softly, a high, piercing sound ululating from her lips as she approached him, came to stand before him as he dangled helplessly, twisting gently in the breeze.

Orka became aware of a sound behind her, turned to see the sea churning, a rippling wake appearing as something approached beneath the waves, as it drew nearer hints of a serpentine body undulating through the flotsam that floated around the *Sea-Wolf*. It was close to the *Sea-Wolf* now, close to where Orka stood. She put a hand onto Breca's shoulder, moving him away from the top-rail, hefting her long-axe, and a reptilian head was breaching the waves, rearing high to peer onto the deck of the *Sea-Wolf*, water cascading from a scaled head, mouth opening to reveal rows of razored teeth.

"Sjávarorm," Orka called out, pushing Breca back and setting her feet, raising her long-axe.

"Let it be," Vol called out and Orka held back her axe swing, stepped away instead.

The sea serpent's head reared above the top-rail, as big as a wagon, staring at Orka with unblinking eyes, then focusing on Vol as she returned to her keening song. The creature's head swayed over the top-rail and lowered onto the deck with a meaty slap, its thick-scaled body slithering out of the sea and onto the deck. As it rippled past Orka she saw that other, smaller, black-scaled serpents were clinging to its body, each as long as a good ash spear, looking like thick woven braids of rope upon her trunk.

A mother with her young, Orka realised.

Vol continued to sing as the serpent approached her, putting out a hand and stroking the creature's head as it reached her. It slithered around the dangling man, head rearing, tongue flickering to caress him. His eyes bulged and he let out a muffled scream.

"You should not have come against the Bloodsworn," Vol said, "should not have slain my friends", and she gave a flick of her hand. The serpent reared high on its muscled trunk and opened its jaws wide, engulfed the man from head to waist. Iva muttered something and the frost-vines around his ankles shattered, releasing him. He fell, his legs dangling from the serpent's mouth, but she did not eat him in one gulp as Orka expected. Instead, she spat the man's body onto the deck, then twisted her head to look back at the young clustered upon her back and hissed at them. They detached themselves from her body and slipped onto the deck, squirming around. One found a pool of blood, its tongue flickering out and it began to drink, sucking and slurping. The adult serpent gently nudged the young serpent away from the blood and towards the man on the deck, who was squirming and wriggling, his arms still wrapped tight to his torso, his mouth still bound with the vines of ice. She slithered around her young, herding them towards the man on the deck, then reared back and darted forwards, faster than Orka thought possible, mouth open, fangs bared, her mouth closing about the man's torso, but she did not bite, her fangs just grazing him. Then she drew back and hissed at her young.

"What is she doing?" Breca whispered.

"She is teaching her young to hunt, like me teaching you to fight," Orka breathed, finding herself smiling. "A mother preparing her children for the world we all live in. See," and as she spoke the young serpents squirmed around the man, letting their tongues flicker upon him. Then one reared back and lunged forwards, bit into the man's thigh. He kicked and spasmed, his eyes bulging, veins and tendons standing thick in his neck as he strained, but the serpent's fangs had sunk deep, and it clung to him. Then the other serpents were darting in, hissing and biting, the man's muffled screams seeping through the ice that bound his mouth, blood leaking and smearing the deck from myriad wounds. All the young serpents joined the attack except one, which slithered up to Vol and coiled around her feet. She looked down at it and smiled. Then the mother serpent was gently grabbing the man's torso and dragging him towards the *Sea-Wolf*'s top-rail, her young all still attached to him, leaving a trail of blood across the deck. She reared over the rail and dropped the man into the sea, Orka looking and seeing the young serpents dragging his body beneath the waves. The mother serpent looked back at Vol and the one young serpent that remained at Vol's feet. It hissed at Vol and with a creak and groan of timber it was rippling over the top-rail and diving into the sea; with a splash and ripple of white foam it was gone. The serpent at Vol's feet coiled around her ankles and began to spiral up one leg, reached her waist and slithered around it, latched onto Vol's forearm, and coiled around it. Vol stroked its head with her free hand.

A silence fell over the *Sea-Wolf*, just the slapping of waves against the hull and the hiss of the wind. Then shadows were rippling across the deck and there was a flapping of wings as the two ravens descended, spiralling downwards. A storm of wind rocked Orka on her feet as the ravens landed, one on the prow and one on the top-rail. The one on the rail looked down at the sea where the serpent had disappeared.

"Grok glad the big snake is gone," the raven squawked.

"Snakes taste good, but Kló not trust the big ones," the other raven croaked. "They bite back." Then she began to preen her feathers.

A flutter of wings and Vesli appeared, the bag at her belt stuffed to overflowing with fresh teeth, blood-smeared and with slivers of flesh still dangling. She flew to Breca and wrapped her arms around his neck, hugging him tight.

"Vesli missed master Breca," she squeaked, "Vesli worried for him."

"I have missed you, too," Breca said, stroking the tennúr's head.

Vesli fluttered back and alighted upon Breca's shield rim. She looked around, at Gunnar and Halja, Lif and Sæunn. "Where Vesli's friend, Spert?" Vesli asked.

Breca's lip trembled, and a fat tear slid down his cheek and he just shook his head.

Vesli's face crinkled and tears welled in her big eyes.

"No," she wailed.

Jarl Orlyg looked from the weeping Vesli to the two giant ravens preening themselves to the young serpent coiled around Vol's forearm.

"Strange company you Bloodsworn keep," he said.

CHAPTER THIRTY-ONE

GUÐVARR

"What is that?" Guðvarr said to his aunt, Jarl Sigrún.

"That is the Jarnvidr, the Iron Wood," Sigrún said.

They were sitting on their mounts before a wide wooden bridge, the River Slågen white-spuming below them, but Guðvarr's eyes were fixed upon the far bank, where a wall of trees stared sullenly back at him, the road they were following disappearing into what looked unsettlingly like a wide-open mouth. For as far as his eyes could see trees reared, north, south and west, a tangled knot of murk and gloom. The forest stood silent and brooding as a cliff, Guðvarr getting the distinct feeling that things hidden within the darkness were staring at him. Just looking at it made his skin crawl. The woodland rolled away to the north, just at the edge of his vision Guðvarr seeing a cluster of hills rearing out of the green-black canopy like the backs of breaching whales.

"I do not like the look of it, do not think we should go in there," he muttered.

"*Like* has nothing to do with it," Sigrún said grimly. "That is where our prey has gone, and we must follow."

Guðvarr frowned.

"Why don't we let Krúsa lead us. Best she and her skraeling go first, in case there is an ambush."

"If there is an ambush, it will come from all sides, not just the front," Sigrún said. "We would be no safer at the rear, or anywhere else in this column. By appearing to lead we win whatever fair-fame is to be had."

If we are still alive to enjoy it.

Guðvarr twisted in his saddle and looked back over his shoulder, saw Skapti sitting upon a horse, looking as relaxed as if he were out for a gentle ride, on his way to a noonday meal, despite the fact that Krúsa and her skraeling stood around him, tennúr whirring above him, and frost-spiders were clustered in the boughs and shadows behind him.

"I do not think we should trust him," Guðvarr said, absently wiping a drop of moisture from his nose.

"Of course we should not trust him," Sigrún said, heaving a sigh. "That word does not exist for the likes of us, people who would be a power in this world. I have not trusted anyone since . . ." she frowned. "I have *never* trusted anyone. But if he is speaking the truth, then this is an opportunity for us. We will use this to climb higher in Lik-Rifa's graces. That is our goal, to be of value to Lik-Rifa, or to Ilska the Cruel. That is how we will survive this war, and how we shall flourish in the new world that Lik-Rifa will rule."

Aye, that is all well and good, so long as in the climbing we are not pushed from the ladder and fall to our deaths.

"But is Skapti speaking the truth?" he said.

Sigrún smiled, though there was little humour in it. "There is only one way to find out," she said, "and if he is not, we will have a fight on our hands. We have been in them before and will be in them again. This is Vigrið, after all." She shrugged, then clicked her horse on.

That is what I am worried about, Guðvarr thought. He hesitated a few moments, then touched his knees to his horse's ribs and followed her. Hooves clattered on wood as they crossed the bridge, the thud of tramping feet and more hooves behind them as Sigrún's *drengrs* followed, then Krúsa led her skraeling across, Skapti with them.

Guðvarr left the bridge and his horse carried him into the gaping mouth of the forest. Boughs wrapped above the hard-packed road, a murky shadow-light engulfing him, the sound of the river fading behind them. He twisted to look back and saw a dark stream of frost-spiders scuttling across the bridge. As the creatures entered the forest, they slipped into the foliage to left and right of the road, climbing trees and spreading through the boughs up above.

His one consolation about his travelling companions now was that, surely, they'd be a match for any other monstrous creature hidden in this forest?

The trees were thick-trunked and far taller than they had seemed from the far bank, looming over Guðvarr, the canopy appearing as a night-vaulted sky far above. From the far bank of the river the forest had appeared silent but, once inside, that could not be further from the truth. There was noise everywhere. Crows squawked, the whirr of insects was all about him, foliage crackled as deer moved through the undergrowth – or at least, he hoped it was deer – foxes barked and shrieked. In the distance he heard wolves howl, and behind it all the wind soughed through branches, leaves rustling and branches creaking and scratching overhead, filling the forest with a swirling fluctuation of sound.

He looked at the trees suspiciously.

"They are not ash trees, are they?" he asked Sigrún.

"No. Birch and alder, mostly," Sigrún said.

Good.

Nevertheless, he watched the trees carefully as they rode deeper into the Jarnvidr.

Sigrún called out, held her hand up and the column rippled to a halt. They were standing before a fork in the road, one path leading straight on, the other curling away to the north, though within fifty paces both paths were engulfed by shadow and gloom.

"Krúsa, bring Skapti up," Sigrún called back down the line.

Her *drengrs* parted to let Krúsa walk through them, the skraeling's long arms dangling, Skapti following behind her. Munni the tennúr flickered in the air above him.

"Which path?" Sigrún asked Skapti.

"That one, straight on," he said without hesitation.

Sigrún looked at him, then back in the direction Skapti had pointed. She nodded.

"Ride with me," she said as she led her horse on, and Skapti drew up alongside her.

They rode in silence awhile, Guðvarr peering into the darkness either side of them.

There could be anything out there, no more than ten paces away, he thought, one hand resting permanently upon the hilt of his sword.

"Guðvarr tells me you were captain of the Grimholt once," Sigrún said, breaking the silence.

"I was," Skapti said.

"And that you were Prince Hakon's man."

"Aye, for a time," Skapti grunted.

"Guðvarr also tells me that Skalk the Galdurman threw you in a cell in his tower."

"Aye, that he did," Skapti said.

"But now you are Skalk's messenger. You are his man now." Sigrún shifted to look at Skapti.

"I am," Skapti said, meeting her gaze and the question in her eyes. "Times change," he shrugged. "I have learned to change with them."

"Why would Skalk trust you?" Guðvarr snapped. He did not like Skapti. Seeing him had reminded him of when Skapti had walked through the door of *The Dead Drengr* in Darl, just as Guðvarr had been winning Prince Hakon's trust over a fine cooked breakfast. A stone of fear had dropped in his belly at the sight of the white-haired warrior, and he had barely evaded a painful death then and there.

"Trust me?" He shook his head. "Skalk does not trust me. I do not think he trusts anyone."

Sigrún glanced at Guðvarr.

"But this was a task that needed doing, and he picked me to do it."

"Why you, then?" Guðvarr said.

"I did not ask him to explain his reasoning to me," Skapti said with a raised eyebrow. "Perhaps because I am expendable." He shrugged. "Perhaps because he knows I am capable. Perhaps he understands that if I want to rise in his estimations then I must perform some tasks with risks. Dangerous tasks, such as this." He glanced down at Krúsa, who walked alongside them, his gaze moving into the trees, where frost-spiders lurked.

"Huh," Guðvarr grunted. "If it is so dangerous, then why did you agree to this task?"

"Because with the likes of Skalk, and most of the powers in this land, you either make yourself useful to them and obey, or you end up with your throat cut, or body broken and stuffed in a barrel."

"Huh," grunted Guðvarr again.

He sounds believable, mostly because he reminds me of how I felt about Skalk, every waking hour. And what we're having to do with Lik-Rifa now.

"Why so far, then?" Guðvarr asked sullenly, determined to catch Skapti out in some lie or other. "Why must we journey so far along this road?"

"You seem to think that I am the chief of their band, to know the answers to these questions," Skapti said. "I am not, that is Skalk and Estrid. Though to meet you on this side of the river is safer than meeting you back on the other side, it seems to me. You have crossed into Jarl Störr's land, so you have no friends here."

"Well, we are on this side of the river now, so where are they?" Guðvarr asked. He wanted this business done, wanted to be out of this forest and see the sky again.

Skapti looked at him and sighed. "I am thinking you are not understanding the words coming out of my mouth," he said. "I do not *know* where they are, or when they plan to meet you. All I know is what they told me. Follow the road into the forest. Do not stray from the road, and you will find us." He raised his hands.

A sound rang out through the forest, off to Guðvarr's left. A frantic rustling of foliage, followed by a high-piercing shriek, and all along the column warriors were stopping and turning, drawing weapons. Guðvarr drew his sword, staring into the murk.

"Munni," Krúsa called out and the tennúr flitted in a circle above Krúsa's head and dropped lower to hover before the skraeling. Krúsa gave a twist of her hand and the tennúr was flying into the forest, disappearing in moments.

"Be ready," Krúsa said, drawing a thick-bladed weapon of dark iron from her belt, shaped like a cleaver but bigger, and with a long, two-handed hilt.

Branches rustled and shook out of sight, the sound of another scream, followed by a thud.

"What shall we do?" Guðvarr hissed to his aunt.

"Wait," she said, "do not leave the road."

I have absolutely no intentions of leaving the road.

More rustling in the darkness, something moving, a deeper shadow within shadows, and then Munni was bursting out of the canopy and gloom.

"A prisoner, a prisoner," the tennúr squeaked.

The shadow in the woods grew denser and closer. Guðvarr could see clustered eyes and jointed legs, a handful of frost-spiders scurrying through the foliage towards them. They burst onto the road where the half-light revealed that they were dragging something behind them, bound around the legs and ankles with blue-tinged web. They scuttled up to Krúsa and dropped their package at her feet.

A small figure, larger than a child, smaller than a man, slender as a sapling. Its hair was a tangle of leaves, skin dark and grained like wax-polished wood, fingers unnaturally long, hooked and curled at the ends like thorns. It glared up at Krúsa with small, dark eyes.

Guðvarr recognised it, had seen something like it before, in Skalk's Galdur tower.

"A faunir," he said.

There were two blue-pulsing lumps on its chest, bite marks, and as Guðvarr watched he could see the skin around the wound shift from wood-brown to ice-tinged blue.

"Why capture that?" Guðvarr said. "Isn't it one of you?"

Krúsa frowned up at Guðvarr.

"No, not one of us," Krúsa said. "Krúsa already told you, faunir made by Snaka, not Lik-Rifa." She crouched down to stare at the faunir as ice began to froth on its lips. "Faunir not nice," she muttered.

"A . . . a . . . a . . . arseling," the faunir stuttered at Krúsa, small eyes glaring. "G . . . g . . . get out of my f . . . f . . . forest."

"See," Krúsa said, looking up at Guðvarr and Sigrún with a big-toothed grin. "Question is, what shall Krúsa do with it?"

"Let the frost-spiders have it for a meal," Guðvarr suggested.

"No, faunir blood is like sap, taste bad, kills frost-spiders."

"Ah, well, just kill it, then," Guðvarr said.

"No. Where there is one faunir, there are many," Krúsa said, scowling at the darkness. "Probably watching us now. If we kill this one, they will not like it. They would attack us." She looked at Guðvarr. "That would not be good," she said.

I agree wholeheartedly with you, Guðvarr thought, nervously looking back into the shadows.

"Keep it as a hostage," Jarl Sigrún suggested. "And release it when we leave the Iron Wood."

"That what Krúsa thinking," the skraeling said.

"Agreed, then," Sigrún said. She barked a command to her *drengrs* and one of them dismounted, pulled a hand-axe from his belt, and, stepping from the road, began chopping at a slim branch on a birch tree. It was not long before the faunir was tied to the new-fashioned pole and hanging suspended between two thick-muscled skraeling.

"On," Krúsa cried out and the column stuttered into movement again, Skapti riding between Guðvarr and Sigrún, the two skraeling carrying the captive faunir marching just behind them.

Wonderful, Guðvarr thought. *We are marching through a forest to meet with a Galdurman who has already tried to kill me and would like nothing more than to see us all dead, while I am riding beside another man who has* already *tried to kill me, and behind me is a nasty little creature with a host of malicious friends who would no doubt like to kill me and could attack us at any moment.*

He sucked in a deep breath and blew out a long, mournful sigh.

I wish I were back in Fellur village.

CHAPTER THIRTY-TWO

ORKA

"Orka," a voice called out and Orka turned to see Jarl Orlyg striding across the blood-pooled deck of the *Sea-Wolf* towards her, his son, Dagrun at one shoulder, and Gösta the Galdurman at the other, a handful of Tainted warriors and *drengrs* spreading behind them.

"Farmer, introduce me to your friends," Orlyg said as he reached her. His white hair was blood-spattered, a rent in his mail across his barrel chest and one shoulder, but he looked well enough.

"Glornir," Orka called, though when she looked for him he was already striding towards her, Vol at his side.

"Well met, Glornir of the Bloodsworn," Orlyg said, looking Glornir up and down. Glornir was blood-drenched, a map of cuts across his face, gore thick around his jaw and dripping in clumps from his fists.

"My thanks for your help," Glornir growled. "Who are you?"

"I am Orlyg of Svelgarth, though Svelgarth doesn't exist so much now, more's the pity, because Lik-Rifa and her *niðing* warband of arselings have torn it to rubble," Orlyg said. "I know who you are, and it was good fortune to meet you on the whale road – more your good fortune than mine, I would add – but where are you sailing to?"

Orka said nothing, knew that Orlyg was testing the tale she had told him.

"I am bound for Snakavik," Glornir said. "Elvar of the Battle-Grim has hired the Bloodsworn for some dragon-killing."

Orlyg glanced to Orka, then back to Glornir and grinned.

"I am sailing to Snakavik, too, to throw my axe in with Little-Elvar. There is more than just a dragon to kill, though. Rotta the rat is with her."

"Rotta?" Glornir said, scowling.

"Aye, Rotta, the *niðing* whore-son," Orlyg spat. "It was Rotta who led the assault on my Svelgarth. But Elvar has a god of her own. She has Ulfrir-wolf, and with a thrall-collar around his neck."

"Ulfrir!" Glornir said, glancing at Orka.

"Did Vesli not tell you of Ulfrir?" Orka said.

"No, she did not," Glornir said slowly.

Orka looked for Vesli and gave the little vaesen a scowl.

Vesli shrugged. "Vesli forgot. Vesli remembered all the important bits . . ." She looked slightly guilty. "Eventually . . ."

"We are living in a skáld-song," Glornir muttered. "To my mind, though, it is best if the dead gods stay dead."

"Aye, agreed," Orlyg said. "But at least we will have one on our side, and I would rather a wolf than a rat and a snake with wings."

"There will be much to see in Snakavik, then," Glornir growled.

Orlyg looked around the deck of the *Sea-Wolf*, at the dead bodies and pools of blood. "And this? What brought Kirill's hounds down on you?"

"Some trouble in Ulaz," Glornir shrugged.

"Aye, well, more trouble for them, as it turned out," Orlyg grinned. "A good fight, though, and good to send Kirill's dogs back to Iskidan with their tails between their legs."

"I am grateful for your help," Glornir said.

"Ah, now that is good to hear. Gratitude." Orlyg pronounced the word slowly, savouring it. "Well, the world is changing, so you never know, I may be in need of some help myself, in the near future. If I am, can I count on you and your *gratitude*?"

"You can," Glornir nodded. "The Bloodsworn are in your debt."

Jarl Orlyg's grin grew wider. "In my debt, ahh, now that is a phrase that brings me joy."

"You have my word on it," Glornir said, and offered his arm to Orlyg, who took it by the wrist in the warrior grip.

"That will do me," Orlyg said. He looked to Vol, and behind her Iva, who was sitting on a barrel, the hulking black warrior handing her a horn full of water. "You have some powerful Seiðr-witches. I would like to buy one from you."

"I am always open to trade," Glornir said with a shrug. "But these two are not for sale. I need a Seiðr-witch on each of my ships." He gestured to the *knarr* still moored to the *Sea-Wolf*. And I see you have a Galdurman to protect you during your voyage."

"Aye, that I do," Orlyg said. "Oh, well, it was worth a try. If you change your mind, let me know. With me," he grunted to his warriors, and strode away from them, back towards his own *drakkar*, which bobbed on the swell of waves, grating hulls with Sulich's *knarr*.

Orka watched Orlyg and his retinue climb over onto the *knarr* and make their way to the ship's stern, towards their own longship. When they had disappeared, she turned and looked at Vol and Glornir.

Vol stepped close to Orka and took her hands. They were blood-slick and throbbing. Orka's whole body ached, exhaustion sweeping her now that the battle was done. She looked at Vol, gave a knotted frown to the serpent coiled around Vol's forearm, as its tongue was flickering out to taste the blood on Orka's knuckles.

"Not for you," Vol said, and the serpent closed its mouth.

Glornir wrapped his arms around Vol and Orka and pulled them close to him, pressed his forehead to theirs.

"Well met, Skullsplitter," he breathed.

"Well met, Glornir Shieldbreaker, Vol Thorn-Tongue," Orka said, little more than a sigh. Memories whirled through her thought-cage, of Glornir and Vol, of the Bloodsworn, of Thorkel, a tide of emotion swelling within her, filling her chest, making it hard to breathe. She swallowed and leaned away.

Glornir stepped back and put one hand on Orka's shoulder and regarded her.

"A hard journey?" he asked, looking Orka up and down, taking in the old, scabbed wounds and the new.

"Aye," Orka said. "But no harder than yours, I do not doubt," she added, looking at the maze of wounds across Glornir, then to the white seam of pinprick scars around Vol's mouth.

"There is a tale or two to be told around the hearth-fire, for sure," Vol shrugged. "Your son?" she asked.

A smile touched Orka's lips.

"Breca," she called. He had been standing close to the top-rail, his eyes never leaving Orka, but at her call he hurried forwards. "Breca, this is Glornir. He is your father's brother. Your uncle. He is kin, and chief of the Bloodsworn."

Breca looked up at Glornir with his dark eyes.

"By the dead gods," Glornir breathed, "but you have Thorkel's look about you." He crouched down, putting one knee on the deck, effortlessly lifted Breca up and sat him upon his other knee. "My brother's son," he said, tears filling his eyes and he ruffled Breca's hair, almost breaking the lad's neck. "Well, it is good to meet you, Breca Thorkelsson."

"It is good to meet you, too. Uncle," Breca said, hesitantly, and brushed one of Glornir's tears away. Glornir smiled, laughed.

"Uncle. I like the sound of that." He looked at Orka. "You got him back, then. Took him back from the dragon, eh. Ah, but there is a song for the skálds to sing of. Thorkel would be proud. You have fulfilled your oath."

"Part of it," Orka grunted.

"The other part?"

"To avenge him."

"The man still lives, then?" Glornir growled, a twist of his lips.

"Aye. He was not at Svelgarth with Rotta's warband."

"Drekr went to Darl with Lik-Rifa," Breca said.

"I will find him," Orka snarled.

"We will find him," Glornir growled.

"Yes," Breca said.

"Lift," Orka grunted to Breca and together they heaved a body over the side of the *Sea-Wolf*, a *druzhina* warrior stripped of his armour and weapons, Breca leaning over the top-rail and watching as his pale body fell into the sea. A white-spumed splash, a ripple and then he was gone.

All on the *Sea-Wolf* and Sulich's *knarr* were doing the same, tending to the wounded, stripping the dead of anything of value, heaving their bodies overboard, mopping and scrubbing the decks of blood. The ravens Grok and Kló were making a noisy meal out of a pile of stripped *druzhina* corpses.

Footsteps, and Edel walked to Orka, her hound at her heel. Breca stroked the hound's head.

"Good to see you again, Skullsplitter," Edel said.

Orka looked at her. "You, too," she nodded.

She looked down at Breca, then back to Orka. "I did not doubt you would find him. And you brought my small crew back to me."

Orka looked to Gunnar Prow and Halja Flat-Nose, who were helping Lif and Sæunn clean a coat of ring mail that had been stripped from a fallen warrior.

"Not all," Orka said, and called Gunnar and the others.

Edel looked at them: Gunnar, Halja, Lif and Sæunn.

"Ah," Edel said. "I counted four, but, having the one eye, I did not look closely enough."

"This is Sæunn," Orka said. "She has been a friend to us in hard times."

Sæunn blinked at that, a tentative smile touching her lips.

"Well met, Sæunn," Edel said. "And Revna Hare-Legs?" she asked Gunnar.

"She fell, at Svelgarth," Gunnar said, a ripple of emotion flickering across his face, muscles twitching in his jaw. "We buried her beside the lake we pulled Breca from," Gunnar added, glancing at Orka.

"This is why I did not want you to join me," Orka said. She looked from Lif to Gunnar. "I know the taste of grief, and I did not want to be the cause of it for you. Lif, your brother, Gunnar . . ."

"Revna made her choice, as did we all," Halja said. "We are the Bloodsworn, not bairns to be protected, or told what to do."

Orka looked at Gunnar. "Do you still agree with that?"

"I do," Gunnar said. "We knew following the Skullsplitter would be a hard road. Revna died fighting to take the Skullsplitter's son back from the dragon and the rat, a blade in her hand. She would be pleased with that skáld-song." He looked Orka in the eye. "But now you are not the only one seeking vengeance. That *niðing* rat-blood will feel my blade before this war is over."

"Biórr, his name is Biórr," Orka said.

"Biórr," Gunnar repeated.

"And you," Edel said, looking at Lif. "If anyone were to die, I thought it would be you. How have you come through so many battles alive?"

"I am not sure," Lif said. He had a new cut from cheek to jaw, blood sheeting below the wound. He raised his battered shield. "Perhaps this has saved me."

"Ah, I told you," Edel said, a rare smile twisting her lips. "A shield will be a good friend to you in battle, if you know how to use it."

"He knows," Halja said, at which Lif blinked, looked at Halja wide-eyed, and blushed.

"Lately I have had plenty of practice," he stammered.

"Ha," Edel laughed. "You will have plenty more, I am thinking, before the dragon is dead."

Glornir put his hands to his lips.

"Gather the dead," he bellowed.

Orka and Breca watched as bodies wrapped in cloaks and linen were rolled over the top-rail of the *Sea-Wolf* and dropped into the green-dark waves.

Eight of the Bloodsworn, ten of Sulich's kin, and Orka could see the grief etched on the faces of friends they left behind. Glornir had said words as each body was given to the sea, calling out their names in his rock-slide voice, remembering their deeds.

All of them bowed their heads as the last body hit the waves, gone in a few moments, and stood there longer, silence thick and heavy as memories. Then Glornir was shouting commands, and all were moving to allotted tasks, blood being mopped from the decks, the damage of the battle being assessed and where possible repaired. Sulich and his crew tended to the horses that had survived the battle and making the *knarr* ready to sail. By the time they were done Orlyg's *drakkar* already had a sail full of a south-easterly wind and was carving towards the coast of Vigrið.

"Sulich, bring your crew to me," Glornir called out. "Iva, Taras," he boomed, "you come, too", and Orka saw Sulich leap onto the deck of the *Sea-Wolf* followed by forty or fifty warriors behind him, men and women, some fair-skinned, some looking like they had been kissed by the fire and others burned by it, black as crow-wings, all with the shaved heads and single braids that marked warriors of Iskidan. The Seiðr-witch and the hulking black-skinned warrior followed after them. He walked stiffly, was bound with bandages, patches of blood marking where he had been pierced with arrows.

"Iva, Taras," Glornir said to them as they reached him, Taras slapping a big hand on Einar's shoulder and squeezing it.

"You are injured," Einar said, worry creasing his brows as he looked at Taras' injuries.

"Do not worry," the bull-man said. "Taras' skin is thick, they have not sunk deep. And Iva always look after Taras' wounds."

Orka and the Bloodsworn gathered around Glornir and Sulich's crew, Breca following Orka, close as a newborn wolf cub to its mother. Even the ravens stopped in their gorging to look at Glornir, heads cocked to one side.

"We are bound for Vigrið," Glornir boomed. "We are Tainted, and much like in Iskidan, in Vigrið if our blood line is discovered, we will be thralled, or killed." He shrugged. "This is the world we live in, but the Bloodsworn have walked this blade edge for many years. We made a choice. You all have a choice to make, too." He held up a thick finger. "To wear a collar, as Vol has done, so that you may use your powers freely, under the guise that you are thralled to me, and I have commanded you to use your blood-gifts." He smiled. "I have never commanded Vol to do anything."

"He would not dare," Vol said with a nod and some of the Bloodsworn chuckled.

"Your second choice," he held up another finger. "To be free of the collar, but to never use your powers where there are witnesses. We only ever use them in public if we plan to kill all who are there. The world can never know what we are, or we are done. We would be hunted, thralled, executed." He looked slowly at all those gathered around him. "This is about our lives; this is about our survival. All of us. Think on what I have said and before we land in Vigrið you must make your choice." He looked at the two ravens perched on the deck.

"My thanks to you," Glornir said. "The Bloodsworn are in your debt."

"FRIENDS," one of the ravens squawked.

"Grok mean friends help each other," the other raven croaked.

"They do," Vol said. "And the Bloodsworn will always help you, if we can."

The two ravens bobbed their heads.

"Grok and Kló fly the skies, look for danger," one of them squawked. "Help friends, look for dragon."

"That would be helpful," Svik called out.

"But we finish eating first," the other raven rasped.

"Always," Einar Half-Troll said with a chuckle.

"Taras like these ravens," the big man said.

Glornir looked at all gathered around him.

"Good, we are done, then. Now prepare your ships. We sail for Snakavik."

CHAPTER THIRTY-THREE

ELVAR

Elvar paced back and forth across the hall of the Galdur tower while her advisers stood and stared at her. She was dressed in her war gear; her bright-gleaming *brynja* that she had taken from the battle plain at Oskutreð, a spectacled helm buckled at her belt and a sword hanging at her weapons belt, along with the slim-hafted axe that Grend had gifted to her. Gold and silver rings wrapped her arms, and she wore a jarl-torc about her neck, a thick rope-twist of gold, twin serpent heads as terminals. The first grey of dawn was seeping through high windows, the dark shadows in the room flame-licked by the hearth-fire. She should be thinking about leading, that was her task as jarl. To be the carer and provider of her crew, of her oathsworn, to be their gold-giver, the bringer of victory. She should be making plans, thinking about tactics, about logistics, using her deep-cunning to win this war, but only one thought swirled around her thought-cage like a savage north wind, forcing all else out.

Where is Grend?

Too many days had passed. She had thought he would return to her in a day or two. She had known that coming back to Snakavik had been hard on him, stirring up the memories of her mother, of her death, and that he had needed some time to sift through those times and lay old ghosts to rest, but it had been five days now, and there was still no sign of him. For the last two days she had sent her *drengrs* out searching for him, sent the Battle-Grim to the docks, to see if they could find word of Grend leaving Snakavik by ship, not that she thought he would ever do that, would ever leave her.

He swore his oath to me, sealed it with his blood. She had a sick feeling in her belly, a pressure in her chest, could not imagine a life without Grend in it, without his steady, reassuring presence at her shoulder.

"We must sail at noon with the tide," a voice said. Uspa, standing wrapped in a cloak of raven-feathers, the tattoos on her hands and forearms looking like swirling veins in her pale flesh.

Elvar stopped pacing and looked at those around her. Uspa, Berak and a half-dozen *Berserkir*. Gytha and some of her *drengrs*, Silrið, standing alone, half in firelight, half in shadow. Sighvat with Sólín Spittle. Hrung on his stone pedestal. Ulfrir, Skuld and a handful of his *Úlfhéðnar* with him. Over the last few days more of his wolf-blood followers had come to her, to swear their oaths, Ulfrir having close to a hundred of the Tainted warriors gathered to him now.

His own wolf pack.

"We must go to the docks, Elvar," Uspa said, "we must sail with the tide at noon."

Elvar glowered at her.

"Is there word of a *Hundur*-thrall?" she asked.

A day ago she had sent word through her followers, her petty jarls and mercenary bands, asking if any had a thralled *Hundur* in their service. She needed one with Hundur the hound's blood in their veins, to track Grend, and not for the first time cursed Biórr for freeing Ilmur the *Hundur*-thrall from the Battle-Grim.

"No word, my lady," Gytha said, stepping forwards. "But all who can be spared are still searching for him." Gytha had dark shadows beneath her eyes, and Elvar knew that she had been one of those searching, knew that she had not slept the last night for searching.

"You are needed at the docks," Uspa said, her voice a grindstone, grating in Elvar's skull.

"The tide waits for no one," Hrung said cheerfully.

"One more day," Elvar said.

"You said that yesterday," Uspa said with a glare.

"I know," Elvar snapped.

"We must leave," Ulfrir said. "If Lik-Rifa came upon us here she would destroy us. We have waited too long already."

Mutters rippled through those gathered in the hall and Elvar bit back a sharp reply. She sucked in a deep breath and walked slowly to her chair, took the bearskin cloak that was draped over it and swung it across her shoulders, pinned it with an iron brooch.

"To the docks," she said, and strode towards the Galdur-tower doors, *Berserkir* guards heaving them open for her, *drengrs* moving to Hrung and hoisting his head into a small cart, two shaggy ponies harnessed to it.

She swept through her father's halls, out into the ruin of his mead hall and into the streets of the fortress. Crusted snow crunched underfoot, the glare of the sun in a pale blue sky reflecting from the snow and making her squint. The fortress was empty, a dead husk, most of Elvar's people already moved down to the town of Snakavik, where her war-host was preparing to sail.

Out through the gates of the fortress and across the snow-covered skull of dead Snaka. The mercenary camps were gone now, just the wind hissing, sifting the snow and scouring across Elvar's exposed flesh like ground chips of ice. She was glad to step into the murk of the Bone Tunnel that bored through Snaka's skull like a wormhole through soil. The wooden walkway was damp and slick underfoot, smoke from braziers of whale-oil thick and claustrophobic. As she had done since a child, she counted the steps as she walked them.

"Two hundred and twelve," she breathed as she stepped from the darkness of the tunnel into the town of Snakavik and paused a moment, leaning upon a thick-posted rail. Beams of sunlight cut through the gloom, pouring down through the empty eye sockets of Snaka's skull, birds swirling in and out of the light.

The town spilled down a slope, pinpoints of flickering flame where torches burned marking the streets like constellations of distant stars fallen from the sky, reeking smoke wafting, buildings sagging and leaning, all leading towards the jaws of the dead god, where Snakavik's harbour and port lay snugged within the serpent's fangs and the steep-sided slopes of a fjord beyond. From this distance the docks were just a smear of silvered light reflected on water, the *drakkars* moored there small and dark as rusted rivets, though Elvar knew they were being loaded with war gear and provisions.

She walked on, looking left and right as she marched down a winding, steep-sloped wooden walkway, peering through Snakavik's gloom-filled half-light, part of her expecting to see Grend appear, emerging from the door of an inn or from the shadows of an alley.

"Where is he?" she muttered.

"My lady?" Berak said, looming at her shoulder, his voice like a slide of gravel.

"Grend, where is Grend," Elvar said, louder, one hand tugging at the troll tusk on a leather cord about her neck.

"All are searching for him, Jarl Elvar," Berak rumbled, and she knew that was true enough. She glanced over her shoulder and saw Ulfrir behind her, Skuld and his ever-growing retinue of *Úlfhéðnar.*

The deeper into Snakavik she travelled the busier the streets became, the lower town boiling like a kicked ants' nest as Elvar's host made ready to sail. Troops of warriors tramped through the streets, mercenaries or *drengrs* sworn to Elvar or her petty jarls, shields slung across their backs and spears in their fists. The crack of whips rang out as loaded wagons rolled, a swarm of traders rushing to sell their goods before Elvar's war-host sailed. The slope levelled and the roads widened, barns looming either side of her as she drew nearer the docks, voices shouting as wagons were loaded with all manner of goods; barrels full of salted fish, whale meat and walrus meat soaked in brine, venison, salted pork, lamb and beef, barrels packed with apples and turnips, cabbages and kale, honey and ale and mead. More barrels full of iron nails, rivets, caulking tar, and water, bundles of spear shafts carved from elm or ash, spear-heads of iron, bolts of cloth and wool and linen for repairing sails, for cloaks, caps, mittens, tunics and *winnigas*. All headed for the docks, and behind it all the screeching of gulls that swirled and swooped. Elvar had never seen such a sight in all her years.

She strode down a pier, past a handful of *knarr* that were sitting low in the water, their decks piled high with supplies, and then she saw the *Wave-Jarl*. It bobbed on the swell, sitting sleek beside the *knarr* as a wolf among sheep, the mast already set in place, the sail furled. The ship had been hauled onto land and damaged strakes repaired, tarred horse-hair wedged into gaps, the hull scraped of mussels and limpets, of algae and seaweed, and fresh-coated in pine tar and resin. Orv the Sneak and Urt the Unwashed stood on the pier, grinning and nodding to her, most of the Battle-Grim already aboard, standing or sitting at sea-chests, oars ready.

The sight of it made her heart swell.

My ship, my crew. Abruptly she longed for the sea, the simplicity of it, away from plots, politics and responsibilities and the need for deep-cunning, to feel the salt spray in her face, the muscle-burn of a shift at the oar-bench and she looked at her hands, the skin tough and calloused from oar-work, from blade work.

"Ah, hello, old friend," Hrung boomed as the wagon his head was secured within rumbled up the pier. He was looking at the deep dark of the fjord, sparkling in the winter's sun. "I must say, I hoped never to see you again. Three hundred years sitting in your embrace was too long for our friendship to endure." He looked at Elvar and winked.

"Load him on to the *Wave-Jarl*," Elvar called out. "Carefully," she added as one of the *drengrs* carrying Hrung slipped as they stepped from the pier onto the top-rail.

The thud of feet on the pier behind her, voices raised, and Elvar spun on a heel, saw her *Berserkir* blocking the pier to a handful of figures.

"Let me through," a voice called out. "Sister, tell them," she heard her brother Broðir calling out and she barked an order at her *Berserkir*. They parted and Broðir burst through, excited as a puppy. He looked like a god of war, dressed in gilded mail, a gold-edged helm tucked under one arm, a five-lobed sword at his belt, though Elvar suspected he had not won any of this gear through victories in the shield wall or battlefield.

Gifted to him by my father, more like.

"I have found one for you," Broðir said, beaming as he bounded up to her.

"Found what?" Elvar frowned, then saw that there were figures following behind her brother. A mouse-haired woman, broad and squat, mail-clad with a shield slung across her back, two bearded axes thrust through her weapons belt.

Runa Red-Axe, one of my father's petty jarls. No, one of my jarls, she corrected herself. A handful of Runa's *drengrs* followed behind her, shields scribed with two crossed bloody axes. A woman walked among them. She was shaven-haired, wore a fine-embroidered woollen tunic and had an iron collar about her neck.

"I found a *Hundur*-thrall for you," Broðir said eagerly. "You asked for one, to find Grend with, and I have found one for you, sister." If he'd had a tail, it would have wagged.

"Red-Axe," Elvar said as Runa drew near. The woman stopped and dipped her head to Elvar.

"Jarl Elvar," she said. "I have a gift for you." She grunted at her *drengrs*, and the *Hundur*-thrall was pulled forwards. "She has a good nose on her, has always led me to whatever scent I have given her to track."

Elvar looked at the thrall, saw she was wearing good leather turn-shoes, clean woollen breeches and a straw-coloured tunic.

She is a prize, for Runa to treat her so well.

"My lady," the thrall said, though she did not meet Elvar's gaze, just looked down at her feet.

"What is your name?" Elvar asked her.

The thrall looked to Runa Red-Axe.

"We call her Ákveðin," Runa said. "Once she has a scent, nothing can sway her from it."

"My thanks, Red-Axe," Elvar said. "I will not forget this gift."

"You are my jarl," Runa said, as if that were all to the matter.

"I need you to find my friend," Elvar said to Ákveðin.

The thrall raised her gaze and met Elvar's eyes.

"If you have something with their scent on, I will find them," Ákveðin said.

"Gytha," Elvar called out. "Something of Grend's."

Gytha hurried forwards, reaching down to a pouch at her belt.

Elvar became aware of noise along the docks and looked to see another troop of warriors emerge from the streets of Snakavik. She saw the knotwork ravens scrolled upon shields that marked the warriors as Hjalmar Peacemaker's and realised that she had not seen him for many days. He led his crew, a tall man in mail with a tangle of black beard. A murmur of voices rippled along the pier as Hjalmar passed by, a crowd falling in behind them and following.

A burst of raised voices at the pier as Hjalmar turned to walk towards Elvar and the *Wave-Jarl*, people shouting and pointing at something within Hjalmar's warriors.

Elvar's *Berserkir* and *drengrs* spread along the pier, blocking Hjalmar's way.

"I have something you will wish to see, Jarl Elvar," Hjalmar cried out through cupped hands.

"Let them through," Elvar said, and her warriors parted for Hjalmar and his mercenaries. They strode down the pier, Hjalmar marching up to Elvar. She felt Sighvat's presence as he stepped closer to her, his hand resting upon the axe at his belt.

"I have a gift for you," Hjalmar said.

"This is a day for gifts, it seems," Elvar said, nodding to Ákveðin. "Runa Red-Axe has just gifted me her *Hundur*-thrall. Do you have one for me, too?"

"A gift, but not a *Hundur*-thrall, there is no need for one," Hjalmar said, a grin splitting his beard. "I bring you what you seek," and he waved a hand at his band of warriors. They parted to reveal a man standing in their midst.

Grend.

Blood sheeted his face and tunic, one eye swollen shut, lips mashed to pulp, half his face a purpling bruise. His hands were bound at the wrist with rope and a strip of leather was wrapped around his neck, two warriors holding the leash.

Hjalmar barked an order and the warriors dragged Grend so that he stumbled forwards and fell to his knees at Elvar's feet.

"What have you done to him?" Elvar hissed, one hand reaching for her sword hilt.

"No less than he deserved," Hjalmar said. "He has deceived you all these years." He grabbed the leather leash from his warriors and jerked it hard, dragging Grend's face up to look at Elvar.

"He is *Tainted*."

CHAPTER THIRTY-FOUR

GUÐVARR

Will this journey ever end? Guðvarr thought as he rode through the gloom of the Iron Wood. Here and there beams of light broke through the canopy high above, mote-filled pillars of gold that dappled the path ahead of him. He rode beside his aunt, who continued to lead their column into the Jarnvidr, Skapti riding in between them. Behind them the faunir prisoner was awake and spouting a constant string of abuse at all who dared look at it. Krúsa had attempted to bind the faunir's mouth, but somehow within a short time the creature had shredded the gag, regardless of whether Krúsa had used linen or leather. Eventually she had given up trying and just slipped further back down the column, so that she did not have to listen to the constant spouting of insults.

No such luck for me, Guðvarr thought as he looked at the faunir.

"What are you looking at, you filthy *niðing Maður* goat-humping pile of maggot-festering steaming troll shite," the faunir spat at him in its rasping, leaf-rustling voice.

Guðvarr sighed and looked away, sitting straighter in his saddle.

"Járn," Guðvarr said to one of his aunt's *drengrs*, a patchy bearded man with ears too big for his head sticking out from his iron cap helm, "I will pay you if you skewer that vermin with your spear."

"Guðvarr, stop," Jarl Sigrún said.

The path before them widened, the trees clearing a little, and Guðvarr rode into a glade.

I have come to dislike glades within woodland, he thought. *They always contain some unpleasant surprise. Froa-spirits. Skapti.*

More light filtered through from above, glittering on a stream that flowed diagonally across the glade before them. A fallen tree lay beyond the stream, desiccated roots grasping at the air like the skeletal fingers of a long-dead giant. As Guðvarr stared he realised that figures sat upon or leaned against the trunk and branches. One of them gripped a long staff in his fist. A fire burned in a scratched-out pit, an iron pot hanging from a hook over it. Behind the tree horses were tied to branches at the glade's edge, the road beyond disappearing into darkness.

"Skalk," Guðvarr hissed, though it came out mostly as a squeak, a spike of fear rising like bile from Guðvarr's belly and choking his voice. He snatched at his reins and reached for his sword.

Jarl Sigrún rode on calmly, Skapti, Járn and a handful of her *drengrs* with her. After a moment Guðvarr cursed under his breath and urged his horse on, taking his hand from his sword and trying to sit nonchalantly in his saddle. He caught up with them as Krúsa and her skraeling entered the glade. Behind him he heard the rustle and scuttle of frost-spiders spreading through the undergrowth around them.

Hooves splashed as Sigrún's horse crossed the stream, Guðvarr's horse shouldering through others so that he rode just behind her.

Skalk the Galdurman stepped away from the tree and stood leaning on his staff, the puckered scar where one eye had been torn from his head just a deeper shadow. A dark-haired woman rose from where she was sitting upon a stump, stirring the pot over the fire. She was dressed in a travel-stained cloak, beneath it what had once been a blue-dyed tunic edged with silver. Now it was mud-spattered and torn. She wore a fine sword at her hip, the gold on the hilt glittering in the sun.

Estrid. Not looking so regal and haughty as the last time I saw you. How wonderful to see that your journey has caused you some discomfort.

"Sigrún," Estrid said to Guðvarr's aunt as she reined her horse in, no more than ten paces between them.

"Estrid," Sigrún said with a nod. "Skalk," she added, looking to the Galdurman. She made no move to dismount. Behind her *drengrs* dismounted, fanned to either side of Sigrún, shrugging shields into their fists, forming a loose line, two rows thick. Skraeling moved to the edges of the *drengrs'* formation, gathered in menacing knots. Krúsa pushed forwards to stand at Sigrún's side, and tennúr whirred in the air above the glade.

Guðvarr saw shadows shift along the glade's edges, glints of mail in dappled light, tattooed heads and iron collars.

Estrid's Úlfhéðnar. He gulped.

One of them stepped out of the shadows, lean and wire-muscled, tattoos coiling on the sides of his shaved head, long hair braided across the top and tied at his crown. He wore an axe and seax at his weapons belt, walked graceful and silent to Estrid's side. Guðvarr recognised him.

Frek the Úlfhéðnar *sent with me into the far north, when I searched for Lik-Rifa's hall, Nastrandir, on Skalk's bidding.* Fear and anger swelled in him. Fear at the memories of being trapped like a fly in a frost-spider's web, bitten, bound and dragged into Lik-Rifa's hall. The bowel-churning terror when Lik-Rifa had burst through the great doors in her dragon form. Anger that Skalk had compelled him to go through that.

I hate that man.

Other figures moved away from the fallen tree, two women. One a warrior, fair and cold as winter's frost, dressed in a fine *brynja*, sword and seax at her belt, a white scar across her forehead. The other with crow-dark hair and milk-pale skin.

Yrsa and Sturla. I hate those bitches as well.

Yrsa looked at him and sneered.

A whirring of wings above them and Munni the tennúr flew around the glade, circling and alighting upon Krúsa's shoulder, who stood beside Sigrún. The vaesen leaned close to her ear and whispered.

"Fifteen *Úlfhéðnar* in the shadows, twenty-two *drengrs*," Krúsa said. She gave Estrid her fang-toothed smile.

Estrid scowled at Munni, but the expression was swiftly chased from her face, replaced with a blank fjord-cliff. Guðvarr repressed a smug smile, knowing now that they outnumbered Skalk and Estrid.

"Estrid, Skalk," Sigrún said again. "You asked for a meeting."

Estrid and Skalk walked a few steps closer to Sigrún, Frek the *Úlfhéðnar* shadowing Estrid, Yrsa and Sturla moving to Skalk's shoulder.

"Aye," Estrid said.

"What do you wish to speak about?"

"Options. A negotiation," Estrid said.

"Mother-Maker does not negotiate," Krúsa growled.

"She means Lik-Rifa," Sigrún said. "Lik-Rifa does not negotiate."

"Aye, perhaps so," Estrid said, "but even Lik-Rifa needs allies, if she wishes to win this war."

"You, *allies*!" Guðvarr blurted, unable to keep his lips together. "Lik-Rifa and her servants have slain your mother, your brother, destroyed your hall, taken your realm. And you expect us to believe you wish to become our allies!"

"The world is changing," Skalk said, "and allegiances can change with it. Look at you, Guðvarr. You were allied to me, once, and to Helka, did us good service, and look at you now."

"I was not allied, I was *enslaved*," Guðvarr spat.

"Guðvarr's question is a good one," Sigrún said. "Why would you ally yourself to Lik-Rifa, after the destruction she has brought down upon you?"

"Survival," Estrid said bitterly. "I wish to survive. When you are attacked, and you lose, you have the choice of fighting to the death, or fleeing, to live, to survive. That is what we have done." She waved a hand at Skalk, and her warriors scattered in the shadows behind her. "We fled, to survive. At first that was our only thought. But then we had more choices. To continue fleeing, which meant leaving Vigrið, or to fight. I will not flee to Iskidan to become Kirill's pet. No, Vigrið is my home, so I thought to fight. And who is left in Vigrið who could challenge Lik-Rifa? Jarl Orlyg and Jarl Störr. Orlyg was at Darl and is most likely dead, so Störr was the only choice left to me."

"Aye, that is much as we thought," Sigrún said with a shrug. "So, why the change of heart?"

"Are we negotiating now?" Skalk said with a fox-sleek smile. "Knowledge is power, especially in a war. We have information that we would use as a jarl uses silver."

Sigrún looked from Estrid to Skalk.

"If your information is useful, I shall speak for you to Lik-Rifa. And to Ilska the Cruel, who is her captain." Sigrún shrugged, looking down at Krúsa. "I cannot make a blood-binding oath to you, as who knows the mind of a dragon."

Estrid looked to Skalk, who gave a curt nod. "That is fair," she said.

"So, my question; why the change of heart?"

Estrid sucked in a deep breath.

"Jarl Störr is dead." she said.

Excellent. One less enemy to fight.

"That would be of interest to Ilska, I am sure," Sigrún said. "To Lik-Rifa . . ." She looked at Krúsa.

"Perhaps," the skraeling shrugged.

"How did Jarl Störr die?" Sigrún asked.

A flickered glance between Estrid and Skalk.

"He was eaten by a wolf-god," Skalk said.

"And the wolf-god is thralled to Störr's daughter, Elvar," Estrid said.

To have a god as your thrall! That thought was intoxicating to Guðvarr.

He heard Krúsa gasp, and Skalk heard her, too. He gave a thin-lipped smile.

"Perhaps that information will be of more interest to your dragon-queen?"

"Yes," Krúsa said. "Mother-Maker hunts the wolf. Where is he?" She leaned eagerly forwards.

"We know where he is," Skalk said, "which we are willing to tell you, and I suspect that the one to give this news to your dragon will be well rewarded. But there is more that we can offer. More we can do. We wish to be useful to your Lik-Rifa in the coming war." He looked at Guðvarr. "If we are not useful, we are dead."

I know that feeling well.

"It is the way of the world," Frek the *Úlfhéðnar* muttered.

Sigrún dismounted from her horse.

"I think we have much to talk on," she said.

Guðvarr stood at Sigrún's shoulder as she sat on a stump and listened to Skalk and Estrid. Part of him liked what they were saying and proposing to his aunt. It sounded like something that he would think of, or hoped that he would think of in these circumstances, sounded like deep-cunning, but his strongest feeling at the moment was hatred. To be honest, he wished them both dead. Especially Skalk. The sight of him, the sound of his voice, it caused a rage to bubble within him.

"This information that you wish to trade with us," Sigrún said. "Where have you come by it? We are far from Snakavik."

"We have met travellers upon the road. Many who have fled the slaying of Jarl Störr. Apparently, his mead hall was destroyed by the wolf."

Guðvarr could imagine that, after seeing the ruin of Helka's hall.

"And how do you know these travellers were telling the truth."

"I had Frek question them," Estrid said, gesturing to the *Úlfhéðnar*. "He was . . . thorough."

That I fully believe, Guðvarr thought.

Sigrún nodded thoughtfully, while Krúsa stared unblinking at Estrid.

"So, you would choose the dragon and the rat over the wolf in this new war of gods," Sigrún said. "Why?"

"We have seen the power of the dragon," Estrid said. "She destroyed the eagle-god, destroyed Darl. A wolf pack is strong." She looked to her *Úlfhéðnar*. "The lone wolf, though, the lone wolf often dies."

I beg to differ, thought Guðvarr, a surge of unpleasant memories of Orka at the Grimholt, the dead piled at her feet, blood on her lips. He shifted uncomfortably and looked around, saw that Yrsa was staring at him.

You niðing, he thought, attempting to return her dead-eyed gaze, but found he had to look away. She snorted. He rubbed at one eye, pretended some insect had flown into it.

Sigrún sat back and blew out a long breath.

"I am thinking this is something that will please Lik-Rifa and Ilska both," she said, looking at Krúsa.

"Agreed," Krúsa said. "We will take your news, and your offer, to Mother-Maker. She will be pleased." Krúsa grinned. "Munni or his people will find you. He will be our voice to you."

"Agreed," Estrid said, and Skalk nodded.

Guðvarr looked to the trees, a faint sound drawing his attention. A hissing through branches, like a distant wind. Then stronger, the rasp of boughs scraping, leaves rustling.

The captive faunir grunted and shifted in its bonds.

"They are coming," it said, then smiled.

Krúsa stood, looked from the faunir to the darkness beyond the glade. She drew her blade of thick steel.

"We must go," she said, her other hand grabbing Sigrún's shoulder and hauling her to her feet. "*Now.*"

The sound in the trees grew louder with each heartbeat, like an approaching storm, and Guðvarr heard other noises within the maelstrom. Voices, screams, hissing.

Tennúr burst into the glade, whirring above their heads.

"FAUNIR," they shrieked.

"Go," Krúsa shouted, shoving Sigrún towards her horse. Guðvarr stumbled backwards, one fist wrapping around his sword hilt, collided with his horse and half turned, grabbing for the reins, got a foot in the stirrup and half jumped, half hauled himself into the saddle. His horse was dancing on the spot, wide-eyed, and he turned it in a tight circle, bringing it back under control.

Figures exploded from the wall of trees and foliage into the glade, small figures as if carved from animated wood with snarling faces and twisted, grasping thorns for hands. Frost-spiders dropped from the boughs above, suspended by threads of blue-tinged web. They snatched at the tide of faunir, long legs grasping, ice-webs spurting. Some scuttled back up their threads, hauling a screaming faunir in a net of ice, some leaped into the swarm, fangs biting, and others fell or were dragged and disappeared into the mass as it seethed across the glade and crashed into a knot of Krúsa's skraeling. The vaesen snarled and swung their crude weapons of iron, hacking and chopping at the tide of faunir, Guðvarr seeing splinters of wood spraying and hearing strange ululating cries and high-pitched shrieks, but in heartbeats the skraeling were engulfed, overwhelmed as the faunir swept on. Guðvarr saw *Úlfhéðnar* leaping from the shadows with their amber-flecked eyes, fighting with axe and seax, tooth and claw, with more success than the skraeling. They were faster, fiercer and more savage, though some fell with faunir swarming over them like ants.

"TO HORSE," Sigrún bellowed as she ran and leaped into her saddle.

Something whipped past Guðvarr's ear, a ripple of impacts up his arm, like gravel hurled at him, something pinging from his mail half-sleeve. A sharp pain in his forearm and he looked down to see a cluster of splinters stabbing into his forearm, blood staining his tunic.

What? How? he thought through the pain that spiked abruptly. Then he saw faunir snarling incomprehensible words and flinging their arms as if they were hurling stones, fistfuls of sharp wood, like splinters or stakes, aimed at him like knives or nails. He swayed and ducked, a handful of splintered spikes hissing through the air where his face had been, heard a gurgled scream and, turning, saw one of Sigrún's *drengrs* clutching at his throat, plucking at splinters, dark blood spurting.

The faunir were close now, falling upon a handful of Sigrún's *drengrs* too late to their horses and attempting to form a shield wall. They slammed their shields together and stabbed over the rims with spear and sword, chopped with axes, the faunir crashing into the linden wood like a wave upon a rock. The *drengrs* fought well, did not break, Guðvarr feeling a fleeting respect for their stand, but there were too many of the faunir, who scrambled up and over shield rims, slithered beneath them, more swirling around the edge of the wall.

"RIDE," Sigrún yelled, dragging on her reins. Guðvarr heard Skalk's and Sturla's voices raised, glimpsed the crackle of rune-magic flickering to life, heard the hiss and sizzle and those high-pitched screams again, smelled the reek of burning sap and wood.

Small hands grasped at Guðvarr's leg and he kicked, dragging his sword free, chopping down, his blow hacking into a faunir's arm. A jarring impact that shuddered through Guðvarr's wrist and the faunir shrieked, Guðvarr's blow carving deep, splinters flying. He wrenched his blade free and booted the faunir in the face, sent it stumbling away, spitting and cursing a torrent of insults. He kicked at his horse and sent it moving, back towards the path where they had entered the glade. Sigrún was surrounded by faunir and Guðvarr heaved on his reins, sent his horse ploughing into them with a crunch, saw a handful of the nasty creatures fly through the air like bundles of wheat. Sigrún's horse reared, hooves lashing out and smashed the remaining faunir out of her way and then she was moving, slicing either side of her with her sword as she rode.

Krúsa was retreating, a handful of skraeling with her, faunir surging around them. One leaped onto Krúsa's shoulders and started ripping into her with its long-taloned fingers, Krúsa bellowing. Sigrún rode past the skraeling and lashed out, hacked the faunir from Krúsa's shoulders in a spray of splintered wood, Krúsa taking the opportunity and turning, running with those around her for the road out of the glade.

Sigrún reached the road and reined in, turned, urging her *drengrs* and skraeling on, hacking at any faunir that followed. Guðvarr galloped past her, out of the glade and into the gloom of the path, looked back over his shoulder and saw Sigrún finally following, beyond her Skalk and his party retreating to the road on their side of the glade. Near the centre of the clearing a knot of faunir were gathered, bending over something. Guðvarr saw they were sawing at the bonds of the captured faunir, saw it stand and shriek an ululating war cry, and then he was turning a curve in the path and the glade was disappearing behind him.

CHAPTER THIRTY-FIVE

ELVAR

Elvar stood at the prow of the *Wave-Jarl*, looking out onto the whale road as her *drakkar* left the fjord of Snakavik. It was oar-work, the *Wave-Jarl* ploughing into a south-easterly head wind as they turned south to shadow the coast. She glanced back, saw her fleet behind her. Fifty longships, and as many *knarr* with them. It took her breath away. Never in all the history of Vigrið had a war-host been so great. Not since the Guðfalla, if the skálds-songs and sagas were true.

She turned and saw Ulfrir, standing at the stern with Skuld, alongside the heaped piles of treasure that had been brought back from Oskutreð. They were looking back up at the rearing jaws and skull of his dead father. She had allowed Ulfrir to keep a handful of his *Úlfhéðnar* with him, but the rest were scattered throughout her *drakkar* crews, all of them put to work pulling at oars. Sighvat was close by, sitting on a sea-chest and beating time for the rowers with the haft of his bearded axe. He was singing a rowing song, those pulling at the oar-bench grunting out their responses.

Close to the mast-post an awning of old sail had been raised, a sheet hanging to act as a makeshift doorway. With a knot in her belly Elvar turned and walked towards it, at the last moment turning away and walking past. She kept walking, until she was standing in the stern. She nodded to Sighvat as he beat time and sang his rowing chant, and came to stand beside Ulfrir.

"Delaying a task does not make it easier," Ulfrir said as he took his amber-flecked eyes from the glowering might of Snaka's skull and looked down at Elvar. "Often it is the opposite. Better to do it than worry over it."

"Huh," Elvar grunted.

"To lead the pack, you must have strong jaws, wolf-cunning and a storm-hardened heart. Do you have those qualities, Elvar Wolf-Tamer?"

"Wolf-Tamer?" she blinked.

"That is what I have heard you called," he said with a twist of his lips, snarl or sneer, Elvar was not sure.

"You are not tame," Elvar said.

"No, I am not," Ulfrir said, a half-breathed growl.

"As for your question," she sucked in a deep breath, puffed out her cheeks and shrugged. "Time and the skálds will be the judge."

"Aye," Ulfrir grunted. "The world changes, even the things that you think strong, unbreakable." He gestured to his father's skull, fading into the fjord mist. "Who would have thought dread Snaka could be slain."

"I only believe it because I can see it," Skuld said beside Ulfrir.

"So, perhaps we can slay this dragon," Elvar said.

"Lik-Rifa will die, her life-blood draining in my jaws," Ulfrir snarled, and Elvar remembered his howl as he had heard of Orna's resurrection and swift death.

Even a god can grieve.

"Your den, this Wolfdales, you are sure you can find it?"

"Yes, I can find it," Ulfrir said. "If the Jarnvidr still stands, then so does my wolf-den."

Skuld turned and looked at Elvar, her hand resting upon the hilt of the sword Elvar had returned to her. "I would ask a . . . a favour," she said reluctantly.

That must have cost your pride, Elvar thought.

"What favour?" Elvar said.

"In the treasure you stole from Oskutreð . . ." Skuld said.

Stole!

Elvar pursed her lips.

"Go on," she said.

"There is a pair of silver-wrought scissors."

"I remember them," Elvar said, "but, scissors? Why would you want . . . scissors?"

Skuld looked away, then back to Elvar, meeting her eyes.

"They were my mother's," she said.

Elvar turned away and walked to the treasure horde, unknotted and lifted the linen sheet that covered the pile of chests and sacks. She knew which chest the scissors were in, remembered packing them herself. She had taken them from the underground forge in the bowels of Oskutreð's roots, where Skuld and Uspa had forged Ulfrir's rune-collar. She sifted through keys upon a ring at her belt and unlocked a chest, opened the lid and saw the scissors. They were bigger than any Elvar had seen, crafted for god-hands, and finely wrought, runes carved into the silver of the handles. Lifting them, they felt light.

Do they have some Seiðr-power? Elvar thought, suspicious of Skuld for a moment. She frowned at the winged woman. *But she is thralled to me, cannot use them or anything against me.*

"Here," Elvar said, holding them out to Skuld.

She took them almost reverently, turned them over in her hands, staring at them. Ulfrir looked, too, his eyes distant, elsewhere. A faint smile touched his lips, the tips of sharp teeth protruding.

"My . . . thanks," Skuld said, and she hooked the scissors onto a leather loop, unbuckled her belt and threaded the loop onto the belt, buckled it back up. She looked up at Ulfrir and smiled.

Elvar turned away and walked to the awning set around the mast-post, where she paused a moment.

Better to do it than worry over it.

She lifted back the entrance sheet and stepped inside.

Gytha stood before her, hand on her sword hilt, and she stepped aside to allow Elvar into the small, makeshift room.

Silrið sat on a barrel, dark tattoos on her jaw. She was talking to Uspa, who sat next to her, Berak looming like a rockfall behind them. Sólín Spittle stood to one side, picking her nails with her seax. And, of course, Hrung, his head back upon his stone pedestal, which was harnessed to the deck with rope and iron rings. Hjalmar Peacemaker was sitting and talking with Hrung, a bundle on his lap. He smiled to see Elvar. At the centre of them all, hands bound and leashed to the mast, was Grend.

He looked at Elvar through one eye, the other one purpled and swollen shut.

Elvar breathed deep, felt a fluttering of emotion in her belly. Relief, that he had been found. Anger, at what she had been told. Fear, at what she might have to do.

When Hjalmar had dragged Grend before her at the pier Elvar had felt frozen, numb. Slowly, as if through a fog, she had become aware of all staring at her, and she knew that this was not something that should be aired in front of all Snakavik. And so she had commanded Grend be taken aboard the *Wave-Jarl*, a makeshift room crafted with an old sail so that she could speak to him with some semblance of privacy. Of course, on the deck of a ship that was not the easiest thing to do.

"Ah, here she is," Hrung said, smiling at her.

Elvar dragged in a deep breath and looked at Hjalmar.

"Tell me," she said.

"Of course, Jarl Elvar," he said with a dip of his head. "You remember the fight on the dock, against that *niðing* thief, Ingvild?" Hjalmar began. "Grend had a cut, on his forehead." He looked at Grend, squinting at the map of wounds on the man's face, all scabs and crusted blood. "It might be hard to find it now."

"I remember," Elvar said, and she did, remembered seeing him wipe the cut with a scrap of cloth.

"My *Hundur*-thrall found the linen he wiped the wound on," Hjalmar said. "He always has a good sniff around after a fight. We've found a few Tainted that way, made good coin from it," he explained with a shrug. His ever-present smile faded, shifted to something hard and cold. "He is Tainted, has the blood of Hundur in his veins. Well, we went after him. Of course, he disagreed with us. There were a few words. Short story is that he put two of mine in the ground, and then he ran. We chased. He led us a merry dance, up the fjord cliffs and onto Snaka's back, but we caught him in the end. Lost another three convincing him he should come back with us, and . . . here we are." He spread his arms wide and smiled.

"These are his," he added, handing Elvar the bundle on his lap. It was Grend's *brynja*, wrapped with his weapons belt, his axe from Oskutreð bound within it.

"Nice axe, that," Hjalmar said.

Elvar waved the mail and weapon away, Gytha stepping forward to take them.

"You shall be recompensed for your losses, shall be paid well for this service," she said to Hjalmar as she stepped closer to Grend, fought the urge to call for water and a cloth, to bathe his wounds, to stitch him up, as he had done for her, so many times. Instead, she stood and stared at him, kept her face a flat cliff, as he had tried to teach her.

"What have you to say?" she asked him.

He looked up at her, his face beaten and bruised, his one eye fixing on her, Elvar seeing a depth of pain and misery leaking from it. He opened his mouth, lips moving.

"I am sorry," he mumbled.

"Ha, still the man of many words, then," Hrung said, laughing, his booming voice making the awning ripple. "Some things never change."

"I am sorry," Elvar said. "*Sorry!* Nothing else? After fifteen years of being my weapons master, my protector, my . . . *friend*." She spat the last word out as if it were an illness. "After all the counsel, the admonishments, you trying to teach me how to survive. Teaching me your code. To never give up, to never back down, to speak the truth in all things. And you give me *sorry*." Her hand snapped up to slap him, but she held it back, trembling. Stood straighter and put her hand back down.

He looked at her with one eye, gave her silence.

"You have lied to me all these years, deceived me," Elvar said. She looked at Silrið.

"Silrið, put an iron collar about his neck, say the rune-binding words."

"Yes, Jarl Elvar," Silrið said.

Elvar turned and swept from the makeshift room, blinking, and hoping that no one saw the tears in her eyes.

CHAPTER THIRTY-SIX

BIÓRR

Biórr led his horse out of a stable into the courtyard of Darl's Galdur tower. Horns were braying throughout the town, a wild cacophony that set Biórr's blood tingling, and everywhere he looked was frantic motion and fractured sound, a building tension and excitement almost tangible in the air.

We are going to war.

He felt it in his blood, a savage blend of fear and excitement coursing through his veins.

Tennúr whirled in the air above the courtyard and warriors were everywhere, and skraeling, too, milling in clustered knots. Biórr saw Raven-Feeders with black feathers in their hair, dragon-born, *drengrs* from Darl who had sworn their oaths to Lik-Rifa, all tending to horses, leading them from stables or tied to rail-posts, putting saddle-rugs on their backs, cinching saddle-girths tight, checking hooves. The sweet scent of dung was thick in the air, along with the nostril-sting of ammonia, horses neighing, stamping on the hard-packed earth of the courtyard. Biórr looked for Red Fain and saw the old warrior hauling himself up onto the driving bench of a wagon, favouring his injured leg. He made for him, leading his horse and weaving through the throng.

"Careful, old man," Biórr said as he reached Fain, who was sitting on the driving bench, grumbling to himself and massaging his thigh, slipping his new long-axe beneath his feet and reaching for the reins. Harek sat beside Red Fain, and another dozen children sat in the back of the wagon. "You do not want to fall from there. It's a long way down for an old man like you, might break your bones."

"Old man!" Fain grunted. "It will be your bones that are broken if you don't watch that mouth of yours."

Biórr laughed as he shrugged his shield from his back and hooked it onto his saddle, climbed up onto the back of his horse. He looked across at Fain.

"This is it," he said to Fain. "After all these years of hardship, it is happening."

"Aye, lad," Fain said. "Time to change the world. Make it right." He looked down at Harek beside him, then back at the children seated in the wagon behind him. "Time to save these bairns from being treated like animals, save them from a life of thraldom."

"Aye," Biórr agreed. "And time to avenge our fallen."

Red Fain's mouth twisted, white moustaches of his beard twitching, and he nodded.

A fresh, raucous blowing of horns and silence descended over the courtyard.

Lik-Rifa strode from the Galdur tower, dark hair braided and bound with gold wire into one thick coil that rested upon her shoulder like a black-scaled serpent. She was majestic in a coat of brass-gilded mail, a red-wool cloak trimmed in white fox-fur about her shoulders, a slim sword in a fine-tooled scabbard at her hip. Ilska stalked at one shoulder, all black-oiled mail and cold-malice glare. Drekr tall and broad and brooding as a sea-storm was at Lik-Rifa's other shoulder, his dead brother's long-axe in one fist. Rotta sauntered out of the tower behind them, wearing a coat of mail and wolf-pelt cloak, one arm about the waist of a woman. A dragon-cultist led his horse to him, and he kissed the woman and climbed into the saddle, looked at the host gathered in the courtyard, his eyes somehow finding Biórr, and he smiled and dipped his head. A tall grey gelding was led to Lik-Rifa, and she swung elegantly onto its back, Ilska and Drekr mounting their own horses, and Lik-Rifa looked at those gathered in the courtyard. Her face rippled and shimmered, her jaw extending, eyes flickering to red-embered life.

"WE RIDE FOR WAR," she bellowed in her dragon-voice, Biórr feeling it reverberate in his chest, his horse dancing backwards.

"WE RIDE TO GIVE THE WOLF A RED DEATH," Lik-Rifa roared, and all in the courtyard yelled their battle cries, the surge of volume sending crows squawking in startled protest from the Galdur tower. And then Lik-Rifa was riding out of the courtyard, through the gates and into the streets of Darl. Tennúr whirled above her like a flock of starlings, and hyrndur buzzed in wreaths and clusters. A clatter and rumble of hooves and all were following her from the courtyard, Biórr's blood thrumming with the power of what they were doing.

Rotta rode past Biórr.

"With me, my young rat-blood," Rotta said and, with a nod to Fain, Biórr urged his horse to keep pace with Rotta's. He fell in beside the rat-god, who rode just behind Lik-Rifa, Ilska and Drekr. Biórr saw Brák and his crew riding close behind Drekr.

More warriors were waiting beyond the courtyard. Hundreds of Tainted, come at the call of Lik-Rifa. Some stood alone, others in clusters, some were clearly families. All had a wild, half-starved, fanatical look about them as they stared at Lik-Rifa.

She has given them hope. Given them the chance to step out of the shadows and live without fear.

They fell in alongside the war-host, and as they rode through the streets of Darl more flocked to Lik-Rifa's side. Biórr saw Glunn Iron-Grip mounted on a dark bay as he emerged from a street, leading a few score *drengrs* on horseback, more marching on foot behind them. Captains of Darl and other petty jarls joined them as they wound their way through Darl's streets, swelling the procession so that when Biórr twisted in his saddle to look back he could not see the end of the column through the winding streets.

Slowly they made their way through the town, the ground levelling as they descended the hill and drew near to the river with its tangle of piers, wharves and barns, the host growing ever larger as more joined them; groups of skraeling in tens or twenties, dragon cultists, petty jarls with their retinues, groups of drengrs, mercenary bands come to the call Ilska had sent out into Vigrið, looking for coin or land promised once Vigrið was conquered and ready to be carved up like a Yule-Blot pie.

Rotta looked wistfully at the multitude of longships moored at the piers and shifted in his saddle.

"My arse would much rather be sailing to Snakavik than riding," Rotta said.

"Why are we riding?" Biórr asked. He had thought it the wrong decision when he had heard the news. "It will take us so much longer to get to Snakavik."

"Aye," Rotta agreed, nodding. "But there are many who follow my dear sister that will not sail. Frost-spiders do not like the water, I am told, and neither do night-hags. Troll's, neither, although I can see the sense of that. Can you imagine two bull trolls fighting over a mate on the deck of a longship." He shook his head. "They would sink the ship."

Biórr nodded at that.

"And Lik-Rifa will not consider splitting her war-host, with those that can sailing, and the rest marching, all of us meeting at some suitable point near to Snakavik. Perhaps that is because she loves her followers and cannot bear to be parted from them," he gave Biórr a knowing smile, "or perhaps she thinks Ulfrir is too wolf-cunning and would make us pay dearly for splitting our forces, fall upon each group with his full strength and destroy them." He sighed. "I think she gives him too much credit, he is a mange-ridden runt after all, but . . ." He shrugged. "You do not tell my sister what to do."

They rode along the river-docks, and ahead of them figures stepped from a pier. A band of warriors, forty or fifty of them, all looking like they were close-kin to battle, mail-clad and grim-faced, shields with a gold eye painted upon them. A warrior led them, lank fair hair tied at his nape, a thin straggle of beard, stepping out towards the head of the column, where Lik-Rifa rode with her head held high. She slowed at the sight of him, looked down at him.

"I come to offer my sword and axe, my oathsworn to your service," the warrior called out.

"Help me slay the wolf and you will have all you seek," Lik-Rifa said.

"I am—" the man began, but Lik-Rifa waved a hand, cutting him off.

"I do not care who you are," she said, and rode on.

Ilska stopped beside the man and looked at him.

"I know you, Sterkur death-in-the-eye," she said.

"And I you, Ilska the Cruel," Sterkur said.

She looked to the man who stood at Sterkur's shoulder, tall and black-bearded, a coat of mail and seax at his belt.

"And you?" she said.

"I am Leif Kolskeggson," the man said. "New to Sterkur's crew."

"And why would you fight for the dragon?" Ilska asked them.

"For coin, for fair-fame," Sterkur said. "To be on the winning side." He gave a wry smile. "What else is there?"

"I fight because I am told the Bloodsworn fight against the dragon," Leif said. "And I wish the Bloodsworn dead."

Drekr overheard and rode to them.

"You are welcome here, then," he growled. "And you have come to the right place. We will see the Bloodsworn in the ground."

Leif looked up at Drekr and gave a curt nod.

"Fall in with us," Ilska said. "You need bring nothing but your warriors and your weapons, we have food and drink enough for all Vigrið." She gestured behind her, to the scores of wagons that filled the roads behind them, then she was urging her horse on, Rotta and Biórr riding past Leif, Sterkur and his crew as they waited for a place where they could join the huge column that wound out of Darl like a dark serpent slithering from a corpse.

Slowly they left the town behind them and rode into open meadows flanked by scattered knots of woodland. Bands of trolls joined them, twenty or thirty of the grey-skinned creatures at a time, each one its own troll-clan. All of them left rough dwellings behind them, hewn from trees, strewn with bones and reeking of troll-shite. Frost-spiders scuttled from the woodlands in great clusters, night-hags floating alongside them like banks of black-winged smoke, spertus clambering from streams to scurry alongside the war-host, until it looked to Biórr like the whole world seethed with Lik-Rifa's followers.

"Surely we are unbeatable," Biórr muttered.

"Ah, but I have heard that before," Rotta said grimly, "and it turned out badly then. Let's not count our dead wolves until they lay bleeding and lifeless before us."

CHAPTER THIRTY-SEVEN

VARG

Varg sat on a barrel, blinked salt spray and rain from his eyes and stabbed a bone needle through one side of a tear in his wool tunic, pulled the thread through and stabbed the needle into the other side of the tear. Pulling the thread tight the rip in the wool closed and Varg tied his thread off and cut it with his eating knife. He had been concentrating on his task, but also on staying in his seat, as the *Sea-Wolf* rose and fell like a horse, trying to throw him from his place. His balance shifted with each swell and lull of the sea.

At least this time I can do something without emptying my stomach over the top-rail, he thought, remembering his first voyage, sailing to Iskidan in chase of Jaromir and Vol.

That feels like a long time ago now. He thought he had been going to die, much to Svik and Røkia's entertainment. He looked up, saw over the starboard side that the coast of Vigrið was slithering by, cloaked in a fine mist of rain, and to the bow, almost at the edge of his vision, he saw the sail of Jarl Orlyg's *drakkar*.

Beside him Røkia was muttering under her breath as she hammered at her *brynja*, which was spread across her sea-chest. She had tongs in one hand, hammer in the other as she repaired a rent across the ribs of the coat with new rings. On the deck of the ship Einar Half-Troll was on his knees, wrestling with Refna Strong-Hands and a few other children. Svik was leaning on the mast-pole, arms folded, watching.

Varg pulled the repaired tunic over his head and stood, let it fall down his body.

"Røkia, come, let's watch Einar," he said.

Røkia looked up, over at Einar and the children.

"No," she said with a scowl.

"Why?" Varg asked her.

"Because Einar lets them win. It is wrong," she said.

Varg walked away, smiling and shaking his head.

"Ouch," Svik said, wincing as Varg joined him. "Duck, Einar, they are too quick for you," he shouted.

Einar was laughing, toppling forwards as Refna and a handful of other children swarmed over him, dragging him to the ground. He lay there like a dead walrus a few moments, then slowly rose to his hands and knees, shook himself like a hound coming out of a stream, and children flew from him in all directions, laughing and shrieking.

"Come then, try again, little pups," Einar said, rising onto his knees and grinning.

"Mama, can I try?" Varg heard a voice, looked and saw Orka with her son, Breca. He was stood with a shield in one fist, a short spear in the other, a leather cap over the blade.

"Half-Troll?" Orka called out.

"All are welcome," Einar said, grinning at Breca as he stepped forwards. He walked towards Einar until he was just out of spear range, then set his feet, raised his shield and lifted his spear, spun it in his hand into an overhand grip, spear shaft just behind the blade resting on the upper rim of his shield.

Svik grunted approvingly.

"He has been taught well," a voice said close to Varg's good ear, and he jumped, saw that Røkia had come to stand beside him.

"I thought you did not want to watch," Varg said.

"I don't want to," Røkia said, "but I cannot stop myself."

Svik snorted.

Einar grinned at Breca and the boy stepped in, a short, quick, well-balanced shuffle of his feet and he stabbed his spear, fast and hard. Einar batted it away with a swipe of his hand, and smiled encouragingly. Breca pivoted left, spun his spear and cracked Einar across the forehead with the butt end, pushed himself back the other way off his left leg, ducked Einar's looping arm and raked his spear blade across Einar's cheek and nose, then stepped back out of range, shield and spear held ready. The big man grunted and swayed back on his knees, put a hand to his forehead and looked at his bloody fingertips. Frowned.

"Now that is more like it," Røkia said with a smile. "I *like* this little wolf cub."

There was a ripple of cheers among the Bloodsworn who were watching, and some laughter at Einar. Then a figure slammed into Breca's side and hurled him to the deck, his shield and spear clattering from his grip across the decking. He rolled on the ground and looked up.

Refna Strong-Hands stood over him, her hands balled into fists, her face white and trembling with rage. Varg saw colours flickering in her eyes.

"You hurt Einar," Refna screamed at Breca, spittle spraying.

Breca's legs kicked, and he scrambled on the ground, surged to his feet, lips pulled back in a snarl, his own eyes glinting amber and green. Refna did not wait for him, but hurled herself at him, fists flying.

"Oh no you don't," Einar rumbled, climbing to his feet and reaching in, Orka moving at the same time, grabbing at Breca. In heartbeats both children were dangling in the air, spitting and snarling at each other. Einar held Refna by her tunic and Orka held Breca by the fur around his neck.

"Enough," she barked at Breca and slowly the flickering lights in his eyes faded, and he slumped in her grip.

"She attacked me," he said sullenly.

"Refna, you can't go around attacking people just because I got a scratch," Einar said to Refna, who was still glowering at Breca. "There are rules, and manners."

"Your head," Refna said. "It's only just got better."

"A tickle from his stick is not going to do me any harm," Einar grinned. "Now, can I put you down?"

"Aye," Refna grunted, giving Breca a last scowl.

Glornir walked through the crowd as Orka and Einar put the children down.

"What's going on here?" Glornir asked.

"Nothing, chief," Einar said, "just a bit of friendly sparring."

Glornir looked at the cut on Einar's forehead and cheek, then at Breca and Refna.

"Huh," he grunted, then he walked over to Varg.

"Here," Glornir said, holding up a bucket of heated pitch to Varg. "Repaint your shield black. Tonight, you take your vow."

Varg sat upon a rock, listening to the surf as it roared up the beach, then the hiss as the silver moon-glint of it slithered back down into the darkness.

The *Sea-Wolf* and Sulich's *knarr* bobbed in a small cove on the south-western coast of Vigrið, where they had dropped anchor for the night. Out in the bay there was a soft glow of light from awnings on the *drakkar* and *knarr*, where a handful of guards watched over the two ships. The bulk of both crews were gathered further up the beach, though, where the shingle turned to soil and stiff grass.

"Frøya, what would you say to see me now," he breathed to the moon and night air, to the stars pinpricking the vault of the raven-cloaked sky. He was wearing his fresh-scrubbed mail, his weapons and helm buckled at his belt, the sides of his head newly shaved with the edge of a sharp knife. The length of his hair was tied at his crown, and when he had combed his beard with a comb fashioned from elk-bone, he had discovered it was long enough to put a braid in it, which he had tied off with a thin strip of leather. His silver arm ring glinted around his left bicep, given to him by Glornir after the battle at Rotta's chamber.

"I am to become one of the Bloodsworn," he murmured to the sea. Their fair-fame was how all in Vigrið knew of them, but that meant nothing to Varg. "They are home," he breathed to the listening moon and stars. "They are kin." He shook his head. "I wish you were here, Frøya, wish you could have known this . . . belonging. This peace."

Varg listened, the sigh of the wind over the sea, hissing across the sea-spume and shingle, rustling through the dry grass, was almost like a voice.

Footsteps crunched on shingle, growing louder, a shadow looming, silhouetted by the firelight further up the beach.

"Varg No-Sense, it is time," Svik said to him, serious for a change.

Varg breathed deep, blew out a long breath and stood. He bent and gripped his new-painted shield, just a darker shadow in the crow-black of night, and nodded to Svik, who turned and led him up the beach towards the firelight.

The sounds of voices grew louder as Varg drew closer to them, people eating, drinking, talking, Varg making out the bulk of Glornir, Vol, Iva, Edel and Taras with them. The conversation faded and died as Varg reached them, Svik leading him through the crowd that now moved to form a circle around the fire pit. Around Varg.

Glornir stepped into the circle, stood before Varg, and gripped him by the shoulders, looked at him for a long moment. Then Glornir smiled, which made Varg blink. He let go of Varg and turned a slow circle, facing out to the Bloodsworn gathered around them, talking as he turned.

"Varg No-Sense has come to us, a wolf-blood stray, a lone wolf. He has eaten with us, drunk with us, sailed with us, bent his back at the oar-bench with us. He has fought in the battle-fray and shield wall with us, buried our dead with us. Risked his life for us." He stopped in his turning, standing to look at Varg again with his green-touched eyes. "Varg No-Sense, why are you here?"

"I would be one of you," Varg said. "I would be one of the Bloodsworn. I would be kin."

"Who here would have Varg No-Sense for an oar-mate?" Glornir called out. "Who here would trust him at their side in the shield wall, who here would give their life for him?"

A long, flame-licked silence, and then Røkia stepped out of the crowd, the fire-glow casting her face in sharp-gleaming angles and deep shadows.

"I would," Røkia said.

"And I," Svik said, stepping next to Røkia, firelight glinting on his oiled beard and sharp-toothed smile.

"I would," Einar Half-Troll rumbled.

"And I," said Sulich, taking a step into the light.

"And I," said Vol, a hint of a smile on her lips as she held Varg's gaze.

"And I," Edel said. And so it went on, each of the Bloodsworn stepping forwards, forty of them, fifty, until finally all had taken the step and raised their voices, all except one, all eyes coming to settle upon Glornir.

"And I," Glornir said, his voice like gravel.

A silence settled, the crackle of flames.

"Give me your shield," Glornir said, and Varg handed it to him.

Vol stepped closer, her serpent draped across her shoulders, a leather cup in one hand, drawing a seax with her other, a slithering hiss as it left its scabbard.

"Give me your hand, Varg No-Sense," she said, and he held his weapons hand out to her. She took it, her grip firm, skin rough, and lifted it, with a swift movement drew the seax across the back of Varg's hand, blood welling black in the night. A moment before he felt the sting of it, then she was drawing the blade across the back of her own hand, more dark blood glistening. She pressed the back of her hand to Varg's cut and held the cup beneath both their hands, Varg seeing their mingled blood drip into the cup.

"Snaka blóð, þekki barnið þitt, Varg úlfsson," Vol said. There was a flicker of light within the cup and, as Varg watched the blood began to rise into the air, two strands of flickering, grease-slick blood spiralling together, around each other, slowly intertwining, twisting, like the iron rods of a sword as they are forged together. A hiss and flare of flame as the two strands became one, dropping back into the cup, swilling there like molten metal.

"Say the words," Glornir said.

"Before you all I swear my oath," Varg began, reciting the words that Glornir had spoken to him upon the beach. "To become kin with you, my brothers, my sisters; to become pack. To fight for you, to die for you, if needs be to avenge you, until the world's ending."

He looked from Glornir to the Bloodsworn gathered around him. "By my blood, bone, flesh and steel I swear it."

"Your hands," Vol said and Varg cupped his hands as Glornir raised Varg's shield. Vol lifted the cup and turned it over, the still-glowing blood dripping and pooling into Varg's hands.

"I seal this oath with my blood," he said and flung the blood at his shield. With a sizzling hiss the blood spattered across the shield, burning and marking it, the reek of charred linen and wood wafting, tendrils of smoke rising from where the blood had kissed the shield.

Glornir handed the shield back to Varg and he took it.

"Welcome to the Bloodsworn," Glornir said, and a great roar of cheering erupted around Varg. He grinned with the joy of it, emotion rising like a wave, and tears ran down his cheeks.

CHAPTER THIRTY-EIGHT

ELVAR

Elvar stood at the prow of the *Wave-Jarl*, Ulfrir at her side.

"Here," he said, "this is the place. This is the river."

"That is the River Falinn," Elvar said to him, looking at a wide estuary that bled into the sea, the banks to north and south of the river cloaked in a snarling tangle of forest.

"I do not know the new names of your rivers, but that is the Jarnvidr, and that river is the path to my den," Ulfrir said. He raised his head, as if tasting scents on the wind. "It is close," he said.

Elvar turned and yelled out orders to Sighvat, who gripped and leaned on the steering oar, and slowly he changed their course, guiding the *Wave-Jarl* in a great sweeping curl until they were rowing into the mouth of the River Falinn. Gytha blew a horn, ringing out across the waves to the fleet behind them and Elvar heard the call taken up, spreading through the war fleet like lit beacons, all shifting to follow the *Wave-Jarl* into the open jaws of the Iron Wood.

As they changed course the headwind they had been rowing into shifted until it was blowing behind them and Elvar barked out more orders, oars coming up in sprays of jewel-glinting droplets and shipped, stowed in oar-racks that ran along the deck's centre, the sail unfurled for the first time since they had left Snakavik, fresh-coated with sheep's fat to protect it from the sea-rot and catch and hold the wind better. The sail snapped and billowed, then grasped a fistful of wind and the *Wave-Jarl* was carving through the estuary, a mist of water spraying over the bow and leaving a spumed wake spreading behind it like white-tipped wings. Elvar grinned for the joy of it, and for a heartbeat or two almost forgot the pain of Grend's betrayal.

The Iron Wood had closed around them, banks drawing nearer, trees rearing tall as towers, boughs reaching like grasping hands across the river, straining to touch one another across the wide swirl of the water as the *Wave-Jarl* sliced through the current. After half a day of sailing upriver, Elvar had ordered a half-crew back to the oar-bench, both to speed their way as the wind began to dip, and to keep the longship from serpent-sly currents that lurked beneath the surface and could snatch the *Wave-Jarl* and toss it into the riverbank.

She strode along the deck, having just left Sighvat at the tiller, and saw Orv the Sneak leaning on the portside top-rail, staring into the gloom and snarl of woodland on the west bank.

"What do you see?" Elvar asked him as she walked to him.

"Shadows," Orv murmured. "Something is stalking us." He pointed and Elvar stared. The forest was a knot-twist of branch and vine, the undergrowth between the thick-trunked trees dense and as impenetrable as the night-dark shadows. And yet, as she stared, she did see movement, layers of darkness, the flicker of shadows within shadows, here and there a moment of dappled light on fur, the glint of eyes as fractured rays of daylight filtered through the canopy above.

"Wolves," Elvar said. "Many wolves." She looked to Ulfrir, who stood at the bow, staring upriver.

"Do you trust him?" Orv said with a frown.

"As much as I trust anyone," Elvar said, then immediately thought of Grend. "Trust is a trap, anyway. But Ulfrir has my collar about his neck. He cannot betray me, or attempt to cause me harm, or incite others to cause me harm."

"Well, that is good, because I do *not* trust him. All you can trust a wolf to do is mischief," Orv said. "Is the collar enough?"

"Well, I am still breathing," Elvar said with a shrug, "which Ulfrir would change if he could, for his freedom. Other than the *blóð svarið*, the blood oath, the Seiðr-made thrall-collar is the greatest insurance of obedience we have. The blood oath, that sneaky piece of shite-born Seiðr-magic, knows your thoughts. The thrall-collar will not allow you to commit an act of betrayal, but with the blood oath you cannot even think about betrayal."

Orv shivered. "Don't like the thought of that," he muttered.

"Anyway, even if Ulfrir managed to come up with some deep-cunning way of slaying me," Elvar continued, "he would still not be free. Broðir would become his master, because he is my blood kin. Just as my father's *Berserkirs* became mine upon my father's death." She glanced back to where longships and *knarr* filled the river, her brother made chief of one of the crews. It swelled her heart to see them, her war-host. Win or lose in this coming war, the skálds would sing of Elvar Fire-Fist's war fleet and how it had sailed to face the might of a dragon.

The howling of wolves shattered her thoughts and Elvar spun around to see that the trees were thinning on the western bank, a great hill rearing out of the forest. Ragged trees and thornbushes grew upon the hill's slopes, here and there what looked like the crumbling remains of vine-crusted towers, and upon the hill's crest wolves had gathered, standing silhouetted against the pale winter's sky. Hundreds of them, and all of them were howling. The sound swirled around the *Wave-Jarl* like a breeze, rising and falling, feeling as if it must fill all the world.

Elvar strode to Ulfrir.

"What is happening?" she snapped at him.

Ulfrir looked at her and smiled.

"They are welcoming me home," he said.

The *Wave-Jarl* turned a bend in the river, coiling around the hill. Elvar shouted for the sail to be furled and the mast taken down, Sólín Spittle hammering the mast-stop into the hole the mast had just been heaved from, and then they were scudding beneath a stone bridge.

The bank along the hill's edge dropped low, with what looked like fallen trees stabbing out from the bank into the river, but as the *Wave-Jarl* passed the first of them she realised that they were ancient, moss-covered piers.

"There," Ulfrir called as the river followed the curl of the hill, and Elvar saw two smaller promontories stretch out from the hill like slumped arms, a vale between them leading to a sheer, cliff-faced escarpment. A stone bridge and pier were set in the river directly opposite the slopes, mooring posts spread along it.

Elvar shouted orders and Sighvat guided the Wave-Jarl towards the pier, oars pulling at a slower rhythm. Skuld spread her wings, climbing into the air and she flew a looping circle above the *Wave-Jarl* and made for the pier, alighting upon it and running to one of the mooring stones.

"OARS," Elvar yelled, and the oars came up, were dragged back through the oar-holes and shipped and the *Wave-Jarl* slithered alongside the dock, hull scrapping on stone. Orv threw a rope to Skuld and she wrapped it around the mooring stone, the *drakkar* snugging up tight to the pier. Elvar took her shield from a rack, shrugged it across her back and climbed onto the top-rail, then leaped onto the ancient pier. She stood there a moment, looking back down the river where other longships were appearing and rowing to the piers that jutted out into the river, then Berak and a handful of her *Berserkir* were leaping from the *Wave-Jarl* to the dock and forming up around her. Gytha came next with a score of *drengrs*, moving down the pier, fanning out to search the undergrowth and shadows.

Elvar looked to Ulfrir, who was still stood in the bow.

"Come, then, Ulfrir-wolf," Elvar said.

Gracefully he climbed onto the top-rail and stepped over onto the pier, his handful of *Úlfhéðnar* following him. As Ulfrir set foot on the ancient stone the howling of wolves stopped, echoes of their song fading to silence.

All from the *Wave-Jarl* were disembarking now, Sighvat, Orv, Sólín Spittle and the rest of the Battle-Grim settling around Elvar. *Drengrs* carried Hrung from his pedestal on thick wooden beams, Hrung's eyes staring up at the hill, looking at the wolves gathered on the hill's brow.

"Noisy bunch, aren't they," he grumbled. "I was having a wonderful dream, about having a body and legs."

Behind Hrung, Silrið emerged from the awning on the *Wave-Jarl*'s deck, leading Grend by a leather leash that was buckled around the iron collar about his neck. Grend looked at Elvar and she looked away, the guilt, despite his betrayal, gnawing at her.

"So this is the home of a wolf-god," Sighvat said. "Just looks like a big hill to me."

"Looks can be deceiving," Uspa said as she came to stand beside Elvar.

Silrið stepped onto the pier, Grend following, and she walked over to Elvar.

"What would you have me do with him, Jarl Elvar?" Silrið asked her.

"Follow us," Elvar said. "Once we are inside this wolf-den we should be able to find a gaol for him."

"You do not need to do this," Grend said to her, looking at the rope that still bound his wrists, and raising his hands to touch the leash that hung from his neck. "You know I will not betray you."

Elvar looked at him, saw that his wounds were healing, his eye still swollen, but he could open it now.

"You already have," she said to him, then walked away, moving to stand beside Ulfrir.

"Lead on," she said to Ulfrir, and he strode down the dock, Skuld falling in at his shoulder, his *Úlfhéðnar* behind him, Elvar and all with her following in their wake.

The pier spilled onto a road covered with vine and a thin layer of dirt, but Elvar kicked at it and saw that beneath the soil it was paved with stone. The road led straight into the vale between the two promontories that arched out from the hill and Ulfrir marched down it, drew up before the sheer escarpment, looking up at its heights at the wolves silhouetted across its heights, looking down upon them.

"Wait here," Ulfrir said and strode on another score of paces. He stopped before the cliff face that rose sheer before him, two huge boulders set at either side of the escarpment. All was covered in creeping vine. He looked up at the steep-sloped cliff, twisted his neck one way so that it clicked, then the other.

"Úlfabæli, mitt forna heimili, opinberaðu varðmenn þína, opinberaðu þín fornu hlið," Ulfrir cried out, his voice unnaturally loud, ringing and echoing, slowly fading to silence.

Elvar felt a vibration in the ground beneath her feet, a wind swirling through the woods, trees rustling and scraping, boughs creaking, the wind rising, whipping white foam across the river and then it was hurtling across the pier, funnelled between the two promontories of the hill and sweeping around her, lashing at her like a sea-storm, tugging and tearing at her braided hair, the hem of her woollen tunic, all those around her swaying and bracing themselves. The ground trembled and the wind hurled itself across the boulders either side of Ulfrir, scouring them of the vine that coated them and continued up the cliff face, the rock trembling and shuddering, vine falling in great clumps, shaken and torn away, a huge cloud of dust exploding, enveloping Elvar and all about her. She coughed, covering her face with her bearskin cloak.

There was a ripple of cracking sounds, like bones breaking but louder. The dust had settled; Ulfrir was standing staring up at the rock face. Now that the vine and layers of dirt were gone, Elvar could see the outline of great stone doors, snarling wolf-heads carved into each one. But that was not where her eyes were drawn, not where the cracking sound was coming from.

The two stone boulders were moving, juddering, unfurling, legs appearing, huge snarling faces and then two stone-carved wolves were standing before the great gates, their lips pulled back, teeth bared, hackles raised, eyes glowing amber in their grey-stone faces.

The outline of Ulfrir shimmered, a pale glow about him as his form shifted, began to grow. A series of popping cracks as he fell to all fours, his muzzle lengthening, fur sprouting, a tail growing, the air about him rippling like a heat haze and he was standing in his wolf-form, big as a mead hall before the gates and stone wolves.

He threw his head back and howled, the sound of it crashing upon Elvar like a sudden summer storm, people around her raising their hands to cover their ears. The two stone wolves raised their heads and howled, too, adding their voices to Ulfrir's, and the wolves gathered at the top of the hill joined in the baying, until the whole world must have rung with it.

There was a great grinding, more dust and stone exploding from the stone gates as they rumbled open, stone grating, unseen hinges creaking until the doors lay wide open, an ancient, musty odour wafting out from within the open doors.

Ulfrir turned and looked down at them with amber-glowing eyes, the wind dying, sifting his fur.

"Welcome to my home," he growled.

CHAPTER THIRTY-NINE

ORKA

Orka leaned and pulled, leaned and pulled, her oar dipping and rowing, rising and dipping again. Sweat dripped into her eyes, ran down her neck and back. It felt good to lose herself for a while in the physicality of rowing. She had watched the oath-taking ceremony of Varg No-Sense, and it had stirred up memories that lurked deep within her, memories that she had tried to bury for the pain that they caused.

She could still hear the words of her old chief, Boðvar-Claw. *"Orka Skullsplitter, why are you here?"*

"To be one of you," she had given her answer, "to be kin."

And yet I walked away, turned my back on them all. I am a niðing oath-breaker.

For our son, she heard Thorkel's voice whisper in her thought-cage.

"Aye, for our son," she breathed out as she pulled.

"What's that, Mama?" Breca asked, who was sitting on the sea-chest beside her, his hands wrapped around Orka's oar, pretending to row alongside her. Vesli the tennúr sat on Breca's lap, eating teeth from the pouch at her belt.

"Nothing," Orka grunted.

A horn blew, signalling the end of Orka's shift at the bench and she raised her oar and stood, a female warrior named Æsa that had not been one of the Bloodsworn in Orka's time moving to take her place.

"My thanks, Skullsplitter," Æsa said to her.

Orka grunted and moved out of the way.

"I want to row, Mama," Breca said.

"No," Orka said.

"Why not?" Breca scowled. "And do not say I am too young. She is rowing," and he nodded at Refna Strong-Hands, who was taking her place on an oar-chest.

"It is harder than it looks," Orka said. "If you're not used to it, you will splinter the oar, throw the rhythm, maybe break the arm of the rower ahead or behind you."

Breca muttered something under his breath.

Orka ignored him, walking towards the water barrel. A shadow flickered across the deck of the *Sea-Wolf*, the beating of air, one of the giant ravens spiralling above them, sweeping down. It croaked and squawked, wings beating, and alighted upon the deck, rocking the *Sea-Wolf*.

"Grok bring news, Grok bring news," the raven shrieked as Glornir passed the steering oar to Einar and approached the raven.

"What news, friend?" Glornir asked the crow.

"The dragon has left Darl," Grok rasped, running his black beak through feathers on his wing.

"Where is she going?" Glornir asked her.

"West. Many walk with her."

"She is not flying, or sailing, then?" Vol asked as she joined them, her serpent wrapped across her shoulders. She was stroking its head.

"No, not fly, not sail," Grok croaked. "They walk."

"Do you know where they are going?"

"Grok not fly close enough to hear them," the raven cawed. "Grok not want to be eaten by dragon. Or spiders, or trolls." He gave what passed for a shrug. "They walk west."

Vol looked at Glornir. "Snakavik is west of Darl."

"Aye. She will have heard that Ulfrir is there, no doubt. It would be hard to keep a wolf-god secret," he said.

"Grok hungry," the raven squawked.

"Follow me," Vol said to the crow. "We have a barrel of pickled herring that I think you might like."

"Grok love tasty fish," the raven said, clacking its beak and hopping after Vol.

Orka scooped a ladle of water from the water barrel and drank deep, then scooped another one and drank again.

"So, Lik-Rifa marches on Snakavik," Orka said, looking to Glornir.

"Aye," he grunted. "That is good. Less time spent sailing and hunting her if she is coming to us." He walked to Breca and put a big hand on the boy's shoulder.

"Aye," Orka agreed. A memory of Drekr filled her head. Now that she had Breca back, the thought of vengeance for Thorkel spiralled in her head like hunting wolves smelling blood.

"Thirsty work on the oar-bench," a voice said behind her and Orka turned to see Svik, his usual smile on his face. By the look of his sweat-stained tunic he had just finished his own shift on the oar-bench. Orka offered him the water ladle. Behind him she glimpsed Røkia sparring with Varg No-Sense. They paused in their axe-work and turned to watch Svik, who took the ladle from Orka and took a deep drink, then followed Orka's eyes to look back at Røkia and Varg.

"You remember the words he spoke last night?" Svik asked Orka. His smile still lingered at the edges of his mouth, though it was not in his eyes.

Orka just looked at him.

"Did you not hear me?" Svik said.

"I heard you," Orka grunted.

"Then the least you could do is answer me," he said. "I—" he paused, swallowed. "I loved you like a son. My heart broke when I thought you dead. I . . . grieved for you." He dragged in a deep breath. "And yet you did not die, you just . . . left. Without any word."

A flash of memory in her thought-cage, of pulling back a gorse bush to find a snarling boy, frightened and fierce, mud-spattered, bruised, red weals on his back from the lash of a whip.

Orka had words she wanted to say to him, had prepared to say, had imagined herself saying many times over, but they turned to ash in her mouth.

"So, do you remember the words of your oath?" Svik asked her again.

"They are carved on my soul," Orka breathed.

Svik blinked at that, nodded.

"Then why did you leave us. Why did you leave *me*?"

She looked at him then, felt the words pile up in her throat, thought of clamping her jaws shut, thought of turning around and walking away.

"For my son," she said eventually. "To keep him safe, to bring him up in peace."

A silence settled over them, Svik looking at her, and Orka became aware that many of the Bloodsworn were gathered close, listening, and those on oar-benches nearby were leaning her way, ears straining.

She puffed out a hard breath. "That did not work out so well. Our steading burned, Thorkel slain, my son stolen by dragon-born, and now we are on the *Sea-Wolf* sailing towards a red war. I chose to leave death behind me, but it seems death has not chosen to let me go."

A few snorts of laughter and agreement around her, but Svik still stared at her. Slowly he nodded.

"So, are you back with us now?" Svik said. "Are you Bloodsworn, are you kin?"

"In here, I always have been," Orka said, touching her chest. She shrugged. "I am Bloodsworn, if Glornir will have me back, and forgive me for leaving."

A silence, all looking at Glornir.

"In here," Glornir said, putting a big hand over his heart, "you never left."

A flapping of wings from above them and they all looked up to see Kló sweeping over them, circling down. She landed on the starboard top-rail, the *Sea-Wolf* listing dangerously low, and she hopped off onto the deck. A raucous squawking and Grok spread his wings, glided over to her and the two giant ravens began preening each other's feathers.

"Kló have news," the raven said, looking up and cocking her

head to fix Glornir with a black-gleaming eye while Grok continued to run his beak through her feathers.

"Ships sail from Snaka's skull," the raven croaked. "Many ships."

"Elvar," Glornir said. "Where are they going?"

"They sailed south, then rowed into the Jarnvidr," Kló said.

"The Iron Wood," Vol said, joining them again. "Why have they sailed into the Iron Wood?"

"Ulfrir's den, the Wolfdale," Grok said, stopping his preening for a moment.

"The Wolf-Dale?" Glornir said.

"The Wolf-Dale, Ulfrir-wolf's den, Ulfrir's home," Kló squawked.

"I have never heard of it," Glornir frowned.

"Does not mean it is not there," Grok cawed.

"And how do you know they have gone there?" Vol asked Kló.

"Kló saw it, Kló heard it. Wolves howling, hurt Kló's ears."

Glornir shared a look with Vol.

"Lik-Rifa is on the move, Ulfrir and Elvar have sailed," Vol said. "This war is close."

"Aye," Glornir grunted. "Grok, Kló, can you tell Jarl Orlyg of this news? Tell him that we have a change of course. Tell him we are sailing for the Iron Wood."

CHAPTER FORTY

ELVAR

Elvar sat in Ulfrir's high-arched, wolf-carved chair, her scabbarded sword wrapped in her baldric and resting across her lap, her fingers tapping on the wire-wrapped hilt. The chair was too big for her, but she was not going to allow Ulfrir to sit in the high seat of this wolf hall. That was her place now. Instead, she had told him to stand at her shoulder, Berak the other side, while her advisers stood before her and tried to work out how they were going to kill a dragon.

Gytha had been talking of tactics, of shield walls and boar-snouts, and now Silrið was talking of Galdur-magic, of rune-spells and the power of god-relics and bones.

"She must come to us," Ulfrir said, interrupting Silrið.

"Come to us?" Silrið said, frowning. "And how do you get a dragon to do what you want it to do?"

"By using me as bait," Ulfrir said. "Lik-Rifa hates me, and fears me, too. But she knows the longer I live, the more dangerous I become. She is fresh from her destruction of Orna, she will want to find me and fall upon me, as she did my wife."

A shudder rippled through Skuld's wings.

"Be careful, my friend," Hrung said to Ulfrir, "or you may end up just a head, sitting upon a pedestal next to me, or hanging from a wall like some hunted trophy."

"It will be Lik-Rifa who has her head ripped from her slithering neck," Ulfrir snarled.

"And you think she will come at you here, in your home?" Uspa asked him.

"Lik-Rifa fled to Nastrandir when she was weak," Ulfrir said. "She will think that is why I have come here, to recover. She will think that I am weak."

"And if we did manage to lure Lik-Rifa here, how would we slay her?" Silrið asked.

"*I* will slay her," Ulfrir said. "Your part is to slay her war-host, which I would suspect is formidable. Her dragon-born, her vaesen, many of the Tainted."

Elvar wanted to interrupt. A thought had been worming its way into her head, an idea, faint as a half-remembered dream. Something that felt important, but was just frustratingly out of reach.

I cannot think straight, since . . . since . . .

"Ach," she snarled and stood from her chair, looked at all about her and strode away without a word, all of them staring at her. Berak hurried to walk at her shoulder, and Sighvat lumbered to her other side.

"Where are you going, Jarl Elvar?" Silrið called out after her.

"I have something I need to do," Elvar called back.

She strode through Ulfrir's great hall, as awestruck by it now as she had been when she first followed Ulfrir through its open gates, two days gone. At the centre of the hall grew a tree, thick-trunked as a mead hall, the bark moss-covered. It shimmered with some ethereal light, emanating from dense clumps of fungus that grew large as shields upon its trunk. Elvar looked up, her eyes tracing the tree by the fungus-glow into the high-vaulted roof of the hall, where, perhaps by some strange Seiðr-magic, light broke through the dome of the hill the hall was built beneath in fractured seams. She walked around the tree and passed between thick wolf-carved pillars that disappeared into shadowed murk, past torches that had burst to life at Ulfrir's word, sending stretching shadows as she strode beneath them.

Much had been done in the two days since they had arrived.

The exploration of Ulfrir's den had to come first, of which this great hall was only a small part. Ulfrir had told her that tunnels spread from this chamber like threads from a spider's web, carving beneath the river and spreading wide to exits and entrances throughout the Iron Wood. The first task she had set had been sending scouts into every tunnel, to secure those entrances. Once that was done, time had been given to organising her forces, where they would sleep, cook, eat, train.

But there is still so much more to do, and, for all I know, Lik-Rifa is only heartbeats away. I need eyes upon her, I need information, so that I can plan. But for that, I need a clear head.

She left the great hall and strode into a torch-lit corridor, high and wide enough for Ulfrir to travel through in his wolf-form.

"Sighvat, you do not need to shadow me everywhere I go," Elvar said.

"You are my chief," Sighvat said.

"I know, but I have *Berserkir* that guard me."

"They guard you because they are thralled to you, forced to guard you," Sighvat said. "I guard you because you are my deep-cunning chief. I guard you because I *choose* to. It is better than a thrall-guard." He glanced at Berak. "I am loyal, as are all the Battle-Grim. One of us will always guard you, wherever you go," he said.

"I know you are loyal," Elvar said, something about Sighvat's words warming her.

"I would guard you through choice, even were I not wearing your thrall-collar," Berak growled, glancing at Sighvat. "Because you go to war to save my son."

"Huh," Sighvat grunted, conceding the point.

Elvar turned into another corridor that sloped downwards, the walls damp, water dripping and echoing. She walked until she saw a figure standing beneath torchlight. Another one of her *Berserkir*, Thorguna Storm-Cloud, on account of her permanent heavy-browed frown.

"My jarl," Thorguna said as Elvar reached her.

"Open the door," Elvar said, and Thorguna took a big iron key from her belt and put it into the lock on the door she guarded, turned it and pulled open the door, light leaking out. She made to step into the room.

"No," Elvar said, "I will go alone", and she stepped through the doorway. Sighvat followed her and she stopped.

"I said alone," Elvar said to him.

"But I didn't think that meant me," Sighvat frowned.

"Alone," she said again, gesturing outside.

"But—"

"Out," Elvar said, stepped further into the room and pushed the door closed on creaking hinges behind her. Then she turned and looked at Grend.

He was seated on a cot, his hands still bound, the leather leash that Silrið had led him into these halls with still buckled at his thrall-collar and tied to an iron ring set into the rock of the wall.

She looked at him a long moment, and he returned her gaze. Elvar felt a flare of sadness, and of anger.

"You have made me appear weak, a *fool*," she snarled at him. "There are whisperings that I should kill you, hang you from a gallows-branch, or put you in a cage to rot. It is what my father would advise, and he would be right. You have caused my jarls to doubt me, to lose their respect for me."

Grend nodded.

"I am sorry," he said.

"Sorry does not change anything," she snapped. Scowled at him, blew out a long sigh.

"Why?" she asked him. "Why did you not tell me? Why did you deceive me all these years?"

He looked down at his bound hands, his brows knotting in a frown, then looked back at her.

"I swore an oath," he said.

"You swore an oath to *me*," she snarled.

"I swore this oath first, and it was about you," he answered.

"What?" Elvar said. "What oath? Who did you swear it to?"

"I swore an oath to your mother, soon after you were born. That I would always protect you. How could I protect you if I had a thrall-collar about my neck and owed allegiance to your father?"

"Did my mother know that you are Tainted?"

"Yes."

Elvar thought about that, let that seep in.

"Please, Grend," she said, "tell me."

He looked up at the pain and questions in her eyes and took a slow, deep breath. "I was born to a thrall in the household of your mother's father," he said, slowly, as if the words were shackled somewhere deep within him. "He was a petty jarl of Jarl Störr, as you know. I grew up as a thrall-servant in his household, working the kitchens, the farm, the forge. Your mother and I were of a similar age. We became . . . friends. Once she saw me being beaten by one of her father's *drengrs*, and afterwards she came with a bowl of hot water and bandages, cleaned my cuts." A ripple of a smile crossed his mouth, disappeared almost instantly, like the moon behind scudding clouds. "She was *always* kind to me. One day, when I had eleven, maybe twelve winters on my back, I was one of many beaters on one of your grandfather's hunts. It was her first hunt and she got lost in the forest. Her father sent all out searching for her. But I was Tainted, though I did not know it, then. Hundur the hound was in my veins, and I knew her scent. I tracked her deep into the forest, and then I heard her crying out, ran through the forest and found her. Three *niðing* outlaws had her. Had torn her from her horse, ripped her clothes from her. They were trying to . . . use her. I picked up a fallen branch and . . ." He spread his hands. "We killed them. I put two in the ground, but the last one, he was Tainted, had *Hundur* in his blood, like me, and he smelled it on me as we fought, as I bled. He shouted it out, told me to join him. I froze a moment, and he made to skewer me with his seax. Your mother cut his throat." He shrugged. "We were bound from that moment. Had saved each other's lives. She swore never to tell of my secret, and when I took her back to her father, she told him of how I had saved her. Her father rewarded me by giving me my freedom, allowed me to enter his household as a freedman. I took to the spear and sword and axe and rose to become a *drengr* in his household." He was silent a while, lost in his memories. "They were good days. But then Jarl Störr came visiting and saw your mother. She was beautiful, of course, but also Störr wanted your grandfather's allegiance, and so he took her for his wife. When she had been at Snakavik a while she sent to her father, asking for me. He gave me a choice: stay and become captain of his household *drengrs*, or go to Snakavik and your mother." He looked up at Elvar and smiled. "That was no choice at all." He raised his bound hands and scratched at a scabbed cut on his face. "You were born, and soon after your father began to . . . mistreat your mother. She asked me to swear a blood oath that I would always look after you." He turned his hand and showed her a pale-ridged scar, and Elvar remembered running her fingers across a similar scar on the back of her mother's hand. "And that is what I have tried to do."

"Am . . . am I your daughter?" Elvar breathed.

Grend looked up at her and gave a sad smile. "No," he shook his head. "Though I wish you were." He looked at her, an intensity in his gaze. "You are not your father's daughter. You are nothing like Jarl Störr. In all else but blood I do consider you to be my daughter." A tear spilled down his cheek and he lowered his gaze. "It grieves me to bring shame upon you."

I am not my father's daughter. Or am I? My greatest fear is to become him, and I can feel it happening.

She stood there staring at him, eventually moved, drawing the axe that Grend had given her from her belt. With a short chop she cut the bonds that bound his wrists, slipped the axe back into her belt and unbuckled the leash that bound him to the iron ring. Then without a word she turned, opened the door and left.

CHAPTER FORTY-ONE

BIÓRR

Biórr sat eating a bowl of porridge, stirring a drop of honey into it with his wooden spoon. The pewter-grey of dawn was leaking into the world, darkness fading, a faint glow at the edge of the world where the sun was clawing over the horizon. Around him the camp was moving, people eating, drinking, tending to horses, packing their kit. He saw a bull troll bellowing at two cubs that were rolling on the ground, punching and kicking, gouging with their new-grown tusks and close by Red Fain was overseeing the Tainted children sparring, saw Harek slam a shield into his sparring partner and send her crashing to the ground.

So much was happening all around him, so many people all around him, and yet he felt alone.

The scrape of footsteps and a figure stepped out of the grey, sat on a barrel beside him.

Ilska the Cruel. She stared at the pot of porridge a moment, reflected flames flickering in her dark eyes. Biórr saw that the lines on her face were deeper, the grey in her hair stronger.

"I have not thanked you," she said with a frown, "for bringing Myrk's body to me."

Myrk's body. The words were like a fist clenching in his gut.

"You do not need to thank me for that," Biórr said. "She was . . . dear to me."

"You brought her joy," Ilska said, "and I thank you for that, too."

"The joy was mutual," Bióṙr said, "and the world is less without her."

"Heya," Ilska agreed.

They sat there in silence a while, Biórr's head full of Myrk, the smell of her, the twist of her smile, the taste of her lips.

"This Orka," Ilska said, breaking the silence. "Tell me what you know of her."

Biórr frowned, thinking on that.

"She is Tainted," he started, "*Úlfhéðnar*. She has a rare weapons craft." He paused, seeing Orka in his head, fighting, snarling, carving her way through all before her. "She prefers the long-axe, though I have seen her fight with seax and hand-axe, with her teeth and claws." He shook his head to dispel the image of Myrk with her throat ripped out. Remembered his conversation with Orka, about the gods. *They do not care for the lives of anyone*, she had said. "She is stubborn," he grunted.

"Anything else? There must be more," Ilska asked her.

Biórr sifted over all that Myrk had told her of Orka.

"She is single-minded and loves her son. She tracked him across all Vigrið. She does not fear death like most do, it is . . . unsettling. She walked into *The Dead Drengr* at Darl to confront Drekr and a dozen others with him, slew most of them. She walked out of the trees and confronted Myrk and a dozen Raven-Feeders at Rotta's camp, would have fought them alone. She walked into our war-host as we attacked Svelgarth, carved her way through frost-spiders, warriors, skraeling, just to get to her son, so she has stones of granite and some deep-cunning." He sighed. "She took pain, would say nothing about Ulfrir despite a beating from Rotta. She only spoke of Ulfrir when Rotta threatened the life of her spertus."

"A spertus? But they are loyal to Lik-Rifa," Ilska said.

"Not all," Biórr said with a shrug.

"And then she attacked Rotta when he slew the spertus. She has no fear, or respect, for the gods."

Ilska nodded, thinking it all over.

"Why are you asking me this?" Biórr asked her.

"Because it is best to know your enemies. And I will meet her soon," she said, a cold twist of her lips. Biórr had seen that before, and he shivered.

"Is there anything else?" Ilska asked him.

"She is bound to the Bloodsworn, somehow. Three of them were with her at Svelgarth. I slew one of them."

Ilska grunted approvingly at that.

"Two of them came for her when we were attacked by Orlyg and his Tainted. They helped her escape."

"There will be a reckoning for the Bloodsworn, too. Sterkur death-in-the-eye has heard news that your Elvar has offered them silver to fight for her, so I think that we shall meet them soon."

Your Elvar. He did not like to think on Elvar, although she was always in his head, lurking in the shadows. His betrayal of her was the one thing he regretted.

"The cost of our war," Ilska said, "it has been high. My father, my brother, my sister." She blew out a long breath, shook her head. "We cannot fail."

"We will not," Biórr said.

Horns blew, marking the call to march.

Ilska patted him on the leg and stood. "My thanks," she said. She drew something from a pocket inside her cloak. A raven's feather.

"It was Myrk's," Ilska said, holding it out to Biórr. "I think she would have liked you to have it."

Biórr took it, watched Ilska walk away as he braided the feather into his hair.

Biórr rode alongside Rotta, close to the head of their column, only Lik-Rifa and Ilska ahead of them. Rolling plains and patches of woodland stretched before them and, in the distance, the sun reflected upon the curl of the River Slågen, sweeping across the land like a silver-touched serpent. Beyond it Biórr could just make out the sweeping darkness that was the Iron Wood.

"That river is the boundary between Queen Helka's land and Jarl Störr's," Biórr heard Ilska telling Lik-Rifa.

"It is my land," Lik-Rifa said, "this upstart Jarl Störr and his pet wolf are maggots festering in a wound. I will cut them from it, teach them the meaning of pain."

As Biórr looked he saw riders ahead, appearing over the rim of a low hill.

A whirring of wings and a handful of tennúr swooped out of the sky, hovering around Lik-Rifa. Biórr recognised Tannbursta, their chief.

"It is your people, my queen," the tennúr said. "Krúsa and those others you sent out."

Jarl Sigrún and her snot-nosed nephew.

As Biórr looked he saw them spill down the hillside, riders and skraeling loping alongside them, a dark cloud of frost-spiders behind them. As they drew nearer Biórr saw there were less of them than had left Darl, and he made out bandages upon some of the riders. He saw Krúsa running at the head of her skraeling, long arms dangling, almost running on all fours, and Sigrún leading her *drengrs*, her nephew Guðvarr close to her.

They have seen some action, then, and they do not appear to have any prisoners. Did they kill Skalk, Estrid and the others, or were they beaten and routed by them?

Ilska turned in her saddle and shouted orders. Horns were blown and like a juddering, dying insect Lik-Rifa's war-host came to a halt, waiting for Krúsa and Sigrún. They were moving at a fast pace and it did not take long. As Biórr watched them rein in and draw up before Lik-Rifa he saw more tennúr in the distance, a handful appearing over the hill that Sigrún and Krúsa had ridden across. These tennúr sped towards them, circling overhead, and one swirled down and landed upon Krúsa's shoulder, began talking animatedly in the skraeling's ear.

"My queen, Ilska the Cruel," Jarl Sigrún called out as she rode up, reining in to a halt before Lik-Rifa and dipping her head to them both.

"Are they dead, then?" Lik-Rifa said. She looked to Ilska. "What were their names, the ones they went after?"

"Estrid and Skalk, my queen," Ilska said.

"No, my queen, they are not dead," Sigrún said.

"Have you been defeated, then," Lik-Rifa scowled, looking at the injured among them.

"No, Mother-Maker," Krúsa said, lopping forwards, the tennúr remaining upon her shoulder. "We fought faunir in the Jarnvidr."

"What of Skalk and Estrid?" Ilska asked.

"We found them," Krúsa said.

"They wish to join you, to swear their oaths to you," Jarl Sigrún said.

"Do they?" Lik-Rifa frowned.

"Why?" Ilska asked, her face cold and hard.

"Things have changed in Vigrið," Sigrún said. "They have offered information to prove their new-found loyalty, and more."

"What information?" Ilska asked.

"Jarl Störr is dead, slain by Ulfrir," Sigrún said.

"So, the wolf seeks to rule," Lik-Rifa snarled.

"No, my queen, Estrid and Skalk have told us that Ulfrir wears a thrall-collar, they say that he is thralled to Jarl Störr's daughter, Elvar, chief of the Battle-Grim."

"What?" Biórr said, in time with Rotta, Ilska and Lik-Rifa.

"This is news indeed," Lik-Rifa said thoughtfully. "My wolf-shite brother, a thrall." She gave a vicious grin.

"You said Skalk and Estrid offered more," Ilska said to Sigrún. "What more?"

"To be our eyes and ears in Ulfrir's camp," Sigrún said.

Ilska nodded slowly, thinking it over. "That would be good, very good, but can we trust them?"

"They say they are better served swearing oaths to the dragon rather than the wolf," Sigrún said.

"Obviously," snorted Lik-Rifa.

"As for trust," Sigrún shrugged. "We trust no one. But so far, their information has been helpful."

"They have sent more news, Mother-Maker," Krúsa said, stepping forwards. "Munni brings word from them." She nodded at the vaesen on her shoulder, who gave a deep bow to Lik-Rifa. "Ulfrir is not at Snakavik, he has fled to his den in the Jarnvidr."

"It is true, it is true," the tennúr said, hopping from one foot to the other on Krúsa's shoulder. "When Maður told Munni, Munni think, be brave, be brave, think he must see with own eyes to be sure, think Mother-Maker would wish Munni to do this. I flew there, saw many ships on the river, saw the stone wolves at the doors of Ulfrir's den. He is there."

"You have done well, Munni, very well, all of you have," Lik-Rifa said as Rotta rode up beside her. Lik-Rifa looked at him and grinned.

"He is weak, brother. If Ulfrir has slunk to hide in his den, then he is weak."

"And he is close," Rotta said, looking ahead at the faded, green-tangled blur of the Jarnvidr in the distance.

"Soon he will be close enough to touch," Lik-Rifa said. "Close enough to kill."

CHAPTER FORTY-TWO

VARG

Varg shipped his oar and the *Sea-Wolf* skimmed across the river, gliding close to Sulich's *knarr*. Ropes were hurled across, men and women heaving, dragging the two ships together.

"It is time for your crew to choose," Glornir called across to them, Vol at his side. He held a sack in one fist, "To wear the collar or not."

Sulich jumped onto his top-rail.

"Only Iva wishes to wear the collar, and Taras, too," he called out.

"Taras do what Iva do," the big man called from where he was sitting on a barrel in the stern. Iva walked to stand close to Sulich.

"If I wear the collar I will be able to use my blood-gifts," she said. "I think where we are going we will need them." She shrugged. "And besides, Jarl Orlyg saw me wielding the runes. My only condition," she added, "is that you do *not* sell me to him."

Glornir grunted a laugh.

"That will not happen," he said. He reached into the sack that he was carrying and pulled out two iron collars and two keys on iron rings, threw them over the ship to Sulich, who caught them both.

"There is the collar and the key, Iva. You have both." He held her gaze a moment. "You are sure about this? Some find it hard to put the collar back on, even like this. It can stir . . . memories."

"It is fine," Iva said with a shrug, "I know in my heart I am free."

"Good," Glornir said.

"There is one other act of deception to be done before we reach Elvar and her war-host," Vol said, stroking the head of the serpent that was draped across her shoulders. She whispered her Seiðr-words to it and the serpent uncoiled and slithered down one of Vol's arms.

"Höggormur vinur minn, skiptu um form, sofðu við mjöðmina, bítu þegar svipan er sprungin," Vol whispered, and the serpent slipped into her fist, coiled in circles, a thin thread of Seiðr leaking from Vol's hand and spiralling around the serpent like silver wire, wrapping tightly around its tail, looking like a handle. The outline of the snake shimmered and rippled, shifting, until to Varg's eyes the serpent came to resemble a whip.

"There, sleep now, my lovely," Vol said, and she wrapped a leather buckle around the serpent's body and buckled it to her belt, where it hung, appearing as a black, thick-coiled whip.

"Release the mooring ropes," Glornir called to Sulich. "To the oars," he bellowed at his crew, "and row hard, we need to catch Orlyg so that he does not arrive at this Wolfdales before us. We will never hear the last of his bluster if he beats the Bloodsworn there."

Varg stepped off the *Sea-Wolf* onto a stone pier. He stood with Svik and Røkia, waiting while all the Bloodsworn disembarked. He felt agitated, a tingling in his blood, and rolled his shoulders to adjust the weight of the shield across his back. The voice that he had heard in his dreams was echoing in his head while he was awake now. He looked at Røkia and knew that she heard it, too.

Hooves clattered as horses were led down a gangplank from Sulich's *knarr*, warriors clothed in their *druzhina* war gear, horse-hair helms, coats of lamellar plate, sabres, arrows, and recurved bows in scabbards at their weapons belts, spears in their fists. Sulich looked to Glornir, grinned and nodded, then pulled himself up into his saddle, all the warriors about him mounting up. Iva and Taras were last to leave the *knarr*, both wearing iron collars around their necks. They approached Glornir and Vol.

He nodded to them, then looked at his crew. All were gathered on the stone pier, wearing their war gear, black, blood-spattered shields slung across their backs. Edel stood with one hand on the head of her hound. Vesli perched on Breca's shoulder, and Grok and Kló were sitting upon the top-rail of the *Sea-Wolf*. They had made it clear that they wanted to accompany the Bloodsworn into the wolf's den, and they had drawn many an eye as the *Sea-Wolf* had sailed along the river searching for an empty space to moor at a pier.

The tramping of feet and Varg looked back along the west bank to see Jarl Orlyg approaching, his son one side of him, his Galdurman the other, his crew of fifty or sixty *drengrs* and Tainted warriors behind him.

Jarl Orlyg halted before the pier that Glornir and Sulich had moored at and gestured for them to take the lead.

"Bloodsworn, with me," Glornir said and strode along the pier, black shield across his back and long-axe in his fist like a staff, the Bloodsworn following him. Grok and Kló jumped from the *Sea-Wolf* onto the pier and hopped after them.

Glornir led them onto a wide path that shadowed the curve of the River Falinn, a steep-sided hill on Varg's right that rose out of the forest like the twisted spine of a giant's back. Varg glanced across the river to its east bank, where the Iron Wood reared tall and dense and ominous, shadows deep as night, although Varg saw that there were people on that side of the river working at clearing the foliage back from the riverbank, so that there was a widening strip between the river and the treeline.

But it was the west bank that he was walking upon that drew his eyes.

They walked past a series of piers, all of them full with moored *drakkars* and *knarrs*, people busy unloading their cargoes. Others were digging ditches and throwing up earth embankments, setting long wooden stakes into the ground, while at the bridge they built wooden gates, short towers and palisades. Many stopped to watch the Bloodsworn pass by, followed by Sulich and his mounted *druzhina*, the two giant ravens and finally Jarl Orlyg's crew.

And then Glornir was turning, walking away from the river upon a stone-paved road that carved between two rearing slopes, leading towards great stone-arched doors that stood open in the side of the hill. Varg had glimpsed it as they had sailed past, looking for a pier to moor at, and just the briefest sight had set Varg's blood thrumming.

Ulfrir is in there. A god is in there.

As they drew nearer Varg saw two huge, stone-carved statues of wolves standing at either side of the doors, each one half the size of the *Sea-Wolf.* Two guards stood to either side of the doors, men and women, all of them thick-muscled and hulking, dressed in fine mail, hair braided and oiled, axes in their fists, rings of silver on their arms. They all wore iron collars around their necks. At the sight of Glornir and the Bloodsworn one of them put a horn to their lips and blew, long and ringing.

"*Berserkir,*" Røkia said beside Varg.

They walked between the stone wolf-statues and Varg blinked, saw that the wind was sifting their fur. Then one of them turned its head with a grinding sound and looked at them, took a deep sniff and curled its lips, revealing huge stone fangs.

"Keep walking," one of the *Berserkir* guards said as Varg's hand went to his weapons belt. Glornir ignored the statues and walked through the open doors, leading the Bloodsworn into Ulfrir's wolf hall.

The room was vast, Varg looking up and feeling dizzy as stone-carved pillars reared up into shadow. Torches blazed in sconces upon those pillars, set around the edges of the chamber, hammered into stone. In the centre of the chamber was the trunk of a huge tree that rose up into the vaulted darkness. It glowed with faint light that emanated from dense clumps of fungus, as if some Seiðr-magic flowed within them, and carved into it, spiralling upward around the trunk, was a wide-stepped walkway. As Varg's eyes followed the tree upwards he saw the glimmer of fractured light speckling the rooftop, much like dappled sunlight filtering through a treetop canopy.

People were everywhere, part of the chamber filled with long tables and benches, fire pits blazing, carcasses of deer and mutton and boar turning on spits, huge cauldrons bubbling. Hammers rang and echoed, Varg seeing the white-hot fire-glow of forge-fires set back in alcoves around the chamber, black smoke belching. Elsewhere he saw warriors sparring, with spear and shield, sword and axe, but as they strode through the hall all that saw the Bloodsworn stopped what they were doing and started to follow them. Varg noticed their shields bore many different insignia.

They are mercenary bands, like us.

The crowds parted as the Bloodsworn strode through them, Varg hearing whispers and nods of respect as warriors saw the black, blood-spattered shields. He saw others scowling at Taras, though, and at Sulich and his riders.

Why? Because they are from Iskidan? Because their skin is a different colour from ours?

Varg scowled at that, felt the wolf in his blood growl and his hackles rise.

Glornir led them around the trunk of the tree and Varg saw a wide dais set at the far end of the hall.

A chair stood at the centre of the dais, a small figure seated upon it, others gathered around it. Further back, upon a stone pedestal, was a carved bust of a huge head.

Glornir led them on and, as they approached the dais, Varg saw that it was a full-grown woman sitting in the chair, and that the chair was oversized. She was a warrior, clothed in fine-gilded mail, a scabbarded sword across her lap, seax and slim axe at her belt, a black bearskin cloak around her shoulders, rings of gold upon her arms. A troll tusk hung on a leather cord about her neck. *This must be Elvar of the Battle-Grim.*

She stood as she saw Glornir and the Bloodsworn approaching. There were others upon the dais. Hulking mail-clad warriors at the woman's shoulder with iron collars around their necks, *drengrs* in mail and gilded helms, Seiðr-women with tattooed arms and jaws, and other figures standing further back, in shadow. Then in a burst of movement a woman was running past Elvar, jumping down from the dais. A fair-haired Seiðr-witch with dark tattoos on her arms and lower jaw, a cloak of raven-feathers about her.

Vol shouted and she was moving, too, the two women meeting

and embracing, squeezing each other tight. Varg saw tears upon Vol's cheeks.

"Vol's sister," Svik said to him as Glornir led them closer.

Vol and her sister parted, both smiling, both weeping, holding each other by the shoulders.

"Uspa," Glornir said as he reached them.

"Ah, Glornir, Glornir," the Seiðr-witch named Uspa said, and wrapped her arms around him.

Varg looked beyond them to the dais, his eyes drawn to a shadowy form behind the chair, and a man stepped into the light. Tall, long dark hair streaked with grey, tied at the nape, a short, grey-streaked beard, and bright amber-flecked eyes.

I see you, wolf-child, I see you, my child, a voice said in Varg's head, and he blinked, grimaced. A grunt beside him and he saw Røkia shaking her head, scowling. He looked back to the man on the dais, saw that he was staring straight at him, a slight smile on his lips that revealed the tips of sharp-fanged teeth. There was another figure behind him and Varg saw it was a woman, red-haired, wearing a fine *brynja*, something hunched over each of her shoulders, some strange armour. She stepped to the tall man, touched his arm and he bent for her to whisper in his ear. She turned as she did so and Varg saw that it was not armour that rose above her shoulders, but that she had wings upon her back, rust-coloured as autumn leaves.

I have stepped out of Vigrið and into a saga, he thought.

Your secret is safe with me, the voice in his head spoke again. *Come to me, when you can,* and Varg looked up to see the tall man staring at him.

You are Ulfrir, the wolf-god! Varg thought.

I am your *god,* the voice said.

"Elvar Fire-Fist, I am Glornir Shieldbreaker, chief of the Bloodsworn, and I have come at your request," Glornir called out. "We will fight this dragon with you."

"Well met, Glornir Shieldbreaker," the woman who had been sitting in the chair said. "Your fair-fame, and that of your warband, is known to all in Vigrið and beyond. I am glad that my message reached you, and that you have accepted my offer. Is Orka with you?"

CHAPTER FORTY-THREE

ORKA

"I am here," Orka said, stepping out of the ranks of the Bloodsworn.

"I am glad to see you," Elvar smiled. She had changed since Orka had seen her last. The lines on her face sharper, a depth and weariness to her eyes that spoke of responsibility and pain. She looked older than her years.

"Did you find your son?" Elvar asked her.

"I did," Orka said, and gestured to Breca, who was standing among the Bloodsworn with a shield almost as big as him slung across his back, a short-hafted spear in his fist, an axe thrust through his belt. Elvar smiled at the sight of him.

"He looks as fierce as his mother," she said. "And Myrk?" Elvar asked.

"Dead," Orka grunted.

"Good. And her brother? Have you had your vengeance?"

"He still lives, for now. He is with Lik-Rifa."

"Then you are with us," Elvar said.

"I am with the Bloodsworn," Orka said, and felt a thrill in her blood at the saying of those words.

You should be with me, Ulfrir's voice said inside her skull.

Get out of my thought-cage, old man, she snarled.

"And the Bloodsworn are with me," Elvar smiled.

"As am I, Little-Elvar," a large voice said, Jarl Orlyg striding around from behind the Bloodsworn, Dagrun at his shoulder. "If you will have me."

"Jarl Orlyg," Elvar frowned. "I did not expect to see you walk into my hall."

It is my hall, Ulfrir's voice corrected in Orka's head.

"The world is upside down," Orlyg said. "Svelgarth has fallen, but I have my Tainted and my *drengrs* about me yet. The warriors of Svelgarth can still bite. I would throw my axe in with you, Little-Elvar, fight with you and your wolf against the dragon and the rat."

"The rat?" Ulfrir said. "What do you mean?"

"Rotta the rat-god is with Lik-Rifa," Orlyg said. "He led the assault on Svelgarth."

"You must be mistaken," the winged woman beside Ulfrir hissed.

"He was chained, punished, worse than dead," Ulfrir growled.

"His chains are broken, then, and he is much healed," Orlyg said. "He looked alive enough to me when I attacked his warband on the banks of the Nidden and he smashed one of my *drakkars* to kindling."

"You must be mistaken," Ulfrir echoed the winged woman, "a rune-wielder, perhaps, some man of Seiðr or Galdur-power?"

"No, Rotta lives," Orka said. "I have seen him, spoken with him."

Ulfrir turned his gaze upon her, and she met it.

You have spoken to him?

Aye, he smelled your scent upon me, knew I had spoken to you.

Slowly Ulfrir nodded.

This time I shall make sure he is dead.

"I accept your axe, Jarl Orlyg," Elvar said. "It seems you have helped us already, with the news you bring."

"There is more news," Glornir said. "Lik-Rifa and Rotta are marching this way."

"What?" Elvar said.

"How do you know?" Ulfrir asked, stepping to Elvar's shoulder.

"Grok told them," the giant raven squawked, hopping from behind the Bloodsworn.

Elvar's eyes flared wide at the sight of the giant raven, and Ulfrir's eyes narrowed.

"Where is the other one," a deep-vibrating voice boomed, and

Orka saw Varg jump at the shock of it, searching for the voice. Orka tracked it back to the giant head upon the pedestal, which she had thought was a bust. Now, though, she saw that there was life in its pale-swirling eyes, that its lips parted in a wide smile.

The tales of Jarl Störr's counsellor are true, then, Orka thought.

"Kló here," the second raven croaked at the giant head, hopping to stand alongside Grok.

"Ha, Grok and Kló, I should have known you two rascals were still alive," Hrung boomed. "And what mischief are you two causing now?"

"None," Kló squawked indignantly. "Grok and Kló help friends. Friends are good."

"You never said that when you served my father," Ulfrir said, a low-rasped growl.

"World different now. Snaka dead, Grok and Kló alone long time, Grok and Kló afraid," Grok said.

"Grok and Kló need friends," Kló said. "Friends help Grok and Kló stay safe."

"Unless your friends are fighting a dragon," Hrung said, his laughter echoing around the chamber. "No one is safe, here," he continued to laugh. "But we can still be friends." His laughter boomed out again.

"I knew these ravens," Ulfrir warned Elvar, "they served my father, spied for him. They cannot be trusted, their only loyalty is to Snaka."

"Snaka dead," Kló said mournfully.

"They have helped me," Orka said. "Saved me twice now, and, Elvar, they took your message to the Bloodsworn. They have proved themselves trustworthy to *me*."

Be careful who you trust, Ulfrir whispered inside her head.

I make my own judgements, do not think to tell me what I should or should not do.

"Orka our friend," Kló croaked.

"And Grok telling truth," the other raven squawked. "Dragon and rat marching here from Darl."

"How long before they are here?" Elvar asked the raven.

"Grok not know," the raven grumbled. "Depend how fast they walk."

"But Grok and Kló can watch them for you, tell you where they are," Kló said. "If you be Grok and Kló's friend."

Elvar looked at the two ravens, and slowly a smile spread across her face. "No matter how strange these times are, there seem to always be new surprises around each new day. I would be grateful to you both if you could watch Lik-Rifa for me, and tell me when she is close," Elvar said. "And I would be glad to call you both friends." She looked from the ravens to Orlyg to Glornir. "You are all welcome here, and by the looks of it you have journeyed far and hard. Please, let us find you rooms to sleep and give you food to eat and ale to drink."

"Good idea," croaked one of the ravens.

CHAPTER FORTY-FOUR

ELVAR

Elvar woke with a gasp, some distant, screeching, ululating noise dragging her from her dreams, which were full of dragons and blood and ash, of a gallows-hanging, a faceless man clawing at the rope around his neck, of walking across a room, only to find that the ground was moving beneath her, seething with rats.

She sat up, realised that the noise was a horn blowing and she stumbled out of her bed. It was huge, as she slept in Ulfrir's old chamber.

Horns. Has the dragon come? A spike of fear in her gut, and also hope. Right now, the waiting was proving worse than the prospect of fighting. Although that opinion could change once the dragon was here.

"Morning, chief," Sólín Spittle said to her as she searched for her weapons belt. Sólín was standing in the shadowed alcove of Elvar's open doorway.

"What's happening? The horns," Elvar asked as she found her weapons belt and baldric slung across a chair, buckled the belt on over her coat of mail, which she had taken to sleeping in.

"More come to swear their oaths to you," Sólín said, looking at Elvar. "It's that one-note call on the horn," she added.

"Of course," Elvar breathed, remembering the different calls for different messages. She stood a moment and breathed, knuckled her eyes.

"Hard work, being chief, or jarl," Sólín said. "For what it's worth, I think you're doing a silver-browed job of it."

"That is worth a great deal, Sólín," Elvar said as she slipped her baldric over her head and one arm, let the weight of her scabbarded sword settle it in place. She found her bearskin cloak and threw it over her shoulder. There were two ways in and out of the chamber, a huge open archway that led into the great hall and a smaller door that opened into the tunnels that wormed through the bowels of the hill. "Let us see who calls upon us today, then."

She walked out through the archway towards the great hall and saw the mailed bulk of Thorguna waiting for her.

"Jarl Elvar," the *Berserkir* said as she fell in beside Sólín, and Elvar paused for a moment. She was standing upon a platform set about halfway up the wall of Wolfdale's main hall. She fought a rising sense of dizziness for a moment, as she did each morning, looking down from this height upon the hall beneath her, people moving on the chamber floor appearing small as ants. She could have had a chamber set along one of the many corridors that wound beneath the ground, but, as with Ulfrir's chair, she had felt that she needed to have his bedchamber, too, so that he did not start to become too used to being in the positions of power again. Not for the first time she was regretting that choice. She sucked in a deep breath and moved on, walking along a stairwell that was carved into a huge branch of the tree that grew within the chamber. Soon she reached the trunk, and the stairwell joined the walkway that spiralled around the trunk, winding steadily downwards.

The smells of food wafted up to her, slices of bacon frying on iron skillets, fresh-cooked bread from stone ovens, cheese and smoked fish and porridge bubbling in pots, and her stomach growled. She had not realised how hungry she felt. As she spiralled down the stairwell, she saw Silrið on the ground, talking with her brother, Broðir, and a handful of her petty jarls, Runa Red-Axe among them. Silrið looked up at Elvar as she walked down and marched towards her, joined Elvar as she reached the ground.

"Jarl Elvar," Silrið said, matching Elvar's pace and they walked past the new training court, the sounds of warriors sparring ringing out, the clack of blades, thud of shields slamming, grunting of warriors and the shuffle and scrape of footwork. She glimpsed some of the Bloodsworn there, and Jarl Orlyg's *drengrs*, too.

"Have you decided on the matter of Grend, my jarl?" Silrið said.

Elvar felt a wave of nausea at the mention of his name, knew that this conversation was coming. Bit back a snarl.

"No," she said, as calmly as she could.

"A decision should be made, and soon," Silrið said. "There are murmurs, among your jarls, among the mercenaries that have pledged to you."

"What murmurs?" Elvar said, although she already knew.

"That Grend has lied to you, deceived you for many years. That if you show . . . leniency to such as he, how can you be trusted to show strength against the dragon, against the war-host that is descending upon us. Your people need to see a strong hand, they need to know that you have the strength to lead them . . ."

"I have seen Oskutreð, fought the Raven-Feeders, thralled the wolf-god, slain my father, what more strength do they need to see? And I have the silver and gold to pay them, so let them keep their mutterings and find someone with more gold and silver if they are not happy with how I rule."

"Gold is little comfort to the dead," Silrið said, "it is only useful if you are alive to spend it. They need to trust that you can bring them through this. We are at war."

"I have heard you," Elvar said.

"Grend should be dealt with before all so that—"

"Enough," Elvar snapped, and Silrið pursed her lips.

They passed around the trunk of the tree and the dais came into view, a knot of people standing before it. She glanced to the open stone doors and saw that the light was soft and grey with dawn.

She looked at the backs of the new arrivals, saw that some of them were *drengrs*, well-armed and in good mail, and there were also Tainted among them in iron collars, *Úlfhéðnar* by the way the sides of their heads were shaved and tattooed. There were two people standing at the head of them, a man and woman, Uspa standing with them in hushed conversation. The woman was fair-haired, and looked as if she had seen some hard travelling, her clothes mud-spattered and ragged, her braided hair frayed. She wore a sword at her hip. The man had a wooden staff in one hand, which set her heart beating a little faster.

A Galdurman.

She strode past them without giving them a backward glance, stepped up onto the dais, saw Ulfrir standing back in the shadows, unseen. She gave him a sharp nod and turned to face the newcomers, and blinked, because she recognised them, though she had not seen either of them for many years. Not since they had visited her father's court at Snakavik, in the company of Queen Helka of Darl before Elvar had fled and joined the Battle-Grim.

Estrid, Helka's daughter, and Skalk, Helka's Galdurman.

Skalk had changed much, one of his eyes a scarred, shadowed socket.

Two women stood close to Skalk, a fair-haired *drengr* and what looked like an apprentice Galdurwoman, bones tied in her dark, matted hair.

Uspa stepped forward.

"Estrid, Queen of Darl, and Skalk, Galdurman of Darl," she said, a twist of her lips as she said the Galdurman's name.

Queen of Darl! You are no queen; you have had your kingdom ripped from you.

"Well met, Estrid," Elvar said. "You are a long way from your home."

"Jarl Elvar," Estrid said, dipping her head. She straightened her shoulders and sucked in a deep breath. "My home is a ruin, destroyed by the dragon. My mother slain; my brother slain. I am hunted, pursued by vaesen, and yet I fight on. I hoped to find a friend in you, as I have heard that you mean to stand against Lik-Rifa and her horde of Tainted and vaesen. You are the enemy of my enemy, and so, I hope, my friend. I offer my sword, my *drengrs* and my Tainted, my friendship. I would fight at your side, and, I hope, build a new world with you once the dragon is dead."

That was well said, no matter that you are on your knees with only a handful of warriors at your command.

Elvar opened her mouth to answer her and then a figure strode before the dais, marching towards Estrid and Skalk. A hulking warrior, bald-headed, grey-bearded, clothed in mail, a black, blood-spattered shield across his back.

Glornir Shieldbreaker. Vol was a score of paces behind him, hurrying to catch him, and more of the Bloodsworn followed her.

"I told you I would see you again, Skalk of Darl," Glornir growled, making the hairs on Elvar's neck stand on end.

Skalk turned and saw Glornir descending upon him, took a step back, raising his staff, and the fair-haired *drengr* stepped forwards, between Skalk and Glornir, drawing her sword with a hiss. She did not have time to shrug the shield from her back, just set her feet and began to raise her sword.

Glornir did not break his stride, one hand snapping out and grabbing the wrist of the *drengr*'s sword arm. She grunted, tried to twist out of his grip and he slammed a fist into her jaw. She dropped like a brained ox and Glornir strode on.

"Rauð reiði, brenna holdið af beinum hans," Skalk blurted, red runes crackling to light at the end of his Galdur-staff. Vol appeared alongside Glornir, shouting her own Seiðr-words, blue flames hissing into life around her hands. Glornir drew the sword at his hip, still not breaking stride, eyes fixed on Skalk.

"Ulfrir, stop this," Elvar called out.

Ulfrir stepped out of the shadows, his body already rippling, the air about him shimmering, and he collapsed onto all fours, bones cracking, muscle growing, fur sprouting. People on the dais scrambled away, Glornir, Skalk and all the others frozen, staring. Elvar walked calmly to one side of the dais as Ulfrir rose in his snarling wolf-glory. He stood towering over them all and padded forwards towards Glornir, Skalk and the others, saliva dripping from his teeth, letting out a low-rumbling growl that made the ground tremor. Elvar felt it rumble in her chest and rise into her body through her feet.

"Stop," Ulfrir said, and they stared up at him, shock and awe on their faces.

"So, it *is* true," Estrid said.

Elvar stepped forwards.

"What is this about?" she said to Glornir.

"Skalk stole my Seiðr-witch, slew one of my Bloodsworn," Glornir growled. "Vol," he said, beckoning to her. "He did this to her", and he gestured to the white scars that ringed Vol's mouth. "He stitched her lips shut, he beat her." A tremor ran through him. "No one steals from the Bloodsworn, *no one* mistreats one of my crew. No one slays one of us and walks away." Muscles twitched in his arms, his fists closing. "He will answer for it."

"No," Elvar said, shaking her head, though she understood all that Glornir had said, knew the code he lived by, remembered the red rage she had felt when Ingvild had stolen a chest of her treasure.

"This is my hall, my war-host," she said to Glornir and Skalk. "If there are grudges held between those who follow me, they must be put aside. Perhaps not forever, but at least until the dragon is slain. After that," she shrugged. "We will have to see."

Glornir looked from Elvar to Ulfrir to Skalk.

"Soon," he growled at the Galdurman, then stalked away.

"And that rule is for all," Elvar said. "We are a host of many, from different places, different countries." She looked to some of the Bloodsworn with their dark skins and lamellar armour, then to the tennúr that travelled with the Bloodsworn, and at Ulfrir, Skuld and Hrung. "Even different species. We will not fight among ourselves, that way lies defeat. We put our grievances and differences aside and win this war together." She gave a hard stare at all before her, her gaze coming to settle upon Skalk and Estrid.

"Estrid, you are welcome here with us, and you, too, Skalk, but I expect the same standards from you both." She looked at Skalk, who was glowering at Glornir's back. "I am *talking* to you, Galdurman," she growled. His eyes snapped to her, a brief flash of contempt flickering behind them, gone in a heartbeat, and he was smiling.

"Of course, Jarl Elvar," he said, dipping his head to her. She looked to Estrid.

"We are glad to be here," Estrid said firmly, "and will abide by whatever rules you wish."

"Good," Elvar said.

A squawking and flapping of wings and one of the giant ravens was flying through the wide-arched entrance to the hall, flying around the edge of the huge chamber and landing in a cloud of dust before Elvar. She glimpsed shocked expressions on Skalk's and Estrid's faces at the sight of the bird.

Wait until they hear it speak.

"Lik-Rifa has reached the Jarnvidr," the raven squawked.

CHAPTER FORTY-FIVE

GUÐVARR

Guðvarr reined his horse in alongside Jarl Sigrún, both of them sitting upon the crest of a hill. They stared at the Iron Wood spread below them, a dark ocean of green, swaying and stretching into the horizon.

Wonderful, the one place I hoped I would never see again.

"There," he heard Rotta the rat-god say, pointing south, into the distance, to where hills reared from the depths of the forest like sea creatures breaching waves. "Ulfrir's den."

Even better, I am going back into that place of nightmares to fight a giant wolf and his hordes of lunatic followers.

They had ridden hard, Lik-Rifa's host of gods, humans, Tainted and vaesen sweeping across the land. They had not retrodden the path of Sigrún's and Guðvarr's journey into the Iron Wood, but instead had crossed the River Slågen further north, skirting the north-eastern boundaries of the forest to move across more open land until they were directly north of the hills that the rat said was Ulfrir's bolt-hole. To reach it they had less forest to travel through now, and the road was wider, more travelled upon.

Faster and easier passage, Ilska the Cruel had said, and it had been her who had chosen this route. To be fair, she had been right, and they had travelled much further in a shorter time, bringing them closer to their destination before they had to risk the dangers of the forest.

Not that I think faunir or Froa will be brave enough to attack us now.

Guðvarr shifted in his saddle and looked back over his shoulder, seeing the sprawling, dark stain upon the land that was Lik-Rifa's war-host. It moved like a huge shadow crossing the sun, creeping inexorably towards the treeline of the forest.

"Ilska, how long?" Lik-Rifa called out.

"Five days, perhaps less," Ilska said, eyes fixed upon the hills in the distance.

"Do you agree with her, aunt?" Guðvarr asked Sigrún, keeping his voice low.

"Aye," Sigrún nodded. She leaned in her saddle and whispered. "Lik-Rifa may be the head of this war-host, but Ilska the Cruel runs it. She has a rare head upon her shoulders, and without her this campaign would be chaos."

Ilska spoke to a tennúr that sat upon the crest of Lik-Rifa's saddle and in a burst of wings the small creature was taking to the sky, letting out a high-pitched, squeaking cry; in moments a flock of the winged vaesen were swirling around it. They climbed higher into the sky, swirled around their heads and then they were flying hard for the forest, spreading wider, fanning out like the wake of a ship as they reached the treeline.

"I do not like those filthy little creatures," Guðvarr muttered, absently wiping a drip of snot from the end of his nose. "They steal your teeth when you sleep."

"You see, she has a head for tactics, using the resources this war-host brings her without prejudice," Sigrún said, giving Guðvarr a hard look. "Tennúr make for excellent scouts."

I still do not like them, he thought.

"Onwards, then," Lik-Rifa called out. Horns blared, and the war-host shuddered into movement, Sigrún and Guðvarr clicking their tongues and guiding their horses on down the hill, towards the Iron Wood.

Hello old friend, Guðvarr thought as he approached the dark, looming wall of trees. *How I have missed you.*

Guðvarr unbuckled his saddle girth and slid the saddle from his horse's back, laid it across the branch of a tree, took off the saddle blanket, too, folded it and laid it down on top of the saddle, then checked his mount's hooves.

It was late and Guðvarr was tired. They had marched for the second day from sunrise until late into the night, the forest around him an impenetrable darkness made denser and deeper by the myriad fires that burned throughout the camp. He set the last hoof down and stood, stretched his back, heard it click.

"Feed her," he said to a thrall and she nodded her head, a shaven-haired woman, one of many who had travelled with the war-host from Darl. Without the thralls to do the cooking, clearing, mending of kit and tending of horses and a hundred other tasks the war-host would have become unglued. Something else that his aunt said Ilska the Cruel had orchestrated.

He threaded his way through the camp with a rising sense of dread in his gut. The crushing, claustrophobic darkness, the exhaustion, the prospect of a giant wolf at the end of his journey, it was all overwhelming, his unease growing into a heightened state of agitation that set every muscle in his body trembling. As he moved around knots and clusters of warriors and vaesen that sat huddled around fresh-scraped fire pits, *drengrs* and Tainted, trolls and skraeling, he heard fractured glimpses of their conversations, sitting, eating, drinking, laughing, the murmur of their conversations rising and falling as he moved among them.

How are they all so calm? They made him feel like a coward.

He saw Drekr moving through the camp and paused to watch him. The big man was stopping at each fire to talk to those gathered there, to sit and drink with them a while. Tainted, dragon-cultists, *drengrs*, skraeling. All of them greeted him with smiles and laughter.

Is he loved, or feared? Whichever it is, he is respected. Why do people not look at me the way they do at Drekr?

He sighed and moved on.

In either direction the fires burned, fading to pinpricks in the darkness as far as he could see. The forest had forced them to stretch the bulk of the war-host along the road, only the frost-spiders, night-hags and tennúr able to filter deeper into the undergrowth of the Iron Wood. Not even the trolls could forge a way through the dense scrub that grew between the trees. Here and there he saw the deeper shadows of guards standing among the trees, not that they probably needed them, with frost-spiders in the boughs and night-hags moving about the war-host's fringes like mist.

He saw Sigrún's small camp, a fire pit with thirty or so *drengrs* around it, an opened barrel of ale and an iron pot hanging over the fire. He helped himself to a bowlful of stew from the pot and a hornful of ale from the barrel, then looked for his aunt. She was sitting a little apart from her *drengrs*, sipping at a cup of ale and he made his way to her, sat down with a sigh.

"The horses are tended to," he said, "fed and watered."

"Good lad," Sigrún said. He looked at her, saw that she was staring into the crow-dark, her face shifting planes of shadow and light in the soft-glow from the fire pit. The scar on her face, inflicted by Orka, looked like some deep dark valley upon a carved map.

"Are you all right, aunt?" he asked her.

"Just thinking," she said quietly. "A year ago, we were worrying about the borders of Fellur village, and of the possible fight between Helka and Störr." She snorted a laugh. "To think I was worried about that. And now we are in the middle of a war between gods."

"I know," Guðvarr squeaked, his voice coming out higher than he had intended.

She sipped at her cup and looked at him. "I know you are scared, but it is all right to be scared."

He blinked at her, swallowed.

"We all feel fear, Guðvarr," Sigrún said to him. "I know I do."

"Huh," he snorted. "Not you. You are the bravest person I know, have ever met. You always know what to do, always keep your head, even when you are fighting. Look at you when the faunir attacked. You saved Krúsa, you did not flee, you stood and fought to protect your *drengrs*." He shook his head. "You are brave. A hero worthy of a skáld-song to me."

Sigrún's face cracked in a smile.

"In that glade, as the faunir attacked us, I was terrified," she said. "I nearly pissed my breeches." She looked him in the eye, firelight reflecting liquid gold. "We *all* feel fear, it is what you do with it that counts. I was scared of the faunir, scared of dying, but I know in here," she put a finger to her temple, "and here", moved it to her heart, "that if I gave in to that fear and fled, then I would lose everything. All that I have spent my life working for, fighting for. I would not stay a jarl long with that reputation. I would lose Fellur village, my *drengrs*, my respect. Any fair-fame I have earned would be snuffed out in a moment. I fear that more than I fear death."

Guðvarr nodded, thinking that through.

"Courage is just a reaction to fear. You cannot show courage without first feeling fear."

"I understand that," Guðvarr said. "But cowardice is also a reaction to fear. It is the not running away part that I still struggle with."

Sigrún laughed at that. "So do I," she smiled. "But remember this: you have come through much. Fought your way out of the Grimholt, fought through Jaromir's attack on Skalk and the Galdur tower, slew one of the Bloodsworn, journeyed into the frozen north to seek out Lik-Rifa's halls, negotiated with her, planned the downfall of Queen Helka and her brood, fought Hakon and Estrid at Darl. Survived the Froa-spirits and faunir of the Iron Wood." She looked into the darkness of the forest, her smile growing broader, and she winked at him. "So far."

"Ha, so far," Guðvarr said, unable to stifle a smile of his own. "To be honest, all of that was just trying to stay alive."

"Well, that is no surprise. This is Vigrið, after all," she said. "The point is, you *have* stayed alive, you *have* come through it all. And look at you now, you have risen high in the ranks of a god."

Guðvarr thought about that, nodded.

This is true.

"My advice to you," his aunt continued. "Eat well tonight, sleep well, and we shall face whatever the morrow brings with . . ."

She looked at him and he smiled.

". . . courage," he finished for her.

Guðvarr woke to darkness. He lay there a moment, eyes open, slowly watching the shifting of shadows above him, the grey of dawn seeping into the world, leaching the black away. Branches creaked overhead, leaves rustled, and with a groan he sat up. He was stiff, had rolled onto the knuckle of a root during the night. It felt like someone's fist was grinding into his back and he cast his wool blanket back, reached about him for his weapons belt, felt soft, damp leaves and earth, then found it. Stood up and buckled it about his waist, cinching it tight, felt the pain of a full bladder.

The camp still slept and he trod quietly, walking towards the treeline, looking for somewhere to empty his bladder. He saw a group of skraeling stirring, Krúsa there, kneeling and blowing on a fire, sparks flaring.

A sound up above and he looked up at the gloom of the forest, saw the fractured glow of dawn through the canopy, heard a whirring, and saw a darker shape flitting through the shadows. A tennúr, he realised, flying down through the canopy.

Is that Munni? he thought, as the vaesen swept over his head.

"WARE," the vaesen shrieked, "WARE, THEY ARE COMING."

Guðvarr turned and ran stumbling back towards Sigrún and her *drengrs*.

CHAPTER FORTY-SIX

ORKA

Orka stood in the darkness, waiting in the shadowed space between the fire-glow that two torches cast. People were gathered around her, Lif and Sæunn close to her, more of the Bloodsworn. All were silent, some drinking from water bottles after their forced march, others checking weapons, loosening blades in scabbards, more habit than necessity. Further ahead Orka could see the torch-glow where Glornir stood at the head of their column.

Soon, Ulfrir's voice growled in her head and Orka felt the wolf stir in her blood, a trembling in her muscles. She paced along the tunnel, Lif and Sæunn following her, walked past Sulich and a score of his kin, all clothed in their lamellar plate, their recurved bows strung and ready in their belt-scabbards. Orka came to a knot of the Bloodsworn gathered behind Glornir. Vol was there, and Røkia, Svik and Einar and Varg. Glornir was stood before a set of stone steps that led up into nowhere, just a crumbling stone ceiling, vine hanging, dripping with damp.

"Soon," she said to Glornir's look and he grunted.

"We have told him, we also heard his voice," Røkia said.

Orka nodded, then looked at Lif and Sæunn. Lif held his shield loose, a spear in his other fist, wore a coat of mail and a steel helm with a wide nasal guard. Sæunn was wearing a coat of ring mail taken from a fallen warrior after the sea battle, and wore a plain steel cap, a leather strap buckled tight under her chin. She held a spear in her fist and had a seax at her belt. She had no shield.

But, then, neither do I. Orka gripped a long-axe in her fist, two seaxes scabbarded front and back on her weapons belt, and a short-axe shoved through it, too.

"You did not have to come," Orka muttered to them both. "You are not warriors. You should have stayed at Wolfdales with Breca." She did not want more death on her hands.

"No mistress," Sæunn said. "I owe you my life."

"You owe me nothing," Orka growled.

"I am coming," Sæunn said, returning Orka's hard gaze.

"Then stay with me. Better yet, stay *behind* me," Orka said.

"I intend to, mistress," Sæunn said. "That is why I have come, to guard your back."

Orka shook her head, buckled up the strap of her helm.

"And you, what is your excuse for risking death?" she demanded of Lif.

"Guðvarr might be out there," Lif said, a cold twist to his mouth. "I owe him."

That I understand. He seeks vengeance for his brother, as I seek it for my Thorkel.

Now, Ulfrir's voice snarled in her head.

"Now," Orka said to Glornir, echoed by Varg and Røkia.

"*Rúnar innsiglaðar hurðir, opnar fyrir vini úlfsins,*" Vol cried out, a flare of red runes crackling from her hands and seeping into the roof of the tunnel. Lines of fire flowed across the roof, there was a grinding, cracking noise, and a hatch-door appeared, made of wood and stone, an iron bolt locking it. Glornir threw the bolt, dropped the torch he was holding into a puddle at his feet where it sputtered, flickered and died, and in the light of the runes fading glow he pushed the hatch-door open.

"With me," he growled as he strode up the stairs, Vol behind him, Einar, Røkia and the others following.

"Remember, stay with me," Orka said to Lif and Sæunn as they climbed the steps and walked out into the Iron Wood. Vol patted

Orka's shoulder as she climbed out of the tunnel, and then Sæunn's as she emerged into the woodland behind Orka.

"I shall guide you back," Vol said to each of the Bloodsworn as they emerged from the tunnel into dawn, silver-grey light leaking through the canopy above, separating the shadows. It was just enough light to see by, though Orka let the wolf trickle through her, sharpening her senses. Off to her right, about fifty paces away, Orka saw the soft glow of many fires. Glornir was already striding towards them. Orka followed, the Bloodsworn spreading wide behind him. Weapons hissed from scabbards, shields in fists, and they moved, silent and stealthy, through the undergrowth. Sulich split his crew into two groups, each one moving to the flanks of the Bloodsworn. Their bows were in their fists, arrows nocked. Glornir pointed to a cluster of boughs ahead, hanging low before the road, and Orka saw it, a darker shadow, the glitter of reflected firelight.

Sulich's bowstring thrummed, there was a *thunk*, and a frost-spider fell from the branch and landed with a thud on its back, legs curled.

In the distance, Orka heard a voice shrieking, heard shouting, followed by the clash of steel and iron, screams.

It has begun.

Glornir let out a growling roar and began to run through the undergrowth, Einar at his shoulder.

Boughs burst to life above them, Orka seeing snatched glimpses of legs and eyes and fangs. Spiders descended on glistening threads, bowstrings thrummed, arrows hissing, and spiders were falling. Orka glimpsed one of the Bloodsworn thrown to the ground, a spider's legs wrapped around him, fangs lunging, other Bloodsworn hacking at the spider's abdomen, gouts of blue-tinged blood erupting. A flash of something to Orka's right and she twisted, bringing her axe round, saw a shadowed form flowing from the trees like mist, a glimpse of a haggard, emaciated face, mouth open wide, skeletal hands grasping at her and Sæunn stepped before the night-hag, swung her spear. It passed through the night-hag as if it were mist, the hag's fingers closing around Sæunn's throat. Sæunn stumbled backwards, gasping, stabbing frantically with her spear but each blow slipped through the hag's body as if it was not there.

Orka snarled as she hefted her axe, but Lif was already stepping in front of her.

"*Skuggar skilja*," he yelled and stabbed at the night-hag with his spear. It sank deep into the creature's side, and she let out a hissing scream, reared back, clutching at the wound as Lif ripped his spear back.

"*Skuggar skilja*," he yelled again and plunged his spear into the night-hag's chest. With a shriek she exploded into a thousand black shards that melted to mist. Orka grabbed Sæunn by her ring mail and heaved her up.

"Remember the Seiðr-words Vol taught us," she snarled. "And what happened to staying behind me?!"

"Aye, mistress," Sæunn rasped, "*skuggar skilja, skuggar skilja*," she repeated, even as the Seiðr-words rang out around them in the forest, more of the Bloodsworn encountering the night-hags.

And then their warriors were crashing out of the undergrowth onto the road.

Tents were everywhere, more than Orka could ever have imagined, filling the road both north and south as far as Orka could see. Figures were emerging from them, blinking, stumbling, dragging on *brynjas*, buckling on weapons belts and helms, but there were others standing ready, clusters of warriors with steel already in their fists, skraeling snarling, crude weapons of iron in their hands, Orka saw the shadowed bulk of a troll behind them.

Glornir charged from the forest, crashing into a knot of skraeling, his long-axe hissing, and blood flew in a dark arc, screams ringing out. Einar and Svik were right behind Glornir, Einar taking a skraeling's head from its shoulders with two blows of his hand-axe, smashed his shield into another that sent them hurtling into a fire. The skraeling rolled, came to their feet in flames and staggered, screaming, arms flailing, and Svik kicked them crashing into a tent. The hiss and sizzle of flames catching, and black smoke billowed. All along the road Bloodsworn surged into the camp, leaving blood and screams in their wake. Orka snarled and ran at the warriors in front of her, all *drengrs*, swung her axe looping over her head and smashed into a raised shield, hacked through it into the meat of an arm and sent the woman holding the shield crashing into the warrior beside them. They both fell and Sæunn stepped in, her spear stabbing in and out, dart-fast, a grunt and scream, fading to a whimper, and blood was staining the forest floor. Orka put one foot on the shield of the fallen woman and wrenched her axe free. Lif shoved past her, catching a spear meant for Orka on his shield, pushing it away and stepping in, a short stab of his spear and a man was falling back, blood spurting from his throat.

"On," Orka snarled, the wolf in her baying for blood, and they waded into the camp, hacking, stabbing, kicking, stamping, all around them the din of war deafening, filling the forest. Flames were spreading, smoke billowing. Orka saw a troll loom out of the murk, heard the snap and twang of bows and the troll stumbled and let out a mournful roar, fell to its knees, pierced with a dozen arrows.

Voices to Orka's left, shouting out in a strange tongue, and through the smoke and gloom Orka saw the crackle of rune-magic. *Dragon-born.* She turned and strode in their direction, two skraeling blocking her path and she gripped her axe two-handed, like a staff, slammed the butt end into a jaw, sliced the blade left to right and both the skraeling were down. Stalked on. Saw shadowed figures through the flame and shadow, glimpsed a warrior, tall and broad, black-haired, heard a snarling in her blood. Was dimly aware of Lif shouting, moving away from her right-hand side.

The smoke parted and Drekr stood there, dark and hulking, raven-feather tied in his hair, silvered scars raking one side of his face. He saw her and stopped, eyes narrowing, the two of them locked. Orka set her feet, hefted her axe in a wide, two-handed grip and gave him a lip twisting wolf-snarl.

And then he was running at her.

CHAPTER FORTY-SEVEN

GUÐVARR

Guðvarr looked around wildly for his aunt, all about him black smoke and red flames, cries eddying on the wind, the clash of steel, grunts and screams, figures swirling in and out of his vision. He held his shield ready, sword half raised, shuffled in a half-circle, searching, stumbled over a dead body. In the chaos and confusion it was difficult to make out friend from foe. The clash of iron and snarl of voices close to him and he saw two figures silhouetted by flame, both wielding long-axes, fighting amidst the carnage as if nothing else existed. Guðvarr watched, open-mouthed, his shield and sword dropping, awed by the savagery and skill he was witnessing.

The long-axes whirled and cracked, the two warriors standing, feet set, axes held like staffs, wood clacking, iron blades grating, sparks flying. Grunts and thuds, the two figures moving now, swirling in and out, around each other, axes swinging, and Guðvarr glimpsed black hair and a raven-feather, realised one of the warriors was Drekr, then the other one stepped into flame-kissed light and Guðvarr took an involuntary step backwards with a whimper.

It was Orka, the *Úlfhéðnar*, just as he remembered her from the Grimholt. Snarling, blood spattered, amber eyes blazing. He stared at her, felt a rush of fear, felt his feet start to take him away.

No. All feel fear, he heard his aunt's voice. *It is what we do with it that matters.*

He stopped his unconscious retreat, began to stalk towards Orka.

Perhaps I could stab her, while she's fighting Drekr. Chop her leg while she's distracted, maybe. In and out, let Drekr do the hard work.

He picked his pace up, his shield and sword rising. Then something hurtled out of the smoke at him, a man, dark-haired, in mail and helm, a short beard, shield and spear, eyes hate filled, lips a twist of rage. Something familiar about him, but there was no time. He had a moment to pivot on one foot, raise his shield, then the warrior was upon him, spear stabbing at Guðvarr's face. He shuffled backwards, clumsily jerking his shield rim up to knock the spear away, swinging his sword at the spearman's waist, but the spearman pushed the sword-blow wide with his own shield, a twist of his wrist and punched the iron boss into Guðvarr's jaw, sent him reeling backwards, biting his tongue, white stars bursting in his skull, crunching into a tree. The spear-point came at him, and he ducked, threw himself to the side, felt a hot-burning line along his cheek and ear where it caught him, stumbled away and put his shield-hand to his face, felt something sticky, looked at his hand to see blood.

The spearman tugged at his spear, which was buried in the tree. Guðvarr saw his opening, snarled and lunged at the man, stabbing, his sword grating on mail, rings tearing as the warrior ripped his spear free and twisted away, took a few steps back and set his feet, raised his shield, spun the spear in his grip into an underhand grip. He looked at the cut on Guðvarr's cheek.

"That is for Mord," the warrior said, and Guðvarr blinked, looked again at this warrior in front of him, recognition sparking.

"Lif? *Lif!* No, it cannot be," he said, then, slowly, he smiled.

"Shield, spear and mail do not make you a *drengr*," he said with a smirk. "You are nothing but a *niðing* fisherman *pretending* to be a warrior," and he walked forwards.

Lif waited for him and Guðvarr darted in, stabbing low with his sword, aiming for Lif's shins beneath his shield rim. He had seen many a *drengr* felled by such a blow.

A flick of Lif's wrist and a sidestep, his shield rim dropping, knocking Guðvarr's sword into the soft earth, stepping right around Guðvarr's shield and stabbing, a sharp pain in Guðvarr's shoulder and he hissed, took a hasty step backwards, out of range, but Lif was coming at him, the spear stabbing at him again, at his eyes, Guðvarr raising his shield, losing sight of Lif, then another hot pain along his calf, a snatched glance and he saw his *winnigas* leg-wrap torn, blood seeping into the fabric, running down his leg. The pain followed and he limped backwards.

No, this cannot be happening. How did he learn this weapons craft? I fear Úlfhéðnar *and Froa-spirits and dragons, not fishermen!* The indignity of it surged within him, turned into a red rage and without thinking he roared, hurling himself at Lif, saw the surprise flare in the fisherman's eyes, and then he was smashing into him, both of them tumbling to the ground, rolling, shields tangled, Guðvarr trying to get his sword free to stab, Lif losing his grip on his spear. They came to a stop, Lif flailing at Guðvarr with weak punches. Guðvarr let go of his shield and sword, twisted and grabbed Lif around the throat with one hand, pinned Lif's spear hand with his knee and heaved himself on top of the thrashing fisherman, wrapping his other fist around Lif's throat and squeezed. Dimly he was aware of battle raging all around him, people screaming, fighting, dying.

Lif struggled and writhed beneath him, eyes bulging, frothing foam on his lips as he spat and snarled and gasped, and Guðvarr felt the strength begin to leak from him. He smiled and squeezed harder, putting all his weight into his grip.

"Tell your *niðing* brother hello from me when you see him," he grunted as he squeezed. Lif gave one last panicked heave, then there was a crunch in the side of Guðvarr's head, the world spinning, an impact and Guðvarr realised he was lying on the ground, leaves and earth in his face. He groaned, rolled, tried to push himself up, one side of his face throbbing, saw that Lif was gasping, flopping, his shield still in his fist, realised that was what had hit him.

He climbed to one knee, found his shield and clambered unsteadily to his feet, the world spinning, heard a voice and focused on Lif, saw a woman standing over the fisherman, tall and slender, short-haired, a spear in one hand. She was gripping Lif's arm and dragging him to his feet. Then Lif and the woman were turning, lifting their weapons and moving at him.

He raised his shield, swayed, his other hand grasping for the seax at his belt.

A huge roar shook the world, all three of them freezing in their tracks, then stumbling as the ground shook, trees trembling. Another roar, louder and closer than the first.

Lik-Rifa, Guðvarr realised.

The sound of wood cracking and a great rent of light ripped through the sky above them, branches falling, splintered wood raining down around them, then the light was blotted out and Lik-Rifa was crashing through the canopy, wings beating, sending flames and smoke and leaves swirling, feeling like a storm raged around them. Lik-Rifa hit the ground like an avalanche, trees torn from their roots, people, skraeling, trolls, hurled through the air. Guðvarr was knocked from his feet. An eruption of dust filled the world, Guðvarr coughing and rolling, losing his shield, saw Lik-Rifa standing with her wings spread, rearing onto her back feet, jaws opening wide, teeth long as spears.

"ULFRIR," she roared and crashed back to the ground, the impact hurling Guðvarr into the air again, crunching down on soft ground and lying there, groaning. He rose, grit in his eyes. He rubbed at them, eyes watering and risking a glimpse, saw the dust cloud was slowly settling, people around him staggering to their feet. He looked about for Lif and the woman but could not see them. Heard a horn calling, off in the forest, saw shadowed figures flitting away from the camp and retreating into the night-dark murk of the forest. Heard a woman snarling and screaming, looked to see Orka thirty or forty paces away, a bald warrior one side of her, a giant red-haired man on the other, both of them gripping her arms and dragging her away from the road, back into the forest while she spat and snarled and raged.

Then he saw Ilska, a handful of dragon-born around her, red rune-shields glowing in their fists. She was crouched on one knee, looking at something or someone on the ground, then a figure rose to one knee, Drekr, Ilska helping him to his feet. A brief exchange of words.

"After them," Ilska yelled, and she was moving.

Guðvarr looked around, saw a shield and snatched it up and drew the seax from his belt.

"Guðvarr!" a voice cried, and he reeled around, saw Sigrún emerge from the smoke and gloom, a dozen of her *drengrs* around her. The relief he felt at seeing her was as a wave sweeping over him.

"Are you injured?" she asked him.

"Well," he said, putting one hand to his cheek, looking down at his blood-soaked calf, pain pulsing from both wounds. They were agony, he felt sick and weak and just wanted to drop to the ground and curl into a ball. "It's nothing, just scratches," he said, stifling his honest reaction.

"Thank the dead gods," she breathed, then looked to Ilska, who was still bellowing commands, leading warriors into the trees after those who had attacked them.

They are fleeing, is there any real need to chase after them?

"With me," Sigrún said and strode towards the treeline.

Guðvarr sighed and followed.

Sunlight broke through the canopy where Lik-Rifa had smashed through it in great pillars of dust-moted gold as Guðvarr threaded through the battle-torn camp. Bodies were strewn everywhere, fires burning, black clouds of smoke billowing, and then Sigrún was leading him between the trees, shadow falling about them like a curtain. Nearby Lik-Rifa thundered into the forest, tearing trees up by their roots as she raged, Guðvarr wincing as splinters of wood flew through the air about him.

"There," Sigrún said and broke into a run, Guðvarr seeing figures ahead of them, silhouetted by a flare of blue light that pulsed in the darkness. He ran limping after his aunt, the undergrowth flattened by the battle, glimpsed bodies lying in the undergrowth, people, frost-spiders. A knot of skraeling overtook him and Sigrún, crashing through the undergrowth and Guðvarr heard the hiss and twang of bowstrings, heard grunts and yells, saw a handful of the skraeling stumble and fall and he raised his shield, felt an arrow thump into it, stumbled on blindly.

Ilska's voice shouting unknown words from ahead of him and a burst of rolling red runes sailed into the air, hovered high above them, just below the canopy, then exploded in a shower of sparks, illuminating the area around him.

He saw a woman standing in the forest, Seiðr-runes flickering and pulsing around her, people running past her and disappearing. She shouted something, the runes flaring to incandescence and exploding, searing Guðvarr's eyes so that he cried out and covered his eyes, and when he could see again, the woman and all the warriors were gone.

Ilska and Drekr ran forward, stopping roughly where the woman had been standing, Sigrún, Guðvarr and her *drengrs* following. The ground was trampled and churned, and then . . . nothing.

"Where are they?" Drekr snarled, turning in a circle. He was bleeding from a cut across one cheek, a flap of skin hanging.

Guðvarr peered into the gloom, wary of another attack from the darkness, saw a flicker of movement and squawked a warning, raised his shield, then saw it was a night-hag floating like mist between two trunks. He heard movement up above him in the branches, looked up at the frost-spiders moving in the boughs.

More figures approached them from the road, Lik-Rifa leading them. She had returned to her human form, her face all strained lines and twitching muscles. Tennúr swirled above her, flitting among the trees and branches, dragon-born and skraeling spread behind her.

"Where are they?" Lik-Rifa said as she neared them.

"Gone," Ilska said.

"Tannbursta, find them," Lik-Rifa snapped, giving a sharp flick of fingers and the tennúr were speeding away, disappearing into the forest.

"There are tracks," Drekr said, pointing his long-axe at the ground, "many tracks, and then," he looked up and shook his head. "They are gone."

There was a crashing in the distance, growing swiftly louder, Guðvarr seeing the bulk of a huge shadow through the trees. Ilska, Drekr and the dragon-born were moving, spreading into a half-circle before Lik-Rifa, voices shouting in their strange rune-tongue, shields of fire crackling to life, and Lik-Rifa began to twitch and shudder.

The shadow among the trees sped at them, branches straining, cracking, a tremor in the ground and Guðvarr hurried to stand beside Sigrún, her *drengrs* moving close, forming a loose shield wall.

The wolf is coming, the wolf is coming. He felt fear flood through him, then, gut-churning, bowel-loosening fear and fought with every ounce of strength to remain standing, to not turn and run wailing into the safety of the darkness. He gripped his shield, knuckles white, raised his seax, gritted his teeth, part snarl, part grimace.

The shadow passed through a column of light from the canopy above and Guðvarr saw a tapering snout, black eyes, a long, hairless tail, and Rotta was skidding to a halt before them, his body shimmering and shrinking, bones crackling and popping, and in heartbeats Rotta the man was standing before them.

"Ulfrir?" he asked.

"He is not here," Lik-Rifa said, her transformation reversing, "with you?"

"No. We were attacked along the line, *Berserkir* and *Úlfhéðnar*, some others, but no Ulfrir."

Tennúr flitted back out of the gloom, one of them circling Lik-Rifa and alighting upon her shoulder.

"No one out there," the tennúr squeaked.

"Those that attacked us, they have disappeared," Ilska said.

Rotta looked at the ground, saw the downtrodden foliage and tracks, then nothing. He crouched, brushed the ground, nose twitching, then looked up at Lik-Rifa.

"Tunnels," he said.

CHAPTER FORTY-EIGHT

VARG

Varg ran, a steady jog, his eyes fixed on Svik's feet before him, using the echoing slap of Svik's feet on stone to set his rhythm, like a drumbeat for rowers. Sweat stung his eyes, was running down his back but he ignored it. He was not sure how long they had been running through the tunnel, all track of time swallowed by the darkness, his head filled with only one thought.

Brák Trolls-Bane. He had hoped to find him during the ambush, had searched for him, felt his frustration rising with each passing moment, because he had known that they were only there for a brief time.

Strike fast, strike hard, get out alive had been the order, and that had been what had happened. They had sown death and destruction until Lik-Rifa had arrived, and then retreated.

But he had not found Brák, which gnawed at his soul.

I will find him. I will kill *him.*

Slowly he became aware that there was more space around him, more light, torches burning in high sconces on the wall. He looked up and saw that they had left the tunnel and had entered the underground corridors of Wolfdales, Glornir leading them on, slowing from a jog to a walk. The ground began to slope upwards, wide steps as the slope became steeper, and soon they were entering the great chamber. The first thing Varg saw was Ulfrir, standing in the shadows of the huge tree that dominated the hall.

Well done, vicious child, he heard Ulfrir's voice in his head.

Elvar was moving among the wounded that were being taken to one corner of the chamber, Varg seeing many carried by comrades, their bodies blue-tinged and rigid, bitten by frost-spider's fangs. Many others were already lying or sitting on cots, thralls tending to their wounds. Varg saw Dagrun, Jarl Orlyg's son, blood sheeting one side of his face, sitting and having a scalp wound cleaned. Elvar's warriors were close to her, watching over her: *Berserkir, drengrs*, the Battle-Grim, Uspa and Silrið. A linen bandage was wrapped around Elvar's forearm, bloodstained and dirty, and others around her bore the marks of battle, but as Elvar walked away from the wounded she was grinning, Varg seeing in her the joy of coming through battle with your life, the joy of a battle fought and won.

Not that we have won the war, or even a great victory, but we have drawn first blood, let our enemy know that we have teeth.

Glornir slowed as he walked into the chamber, Vol at his side. Elvar saw them and strode over. She looked at the Bloodsworn filing into the chamber, saw two wounded being carried, one slung over Einar's shoulder, another frost-spider-bitten and carried between two warriors. Varg saw Elvar's eyes taking it all in, counting those on their feet and those being carried.

"You did well," she said to Glornir, "brought all your crew back, none left behind."

"Aye," Glornir said, weariness in his voice, part of the exhaustion that filled you once the fighting was done.

"And Lik-Rifa has learned she cannot just walk right up to us without a care in the world."

"Aye," Glornir grunted again. "We have bloodied her nose, for sure." He paused. "We saw her," he said.

"Lik-Rifa?"

"Aye. The dragon. She was . . . angry." A smile touched his lips, and Elvar grinned.

"Good," she said. "Tend to your wounded, eat and drink." She gestured to long tables and benches that were set out before the dais, looking like a mead hall before the jarl's seat. Carcasses of deer and boar and cattle were turning over spits, fat dripping and sizzling, cauldrons bubbling, the tables set with jugs of ale and mead, bowls of creamy skyr and thick curds, trenchers of hare and goose, salted cod, herring in brine, platters of fresh-cooked bread and steaming vegetables being carried over. Varg's belly growled.

Varg sat with a wooden plater piled high with food. Warm, fresh-buttered bread, thick slices of venison and pork, turnips and cabbage and onions, a cup of juniper-spiced mead in his hand. He took a long drink and breathed out, feeling its warmth seep through him.

Røkia sat one side of him, Svik the other side and Einar opposite him. Most of the Bloodsworn were sitting at the food benches around them, though Varg saw Orka walking away with her son Breca, both carrying platters of food and drinking cups. They left the chamber, walking into the corridor that led to the Bloodsworn's sleeping chambers.

"A good scrap," Einar said cheerfully as he ripped into a chunk of bread, butter dripping into his beard.

"Aye, it was," Svik agreed, using his eating knife to neatly cut and skewer a slice of meat. He looked up at Varg.

"We will find him," he said.

Varg looked at him. Nodded.

"Find who?" Einar said.

"Brák," Røkia said.

"Ah, that *niðing*," Einar grunted. He looked at Varg and shook his head. "Now that is one who will not meet old age."

"No, he will not," Røkia growled.

Varg looked around at them all, touched by the emotion in their voices, the way they would make his task their own.

"I am fortunate, to have such friends as you," Varg breathed.

"Friends?" Svik said. "We are more than that, brother, far more."

We are Bloodsworn, closer than kin. We are pack.

"That is a truth," Røkia said beside him. On impulse Varg reached out and squeezed her hand. She tensed but did not pull away.

Svik raised an eyebrow and smiled.

Einar leaned forwards, his bench creaking, and wrapped one huge hand over Varg's and Røkia's.

"Friends. Kin," he said. "We look after our own."

Varg saw servants bringing fresh food to the table, all with thrall-collars on their necks, and up on the dais *Berserkir* guards stood around Elvar. Ulfrir in the shadows, the glint of iron about his neck, too.

"We do. And yet we are fighting for those who would enslave us," he muttered.

"Be careful," Svik said, glancing around.

"We fight for Elvar and yet, just by being here, we risk being thralled. The Tainted fight with the dragon for their freedom. Should we be fighting for a slaver?"

"I understand why you say this," Svik said. "But it is more complicated than that."

"Lik-Rifa is insane," Røkia said.

"Lik-Rifa has stolen Tainted children, as good as thralled them," Svik said. "Speak to Orka's son."

"They took Refna and the others. And they still have Bjarn, Uspa and Berak's boy," Einar rumbled. "I do not like people who steal children and use them as slaves." His brow knotted in a thunderhead scowl.

"They slew my Revna," a new voice said, Gunnar Prow, who was sitting close to them.

"And my brother," Halja Flat-Nose said. "They slew Vali."

"And Thorkel," Svik said.

"We owe them a blood feud," Røkia snarled.

"Aye, fair enough," Varg said, "Lik-Rifa is not one to fight for, as you say." His eyes tracked an *Úlfhéðnar* with an iron collar about his neck walk to the food bench and fill a trencher. It was Frek, the warrior who had been assigned to guard Prince Hakon when the Bloodsworn had taken him as hostage.

"Much has changed in Vigrið, Hakon dead, Helka dead, Jarl Störr dead. We sit here and eat with a severed head and talking ravens and a resurrected wolf-god." He looked at the iron collar about Frek's throat.

"Why can there not be a way for that to change, too," he muttered.

"Change how, though?" Svik asked him.

"Thrall-collars," Varg said, resisting the urge to put a hand to his own neck, where he knew the old scar was, faded, but never gone. "They are a curse. Vigrið is changing, all are saying, the world upside down. So why can the thrall-collar not change, too? Why can we not just . . . throw them away."

"What, and make the Tainted free and thrall everyone else?" Svik said with a half-smile.

Varg thought about that.

"No," he said, "why not make all freedmen, and just pay those who labour for a task. Like we pay a blacksmith, or a farmer."

Einar frowned.

Svik and Røkia just looked at Varg.

The tramp of many feet and they all twisted on their bench to see a handful of *Berserkir* leading a large group of warriors through the chamber towards the dais, over a hundred of them. They carried blue shields with red sails painted upon them. A man strode behind the *Berserkir*, ahead of the warriors, a gold torc around his neck, silver rings on his arms, grey hair and beard braided, his barrel chest and wide belly straining his brass-gilded *brynja*, a shield slung across his back. With a scraping bench Glornir was rising and striding over to him. The *Berserkir* parted for him and Glornir grinned, offered his arm to the grey-haired man, who laughed and gripped Glornir's arm.

"I should have known *you* would be here," the man said, "now I know I made the right choice."

Glornir turned and led the old man before Elvar, who was seated on her chair upon the dais, Ulfrir at her side.

"Jarl Elvar, I bring before you Jarl Logur of Liga. He has been a good friend to the Bloodsworn."

"And I shall be a good friend to you, if you will have me, Jarl Elvar," Logur said. He looked around, saw Ulfrir standing behind Elvar.

"I am in need of friends," Elvar said.

"You can never have too many friends," Hrung called out, startling Jarl Logur.

"Ah, I have heard tales of Störr's talking head," Logur said as he stared at Hrung.

"I would like to hear them," Hrung said with a wide grin. "Perhaps over a jug of mead or two."

"I like you already," Jarl Logur grinned. His eyes moved on to the others on the dais.

"Is this the wolf?" he said.

"He is," Elvar said, Ulfrir regarding Logur with his amber eyes. Logur stared at him, looked him up and down, then his eyes flickered to Skuld and her red wings, and on to Grok, who had his beak in a barrel of pickled herring, and finally back to Ulfrir.

"Well, it looks like Vigrið is caught up in a skáld-song saga, the father of all family feuds, and all of us along with it." He rolled a shoulder, bones cracking and grinned. "I understand, I always *hated* my sister, though I never had a war-host this big to help me kill her."

"It will be a skáld-song," Elvar said, "of that there is no doubt."

"Well, I would like to be in it," Logur smiled.

"If Glornir Shieldbreaker speaks for you then you are welcome," Elvar said. "We have just bloodied Lik-Rifa's nose and are celebrating. You and your oathsworn are welcome to join us. Please, sit and eat."

"With pleasure," Logur grinned. "It's been hard rowing since we sailed from Liga, so we have worked up an appetite."

Glornir led Logur and his crew to the food benches, and all returned to their seats.

A beating of wings and Kló flew into the chamber, flying to land on the dais close to Elvar.

"Kló has news," the raven squawked, then she saw Grok feasting on his barrel of pickled herring. "Kló hungry, too," she rasped.

"News first, then food," Elvar said.

"Good news and bad," Kló said, bobbing her head. "Good news, many dead from your attack, make Lik-Rifa angry. Make Lik-Rifa very angry. Make trees shake."

Laughter and cheers rippled through the hall at that.

"Bad news, Kló see new warriors joining Lik-Rifa."

"What new warriors?" Elvar asked.

"Tainted. Many Tainted."

CHAPTER FORTY-NINE

ELVAR

Elvar walked out through the stone gates of Wolfdales and into the pale blue of winter. She pulled her bearskin cloak tighter about her. Ulfrir and Skuld walked with her, along with Uspa, Vol and Iva, a Seiðr-witch thralled to the Bloodsworn. Also with her were the *Berserkir* Thorguna, Orv the Sneak from the Battle-Grim, and a hulking, black-skinned man called Taras, another thrall of the Bloodsworn, though he seemed to be tasked as Iva's guard, as he followed wherever Iva the Seiðr-witch went.

The river was choked with longships and knarr, made up of her fleet and those like Jarl Logur who had joined her since they had come here. Elvar strode to the stone bridge that arced across the river. A timber gate with a palisade and towers had been built across the bridge, and Elvar walked to it, stepping over small trenches that been dug into the earth. Thick timber struts had been sunk into the ground and tied; the gate closed with two heavy bars of oak. Elvar climbed a stairwell up to the palisade, walked past a pile of head-sized rocks that had been stacked neatly, and stood there, looked across the bridge and river to the forest beyond.

Somewhere out there is a dragon, coming to try and kill me. Somewhere out there my warriors are fighting for me, dying for me.

She had sent more warriors into the tunnel, more groups to snap and claw and bite at Lik-Rifa's war-host as they wound their way through the Iron Wood towards her. These new attacks were charged with burning the supply wagons. For a moment Elvar thought she could hear screams and smell smoke drifting on the wind.

"A good spot to put some arrows in the enemy," Orv the Sneak said, standing on the walkway and looking out over the palisade and bridge. "Or drop some rocks on their heads," he added, looking at the pile of rocks beside them. There was another pile on the far side of the walkway, and larger piles set on the ground behind the gates.

"Aye," Elvar agreed.

The bridge would be a chokehold for any who tried to cross, and the gates looked like they would hold out against the thickest of rams.

She looked left and right, a new ditch dug running along the riverbank, all of the earth from it thrown up into embankments that were piled against a new timber wall, all built since they had arrived here. It was a considerable achievement and looked formidable.

"It is impressive," Elvar said.

"It will hold Lik-Rifa's war-host, at least for a while, and allow you to slay many of them," Ulfrir said.

Elvar nodded, imagining the far banks seething with her enemy, imagined them swarming across the bridge, building rafts to cross the river, could almost see her warrior's hurling spears, loosing arrows and dropping rocks onto their attackers. Could almost hear their screams.

She also remembered Glornir's description of Lik-Rifa, of the destruction she had caused in the Iron Wood.

"But it will not stop a dragon. If she can rip trees up by their roots, one swipe of her claws would tear this gate to kindling."

And Skalk and Estrid have told me what the dragon did to the hall and fortress of Darl. Smashed it to splintered wood and rubble. She could do the same to these gates, these walls.

"She would destroy this gate, the towers and wall in as much time as it takes for me to speak these words," Ulfrir said.

Elvar looked from Ulfrir to Skuld, Uspa, Vol and Iva.

"Can you do what I have asked?"

"We can," Ulfrir said.

Uspa, Vol and Iva walked down the stairwell to stand behind the gates, within the carved circle, Ulfrir and Skuld remaining on the walkway. With a snap Skuld beat her wings and took to the air, hovering over the gates, leaving Elvar standing with Ulfrir, Taras and her guards.

"*Guð blóð, úlfablóð, heyrðu kall okkar, finndu mátt okkar,*" Ulfrir called out, Skuld and the others echoing Ulfrir's strange Seiðr-words, and Elvar felt a tingling shift in the air around her, making the hairs on her arms and neck rise. Sparks crackled in the air around Skuld and Ulfrir.

Vol stepped over the new trench dug in the ground, no more than a handspan deep.

"*Snaka, alfaðir í mínum æðum, fylltu þennan staf af krafti þínum,*" she cried out, and a sharp-angled rune flickered to red light around her fist, like a glove. Vol dropped to one knee and punched it into the trench. A flare of sparks and hissing, and red flames ignited and crackled along the trench like red-molten metal poured into a cast. Elvar saw a pattern appearing from her position over the gateway, a half-circle of flames hissing along the shallow ditch, forking into new channels and ruts, red runes appearing, like spokes in a wheel leading to the centre of the wooden gate, passing under it and flaring into red-flamed life on the bridge beyond the gate. More lines of fire ran into the fresh-dug ditch to either side of the gate, running before the new earthworks and palisade that spread along the riverbank.

"*Blóð Snaka, kraftur í æðum okkar, heyrðu okkur núna,*" Vol called out, more runes appearing around both of her fists, and still kneeling she plunged her hands into the molten stave-line.

"*Blóð Snaka, kraftur í æðum okkar, heyrðu okkur núna,*" Uspa called out, a sparking of flames in the air around her fist, and she knelt, too, pushed her fist into the red-hissing ditch.

"*Eðlur blóð, kraftur í æðum mínum, heyrðu okkur núna,*" Iva chanted, runes of pale fire bursting to life, then bent to one knee, thrust her rune-glowing hand into the molten channel.

"*Snertu þessa veggi úr furu,*" they called out together, "*þessi hlið af eik, gefðu þeim styrk, gefðu þeim kraft til að standast afkvæmi þitt. Kraftur til að standa á móti drekanum og rottunni.*"

Ulfrir pulled a seax from his belt and drew it along his palm, cupped his fist until blood welled. Skuld did the same as she hovered over the gateway.

"*Úlfablóð, guðsblóð, verndar okkur fyrir drekanum, verndar okkur fyrir rottunni. Verja þessi hlið, verja þessa veggi,*" the two of them cried out as Ulfrir cast his blood into the air, Skuld, too, red droplets glistening. In a flare of white light, they burst into bright incandescence above Elvar and fell in a shower of sparks.

Taras gasped as the droplets floated down around them like snowflakes, laughed as some of them settled on his skin.

"They do not hurt Taras," he said, even as some of them touched Elvar's cheek. They felt warm, almost comforting, as they melted away. When they touched the timber of the gateway, though, they flared bright, hissing and crackling, and Elvar watched, mesmerised, as they floated down into the rune-channels. Where they touched the carved rune-wheel ditch they burst into bright light, rippling through the rune-channels and flowing out into the ditch before the embankment walls.

Slowly the rune-fire faded, became a soft glow like embers cooling in a fire, a final flicker and they were gone.

"It is done," Ulfrir said, looking at Elvar, "the gate and wall will hold against my sister and brother now."

"My thanks," Elvar said.

"Perhaps it will even give them a bite or two," he grinned.

CHAPTER FIFTY

BIÓRR

Biórr walked among the dead, and threaded his way through the destruction, searching. Here and there flames still licked and crackled, though most were doused or burned out now, leaving the black-charred carcasses of wagons behind, looking like long-dead skeletons of some unknown, forest-dwelling creatures. People were all around him, going through burned-out wagons as they searched for anything that had survived the flames. Any barrels or chests that were still intact were being heaved out and set in piles. The rustling of forest litter in the shadows and Biórr spun on his foot, raising his shield and hefting his sword, but it was just a spertus, legs scuttling as it slipped into a stream with hardly a splash. He studied the deeper shadows, wary of another attack, but saw nothing. Skraeling and tennúr were all around now, and he saw trolls wading through the shadowed undergrowth.

They will not be back now, there are too many of us here, and we are ready. He slipped his shield over his back and sheathed his sword, put his hands to his mouth and shouted.

"FAIN," he called, and strode on through the devastation, walking past a cluster of seared wagons, some of the beams still smouldering, and then he saw him.

Red Fain was walking through the ash-covered ground, carrying a child in his arms. Biórr ran to him.

"Thank the dead gods," Biórr breathed as he reached Fain. The old man was covered in black streaks of ash, and there was a long cut on his forearm, but he gave Biórr a hard grin.

"Take more than a few *niðing* goat-humpers to send me onto the soul road," Fain said.

"Well, I know that," Biórr said, taking the child from Fain's arms. It was a girl named Aila. She was unconscious, thick with ash, her breathing steady.

"This way," Fain said and led Biórr around a curve in the road, and he saw them, a score or so children, huddled around a small fire, a pot suspended over it. Some of the children were lying down, others tending to them, cleaning wounds, giving them water to drink. Some stood guard with oversized shields and spears, or axes. Harek called out as he saw Biórr and Fain.

Biórr laid Aila down on a bed of rough-cut branches, a lad coming over with a linen cloth and a bucket of water. He knelt beside Aila and started washing the ash from her face.

"I was about to come looking for you," Harek said to Fain. "I thought . . ." he stuttered to a halt.

Fain scowled. "Seems like everyone round here thinks I can't look after myself," he grunted. His face softened and he tousled Harek's red hair. "You need not worry about me, lad. I'm not going anywhere. How are they all?" he asked, looking at the wounded.

"All right, I think," Harek said. He twisted round to look at another lad who sat with his knees hunched up. Biórr realised it was Bjarn. "No thanks to your *niðing* friends," Harek snarled at him.

The lad scowled up at Harek and stood slowly, Biórr surprised to see how broad and thick-limbed Bjarn was becoming.

"Shut up," Bjarn snarled, his fists balling, and Biórr saw the flicker of green in his eyes.

"Enough of that," Fain said, stepping between them. "No fighting." He pointed a finger at them both. "There is enemy enough without fighting among ourselves."

"He *is* the enemy," Harek grunted.

"No, lad, he is not," Fain said. "Bjarn is just . . . confused."

"What's to be confused about? We are fighting those that try to thrall us, it is simple enough," Harek muttered.

"I am thralled here, the same as you," Bjarn said. "Even though I do not wear the collar I am kept a prisoner, not allowed to go. We all are." He glowered at Fain. "No different from a thrall."

"The difference, Bjarn," Biórr said, stepping close to the lad, "is that we do this to keep you safe. The people we fight, they will thrall you to be their tool. They will treat you like an animal, no different from a hound, or a good milking goat. All they see is your usefulness, how you could serve them, make their lives better."

"And I was taken to be used by you Raven-Feeders, we *all* were," Bjarn said. "You used us to cast your Seiðr-spell and set Lik-Rifa free. You didn't *ask* us. We weren't given a *choice*. How is that any different?"

Biórr just looked at Bjarn, had nothing to say to that.

"I want to go back to my family," Bjarn said. "My mother. Those Bloodsworn, they were going to take me to her."

"Your mother is a thrall," Biórr said. "A powerful thrall, but still a thrall. She is of use to Elvar and the Battle-Grim. If you went to them, you would become a thrall, too."

"You do not know that," Bjarn said, "and, anyway, if I am free, like you keep saying, then it would be my choice to make. Stay or go." He looked from Biórr to Fain. "Can I go?"

They did not answer him. Bjarn took a step towards the road.

"Stop," Fain growled.

"Exactly," Bjarn said, stopping and glaring at Fain. "You are no different from a slaver, no better," and he turned and walked away, sat down away from the rest of them.

"Don't listen to him, he is a halfwit *niðing*," Harek growled. "We all know what you have done for us. We are grateful."

Biórr shook his head, remembering the Bjarn he had first met, remembered playing tafl with him in the inn at Snakavik.

"Give him time," he said to Harek, then he looked at Fain. "Let me see that cut on your arm."

Biórr sat upon a stump and sipped from a horn of mead while he listened to Lik-Rifa's captains.

They were seated in a wide glade, long shadows stretching as the sun sank below the treeline, a fresh-scraped fire pit burning.

Lik-Rifa sat with Rotta beside her, Ilska and Drekr on her other side, listening as her captains reported to her: Krúsa of the skraeling, a huge bull troll called Heðin, leaning on a club the size of a small tree and wearing a cloak of bearskins stitched together, Tannbursta of the tennúr, a spertus whose name Biórr could not pronounce, the petty jarls sworn to Lik-Rifa, Glunn Iron-Grip and Sigrún among them, and a handful of mercenary captains, Sterkur death-in-the-eye and others.

All of them were talking of the night raids. They had suffered the worst casualties on the first night; since then their guard and vigilance had increased, but the war-host was spread along such a distance that the guards were stretched too thin, and each night had seen new attacks and new casualties.

"Some of the mercenary bands have deserted," Ilska reported, her voice flat and emotionless.

"What?" Lik-Rifa growled, low and chilling.

"How many of these bands have deserted?" Rotta asked Ilska.

"Two, my lord," Ilska said.

"They will regret that," Lik-Rifa hissed. "Have they gone to my brother?"

"No," Ilska said. "Following their tracks, they are headed north, out of the Iron Wood."

"When this war is done, I will track them down for you, my queen," Drekr said.

"Thank you," Lik-Rifa said. "Try to bring as many of them back to me alive as you can."

Biórr shivered at that.

"Heðin will squash them for Mother-Maker," the troll said, his voice deep as a fjord. "Heðin will turn them to gruel."

"How good of you," Rotta said.

"Food is also low, my queen," Ilska said, continuing her report.

"Perhaps Heðin can find these runaways soon, then," Rotta smiled. "Ilska, how much food do we have left?" he asked.

"Three days, perhaps four," Ilska said.

"Tannbursta, how long until we reach my brother's lair?" Rotta asked the tennúr.

"Two days until we reach the wolf-den," Tannbursta said.

"That is fine then," Lik-Rifa said. "We have more than enough."

"Not if we have to undergo a siege," Rotta explained. "It may take a while to dig Ulfrir out of his hole."

"We will not be at Wolfdales long," Lik-Rifa said.

"Why—" Rotta began, but Lik-Rifa cut him off with a raised hand and a dark look.

"If needs be I shall hunt for you," Lik-Rifa said. "I will not see those loyal to me go hungry." She waved a hand, dismissing the subject. "Is there anything else?"

"Yes, my queen," Ilska said.

"What?" Lik-Rifa asked. It was clear that she did not want to be talking of logistics, of food shortages and desertions.

"More Tainted have joined us."

"Excellent," Lik-Rifa said.

"Make sure that they are fed and cared for, given clothes and war gear, if they are needed," Rotta said.

"Yes, do that, of course," Lik-Rifa said.

"And Ilska," Rotta said, "if any have my blood, bring them to me later."

A tennúr winged down from the darkness and alighted upon Rotta's shoulder. It leaned and whispered in his ear.

"Ilska, is there anything else to discuss?" Lik-Rifa asked.

"No, my queen."

"Good," Lik-Rifa said and stood. "Two days, and then," she gave an unsettling smile, her sharp teeth too large for her mouth, "my brother shall regret being reborn into this new world. Into my world. I long to tear him into lifeless strips." She licked her lips with a long, serpent-like tongue. "I will not forget your loyalty, all of you. You shall be well rewarded. Now, if that is all, go to your people, your kin, and be ready for Ulfrir's rabble. They will undoubtedly come again tonight, though he is too weak or too scared to join them."

The glade emptied and Bióрr stood to leave.

"Not you, Biórr," Rotta said, and he sat back down.

"Munni brings news, my sister," Rotta said.

"What news?" Lik-Rifa asked.

"This Elvar has built gates and towers, a wall around Wolfdales."

"Perhaps I shall pay these towers a visit. I will smash them to kindling," Lik-Rifa sneered.

"I am sure you will," Rotta said.

"This Elvar. Who is she to think that she can stand against a god?" Lik-Rifa snarled. Biórr could see the rage building within her. She turned her gaze on him, which he found uncomfortable. "You know this Elvar, Biórr, how does she dare?"

"She was always . . . ambitious, my queen," Biórr said. "She rose high in the Battle-Grim, and quickly. She is a fine warrior, too, has good weapons craft. But to become chief of the Battle-Grim, to resurrect and thrall Ulfrir, to return to Snakavik and slay her father," he blew out a breath and shook his head. "She has surprised me. Shown she has deep-cunning, too. She is a jarl's daughter, grew up in his court, and Jarl Störr was known for his cunning and his ruthlessness. He had an arrogance, as if he were fated to rule, and no doubt Elvar has inherited some of that from him."

"More than her father would have hoped, I imagine," Rotta smiled, "considering what she did to him."

"If this woman is so formidable, why are you smiling?" Lik-Rifa growled.

"Because knowledge is power, and I know something," Rotta said.

"What?" Lik-Rifa said.

"Patience, my sister."

"I have been *patient* for three hundred years," Lik-Rifa said, her voice cold, a tremor in it.

"True, true," Rotta said placatingly. "Our friends at Wolfdales have told Munni that not all love this Elvar. That there are some among her followers who are . . . disappointed with her leadership. And they have told Munni that if Elvar were to die, perhaps the doors of Wolfdales would be open when we arrived."

"And how will Elvar die, when we are here and she is there? Will our friends there kill her for us?"

Rotta smiled.

CHAPTER FIFTY-ONE

ELVAR

Elvar woke to a voice, saw a shadow looming over her and reached for a blade.

"Don't panic, chief, it'th me," Sólín Spittle lisped.

"What is it?" Elvar breathed.

"You have a vithitor," Sólín said, looking towards the entrance of Elvar's chamber.

Elvar sat up, saw Ulfrir standing silhouetted in the entrance.

"I must show you something," Ulfrir said.

"What?" Elvar said, splashing cold water from a bowl into her face and rubbing the sleep from her eyes.

"It is best if you see," Ulfrir said. "Come." He turned away and walked out of the chamber.

Buckling on her weapons belt and snatching up her baldric and scabbarded sword, Elvar hurried after him, Sólín Spittle falling in behind her. She stepped out onto the platform and stood there a moment, was pleased that she did not sway with dizziness, saw Ulfrir walking onto the stairwell carved into the branch and followed him.

"Jarl Elvar," Berak said. He had been standing guard at her chamber door and he fell in beside Sólín.

Elvar caught up with Ulfrir as he reached the trunk of the tree. He turned and waited for her.

"They must stay here," he said, nodding at Berak and Sólín.

"Why?" Elvar said.

"I have something to show you, but it is for your eyes only."

She looked at him a moment.

"I could just command you," she said.

He dipped his head in acknowledgement. "I am trusting you with what I will show you. Trust me when I say no one else can know." A silence passed between them.

"Berak, Sólín, wait here," she said.

Ulfrir turned and walked away, Elvar following, slipping her baldric over her head and left arm, shifting her scabbarded sword so that it hung at her hip. She was surprised when Ulfrir turned left to climb the stairwell that wound higher around the trunk, rather than right, to descend to the great hall's floor.

"Where are we going?" Elvar asked him.

"Up," Ulfrir said.

As they spiralled upwards around the huge tree Elvar saw other chambers around the hall's curving walls, each one at the end of a thick-limbed branch. Some had the soft-glow of firelight, where people had taken up residence in them, others were dark shadows, like black eyes gazing out into the chamber. Elvar saw movement in one of those chambers, the flare of a torch, shadowed figures. She saw Silrið with a handful of others, glimpsed Runa Red-Axe, along with Hjalmar Peacemaker and Estrid Helkasdottir. There were others, but they were cast in shadow. Elvar paused for a moment, but then Ulfrir was disappearing around a curve in the path and she hurried after him.

Meeting to discuss Grend and his fate, no doubt, she fumed. And then Grend was rearing up in her head, looking at her with his expressionless face, only his eyes hinting at what he felt inside. A swirl of emotions at the thought of him. Hurt, that he had deceived her, anger, at the position he had put her in, unease, at what she should do.

He has made me appear weak, has made many doubt me.

Appearing weak is a jarl's greatest enemy, he heard her father's voice whisper.

She knew what she should do.

"Why are you taking me up here," Elvar snapped at Ulfrir, agitated and tired of the mystery.

"This was my home," Ulfrir said. "Orna my wife had her own hall, further north, a great eyrie where you felt like you could see the whole world. All of us children of Snaka had our own halls, but Orna visited me often here. She loved to perch in this tree."

Elvar saw a smile touch Ulfrir's lips as he thought over some distant memory.

"I am sorry," she said.

Ulfrir looked at her.

"Sorry that Orna is dead."

He sighed. "When you brought me back, and I found out that Orna was long dead, it was like the twist of a knife in my belly," he said. "But to hear that she had been brought back, too, like me, that she had felt new breath in her lungs, felt the same wind that blows on us on her face. That she had looked at the same sun and sky . . ." he shook his head, let out a low-rumbling growl. "I do not know why, but that pain, it is worse."

Elvar nodded. A look of such despair swept his features. In all of her grand schemes she had not thought about the feelings of a god, certainly not cared about them, but looking at him now, seeing a glimpse of the depths of his pain, it was impossible not to feel something.

"I am sorry," she said again. "I know that words change nothing, heal nothing. All that they do is tell you that someone cares, even if only for that moment."

Ulfrir nodded. "You are right, it changes nothing. But, it is still . . . something."

They walked on in silence and Elvar saw that they were approaching the domed roof of the chamber, branches thinner and denser up here. She felt something upon her face, a gentle caress, stared at the roof, then stopped, gasped.

"It is open," she said. "I can see the sky, the sun." From the chamber's floor she had been able to see some kind of fractured light that rippled across the roof, but she had thought it was more Seiðr-magic. Now she saw that it was daylight filtering through the canopy of branches, and that sensation upon her face. It was the wind.

"But are you insane," she hissed. "We are open to attack. Lik-Rifa could just *fly* into this chamber with nothing to stop her but a few branches. We must do something." She felt an overwhelming urge to grab Ulfrir and shake him, to push him tumbling from this great height.

"You told me we were protected from Lik-Rifa here, that it is safer than Snakavik."

"It is safer," Ulfrir said, holding up a hand to halt the words gushing from her mouth. "Walk on."

Elvar scowled at Ulfrir and took a hesitant step on up the spiral stairwell. Her head was almost level with where the roof should be, but instead it was branches, leaves and air. She took another step, lifted her hand to brush leaves out of her way and . . . hit something. She frowned, pushed at the leaves again, saw that before she touched them her hand hit something solid. There was a ripple of blue light. She pushed harder, but met an invisible resistance, then punched with the bottom of her fist. A crackle of blue light, rippling away and fading.

"It is a Seiðr-spell," Ulfrir said as he climbed to stand next to her, "much like the protection that we put on the gates and wall at the bridge. Nothing can get through."

"Nothing?" Elvar said.

"Well, sunlight, wind, sound, but nothing of flesh and bone."

"Nothing?" Elvar echoed.

"Nothing, unless you know the words," Ulfrir said. "I crafted this for Orna, so that she could fly to my halls, but could still feel the wind in her feathers and land here, watch the world from this high place."

He touched the invisible barrier with his fingers, blue pulses of light around each fingertip.

"*Úlfavinur, opinn,*" he said, the blue light flared and rippled through the dome and Ulfrir strode on, passing through the leaves and branches. He looked back, peered down to her. "Come on," he said, as he disappeared through the canopy.

Elvar stood there a moment, then followed him.

She stepped into daylight, a cold wind stirring around her, blowing through the branches of the treetop as it reared above the dome of the hill. She saw grass and stone around her, realised that she was standing where the wolves had been when she had arrived at Wolfdales.

"*Úlfavinur, náinn,*" Ulfrir said, and Elvar saw the blue light shimmer for a moment beneath her feet, then it was gone.

"It is back, impenetrable again," Ulfrir said. "The only way back into the chamber now is to walk down the hill and use the front door. Unless you know the words." He grinned at the expression on her face, then became serious. "You understand that I am *trusting* you a great deal, here. You have heard the words now."

She nodded.

"But my guards can be trusted," she said.

Ulfrir shrugged at that. "They are loyal to you, perhaps. Even so, people talk. Whispers spread, and ears listen." He looked at her intently. "Rotta will have people here, of that I am sure."

"What?" Elvar hissed.

"He is cunning, a deceiver, a liesmith. Lik-Rifa has her own cunning, but she is insane, and impatient. Although perhaps three hundred years in the bowels of Oskutreð has taught her some measure of patience."

"Spies in my camp, we must find them, root them out."

"If you can," Ulfrir said. "Until then, speak only what you must. But this is not why I have brought you here." He stepped off the stairwell into what appeared to be thin air, but Elvar saw the slight crackle of blue light where his feet touched the barrier.

"Come, it is quite safe," he said.

Elvar looked down, saw leaves and branches, and air, the ground of the chamber a very long way down. She felt a wave of dizziness, swayed.

"Trust me," Ulfrir said, and Elvar took a step from the branch, stepped out into the air, and felt a firmness underfoot. She walked across the dome to Ulfrir.

"Orna liked to sit in the branches of this tree and look out at all Vigrið," Ulfrir said, and Elvar gazed at the view from the hill. All Vigrið lay before her, rivers glinting in the pale sun like serpents slithering across the land, the dark, green-black ocean of the Iron Wood spread all around the hill of Wolfdale. She saw Snaka's skull and the curving line of the Boneback Mountains, far closer and clearer than she would have thought, could even make out her father's fortress upon the skull. Her eyes followed the fjord out to the sea, took in the coast of Vigrið and estuary of the River Falinn that they had sailed up, her eyes coming to rest on the river full of longships far below, the trees of the Iron Wood thick on the far bank.

"It is . . . beautiful," Elvar breathed.

"Yes," Ulfrir said. He was smiling, a sharp wind soughing through the branches and sifting his wolf-grey hair. "You see those trees down there, on the far bank of the river?"

"Yes," Elvar said, peering.

"Many of them are ash trees."

Elvar blinked at that. "Ash trees," she echoed.

"Aye." Ulfrir grinned. "Ash trees mean Froa-spirits."

Elvar nodded, a slow grin stretching across her face.

"Froa-spirits will not like a war-host trampling around their trees."

"A warm welcome," Elvar said.

Ulfrir looked at her.

"You have done well," he said, "to raise such a host, to keep it together, to strike against Lik-Rifa and Rotta as you have done. It has been no easy task, to reach this point."

"Well, I have had some help," Elvar said, surprised by his words.

"Heya," Ulfrir agreed with a shrug. "Having a wolf-god at your shoulder may have helped a little." He gave his half-smile. "Although I am thralled to you, so I have no choice in the matter." An altogether different twist of his mouth. "But many would have failed where you have succeeded. It has taken some courage and deep-cunning to get this far. I understand why you gave me my life, why you thralled me. A risk, to anger a god, which is why I say you have courage, but I probably would have done the same in your position. And you are no tyrant, you do not seek power for power's sake. You have a vision."

She looked at him.

"Once, my vision was to climb high, to win battle-fame, to live on in a skáld-song. All to show my father that he was wrong about me. That I am better than he thought." She shook her head. "None of that matters now. I do not like power, I do not like leading. It is a weight about my neck, but for now I must lead, because my vision is to survive, and to do that I must get Bjarn back for Uspa," she said. "And for that to happen Lik-Rifa must die, it is as simple as that. I am no brave saga-hero, I am more a thrall than you, it is the *blóð svarið* that drives me."

Ulfrir nodded. "I think we understand each other. Perhaps we should learn to trust each other."

A slow smile spread across Elvar's lips.

"Now that would be brave," she said.

He smiled, too. "I have trusted you with the secret of my home," he said. "Outside my family, you are the only one to hear the words that open this rooftop gateway into my den."

Elvar nodded, acknowledging that.

"Is this the only other entrance to your home, then?" Elvar asked him.

"No," Ulfrir said. "There are the tunnels, though we have sealed all except the one we have been using for the night raids, and that is well guarded, both by flesh and blood and by Seiðr. And there were entrances in those towers," Ulfrir gestured to the crumbling, vine-wrapped ruins that Elvar had seen upon the slopes of the hill when she had first seen Wolfdales from the deck of the *Wave-Jarl*. "But they are collapsed, and even if someone took the time to dig their way through, there is a Seiðr-wall in each tower, just like this one." He tapped his foot on the invisible barrier they were standing upon.

"Are they the same Seiðr-words to open them?" Elvar asked.

"No, I shall teach you them, if you wish. Trust you with the words of power, though we will not use them."

Elvar nodded.

"And I will trust you with another, greater secret," he said. "My father, Snaka, planted this tree, a seed of Oskutreð. The first seed of the Jarnvidr, and he gave me this land about it, sowed the Jarnvidr for me to roam within. I built my hall about the tree, dwelt among the woods. But Oskutreð is an ash tree, and ash trees have their Froa."

"They do," Elvar said, remembering the Froa-spirit she had encountered at Oskutreð.

"The building of my hall, the carving of the stairwell into the tree, the Froa-spirit did not . . . approve," Ulfrir said. "She resisted. So, at my request, my father sang her to sleep." He strode to the trunk of the tree and laid a hand upon it, stroked a deep line in the bark. Elvar stared, and gasped.

There was a huge face carved into the tree, Ulfrir tracing the line of its jaw. A woman, hard-faced, long hair like vines wrapped around the trunk, limbs of knotted wood winding about the tree.

"Snaka taught me the words to wake her, which I would have sung a long time ago, but then my daughter, Valkyrie, was abducted . . ." he paused, a twitch of muscle in his cheek. "And war erupted. You call it the Guðfalla, the god-war." He spread his arms. "And I died." He shook his head. "It has been a long time, a deep sleep for her, but I think it is time for Gelta to wake." He looked at Elvar. "Are you ready?"

"Why are you telling me this?" she breathed.

"We both fight Lik-Rifa and Rotta, we are on the same side," he said. "I think it is time we trusted each other. And if anything happens to me, Gelta should know you. She should know that you mean her and her tree no harm, otherwise," he smiled, "an angry Froa-spirit is the last thing you need."

Elvar nodded.

"Good," Ulfrir said, and opened his mouth, began to sing.

CHAPTER FIFTY-TWO

ORKA

Orka sat on a stool with Breca in a shadowed alcove of Ulfrir's hall, dipping a chunk of hard bread into a beef and turnip stew as her eyes skimmed across all who sat in the eating hall before Elvar upon her dais.

The scrape of feet and Orka saw a man walking towards them: Dagrun, Orlyg's son.

"Ahh," Orka murmured.

I wondered when he would seek me out.

"Farmer," Dagrun said as he reached them. He pulled a bench closer and sat on it.

"What do you want?" Orka said to him.

"Just to talk," Dagrun said. He looked from Orka to Breca. "No need to be so hostile. I told you, your secret is safe with me."

"What is your price?" Orka said.

"Price? None, really. You saved my life, remember."

"Aye, and you paid me blood-price for that with this *brynja*."

"My life is worth more than a *brynja*, no matter how fine it is," Dagrun said. "At least, to me it is. I saw the beast in you when you fought Myrk." He smiled and nodded approvingly. "You fought well, just that *holmganga* alone should be a skáld-song."

"What is your price?" Orka asked him again.

"Keep asking me that and you may well offend me," Dagrun said, his smile fading. "All I ask—"

"Ah, now we have the meat of it."

"All I ask is that you be a friend to me. As those ravens say, we *all* need friends. One day I may need your help, may ask you for a favour." He shrugged. "That is all. And it will work the other way. If you ever need help, only ask and I will do what I can."

"I am Tainted," Orka said carefully. "You could have me thralled. I would become your enemy then, and one day I would kill you for it, but you could still expose me. Use me."

"I judge people by their deeds, not what or whose blood flows in their veins." He stood up, looked at Breca. "She has fought her way through a war-host to get you back."

"I know," Breca said.

"Never forget it," Dagrun said as he turned and walked away.

"I will not," Breca whispered.

Orka watched Dagrun and saw another figure separate from the crowds and approach them, Glornir, broad and hulking.

"Why are we hiding in the shadows?" he asked them as he pulled up a stool, the wood creaking with his weight, a horn of mead in his fist.

Orka slurped stew from her bread.

"Because there is a man out there who knows that I am Tainted, and if he saw me it would go badly for Breca and me," she said.

"Skalk," Glornir growled.

"Aye, Skalk, the Galdurman with Estrid," Orka said to Breca's questioning look. "I crossed paths with him at the Grimholt, when I was looking for you. I thought you were a captive in their outbuildings and . . ."

"And what?" Breca asked her.

A twist of her lips, a shrug.

"I loosed the wolf in my blood."

"Ah," Breca murmured, thinking it over. "We could kill him," he said.

"Yes," Glornir growled, patting Breca's shoulder. "I should have killed him when I saw him, but he will die, and soon."

"We could kill him now. Vigrið would be a better place without him," Orka said. "But I have been watching him and he is never alone, always with his *drengr* and Galdurwoman. I could kill them, too, but without being seen. That is not so easy."

"You could put on one of uncle Glornir's collars," Breca said. "Like the ones he gave to Iva and Taras, pretend that you are thralled. Then you can use your blood-gift without fear."

Glornir grunted approvingly.

Orka looked down at Breca. "That is some deep-cunning thinking," she said.

"I have been thinking a lot," Breca said.

"About what?" Orka asked him.

"Many things. About our home at Fellur, about Spert. About Papa," he said, and tears welled in his eyes.

"You remind me of him," Glornir said.

Breca gave him a half-smile, a tear spilling down one cheek.

"Not just the look of you, Thorkel is in the way you speak, the way you walk," Glornir said. He leaned closer. "When you feel anger, do you hear the growl of the bear, or the howl of the wolf?"

"Both," Breca said.

Orka blinked at that, and shared a look with Glornir, who nodded, tugging at his beard.

"The wolf and the bear," he murmured. "Well, that is a rare thing." A smile split his beard. "I would not want to stand in the shield wall against you when you are grown. There were few who could stand against Orka and Thorkel together." He was silent a moment, eyes distant with memory. "None, actually, that I remember." He looked down at Breca. "Ah, lad, but you should have seen them. My brother and sister were a rare sight."

"Sister?" Breca said.

"We are Bloodsworn. Thorkel was my brother by blood, but Orka was my sister through our oaths. Oaths bind us."

"But I walked away, turned my back on my oath," Orka whispered.

"Ach, no more of that," Glornir said. "You had your reasons, but you never stopped being my Bloodsworn sister. And I do not believe you ever stopped thinking of us as your kin." He looked into Orka's eyes, held her gaze.

"No, I did not," she said. "My brother."

Glornir reached out and patted her hand.

"I wish my father were still here," Breca said.

"So do I, lad, so do I," Glornir murmured.

Breca looked up at Orka. "Do you think about him, Mama?"

Orka closed her eyes, could see Thorkel in her head, his eyes that always seemed to look into the heart of her.

"Every moment of every day," she breathed. Blew out a long sigh. "Glornir is right, your father would be proud of you, his fierce, deep-cunning son. You have a temper, though, and that can get you into trouble."

"Ha, you are a fine one to talk. I think perhaps I got that temper from you," Breca smiled.

"Ha," Glornir grunted a laugh.

A smile twisted at Orka's lips, and she ruffled Breca's hair. "Heya," she acknowledged.

"And what else have you been thinking on, in this thought-cage of yours," she asked Breca, tapping his head with a finger.

"About this war," he said. "I have heard people say that we are fighting for a slaver, that Lik-Rifa would set the Tainted free. That *we* could be free."

"Heard who?" Orka said, frowning down at Breca.

"Ákveðin," Breca said. "She is a *Hundur*-blood, thralled to Runa Red-Axe. But not just her."

"Huh," Orka grunted. "Well, it is not as simple as that. You will hear one person saying they fight for this freedom, another that they fight to right a terrible wrong. It is all talk. People fight for themselves. Lik-Rifa fights her brother because of grudges centuries old. Ulfrir would fight Lik-Rifa because of the slaying of his daughter." She rolled her shoulders. "That I understand. That is the truth. People fight to survive, or fight for blood feud, or fight for power. There is nothing else, no matter what pretty words come out of their mouths."

"Heya," Glornir agreed.

Orka woke with a growl, a rumbling echoing all about her, clouds of dust shaken from the walls. It felt like the world was breaking apart.

"SHE IS HERE," Ulfrir's voice howled in her head and Orka was on her feet, Breca blinking and pushing himself up.

They slept in a chamber with all of the Bloodsworn, and all around Orka warriors were jumping to their feet, buckling on belts and helms, grabbing spears and shields. Varg and Røkia were already standing, but all in the room were close behind them.

The chamber echoed with the sounds of destruction. A roaring that filled the world, the sound of timber splintering, smashing.

"What?" Einar said with a thunder-cloud frown.

"Lik-Rifa," Glornir growled. "Weapons," he said as he buckled up his weapons belt and shrugged his shield over his back, and then he was moving, leading them out from the chamber.

"Stay close," Orka said to Breca as she swept up her long-axe and followed after Glornir, who led them through high-vaulted corridors until they were bursting into the great hall.

All was movement, warriors pouring into the chamber from corridors that fed into the hall, and Orka saw Ulfrir with Elvar, her *Berserkirs*, *drengrs* and Battle-Grim about her, all of them striding to the great stone doors. Glornir led them after her, the Bloodsworn shouldering through the gathering crowd. Ulfrir glanced at Orka.

She is here, the wolf-god said inside Orka's head.

Beyond the doors it sounded like the world was ending, a great beast roaring louder than the mightiest of storms, the sound of timber splitting, torn, smashed.

Elvar walked to the doors, shouted a word of command and with a grating creak they began to open, dawn's milk-pewter light seeping in. There was an eruption of blue-tinged light that seared itself across Orka's eyes, an earth-shattering roar edged with pain and a turbulence of air surging through the opening doors, rocking people back on their feet, and then the sounds of destruction were fading.

Elvar strode out into the dawn, Ulfrir and all following her. Orka heard bellowed commands, some troops drawing up into shield walls, but Glornir just led the Bloodsworn in a loose formation. Orka looked, checked where Breca was and was pleased to see him close to her, clutching his shield and spear, eyes wide.

The two stone wolves were crouched and snarling, glaring up at the pale sky beyond the river and Orka saw the black stain of dragon-wings over the forest, beating slowly, heard the distant heartbeat like a pulse, Lik-Rifa fading into the distance.

Elvar led them on, through the vale flanked by steep slopes and onto the road that led to the bridge, warriors spreading wide as they passed beyond the reach of the two hillside promontories, moving along both strands of the riverbank as Elvar approached the gates built across the bridge.

The gate and towers were intact, fractured ripples of blue light flickering through them. Elvar reached them and strode up a stairwell beside one of the gate towers. Orka saw others heading for the other stairwell, Elvar's brother, Broðir, with one of Elvar's jarls, Runa Red-Axe and a handful of her drengrs. Glornir led the Bloodsworn behind them and climbed the stairwell, Vol beside him, Orka following close. She heard gasps as she stepped out onto the walkway and palisade, felt her heart lurch in her chest.

The fleet of longships and *knarr* was gone, the river choked with shattered strakes and timber, with masts and oars and broken prow-beasts. Half-submerged sails floated by, the current slowly carrying smashed hulls and splintered bows away. Half a longship had wedged against the riverbank close to the bridge, snaring more ruined timber, the water frothing white as the current swirled around it.

All along the riverbank Orka heard warriors crying out as they climbed up onto the palisade built upon the new embankments. Some warriors scrambled over the palisade and slid down into the ditch, clambering back up the other side in a vain attempt to salvage something from the wreckage.

"Why has she done this?" Orka heard Elvar say.

"So that we cannot flee," Silrið said, who stood close to her.

"She is a child having a tantrum," Ulfrir snarled. "She came to destroy the gate, and, when unable to, she lashed out in rage at the closest thing."

All along the walkway above the gates people just stood and stared in shock, frozen at the sight of such destruction. Never had

Orka seen so vast a fleet, and in moments it had been reduced to a river of splintered matchwood. People were weeping.

"Mama," Breca whispered, tugging at the mail sleeve of Orka's *brynja*.

"What?" Orka said, still gazing in horror at the wreckage in the river.

"Something's . . . wrong," Breca said, and Orka tore her eyes from the carnage to look at him.

"There," Breca said, pointing, and Orka saw someone walking along behind all those gathered above the gates, making their way to Elvar. Broðir, her brother. It looked strange, out of place, because all else were fixated upon the ruined fleet. As Broðir drew near to Elvar, Orka saw his hand reach inside his cloak, saw the glint of steel.

"ELVAR, WARE," Orka cried out as she reached for the hand-axe at her belt. Elvar was turning, eyes flaring wide as she saw Broðir, his seax stabbing at her. Gytha lunged at Broðir, and a body slammed into her, Runa Red-Axe, a sword in her fist. Gytha grabbed Runa's wrist and the two of them stumbled against the palisade wall and toppled over.

Elvar twisted and Broðir's seax stabbed at her, the blade grating along the waist of her *brynja*, Broðir snarling, punching Elvar with his other fist, sending her reeling back, Broðir's wrist coming back for another strike with his seax.

A handful of Runa's *drengrs* were there, had filtered among Elvar's *drengrs,* and now were stabbing and chopping, stopping her guards from coming to her aid. A *Berserkir* growled, Thorguna Storm-Cloud, drawing the twin axes at her belt and with a wet slap she buried one axe in the skull of a *drengr*, severed a wrist with her other axe.

Ulfrir roared, his body rippling and people ran or leaped from the walkway.

"*Kraftur öskunnar, kraftur guðanna, brenndu hana, svíðu hold af beinum,*" a voice cried out and red runes crackled to life at the tip of Silrið's staff, the Galdurwoman pointing it at Elvar and Broðir.

"*Snákur svipar, vakandi og bítur djúpt,*" another voice called out, Vol reaching down to the black whip at her waist, grasping the handle, the serpent-end rearing up, hissing, fangs bared. With a crack she snapped the whip out and Silrið screamed, reeling away with the serpent-headed fangs of the whip embedded in her cheek. Vol ripped her arm back and the serpent came free, a chunk of Silrið's cheek still in its mouth. The Galdurwoman screamed, stumbling away.

Orka ran along the walkway, long-axe in one fist, hand-axe in the other.

Broðir had pushed Elvar back against the wall, was trying to bring his seax up to her throat, but she had his wrist in her grip. Orka drew her arm back and threw, her hand-axe spinning through the air. It slammed into Broðir's back, sliced through his mail shirt and deep into his back and shoulder. He reared back, screaming, grasping at the axe, and Elvar head-butted him in the face.

Silrið reeled into Broðir, grabbed a fistful of his tunic, and she leaped over the wall, dragging Broðir with her.

Orka ran to the wall, Elvar leaning over it, Ulfrir leaping as he transformed into his wolf-form. The ground and gates shook as he landed, Silrið clambering to her feet, one side of her face blood-drenched, dragging Broðir across the bridge. Ulfrir padded after them, lips drawn back in a snarl. Broðir saw him and screamed, high and terrified, and he turned and leaped from the bridge into the river, Silrið stumbling after him. With a splash they were both gone, disappearing amidst the ruin of longships that were being swept by the current.

People ran to Elvar, who snarled and spat curses, one hand going to her waist where Broðir had struck her. Runa's *drengrs* had all been slain on the walkway, but Gytha stood on the bridge with one foot on Runa's wrist, her sword tip touching Runa's throat.

"Alive, I want her *alive*," Elvar shouted down to Gytha.

Orka leaned on the wall, staring at where Broðir had flung himself into the river. Svik came to stand beside her.

"What's wrong?" Svik asked her, looking at the scowl on her face.

"He's got my axe," she snarled.

CHAPTER FIFTY-THREE

BIÓRR

Biórr grunted approvingly.

"Although unable to walk properly you are doing a fine job with these children," he said to Red Fain as they watched them training and sparring.

They are no longer children. They had gone from children to warriors, all of them moving well with shield and spear.

"I would rather be in the front row of the shield wall," Fain grunted. "That is where I will find my vengeance for Storolf. Not teaching bairns their weapons craft."

"Your wound has not healed," Biórr shrugged. "Besides, we each play our part," he said. "And these bairns are looking to you like a father now."

Fain grunted at that, but Biórr saw the glimmer of a smile twitch his braided moustaches.

Lik-Rifa's war-host had just finished another long day of riding and marching through the forest, Biórr travelling with Red Fain and the Tainted children. They were all mostly recovered from the attack on the wagons two nights ago, though some of the children were still vomiting and complaining of pains in their head, suffering the after-effects of the fires.

Biórr and Fain had seen to the horses while some of the more able of the Tainted children had set about making their camp. Setting a perimeter, fetching water, scraping a fire pit and starting a fire, boiling water, going to the food stores to be given supplies for their evening meal. Biórr was impressed with how Fain had been teaching them, almost as if they were their own small crew among this fractured, many-faceted war-host. And every evening after their meal Red Fain trained them in weapons craft. Their small camp was set among many others, the Raven-Feeders close by, and a handful of them watched the Tainted children as they sparred.

Fain had set them to practising their spear and shield-work, leather covers over the spear blades, and he was demonstrating the overhand and underhand grips, showing them how to move from one grip to the other.

"The overhand grip gives you a longer reach," Fain was saying, "so is useful in a shield wall, or whenever you need that length of attack. The underhand grip," he spun the spear in his fist, reversing his grip, "though shortening your striking range, gives you a stronger grip, so you can strike more powerful blows. You must use your thought-cage, to decide which grip will help you survive the fight you are in."

The children had trained in two shield walls, and had now broken down into melee practice, one on one. As always, Harek and Bjarn had gravitated to each other, and were both doing their best to shatter each other's shield and bones with their spear and shield strikes.

"Best stop them before one kills the other," Biórr grunted to Fain.

Biórr became aware of noise rippling through the camp, and he looked up, saw tennúr whirring through the air, flitting to each fire pit, talking to those gathered around the fires, and in their wake people were standing, hurrying to tents.

"What is it?" Red Fain said, hand dropping to rest on the short-axe at his belt.

"Another ambush?" Biórr said, and then a tennúr was flying down out of the dark, hovering in the air before Biórr and Fain.

"Prepare to ride," the tennúr squeaked, "and leave your campfires burning."

"What?" Fain frowned.

"PREPARE TO RIDE, LEAVE THE FIRES," the tennúr

shrieked. "Old *Maður*-man deaf," it muttered as it flew away, and Biórr saw that all along the road warriors were breaking camp.

"Break camp," Fain shouted to the children, though he glowered at the disappearing tennúr.

Come to me, Biórr heard Rotta's voice in his head.

Biórr rode along the column at a fast trot, passing warriors marching or riding, all of them grim-faced and dressed in their war gear. Many glanced to shadows either side, searching for signs of the raid that might come with the darkness, but all Biórr saw was the shifting shadows of night-hags and the deeper shadows of frost-spiders in the boughs.

We are so close now. Biórr knew that with the coming of dawn they would most likely see the slopes of Ulfrir's lair. Battle was coming. He could feel the fear and excitement building, felt it in his own blood, thrumming like a new-strung bowstring, but he could also feel it in the air around him, see it in the faces of all those he passed by.

Soon we fight. Soon we will stare death in the eye. Live or die, all decided by the edge of a blade.

Rotta was ahead. The rat-god rode alongside Lik-Rifa, a handful of new guards around him, rat-blood Tainted, like Biórr, who had joined the war-host. One of them nodded to Biórr as he rode up alongside them.

"Well met, brother," the man said, tall and wiry, like an old rope, a straggle of beard on his chin, his skin pockmarked.

"Skadi," Biórr said, nodding back to the man.

It takes more than sharing some god-blood before I will think of you as brother, he thought as the warrior dropped back to allow Biórr closer to Rotta. The rat-god was listening to his sister, who was not best pleased.

"Set a Seiðr-spell that bit me when I tried to smash their wall," Lik-Rifa was snarling. "Still, I have wiped the wolf-grins from their faces. I turned their longships to firewood."

"You have told me, sister," Rotta said, looking to Biórr and rolling his eyes. "Many times," he breathed.

"Why are we riding now?" Biórr asked.

"To reach our enemy sooner, of course," Rotta said. "Munni has reported that Ulfrir and this Elvar have eyes in the sky, reporting on our progress, which no doubt has helped them pinpoint their night raids. Travelling through the dark, and leaving our campfires lit may well deceive those spying on us, and we shall give Ulfrir and Elvar an unpleasant surprise, when they find us knocking at their door with the dawn."

Biórr nodded.

"Soon, brother," Lik-Rifa said to Rotta. "Soon we shall face Ulfrir."

"I know," Rotta said. To Biórr he did not look so happy about that prospect. Lik-Rifa heard it in Rotta's voice, too, and gave him a sidelong glance.

"You fear him," she said, quiet as the wind sighing through the trees.

"Aye," Rotta said. "My last meeting with him was . . . unpleasant."

I am sure it was, Biórr thought. *If the skáld-songs are true, then Ulfrir beat you half to death, chained you to a rock, and dripped the venom of serpents over you.*

"He is weak, brother, hiding from us in his den."

"Or perhaps he wishes us to think that," Rotta said. "He is wolf-cunning, remember."

A snarl spasmed through Lik-Rifa's lips. "Aye," she growled. "If that is the case, we shall do it. Do what you suggest. But only if things go bad for us." She shivered, shook her head. "That road is more dangerous than Ulfrir. It could see us eaten . . ."

They rode in silence awhile, and then Biórr saw figures on the road ahead, emerging from the darkness. Brák Trolls-Bane led them, a small crew of scouts made up of Tainted and skraeling. They were spread in a loose circle around two figures.

Lik-Rifa called out and held a hand up, the column juddering to a halt behind her, and Ilska and Drekr rode forward, spoke with Brák a few moments and they all approached Lik-Rifa and Rotta together.

"Look what we found stumbling around in the dark," Brák said, and his crew parted to let two figures step forwards. A man and a woman, both soaked to the skin, hair bedraggled and dripping, both wounded. The woman walked with a staff and appeared to have half her face missing, a red wound leaking blood where her cheek should be, and the man walked with one shoulder slumped, his tunic blood-soaked and a red wound across his back.

"Silrið the Galdurwoman, and Broðir, brother of Elvar," Ilska said.

"Broðir, aren't you supposed to be slaying your sister and opening the doors of Wolfdales for me?" Lik-Rifa frowned.

"I . . . I tried," Broðir mumbled.

Lik-Rifa curled her lip.

"What shall I do with them?" Brák said.

"What use are they, now they have failed?" Lik-Rifa said with a shrug. "Kill them."

"Perhaps hold on that order," Rotta said. He leaned closer to Lik-Rifa, whispering, though Biórr could hear him.

"If Elvar dies, for any reason – battle, assassination, hunting accident, overeating, the ale-death, if she falls from her horse and bangs her head – the power of controlling Ulfrir will pass to Broðir. Think about that. He would be able to command Ulfrir to lie at your feet."

A moment's silence.

"Tend to his wounds," Lik-Rifa said to Brák and Ilska, and they led Broðir and Silrið away. The column stuttered into motion again.

"I want Elvar dead," Lik-Rifa said to Rotta.

"I know," Rotta said. "So do I." He let out a long sigh. "I suppose if you want a job done properly, you must do it yourself."

CHAPTER FIFTY-FOUR

ELVAR

Elvar dropped her *brynja* in a heap of rings on the floor and lifted her wool and linen under-tunics, saw a purpling bruise spreading along the length of her waist.

"A good blow from Broðir," Urt the Unwashed said with a whistle. He was her guard from the Battle-Grim today.

"Aye," Elvar grunted. She knew that it would have punched through any ordinary coat of mail.

"I am sorry, Jarl Elvar," Thorguna Storm-Cloud said.

"For what?" Elvar asked.

"Letting that happen," Thorguna growled. "I should have been more vigilant."

"You fought, risked your life for me, defended me," Elvar said. "You have nothing to be sorry for."

Thorguna blinked at that.

"What?" Elvar said.

"You . . . you are not your father," Thorguna said. "He would have punished me."

"I am not my father," Elvar echoed. She lifted her *brynja* and slithered her way back into it. Buckled on her weapons belt with her seax and long-handled axe suspended from it and threaded her baldric and sword over one arm and shoulder. Grabbed her bearskin cloak and wrapped it around her shoulders.

"Come," she said, and strode from her chamber.

After throwing Runa in a locked gaol and sending scouts out to search for Broðir and Silrið, most of the day had been spent searching the wreckage on the river for anything that could be salvaged. One longship and two *knarr* had survived total destruction, though they all needed work on their hulls before they could sail again. She had noticed Orka and Breca searching long hours, and eventually they had left the riverbank with Orka carrying a barrel across one shoulder.

Now, though, she had work to do. Work that all who followed her must see.

She wound her way down into the main hall and walked towards the dais, where Runa Red-Axe stood, hands and feet bound, Sighvat with one big hand on her shoulder, a loop of wound rope in his other hand. Gytha was there, too, with a handful of Elvar's *drengrs* and Berserkir around her. It was after dark, the evening meal already finished, and Elvar saw the hall was full, all her captains gathered with their crews, their oathsworn. She strode through them all, seeing Glornir, Jarl Logur, Hjalmar Peacemaker, Jarl Orlyg, and all the others, and made her way onto the dais, walked up to Runa, who looked worse than when she had seen her last. Her lips were pulped and swollen, one eye closed, a cut over one eye. Some of those injuries Gytha had given her, some had come during the long day of being put to the question.

Elvar strode up to Runa and looked at her.

"Why?" Elvar asked her.

"You are weak," Runa said, shrugging and smiling through bloodied lips.

Sighvat pulled his arm back, his fist clenching.

"No," Elvar halted him. "Weak? How?"

"Grend. He still lives. A man who deceived you, *betrayed* you. A *Tainted*." She spat blood on the floor. "And what have you done? You have led us to run and hide, to wait here in a hole for our deaths. How can I respect you, follow you, trust you?"

A long silence, Elvar staring at her.

"Who else is with you?" Elvar asked.

"No one," Runa blinked. "My *drengrs* are all slain, Broðir and Silrið gone."

I have seen you in secret meetings with Broðir and Silrið, Elvar remembered. *But there were others there, too. I saw Estrid Helkasdottir with you.* She glanced at the hall, at all those watching her, knew that Estrid was out there, and the others, whoever they were, watching her, judging her. Knew that she had brought this upon herself.

I was a fool, allowing Broðir to live, she thought. *My father would have slain him without a moment's hesitation. I should have been more ruthless. I should be more ruthless. But, for better or worse, I am not my father.*

She looked back to Runa.

"Hang her," she said.

Sighvat unwound the rope in his hand, Elvar seeing that he had already made a loop and hanging knot at one end. He slipped it over Runa's head down to her neck, pulled it tight, then reached for the rest of the rope, swung it around his head three times and hurled it high. It arced into the air, up, over a branch of the ash tree and then it was falling. Sighvat grabbed it, held it, and looked at Elvar.

"You are an oath-breaker," Elvar said to Runa, "thrice cursed."

"Do it," she said to Sighvat and he heaved on the rope, hauling Runa into the air. She gasped and squawked, Sighvat heaving her until her legs kicked just above Elvar's head. Runa bucked and writhed, gasping, her eyes bulging, veins protruding, her face turning red, then purple. And slowly her kicking lost its strength, became less frantic, gave way to a series of twitches and she slumped, still, the rope creaking as she turned in a slow circle.

Elvar turned to face the hall.

"This is what happens to those who break their oath to me," she said. But today had made her realise the extreme risks of her situation. While Broðir lived the event of her death would be catastrophic. He would command Ulfrir, command her *Berserkir*. If she died, Vigrið would fall to Lik-Rifa. She remembered all the conversations with Uspa, how she had spoken of releasing the Tainted from thraldom, of freedom for all. How Elvar had thought her insane.

"Ulfrir, step forward."

The wolf-god padded out of the shadows, a questioning look in his eyes.

"Ulfrir Snakasson, if I were to free you, would you swear the blood oath, the *blóð svarið*? Would you swear to never use your blood to gain power unjustly over another? That you would protect the Tainted and untainted alike? That you would treat *all* fairly? That you would enforce justice in all Vigrið? That you would punish the murderer, the thief, the oath-breaker, that you would defend those who are wronged?"

He blinked, just stared at her. Gasps rippled around the hall, the murmur of voices. Elvar ignored them, knew she could not stop, *would* not stop now. She had taken the first step into the abyss and there was no turning back.

"What are you doing?" he whispered.

"It is time we trusted one another," she whispered back to him.

"Would you swear it?" she cried out, loud enough for all to hear.

He stood straighter. "I would swear it," he said.

"Uspa," Elvar called out and the Seiðr-witch stepped forwards.

"Do you mean this?" Uspa asked her.

"I am not my father," Elvar breathed. Uspa reached out and squeezed Elvar's hand, her eyes shining with tears.

"Do it," Elvar said, "and use Ulfrir's chair for the runes."

Uspa drew her seax from her belt and set to digging and chopping at the arm on Ulfrir's seat, carving a series of sharp-angled runes. Two, three, then a fourth.

A silence fell upon the hall, deep and dark as a fjord.

"Líf, giver of life," Uspa said, pointing to the first rune carved into the chair. She drew her seax across the heel of her hand and let her blood drip into the rune, filling it.

Elvar sensed a change in the air, a tingling skittering across her skin, oppressive as a storm.

"Dauða, bringer of death," Uspa said, letting her blood fill the second rune.

All in the hall were silent, shocked, stunned, staring.

"*Blóð svarið*, the blood oath that binds unto death," Uspa called out as she moved to the third rune, holding her palm so that her blood dripped into it, and then she moved to the next.

"Kvöl, torment to the oath-breaker," she called out as her blood filled the last rune carved into the chair. She looked at Ulfrir and held the seax out to him. "Join your blood to mine," she said.

Ulfrir took the seax and dragged his wool sleeve up, drew the blade across the palm of his hand and held it over the runes, his blood dripping, falling into each rune-carving, mingling with Uspa's.

"You know the words," Uspa said to him. "Say them."

Ulfrir looked at her, looked at his blood dripping into the runes, then looked at Elvar. He held her gaze as he said the words.

"*Blóðeið eg gjöri, binda mig orðum mínum með valdsrúnum, dyr til gamla hátta,*" he cried out.

"Blood oath I make, binding me to my words with runes of power, door to the old ways," Uspa called out for all in the hall to hear.

"*Ég sver að nota aldrei blóðið mitt til að ná völdum á óréttlátan hátt yfir öðrum. Ég sver að ég mun vernda hina menguðu og ómenguðu jafnt. Ég mun meðhöndla alla sanngjarnt. Ég mun framfylgja réttlætinu í öllu Vigrinu. Ég mun refsa morðingjanum og eiðsbrjótanum og þjófnum, ég mun verja þá sem beitt er órétti,*" he called, his voice filling the hall, his eyes fixed upon Elvar.

"I swear never to use my blood to gain power unjustly over another," Uspa cried, translating Ulfrir's Seiðr-words for all to hear, for all to know the oath he was taking. "I swear that I will protect the Tainted and untainted alike. I will treat all fairly. I will enforce justice in all Vigrið. I will punish the murderer and the oath-breaker and the thief, I will defend those who are wronged."

Ulfrir clenched his fist, more blood dripping.

"*Ég innsigla þetta með blóði mínu, lífi mínu, megi dauði og kvalir taka mig ef ég brýti það,*" he cried.

"I seal this with my blood, my life, may death and torment take me if I break it," Uspa translated.

A silence fell over the hall. The stone doors slammed open, the walls shaking, a chill, ice-touched wind sweeping into the room, shaking the branches of the tree, swirling around them, and the blood in the runes began to hiss and sizzle. It rose into the air, looking like red strips of tendon, keeping the shape of the sharp-angled runes. With a crackle the blood-runes merged, fusing into one long strand, spiralling upwards towards Ulfrir's outstretched arm. It wrapped around his hand, his wrist, his forearm, drawing tight with a sizzle and hiss, the stench of burning flesh, and Ulfrir grunted. Then the red line was fading, evaporating, leaving a raw, spiralling scar around Ulfrir's hand and forearm.

"*Svo sé,*" Ulfrir snarled.

"So be it," cried Uspa and the wind was gone, all in the hall staring.

Elvar reached into her cloak and took out a large iron key, placed it into the lock in Ulfrir's collar, and turned it. A click, and the collar opened, Elvar taking it from his neck and holding it high.

She looked into Ulfrir's eyes.

"I SEE YOU," she cried out, saying the ancient words for when a thrall was given their freedom. Then, more quietly, "You are free."

Ulfrir looked at the collar, and a slow smile spread across his lips.

"Skuld," Elvar called, and she stepped forwards, shock in her eyes, and something else. Elvar took out the key to Skuld's collar and unlocked it, took the collar from her neck.

"I see you," she said to Skuld.

"What, no blood oath for me?" Skuld said.

"There is no need," Elvar said. "Abuse your power and your father will deal with you." She smiled as she saw the fullness of Ulfrir's oath register in Skuld's eyes.

"That is some deep-cunning," Skuld muttered, but she smiled in return. "Thank you," she said, dipping her head.

Elvar sucked in a deep breath.

See this through.

"Berak, Thorguna, all my *Berserkir,*" Elvar called, and they came to her, muscled and mail-clad, brooding and iron-collared, they all stood before her. "Uspa, their keys", and Uspa came forward, producing an iron ring with many keys upon it. One by one Elvar unlocked their collars and took them from their necks, looked into each one's eyes as she did it and repeated the ancient words.

"I see you."

"I see you."

"I see you," until they all stood before her, free.

"You are free," Elvar said to them. "Free to stay, free to go. I would ask you to stay and fight at my side, fight against the rat and the dragon, fight to keep our land free from a new tyrant. Fight to rescue Berak's son from their grasp. But I only ask, I do not command. And if you wish it, you may swear your oaths to me, become my *drengrs*, and I will provide for you as any good jarl does for their oathsworn. I will be your gold-giver, give you hearth and home in return for your service." Then she turned to face the crowd gathered before her.

"There are jarls out there with Tainted in their warbands. If you wish to remain here, wish to fight alongside me against Lik-Rifa, then you must set your Tainted free. If not, you are free to leave, I will not hinder you. But leave you must."

She stood there and waited, knew that this was the knife-edge, when the world could turn on her.

A long, drawn-out silence, and then there was movement in the hall, a figure pushing through the crowds, others behind him.

Jarl Orlyg stepped up onto the dais, a score of warriors behind him, all with collars about their necks. He frowned as he approached Elvar.

"You are either insane, or the deepest-cunning thinker I have ever known," he said. "For my sake I hope it is the latter, but, either way, Little-Elvar, I stand with you." He turned to his Tainted thralls and unhooked a ring of keys from his belt.

"I see you," he said as he took the first collar from a warrior. Then he went to the next, and the next, repeating the ritual.

"I make you the same offer as Elvar made to her thralls . . . I mean, freedmen," he said. "I would welcome your oaths. I know your bravery, your weapons craft, and the dead gods know I would be happy to have you as my *drengrs*. Though Elvar will have to help me win some more silver so that I can pay for you all."

"I'll drink to that," one of the released Tainted said with a laugh.

Other jarls and mercenary chiefs came to the dais, all going through the same ritual, setting their Tainted thralls free. Elvar stood and watched, feeling detached from it all now, elated and exhausted. She had known this was coming, had feared it, feared the relinquishing of her power over her Tainted, feared how her jarls and chiefs would react, feared what could happen.

All came to stand before her, even Estrid stepping onto the dais and releasing her *Úlfhéðnar*, which was unexpected. And at the very end she saw a group of people pushing through the crowd like the prow of a *drakkar* through ice-crusted sea. Glornir and the Bloodsworn. Glornir stepped onto the dais, with his two Seiðr-witches and the thick-muscled black man at his shoulders. Strangely, all the Bloodsworn followed behind them, including all those wearing the *druzhina* kit of Iskidan.

Glornir walked to Elvar.

"A bold decision," he said. Then he turned to Vol and nodded.

She took a key from her cloak and unlocked the collar around her neck, took it off and dropped it on the dais. Iva and Taras did the same, and Elvar frowned.

"They were not thralled to you?"

"Never," said Glornir.

"Why?"

Glornir waved a hand to take in the Bloodsworn and looking at them Elvar saw the flicker of eyes changing colours, of teeth growing, claws extending. Even the lad Breca.

"You are *all* Tainted," she breathed.

"Aye," Glornir said. He stood straight and drew in a deep breath looking back at his people. "You taste that," he said to the Bloodsworn, "that is the taste of freedom."

Elvar shook her head. "The mighty Bloodsworn, Tainted," she said.

"Elvar Fire-Fist, you have done a remarkable thing," Glornir said, "and you will have our loyalty for as long as we draw breath", and then he led the Bloodsworn from the dais.

Elvar called for barrels of ale and mead to be opened, and, once the celebrations began, she left the dais and slipped through the crowd, made her way into one of the tunnels that led from the great hall. She heard the soft-scrape of feet behind her and turned quickly, hand reaching for her sword, but it was Thorguna and Berak, Sighvat and Urt with them.

"What are you doing?" Elvar said.

"We are your guards, we are guarding you," Berak rumbled.

Elvar paused, looked at them.

"We give you our oaths, freely," Thorguna said, and she had tears in her eyes.

Elvar smiled and nodded, then turned and walked on. They passed through corridors until Elvar reached a door with torch-glow leaking from it. Unbolted a lock and opened the door, stepped inside and closed it behind her. She turned to face Grend, who was sitting on his cot. His wounds were mostly healed now, though he looked older, the lines in his face deeper, and there was more grey in his dark hair.

"I have set Ulfrir free, set Skuld free, set all the Tainted free," Elvar said as she took the last key from her iron ring and stepped close to Grend. She placed the key in the lock and turned it, a click and it opened, and she took it from his neck. "And I set you free, too," she said, and he looked up at her with questioning eyes. She took his hands and pulled him to his feet.

"There were many wise reasons to do it," she said, "deep-cunning reasons, you may say, some practical, some ethical, but the truth of it is", she leaned forward and put her hands around him, hugged him tight. "I did it for you," she breathed.

CHAPTER FIFTY-FIVE

GUÐVARR

Guðvarr heard the horns blowing and reined his horse in. Followed Sigrún and her *drengrs* as they found a space to tie their mounts and make camp. Dawn was bleeding into the world, the shadows parting and separating into shades of grey. Tennúr whirred through the camp, calling Lik-Rifa's captains to her.

"Guðvarr, with me," Sigrún said as she slung her shield across her back, checked her weapons, took her helm from a saddle-hook and buckled it onto her belt. He felt a glow of pride as he walked behind her, and of love, for she had picked him, always raised him up. He felt a ripple of fear, too, as they threaded through this new camp.

Not just a new camp. Our final camp. We are at Wolfdales. At the site of our great battle. The fate of Vigrið shall be decided here. The wolf or the dragon. Fear and excitement shivered through him. To be part of this momentous moment, to become part of the greatest saga, to be a part of skáld-songs that would surely be sung throughout the ages. It was every warrior's dream.

Yet there is also the very real possibility of death, and not a kind one in my sleep, or a pleasant one with a whore bouncing on top of me, but an extremely painful one at the end of a sharp blade, or on the tips of some Úlfhéðnar's *sharp teeth or claws.*

He gulped and adjusted the shield on his back.

Sigrún led him on and he saw daylight filtering through the canopy, coming now in great columns and swathes of light as the branches thinned. They walked upon an old stone road, stepping out from beneath the trees into a strip of green land that spread either side of him, the sky a pale blue, a cold wind cutting into him. There was a wide river before him, and a towering hill beyond it. But it was not the river or hill that drew his eyes. The stone road led to a bridge that arched across the river, and at its far end was a tall timber gate and wall, gate towers rearing at either end. And on the far riverbank, spreading either way beyond the bridge gate, he saw a deep ditch had been dug, leading up to a steep-sloped earth embankment, upon which a timber palisade ran. Upon the gate and embankment palisades were warriors. Many warriors in gleaming helms and *brynjas*, spear-tips glinting in the first light of dawn like a forest of diamonds. All still, all silent, seeming as if they all stared at Guðvarr. The sight of it made him stop, and stare, and swallow nervously again.

"Guðvarr," Sigrún called to him, and he hurried to catch up with her.

Lik-Rifa stood with Rotta, a score of her captains about her.

"We shall carve a ram to break those gates," Drekr said, glowering at the gate on the bridge.

"No rams," Rotta said. "The gates are Seiðr-bound, there will be no smashing them down. The walls on the embankments are protected, too. We can, however, still climb over them."

"Ladders, then," Drekr said.

"Aye, lots of ladders," Rotta said.

"And rafts to cross the river," Ilska added.

We have a dragon, why can she not just fly over there and destroy them all? Guðvarr thought, though speaking that aloud in Lik-Rifa's earshot did not seem like deep-thinking to him.

Lik-Rifa just stood and glared at the hill behind the gates.

"He is in there, brother," she said to Rotta.

"Aye, sister, and we shall dig him out."

"What does he plan?" Lik-Rifa snarled. "He is wolf-cunning, remember?"

"Oh, I remember," Rotta said. "He chained me to a rock and dripped snake venom upon me."

"You did skin his daughter alive," Lik-Rifa said, looking at Rotta, and she sniggered.

Rotta looked around at the captains gathered around them, as if he had forgotten they were there.

"Ladders and rafts," he said, clapping his hands, and they all turned and walked back to the forest.

Sigrún led Guðvarr back to her *drengrs* and they went to the supply wagons, where wood-axes were being handed out, along with great rolls of rope and twine. As they made their way off the road into the forest the rhythmic sounds of axes hewing wood began to ring out, the war-host spreading through the forest. Guðvarr saw skraeling climbing trunks and hewing at branches, saw warriors hacking at trunks, wood splintering.

"Here," Sigrún said, leading Guðvarr and her *drengrs* to a thick-limbed elm tree. Járn clambered up the trunk and used a hand-axe to chop at branches, dropping them down to other *drengrs* who trimmed the branches of leaves and chopped them to size, set about tying them together with twine, making ladders. Guðvarr and another *drengr* hefted long-shafted wood-axes and set about chopping into the base of the trunk, the thicker timber needed for raft-building.

A sound behind Guðvarr, and he turned to see a dozen dragon-cultists stripped to the waist and hacking at a tree, their dragon-tattoos swirling across their bodies, glistening with sweat despite the cold wind that soughed through the forest.

The branches of the tree were quivering, began to shake violently.

Oh no.

"You *dare*," a voice said from somewhere above, ancient as time, sounding like the scrape and scratch of branches in the breeze, the rustle and crackle of leaves, and then Guðvarr saw a figure drop to the ground, one knee and fist on the ground, slowly rising. A woman, carved from wood, hair trailing and shifting like vines, her face sharp-carved lines, contorted with rage.

"YOU DARE," she cried, raising her hands, and the dragon-cultists fell back before her.

"*Rætur skapara míns, binda og snara, rífa og rífa,*" the Froa called out and the ground shook, began to buck and heave, and roots burst from the earth, snaking around the ankles and legs of the dragon-cultists, snaring them, dragging them to the ground. Guðvarr saw three, four, five of them caught and pulled to the ground, others turning and running, roots whipping after them, lashing at them. Those on the ground twisted and struggled but the roots wrapped tighter around them, pinning them, and still the roots flexed tighter. Screams pierced the air, terror-filled, and Guðvarr stared in fixated horror as flesh began to rip and tear, blood welling, spurting, cracking sounds as bones broke and shattered, the screams rising in pitch, and one of the warriors who had evaded the roots ran back in, began chopping with an axe at the roots that snared a woman.

"*Vínviður af safa-blóði mínu, stinga og stinga, drepa og slátra,*" the Froa screamed, rage- and malice-filled, and the vines that were her hair snaked out, each one thorn-barbed, piercing her attacker, stabbing into his limbs and body, blood spurting. She raised him up into the air, threw him screaming into a tree with a bone-splintering crunch. He dropped to the ground, whimpering, blood staining the forest litter.

Guðvarr heard more screaming, more branch-scraping voices crying their Seiðr-words. He turned in a slow circle, saw the forest shaking all around him, saw people running, screaming, saw vines and roots whipping, snaring, impaling, blood spraying. He held his axe, backed away until he bumped into the tree at his back.

Sigrún was shouting orders, her *drengrs* moving to her, forming a circle, axes and weapons ready, but Guðvarr could only stare at the savagery all around him. There was a greater roaring, drowning out the sounds around him, a shadow above the forest canopy, a great wind from beating wings and Lik-Rifa was crashing through the canopy above, splintered branches and leaves raining down, the dragon descending, her jaws wrapping around the trunk of an ash tree close to Guðvarr. The dragon's feet hit the ground and the world trembled as Lik-Rifa heaved, straining. The Froa-spirit turned and shrieked, whipped at Lik-Rifa's hide with her roots and vines, tore red wheals along the dragon's skin, blood welling in long streaks, but Lik-Rifa ignored the Froa, and pulled. There was a ripping, tearing sound and the ash tree tore loose from the ground, an explosion of earth, roots flailing in the air like grasping fingers, and Lik-Rifa spat the tree from her mouth, threw it to the ground with a crash, a cloud of dust. The Froa-spirit screeched and stumbled, fell to one knee, gasping and sucking at air, her hands rising to her throat. She toppled to her side, chest heaving, limbs and vines thrashing, her breath wheezing, mouth open wide, choking. A spasm wrenched through her, a lingering shudder and she was still, eyes wide, mouth frozen in a rictus scream.

Lik-Rifa stood over the fallen ash tree and Froa, opened her jaws and roared, Guðvarr falling to his knees and clasping his hands over his ears. Then Lik-Rifa was crashing through the forest, jaws snapping and crunching about the next ash tree.

CHAPTER FIFTY-SIX

VARG

Varg stood on the walkway over the bridge gate and looked out at Lik-Rifa tearing trees from the Iron Wood like so much kindling. Varg had seen her appear, wings beating, raising her up above the forest canopy, and then she was plunging down again, disappearing, wood splitting and cracking. The sight of her had filled him with awe and fear, and the wolf in his blood snapped and snarled, hackles raised.

The dragon roared, setting the world to shaking, but Varg could also hear other sounds, people shouting, screaming, and other, ethereal, inhuman voices, shrieking in horror and rage, in pain and terror.

"She is killing the Froa," Vol said, a tremor in her voice.

"We must stop her," Iva hissed.

"How? We cannot go out there."

"Poor trees," Taras murmured.

The roaring and tree-splitting continued for a while, all on the gate and embankments staring on in silence, and finally, slowly, the sounds of destruction faded, and Varg heard the rhythmic chopping of wood resume, began to see movement within the trees, shadowed forms.

Out of habit he checked his weapons. His shield and spear were leaning against the wall in front of him, his spectacle helm buckled and hanging at his belt. He half drew his seax in its scabbard, brushed the poll of his hand-axe, and felt for the hilt of his cleaver.

"Soon, No-Sense," Røkia said beside him.

He felt the tension in the air, felt the fear and thrill that came with the threat of violence, with the promise of battle, as he had felt it many times before. But this day was different. This day he was free. He looked at the Bloodsworn around him, Røkia and Svik either side of him, at Sulich and his archers spread along the wall, at Glornir beside Vol, Orka with Breca, the tennúr Vesli perched on the battlements. As he looked at them he saw Vesli wrap her slim arms around Breca and hug him tight, kiss his cheek. Orka's own small crew were about them, Gunnar, Halja, Lif and Sæunn. Elvar stood with Grend at her side, broad and solid as a cliff in his mail, axe at his belt. A handful of *Berserkir* spread around her, all without their iron collars.

All of us Tainted, all of us, free. It felt incredible, breathtaking, surreal. *Elvar, you have changed the world.*

He looked at the horde mustering beyond the river.

Though perhaps only for a day. You have given us something to fight for, something other than revenge.

There was movement on the far bank, people emerging from the treeline. Groups of warriors carrying wide rafts bound with knotted rope between them, taking them down to the river's edge. Others emerging from the trees with rough-hewn ladders tied with twine. Hundreds of people, clothed in mail, shields on their backs, spears in their fists, steel hanging from their weapons belts. Varg saw many sigils on shields. The dragon of Lik-Rifa's cultists, a black raven on a grey field marking Ilska the Cruel's Raven-Feeders, a clenched fist, an open sail, crossed axes, and then Varg saw a shield he recognised, a golden scrollwork eye upon it.

He hissed and nudged Svik, pointed.

"Ah, the arselings Leif Kolskeggson and Sterkur death-in-the-eye," Svik said.

"So, the *niðings* got away from Ulaz, then," Røkia said.

"I am glad," Svik said. "I owe Sterkur a red death."

"And I owe Leif," Varg growled.

The far embankment was seething with movement now, Varg seeing shapes that were obviously not human among the various warbands of warriors. Great clusters of skraeling with their long-limbed, thick-muscled gaits, rusted mail and crude iron weapons, the bulk of trolls lurking in the shadowed eaves of the forest. Things with many legs scuttled through branches, and tennúr flitted in swirling flocks in and out of the treeline. More people and creatures than Varg had ever seen gathered in one place. The sight of the frost-spiders made his skin crawl. He heard Svik chuckling beside him.

"What is so funny," Varg asked him.

"Look how happy she is," Svik said, nodding at Røkia, and he was right: Røkia had a smile on her face. "Never has she had so many enemies to kill."

"It will be a red day," Røkia said.

Voices and footsteps behind them and Varg looked back behind the gates. Half of the Bloodsworn were down there, Einar with them, along with many other warbands, all of them held in reserve for the wall. A group of warriors were passing through them, heading for one of the stairwells at the gate tower. The sides of their heads were shaven, the long hair on top braided. Varg had seen them before, though this was the first time without their collars of iron. Helka's *Úlfhéðnar*, passed on to Estrid at Helka's death. A warrior Varg recognised led them up the stairwell, Frek, the man who had sailed with the Bloodsworn to Liga as Prince Hakon's guard. He called out to Elvar, and she turned, greeted him and all those behind him.

"We would swear our oaths to you, Jarl Elvar," Frek said.

"You are *Úlfhéðnar*, would you not feel better swearing your oath to your wolf-god?" she said. "You are free to do so."

"*You* set us free, not Ulfrir," Frek said.

Elvar nodded at that. "I will gladly receive your oaths," she said.

"And we would tell you something of import," Frek said. "Estrid and Skalk have been meeting with messengers of Lik-Rifa, sending them information. They were part of the plot against you, with Broðir and Runa Red-Axe. Hjalmar Peacemaker was with them."

Elvar looked at them, her face hard and cold. Grend beside her made to step past her.

"Where are you going?" Elvar asked him, putting a hand on his wrist.

"To find them," Grend grunted.

"We have already searched, they are gone," Frek said. "We meant to bring them to you, some small measure of thanks for the gift you have given us. But by the time we had discussed it and agreed," he raised his hands, "they had fled."

Elvar looked to Gytha. "Search all of Wolfdales, we do not want them hiding in some dark corner causing trouble."

"Yes, my jarl," Gytha said and called out orders, *drengrs* held in the reserve behind the gates turning and heading back towards the great hall.

"You are welcome to fight with us then," Elvar said to Frek. She gestured to the wall.

"Wait in the reserve, here at the wall or on either embankment, and go where you are needed."

"My jarl," Frek said, dipping his head to Elvar.

Horns blew from the other side of the river and Varg turned to see three figures emerging from the swell of bodies on the far embankment, walking along the road and onto the bridge. Varg heard Orka growl, a low tremor at the edge of hearing, and guessed that one of them was Drekr. A dark-haired man, tall and broad, mail-clad with a long-axe in his fist, a raven-feather tied in his hair and white scars like claw marks down one side of his face. He bore fresher, scabbed wounds as well. Beside him a man walked who was taller than Drekr, though slimmer. His brown hair was braided and pinned, a short beard oiled and gleaming, dark eyes bright with intelligence, face long and handsome. He wore a gilded *brynja* and had a seax at his belt. On his other side a woman strode, mail-clad, dark, grey-streaked hair braided and pinned at the nape, a raven-feather tied in it. Her face was all sharp lines, hard and cold as winter, a sword and seax at her weapons belt.

"Ilska," Varg heard Elvar snarl.

"Cold, isn't it," the tall man said conversationally when he came close to the wall. He stood and looked at the line of faces peering down at him and stamped his feet against the chill.

"Where is my brother, then?" he asked good-naturedly, the edges of a smile hovering on his lips.

"To know your brother, I must know who you are," Elvar said. "And as you appear wholly unmemorable, you will have to give me your name."

The tall man laughed at that, seemed genuinely amused.

"I am Rotta, cleverest and most handsome of the gods," he said, giving her a deep bow. "I am guessing you are Elvar, who leads this rabble." He peered more intently at her. "Yes, from Biórr's description you are *definitely* Elvar."

Varg saw Elvar blink at that, a flicker of emotion that rippled across her face and was gone.

"You see, I knew it," Rotta said, another smile.

"You are Lik-Rifa's messenger, then," Elvar said. "And where is she?"

"Lik-Rifa is as far above you as you are above an ant," Rotta said. "She does not converse with ants."

"But you do," Elvar said.

"I love all creatures that my father created," Rotta said, rubbing his hands together and blowing into them. "Though sometimes I wonder why he bothered." His eyes flickered along the wall, and he saw Orka.

"Ah, so you found your way here, then. Good. It will save me having to hunt you down once this is done."

Orka just stared at him.

"I believe you have met Drekr, the man who slew your husband," Rotta said, really grinning now.

"I shall meet him one more time," Orka said, her voice hard as iron.

"Today I will kill you, and your son, too," Drekr growled at her.

"Hard words break no bones," Svik called down at him.

Rotta looked at Svik. "You appear to have made some friends, Orka. A shame that they shall all be dead before the day is done."

"Do you have anything of worth to say?" Elvar said. "Your words are starting to drone in my ears like the buzzing of a fly."

"I like you," Rotta said with another grin, "and I am feeling uncommonly kind-hearted today. I am here to offer you your lives, and your freedom."

"Generous of you," Elvar said. "Which is why you have marched a war-host to my door."

"Not your door," Rotta said, "my brother's. And, yes, it is a generous offer, one of my many failings." He shrugged. "Give me the wolf, and you may go free."

"Ulfrir is not mine to give," Elvar said.

"Ah, and I thought better of you," Rotta said. "This is no time for lies among friends. All Vigrið knows that you are the one who thralled the wolf-god."

"I did," Elvar said. "And now I have set him free."

Rotta's expression shifted, his smile wavering, just for a moment.

"Either you lie, or you are a fool. For your sake and all those who follow you I hope you are lying. You are familiar with the expression a wolf among sheep?"

"I have set Ulfrir free, and all the Tainted, too. This is a new world, and we shall rid it of gods who would rule us all."

"Oh no, you are a zealot," Rotta sighed. "You do not look like one, but looks can be deceiving." He shook his head. "Well, I can see that this is pointless, there is no getting through to zealots. But do not say I did not try to help you. Ilska, Drekr, come," he said and turned away. With one last glower at Orka, Drekr followed him, but Ilska stayed where she was, staring up at Orka.

"This is your last day," she said, looking up hard and cold at Orka. "Once this begins, I shall find you, and end you. For Myrk." Then she was turning and striding away. As they reached the embankment Rotta raised his arms and horns blew out, loud and strong. The war-host lurched into motion.

Varg watched them come forwards. On the riverbanks rafts were dragged to the water, thirty, forty rafts, more of them emerging from the treeline, skraeling and dragon-cultists clambering onto them with crude-carved oars. On the road warriors holding ladders appeared, other warriors flanking around them, holding shields high. They reached the bridge, six wedges fitting onto the bridge, more forming up behind them, an endless procession filling the embankment, and on the riverbanks the rafts were pushing off, oars slapping into the water, skraeling spitting and snarling as they drew nearer to this side of the river, eyes fixed on warriors standing on the palisade walls.

"This is it, then," Svik said. Varg slipped his nålbinding cap onto his head, then took his spectacle helm from his belt and buckled it on tight, shook the mail neck guard across his shoulders. He remembered Jökul and his ritual of taking a handful of earth and rubbing it between his hands, remembered Tjorvi and Vali Horse-Breath and Ingmar Ice and all the Bloodsworn who had fallen since he had joined them. And he remembered Frøya, his sister, stabbed and pinned to a tree by Brák Trolls-Bane.

Hands grabbed his shoulders and turned him, and he was looking at Røkia, her helm buckled on, eyes wolf-touched and fierce.

"Stay alive, Varg No-Sense," she growled at him and gently butted her helm against his, soft as a kiss, then she was turning and hefting her shield and spear, and the warriors surging towards them were roaring.

"Nock," Sulich cried out and all along the gate-wall his *druzhina* warriors nocked arrows to their bows.

"Draw and loose," he yelled, and arrows were hissing and buzzing through the air. The splatter-ripple of arrows piercing shields, finding gaps and piercing flesh, punctuated by screams.

Along the far embankment voices cried out, Seiðr-words ringing, and runes crackled to life, blue and red flames and they were spinning slowly through the air, arcing high over the bridge and gathering speed, curling down towards Varg and those on the wall.

"*Guðsblóð,*" Vol called out, runes sparking to life before her.

"*Rúnakraftur,*" Uspa yelled, more runes crackling into existence.

"*Fornar háttur,*" Iva chanted, and fresh runes flared.

"*Verndar okkur nú. Eldur, logi og ís, verndar okkur núna,*" they all cried in unison, and their runes merged, hissing and crackling, spreading high above and along the bridge, over the heads of Varg and all those standing upon the bridge palisade.

The enemy runes crashed into them, and both exploded in a

fountain of red and blue, Varg feeling heat as they showered over him, melting into his mail. And then the ladders were at the gate. Taras let out a great roar, picking up a rock the size of a skull and hurling it over the wall, Varg seeing it shatter a shield, the warrior beneath stumbling, dropping to the ground. A spear was thrown through the gap and the warrior toppled with a scream. Arrows rained down, rattling like hail, more rocks were thrown, and spears were hurled.

Roars to the left and right and Varg caught a snatched glimpse of the rafts reaching the riverbank, of warriors and skraeling bellowing as they surged onto the bank and down into the ditch, clawing their way up the earthwork embankment. People were falling, pierced with arrows, spears. A ladder slammed onto the wall immediately in front of Varg, two, four, five more thudding along the top of the palisade, and he glimpsed more shield-guarded ladders being carried onto the bridge. And then it was spear-work as bodies climbed the ladders. Faces appeared, helmed and snarling, lashing out with axe or seax. Varg took an axe blow on his shield, stabbed his spear into a face and the man fell away, screaming, replaced by another. A seax stabbed at him and he batted it aside with his spear shaft, slammed the iron boss of his shield into this warrior's mouth, a spray of teeth and blood as the warrior reeled back, one hand still clinging to the ladder, Varg stabbing with his spear, raking it across the warrior's hand and severed fingers spun away, the warrior disappearing with a shriek, blood spurting from his ruined hand. Either side of him Svik and Røkia stabbed and hacked, mists of blood exploding, the whole world becoming a snarling, grunting, blood-soaked haze. Spears were hurled up at them from the bridge, some hissing overhead, some thumping into the linden-wood of shields, the wet-slap of others piercing flesh. Screams along the wall, the crash of bodies falling to the ground behind the gates. Another face reared from a ladder, a fair-haired woman hacking at Varg with a hand-axe. He took the blow on the boss of his shield, a clang that shivered up his arm, and he stabbed with his spear, the blade bursting through mail links and on, grating through ribs deep into the warrior's chest. She fell away and he tried to rip his spear free, felt it snag on bone and was dragged slamming into the wall with a grunt. He let go of his spear rather than be dragged over the wall, drew his hand-axe and hooked the beard of the blade around the ladder shaft, dragged it to his right, heaving at the weight of bodies climbing the ladder, and it toppled sideways, slowly building momentum until it crashed into the next ladder, splintering it and both of them fell away, the people climbing it shrieking, jumping clear.

"Good thinking for a man with no sense," Svik gasped at him, and then the next ladder was slamming against the wall.

CHAPTER FIFTY-SEVEN

GUÐVARR

Guðvarr starred in horrified fascination.

He was standing with his aunt and her *drengrs* a few paces beyond the treeline, close to a stream that fed into the river. His shield was slung across his back and he held his spear in a white-knuckled fist. Warriors stretched to left and right, all waiting their turn to march into the steel-storm that was raging before them.

Just the sound of the battle made him want to cover his ears, made him want to take a few quiet steps backwards, into the treeline, then turn and slip away. The din of war filled the forest. Screams drifted on the cold wind, battle cries, death shrieks, the clash of steel and iron, the drum of feet.

No. Face your fear, find your courage.

As Guðvarr watched he saw a fresh wave of rafts rowing across the river, saw warriors and skraeling leap from them onto the far bank, disappearing as they descended into the ditch, then reappear as they scrambled up the far side. Arrows, spears, rocks, all came hurtling down at those warriors and Guðvarr marvelled at their courage, how they kept climbing, despite the death raining down upon them, despite seeing their comrades' corpses tumbling or sliding back down into the ditch.

How can they do that? Keep on going in the face of such death? He swallowed, feeling scared and then ashamed.

He saw a warrior reach the embankment wall and heave himself over, saw him set upon by foes to either side, saw him fall. A handful of others reached the wall, another wave from the rafts scrambling and slithering up the ditch behind them.

A new roar drew his eyes to the bridge, where he saw a knot of skraeling were gathered, preparing to assault the gates. They were snarling and growling, thumping their chests, ripping at their tattered mail shirts, the sound of them rising to a frenzied roar, and then they were running in great leaps and bounds, warriors moving from their way. They reached the press at the gates, where warriors stood with shields raised and locked, protecting those carrying new ladders. The skraeling leaped onto the tops of the shields and leaped again, reaching the top of the wall with long-armed, grasping hands, hauling themselves over the palisade and onto the walkway beyond. Guðvarr saw snatched glimpses of furious combat, spears and swords stabbing, skraeling swinging their crude iron weapons, a huge, black-skinned man lifting a skraeling over his head and hurling the vaesen back over the wall at those carrying ladders at the gates, smashing a knot of warriors to the ground.

He swallowed again, a fresh wave of fear swiftly followed by shame.

To Guðvarr's right there was a splash and a ripple of movement in the stream, and he looked closer, saw a glimpse of a black-shining, chitinous body, antennae, a curving tail and sting. A spertus, swimming down the stream towards the river. Then more movement, another spertus, and another, and another, until the stream looked crammed with them as salmon in breeding season.

The rustle of movement behind him and he twisted, saw that Rotta was passing within the shadows of the forest, the warrior Biórr and a dozen others behind him.

"Where are we going?" he heard Biórr say.

"I told you, if you need a job done properly, you must do it yourself," Rotta said, and then they were gone, merging with the gloom of the forest.

An impact on his arm and he jumped, wild-eyed.

It was his aunt. She was slapping his arm with the back of her hand.

"Guðvarr, make ready," she said.

"What?" Guðvarr squeaked.

"Make ready," Sigrún said to him as she buckled her helm tighter, nodding towards where her *drengrs* were lifting two rafts. "Time to earn our place in this skáld-song," she said to him.

The *drengrs* began to carry the rafts down the bank towards the river, Sigrún yelling for her *drengrs* to follow her.

Guðvarr swallowed and took a slow step after her.

CHAPTER FIFTY-EIGHT

ORKA

Orka fought with her two seaxes. They were both red to the hilts. She ducked beneath the sweep of a skraeling's long arm, snarled as she came back up and slashed one of the blades at the creature's thigh, flesh parting, blood streaming, sent it stumbling backwards, crashing into Halja, who slammed her shield into the vaesen and sent it tumbling off the walkway, falling to the ground where the warriors waiting in reserve at the gate pierced it with a dozen spears.

Two more skraeling before her on the walkway, their backs to her, raking claws and hacking at Breca. He took a blow on his shield and stumbled back a pace, set his feet and jabbed at the vaesen with his spear. One swept the spear away and lunged at Breca. As Orka charged she saw Vesli sweep down from above and wrap her claws around the head of one of the skraeling, biting and ripping with her long-taloned nails. The skraeling shrieked, staggered and fell from the wall. Orka took two, three steps, and leaped, crashing into the second skraeling, the two of them falling to the floor, rolling, snarling, biting. Orka twisted and heaved herself on top of the creature and stabbed with both blades, a flurry of blows, blood flying in arcs. She growled and snarled, stabbed again and again and again, slowly realised the skraeling was no longer struggling, limbs flopping. Realised Breca had been stabbing it with his spear, too, his lips drawn back in a snarl. She rose, blood-spattered, breathing hard, saw a face loom at the wall, a socketed helm and red beard. She stabbed, a seax grating along the socket guard of the helm and into red-beard's eye. A rising shriek cut short, and he was falling away, Orka pulling her seax free. She stabbed both seaxes into the timber of the wall and swept up her long-axe, which she had laid down, the fighting too close for long-axe work. Setting the top curve of the axe blade against the strut of the ladder she pushed, felt it move back away from the wall, bent her back to it, but the weight of bodies climbing the ladder was too great and she reached a sticking point, grunted and strained, every sinew bulging. Her feet began to slip, and she was sliding back. Breca grabbed the axe and heaved, too, but still they were sliding backwards. A shadow behind Orka, someone else grasping the haft of her axe and she stopped sliding. A snatched glance over her shoulder and she saw Einar Half-Troll there.

"Together," he said, and all three of them pushed at the blade, sent the ladder toppling back. It teetered a moment in the air, standing upright, then Orka, Einar and Breca shoved again and the ladder was falling away from the wall, screams echoing up.

"My thanks, Half-Troll," Orka grunted.

"You're welcome," Einar said, then went back to restocking the pile of boulders on the walkway. He was able to carry twice as many as any other warrior, so the task had fallen to him.

All along the walkway above the gates battle raged, Orka seeing Elvar fighting with shield and sword, Grend beside her hacking a shield apart with his hand-axe, timber spraying, the warrior behind it half over the wall, one leg still on the ladder. Grend chopped again, his axe smashing through the splintered shield and into the arm of the warrior holding it, ripped his axe free and slashed it across the warrior's face, dented the man's helm, scraped along it and carved a bloody line across cheek and through his nose. A scream and the warrior toppled backwards. *Berserkirs* around Elvar hacked at two skraeling that had made it over the wall, carving them to pieces.

A lull in the combat, a hesitation from those heaving the ladders against the wall and scrambling up them, and Orka glanced over the palisade, saw the dead piled in heaps before the gates. More warriors carrying ladders were stepping onto the bridge, beyond them mercenary warbands were moving into position, shields lining up. In the eaves of the forest Orka saw huge shadows gathering, twenty, thirty trolls, more, growling, gnashing their teeth and yellowed tusks, spears thick as saplings and clubs banded with iron in their fists. And behind them Orka saw the scuttling, angular movement of frost-spiders, scores of them spreading out from the treeline into the pale day.

"Be ready," Elvar yelled, and all along the wall warriors reset themselves. Glornir stood with Sulich and Æsa, all of them blood-spattered. Sulich had sheathed his bow and had a sabre in one fist, a slim-handled axe in the other.

A rush of movement on the riverbank to Orka's left, beyond the bridge, more rafts being launched. Crowded with *drengrs*, skraeling and mercenaries, and Orka saw creatures emerging from the water on this side of the river, a line of black-scuttling, segmented creatures, curved tails and stings arching over their backs.

"WARE SPERTUS," Orka cried, ripping her seaxes out of the timber where she had stabbed them and pointing one of her blades.

The cry was taken up, and arrows fizzed and buzzed as the spertus swept up the riverbank and down the other side, into the ditch. Some of them opened their shells and wings spread wide, lifting them into the air. Arrows punched into them, black blood flowing, and many fell crashing to the ground, others pinned to the earth as they scuttled up the embankment. But there were too many and soon scores of them were reaching the embankment wall. Spears stabbed down, slicing into them, but many of the spertus were scrambling over the wall in a flurry of wings and barbed limbs. Then the screaming began.

Warriors walked towards the bridge carrying more ladders, Orka seeing the mercenary bands moving forwards, trolls and frost-spiders following them, and far to her left rafts were skidding onto the nearside riverbank, warriors and skraeling leaping into the shallows and clambering ashore. They ran forwards, up a gentle slope and down into the ditch, disappearing and reappearing again, clambering up the embankment. A handful of arrows flitted down at them, spears stabbing, some falling, and then they were at the wall and heaving themselves over. On the palisade Orka saw black clouds of spertus poison floating in the wind, saw the creatures scuttling, flying, their black stings stabbing, and corpses lay heaped upon the walkway. The resistance on the embankment was fraying, close to breaking.

A thunderous roar drew her eyes and Orka saw the warriors on the bridge parting, a handful of trolls lumbering forwards, bellowing as they came. They all gripped huge, thick-shafted spears or wickedly curved axes, and threw them as they ran. Some hissed over the gate wall, a *Berserkir* skewered by a spear and hurled from the walkway. Many of the spears and axes thudded deep into the timber of the gates and wall. Orka heard a warrior near to her laughing, mocking the trolls' poor aim, but then the trolls were at the wall, leaping, grabbing hold of the axe and spear shafts and hauling themselves up, roaring as they came. Warriors around Orka stabbed down with spears and swords, dropped rocks, chopped with axes, a troll crying out and falling away, squashing people as he hit the bridge, but others heaved themselves tumbling over the wall, falling onto the walkway and lashing out, sending warriors flying, falling, toppling back into the courtyard behind the gates. And behind the trolls came a swarm of tennúr, whirring out from the Iron Wood and falling upon the defenders of the wall, slashing and raking at faces with their long-taloned hands. Orka cut one from the air with a seax in a spray of blood, turned and stabbed her seax deep into the meat of a troll's thigh, heard it bellow in pain as she ripped the blade free, saw Vesli skewer another tennúr with her small spear. More ladders crashed against the wall, warriors scrambling up them and throwing themselves onto the palisade.

Screams drifted across to her and she saw warriors from the embankment walls falling back, shield walls forming in knots, black clouds of spertus poison hanging in the air.

"The wall is breached," Orka shouted. She looked along the line on the gate-wall and saw trolls, warriors and tennúr everywhere. Kneeling, she wiped her seax blades clean on a corpse's tunic, sheathed them and gripped her long-axe.

"FALL BACK," Elvar bellowed.

CHAPTER FIFTY-NINE

GUÐVARR

Guðvarr leaped from the raft towards the riverbank, splashed into ice-cold water that soaked his legs to the knees and snatched at his breath, waded through water and reeds and onto the riverbank. Looking around for Sigrún, he saw her to his right and made for her as she surged on, her shield held high, sword drawn in her other fist. On, up a gentle slope. A flicker of movement and an arrow hissed past him, and he twisted, saw the arrow slam into a warrior's throat, saw them tumble backwards into the shallows, grasping at the shaft, blood spreading like oil in the water. Guðvarr stumbled on, using his spear as a staff to keep his footing on the slippery ground, lost sight of Sigrún, found her again and then the ditch was before him. A steep slope down and Guðvarr hesitated, death's reek wafting up to him, of blood and voided bowels, a sight of nightmares before him.

The ditch was piled thick with corpses, limbs tangled in a macabre embrace, mouths open, flies already crawling in them, empty, lifeless eyes staring. Guðvarr took a step backwards, then another. Someone slammed into his back, shoved him forwards and he was stumbling down the ditch, lost his footing in the slick mud and falling, tumbling, losing his grip on his spear and slamming into something, his head crunching into his shield. He tried to move, turned his head into a skraeling's dead face. Opened his mouth to shout for help but sucked in a mouthful of hair instead. There was a foot on his back, a weight pressing him down and panic filled him, struggling and flailing, he grabbed hold of the top rim of his shield and dragged himself to his knees. Stayed there, gasping in great lungfuls of air. The twang of bows and arrows hissed, a woman falling back down the slope, crashing to the ground beside him, an arrow through her eye.

The only way out was up, was forwards. He staggered up the mud-churned slope, dragging himself with his shield, slid back a step, climbed two more. Slid back another step. Shouts and screams filtered down to him. A body rolled down the embankment towards him and he tried to avoid it, fell, dug his fingers into the mud to stop himself slithering back down into the ditch, and dragged himself up, slamming the shield rim into the soft earth, his arms burning with the effort. He began crawling up the slope, fist in the earth, then shield, fist in the earth, then shield. A shadow before him and he looked up, saw the wall. Clambering to his feet, the wall reared before him up to chest height. There were no warriors facing him, which he thanked the dead gods for, though he saw blurred figures on the walkway, heard the clash of weapons, saw black clouds of spertus poison hovering in the air, and the rapid scuttle of their segmented bodies. Hoping they'd know he was on their side, he heaved his shield up and over the wall, anchored it, grabbed the wall with his other hand and, with a gargantuan effort, hauled himself up and flopped over onto the walkway. Lay there, his chest heaving.

The dead were all about him, men and women in mail, some with black veins threading their faces, mouths open, black tongues swollen, skraeling with great rents in their flesh, spertus leaking pools of black blood. He saw feet and legs moving in shuffling, juddering dances, heard steel striking shields, clanging on metal, heard the sound of blades hewing flesh.

I have no strength left, am too weak to stand, let alone fight. Death, take me if you will.

A spertus scuttled towards him, its black sting twitching and Guðvarr found new strength, flopped onto his front and pushed himself up, staggered away, hefted his shield.

"Friend," he cried to the spertus, holding his shield before him. "I am on your side."

The spertus regarded him a moment, its antennae twitching, a ball of fluid glistening at the tip of its sting. A hand grabbed Guðvarr's shoulder and dragged him around. His aunt, shield and blood-slick sword in her hands, and he felt a wave of relief to see her. The spertus scuttled away.

"With me," Sigrún said to him, "and draw your sword," she grunted, then she was moving, *drengrs* falling in behind her. Guðvarr thumped down a handful of timber steps off the walkway, drawing his sword and they were on a wide track that skirted the steep slope of the hill. He saw that all along this embankment warriors and skraeling were clambering over the wall, the defenders retreating down the path before them.

Jarl Sigrún led them around a black cloud of spertus poison that hovered in the air, people lying dead within it, beneath it, bodies twisted and black-veined. Guðvarr saw a knot of combat raging on the path before them, skraeling and dragon-cultists hurling themselves against a small shield wall, wolf-heads painted on the shields. Guðvarr seeing a white-haired, barrel-chested warrior with a braided beard shouting and bellowing insults. They were retreating slowly, swords and spears stabbing out at the skraeling and dragon-cultists who hurled themselves at the linden wall, axes chopping, leaving a tide of the dead behind them.

"Come," Sigrún said to Guðvarr, and she was lifting her shield, locking it with Guðvarr's. "Warriors of Fellur, to me," she yelled and *drengrs* ran to her, shields slamming together, a wall ten men wide forming, other warriors stepping into a second line. Sigrún punched her sword hilt into her shield, setting a rhythm and her warriors echoed her, marching in time to her beat.

Guðvarr's heart slammed in his chest, beat in his mouth. Skraeling saw them coming, made way. Guðvarr and Sigrún were ten paces from the enemy shield wall, five paces, then with a roar they were crashing together. Shields scraped, Guðvarr pressing his shoulder into his, feeling the weight of the enemy against it.

I am in the battle-fray, the storm of steel, he realised.

He gritted his teeth, peering over the rim of his shield, saw a snarling growler of a man, all black beard, frothing lips and blood-crusted axe. Guðvarr stabbed his blade over his shield rim, slithering out to ping off black-beard's helm. The man hooked his axe over Guðvarr's rim and dragged it down, Guðvarr seeing a spearman in the second row, the spear snaking towards him.

He felt a moment of gut-churning, bowel-loosening fear and opened his mouth to scream.

A spertus dropped out of nowhere, its tail flicking out, and the spearman was gasping, black veins spreading from a swelling lump on his cheek, the spear falling from his grip as his hands went to his throat and he was reeling away, choking, gasping, collapsing to his knees.

Then other spertus were flying over the wall of shields and dropping low. Screams rang out, warriors dropping shields and weapons, black veins spreading through them, and the shield wall was breaking apart, splintering in a dozen places. The white-haired warrior yelled, and then the warriors were turning and running in a knot around him.

Guðvarr felt a wave of relief as he saw the backs of his enemy, then a flush of elation.

I have stood in the shield wall and my enemy have broken and fled before me.

He glanced at the spertus.

Before us.

"On," Sigrún said, and they moved forwards, maintaining their wall of shields. His enemy ran before him, merging with more warriors who were retreating from the embankment walls. Guðvarr saw archers stopping to nock and loose arrows, then running on again, other warriors slowing to lock shields and retreat in a more orderly fashion. Other warriors lagged behind, some locked in combat as skraeling ran around Sigrún and her small shield wall, leaping at the straggling warriors, and the spertus scuttled after them, spreading the pestilence from their mouths, stabbing with their stings.

Sigrún led Guðvarr on, more of her *drengrs* finding her, other warriors joining them.

He could see the bridge and gates now, heard horns blowing. Saw warriors streaming down the stairwells above the gates, forming a thick wall of shields and retreating slowly, the warriors retreating from this embankment joining them, slipping into the wall and locking their shields. They retreated backwards, moving out of Guðvarr's sight, hidden by a promontory of the hill. Other figures were swarming over the gate wall now, skraeling and other warriors, the skraeling leaping from the walkway and clustering at the gates, heaving great bars up and casting them down with a resounding crash. Then the gates were swinging open on their iron hinges.

A wave of warriors poured through the gates, Ilska and Drekr were there, marching through the open gates at the head of the Raven-Feeders, Drekr with his long-axe in his fists and shield slung across his back, Ilska with her sword and shield in her hands. A host followed behind them, and as Guðvarr drew nearer he saw that the other embankment must have fallen, too, for there were more of Lik-Rifa's war-host surging along the path that shadowed the hill.

Sigrún led her warriors towards Ilska and the Raven-Feeders and, as they moved into the area behind the gates Guðvarr saw that the bridge road continued on, flanked by two steep-sloped spurs of the hill, towards a huge-arched doorway set into the hill-side. It towered above them, large enough for Lik-Rifa to walk through in her dragon form.

And before it stood Elvar and her war-host, a wall of shields spread across the road like a great dam before a river.

CHAPTER SIXTY

ELVAR

Elvar walked behind the lines of the shield wall, bellowing commands, Grend, Gytha, Sólín Spittle and Berak shadowing her. The stone gates of Wolfdales were open a crack, the wounded limping or being carried into the great hall, the two stone wolves crouched either side of the gate with their hackles up, lips pulled back in savage snarls, eyes fixed on Lik-Rifa's war-host as it flowed through the bridge gate.

Berserkir and *Úlfhéðnar* prowled back and forth behind the bulwark of the shield wall, eyes of amber and green glowering at the oncoming horde, rumbling, snarling, growling. Between the *Berserkir* and the shield wall stood Vol, Uspa and Iva, heads together in conversation. Taras the Bull stood close to them, clothed in a steel skull-cap and a coat of mail, two hand-axes thrust into his belt.

A hand cart was pulled out from the open gates of Wolfdales full of bundled arrows, Sulich and Kesha pulling it at a half-run. They passed through the ranks of *Berserkir* and *Úlfhéðnar* to where Sulich's warriors in their *druzhina* kit waited, who fell upon the contents of the cart like the starving upon fresh-cooked bread. Sulich barked orders and they formed a line behind the shield wall.

Elvar stood assessing the war-host gathering in the space this side of the gates, saw Ilska marshalling her troops, shouting at warbands. A shield wall was forming, deeper than Elvar's, and behind it the vaesen milled in an ever-growing horde. Trolls lumbered, growling and roaring, skraeling gathered in tight clusters, frost-spiders spread like the sea, tennúr whirring and flitting in the air like starlings, many of them perching on the gate-wall, and behind them all Elvar glimpsed through the open gates the wraith-like bodies of night-hags.

The immensity of Lik-Rifa's war-host hit her, despite the hundreds, maybe thousands, that had already fallen in the assault on the gate and embankments, and a wave of fear washed through her, clouding her thinking for a moment.

"Where ith the dragon?" Sólín Spittle lisped.

"Out there somewhere," Elvar said, gazing at the dark wall of the forest. "Watching us."

But she hesitates, has not come to join the battle. Ulfrir was right, thank the dead gods. Because if she had joined the battle-fray this would have gone badly wrong already.

"Why hath she not come at uth?" Sólín asked.

"She fears Ulfrir," Elvar said. "Fears his wolf-cunning. Fears a trap. She will not risk herself. Wants to see us broken, first."

"Let her try," Grend snarled, and Elvar smiled at him, the spell her fear had cast over her shattering like ice under a stamped heel. It felt good to have him back at her side.

"It is time," Elvar said. "Gytha," and her captain lifted a horn to her lips and blew, long and ringing.

The gates of Wolfdales creaked and began to grind, closing with an echoing crash.

We are locked out, enemies ahead, a cliff behind, Elvar realised. *Ulfrir better pass this test of trust, or it is our lives on the line.* She looked at her war-host. *All of us.*

She strode through the *Berserkirs* and *Úlfhéðnar*, paused to look at them, Thorguna and Frek stepping forwards, their chosen captains.

"You know what to do, remember the plan, keep your beasts on a tight leash," she said, to which there were grunts and heyas and nods, and then she was striding towards Sulich and her shield wall beyond.

Orv the Sneak ran up to her, bow in hand, his quiver full to bursting with arrows.

"Thought I might be of better use with this than in the shield wall to start with, chief, if that's all right with you," he said to her.

"That's fine with me," Elvar said. "Come and join us when you run out of arrows."

"Aye, chief," he said, bobbing his head and moving to join Sulich and his crew.

Elvar shrugged her shield from her back and hefted it, a new shield taken from the supplies brought out from Ulfrir's chamber, as the shield she had been using on the wall was too battered and splintered to last long in the coming clash of shields and steel.

"Make way for Elvar Chainbreaker," Berak called out as they reached the rear of the shield wall. A great roar rose up, her warbands cheering her, ringing and echoing between the stone doors and two spurs of hill as warriors parted and Elvar looked up at the hulking warrior.

"Chainbreaker?" she said as the din faded.

"Aye," Berak grunted, "you have broken our chains, set us free. Your fair-fame will live on forever."

If any of us survive this day to remember it, Elvar thought.

She strode through the centre of the shield wall, warriors parting before her, opening a path.

"Jarl Elvar," Gytha said quietly, leaning closer, "you should rethink your position. If you are lost, your host will crumble."

"No," Elvar said. She knew that what Gytha said made sense, from a tactical point of view, but the tactics were all spoken of and finished now. This next part was about will and heart, about muscle and steel, about strength and courage, and she knew that she was the beating heart of her war-host. She had led them here, and she would fight with them here. Perhaps die with them here.

"I knew you would say no," Gytha said, a smile twitching her lips, "but as your captain I had to say it." Her expression shifted, became serious. "I am honoured to serve you, fight by your side," she said. "You are not your father."

Elvar faltered in her steps, and she looked at Gytha, nodded to her.

And then she saw her Battle-Grim ahead of her, two rows deep set at the front and centre of the shield wall. Sighvat turned and grinned at her, gave her a mock bow, offering her the space in the front row, and she took it with a smile. Grend slotted in on her left, Sighvat on her right, Berak and Gytha and Sólín behind her. She set her shield on the ground, resting her arm, and looked along the line. Saw chiefs and their crews from her mercenary bands either side of the Battle-Grim, beyond them Glornir and his Bloodsworn drawn up on her right flank, on her left flank Orlyg and Dagrun with his *drengrs* and Tainted. She turned her head and saw her *drengrs* lined three deep behind the Battle-Grim.

"Drink," Grend said, thrusting a horn of water to her and she took it and drank deep, knew that the battle-thirst would be on her soon with no chance of slaking it. Other warriors around her drank from cups and waterskins.

Horns blew and Elvar turned again to face Lik-Rifa's war-host. She lifted her shield and drew the slim-hafted axe from Oskutreð at her belt that Grend had given her. Set her feet. Began to pound her axe-haft on the planks of her shield, Sighvat and Grend taking up the rhythm either side of her, until all her shield wall rang with the pounding, beating like a great beast's heart.

Lik-Rifa's war-host flowed into the road between the two hills, coming on like a wave of wood and iron and flesh, and Elvar saw that the Raven-Feeders were at the front and centre, their grey shields and black ravens, and Ilska led them, Drekr snarling in the second row behind her, his long-axe in his fists.

Biórr rose up in her head, dark-haired and sad-eyed, and she felt anger and sadness coil around one another. She searched their ranks, but could not see him.

A hundred paces separated them, and Elvar saw movement at the feet of the Raven-Feeders, saw spertus come scuttling out from between their feet, a black-glistening tide of them, antennae twitching, tails and stings arched high over their backs. They swept forwards and Elvar felt a jolt of fear. In the crush of the shield wall there was no escaping the poisonous creatures. Some of them opened their carapaces and their wings blurred, lifting them into the air.

A hissing from far behind Elvar, like the rising of a strong wind, and arrows were arcing over the warband, falling like hail into the wave of spertus, puncturing their black shells, black blood spurting, skewering them and punching them from the air to fall screeching. Another volley, and another, and another, and the ranks of the spertus thinned.

A score or so were left and they surged forwards, almost on the shield wall now, stings twitching and spasming. A handful were running at Elvar and her part of the wall. One seemed to be looking straight at her, ran at her, its sting darting forward like the lash of a whip. She dropped her shield to stop it running beneath the shield rim and stinging her legs and the spertus' sting cracked into the shield, stuck in the timber, and then Grend was leaning over and chopping with his hand-axe, a fountain of black shell and tar-slick blood and the creature was twitching on the ground. Grend wrenched his axe free and Elvar hacked the sting from her shield and raised it up. Saw another spertus to her left rise into the air on wings, its mouth open, a black cloud like flies issuing from its mouth, and warriors began to scream. One stumbled from the wall, dropping to her knees, clutching at her throat. Elvar saw black veins spreading through her face and the warrior toppled slowly to her side, feet twitching. The cloud of pestilence began to spread along the line and Elvar sucked in a deep breath, held it, heard raised voices behind her.

"*Vetrar vinda, tæta og tæta svarta skýið, dreifa því.*"

A wind surged from behind her shield wall, hissing across her, tugging at her warrior braid, and the black cloud was shredding, whipped away like clouds in a storm. Spears snaked out from the shield wall, punching into the spertus' segmented belly and it was screeching, dropping to the ground.

A horn blast from the rear of Lik-Rifa's shield wall and the last of the spertus were veering away, curling around to scuttle back to the safety of the approaching war-host.

Sulich's archers continued to loose volley after volley, Lik-Rifa's war-host in range now, Elvar hearing the rattle of arrows striking wood, heard screams as some found flesh, saw shields drop in the front row, warriors from the second row stepping forwards, trampling their fallen comrades as they filled the gaps in the wall. They were close, the tramp of feet stirring up a cloud of dust, snarling faces, sharp steel glinting, filling the whole of Elvar's world.

"Chief," Sighvat said, frowning at the onrushing shield wall, "are you sure this is part of your deep-cunning plan?"

Elvar laughed, feeling the surge of fear and excitement, the battle-joy flooding her.

"Elvar," Grend said to her, and she looked at him. "I'll see you after," he said, and grinned at her.

Then with a roar Lik-Rifa's host surged forwards and the shield walls were crashing together.

CHAPTER SIXTY-ONE

VARG

Varg checked his shield was locked with Svik's and Røkia's, set his feet firmly and braced his shoulder into his shield, looking over the top rim to see a wall of linden wood, steel and flesh crashing down upon him.

Brák Trolls-Bane is out there, in that shield wall. May the dead gods grant that he comes against me.

A concussive crash rippled along the line like thunder, clouds of dust swirling up, Varg rocked back by the weight pressing down upon him. Svik grunted beside him, staggered back a pace, Røkia's feet scraping as she slid back.

"No," Varg heard Røkia growl, as if by her very words and will she could resist the mountain crushing down upon them. The weight of the shield wall behind Varg pushed back, steadying him, helping him find his balance. He thrust back, the dust cloud of their collision settling, and he stabbed blindly with his seax over the top rim of his shield, felt the blade scrape off a steel helm. Above him he glimpsed the streak of rune-spells arcing overhead. Grunts and snarls everywhere, thuds and the screech of steel on iron, axes chopping into wood, steel stabbing into flesh. A face loomed before him over a shield rim, a dark-haired woman, a seax snaking out at him. He twisted his head and the seax blade grated on his helm. A twist of his wrist and he knocked the seax to his left, flicked his own blade out and scored a red line down the warrior's forearm. She grunted and drew her blade back, locked eyes with him and they shoved and pushed their shields, each trying to gain an advantage. He felt a burning line of flame across his calf, realised she had stabbed at him beneath his shield and sliced through his leg-wrap and wool breeches, knew that she was a veteran of the shield wall. Gritting his teeth, he ignored the pain that pulsed from his wound, kept his shield locked, holding against hers, with a grunt and shove he pushed, twisted her shield open a handspan and saw Orka Skullsplitter's long-axe hiss over his shoulder and chop into the gap, hacking into dark-hair's shoulder, mail links and blood exploding as Orka ripped the axe back. Dark-hair's shield wavered and dropped as the shoulder wound sapped her strength and Varg stabbed out with his seax, piercing the soft flesh of her throat, a gush of dark blood and she was falling gurgling away, someone stepping forward, filling the gap. Varg snatched a glimpse over his shoulder and nodded his thanks to Orka, who stood with no shield, her long-axe held high, Breca holding a shield to cover her left, Lif with him, and Sæunn to Orka's right. Orka grunted at his nod and then he was facing forwards again. To his right he glimpsed Røkia stab her seax into an eye socket, a shriek cut short, and to his left Svik punched his sword hard at the top rim of a shield, tipping it backwards into a warrior's jaw, Einar's axe snaking out from the row behind Svik, hacking into the warrior's face. An eruption of blood and the warrior was falling.

Another warrior before Varg, a tangle of red beard and a hand-axe chopping at him, grating off the front of his helm, the warrior dragging the axe back, hooking Varg's shield but, anticipating it, he lashed at the axe blade, knocking it loose so that his shield was not pulled down for the spearman in the row behind red-beard to skewer him. Varg crouched behind his shield, stabbing low under the rim, and up, felt his blade find flesh, warm blood sluicing onto his hand as he sawed the blade out, watched red-beard's face drain of colour, mouth opening and Varg realised he'd stabbed the man in the artery in his groin. Red-beard swayed and slumped, hands dragging him back, another figure filling his place, Varg hoping this one would be Brák Trolls-Bane.

The flit and flicker of arrows overhead falling into Lik-Rifa's host, more screams echoing up. The next warrior was growling and hacking at Varg, broad-shouldered and fair-haired, not Brák. Varg snarled in frustration, lashed out with his seax, saw the man twist his head away, realised he was tiring, his limbs heavy, tendons in his wrists burning, eyes stinging from sweat and blood. The wolf in Varg's blood was snapping and snarling, begging to be set loose, and he allowed it to filter through him, sharpening his senses, flooding his muscles and sinews with new strength and speed, and he fought on, pushed, stabbed and chopped, and fair-hair was falling away, replaced swiftly by another. Not Brák. Varg lost track of time, stabbed, and hacked, and sliced, grunting, snarling, spitting, cursing, lost himself to the fog of war. Each attacker, killed in the hope that he'd eventually come face to face with his sister's murderer. An axe chopped over his shield at him, crunched into his shoulder and mail rings tore, a line of blood welling, Varg flicking his seax high over his shield, stabbing down, saw the blade slice along the warrior's jawline, cut through the helm's leather buckle, the helm slipping down, over the warrior's eyes, and Orka's axe crunched down, denting the helm and the warrior dropped. Varg glanced up, saw the sun was dipping above the Iron Wood, became dimly aware that warriors along his front line were stepping back from exhaustion, being replaced by warriors moving up from the third row, but he refused to step away. Brák Trolls-Bane could be the next face to fill the gap in the shield wall before him.

The sound of horns braying, swirling above the combat, and Varg realised it was coming from beyond Lik-Rifa's war-host. A ripple passed through the dragon's shield wall, and then they were disengaging, taking a step back, and another, and another, a gap opening between the two shield walls. Lik-Rifa's host stepped back steadily now, retreating, and all along Varg's line warriors cheered, hurled insults, and jeered. Varg's mouth was too dry for words, no saliva in it. He rested his shield on the ground and reached for the flask of water on his belt, drank deep, wiped blood and sweat from his face, looked at Røkia.

She grinned at him, wild and feral, gore-spattered.

More horns ringing out and Lik-Rifa's shield wall was parting at the middle, a wide path opening up. Creatures scuttled down it, a multitude of angular, sharp-barbed legs, of clustered shining eyes and long, twitching fangs glistening with ice-tinged venom. A tide of frost-spiders flooded through the gap in the shield wall like maggots from a pus-filled wound, spreading along the length of the shield wall, filling the gap between the two hosts. And behind them Varg saw the tall, thick-muscled silhouettes of trolls come lumbering forwards.

He stoppered his waterskin and buckled it back onto his belt. Rolled his shoulders and clicked his neck. Sheathed his seax and drew his cleaver. The day wasn't over yet.

CHAPTER SIXTY-TWO

ORKA

Orka stared at the sea of frost-spiders and the trolls lurking behind them.

"Remember, do *not* let those spiders bite you," she said to Breca, who stood at her side, staring.

"I think that is some advice you should remember, too," Breca said with a small smile.

"Heya," Orka grunted in agreement. The sensation of ice-venom flowing through her veins, numbing her limbs, fogging her head was not one she wanted to repeat.

Some of the spiders took a slow, tentative step towards them.

Orka heard Elvar shout something, and then a horn was blowing, sounding the call to retreat. Somewhere a hilt punched onto a shield, and again, and again, setting a rhythm, and as one Elvar's shield wall began to move backwards, stepping in time to the pounding rhythm.

"Whatever happens, stay with me," Orka grunted at Breca.

"I will, Mama," Breca breathed, clutching his battered shield and spear, a short-axe thrust into his belt.

Voices from the rear of the line, rune-words, and Seiðr-spells of frost and flame arced overhead, exploding amidst the spiders. Limbs and ichor erupted, but there were so many of the spiders that the spells disappeared like pebbles cast into a pool.

A frost-spider scurried forwards, raised its forelegs and bared its fangs, let out a high-pitched, ululating screech, and the sea of spiders was lurching forwards in a stuttering surge. The twang and hiss of arrows from behind Orka, a volley arcing overhead and curving down, another volley loosed before the first one hit, then another, the waves of arrows punching down into the horde of spiders, more Seiðr-spells hissing overhead and crashing into the spiders in eruptions of flame and frost. High-pitched shrieks, spiders rolling and curling, and then they were on the shield wall. Leaping, legs grasping with sharp barbs, fangs clacking. Spears snaked out, axes chopping, swords stabbing, shields punching, and spiders fell.

Spiders hit the wall before Orka, leaping at Varg, Røkia and Svik. They were stabbing and chopping with their blades, spiders falling away in eruptions of blue-tinged fluid, but more scrambled over their corpses, hurling themselves at their shields. A spider wrapped its legs around Varg's shield, one barbed leg snaring Varg's coat of mail and heaving him off balance. Orka's long-axe and Røkia's sword pierced the spider at the same time, and it fell away like a stone, Varg stumbling back into line.

A new horn call and the shield wall retreated faster, the rows at the back peeling away, turning and running, leaving the front few rows to stem the tide of spiders. Warriors were screaming, some dragged from the front row by spiders that clung to them, their shields and all, dragged crashing and rolling to the ground, spider's fangs stabbing. Lif and Sæunn stabbed a spider as it leaped at Breca, skewering it and throwing it from their blades. Another horn call and the shield wall was splitting through the centre, the *Berserkir* and *Úlfhéðnar* striding through them towards the frost-spiders, fists filled with sharp-edged steel, their bodies twitching, muscles bunching, eyes glowing. They broke into a loping, slavering, growling run and hit the frost-spiders like an avalanche, hurled bodies flying into the air, hacked and chopped and sliced and stabbed all about them in a savage frenzy, carving through the spiders, severing limbs, puncturing abdomens, ripping bodies apart with their hands.

"Run for the gates," Orka said to Breca, and he set off, Sæunn and Lif keeping pace with him. About to follow, she saw Varg still staring forwards, even though the press of spiders was gone, all of them turning to their new foe. Orka grabbed Varg's shoulder. "You need to run, *now*," she said.

He looked at her, a fierce, primal twist to his features.

"I think I see him," he snarled, pulling away, staring at the enemy shield wall, Orka following his gaze to where Ilska stood in the front row of the shield wall. She saw Brák Trolls-Bane beside her, Drekr in the row behind.

"If that is Brák Trolls-Bane, he killed my sister," Varg growled, and Orka could see the wolf prowling through Varg's blood.

"Aye, that is Brák," Orka said. "He gave my son the scar he carries beneath his eye." She drew a line with her finger across one cheek. "And you see that man behind him, dark-haired with the long-axe. He is Drekr and he slew my husband." She felt her own wolf growl and snarl, felt a rush of rage, the need for blood and vengeance almost pulling her towards them. "But if we go at them now, we will die, and they will live. That is not vengeance for those we love. That is foolishness." She glowered at Drekr and Brák. "Soon, but not now," she growled.

"The Skullsplitter is right," Svik said, putting his hand on Varg's arm, and Røkia grabbed his wrist.

"Live, No-Sense, and stand over his corpse later," Røkia snarled.

Varg stared at Brák a long moment, then nodded.

"Aye," he said.

A buzzing sound, growing louder, and Orka looked up, over the frost-spiders and Lik-Rifa's shield wall, saw a cloud swirling towards them. Realised what it was.

"HYRNDUR," she yelled, and then she was turning and running with Varg, Svik and Røkia on her heels.

The buzzing grew louder, and Orka felt the ground shaking, snatched a look over her shoulder and saw the trolls lumbering, breaking into a run, roaring.

Then the hyrndur were overhead, swirling in looping circles, some sweeping down upon the *Berserkir*, *Úlfhéðnar* and fleeing warriors from the shield wall. Orka saw a cluster of the giant hornets swirl around a warrior's head as they ran, flying into the gaps in their helm, the warrior stumbling, ripping at the helm, tearing the leather strap and hurling it away. It was a fair-haired woman, huge swollen lumps already showing on her face and neck. She opened her mouth to scream and a hyrndur flew into it, the sting on its abdomen striking at her tongue. She staggered and fell, batting at her face, eyes bulging. More screams rang out throughout the fleeing warriors, even *Berserkir* roaring and frothing in agony.

"*Eldnet, gríptu þá, brenndu þá, breyttu í ösku,*" Orka heard voices cry out and runes were crackling to life ahead of her, before the stone doors of Wolfdales. They spun in the air, rolling slowly forwards like wheels of fire, growing, merging, turning into a net of crackling flame that stretched across the length of the road, protecting the retreating shield wall. It scythed through the hyrndur in the air, a ripple of sizzling hisses and pops as the hyrndur were incinerated, reduced to flakes of ash. The first of the trolls was almost upon them and it swung its great club at the rune-net, wrapping it around the club and dragging it from the sky. The stench of scorched wood, the club burst into flames, and strands of the net draped across the troll's head and shoulder. A hiss and sizzle of burning flesh, the troll bellowing its pain, throwing the burning club to the ground, pulling the remnants of the net with it, ripping great tracks of blistering flesh from the troll's head and face. It dropped to its knees, thrashing in a frenzy of pain, and slowly toppled to the ground, flattening a handful of frost-spiders beneath it, a cloud of dust and charred smoke erupting around it.

Orka ran on, Breca ahead of her, Lif and Sæunn with him and Vesli winging above them, a short spear in one of her long-fingered fists. There were shouts and screams behind her, and glancing back she saw a troll stabbing at Svik with a spear as thick as a sapling. He swerved, the spear grating sparks on the stone road, Svik leaping over a fallen warrior, snaring his foot and falling, the troll rearing over him, raising its spear.

Orka snarled, hefted her long-axe and ran back.

Varg hit the troll first, dropping his shield and leaping, swinging his cleaver two-handed over his head, burying it deep into the meat of the troll's knee. It bellowed and swung the spear at Varg as he dropped to the ground and rolled, the spear hissing over his head, then Røkia was there, scoring a red line with her sword down the troll's calf, turning and slashing at its hamstring. The troll took an unsteady step and stumbled, dropped to one knee as Orka swung her axe two-handed, chopping into the meat of its waist, carving deep. She ripped the axe free, a gush of blood and the troll roared its pain, swiped at her with a fist large as a boulder. Orka threw herself away, crunching on the ground, rolled, came to one knee and saw Røkia clambering up the troll's back. The troll flailed at her but Røkia evaded the grasping hand and climbed nimbly onto its shoulder, stabbed with her sword deep to the hilt into the meat between neck and shoulder, ripped her sword free and leaped from the troll's back. It stumbled a few steps, swayed, let out a roar and toppled to the ground, blood pooling around it.

Svik scrambled to his feet, looked at Orka, Varg and Røkia and grinned, "My thanks, but I could have taken him."

Røkia rolled her eyes and they all ran for the gates.

CHAPTER SIXTY-THREE

ELVAR

Elvar strode between the two stone wolves that were still crouched and snarling on guard, and made her way to the doors of Ulfrir's hall, Grend, Gytha and Berak at her shoulder, the Battle-Grim around her. She turned, looked back.

The vale of Wolfdales seethed with combat. Her shield wall was broken now, in full retreat, many running for the gates. She saw *Berserkir* and *Úlfhéðnar* holding the tide of frost-spiders at bay, saw trolls lumbering towards her, bellowing and swinging their clubs and spears. Watched one roaring as a handful of *Úlfhéðnar* swarmed around and over it, like a wolf pack bringing down a bull elk, saw Sulich and his archers releasing one more volley at a troll before turning and sprinting for the gates. And behind them all the ringing of horns drifted on the ice wind, and Lik-Rifa's shield wall lurched into motion, marching at a steady beat towards them. Elvar glanced at the stone gates and sheer slope behind her.

They will seek to crush us, like wheat between two quern stones.

"Gytha, now," she said, and Gytha raised the horn from her belt and blew, three sharp blasts echoing off the stone doors that reared above them.

Open.

The doors remained closed, still and silent and brooding.

"Open," Elvar snarled. Heard the cries of battle, the rumbling thunder of the approaching war-host, knew that if they remained closed any longer her war-host would be crushed.

"Open," she pleaded. "Ulfrir, open the doors."

A shiver ran through the stone doors, a creaking rumble, and they lurched into movement, opening a crack, then wider. Skuld came swooping out, her red hair and wings blazing in the light of the sinking sun, and she swept up into the sky, looped and sped down, Elvar seeing her bow drawn in her fist. The thrum of an arrow loosed, and it punched down to the fletching into the eye of a troll. The huge vaesen ran on a few steps, legs faltering, abruptly loose, and it crashed to the ground, people leaping out of its way.

Elvar's warriors were pouring through the gates now, into the chamber, a river sweeping past her, Elvar urging them on. Her *Berserkir* and *Úlfhéðnar* disengaged from their frenzied attack and started to retreat, overtaking trolls, hacking at them as they sprinted past.

A knot of trolls was close, hammering with clubs at whoever was in reach. Elvar saw a troll skewer a *Berserkir* with the blade of its spear, lift him into the air and hurl him into the slopes of the hill. And then, with a sound like rocks grinding, the two stone wolves either side of the doors were moving, first pacing forwards, then loping, then running, snarling, leaping as their jaws opened wide. They crashed into the knot of trolls, one's jaws clamping around the head of a troll, both of them crashing to the ground and rolling, the other one latching onto a troll's arm and dragging it spinning around, shaking its head like a dog with a rat and there was a wet, tearing sound as the troll's arm was ripped from its shoulder. It bellowed in agony, blood jetting, and crashed to the ground. The other stone wolf was on top of the troll, snarling and ripping great chunks of flesh in bursts of blood, the troll's limbs flailing, then flopping, and the two wolves were turning, crouched, leaping again.

One troll clubbed one of the wolves across the head, sent it crashing to the ground in an explosion of grey stone and dust, the wolf tumbling, coming up on all fours with one ear and part of its head gone. Another troll came up on its side, club swinging, crunching into the wolf's ribs, another explosion of stone and dust, the wolf whining. Then the second wolf was leaping onto the back of the troll, ripping at its neck, blood spraying, the troll staggering, arms and club flailing, trying to reach the wolf on its back, its club striking another troll in the shoulder, sending it toppling to the ground.

The bulk of Elvar's warriors were through the open doors now, the last of the Bloodsworn passing through, *Berserkir* and *Úlfhéðnar* close, some in running battles with frost-spiders, and Elvar saw hyrndur flitting and skimming into the hall. Lik-Rifa's shield wall was looming close, only two or three hundred paces away, and between them and the doors the trolls and stone wolves were savaging each other.

More trolls had circled the stone wolves, clubbing and stabbing at them, the wolves snapping, snarling and leaping, jaws crushing flesh, but the trolls were penning them in. A blur of red wings and Skuld swooped out of the sky and flew among them, her bow thrumming, arrows sprouting from a troll's chest, another from a throat, another in a troll's belly, and Elvar saw a blue-glowing arrow streak through the air, punch into a troll's mouth as it opened it to roar, traced it back and saw Orv standing close to her, his rune-bow thrumming.

She glanced from the wolves and trolls to the oncoming shield wall.

"Inside," Elvar said to her guards about her, "Ulfrir must close the doors."

"The wolves?" Sighvat said.

She glanced at them.

"Inside." She said and led her guards through the open doors. Knots of battle were raging, Elvar seeing frost-spiders, and hyrndur swirling in small clusters.

Ulfrir was standing in his wolf-form at the foot of the ash tree's trunk, cloaked in shadow, eyes glowing amber, still and menacing. A few score *Úlfhéðnar* stood at his feet. He saw Elvar, raised his head and howled, and the doors shifted, began grating closed. The sound of wolves snarling from beyond the gates, a crash, trolls bellowing, the two stone wolves leaping through the closing doors, Skuld skimming above them in a blur of wings, a troll lumbering through after them as the gates slammed shut with a resounding crash.

The troll stumbled to a halt, looked about it and began hammering at people with its club, an explosion of blood and bone as it squashed one of Elvar's *drengrs* to pulped gruel.

Ulfrir snarled and padded forwards, leaped and swept the troll up in his jaws, shook it like a rat and blood rained down in a fountain, one of the troll's severed legs landing with a wet splat.

Elvar looked around her, saw her warriors surrounding the frost-spiders that had slipped into the great hall, saw Vol, Uspa and Iva using their rune-spells to finish off the hyrndur that were buzzing around the chamber. And then she heard a deep-rumbling scream, loud and echoing.

Hrung.

She broke into a run, sprinted around the bulk of the ash tree to see Hrung upon his pedestal on the dais, a frost-spider wrapped around his head, fangs striking at his pale flesh.

She rushed forwards, her shield in one fist, her slim axe in the other, heard the thud of footsteps behind her, reached the dais and leaped onto it, raised her axe, but before she reached it the frost-spider crumpled and fell away from Hrung's head, landing on its back with its legs curled. Elvar skidded to a halt and looked down at it.

Grend reached her side and poked the spider with his axe.

"Dead as a stone," he pronounced.

"That's it," Hrung said, "everyone worry about the spider. W . . . w . . . what about me?"

Elvar noticed two blue-tinged lumps on Hrung's cheek and saw that his lips were starting to turn blue.

"You?" Grend said. "You're going to start feeling numb soon. So numb that you won't be able to talk." He smiled.

"Well, th . . . th . . . that's nice," Hrung said, then his eyes glazed over with ice.

"Can we keep one of those things alive," Grend said, nudging the dead frost-spider with his boot.

CHAPTER SIXTY-FOUR

BIÓRR

Biórr stepped onto a raft and pushed off from the riverbank with his spear, others dipping rough-shaped oars into the water and beginning to row. The current dragged them downriver, but it was not long before they were at the other side, the raft sliding into a silted bank and Rotta was jumping onto soft earth and striding up the riverbank.

They had passed through deep forest, shadowing the curve of the river around the great hill of Wolfdales and, as Biórr leaped from the raft onto the riverbank, he heard screams, faint on the wind. The sun was a red line above the forest now, day leaking from the world, and shadows stretched and merged all about him.

Rotta was standing at the foot of a steep slope, the others already gathered about him. A dozen warriors, all with Rotta's rat-blood in their veins.

"Well, no point just staring at it," Rotta said as he looked up at the slope. "We've got to get up there, so we might as well be doing it as thinking about it." With that he set off, scrambling through thick grass.

Biórr looked up at the slope, saw that it climbed steadily for a while, then steepened again, became almost a sheer cliff. He rolled his shoulders, settling his shield on his back and set off after Rotta.

Darkness fell about them swiftly, but there were few clouds and the winter's moon was bright, so Biórr could see his way well enough. By the time he reached the point where the slope steepened again, he was breathing hard, and he paused for a moment.

Rotta was already scaling the cliff, a darker shadow in the encroaching night zigzagging his way up the almost sheer wall as he found seams in the rock. Biórr bent and untied the knots on his turn-shoes, took them off, and his nålbinding socks, too, and stuffed the shoes and socks into his belt. He would need bare feet for this. He focused on the rat in his blood.

Help me, old friend, to find the safe way, to be nimble and deft, to cling, to climb.

He felt a wash of strength flood through him, felt the bones and nails of toes and fingers lengthen and harden. He started climbing the rock face, finding variations in the surface that would have been invisible without his god-blood, clinging to them with his long fingers and deft toes, slowly winding his way up the cliff. He paused at one point, looked back down and saw the shadowed forms of those other rat-blood infused warriors with him, a breadcrumb trail winding up the rock face. Glancing up, he could see the dark line of the cliff-top, a silver glow of moonlight shimmering above it. He climbed on, the cold wind swirling, tugging at his braided hair and the hem of his tunic beneath his *brynja.* His sword hilt snared in a knotted clump of rock and dragged him back, one hand slipping free. He hung suspended a long, timeless moment, and then a hand was reaching down to him, long, strong fingers wrapping around his wrist and hauling him up.

"Would be a shame to fall when you're almost at the top," Rotta said to him with a smile.

Biórr moved to take his socks and shoes from his belt.

"Wait for that," Rotta said, and Biórr nodded, looking around while they waited for the others to reach them. The wind blew harder and colder up here, hissing, ebbing and flowing in his ears like the lapping roar of the sea. He was standing upon the gently slopping crown of a hill, the dark ocean of the Iron Wood spread around them. As he looked, he saw pinprick fires flicker into life along both edges of the riverbank, realised that it was Lik-Rifa's war-host making camp.

Well, we are not beaten, then. Although we have not won, either, or Lik-Rifa would be inside this dark hole of a wolf-den already.

Skadi's slim face appeared over the edge of the cliff, and he scrambled up to join them, the last of Rotta's hand-picked rat-blood crew.

"Well, as much as the view is wonderful, we should be moving on," Rotta said, and he led them up the gentle slope of the hill. The grass was stiff and damp beneath Bíórr's feet and he saw the peak of a large tree ahead, Rotta leading them around it in a wide circle, until they had moved from one side of it to the other. Rotta was crouched now, eyes bright in the moonlight, nose twitching as he chose his path with care. Bíórr and all those behind him emulated Rotta, moving swiftly, then crouching still and silent for long moments, the grass sighing about them.

Another swift scuttle through the grass and Rotta stopped in the shadows of a ruined, vine-wrapped tower. Crawled around it, stopping at what Bíórr saw must have been an old entrance. It was piled with fallen rubble now, clogged with earth and grass growing in thick tufts. A dark shadow marked a ragged seam no wider than a man's open hand. Rotta unbuckled his weapons belt and slithered out of his *brynja* and handed them to Bíórr.

"Pass them through to me in a moment," he said, and he stuck his nose into the seam, sniffing and snuffling, his long-clawed rat-hands probing the edges. He pressed his body into the seam, stretching, elongating, his new form squashing through the impossibly narrow gap. Then he was gone.

Bíórr shrugged off his shield, unbuckled his weapons belt, wrapping it around his sword and seax, wriggled out of his *brynja*. Began to feed Rotta's kit and his own through the gap and saw Rotta's long-fingered hand reach out from the darkness for them.

"Come on," Rotta hissed from the darkness once Bíórr had passed everything through.

Bíórr closed his eyes and felt the rat in his blood. Gave it full sway, felt it surge and run and scamper through his veins, felt the tingling power, the fear and savagery, inextricably bound, and moved, sliding into the ragged slash of darkness that separated the rubble and grass, felt his flesh squeezing into the gap, felt his bones soften and compress, ribs bending like saplings, a pressure building within him, every part of him becoming more pliable. The world pressing in upon him, a claustrophobic darkness squeezing him, and with a gasp he was through, falling into blackness, his bones springing back into place, the rat in his blood exultant.

We are safe in the dark, the rat whispered to him.

Biórr blinked, the rat in him filtering and sifting the darkness until he could see outlines, the black shifting to grey. Rotta's sharp-lined face appearing. He was holding out Biórr's kit and he took it, looked around and saw he was in a small space, not quite large enough to stand straight, just wide enough for Rotta's crew to squeeze into. He dressed as the others crammed into the space, putting his woollen socks and turn shoes back on, his *brynja* and weapons belt.

"You all may be wondering why you are here," Rotta said to them, once the last warrior had made it into this tight space.

Some grunts and heyas.

"Ulfrir's lair has a number of entrances, but all of them are sealed with some Seiðr-rune or other," Rotta said. He crouched down to the rotted frame of a huge trapdoor, Biórr seeing the hint of steps in the shadows beneath it, and rapped his knuckles on what should have been open space. A crackle and flare of blue light rippled out from his knuckles, like waves from a stone cast into a pool. "You see, this entrance is barred by Seiðr."

"So why are we trying to sneak in, if every way is barred?" Skadi asked.

"Ulfrir is very big on *pack*," Rotta said. "On family. Orna his wife and their children together spent much time with him here, perhaps that is why he has returned here," he mused. "Anyway, all of Ulfrir's pack, all of his family knew the words of power that would give them access to his home." He was silent, eyes looking elsewhere.

"So how does that help us get in?" Skadi asked him.

Rotta's eyes snapped back into focus, and he smiled.

"I flayed the skin from one of his daughters while she was still alive," he said. "You would be surprised at what comes out of a person's mouth when they are subjected to such . . . extremes."

He placed his splayed fingers upon the Seiðr-barrier, crackles of blue light around each of his fingertips.

"*Turn úlfsins, opinn fyrir úlfaflokkinn,*" Rotta whispered, and the Seiðr-barrier flared and melted away. Rotta grinned at them and took a few steps down the stairwell beneath the trapdoor.

"Skalk, Estrid?" Rotta hissed.

A silence, then a voice whispered back.

"Here."

CHAPTER SIXTY-FIVE

ELVAR

Elvar sipped from a horn of mead as she sat in a new chair that had been brought up onto the dais for her. It was smaller than Ulfrir's which, truth be told, was far more comfortable for her. She no longer felt like a child sitting in a chair where her feet did not reach the ground. And now that Ulfrir was free, it felt redundant and petty for her to continue to enforce her authority through such gestures. She did not need to worry about his rebellions. The blood oath would look after that for her.

"It has gone well," Ulfrir said to her as he sat in his own chair with a plate of roasted salmon, fried potatoes and onions, Skuld standing at his shoulder. She had a cut beneath one eye, but other than that had returned to the chamber uninjured. Elvar's jaw throbbed, a bruise swelling there from a shield rim smashed into her face. Every part of her ached, every muscle, every joint, every sinew was pulsing, exhaustion lying upon her limbs like a heavy cloak.

"Aye," Elvar said, though she looked towards the section of the chamber that had been turned into a bay for the wounded, and then she glanced to the stone doors. It was a weight that sat heavy in her soul, knowing that warriors lay dead in the vale, and that it had been her decisions that had caused those deaths.

"You think she will come tomorrow?" Elvar said.

"I do," Ulfrir growled, Elvar feeling the hairs on her neck stir. "Lik-Rifa thinks me weak, thinks I have come here to recover, but she will have suspected a trap. And now she has seen our forces pushed back by her war-host and I have done nothing to stem that. Done nothing to help them." He shrugged. "She will feel . . . reassured, that she was right, that I am not strong enough to fight, that I fear her. So, tomorrow, if you march out and set your wall of shields, then retreat, pretend to be broken and run, and we leave the doors open longer, allow her forces to push into this chamber. She will come, I am sure of it, and then . . ." He smiled, a sharp-toothed grin. "She will die."

"Tomorrow, then. Good," Elvar said, although it was late now, must be almost tomorrow already. Absently she ran a hand over her forearm, could feel the coiled ridges of the white scars of her *blóð svarið* beneath her woollen tunic. She looked to Uspa, who stood close by, tending to Hrung, who was still blue-tinged, water dripping in pools from the tattered flesh of his neck.

"Uspa, is there any word? Any sign?" The ravens Grok and Kló had been searching for signs of the Tainted children among Lik-Rifa's war-host. Searching for Bjarn, who was the grindstone that had set this war-mill into motion.

"No," Uspa said, a weight of feeling behind that one word.

"We shall find him," Berak growled, who stood with Uspa.

"We shall," Elvar echoed. "Tomorrow, when the dragon is dead."

Ulfrir stood and stretched like a hound, or a wolf. "I am for my bed. Even a god must sleep, and tomorrow shall be a hammer-hard day. A red day." He paused. "I am free," he said, gave a gentle smile. "Sometimes I forget, think that the collar is still about my neck." He looked at Elvar. "You have done a rare thing. Though there is a sharp sword-edge to it," he added, tracing the outline of the blood-oath scar that wound around his arm. "That was some deep-thinking, and it will no doubt give me a lifetime of inconvenience and trouble, *treating all fairly, enforcing justice*." He nodded to himself, "But it was a good thing, and much better than a life with the iron collar."

"Heya," Berak grunted.

Elvar looked around at them all. "I did what I must," she said.

"No," Ulfrir shook his head. "You did not have to do it, and I thank you for that."

"We all thank you for that," Skuld said. And then they were walking from the dais, *Úlfhéðnar* drifting from the shadows of the chamber to follow Ulfrir to his den.

"Sleep, that sounds good," Elvar said. She stood, felt the ache of muscles and joints that only a fjord-deep sleep would cure. Hrung groaned, his eyes blinking.

"So c . . . c . . . cold," he mumbled.

Elvar paused, walked to Hrung.

"*Hlýju,*" Uspa said and Elvar saw a soft-glow of heat ripple around her hands. The Seiðr-witch placed them upon Hrung's face, heat radiating.

"Ahh, but that f . . . f . . . feels good," Hrung shivered. The opaque swirl of his eyes focused on Uspa. "Did I ever tell you that I love you, Snaka's child? If I had arms, I would wrap them around you and kiss you."

"Ha, you are making me glad that you are just a head," Uspa said, shifting the position of her hands and massaging warmth into him.

"And if you had arms and tried to do that, then I would chop them off," Berak rumbled.

"Ha, well, it is best for all that I do not have my arms then," Hrung said, a deep-rumbling laugh echoing from his wide lips. He glanced down at the dead spider still curled at the base of his pedestal and scowled.

"I am glad to see you awake," Elvar said. "There is something I would talk of with you."

"Well, then, let us talk, dear Elvar. These days it is all that I can do."

"I am not so sure of that," she said.

Elvar strode through the great hall. Many warriors were still eating, others sitting around fires, drinking, talking, laughing, some staring silently into the flames. She saw the Bloodsworn and Battle-Grim sitting together, Sighvat locked in an arm-wrestle with Einar Half-Troll, warriors around them shouting encouragements and swapping coin and hacksilver. Veins bulged on both of them, muscles bunching, straining, and Taras stood laughing behind Einar, the sound of it booming through the chamber. Glornir sat talking with Vol and

Orka, Breca sat upon the big man's lap, and Vesli the tennúr was sitting on Breca's shoulder.

Elvar passed through it all and made her way up the stairwell about the great tree, stepped into her bed-chamber, felt each step was like dragging a weight of iron wrapped around her legs. Torches burned in sconces hammered into the stone walls, sending shadows stretching. She unpinned the brooch of her bearskin cloak and draped it across the back of a chair, slipped off her baldric and scabbarded sword, hung it over the same chair, unbuckled her weapons belt with seax and the axe Grend had given her and set that over the chair, too, then sat on her bed. Grend and Gytha were with her, and Sólín and Thorguna.

Elvar was talking tactics, of rising with the dawn, of which warbands and crews to set in the shield wall and where to put them.

Grend took her hand in his, smiled at her, which was a rare thing for him.

"What?" Elvar said.

"You have changed the world," he said, squeezing her hand. To her surprise she saw tears well in his eyes. "Though it counts for little, I am prouder of you than words can express."

"It counts for much," she whispered.

"As for the morrow, you have done all you can. Sleep, now, Elvar," Grend said. "And when you wake we shall slay a dragon."

"Aye," Elvar said.

Grend leaned forwards and kissed her gently on the cheek, like a father settling his child before bed, and he and Gytha left by the door in the rear of Elvar's chamber, leading into the tunnel where Gytha's rooms were situated.

Elvar stared after him a long moment. Nodded and let out a long sigh.

"Sólín, Thorguna, you have fought well, made a song for the skálds," Elvar said to her guards.

"Retht, chief," Sólín said, and Elvar lay back, glimpsed Thorguna taking up her place of guard in the shadows of the tree-branch entrance, and Sólín moving to stand near the rear door. Then sleep was sweeping over her like a great wave.

CHAPTER SIXTY-SIX

BIÓRR

Biórr crept through the corridors of Wolfdales, scurrying to the shadows that nestled between the glow and flicker of wall-mounted torches. Some of the tunnels they had travelled were huge, big enough for Rotta to pass through in his rat-body, but now they were moving along smaller tunnels, fashioned for more human-sized bodies. Ever downwards they had crept, Biórr, Rotta and the other rat-bloods, led by Skalk and his fair-haired *drengr*, passing by open entrances to other tunnels and closed, thick-carved doors. Most of the tunnels were empty, rooms and chambers uninhabited. They had only come across two people so far, and they had been in a chamber with the door open, two naked bodies thrusting and groaning, perhaps celebrating surviving the first day of this battle. They had not survived into the second, Skadi and another staining the bed with their blood.

Biórr's rat-senses were twitching and tingling now, every sound shuddering through him, every scent that drifted through the damp corridors causing him to shiver.

We are in the lair of the wolf, he thought, *and the wolf is no friend to rats.* He knew that to be seen now, to be discovered, would mean his death, and the rat in his blood was just as aware of that possibility. Its instinct was to flee, to seek darkness and safety, but Biórr knew there was a savagery to the beast in his blood, too, a courage of sorts, especially when the rat was cornered. But to walk willingly into the lair of his enemy, that took a different type of courage. Biórr tried to speak that courage to his beast, encourage it to overrule the almost overwhelming instinct to flee. So far he was managing to do that. Just.

"I know your struggle," Rotta whispered to him as they paused in the shelter of shadow between two torches, Skalk and his *drengr* moving on ahead. "This is not what I want to be doing, either. The last time I saw Ulfrir he was chaining me to a rock and dripping serpent venom onto my face." Rotta grimaced and snarled. "But sometimes the only way to get a job done properly is to do it yourself."

"Yes, lord," Biórr whispered.

"And besides, I am sure that you will enjoy seeing Elvar one last time. It will be fitting that you strike the blow that will end this war, strike a blow into the slaver's heart."

"Aye," Biórr growled.

Elvar. He remembered the last time he had seen her, the anguish of his betrayal reflected in her face, then the anger.

But she had no right. She was the one happy to hunt down and enslave us Tainted, happy to sell us for coin or hacksilver to the highest bidder. She is the one who has thralled a god.

Yet he also remembered the brush of her lips on his, the touch of her hand upon his scars. The warmth in her eyes as she had lain with him, looked at him as if he *mattered.*

Skalk beckoned to them, and Rotta ran light-footed and silent through the torchlight, passing another oak door and on to the next patch of shadow, Biórr and the other rat-bloods following him. Estrid, her *drengrs* and the mercenary chief named Hjalmar had been sent elsewhere in this underground nest of tangled tunnels.

"There," Skalk hissed, pointing. He stood at a curve in the tunnel and Biórr leaned to see a wide-arched door that sat at the end of the corridor. "She is in there."

Rotta waited for the other warriors to reach them, and then he was leading them down the corridor. They reached the door and Rotta turned to Biórr.

"The honour is yours," Rotta whispered. "Do this and your name will live forever in your skáld-songs, a saga greater than the Guðfalla. Do this and you will change the world."

Biórr drew his sword, almost without sound because of the sheepskin and grease that lined the leather scabbard, and he put his hand on the ring-handle of the door.

Turned it. A soft click, and he pushed the door. It slid open.

Shadows in the chamber, the flicker of torchlight, at the far end of the room a wide-arched opening, the exit from the bedchamber that Skalk had told them of, that led into the great hall. Faint light pulsed beyond the circular exit, the movement of air and sound suggesting a vast open space beyond it.

He took a slow, careful step into the room, let his rat-blood adjust his vision. He saw a wide bed, a chair beside it, a dark cloak slung over it, belts and weapons draped over the cloak. He blinked, stared, recognised that cloak.

Agnar's bearskin. It is true, then, Elvar became chief.

A dark shape spread on the bed, a deeper shadow, Biórr seeing arms and legs, the glint of a mail coat, a shock of blonde-braided hair.

He lifted his sword.

"CHIEF," a voice screeched as a figure lunged at him from the shadows, a bright spear-point slicing towards him.

CHAPTER SIXTY-SEVEN

ELVAR

Elvar woke with a jolt, not knowing where she was. Sounds filtered through to her. Shouting, the clash of steel. The world came crashing in and she heard Sólín's voice, lunged for the chair with her weapons, grabbed her sword and ripped it from its scabbard, gripped the slim-hafted axe with her other hand, turned.

Flickers and crackles of blue light as Sólín traded blows with a shadowed form, her Oskutreð-spear illuminating the room in stark, fractured bursts with each strike and swing of the blade. She was pushing a warrior back towards the open door, other, shadowed forms pressing through and around the figure and then Sólín was stepping forwards, stabbing. A gurgled gasp, Sólín ripping her spear from a warrior's throat, dark blood spurting. Elvar jumped onto the bed, heard Sólín grunt and saw her crumple around a sword in her belly, saw her drop to her knees as the sword was ripped free in a spray of *brynja* rings and blood.

"SÓLÍN," Elvar yelled and leaped. Glimpsed Thorguna come roaring across the room, an avalanche of muscle and mail, an axe in each fist. Elvar crashed into the knot of figures, sent them falling as Sólín sagged to the floor. Elvar struggled with someone, her sword arm pinned beneath the figure, snarled and raised her hand-axe, chopped down hard and felt it crunch into bone, a splatter of blood across her face, a form slumping beneath her, Thorguna roaring above her, the sound of steel chopping through mail into flesh, screams and a hand was grabbing Elvar and hauling her to her feet. She stood there gasping, took a step back to stand shoulder to shoulder with Thorguna, saw Sólín on the ground, lying in a pool of her own blood, lifeless eyes staring. Felt a flush of rage at that. Other bodies lay tangled on the floor, great red wounds in their flesh from Thorguna's axes, just one figure rising from the heap. A dark-haired man, a sword in his fist. Elvar raised her sword and axe, and froze.

It was Biórr.

He looked at her with his dark, sad eyes, more beard on his face now, his hair braided, two black raven-feathers tied into it with silver wire. Still handsome.

"Kill her," a voice from the shadows snapped. Figures loomed behind Biórr, pressing through the open door in a cluster, and he lunged at her. She swept the blow away with her sword, took a step back as he backswung at her head, and Thorguna did not wait for the others. With a ravening, blood-curdling howl she threw herself in a spitting, frothing frenzy at them, axes swinging. Voices screamed, shouting, Elvar stepping to her right and slashing her sword at Biórr's shoulder, saw him move to block, which opened up his right side, and Elvar snaked her hand-axe out, so light it was adder-fast, scoring a red line across Biórr's cheek and neck, chopping through *brynja* rings as if they were leather, and she was stepping back.

"I am going to bleed you, for Agnar," Elvar snarled at him.

"Agnar the *slaver*, you mean," Biórr hissed, a new glint in his eyes, flecked colours spiralling, and his sword was stabbing at her, faster than she thought possible, forcing her back, step by shuffling step. A lunge, followed by an overhead swing, Elvar stepping away, the blade catching her shoulder and arm, her coat of mail holding, a flicked wrist and the sword tip was coming for her throat, a frantic sweep of her arm to deflect it, swung with her axe but Biórr was no longer there, pivoted on her left foot to take herself out of range, but he was on her. A flurry of blows, Elvar's sword and axe just blocking each one, and they were stepping apart, both breathing heavily, Elvar almost at the doorway to the tree branch that led out of her chamber into the great hall.

Behind Biórr Elvar saw that Thorguna was carving red ruin, holding all who were trying to press in through the doorway.

"Oh, this is ridiculous," she heard a voice say. "Skalk, end this."

She saw a flicker of red flames around the tip of a wooden staff. Heard a voice.

"*Færa, kasta,*" the voice cried out. There was a crack that rippled through the floor and Thorguna and all those in the doorway were hurled into the room, falling and tumbling, Elvar and Biórr staggered, too, stumbling back a handful of paces onto the platform beyond her room. More warriors swept into the chamber, five or six of them, followed by two men. Skalk, and Rotta, tall and smiling.

"For goodness' sake, get up," he said to the warriors who had fallen, then looked at Biórr. "We do not have time for this, I have things to do. End her."

Thorguna was clambering to her feet, stepping back and sweeping her axes up, growling and beckoning at the warriors surrounding her, stabbing at her and stepping away, worrying at her like hounds around a bear. Biórr came at Elvar again. The clash and grate of steel, sparks flying, and Elvar was forced back one step at a time, off the platform and into the stairwell carved into the tree, heard voices shouting from far below. A horn rang out.

Biórr's sword snaked through her defence, stabbed into her belly, but her *brynja* held, though the wind was knocked from her, and she stumbled back, gasping for air. Behind Biórr she heard Thorguna roar, saw blood streaming from a wound in her shoulder, Rotta leaning against a timber column with his arms folded, and then the warriors spread around her were turning, shouting, Elvar glimpsing Grend and Gytha burst through the doorway behind them, both of them mail-clad, shields and sharp steel in their fists.

More voices from below, more horns blowing in the great hall.

"Finish her, or I will," Rotta shouted at Biórr.

Elvar shuffled back, one step, two, put her weight on her back foot. Biórr stepped after her and she pushed off hard from her back foot, straight at Biórr, raised her arm as he swung at her, trusting her Oskutreð *brynja* to hold. Felt a crunch in her side and a rib crack, maybe two, swept her arm down to wrap around Biórr's sword arm, trapping it, stepped in close and head-butted him across the bridge of his nose, a burst of blood, and she was leaning, hooking her axe behind his leg and wrenching it back, slicing it through muscle and sinew. They staggered together, locked in a grip, turned half a circle so Biórr was stumbling back down the branch towards the trunk of the tree, and he was tripping, falling, slamming onto his back. Elvar kicked his sword from his grip, sent it tumbling off the branch and into air and stamped on his wrist, touched her sword point to his throat.

"You *niðing* betrayer," she snarled.

"You have betrayed us all, thralled a god," he shouted back at her. "You are worse than Agnar, worse than all of them."

"I have set Ulfrir free, set *all* the Tainted free," she growled down at him, hating him, and yet something stayed her hand.

"You have done what?" he said, eyes widening.

"Did your rat-god not bother to tell you? Ulfrir and the Tainted are free."

The soft scrape of swift footsteps behind her, she half turned, felt a hand across her forehead, a grip like iron, twisted.

"You should have chosen the rat, not the wolf," a voice snarled into her ear. There was an impact on her neck, like a punch.

"No," she heard Biórr's voice shout.

She opened her mouth to speak, but could not, choking on something in her throat. She coughed, hot blood gushing out in an explosion from her mouth. Then the hand holding her head was gone, other hands pushing her, and she was stumbling towards the edge of the stairwell, legs weak, falling. Distantly, as if from a far way off, she heard Grend scream.

CHAPTER SIXTY-EIGHT

VARG

Varg ran from the Bloodsworn's sleeping chamber, still blinking sleep from his eyes and slipping his shield across his back, horns ringing and echoing. He followed Glornir and a handful of others, the rest of the Bloodsworn behind him, sprinted through a wide corridor and hurtled into the great hall. Skidded to a stop behind Glornir and Vol and looked around, trying to make sense of it all.

"There'd better be a good reason for waking me," Svik growled as he ran up to stop beside Varg. "I haven't even had time for a mouthful of cheese."

Warriors were fighting before the doors, steel clashing, screams and battle cries. Varg saw Elvar's *drengrs* with their backs to the doors, and many of those fighting against them bore shields with two black-scrolled ravens upon them, others with the eagle of Darl.

"Hjalmar's Fell-Hearted," Glornir growled and hefted his long-axe.

"Estrid and her *drengrs*, too," Svik grunted. "Oath-breaking scum."

A scream from high above, Varg watching as a body fell from one of the thick branches of the great tree. It plummeted, limbs loose, spinning, and crunched to the ground before Varg and Glornir, the crackle of bones shattering, blood exploding, spattering in a wide circle. A warrior in mail, blonde braided hair. One arm twisted unnaturally, the woollen sleeve pulled up. A white-coiling scar on her forearm.

"Elvar," Glornir breathed.

No. A wave of shock tremored through Varg, horror sweeping him at the sight of her. Elvar, who had brought this war-host together, who had stood against the dragon and the rat, led them against Lik-Rifa's war-host, set the Tainted free.

A man screaming high above them, Varg letting the wolf filter into his blood, his vision and hearing sharpening. He saw Grend standing on the branch high above, staring down at Elvar's corpse, others behind him fighting on the platform of Elvar's bed-chamber. Warriors running at Grend. Movement on the stairwell, a cluster of figures hurrying down towards the chamber's floor.

The din of battle from before the doors grew higher, more frantic.

"We are betrayed," Røkia said as she stepped close to Varg.

"They seek to open the doors," Vol said.

"Well, let's put an end to that," Glornir growled, the Bloodsworn moving behind him at a loping run. The combat was too dispersed for the shield wall, so they formed a loose line, Glornir yelling orders, Varg shrugging his shield from his back and pulling his hand-axe from his belt, and then they were upon them, carving through Hjalmar's Fell-Hearted and Estrid's *drengrs*, warriors falling as the Bloodsworn scythed through them like the north wind. Varg swept around a warrior who sought to cave Varg's skull in with an axe swing, hacked into the back of the warrior's neck as he ran past him, ripped the blade free and the warrior spun in a circle, hands going to the blood spurting from his wound, fell to his knees as Varg ran on, punching with his shield, chopping with his axe, and he was at the doors, no more warriors before him. He skidded to a halt and turned, saw Glornir fall upon Hjalmar Peacemaker, the chief of the Fell-Hearted setting his feet and raising his shield, sword hovering in his fist.

Glornir did not break his stride, lifted a leg and straight-kicked Hjalmar's shield, sent the warrior tumbling and crashing to the floor. Glornir strode after him, raising his axe. Hjalmar lifted his shield over him and Glornir hacked down, his axe chopping into the shield, burst through it in an explosion of splinters, the blade carving on into Hjalmar's chest. Glornir put a boot on Hjalmar's shield and wrenched his axe free, blood and bone erupting, and Hjalmar gasped, blood-flecked foam on his lips, and died.

"Oath-breaker," Glornir growled and spat on Hjalmar's corpse, then turned away, looking for the next warrior to kill.

Varg saw a spurt of red flame around an ash-wood staff, saw Sturla the Galdurwoman apprentice snarling runes, fire licking at one of Elvar's *drengrs*, the warrior bursting into flames like an oil-soaked torch, screaming, arms flailing as he blazed. Estrid was close to Sturla, shield and sword in hand, a handful of her *drengrs* with her. There was a crackle of Seiðr-runes in response as Vol's voice commanded a rune flicker into blue, ice-flecked life before her, spinning slowly, expanding and spreading like a tapestry upon a loom, sharp lines flowing, becoming a net of ice, and Vol was flinging it at Sturla. The Galdurwoman saw it coming, shouted words, and fire leaped from her staff at the net, exploded into it, a fountain of red sparks, steam hissing, but the ice-net rolled on, consuming the flame. Sturla stumbled back, turned to run and the net was upon her, wrapping about her, shrinking, pulling tight, and Sturla was screaming, frost crackling across her body, ice crusting on her and she slowed, as if wading through a bog, and she stopped, frozen in mid-stride, the net tight and constricting about her.

"*Mylja hana, brjóta hana í sundur,*" Vol cried out and the net shuddered and tightened again, and Sturla broke apart, ice-shards exploding, cutting into those about her.

"To me," Estrid was crying, a score of her *drengrs* around her, and Varg saw the survivors of Hjalmar's crew fighting their way to her.

A howl echoed from one of the huge tunnels that fed into the chamber, many disengaging from their combat, turning to look, and Ulfrir came loping from the tunnel in his wolf-form, Skuld in the air behind him, the two stone wolves at Ulfrir's feet and a warband of *Úlfhéðnar* following him. He padded up to Elvar's corpse, stopped and looked down at her, sniffed her, whined. Then he looked to the tree, to the stairwell, where figures were hurrying, almost at the chamber's floor now. And Ulfrir growled, the sound of it echoing through the hall, thrumming through Varg's bones and blood, and the figures on the stairwell paused, stopped. One of them was far taller than the rest, lean, dark-haired and handsome, clothed in mail. He held a seax in his hand, red with blood.

"Brother," he said, smiling at Ulfrir. "How I have missed you."

"I should have killed you when last I saw you," Ulfrir rumbled.

"You should have," Rotta agreed. "It would have saved you a lot of trouble, and me a lot of pain." His face flickered, and Varg saw the smooth skin of Rotta's face disappear for a moment, revealing a red smear of scarred tendon and pitted, red-raw flesh. A shimmer and ripple in the air and the smooth, handsome face was back.

"But, if I were dead, then I would have missed out on this warm-hearted reunion, and that would have been a shame."

"Uncharacteristically brave of you to come here," Ulfrir growled.

"I have hidden depths," Rotta shrugged, still smiling.

"Brave, but a mistake. You have committed your last atrocity," Ulfrir snarled.

"Oh, far from it," Rotta said, and opened his mouth, lips and jaws expanding, elongating, teeth growing.

"*Hurðir úr steini, heyrðu orð Úlfris og opnaðu mér úlfagryfjuna,*" Rotta cried out, his voice ringing, filling the chamber. The echoes slowly died, replaced with silence. And then there was a grating, grinding sound and the doors began to open.

A crow-black line between the doors, the darkness before dawn, and a black mist flowed through the opening gap, night-hags screeching and wailing.

CHAPTER SIXTY-NINE

BIÓRR

Biórr stood on the stairwell behind Rotta and stared as the doors of Wolfdales ground open, a black tide pouring out of the night and washing into the hall. Night-hags came first, floating like mist, screeching and grasping with their long-fingered hands, then the frost-spiders were scuttling through, sweeping across the ground like spilled ink. Trolls lumbered behind them, skraeling swirling about them, and then came the steady rhythm of the shield wall, loosely formed up, Ilska leading them at their front and centre with her Raven-Feeders.

Chaos exploded, horns blasting, voices yelling. Biórr saw the Bloodsworn with their black, blood-spattered shields falling back, forming up into their own shield wall, mercenary chiefs marshalling their warriors, saw *drengrs* gathering to their jarls, heard the clatter of hooves as mounted warriors burst from one of the corridors, clothed in lamellar armour and horse-hair helms, recurved bows in their fists. They crashed into the chamber, hooves trampling frost-spiders, arrows hissing, spears slashing. And among it all Biórr saw the wolf-god standing before him, lips curled in a gut-loosening snarl, giant stone wolves at his side, a small host of *Úlfhéðnar* gathered behind him. Despite the fact that he was in a room with two war-hosts and two gods, all Biórr could look at was the broken, mangled body of Elvar, still and lifeless upon the ground before him.

He had come here to kill her, knew that she deserved death. Or he thought that she did. Her words still rang in his head.

I have set Ulfrir free, set all *the Tainted free.*

"A lie. She must have been lying, to save herself," he muttered to himself.

But she had me down, her sword at my throat. She did not need to lie to save herself.

"What are you muttering about?" Skalk snapped at him, the Galdurman stood on the stairwell beside him, Rotta ahead of them. The Galdurman's fair-haired *drengr* was with him, all the others still fighting in the chamber and on the platform, or they had been, when Rotta hauled Biórr to his feet and led him down the stairwell.

Biórr looked at Skalk, then Ulfrir was roaring, bunching his legs to leap at Rotta. The winged woman with the red hair swooped over Ulfrir's head, loosed an arrow at Rotta, who dived to the side, the arrow thunking into the tree. A drumming sound of footsteps behind Biórr made him turn; he saw Grend hurtling down the stairs, half running, half falling, his face twisted in rage, lips drawn back, teeth bared, eyes mad with fury, an axe in one fist, seax in the other. Biórr took one look at him and leaped from the stairwell, his rat-instinct for flight and survival taking over. He fell the last distance to the ground, grunted with the impact and rolled, saw Grend slam through Skalk and his *drengr*, sending them falling, saw Grend almost fly from the stairwell, leaping and crashing into Rotta's back, chopping and stabbing as they fell. Heard Rotta crying out, screaming in pain as they rolled, Grend's blades rising and falling, spraying great gouts of blood in red arcs. They rolled to a stop, Grend grappling on top of Rotta, raised his axe and chopped it into Rotta's chest, Biórr hearing the sound of bones cracking.

"NO," Rotta roared, a spasm convulsing through him, and he shook, the air shimmering and rippling around him, limbs lengthening, body thickening, tail and fur sprouting, and Grend was thrown through the air, crashed into the trunk of the tree where he fell to the ground, slumped, stunned and groaning.

Rotta stood there in his rat form, all thick fur and lashing tail, clawed feet and sharp, yellowed teeth. Patches of his fur were slick and matted with blood.

Then Ulfrir was leaping, Rotta scurrying out of his way, Ulfrir's jaws snapping shut with a sharp crack, twisting, turning, hunting for Rotta. All about them the hall rang with combat, warriors stabbing and hacking at frost-spiders, night-hags squeezing necks, here and there bursts of black light as Seiðr-words were shouted out by warriors who remembered them, night-hags exploding, trolls lashing about them with their thick clubs and spears, *Berserkir* frothing and roaring, *Úlfhéðnar* snarling and tearing at flesh with steel, tooth and claw, warbands forming shield walls and standing like boulders in the blood-fray against the swirling tide.

Biórr clambered to his feet, reached for his weapons belt and realised his sword was gone, kicked from his hand by Elvar, only his seax still sheathed at his belt. He looked about him and saw a shield, swept it up, two black ravens upon it, one of Hjalmar's Peacemakers, and then he saw an axe on the ground, slim-shafted with a small blade, and he remembered it.

Elvar's. She had used it against him, sliced through the rings of his mail as if it was flesh, and he bent and took it, tested it in his hand. It was as light as a feather, the balance exceptional.

HELP ME, Rotta's voice screamed in his head, and he turned to see Ulfrir chasing Rotta around the trunk of the huge tree, Skuld swooping and loosing arrows at the rat. One hissed past Rotta's head, and the next punched into his back leg, and he squealed, fell, and Ulfrir's paw slammed down onto Rotta's tail, pinning him.

Biórr ran.

Ulfrir's jaws opened.

Biórr leaped, brought the axe down on Rotta's tail, sheared through it, fur, muscle, gristle and bone, left the tail hanging by a shred. Rotta screamed, his claws scrabbling on the ground and the shred of tail ripped and tore away, Rotta running, leaving half his tail beneath Ulfrir's paw.

The wolf snarled down at Biórr, saliva dripping from teeth as long as swords, and Biórr looked up at him, his back to the trunk, nowhere to run. He felt that savage flare from his rat, cornered and fierce, and set his feet, raised his axe defiantly.

A deafening roar resounded behind Ulfrir, from beyond the open doors of his hall, and a great wind swept into the room, Ulfrir turning, crouched and snarling.

Lik-Rifa burst out of the darkness and through the open doors in a maelstrom of wings and jaws and snapping teeth, of scales and talons and razored, lashing tail, a hurricane of destruction riding the winds of a great storm. She beat her wings and slowed, descending, sending people flying with the turbulence of her landing, others running, leaping to escape her as she alighted in the great hall before Ulfrir. Almost gently she landed, and a silence settled over the hall, all those in combat pausing, stepping apart.

"Three hundred years I have waited for this," Lik-Rifa said, her voice deep as the sea, rumbling as distant thunder.

Ulfrir looked at her, snarled, but said nothing.

"I tore Orna to bloodied shreds," Lik-Rifa said and licked her lips with a black, serpentine tongue. "She tasted good."

Ulfrir trembled, muscles bunched, quivering, but still he did not move or speak.

"You seem awestruck by my appearance, which I understand," Lik-Rifa said. "I have a gift for you, brother." She opened one of her great-taloned claws, gently dropping something that she had carried.

A man rolled out onto the ground, and slowly stood. Dark-haired, lean, heavy browed. He stood with one shoulder slumped, bandages around his back.

Broðir, Biórr realised.

"Speak it," Lik-Rifa growled, setting Biórr's bones trembling.

"Come to me," Broðir said, his voice cracking, then, louder. "Come to me, Ulfrir-wolf. Come to me, my thrall."

Ulfrir stood straighter, cocked his head to one side, staring down at Broðir, and then he laughed.

"Come to me," Broðir shouted this time, louder, trying to be more commanding, though there was an edge of panic to his voice.

Ulfrir stopped laughing.

"I am no one's thrall," he said, voice a rumbling growl, and he lifted his head, showed the thick fur on his neck, where the iron collar had once been. "Elvar set me free."

Biórr felt the strength drain from him at those words, at the sight of Ulfrir's collarless neck, and he stumbled back against the tree.

It was no lie. Elvar spoke the truth.

Lik-Rifa looked from Ulfrir to Broðir.

"Useless, lying human," she snarled, her serpentine neck lunging forwards, her jaws opening, and she swept Broðir up, bit down, the crunch and crackle of bones splintering, a few droplets of blood dripping from her lip, and Broðir was gone. She looked at Ulfrir.

"I shall have to do this the old-fashioned way then," she said. Her wings snapped open, beat and she was leaping at the wolf.

CHAPTER SEVENTY

ORKA

Orka stood with her long-axe, blue slime and shattered shell from frost-spiders dripping from its blade. Breca was close to her, Lif and Sæunn to his left and right, a handful of skraeling dead around them. Vesli had one foot on a skraeling's jaw, grunting as she ripped long, yellowed teeth from its mouth. The Bloodsworn had formed a shield wall against the first rush of Lik-Rifa's horde through the stone doors, but with the coming of the dragon all had broken apart. Orka just stood with everyone else and stared as Lik-Rifa rose into the air and flew towards Ulfrir, who stood before her, crouched, muscles bunched, and then he was leaping into the air, jaws wide, the two gods slamming together, a concussive explosion that shook the chamber, all swaying and staggering, and the two gods were crashing to the ground, bodies hurled into the air as the ground rippled and tremored. They came scrambling to their feet, ripping and tearing, jaws crunching, Lik-Rifa's wings beating, claws tearing at Ulfrir's belly. His jaws sank into her shoulder and the dragon roared, Ulfrir twisting, thick muscles of his neck dragging her, and he threw her crunching into the trunk of the tree.

Lik-Rifa shook herself, wings flicking wide, and set her feet under her, turned to face Ulfrir, but he stepped back a few paces.

"Gelta, come," Ulfrir said.

There was a ripping, tearing sound, and a shape tore away from the trunk of the tree, a woman, grey-skinned, tall as a mead hall, her face hard lines and knotted hollows, hair flowing like vines, her eyes swirling green and amber.

"You are not welcome here, Lik-Rifa, despoiler, malignant deceiver," the Froa-spirit said, her voice like the scrape of a thousand branches.

"*Rætur kjarnaviðar míns, rís upp, bind hana, fanga hana, rífa hana, mylja hana,*" the Froa cried out, and the ground trembled. Roots thick as trees burst from it, snaking out, wrapping around Lik-Rifa's legs. She beat her wings in a great flurry, rose into the air, but the roots held her tight and dragged her back down with a crash. More roots swept over her, across her long neck, criss-crossing over her body, binding her, and Lik-Rifa roared, loud and deafening, edged with fear.

The chamber exploded into motion. Orka saw Ilska break from the line of her shield wall and run towards Lik-Rifa, hacking at all in her way with her sword, smashing them aside with her shield. Drekr followed her, roaring and swinging his long-axe, and more of the Raven-Feeders followed, fighting their way to the dragon.

Without thought Orka stalked after them, smashed a skraeling that ran at her in the jaw with the butt of her axe, chopped into it as it fell with the blade, swung the axe over her head and hacked into a frost-spider that scurried at her, ripped the blade free in a burst of shell and blue-tinged ichor, strode on, dimly aware that others were with her.

Lik-Rifa was thrashing and heaving, writhing, wings beating, jaws snapping, tail lashing, sending people and creatures hurtling through the air, the ear-splitting sound of roots tearing from the ground or bursting apart in explosions of splinters, but the Froa stood before Lik-Rifa and shouted her words, more roots appearing, whipping out from the ground, thick as trees, and the stone wolves leaped onto Lik-Rifa's back and began savaging at her with their jaws of stone, Lik-Rifa roaring in pain and rage and fear.

Orka saw Ilska reach Lik-Rifa, began hacking with her sword at a thick root, Drekr right behind her, raising his long-axe and chopping, splinters flying. More of the Raven-Feeders joined them, weapons rising and falling, Lik-Rifa bucking and writhing and as one root tore apart, Ilska and the others ran to the next one.

No.

Orka ran, smashing skraeling and warriors out of her way, heard a howl ringing out and realised it was her. Ilska paused in her hacking at roots, saw Orka and whoever was behind her coming and barked orders, the Raven-Feeders falling in around her, a loose wall forming, shields rising.

Orka slammed into them before they had time to lock their shields and set their feet, all of them scattering, Orka stumbling, falling to one knee and rising again, furiously swinging her long-axe in a looping arc and chopping into the shield of a Raven-Feeder coming at her, smashing through the linden boards and on into the warrior's chest, sent the warrior crashing to the ground, ripped her axe free. A roar behind her and Gunnar and Halja scythed through the gap Orka had made, Glornir there, too, swinging his long-axe and splintering shields, Halja and Lif and Sæunn there with her, chopping and slashing, Breca snarling and stabbing with his short spear, and the wave of the Bloodsworn pushed the Raven-Feeders back between and around the legs of the Froa-spirit until their backs were against the trunk of the great tree.

"*Eldur íss og loga, brenna og frjósa, brenna og bíta, sprunga hinn forna við,*" a voice called out, and Orka heard the crackle and hiss of rune-flames, glanced around and saw Rotta, back in his human form, bleeding from a dozen wounds. He was facing the Froa and her roots and vines, runes of fire kindled in the air before him. And then turned and hurled the runes at the trunk of the great tree. They exploded in a conflagration of flames, licking at the tree, spreading across the ground, the stench of charred wood and hissing sap spreading through the hall.

The Froa-spirit let out a great wail and lashed out at Rotta, but he leaped nimbly behind the trunk, disappearing. The Froa turned her vines upon the flames that were crackling and climbing, whipping at them, but flames sparked into life on the vines, swiftly racing along them, charring and blackening them. The Froa-spirit screamed.

Vol's voice rose high as she summoned runes of frost and ice, hurled them at the flames upon the tree, but they burst into clouds of steam at their first touch of Rotta's rune-cast flames.

"SKALK," Orka heard a voice roar, saw Glornir standing over a dead Raven-Feeder, pointing his long-axe past Orka. She turned and saw Skalk standing on the lower steps of the stairwell carved into the side of the great tree, his fair-haired *drengr* with him. He stumbled back a few steps, up the stairwell, clutching his staff, his mouth moving, forming words that Orka could not hear as Glornir started carving a way towards him.

Orka ducked the arcing slice of a spear, came up and kicked the shield of the warrior attacking her, a fair-haired man in a nasal helm with a rope-knot beard, sent him stumbling back, crunching into the tree. He tried to right himself as Orka's long-axe slammed down onto his helm, caving it in, blood sluicing down his face and he dropped like a cut puppet. Orka curled her lip, hefted her axe, and then she saw him through the flames. Drekr, standing with Ilska and a knot of the Raven-Feeders before the first steps of the tree's stairwell, fighting a handful of the Bloodsworn and Ulfrir's *Úlfhéðnar*. She broke into a run, leaped through the flames that were spreading about the base of the trunk and threw herself at him. He saw her coming, turned and twisted away from her axe swing and she was smashing into him, sending him tumbling up the stairwell, falling, rolling, coming back to one knee as she staggered and crunched into the tree, felt movement behind her and ducked, a sword chopping into the trunk where her head had been. Twisted and saw Ilska, cold-eyed, her face a cliff. She smashed her shield into Orka's face, sent her stumbling up the stairwell, ripped her sword from the trunk and strode after Orka.

CHAPTER SEVENTY-ONE

GUÐVARR

Guðvarr stood just inside the open doors of Ulfrir's chamber, the first grey light of dawn seeping into the world, his mouth open in shock as he stared at Lik-Rifa. She bucked, heaving and writhing, roaring loud as a storm, snared by a multitude of vines, each one thick as a tree. Flames were spreading across the chamber, licking at the ash tree, black smoke billowing, the Froa-spirit roaring, one of its long arms aflame.

"Forward," Sigrún shouted, leading her *drengrs* away from the stone doors and deeper into the chamber, Guðvarr slipping and almost falling in the blue-touched ichor of a dismembered frost-spider. It was chaos everywhere, battle raging wherever Guðvarr looked. Frost-spiders were scuttling, leaping and biting, people lying on the ground frozen, blue ice crusted around their lips, night-hags swirled throughout, throttling the life from warriors with their mist-wraith hands, trolls were clubbing and stabbing indiscriminately, squashing people into gruel, and jarls like Sigrún and chieftains were leading their small warbands and shield walls deeper into the chamber. The noise was overwhelming, Lik-Rifa roaring, the giant Froa-spirit sounding like a storm raging in the boughs of a forest, Ulfrir growling and snarling, a group of mounted warriors galloping and clattering around the chamber, yelling and loosing arrows at any target they could find, *Berserkir* and *Úlfhéðnar* slavering and snarling, ripping and tearing, and everywhere warriors shouting, screaming, dying, the clash of steel ringing louder than a thousand blacksmiths hammering in a thousand forges. But the worst thing for Guðvarr, despite the numbers of Lik-Rifa's horde, was his growing suspicion that they were losing.

Everywhere he looked he saw the fallen, whether they be human or vaesen, and it looked like the dead of Lik-Rifa's war-host outnumbered by far the dead of Elvar's war-host.

And our illustrious leader, the supposedly indestructible dragon, is wrapped like a goose for the winter blot feast, while the giant wolf runs free. And where is the rat? Maybe he's had the right idea and fled this chaos . . .

He looked back over his shoulder at the grey light beyond the doors, getting further and further away as Sigrún led them into the torch-lit chamber.

Why can we not just stay close to the open doors? Then, if things do go wrong, we won't have as far to run.

They moved alongside another shield wall, thirty- or forty-strong, three rows deep, Guðvarr seeing the eagle of Darl upon their shields, and another emblem, two black ravens. He knew the eagle, recognised Estrid in the front row. Sigrún led her smaller band to them and joined them, shields slotting together.

Well, strength in numbers, I suppose, Guðvarr thought.

"SHIELDS," Sigrún and Estrid yelled together, and Guðvarr looked over the top of his shield to glimpse two or three warriors running towards them, one with skin as black as raven-feathers, a coat of mail that was stretched tight over thick slabs of muscle. He was much closer than the others.

There must be sixty of us, why do they sound so panicked? Guðvarr thought, then, as he focused on the warriors charging at him, like a stone dropped in his belly, he understood. The warriors charging at him were *Berserkir*, and the black-skinned one was not closer, he was running in line with the other two *Berserkir*: he was just much, *much* bigger than them.

And Berserkir *are not exactly small. No, never small.*

"Guðvarr," Sigrún grunted at him, and he blinked, felt a rush of fear, raised his shield and slotted it tight to Sigrún's, made sure his shield rim was tight to Sigrún's boss, the warrior to his left doing the same to his shield. Felt a pressure behind him as the warriors in the second row set their feet and put their shields to his back.

"READY," Sigrún yelled and Guðvarr set his feet and tucked his left shoulder tight into his shield, bracing it. He heard the thumping footsteps of the *Berserkir*, heard a wild-bull snorting, heard frothing, savage-bear growling roars growing louder. He gripped his sword tight, ready to stab over the top of his shield as soon as the *Berserkir* hit the line and were checked by the weight of the shield wall.

A crunch, an impact, and he was weightless, flying through the air. Spinning, the ground rushing up at him. A crunching, bone-rattling impact and he lost his shield, rolled, slammed into something and lay there, dazed, looking up at branches high above. Heard battle cries, the sound of flesh being cleaved and torn, screams, warriors crying out. He groaned, heaved himself over and used his sword like a staff, wedging the tip into the ground and hauling himself up by the hilt. Thirty or forty paces away the black bull-man and *Berserkir* were tearing warriors apart, hacking at them, biting, the bull-man ripping an arm from one of Sigrún's *drengrs* and beating him to the ground with it.

Is that Járn? he thought.

The shield wall was gone, broken and smashed like a splintered dam, bodies lying strewn and sprawled all around Guðvarr. Some were trying to climb back to their feet.

Then the bull-man and the two *Berserkir* were moving on, running at a cluster of frost-spiders who were scuttling towards the mounted warriors, who were loosing their arrows at Lik-Rifa.

A groan and Guðvarr saw Estrid lying on the ground close to him. She was moving, blood seeping from a cut on her forehead, eyes flickering.

Not so regal and haughty, now, are you? And you thought to fight me at Darl. He remembered the flush of fear and shame when she had bested him with her weapons craft, knocked him on his arse. Looking around, he saw that all her warriors were down, and he stepped closer and pressed his sword against her throat. Leaned on it as if he was using his sword for balance. Her eyes snapped open as the blade slid into the soft flesh at the base of her neck, and she jerked and spasmed. Guðvarr slipped the sword free, a gush of dark blood and he dropped the sword and fell to his knees, cradled Estrid's head in his hands while pinning one of her arms with his knee.

She gasped and spluttered, coughing up gouts of blood, tried to grasp and claw at his face, but he held her hand and gripped it as if giving her comfort, pretended to stroke her brow, while holding her down. Her eyes fluttered, rolling white, her strength failing. A cough of blood and a spasm through her legs and she was gone.

That'll teach you, you niðing, Guðvarr thought.

He wiped his bloodied hands on Estrid's breeches, reached for his sword and stood. Smiled. Felt a wash of heat and saw that flames were spreading through the chamber. They were thick around and upon the base of the great tree now, and the Froa-spirit was shrieking and flailing her arms, one of them ablaze, the flames crackling onto her torso. Guðvarr saw people fighting on the stairwell that wound around the tree, the flames forcing them higher as they spread hungrily up the trunk. Lik-Rifa was half bound, many of the roots that had held her charred and splintered. She was beating her wings frantically, trying to rise while the stone wolves tore at her. Dragon-born and trolls were spread around Lik-Rifa, trying to hold Ulfrir at bay, dragon-born casting flickering rune-spells at the wolf and the trolls were hurling themselves at him, smashing and stabbing with clubs and spears while he swiped at them with his claws, eviscerating flesh and cracking bone.

Guðvarr saw the bull-man and a *Berserkir* standing at the side of two women, one lean and short-haired, the other fair-haired and tattooed, both with their arms raised, fists glistening with ice-crusted Seiðr. The bull-man and *Berserkir* hacked with axes at any who came near the women. They were crying out, hurling frost-crackling Seiðr-spells at the flames that were consuming the Froa, clouds hissing where ice and fire met, but the flames were engulfing the frost, melting and evaporating it in greats gouts of steam.

A rasping, branch-shaking shriek echoed through the chamber and the Froa-spirit toppled to her knees. Flames were engulfing her now, spreading through the vines of her hair, across her torso and up her head. Sap hissed and bubbled, smoke billowing, and with another roar she crashed to the ground, sparks exploding.

The roots binding Lik-Rifa fell away, and the dragon winged into the air, roaring, blood falling from her like rain. Ulfrir swept half a dozen trolls away with the swipe of a paw and leaped at her, claws gouging into her, jaws fastening on her chest. The dragon screamed, slewed in the air, wings batting frantically, and she turned, smashed into the burning tree and Ulfrir fell into the flames, howled and rolled free, fur singed and smoking.

Rotta appeared in his rat form, scurrying out from between the flames.

"SISTER," he bellowed, and Lik-Rifa hovered in the air, saw him and dived down, swept him up in both her huge-taloned claws, and then she was beating her wings again, the two of them rising, spiralling up into the chamber, around the burning tree, higher and higher.

CHAPTER SEVENTY-TWO

ORKA

Orka ducked a sword-swing from Ilska and chopped at her ankles, the Raven-Feeder's chief leaping back, shuffling away and climbing another step on the stairwell, a pair of warriors crashing in between them, pushing Orka down a step. She looked around quickly, searching for Breca.

"I'm here," Breca called out, a dozen steps behind her at the rear of the Bloodsworn, Sæunn and Lif protecting him. The stairwell was wide, wide enough for Ulfrir in his wolf-form to pad along it, and all around Orka warriors fought, Bloodsworn and Raven-Feeders, both warbands filled with the Tainted. Frost-spiders and skraeling were there, too, the spiders scuttling up the trunk, swinging on webs from branches. Every step of the way Orka had been trying to reach Drekr but had been hindered by Ilska and her followers. She had left a trail of the dead on the stairwell behind her. Glornir and Vol were trying to reach Skalk, who cast Galdur-spells at them with a frantic intensity, Vol countering them with her Seiðr-runes. They had climbed high around the tree, the flames and smoke forcing them up, passing Elvar's chamber where Thorguna the *Berserkir* had been falling back against three Tainted warriors, many others dead around her. Gunnar and Halja had gone to her aid, and now Thorguna fought with them against Ilska and her score or so of Raven-Feeders, all of them Tainted, fast and strong, though the Bloodsworn pushed them ever back, ever higher, and now they were almost at the vaulted ceiling of Ulfrir's chamber, Orka glimpsing the pale glow of dawn in the sky above her, through the swaying branches.

One of the retreating Raven-Feeders cried out, a red-haired woman with a splintered shield in one fist, a bearded axe in the other, Orka seeing that she had backed into some invisible object. She tried to climb the stairwell again, and Orka saw her stumble back, a crackle of blue Seiðr-light rippling above her.

A Seiðr-barrier, Orka thought. *Good, we have them now, then.* She looked for Drekr and saw he was close to the red-haired warrior, and she climbed another step up the stairwell.

A roar, ringing and echoing, and a tremor passed through the stairwell, the branches above and below quivering. Orka looked back, down at the chamber floor, so far below. She could see the orange flicker of flames and great banks of black smoke, but could make little else out from this height, even with her wolf-eyes. Then Lik-Rifa appeared from out of the smoke and flame, circling higher around the tree, growing larger and larger until she was almost upon them. Blood flowed from a hundred wounds, great rips and rents in her scaled hide, and she held the rat in her claws; his fur was blood-crusted and matted, too.

Lik-Rifa reached the Seiðr-wall and blue light flared across the entire ceiling, knocking the dragon back.

"The way is blocked, brother," Orka heard Lik-Rifa roar.

"*Úlfavinur, opinn,*" Rotta cried out and with a flare and crackle of blue light that rippled across the domed roof, the spell faded to nothing. Lik-Rifa beat her wings and rose higher, passing through the space where the barrier had been and on into the pale pewter sky.

Raven-Feeders turned and ran up the stairwell, Drekr disappearing around a curve in the trunk, and Ilska kicked a Bloodsworn tumbling down the stairwell, then turned and ran as well. All of the Raven-Feeders and skraeling disengaging and backing or running away. The frost-spiders scurried to the trunk and climbed it, fading into the foliage. Orka strode to Glornir. He glanced over the stairwell, down at the chamber far below.

"Halja," he called out, "what do your eagle-eyes see?"

"The Froa is dead," Halja said, "the tree and hall burning. We will not be getting back into the chamber by this path."

"There are other ways," Glornir said. He looked at Orka and Vol. "But not until we have our vengeance", and then he was striding up the stairwell after the fleeing Raven-Feeders, Orka and the others a step behind him.

They emerged through the branches into daylight, a cold wind stirring Orka's hair, scouring her face, and followed the stairwell to its end. Orka felt like she was standing on the top of the world, the snow on the peaks of the Boneback Mountains bright in the first touches of dawn, Lik-Rifa a great silhouette against the diffuse sun, almost blotting it out, retreating to the north-west, towards the gaping jaws of Snaka's skull. To the west and south the ocean shimmered like beaten silver, dark shadows scudding across it from the clouds above. Orka saw the Raven-Feeders gathering together, their backs to Orka and the Bloodsworn, staring out at the ocean.

"What are they doing?" Gunnar Prow grunted. "What are they looking at?" and Halja stepped up, looked with her gold-flecked eyes.

Her mouth dropped open and she blinked.

"A fleet," she said.

"Where?" Glornir grunted.

"Everywhere," Halja said. "You do not need my eyes to see it. Look", and she gestured to the ocean.

Orka used the wolf in her blood and focused, and realised it wasn't the shadow of clouds she'd seen upon the ocean, but great swathes and clusters of ships. Hundreds of them. Many hundreds, perhaps thousands, split into different fleets. Elvar's fleet had been fifty or sixty *drakkar*-strong, and it had been the greatest gathering of ships Orka had ever seen, or heard a skáld sing of. This dwarfed Elvar's fleet many times over. And the more she looked, the more Orka could see them spreading around the coast of Iskidan. One fleet was sailing for Snakavik, another for Liga, one for Darl, and another was sweeping into the estuary of the River Falinn and sailing upriver through the Iron Wood to Wolfdales.

"Has all of Iskidan sailed after us?" one of the Bloodsworn said.

"It is Rurik's fleet, the invasion he and Jaromir were planning," Glornir said.

"They are too many," someone else said.

"One battle at a time," Glornir grunted leading them along the stairwell. "Let's live through this one before we think about the next."

Skraeling were clustering where the stairwell met the thick-tufted grass of the hill, and behind them the Raven-Feeders were turning away from the sea and forming up, Skalk and his *drengr* with them.

"Thorguna," Glornir called out and the *Berserkir* limped towards him. The two of them walked on ahead of the Bloodsworn, muttering and growling, their shoulders and backs hunching, muscle swelling, and then they were breaking into a run, roaring, Glornir hefting his long-axe and Thorguna her two hand-axes. Orka and the Bloodsworn broke into a loping run behind them. Ahead of them the skraeling grunted and snarled, hefted their crude-iron blades. One set its feet and dug a spear-butt into the ground, angled it at Glornir as he surged along the stairwell. Halja hefted her spear without breaking stride and cast it, Orka seeing it fly high, the shaft shivering, and stoop into its dive. It struck the skraeling in the chest, threw it to the ground in a burst of blood, its spear falling from its grip, and Glornir and Thorguna hit them like a rockfall. Bodies flew in different directions, Glornir frothing and slavering, swinging his long-axe in great arcs, a severed head spinning through the air, Thorguna hacking in a blood-mad frenzy with her hand-axes, and the skraeling scattered and broke apart squealing. Orka and the others hit the skraeling a few moments later, smashing them down with their shields, stabbing, chopping. The skraeling tried to rally, but Glornir and Thorguna had carved through them like wheat, split and scattered them, and then they were charging at Ilska, Drekr and the Raven-Feeders, crunching into their wall of shields.

CHAPTER SEVENTY-THREE

VARG

Varg stared about the great hall of Ulfrir, everywhere seething fire and flame and billowing clouds of smoke and ash. The fallen Froa-spirit lay spread across the ground, its body consumed by fire, and looking up at the great tree he saw the inferno crackling up its trunk like fast-growing vines, spreading along the first branches now. He stared up at the roof, where Lik-Rifa had flown, or fled, and glimpsed tiny figures on the stairwell.

"Have we won?" he said to Svik. "Is the dragon beaten? Routed?"

"Routed, yes. Beaten, no. Not until she is dead," Svik said, then he grinned. "But it is a good start. And while she is gone we need to put her war-host in the ground."

They were standing with Røkia and Einar, Æsa and Edel and a handful of the Bloodsworn, cut off from following Glornir and the others up the stairwell by the spreading flames.

"Where shall we start?" Varg asked. The hall was in chaos. Flames were spreading, and clouds of choking smoke were obscuring much of the chamber. Frost-spiders scuttled in and out of the smoke, warbands were formed in small shield walls, both Elvar's mercenaries and Lik-Rifa's. Varg glimpsed the locked shields of Elvar's Battle-Grim, Sighvat at their centre, fighting alongside Jarl Orlyg's warband, pushing a seething mass of skraeling away from the dais and back to the open doors. Ulfrir was beset by trolls and dragon-born, their rune-fire crackling, forming walls of fire in an attempt to herd

Ulfrir back to the flames that were consuming the great tree, a swarm of trolls trying to hem the wolf in. A handful of the trolls were clubbing one of the stone wolves, great chunks of rock smashed to powder, the wolf limping, one of its legs shattered, half of it missing.

"There," Svik said, pointing to the stone wolf, and without waiting for an answer Svik was moving through the hall, shield and sword in his fists. Varg followed, automatically going to Svik's left to protect his flank, Røkia moving to Svik's right. The rest of the Bloodsworn followed, spreading like a wedge, and they cut their way across the hall. Varg smashed skraeling to the ground, hacked at frost-spiders as they scuttled at him, punched warriors with his shield, and then they were emerging from a cloud of smoke, the stone wolf fallen to the ground before them, trolls raining blows upon it.

Edel took three quick steps and hurled her spear, Varg seeing it slam into the lower back of a troll as it lifted its club two-handed over its head. It let out a great bellow and staggered back, reaching for the spear in its back, grabbed it and ripped it free. Then Einar was there, the troll swinging its club at him. Einar stepped away, gave the club a glancing blow with his shield, steering it into the ground, and his axe was swinging, chopping into the meat of the troll's wrist, half severing it with his bearded axe. The troll lifted its arm, blood spurting from the wound, its wrist dangling by a strip of skin, and Einar chopped his axe into its knee, wrenched the blade free and the troll swayed and toppled, Einar burying his axe into the back of its neck, ripped the blade free in a spurt of blood.

Two of the trolls turned on them, roaring, one swinging a club, another stabbing at Æsa with a huge spear. She leaped away from it, the spear blade stabbing deep into the ground in an explosion of earth and Æsa leaped onto the spear, wide as a sapling, and ran up its shaft nimble as a goat. Laughing, she leaped from it and stabbed her seax into one of the troll's eyes. It roared and fell backwards, a great cloud of dust rising around it, Æsa landing, striding to the troll and ripping her seax free. The injured stone wolf threw itself at the last troll, knocking it to the ground, and the Bloodsworn surrounded it, stabbing and chopping until it was dead.

A cry behind them, Varg turning, his wolf-ears catching it.

"Refna and the children," he said.

"Where?" Einar said and Varg pointed. Einar broke into a lumbering run, Varg and the others following, swerving around flames, holding their breath as they ran through clouds of smoke. They burst into clean air and Varg saw Refna and the other children. They were being herded from one of the huge corridors that led from the chamber, warriors and skraeling around them, and Varg skidded to a halt, a cold fist clenching around his heart.

Brák Trolls-Bane led them, and he was dragging Refna by her hair, a seax in his fist. Refna was spitting and snarling and screaming for Einar. The wolf in Varg's blood growled, low and menacing, and Varg felt the hairs on his neck stand on end.

Einar roared and ran at them, Varg a few paces behind.

Brák saw Einar coming and stopped, raised his hand to the crew behind him and they stuttered to a halt. Brák held Refna up and put his seax to her throat. Einar skidded to a halt, just ten paces from Brák, Varg halting beside him, Svik, Røkia and the others spreading in a line, snarling at Brák and his crew.

"Let her go," Einar said.

"Now, why would I do that?" Brák said. He was narrow-featured, a sharp nose and a scraggly beard, his skin weathered as bark. He wore leather, fur and mail, a necklace of troll tusks around his neck, a slim sword at his weapons belt, and Varg saw a multitude of seaxes and knives upon him, some hanging on his belt, more strapped to arms and legs.

"It will go better for you if you do," Einar growled.

"Ah, do not be making threats at me, big man. I've fought bigger than you and lived to tell the tale." He brushed the blade of his seax across the tusks on his necklace. "They do not call me Trolls-Bane for nothing." His gaze swept those with Einar, settling upon Varg. He smiled.

"Now there's an angry man, if ever I saw one," he said. "What did I do, kill your mother?"

"My sister," Varg said, a grating growl.

"Ah, well, I'd like to say I'm sorry, but I'm not. This is Vigrið, after all, and I'm sure your sister deserved it."

Varg took a pace forwards, and Brák put his seax back to Refna's throat, held a fistful of her hair in his other fist. Refna's eyes flickered green, her mouth twisting in a snarl and her hands grasped up, Varg seeing the nails grow long and dark as she raked Brák's hand and wrist, blood welling. He cried out and let go, stabbed with his seax. Refna dropped to the ground and rolled away, came up on crouched legs, hands curled into claws.

"I'll gut you for that, you little troll-shite," Brák snarled. Then Einar was roaring and running, Varg, Svik, Røkia and the rest of the Bloodsworn a pace behind him.

Brák danced away from Einar's axe swing, sliced with his seax, drawing a red line across Einar's forearm, then stepped away, calmly drew his slim sword.

Varg charged, shield and hand-axe in his fists, saw two skraeling running at him, twisted and took a hammering blow on his shield, pushed the skraeling away, ducked the second's hacking blow at his head and chopped his hand-axe into the skraeling's belly, ripped the blade left to right, spilling the creature's intestines in a steaming heap. Glimpsed Røkia, Edel and Æsa locked in combat with Brák's crew. Einar and Svik were attacking Brák, Tainted warriors and skraeling spreading wide around them, a handful of them circling Svik, moving him away from Einar.

They fight like wolves separating an elk from the herd.

Einar roared and swung at Brák, a flurry of blows, axe swing, shield rim, backswing with the axe, punch with the shield boss, Brák retreating, stepping away, Einar's blows hissing past him. Brák struck back, short, fast blows with sword and seax, grating on Einar's shield, stabbing under, slipping around the rim and Einar shuffled back, blocking, grunting, chopped with his axe as Brák moved in, but then Brák was stepping away, a shuffle of feet to place him behind Einar, slashing his sword across Einar's calf, the big warrior crying out, stumbling.

"NO," Varg yelled, saw Svik hacking his way out of the ring around him, heard Røkia's snarl, and he was running.

There was a blur of movement to his left, an impact on his shield, and he stumbled, falling to one knee, a spear stabbing at his neck. He dropped to the ground, lost his grip on his shield, rolled away, came up in a snarling crouch, axe in one hand, his other reaching for his cleaver.

A dozen warriors spread before Varg, Røkia, Edel and Æsa, cutting them off from Einar and Svik. Two men led them, coming at Varg, one dark-haired and bearded, gripping shield and spear, the other with lank fair hair, shield and sword in his fists.

"It feels like I have travelled the whole world to find you, Varg Kolskegg's-thrall," Leif Kolskeggson said. Another dozen warriors came from behind Leif and Sterkur and hurled themselves at the Bloodsworn, all holding shields with a golden eye upon them.

"I do not know you well," Sterkur said, "but I hate you already for the dance you have led me." Leif and Sterkur stepped wide around him, one to Varg's left, one to his right. The rest of Sterkur's crew were spreading around Røkia, Edel and Æsa, and beyond them Varg glimpsed Einar limping after Brák, who stepped away from him, just out of range. Then he was lunging in, stabbing beneath Einar's shield. Einar slammed his shield rim down onto Brák's sword, trapping it, punched the shield boss into Brák's body, hurling him to the ground and Einar was stepping after him, raising his axe. Another warrior behind Einar stabbed a spear into the meat of his leg, Einar roaring, twisting as he fell and hacking at the warrior, burying his axe in the man's side, ripped his axe out in a spray of rings and blood even as he fell to one knee. Brák was back on his feet and dancing swiftly in as Einar turned to face him, stabbed his sword over the top rim of Einar's shield, the slim blade plunging deep into Einar's throat, the tip bursting out from the back of Einar's neck, dark blood welling. Svik's wild scream, Røkia's savage howl.

"Get out of my way," Varg snarled and ran at Sterkur.

CHAPTER SEVENTY-FOUR

ORKA

Orka crashed into the gap that Glornir and Thorguna had made in the Raven-Feeder's shield wall, holding her long-axe in both fists, ripping the blade across a belly, rings spraying, blood welling, punched the butt end into a face, mashing lips, knocking teeth out, bursting a nose, and then she was through, spinning. She swung her axe two-handed and chopped it into the back and shoulder of a warrior, carving through his mail, snapping bone, the warrior crying out and falling. Orka ripped the blade free and stumbled on, saw Thorguna on the ground, a spear blade protruding from her back where it had pierced her belly, two corpses lying beneath her with their throats mangled, other dead piled around her.

Beyond Thorguna, Glornir was on the ground, Drekr on top of him. Both were holding Glornir's long-axe, Drekr trying to crush the haft into Glornir's throat, both with their beasts raging through their bodies, eyes blazing, frothing and snarling, muscles bunched in great straining knots. Shouts and screams behind Orka, the Bloodsworn slamming into the Raven-Feeders to reach their chief, heard Vol and Skalk shouting their Galdur- and Seiðr-spells at each other. Orka righted her balance and ran at Drekr, saw Glornir crunch his knee up into Drekr's groin, Drekr sagging as Glornir twisted, throwing him onto the turf where he rolled, came up onto his feet, pulling a hand-axe from his belt in one fist, seax in the other.

Glornir was on his feet, moving on Drekr, who did not wait for him, striking a flurry of blows, Glornir raising his long-axe and blocking them with the shaft of his axe. A spray of splinters, a crack, and Glornir's axe-haft snapped. Glornir threw the blade at Drekr's head, shrugging his shield from his back and drew his sword. Then Orka shoved past Glornir, her long-axe swinging, a diagonal blow from right to left, chopping down at Drekr. He twisted away, struck Orka's axe blade with his hand-axe, knocking it wide and Orka's momentum carried her on, the axe blade chopping into turf. Drekr lunged with his seax at Orka's belly. She arched her back, Drekr's blade grating on rings, let go of her axe-haft and grabbed Drekr's ring mail, dragged him towards her and bit at his throat, felt flesh tearing, blood bursting into her mouth, heard him scream, shouting unheard words, and then heat was washing through her body, pain a heartbeat behind it and she was hurling herself away, rolling in the turf. Glornir's voice, the clash and grate of steel over her, Glornir's legs planted before her and she was pushing herself up, saw Drekr with blood matting his beard where Orka had bitten him, sluicing down his neck. His eyes were glowing red, Orka realising he had spouted some Seiðr-spell at her, scalding her.

Glornir and Drekr were trading blows, Glornir's feet set, shield raised, sword slicing out, Drekr moving around him, chopping and stabbing with axe and seax. Orka saw her long-axe and scrambled to it, ripped it out of the turf as another figure ran at Glornir's side, Ilska the Cruel with her sword and shield before her, snarling at Glornir. Orka stepped before her, Ilska twisting and slicing at her, Orka deflecting the blow with the haft of her axe, knocking it wide and slamming her axe blade into Ilska's shield, sending her stumbling to her left. Orka followed, chopping with the blade of her axe, then punching with the haft of the axe, denting and splintering Ilska's shield. Ilska found her balance, set her feet and she was stabbing and slicing at Orka, pushing her back across the turf until Orka was standing back-to-back with Glornir. They stood there, Drekr and Ilska slipping around them, stabbing, chopping, probing, Glornir and Orka blocking and countering, the world shrinking to the edge of steel, rasp of breath, shuffle of feet.

Orka was dimly aware of combat swirling around them, Bloodsworn and Raven-Feeders, frost-spiders and skraeling, the sound of Breca's bear-cub growl, his wolf-cub snarl, the clatter of weapons on shields as Lif and Sæunn swirled around him. Vol and Skalk in their duel of runes, flames of frost and fire crackling around them. A snatched glimpse of Skalk staggering, blue flames consuming his Galdur-staff. A crack and it burst apart, splinters exploding, and Skalk was hurled from his feet, raised up into the air, his arms stretching wide. He started screaming. Vol shouted and Skalk convulsed, the sound of bones cracking, and he dropped to the ground, limbs twisted, neck broken.

A frost-spider threw itself at Orka and she twisted, hacked it out of the air with her axe, sent it slamming to the ground in an explosion of dark ichor and fragments of exoskeleton, ducked low under Drekr's axe swing and pushed forwards, punched her axe-haft into his gut, doubling him over, slammed the haft up into his face, sending him reeling back a few steps, tripping over the body of the frost-spider, Orka striding after him, raising her axe.

"NO," Ilska cried, seeing Orka and chopping hard at Glornir, trying to get through him to Drekr's side. Glornir took a step back and to his right, moving between Ilska and Drekr, stabbed low, under Ilska's shield, and she dropped the shield to trap his blade, but he had already pulled it back, a feint, and he stabbed high, into the space her shield had just left, his sword punching into the soft flesh just above the line of Ilska's *brynja*. A grunt and gasp from her and she staggered back two paces, blood spurting, tried to pull her shield up and sword back, but her strength was failing. Glornir ripped his blade free and slammed his shield into her, sending her sprawling on her back, stepped over her and chopped down, blade hacking into her neck.

"ILSKA," Drekr roared, deflecting Orka's axe as it swung down at his chest, batting it away with his hand-axe, eyes blazing red, new strength in his limbs. He kicked at Orka's legs, sent her staggering back, surged to his feet and threw himself into Orka, lifting her from the ground, both of them flying through the air, crashing down and rolling. Orka lost her axe, punched and snarled and bit at Drekr, rolled free of him and came to her feet, snarling, hands reaching for the seaxes at her belt.

A distant rumble, and a heartbeat later Orka felt the ground shift beneath her and staggered. A pressure, inside her head. Another rumble, louder, followed by a stronger tremor, all left standing on the hilltop stumbling and swaying, combatants parting, searching for the source of the tremors. The pressure inside her head growing, like a wind rising, hissing. Another rumble, louder, the ground shuddering. A tearing sound and a crack opened in the earth between Orka and Drekr.

She staggered away, shaking her head, saw others about her doing the same. Looked around, stared into the distance. Narrowed her eyes. Something was wrong with the Boneback Mountains. They were . . . moving, great avalanches of snow rolling down the towering slopes, huge eruptions of snow and ice exploding, rising high as the clouds.

The wind inside her head became a howling gale, an almost discernible voice swirling within it.

"Snaka," Vol hissed, and Orka looked to the north-west, to Snakavik. Blinked, grimaced and shook her head.

The skull of Snaka was shifting, moving, a cloud of dust rising around it. And an amber light flickered and blazed in those long empty sockets.

"No," Orka breathed. "What has Lik-Rifa done?" As she stared the skull rose from the rock and sea, no longer the grey-white of old bones, new scales growing, spreading, rippling across the contours of the skull, grey and green, the jaws rising up, teeth long and glinting, gums showing pink with fresh blood, a blue-black tongue flickering out. The serpent twisted its head left and right, thick muscles on a sinuous neck flexing, rippling as dread Snaka rose from his long death, and a wordless voice roared in Orka's head, loud and fierce as a winter storm.

Snaka looked down at the fjord before him, glowering at one of the fleets from Iskidan as it sailed into the fjord. He stretched his mouth wide, revealing teeth as thick and long as the trees of the Iron Wood, his black tongue flickering out. The rock and earth of the mountain, hundreds of years and layers of sediment that had settled about Snaka's bones, began to fall away from him like water flowing from a dog emerging from a stream. A huge, roaring crash as the weight of a mountain smashed into the fjord of Snakavik, a wall of water rising up, exploding away from Snaka and sweeping the fleet up and away like leaves, crashing down on the longships and crushing them, smashing them, and in a few heartbeats the fleet was gone.

All along the line of the Bonebacks the mountains were rippling and heaving, snow and rock sliding in great jagged sheets, huge clouds of earth erupting into the air, and Orka saw the ground rippling and tremoring like someone shaking a rug, undulating across the land of Vigrið in an ever-growing roar.

Snaka rose up higher, his great head blocking the sun, huge, razored scales spreading wide upon his skull and flowing into knotted ridges upon his back. He reared, tall as the sky, and then dived, head crashing into the sea before him, his long, sinuous body slithering into the ocean, the water exploding, another great wave forming, rearing high and sweeping out into the great-green, storming along the coast of Vigrið, submerging it. And Orka saw the silhouette of Lik-Rifa flying in the air, following the line of the coast. Snaka's head emerged from the sea in a great burst of water, salt spray sparkling in the sun, another fleet of Iskidan's longships hurled into the air and smashed to splintered flotsam. Lik-Rifa flew to Snaka's head, swirled around it, and then she was flying inland, across land, back towards Wolfdales.

And Snaka followed her, his body slithering out of the sea and undulating across the land, tearing up forests, crushing hills in his passage.

Orka put a hand to her head, squeezed it, trying to shake free the storm that was Snaka, his presence like wasps in her thought-cage, like the weight of the deep ocean pressing down upon her.

Through the fog she realised one thing.

Lik-Rifa is bringing him here.

The ground beneath Orka's feet was shuddering now, throwing people from their feet, great rents opening up, clumps of rock and earth falling away, tumbling into the chamber below them. Orka looked around, searching for Breca, saw Glornir grimacing, sheathing his sword and stumbling to Vol, grabbing her wrist and pulling her with him. A flash of movement to Orka's right and she saw Drekr was on his feet, snarling, axe raised, running in a swaying stumble at her, the rumble of Snaka's rising masking his approach. Orka tried to turn and pull a seax from her belt, but the world was moving, bucking and heaving. A shape swept down out of the sky, small and hairless, Vesli, teeth bared in a snarl, long-fingered hands and claws reaching. She crashed into Drekr's head and wrapped her arms around him, claws raking at his flesh, teeth biting into his head. Drekr cried out, stumbling away and he was falling, rolling down the hill with Vesli still clinging to him, disappearing.

"BLOODSWORN," Glornir cried out, the bear in his voice roaring loud as Snaka's approach. "WITH ME," he bellowed and set off at a lumbering, drunk-swaying run across the hilltop. Orka saw Breca with Lif and Sæunn, the three of them trying to reach her and Orka stumbled to them, swept Breca up in her arms and they were all following Glornir, zigzagging across the hill, huge tears and holes opening up in the ground and falling, spinning away into the vastness of the chamber beneath them. Glornir had stopped, Orka reaching him and seeing that he stood at the edge of a great cliff, the River Falinn far below. Halja skidded to a halt beside them, looked over the edge and grinned.

"Wolves behind, a cliff ahead," she said.

"JUMP," Glornir shouted and then he was leaping from the cliff, hand in hand with Vol.

Orka looked at Breca, squeezed him tight.

"I love you with all that I am," she snarled, and leaped from the cliff with Breca in her arms.

CHAPTER SEVENTY-FIVE

VARG

Varg fell to his knees, a wordless voice roaring in his head, the world crashing down around him, the ground shaking beneath him. Leif and Sterkur were on the ground, too, Leif with a huge gash down one shoulder from Varg's cleaver.

He is keeping me from Einar.

A great wave of rage rose up in him, sweeping the voice in his head away and he launched himself from the ground, through the air and crashed into Leif, rolling with him.

"I am no *thrall*," he snarled, and then he let the wolf run free through his veins, opened his mouth and bit down, flesh tearing, blood spurting. Leif screamed, trying to break free, but Varg clung to him, Leif's arms flailing, and they rolled, were thrown into the air together as the ground bucked, then slammed back down. Leif was flopping now, and Varg opened his jaws, spat out blood and chunks of flesh. A strong hand grabbed his arm, dragging him up and he turned, snarling, but it was Røkia.

Røkia looked down at Leif and curled her lip, above her great strips of daylight appearing in the dome of the chamber's roof as huge sections fell crashing down around them.

Leif was dead, blood leaking from his torn throat, Sterkur nowhere to be seen. Varg checked his weapons, felt his seax still in its scabbard on his belt, saw his cleaver and axe and staggered to them, swept them up, and ran stumbling across the room.

Svik was kneeling beside Einar's body, tears streaking his cheeks, Røkia moving to stand beside him. She rested a hand upon his shoulder, both of them looking down at Einar. He lay on his back, a red wound in his throat, blood slick and pooled around him. He looked smaller, in death. Refna had cast herself onto Einar's body, was weeping, and a dozen children were standing around the big man, heads bowed, the rest of the Bloodsworn gathering about them. Edel stood and stared, her hound licking Einar's hand, and Æsa let out a great wail. Varg remembered his first day of meeting the Bloodsworn, when he had fought Einar and bitten his leg. A wave of grief and rage swept him, and he lifted his head and howled, long and echoing.

A lump of stone and earth the size of a longship crashed to the ground about fifty paces from them, shattering and raining earth and shards of rock, throwing people off their feet and dragging Varg back to the now. Flames were sweeping the room, great fissures opening in the ground like sailcloth tearing in a storm.

"Brák?" Varg growled.

"Gone, the *niðing*," Røkia said. "When the world decided to break, he ran like a rat."

Another boulder fell from above, staggering them all.

"What is happening?" Æsa growled, staring up at the collapsing hall.

"Snaka," Edel snarled, her lips twisting in a grimace. "I hear him in my soul."

"We need to get out of here," Svik said.

Everywhere, people were running, a great river of life trying to reach the gates, warriors, spiders, trolls, skraeling, the battle forgotten, all joined together in a desperate flight for survival, all running for the light. Rocks and clumps of earth the size of boulders were falling from the roof high above, crushing many, knocking many more from their feet, and the walls started to crumble. One of the great doors cracked and collapsed, an avalanche of stone sliding across the opening and blocking the way.

"Get out how?" Varg said.

Ulfrir came padding across the hall, weaving and staggering

around great banks of flame and huge rents in the ground, Skuld swooping through the air above him, his stone wolves with him. He was leading many across the hall, trying to cover them with his body. His *Úlfhéðnar* were running beneath him, and Varg saw Sighvat leading the Battle-Grim and Elvar's *drengrs*. Jarl Orlyg was there with the survivors of his warband, and behind them rode the remnants of Sulich and his mounted warriors, Taras running with them, carrying Iva in his arms. Varg saw Sighvat break away from the Battle-Grim and run staggering across the floor, disappearing behind a swathe of flames. Ulfrir saw the Bloodsworn and made for them. He looked to the gates.

"No escape that way," he snarled.

Sighvat emerged through the haze, carrying someone in his arms. As he reached them Varg saw it was Elvar's body. Tears had streaked lines through the blood and grime on Sighvat's cheeks.

A splintering, tearing sound and one of the branches of the great tree fell to the chamber floor, leaves and flames exploding around it, clouds of dust and smoke billowing.

"This way," Ulfrir growled, "to the tunnels", and he padded away from them.

Varg was about to turn and follow Ulfrir when he saw a handful of people stumbling through the hall, disappearing for a moment behind cloud and flame.

"WAIT," Varg shouted and Ulfrir turned.

"We must go," Ulfrir said, glancing up. The roof was a ragged hole, light leaking through in great patches and columns.

"There," Varg pointed, and began to run back into the hall.

Grend was leading a small band of people across the chamber, Varg seeing Uspa and Berak there, Gytha, a handful of *Berserkir* and *drengrs*. Between them they were carrying something, a great weight swaying within a strip of sailcloth.

It was Hrung.

"Go back," Ulfrir snarled at Varg and then the wolf was leaping across the chamber, a huge tremor ripping through the ground and bucking him from his feet, claws scrabbling, and he was upright again, leaping and reaching the small band, sweeping up the cloth that Hrung was suspended within in his jaws, protecting Grend and the others with his body, and they were heading back towards Varg and the others, who were swerving and stumbling across the hall.

Ulfrir padded up to them as they reached the entrance to the tunnel, pausing for a moment, turning and looking back into the chamber. The tremors were growing in intensity, the ground permanently shaking, and another huge chunk of the roof came tumbling down, crashing and erupting. An impact against the far wall of the chamber, beyond the tree and dais, a great fissure running down its entire length, from roof to ground, a seam of light appearing. The whole wall exploded inwards, crashing to the ground, light streaming in, a great cloud of dust erupting and expanding.

Varg, Ulfrir and all of them stood there, staring, frozen. The dust settled, but something blocked the light from pouring through the shattered wall. Something huge beyond all imagining. Varg saw the glow of two great fires high in the air. They blinked. A reptilian head formed around those eyes, grey-green scales, horned and barbed, fanning wide back to a neck thick with muscle and razored scale. The mouth opened, teeth long and sharp, curved fangs, saliva dripping, and a black-blue tongue flickered out, tasting the air.

"Ulfrir, my son," the serpent hissed, Snaka's voice filling the chamber, sibilant, his head swaying, moving from side to side, searching. Varg felt the words rattle and tremor through his bones, felt a pressure constrict around him like a fist squeezing him.

Ulfrir stared up at his father, let out a high-pitched whine, lips curling in a silent snarl, and then he turned and padded into the tunnel, Varg and everyone else following him.

CHAPTER SEVENTY-SIX

ORKA

Orka dragged herself from the river, coughing and spitting, her mail and woollen underclothes a sodden weight. Breca was on the bank above her, hacking up half of the river, or so it sounded.

"Don't stop here," Orka said. "Into the trees", and she gripped his hand and led him on, half dragging him into the shadowed safety of the treeline. Others of the Bloodsworn were already there, Halja and Gunnar, Lif and Sæunn, Glornir and Vol. Lif was chopping at deadwood for a fire. The river curled here, the current sweeping wide into the riverbank and spitting its contents into the weeds and shallows. More of the Bloodsworn were crawling from the river behind Orka.

They had plummeted into the Falinn from the top of Wolfdales, crashed into the icy water like a boulder, and Orka had used every ounce of strength the wolf in her blood could give her to stop her coat of mail from dragging her and Breca to the riverbed. They had burst above the water, gasping in great mouthfuls of air, and the current had grabbed them and swept them downriver until it spat them out on this deep curl.

Orka leaned against a tree and checked her weapons belt, brushed her fingertips across the two seaxes. Felt a wave of anger that she had not returned them to Drekr, had not buried them to their hilts in his flesh.

At least that niðing *Ilska is dead.*

"He might be dead," Breca said, looking up at Orka.

"Perhaps," she said. She hoped not.

Glornir came to stand beside her, Vol going to the deadwood that Lif had piled and speaking Seiðr-runes to start a fire. Breca shuffled close to Glornir, leaning against him, and Glornir put a big hand around his shoulder. Together the three of them looked back along the river, saw the slope of Wolfdales in the distance, half of the hill gone, just a ragged line. Snaka reared above it, his head striking down into the hall, the force of it felt in the ground beneath Orka's feet, smashing the side of the hill to rubble. The roar and rumble of the hill collapsing echoed through the forest, Snaka's head pulling out from the devastation and ruin, silhouetted before the sun.

"Can you feel him?" Glornir asked Orka.

"Aye. Like hornets in my thought-cage. A hand squeezing my bones."

"Aye," Glornir grunted.

"How do we fight that?" Breca whispered.

"One battle at a time," Glornir growled. "First the dragon and the rat."

"Heya," Orka agreed, and stamped her feet, puffed misting breath into her hands. The sun had started to sink towards the treeline of the Iron Wood, just a diffuse glow behind heavy cloud.

"Looks like snow," Halja Flat-Nose said as she joined them.

No more Bloodsworn had clawed their way out from the river for a while, but other bodies were floating past them now. Pale-bodied skraeling floating face-down, a young troll, a horse spinning slowly, warriors, thick-haired legs and other dismembered parts of frost-spiders. Shields floated, barrels, carts half submerged, shattered tables and chairs, flotsam from Ulfrir's great hall.

"Well, chief," Gunnar said. "What do we do now?"

"First, we shall dry our clothes and warm our bodies, else we will be frozen solid by dawn, and that will be the end of us doing anything. Then, we must see if we have friends left alive."

There was a whirring of wings in the boughs up above and they all reached for weapons.

"It's me," Vesli squeaked, and Breca cried out for happiness, held his arms out and Vesli flew into them, Breca wrapping the little vaesen tight.

"Vesli happy to see master Breca," the tennúr piped, looking around at them. "Happy to see mistress Orka, happy to see all of you."

"My thanks," Orka said, dipping her head to her, remembering how Vesli had hurled herself at Drekr as he was charging at her.

"Mistress Orka welcome," Vesli said. "Bad man got away," she said with a scowl. Then smiled. "But not all of him", and she reached into the pouch at her belt and pulled out a long tooth, flesh dangling from the root.

Orka smiled at that, and Vesli popped the tooth into her mouth and crunched it.

"Can you help us," Glornir asked Vesli.

"Vesli try help her friends," she said. "How?"

"Search for our friends, find survivors of Elvar's host if you can. We need to regroup. If there are any who have survived that." Glornir nodded at the jagged silhouette of Ulfrir's hall and Snaka, stark against the sinking sun.

As Orka followed Glornir's gaze she felt a snowflake fall and land upon her cheek, soft as a winter's kiss.

CHAPTER SEVENTY-SEVEN

VARG

Varg emerged from the tunnel into the last light of day to see snow falling, sifting through the boughs above him, settling soft and silent upon the ground. Ahead of him Ulfrir laid the sail-cloth he was carrying gently down, Hrung's muffled voice calling out his thanks. Ulfrir stepped away, and his wolf-form began to ripple and shimmer, shrinking in a series of judders and snaps, bones crackling, joints popping, fur disappearing, turning to skin, and then he was standing among the trees, dark-haired and amber-eyed. His *Úlfhéðnar* spread out wide, scouting the surrounding woodland, Skuld winging up into the branches and disappearing. The two stone wolves limped out from the tunnel and sat with their backs to Ulfrir, both searching the gloom of the forest, still guarding him.

The remnants of Elvar's war-host stumbled from the tunnel behind him, battered, bruised, bloodied.

The survivors of the Bloodsworn emerged first, a little more than a score of them led by Røkia and Svik, Edel and Æsa, all of them curled around Refna and the children like a protective hand. Hooves clattered and Sulich emerged, Kesha riding beside him, twenty or thirty survivors of his crew following after. Most of their quivers were empty. Taras walked with them, Iva cradled in his arms, a gash on her forehead crusted with blood. Jarl Orlyg and Jarl Logur stepped from the tunnel together, what remained of their warbands following them, perhaps a hundred warriors. Last came Sighvat carrying Elvar in his arms, Grend and Gytha either side of him, Uspa and Berak, the survivors of the Battle-Grim, Orv the Sneak there walking with Urt the Unwashed, a few score of Elvar's *drengrs* and *Berserkir* with them, and Frek leading the *Úlfhéðnar* who had once been thralled to Estrid of Darl, and had sworn their oaths to Elvar. Along with Ulfrir's *Úlfhéðnar* they numbered maybe five hundred, perhaps less.

They spread into the woodland around the tunnel, drawing axes and chopping at branches and undergrowth, clearing a space for a camp, searching for streams and water, tending to the wounded. Grend, Gytha, Uspa and Berak went to Hrung and unwrapped him from the sailcloth, heaved and pushed until he was sitting upright.

"Well, I did not expect to be thanking you for the saving of my life, not that it is much of a life," Hrung said to Grend.

Grend paused and looked at Hrung a long moment.

"Elvar liked you, she would have wanted you saved," he said with a grunt.

"Ach, Elvar, but that is a terrible loss," Hrung said. "She was a rare one. A terrible, *terrible* loss."

Grend said nothing, his face pale, tear-streaked, and he walked to Sighvat, who was wrapping Elvar's corpse in a cloak and helped the big man bind it about her with strips of leather.

Ulfrir walked across the clearing, Skuld and his *Úlfhéðnar* with him, stopping to look at Grend and Sighvat, gazing down upon Elvar's body. Varg saw others walking over to them, and without thinking he was joining them, all of them gathering to form a circle around Elvar's body, standing in silence.

"Elvar, you were a great woman," Ulfrir said, his voice a rasp. "You thralled a god, and that took some stones." A hint of a smile twitched his lips, replaced slowly with a look of sorrow. He looked around the clearing, meeting the eye of all gathered there. "She set me free. Set many of you free," people nodding, muttering heyas of agreement. Varg saw tears streaking Uspa's cheeks, many more around her weeping.

"We shall mourn you, Elvar," Ulfrir said. "But first we shall avenge you."

Grend made a growling, guttural sound in his throat.

"Elvar Chainbreaker," Ulfrir said, and all those around him echoed him, startling birds from boughs in the canopy above.

"ELVAR CHAINBREAKER."

A silence settled among them, punctuated by the crying of a child. Refna stepped forwards and took Uspa's hand, red-eyed, tears streaking lines through the blood and grime caked on her cheeks.

"Raise her," Refna said between her sobbing. "And raise Einar, bring him back to us. Please."

"I cannot, little one," Uspa said.

"But you raised Ulfrir, that is what everyone has told me."

"I did. But the power was locked within him, in his bones. He is a god. My Seiðr-spells released that power. Elvar is not a god, Einar is not a god. I cannot bring them back, much as I wish I could."

Uspa dropped to her knee and hugged Refna, the girl sobbing into Uspa's shoulder.

Slowly people began to walk away, going about the tasks of camp-making. Sulich was going through the saddle bags strapped to his horses, searching for food. They found some, oatcakes and biscuits, hard bread and cheese, though not even cheese could cheer Svik after the loss of Einar. And there was not enough to feed all the survivors.

A branch creaked above them and Varg looked up, thought he saw the shadow of movement, heard the faint whirr of wings.

"Come, No-Sense," Røkia said, "let us go and see if we can hunt some food." She walked through the survivors, tapping warriors on shoulders, picking those she thought best suited and least injured to go hunting, and then Varg was loping into the dark woods, letting his wolf-sense guide him.

Varg sat beside Røkia and sucked the marrow from the thigh bone of a rabbit, hot fat burning his fingertips. He welcomed the warmth. They had risked a fire, cutting slim branches and weaving them into fences to mask the light. Varg was too tired to speak, exhaustion sitting deep in his bones, fractured moments of the past day swirling through his head. Of Elvar falling, of the sword stabbing into Einar's throat, of Brák Trolls-Bane's words.

I'm sure your sister deserved it.

The wolf in his blood raised its head and gave a low snarl. Even his wolf was exhausted.

And where is Glornir? Vol? The Skullsplitter and the others?

Varg and the others had seen them fighting on the stairwell of the tree, had tried to follow them but had been cut off by the flames.

They must have reached the rooftop, maybe escaped out onto the hilltop. But then Snaka came . . . He did not want to think about that, wanted to hope that somehow Glornir and the others were still out there. He blew out a long breath, just sat and listened to Ulfrir talk with Elvar's captains. Gytha and Uspa, Sighvat, Orlyg and Logur were there, Frek, and Svik and Sulich speaking for the Bloodsworn. They sat close to Hrung, who was uncharacteristically silent, his eyes downcast, as if deep in thought.

"Well, quite a day," Orlyg was saying. "I think we were winning, right up until that arseling serpent decided to smash the hall in around us." Grunts and heyas of agreement around him. Ulfrir surprised them all by chuckling.

"I have never heard my father called an *arseling*, before," he said, eyes shining. "It suits him."

Varg could still feel the presence of Snaka, like a distant whisper in his blood.

"But what do we do now?" Jarl Logur said.

"We must kill Lik-Rifa and Rotta, and quickly, while they are hampered by their wounds. They will not expect us to attack them now. They will think we are fleeing, putting space between us to regroup," Ulfrir said. "And we must kill my father, too, if that is possible."

"He died once, he can die again," Hrung muttered.

"We need information," Uspa said. "We need to find them, know their plan, and work from there. We need Grok and Kló."

"No," Ulfrir said. "Not now that my father is back. They are his, heart and soul. They would betray us to him. I would not be surprised if they are searching for us now, at Snaka's command."

"I will fly, I will search, be our eyes in the sky," Skuld said.

"No, I will not risk you," Ulfrir said. "You are too easily seen, too easily recognised."

"Then what do you suggest?" Svik asked him.

"Uspa is right, we need information," Ulfrir said. "But we also need allies." He looked around the camp, at their battered warriors. "We are too few now."

"That sounds wonderful," Orlyg said, "but we are in a forest with only trees for company, and a dragon, a rat and a serpent the size of a mountain not too far away, along with whoever and whatever of their host survived your father's visit." He looked at Ulfrir. "What allies do we have left?"

Ulfrir smiled at Orlyg.

A fluttering of wings from the darkness above and they were all moving, weapons hefted, what few arrows left to them nocked and pointing.

"Don't hurt Vesli," a high-pitched voice squeaked above them, and the vaesen whirred down out of the darkness.

"Well, there is our eyes in the sky," Svik said with a smile.

"Vesli bring friends," she said, and footsteps were crunching on snow, all of them turning to see some of Ulfrir's *Úlfhéðnar* guards escorting a group of warriors into the camp.

Glornir walked at their head, Vol and Orka Skullsplitter at either shoulder, and a score or so of the Bloodsworn followed after them. Svik leaped to his feet, cheering and grinning.

"Ah, the Shieldbreaker and the Farmer. I feel better already," Orlyg said with an expansive grin.

CHAPTER SEVENTY-EIGHT

GUÐVARR

Against all the odds, I am alive, Guðvarr thought as he dropped his shield with a clatter, unbuckled his weapons belt, slithered out of his coat of mail and collapsed onto his cloak on the ground, exhaustion dragging him down like a current in his veins. His woollen tunic and linen under-tunic were sweat-stained and stinking, but he did not care, did not have the strength left in him to seek out his kit and change into clean clothes. He was sat close to a fire, snow falling steadily now in flakes big as leaves and he watched fires flicker into life about him as they were kindled across the great swathe of their camp. The ground had changed with Snaka's coming, great ridges of earth running through the camp, trees snapped or fallen, roots grasping at the sky so that all above them was cloud and falling snow. Huge fissures and rents had scarred the ground, but enough of the camp and supplies were left that they could cook and eat.

And sleep, Guðvarr thought. *And there is only enough food left because more than half of Lik-Rifa's war-host have been slaughtered, crushed, or hurled into the river.*

He looked around at the survivors of the last battle, a pitiful few compared to the war-host that had assembled upon these banks only two days gone. He saw warriors limping, the wounded being carried, heard skraeling mourning their dead in their strange, ululating cries. Heard a troll cry out as their leader, Heðin, cauterised a wound with a strip of iron that had been left to heat in the fire. Guðvarr knew that there were frost-spiders and night-hags still lurking in the darkness of the forest, but he had seen so many of their dead piled in heaps that he knew their numbers must be vastly reduced.

At one point of the battle, as Lik-Rifa and Rotta had fled, he had been certain that the battle was lost, and that he was going to die.

Thank the dead gods that we have Snaka on our side, he thought, although even the thought of Snaka set his limbs to trembling. At the sight of the father of the gods' serpentine head crashing through the wall of Ulfrir's chamber Guðvarr had almost lost control of his bladder and soiled his breeches. He leaned forward and sniffed, grimaced.

Perhaps I did lose a little control of my bladder.

He chose to turn his thoughts away from Snaka and watched as haunches and joints of meat were pulled from barrels and put onto spits over fires or set into pots that bubbled with boiling water.

"Get me some mead, or ale," he said to one of Sigrún's *drengrs*, a dark-haired woman with a red wound across her jawline who had kindled the fire he was sitting at and was turning a spitted leg of venison. She looked at him a moment, her lip curling, then Jarl Sigrún was heading towards them, walking away from Drekr, Krúsa and Glunn Iron-Grip, the only captains of Lik-Rifa's war-host who had returned to camp so far. The *drengr* lifted a jug and poured a cup for him, leaned and handed it to him.

"My thanks," he said with a smile and sipped as Sigrún sat beside him.

"Ilska is dead," Sigrún said.

"What?" Guðvarr gasped. Despite the fact they had just passed through two days of war he could not conceive of Ilska actually falling in battle.

"Glornir Shieldbreaker slew her, on the hill," Sigrún said. She looked at him and put her hand on his wrist. "And Skalk is dead, too."

Guðvarr sucked in a breath and stifled the smile and shout of joy that rose up within him.

Skalk, dead. That niðing, *torturing, deceitful, goat-humping arseling. Oh, what a day this has been.*

"And Estrid, too," Guðvarr said, as if in passing. "She was slain when the bull-man and *Berserkirs* smashed our shield wall."

Sigrún nodded.

"Well, there is still a wolf to slay, but it looks like we have chosen the winning side, Guðvarr, and we have lived to reap the rewards. All has changed with the arrival of Snaka. A new world is dawning, and new powers." She squeezed his wrist. "And we shall be among those powers."

A ripple went through the camp, a hush falling, and Guðvarr felt a shift in the air. Abruptly heavy, like a thunderstorm. He looked up, saw Lik-Rifa and Rotta walking into the camp, back in their human forms now, thankfully. Both of them bore the wounds of battle, walked stiffly, blooms of blood on their tunics. Rotta limped and held one arm protectively to his left side. Lik-Rifa had new red wounds across her head and body, one side of her face crusted with dried blood. They walked a step behind a man, taller by head and shoulders than both of them. A milk-pale face, mottled like scales, a sharp ridge of a nose, dark hair tied severely at his nape and eyes that flickered with red-gold fire. The tips of teeth protruded from his dark-veined lips. He wore a grey wool tunic embroidered in gold-swirling serpents edged with red-dyed fur, a belt of leather and gold buckled about his waist.

Dread Snaka, father of the gods.

Guðvarr felt a compulsion to stand and walk to him, to throw himself upon his knees and bow, to swear oaths of loyalty.

Snaka stopped and looked around the camp and everything in it as if it all belonged to him. As if the whole world belonged to him.

Which it does, I suppose, Guðvarr thought, feeling a flutter of fear in his belly.

I am bored of this feeling; fear is distinctly overrated. I long for a day when I awake and live from dawn to sleep without one moment of fear.

All had stopped what they were doing and turned to look at the gods walking among them as they strode into the camp, came to a stop at its centre. All eyes were fixed upon Snaka, drawn like iron filings to a lodestone. The sense of fear and awe was palpable, a shimmering in the air.

"Kneel before your maker, your master, your king," Rotta cried out, sinking to his knees before Snaka, and Lik-Rifa dropped to one knee, bowed her head.

"My father, my king," her voice tremored through the camp.

Snaka stepped forwards, looking at all those gathered before him, at the hundreds of lives, as if they were his, too.

I suppose we are, Guðvarr thought as he stumbled to his feet and knelt before dread Snaka, maker of the world.

CHAPTER SEVENTY-NINE

VARG

Varg used sand, oil and a crumpled ball of wire to scour the blood and grime from his weapons, axe, cleaver and seax laid out on the ground before him. He was sitting with a handful of the Bloodsworn, Røkia and Svik, Gunnar and Halja and Edel, Lif and Sæunn, Orka and Breca, all of them going about the cleaning or repairing of their battle kit. Orka was casting a whetstone across the blades of the two seaxes at her belt. Varg did not think they were blunt, or indeed could be any sharper, but the look in Orka's eyes stopped him from mentioning that to her. Many in the camp were doing the same, tending to their kit, or sleeping. It was late into the night, though the snowfall gave off a soft-sheened glow, reflecting the flicker of dappled firelight.

Glornir and Vol were huddled with Ulfrir and the other captains, trying to navigate some plan that would give them even the smallest chance of surviving the next few days. Vesli flew out of the night, spiralling above Ulfrir and the others, squeaking with excitement.

"I have found them, I have found them," she blurted, flapping down to alight upon Ulfrir's shoulder. He looked at her with one raised eyebrow, but she did not seem to notice.

"Well done, Vesli," Ulfrir said. "And where are they?"

"Spread close to the riverbank before your hall. Or what is left of your hall," the tennúr said. "They have guards, but not as many as they did. The rat and the dragon are there," she paused and shivered. "And the serpent. Vesli not like him."

"I do not like him, either," Skuld said.

"We are in your debt," Ulfrir said, "and one day I hope to repay you for your courage and loyalty."

"Teeth. Lots of teeth," Vesli said without a moment's pause.

"If it is in my power, you shall have a mountain of teeth," Ulfrir said with a smile.

Vesli grinned, revealing her two rows of teeth, and flickered into the air whirring over to Breca, landed on his legs.

"Vesli tired," she said, and curled up on Breca's lap, wrapping a wing over her shoulder and head, Breca stroking her.

Footsteps and Varg looked up to see Frek the *Úlfhéðnar* approaching them. The sides of his head were shaved, like Varg's, and the long hair above it was braided and tied at his crown. He wore a blood-crusted coat of mail, sword and seax at his belt. Walking into the circle of the Bloodsworn he looked down at Svik.

"The last time I sat with you Bloodsworn I was a thrall," he said, his voice a rasping snarl, like sand scraped over mail.

"And now you are free," Svik said to him.

"I am," Frek said, rubbing his hand across the stubble growing on the sides of his head. He squatted down beside Svik.

"You told a tale, when I travelled with you. About the way of the world."

"I did," Svik said with a smile, which faded. "Einar liked that tale."

Varg remembered Einar laughing. It had been about a troll stuck under a rock, and Svik had named the troll Einar.

"I liked it, too," Frek said. "I especially liked the part at the end, where the young lad set the wolf free, and told the wolf that we decide the way of the world. In our thought-cage." He tapped the side of his head with one finger. "I liked it, but I thought it was no more than a tale, never to come true. But Elvar did that. She changed the way of the world, by thinking it," he tapped his head again, "and deciding to do it."

Heyas of agreement rippled around the Bloodsworn.

"Our choices matter," Frek said. "I did not think they did, I did not think one decision could change anything, but I was wrong."

"We just need more people to make the right choices," Varg murmured.

"Come, sit and drink with us, Frek the Free," Svik said, and offered him a cup of ale. Frek took it and sat with them.

"Orka set me free," Sæunn said, and eyes turned to her, moving on to Orka, who just continued to scrape the whetstone across her blades. Voices murmured approval.

"I am free," Sæunn said, as if she whispered of finding treasure. Then she stood and strode into the shadows of the trees to relieve her bladder.

Lif began to sing, a slow, mournful song telling a tale of love and loss, of family and tragedy, of good times shared. His voice was sweet, ebbing and flowing like the tide, making Varg think of rare memories with his sister, when they had shared a stolen honeycomb on Kolskegg's farm, and had to scrub their fingers for fear of giving themselves away, of when she had pushed him over an anthill in the grass and when he had screamed as the ants bit him she had laughed so hard she fell over. Lif's voice trailed off, singing of love between sweethearts, fading slowly. He glanced at Halja.

"No," Halja said, not taking her eyes from her sword, where she was working at a notch in the blade with a whetstone. She paused and looked up at Lif. "You have proven yourself in battle, you have a warrior's heart, and I have no doubt that you will find the vengeance you seek. But I am not for you," she said. He blinked at her, then looked down, his neck and cheeks flushing.

"It is not because I find you weak, or foolish, or irritating," Halja said, continuing to run the whetstone rhythmically across her blade. "Well, perhaps sometimes irritating. It is because you are a man. Men are not for me." She shrugged and Lif nodded. "But you have my respect, and my friendship, always. And if you wished to join the Bloodsworn, I would gladly call you brother and trust you to stand beside me in the shield wall. I hope that counts for more than a hump in the bushes."

A smile spread across Lif's face at that, and laughter rippled among their group.

Sæunn walked back out of the gloom.

"Her, though, I think she would enjoy a good hump in the bushes with you. I have seen the way she looks at you."

Lif blinked rapidly. And flushed red again, glancing sideways at Sæunn.

"What?" Sæunn said to those looking at her as she returned.

"Ask Lif," Gunnar Prow said, and smiled. It was the first time Varg had seen him smile since he had returned without Revna.

Varg went back to cleaning his kit, tested the blade of his cleaver and slipped it back into its leather cover at his belt. He felt a prickling in his skin, the wolf in his blood stirring, and he turned to see Røkia looking at him, an unsettling intensity to her gaze, amber flickering in her eyes.

"What?" Varg said, looking around, thinking there must be some danger somewhere.

"I am not like Halja," she said.

"Huh?" Varg grunted.

"I do not prefer women to men," Røkia said.

"Oh. I see," Varg said.

"No, you do not see, No-Sense," Svik chuckled, sitting close to them.

"I thought . . ." Varg said, and Røkia continued to look at him with that burning intensity. "That you did not like men."

"Most of the time, that is true," Røkia said with a shrug. "Most men are idiots. Especially men like Svik. But you, Varg No-Sense." She leaned forwards and put her hand upon his, her skin rough and calloused from years of blade-work. Squeezed his hand. "I choose you."

"Choose me?"

"Yes. I choose you." She stood, pulling him up, and he rose to his feet, his heart abruptly hammering in his chest, in his head, in his throat. Røkia turned and led him away from their group, walking past Ulfrir and their captains. As they drew near Ulfrir rose.

"Where are you going?" Orlyg asked him.

"To see what I can do about finding an ally," Ulfrir said.

"Before you go," Hrung said, "I must tell you something." Ulfrir and all the others looked at him. "Elvar had a plan," he said, slowly, as if the words were sticking in his throat.

Ulfrir sat back down, and Røkia was leading Varg out of earshot, into the gloom of the trees.

"Where are we—" Varg mumbled and then Røkia was turning, pushing him hard against a tree.

"What are you—" he said but forgot the rest as Røkia's lips were close to his, her eyes dark, shining with flecks of amber and reflected snow, her breath smelling of apples and mead.

"I choose you, Varg No-Sense," she said, and her lips were on his and he was kissing her in return, her hands rising to his waist, finding his weapons belt and unbuckling it, dropping it with a thud in the snow, tugging at his breeches.

"I choose you," he whispered back to her, and then they were sinking to the ground.

CHAPTER EIGHTY

BIÓRR

Biórr trembled as he knelt before Snaka, his knees crunching through the ice-ream crusting on the snow. He could feel Snaka's presence within him, like mead in the blood. All else except Snaka was blurred, all sound except Snaka's voice a dim, muted whisper. He looked up at the maker of the world. Snaka was tall, towering over Biórr, looking down at him with a sharp-boned face, his dark hair pulled back tight, the points of teeth protruding from beneath dark, bluish-black lips. Biórr took his hand and pressed his lips to the pale-mottled flesh. The smell of something long dead wafted around him.

"You are descended from Rotta," Snaka said, his voice a sibilant, rasping hiss.

"Yes, my king," Biórr said, his voice cracking.

I created Rotta. I created you, Snaka's voice slithered inside his head. *You are mine.*

"Yes, my king," Biórr repeated. A flick of Snaka's hand, long-fingered with nails black as blood spilled in the night, and Biórr was dismissed, rising and moving away, another warrior moving forward to drop on the ground before Snaka.

Biórr looked for Fain and saw him standing with the Tainted children, walked over to him. His legs felt like lead weights were strapped to them, every step an effort, and every muscle and sinew in his body ached. The climb to the summit of Wolfdales, sneaking into the hall's dark corridors, the fight against Elvar and all that happened after. Exhaustion was his constant companion now, and alongside it the weight of Snaka's presence, a sibilant voice whispering indiscernible words inside his head, a pressure within and without, as if the very air had changed. He blinked, his eyes stinging, and in his head he saw a fractured image of Elvar, standing over him, her sword point at his throat. Shook his head, tried to scatter the memory as a horse scatters flies.

He reached Red Fain and smiled at the old warrior.

"Snaka stands among us," Fain said, awe and fear in his voice.

"Aye," Biórr nodded. He knew the battle had hovered on the brink of ruin before Snaka's arrival, knew that Snaka had changed everything, but still he felt a deep foreboding in his gut. The rat in his blood was whispering for him to flee, though he knew not why.

"I am glad to see you still breathing," Fain said to him, clapping a big hand on his shoulder and squeezing.

"So am I," Biórr said, managing a smile, through the fear and heaviness in his heart.

I should be rejoicing. We have almost won. Though there is still a wolf to slay, out there somewhere. If he survived the fall of his hall.

"I wish I had been there, wish I had fought in the greatest battle of our time."

"Of any time, I think," Biórr said, remembering the din of the battle-storm, the warriors and vaesen screaming, the Froa, the dragon, the wolf. The oceans of blood.

"You are injured, Fain, there is no shame in that. And you have had perhaps the most important task, looking after these." He gestured to Harek and the Tainted children.

"Aye," Fain said. "They are the ones we are fighting for. They are the ones who will live in a world made free by our sacrifice."

Biórr said nothing, but frowned, Elvar's words echoing in his head.

Footsteps and Rotta appeared. His face was bruised, dried blood streaking it, and Biórr saw that he walked with his left arm tucked tight to his side, blooms of blood on his wool tunic. He remembered Grend hurling himself at Rotta and stabbing him in a frenzy of blows.

"You are injured, my lord," Biórr said to him.

Rotta scowled at Biórr. "That is the understatement of the year," he said. "And no thanks to you. You chopped off my tail, if I recall correctly."

"I did, to save you," Biórr said. His hand brushed the top of Elvar's axe, thrust through his belt.

"Fair comment, I admit," Rotta said. "The wolf had me pinned and was likely to have eaten me, so, it would seem I owe you my thanks for saving my life." He dipped his head to Biórr, gave his charming smile, then looked at him more intently.

"What is it?" he asked.

Biórr heard Elvar's voice in his head.

Has Rotta not told you? I have set the Tainted free. Heard Ulfrir's words before Lik-Rifa and Broðir. *Elvar set me free*, the wolf-god had said.

"You knew," Biórr said.

"Knew what?" Rotta asked him.

"That Elvar had set Ulfrir and the Tainted free."

"What?" Fain said, a gasped splutter.

Rotta shrugged. "She did tell me," he said, "but I did not believe her. I was as surprised as you when Ulfrir did not bow to Broðir's command."

"She told you?" Biórr said, echoing Rotta's words.

"Aye, when I spoke to her on the bridge, before the battle began. But you know the lies and bluster people talk at moments like that. All threats and insults." He shrugged again, looked at Biórr.

"Regret is a luxury we cannot afford," Rotta said quietly. "Put it from your head, else it will eat at you. It is pointless, will change nothing."

Biórr nodded, though Elvar's face still swirled through his head, her words echoing. *I set them free, set them free, free, free.* He scowled at Rotta but saw that the rat-god was staring at Snaka.

"What have we done," he heard Rotta breathe.

"Rotta, Lik-Rifa," Snaka's voice rang out, soft and sibilant, yet filling the whole camp. Biórr looked to see that the entire war-host had finished in their obeisance to their risen maker and king.

"Come, my son, my daughter, we will talk of wayward Ulfrir," Snaka said. "And I am hungry. Three hundred years of death has given me quite an appetite."

"Of course, Father," Rotta said. "Sit, and we shall serve you."

Lik-Rifa ushered Snaka to a table set at the centre of the camp, chairs arranged before it, platters of steaming vegetables and fried potatoes, cups, eating knives and jugs already laid there, and he sat in Lik-Rifa's tall-backed chair.

"Yes, Father, we should talk of Ulfrir," Lik-Rifa said. "We must find him and kill him."

Snaka turned his black-eyed gaze upon Lik-Rifa.

"Mussst?" he said, voice soft, tongue flickering. "You do not say *must* to me."

"No, Father," Lik-Rifa said, her voice shaking, "no, no, I am sorry. Forgive me, please," and she dropped to her knees beside him, lowered her head.

Snaka stared at her for long moments, a dread silence filling the camp, then he placed a hand upon her head.

"You have tried to slay the wolf, and you could not," Snaka said. "Do not think me a fool. I know why you have raised me, wrapped my bones with flesh, put blood pulsing through my veins." Biórr saw Snaka's grip tightening around Lik-Rifa's head, saw rivulets of blood run from where his black fingernails dug into her scalp. "It is not love for a father that has driven you, it is fear of defeat. Fear of death. You need me to turn the balance, to save your scaly skin. Is this not true?"

His nails dug deeper into Lik-Rifa's head.

"Yes," she whimpered.

"But I am not your pawn to be used. I am your father, your *king*. And this is my world, not yours. Everything in it belongs to me, all that breathes, all that grows, including you and your brothers," he hissed. "You belong to me."

"Y . . . y . . . yes, Father," Lik-Rifa groaned.

Snaka stared at her with his baleful eyes, a tremor running through the muscle and tendon of his wrist and into his hand.

"Rise," he said contemptuously and gave a flick of his wrist, sending Lik-Rifa falling onto her back. She stood shakily.

"Father, you must be hungry," Rotta said, hurrying forwards with a trencher full of carved meat, steam rising from it. He set it down on the table, drew a knife from his belt and skewered a slice of meat, setting it on the plate before Snaka.

"And thirsty, too, I do not doubt," Rotta said, setting down a silver cup before Snaka, mead spilling from it.

"Sister, sit, and we shall all eat and drink together," Rotta said, skewering another slice of meat and putting it on a plate set before an empty chair.

"Y . . . yes, brother," Lik-Rifa said. She sat in the empty seat beside Snaka and picked up her long-bladed eating knife. Thin lines of blood trickled from her scalp and down her face.

Rotta poured mead from a jug for Lik-Rifa, and another cup for himself, then moved around the table to sit in the other empty chair at Snaka's side. He lifted his cup.

"To the return of our king. To father, son and daughter, a family reunited," he said and drank from his cup.

Snaka and Lik-Rifa raised their cups and drank deep, Lik-Rifa's hand shaking, drinking so fast that mead ran down her chin. She emptied her cup and refilled it, drank some more as Rotta skewered slices of meat and set them on her plate.

"Come, Rotta," she said, "be quick, I am so hungry I can hardly wait." She licked her lips with her thick, blue-black tongue and Biórr saw her jaw shimmer for a moment, saw the hint of her dragon teeth and elongated muzzle.

"Yes," Snaka rasped as he set his cup down. He looked down at the meat on his plate.

"What is for our meal?" he asked.

Rotta looked at Snaka, a sly smile spreading across his face.

"You are, Father," he said.

Snaka's face twisted, and Biórr saw a tremor run through him, a grimace twisting his features. He opened his mouth to speak, but only a rasping grunt came out. His body began to shake.

"What—" he gasped, prickles of sweat beading his forehead. Black lines appeared across his face, as if his veins were filling with ink. His fingers clawed at the table, nails gouging splinters of wood.

"You are right, Father," Rotta said, standing, "there was no fatherly love involved in our raising of you. Quite the opposite, in fact. We despise you. Of course we raised you to help us win this fight. But not in the way you think. Not by asking you to defeat Ulfrir for us." He tutted. "No, you are far too unreliable to trust that task to. And in truth we do not need all of you to complete the task ourselves. We just need your heart."

Tremors were spasming through Snaka's body now, sweat running down his face, staining his tunic, black veins threading down his forearms and across the backs of his hands. He fell from his chair onto his knees, white-knuckled hands and black nails clawing into the table, keeping him from toppling into the snow.

Lik-Rifa stood and smiled.

"Who is the one on their knees now?" she snarled at him.

Snaka's whole body was shuddering, rasping breath and spit leaking and foaming on his lips, a string of saliva hanging from his mouth, pooling on the table. Biórr heard the echo of words on Snaka's breath, and slowly the convulsions began to subside. The black ink in Snaka's veins stopped spreading, began slowly to retreat, climbing back up his arms, as if someone were sucking the poison from him.

Rotta and Lik-Rifa stared in frozen, horrified terror.

Snaka coughed and retched, his body heaving, a convulsion rippling through him, another wracking cough and he spat something black onto the table. A viscous mass, sticky and malleable. The table hissed and blackened where it landed. Snaka looked up, eyes fixing Rotta, and he began to stand, still coughing, his stomach contracting, spitting out more black mucus onto the table.

"NO," Lik-Rifa screamed and stabbed her eating knife into one of Snaka's hands, slicing through meat and tendon, passing between bones to sink deep into the timber of the table, pinning him there.

Snaka let out a hissing scream and half rose, his face rippling, juddering, body shimmering, and then Rotta was moving, his paralysis broken, grabbing a fistful of Snaka's hair and plunging his knife into one side of Snaka's neck, the tip bursting out the other side, Rotta sawing the blade away from him, carving through the meat and gristle of Snaka's windpipe. A jet of black blood exploded onto the table, Snaka slamming himself back into Rotta, his head crunching into Rotta's face as he coughed great gouts of blood, Lik-Rifa hanging onto the blade in Snaka's hand, her other hand gripping his arm, long-taloned fingers sinking into his flesh, holding him tight. And slowly Snaka slumped back into his chair, blood pulsing from the great wound in his throat, then toppled face down onto the table, blood spreading in a pool. A thunderclap of sound, a ripping, tearing and the ground shuddered, a fissure tremoring through the earth, zigzagging out from Snaka's feet.

A silence settled, filled the whole camp, Biórr staring, mouth open, all staring in stunned shock and horror, snow gently falling about them.

Lik-Rifa ripped the knife free of Snaka's hand and Rotta grabbed him beneath the arms, heaved him up, turning him over and slammed him down onto the table, ripped Snaka's tunic open and put his knife to his chest. Stabbed hard, punching through the breastbone and began to saw. Lik-Rifa leaned over her father's body, slavering, saliva dripping from her lips, dipping her fingers into the pool of Snaka's blood and licking them.

"His heart, Rotta, we must feast on his heart," she said.

Rotta grunted, cutting and sawing, Biórr hearing bones snapping, flesh tearing, and then Rotta was reaching into Snaka's chest. Heaving at bone, snapping it, forcing his hand deeper into the cavity. A wet tearing sound and Rotta ripped Snaka's heart free, held it up in his fist.

"Give it to me," Lik-Rifa snarled at Rotta.

Rotta smiled at Lik-Rifa and opened his mouth wide, his jawline shifting, teeth growing.

A shape flew down from out of the white blur, a tennúr, arms grasping, snatching Snaka's heart and winging away, speeding back up into the gloom.

Rotta and Lik-Rifa roared and bellowed, their bodies juddering, the air about them shimmering as they began to change.

A flicker of wings whirred above Biórr, another tennúr flying out of the forest, more of them appearing.

"WARE," they were shouting, "WARE THE WOLF", and behind Biórr a wolf howled, the sound filling the forest, filling the world, ringing out, echoing. Biórr spun around and saw figures charging from the gloom, roaring and howling as they came.

CHAPTER EIGHTY-ONE

VARG

Varg ran howling from the cover of the trees. He had no shield, had lost it in the chaos of Ulfrir's hall, had his hand-axe and seax in his fists. His mind was still reeling from what he had just witnessed: the murder of Snaka the god-king, maker of the world, his heart carved from his chest and held aloft for all to see.

Varg had been standing close to Ulfrir, and the wolf-god had been transfixed, staring in frozen, horrified shock as Rotta had held his blood-drenched fist aloft.

"No," Ulfrir had snarled, "they *cannot* eat his heart, the power it will give them," and he was transforming from man to wolf in a series of cracks and spasms and judders.

The connotations of Ulfrir's words burst like bright lights in Varg's thought-cage.

They did not resurrect Snaka to win the battle for them, they brought him back so that they could eat his heart and steal his power.

Ulfrir had already shifted into his wolf-form and burst howling from the trees, his two stone wolves loping at his side, hackles raised and snarling, Skuld winging overhead. All followed him, warriors exploding from the ragged treeline in a roar, no organised shield wall here, half of the Bloodsworn were without shields now, just a savage charge to the blood-soaked end of this conflict, Glornir and Orka leading them. Even Orlyg ran at the head of his warriors, Jarl Logur with him, Sighvat lumbering at the head of the Battle-Grim, Grend charging with Gytha and Elvar's oathsworn *drengrs*, *Berserkir* and *Úlfhéðnar* frothing and snarling and growling alongside them. The pulsing thunder of hooves and Sulich led his mounted warriors from the trees, their hooves hammering in time, the drumbeat of war. A few arrows flickered from bows but most of them had spent their arrows, held their spears high, lowered them as they approached the first ranks of their enemy. Screams rang out as they skewered skraeling and warriors, the thud and crunch of horses colliding with flesh, breaking bones as they thundered through the unprepared camp, leaving their spears in the bodies of their enemy, blood splattering the snow, a glitter as they drew their sabres.

And then Varg was among them, chopped and stabbed with axe and seax at a skraeling, ducked the sword-swing of a Raven-Feeder, twisted around their shield and hacked into the woman's hamstring, dropping her to her knee, Røkia finishing her with a thrust of her sword into the woman's throat, and they were moving on.

A deafening roar as Ulfrir reached Lik-Rifa and Rotta, both of them shifting into their dragon and rat forms, people running, jumping to escape the destruction of their transformations, Ulfrir leaping, slamming into Lik-Rifa, jaws snapping, ripping, both of them crashing to the ground. Rotta bit at Ulfrir's haunches, raked one claw through fur. Skuld came hurtling screeching from the sky, hurling a spear that punched into Rotta's back. He squealed and reared up onto his hind legs as the two stone wolves hit him. They fell together, snapping at Rotta as he rolled on the ground, tearing out chunks of flesh and fur. Trolls came roaring out of the darkness, rushing to Lik-Rifa and Rotta's defence, clubs swinging, spears stabbing, and Ulfrir's *Úlfhéðnar* surged around them like surf washing around boulders on the shore.

Varg moved with Røkia and Svik, Edel and Æsa, trying to keep Glornir in his view, staying tight with the Bloodsworn, but even as he fought and killed his eyes were ever searching, seeking a weasel-sharp face with weathered skin and a necklace of troll tusks.

A knot of Lik-Rifa's warriors were rallying against the first rush, Varg seeing shields with wings upon them, the emblem of Darl, a fair-haired warrior barking orders at them, sword and shield in hand. An image in Varg's head, of the same warrior standing over him and Torvik, back in Rotta's chamber. Of her sword stabbing almost casually into Torvik's throat.

Torvik, the first person who ever called me friend.

Varg touched Røkia's arm with his seax, pointed.

"Yrsa, Skalk's *drengr*," he said.

Without words they were both moving, weaving across the battleground, Svik and Edel and Æsa following them.

Yrsa must have glimpsed them because she set her feet, raised her shield. A warrior stepped in either side of Yrsa, shields slamming together, others looming behind, but Røkia was on them before they had time to lock together, using her shield as a ram, driving a wedge between Yrsa and the warrior on her right, crashing through. Røkia's sword snaked out, slicing across the man's throat, sending him spinning away, gurgling and frothing blood, another handful of warriors coming at Røkia and she was snarling and moving around them.

Varg let the wolf filter through him, felt its strength and speed, snarled at Yrsa and twisted around the spear that darted out at him from behind the shield of the warrior still standing beside her, a dark-haired woman in a nasal helm. Varg hooked his bearded axe over her shield rim, stepped around her, dragging her shield down, pulling her stumbling to her side and buried his seax in her eye. Ripped it out and she fell, dead before she hit the ground.

Other warriors were moving on him, four or five with eagles on their shields. A hound leaped at one, crashed into its shield and hurled them to the ground, Edel stepping in and finishing him with her spear, and then Svik and Æsa were there, sweeping the others away in a tide of steel and linden-wood.

"I remember you," Yrsa snarled at Varg.

"Do you remember my friend? His name was Torvik," he growled back as he chopped at her head, Yrsa blocking the blow with her shield. Then she was coming at him, sword stabbing, shield punching, all short, fast, efficient movements and Varg realised instantly that she knew her weapons craft. Was possibly better than him. But Varg was faster, and stronger, and wolf-cunning. He backed away, let her come at him, feinted a slip in the snow and she was stepping in, sword stabbing at his throat. Varg swept her blade away with his seax and lunged his axe under the rim of her shield, hooked it around her ankle and heaved, dragging her leg into the air, toppling her onto her back. She grunted, raised her shield over her and sliced her sword at Varg's leg. He stepped away, then darted in before she could catch him with her backswing and stamped hard on her sword-wrist. The crack of bone breaking, and she cried out.

"For Torvik, for friendship," Varg snarled, and he chopped his axe down into her face. The crunch of bone breaking, blood spurting, and he ripped the blade free, teeth spraying, Yrsa's limbs flopping.

He stood there, chest heaving, and heard shouted Seiðr-words, saw the flicker and crackle of Seiðr in the air, heard the bull-throated roar of Taras and looked, saw Iva locked in Seiðr-battle with a fair-haired Galdurwoman wielding a red-rune blazing staff. Taras was trying to get to the Galdurwoman, but he was surrounded by a ring of warriors, darting in and out, stabbing at him with spears, Varg recognising this crew in their hunting leathers and furs. And then he saw him. Brák Trolls-Bane, slim sword in his fist, darting in behind Taras.

The wolf in Varg surged hard through his blood, growling and snarling.

"BRÁK," Varg bellowed.

CHAPTER EIGHTY-TWO

GUÐVARR

Guðvarr hurried close to Sigrún, who was calling her *drengrs* to her, a small bedrock of safety in a swirling sea of sharp steel. When Guðvarr had heard the wolf howl his guts had turned to water and he had scrambled for his *brynja*, tried to slither so quickly into it that mail rings had snared in his beard ring and he had become stuck, become even more terror-filled as the muffled screams of battle had grown ever closer. His aunt had saved him, dragging the *brynja* up and freeing it, then helping him wriggle back into it.

Now he was keeping as close to Sigrún as he could, as all around him Ulfrir and his warband charged snarling out of the darkness. It was impossible to know what was happening, who was winning, snow falling in great swirls and gusts, veiling everything. Close by Ulfrir and Lik-Rifa were roaring, Rotta squealing, the stone wolves growling. Through the snow Guðvarr glimpsed one of the wolves finally drop beneath a barrage of blows from Heðin and his trolls. Chips of stone and clouds of ground dust were erupting from the stone wolf as it lay on one side, one of its rear legs completely gone, its side crushed, still snapping and snarling as blows rained down upon its head. Heðin roared and smashed his club down two-handed, and finally the wolf was still, its head turned to rubble.

"SHIELD WALL," Sigrún cried and Guðvarr looked away from the trolls and wolf, saw a knot of mail-clad warriors coming towards them in a loose pack, a black axe and spear on their red-painted shields. Guðvarr stepped in close to Sigrún, locked his shield with hers; looking over his shield rim, he saw the red shields tightening up, locking together.

"Who are they?" Guðvarr grunted at Sigrún.

"The Battle-Grim," she said.

Guðvarr swallowed. He had heard of them, had enjoyed the tales that skálds told of them. But it was an altogether different thing to be standing in a shield wall against them. He looked over the rim of his shield again.

A huge, red-bearded warrior stood at their centre, a bearded-axe in his fist. To one side of him stood a lean, unkempt man with thinning hair, but it was to the other side of the red-haired warrior that Guðvarr's eyes were drawn. An older warrior in a nasal helm, black hair sprinkled with grey. His face was as flat and emotionless as a cliff, but his eyes blazed with a depth of hatred that chilled Guðvarr's blood. And he was coming straight at Guðvarr.

Warriors set their feet, Guðvarr's knuckles white as he gripped his sword. The shield walls clashed together, wood grating, voices grunting, snarling. Guðvarr made an attempt to stab over his shield rim and saw the warrior with the hate-filled eyes glowering at him, had his sword contemptuously swatted away and he pulled it back, twisted his head to avoid the savage axe blow that followed it, the blade grating on Guðvarr's helm, jarring his neck and setting his head ringing. He decided it was safer to stay behind his shield and just let the man on the other side of his shield wear himself out or get killed by someone else.

Beside him Guðvarr glimpsed his aunt snarling and stabbing, saw an axe chop over her shield and she jerked her head away, sliced at the axe haft with her sword.

A blow crunched into Guðvarr's shield, shivering through his wrist and up his arm. Another blow, and another.

He must be getting tired, Guðvarr thought. *Please . . .*

On the fourth blow a crack twisted up the inside of Guðvarr's shield, and on the fifth splinters exploded inwards, stabbing into Guðvarr's cheek and he yelped. On the sixth there was a ripping sound and Guðvarr's shield began to tear apart. The blows came harder and faster now, Guðvarr whimpering with each one, his shield splintering, wood spraying, until the axe burst through, and the beard of the blade snared in the iron of the boss. With a roar Guðvarr's shield was ripped from his grip and he stood there, staring at the cliff-faced man, who was dragging his axe from the remnants of Guðvarr's shield and raising it again.

Guðvarr threw himself to the side, crashed into the warrior beside him and sent them both stumbling out from the wall, Guðvarr falling to the ground. A spear struck out, stabbing into the throat of the warrior Guðvarr had pushed, and the warrior fell, the Battle-Grim stepping over him, pressing into the gap left by Guðvarr and the dead warrior, and Sigrún's shield wall was breaking apart.

Guðvarr lay on the snow-churned ground, holding the remnants of his shield over him, heard shouts and grunts and screams, glimpsed Sigrún trading blows with the huge, red-haired axe man. Saw Sigrún fall in a spurt of blood, the axe chopping into her shoulder. Heard the thud of running feet and battle cries and a handful of skraeling were there, Krúsa leading them. Krúsa standing over Sigrún and swinging her thick-iron weapon, half sword, half cleaver. Saw Krúsa smash a warrior's shield to kindling, the one Guðvarr had seen with the lank, thinning hair, and Krúsa was hacking into the warrior's chest, the man falling to the ground close to Guðvarr, his breath rasping, blood foaming on his lips as each breath grew fainter and wider apart. A gurgle that faded to nothing. Another roar, the sound of an axe splitting wet wood and Krúsa's head was spinning through the air, the red-haired warrior smashing her still-standing body to the ground and striding over her corpse, the battle moving on.

Guðvarr lay there, hiding, clinging to his shield, the sounds of battle growing fainter, moving away from him. He scrambled up onto all fours, crawled over to his aunt and saw that she was still breathing, a red gash in her shoulder, mail links of her *brynja* gleaming wetly in the wound.

"Come, aunt," Guðvarr said, making his decision. He hooked his hands underneath her arms and lifted her. "We are *going*. I am getting you out of here and taking you home."

Battle is not for me. I've tried it, and I've had enough. A man can only take so much terror.

He hauled Sigrún a dozen paces, slipped and dropped her. Sucked in deep breaths. Looked at the treeline, not so far away, then at the battlefield, where the steel-storm was raging, warriors fighting, screaming, dying.

No, definitely not for me. He looked down at his aunt, groaning, semi-conscious.

If Lik-Rifa wins, someone will find her, tend to her wounds.

He looked around, found his sword, picked it up, and saw a shield that looked intact enough and swept that up, too. One last glance at his aunt and he began to walk towards the trees.

A figure stepped before him, a man in mail and a steel cap, a shield and spear in his fist. Guðvarr recognised him.

"Oh, not you again," Guðvarr breathed.

"Guðvarr, I am going to slay you for the murder of my father and my brother," Lif said.

CHAPTER EIGHTY-THREE

ORKA

Orka stalked through the battle, a seax in each fist, striking at any who dared come close enough. Skraeling, dragon-cultists, frost-spiders, a troll, all fell before her. Breca was at her right shoulder, Sæunn with him, Gunnar and Halja at her left.

Lik-Rifa and Ulfrir loomed out of the swirling snow and darkness, Lik-Rifa half flying, Ulfrir hanging onto her, his jaws clamped in the flesh of her shoulder, dragging her crashing to the ground, tearing up great rents in the earth, snow and mud spraying. She roared and twisted, Ulfrir's jaws ripping free in an explosion of scales and flesh and blood, the wolf rolling, coming to his feet crouched and snarling, Lik-Rifa's razored tail lashing him across the chest, opening up red lines across his fur, throwing him to the ground. Lik-Rifa roaring and leaping after him.

Skuld swept out of the snow-veiled sky, hurled herself at Lik-Rifa's head and Orka saw her reach to her belt, grasp a pair of long-bladded scissors.

"For my mother," Skuld shrieked as she crashed onto Lik-Rifa's head, one hand grasping onto horned scales, the other stabbing the scissors into one of Lik-Rifa's eyes. There was a wild, frenzied roar and Lik-Rifa shook her head, great muscles of her neck bunching and Skuld was hurled into the darkness.

Then Ulfrir was back on his feet, snarling and slavering, blood leaking from the long wound across his chest and he and Lik-Rifa were leaping at each other again.

Orka strode on, searching. Saw Jarl Orlyg and his *drengrs* locked in a press of shield walls, saw that the warriors striving against him carried grey shields with black ravens upon them, and wore raven-feathers in their hair.

Orka turned towards them.

A handful of frost-spiders appeared scuttling across the snow, ran at Orka and her group, one leaping into the air, hurtling towards her, fangs twitching. It crashed into her, Orka stabbing as they fell together, a flurry of punching blows. Orka slammed into the ground, twisted her head, the frost-spider's fangs biting into the snow where Orka's head had been. Her blades were both buried deep into the abdomen of the spider, her hands and arms pinned by the creature's weight, and the fangs reared back, over Orka, blue-tinged venom dripping from them. Then Breca was screeching and stabbing his short spear into the spider's clustered eyes, ripping the blade out and stabbing again and again, ice-crusted ichor spraying. The spider shuddered and died and Orka pushed it off, dragged her blades free, crouched and wiped both seaxes across the glistening, venom-soaked fangs. She sheathed one of the blades and swept up a hand-axe lying on the ground. Then she was standing and moving on, breaking into a jog as she weaved across the battleground, making her way to Orlyg and his warband. Drew closer and then she saw him.

Drekr.

He was leading a handful of Raven-Feeders, approaching Orlyg's shield wall from the rear. Had his long-axe in his hands, the warriors around him all with shields and spears, axes, swords. With a roar they hit the back of Orlyg's warriors, carved into them.

Panic spread through Orlyg's warriors and Orka broke into a run, saw the wall was bursting apart, Orlyg bellowing orders, Dagrun and a handful of *drengrs* left about him. Drekr raised his long-axe and swung it down, smashing into Orlyg's shield, carving through it, hurling Orlyg to the ground. Drekr stamped on the shield, ripped his axe blade free and smashed his axe-haft into Dagrun's jaw, hurling him to the ground. He stood over Orlyg, one foot on his shield, pinning him, swung his axe high and chopped down into Orlyg's head.

CHAPTER EIGHTY-FOUR

VARG

Varg ran at Brák Trolls-Bane, swift and silent as the hunting wolf. He saw Iva and Silrið battling with Seiðr and Galdur-runes, saw a ball of flame engulf Iva, only to be extinguished by an ice-carved rune, saw Iva hurl a rolling wheel of ice at Silrið, who slammed her staff into the ground, red flaming vines snaking out from its base and wrapping themselves around the ice-rune, snaring it, evaporating the ice in a hissing burst of steam.

Taras was bellowing, turning in a slow circle as warriors darted in and out at him, bleeding him with small wounds and darting back out again. Varg knew how those wounds would slow the bull-man, the loss of blood, the damage to muscle and tendon. He had seen Kolskegg do it to a troll that had wandered inside the boundaries of Kolskegg's farm. Brák stepped in behind Taras and slashed his sword across Taras' calf, just as he had done to Einar, Taras bellowing and twisting around, roaring, muscles bunching, veins bulging as he gathered himself to charge, and then another warrior was moving in behind him, jabbing at him with a spear.

Varg hefted his axe and seax and smashed into the ring around Taras, chopped his axe into a man's ribs, heard them crack, saw blood spurt as he ripped the blade free, stumbled on into the next warrior, a dark-haired woman in trapper's furs, Varg burying his seax in her belly, shoving her away and she fell onto her back. Then he was at Taras' side, Røkia, Svik, Edel and Æsa tearing through the rest of Brák's crew.

"Are you all right, big man?" Varg asked Taras.

"Little man wouldn't fight Taras," he said, "kept stabbing Taras from behind." He glowered at Brák over Varg's shoulder. "Cowards," he said.

Behind Taras Iva clapped her hands, stamped one foot and the ground shook, a fissure opening up and Silrið fell into it with a wail. Runes glowed within the fissure. Another shouted word from Iva, and another stamp of her foot, and the ground shifted, the crack closing, earth falling into it, burying Silrið. A wail that became muffled, followed by a choking gasp and then nothing.

Iva walked over to Taras, and he put his head on her shoulder.

Varg turned, faced Brák.

"Brák Trolls-Bane, it is your time to die," Varg said, hefted his axe and seax and stepped towards him.

"Many have tried, lad," Brák smiled, then his mouth twisted in a wicked snarl, his eyes shifting colour, turning completely black and he danced a little on his toes. "None have succeeded." He set his feet with his slim sword in his fist, drew one of the many knives from his belt, long and needle-sharp. "Come on, then, let's see what you've got."

"He has the blood of Væsa the weasel," Røkia shouted out to Varg. "Swift, vicious, cunning."

Varg closed his eyes for a heartbeat, Frøya's face filling his head, her screams as Brák pinned her to the tree, as he opened her belly.

The wolf in Varg's blood snarled and Varg allowed it to filter through him, felt the strength and speed ripple through his muscle, a tingling energy, and he stepped slowly towards Brák, saw Røkia, Svik and the others spread in a ring around the huntsman, who looked over his shoulder at Svik behind him.

"Do not worry, you little weasel," Svik said. "We'll not be stabbing you in the back, just here to make sure you don't decide to try and sneak off."

Then Brák was moving, a short-stepped shuffle at Varg, moving left, stabbing with his sword, and Varg swept the blade aside with his hand-axe. Brák pushed right off his back leg, slashed with his knife at Varg's face and Varg leaned back, checked it with his own seax, then Brák was moving around to his left, fast, out of range and back in, stabbing with the sword, straight at Varg's chest. Varg blocked it but stumbled back a step. Brák coming after him, sword stabbing high, blocked, knife stabbing low, up at Varg's groin, slashed away, a spin and Brák was at Varg's side, cracked his sword hilt into Varg's head as Varg swung his hand-axe, slicing Brák's side as Brák was stepping away, cut through leather, a red line welling. Brák brushed the back of his hand across the wound, knuckles coming away red, a twist of his lips. Varg stumbled back a few steps, knees abruptly weak, limbs loose, trying to put some space between them, give his head time to recover from the blow. He shook his head, snarled as Brák came in again, sword and seax a blur and there was a hot line across his forearm, another along the inside of his thigh, just below his *brynja*. He slashed at Brák with his seax but cut only air, turned as Brák danced away, moving to Varg's left, a heartbeat and Brák was coming back in again, a flurry of blows with sword and knife, Varg stepping back before him, blocking more and more wildly, another line of fire across the back of his hand and he grunted with pain. The wolf in him snapped and growled.

Let me rip and tear and rend him, the wolf snarled.

No, Varg told the wolf.

He is controlling this, fighting his way, Varg thought. *Remember the pugil ring*. And then he was moving, stepping after Brák rather than waiting for him, using his axe and seax like fists, stabbing at Brák to keep him off balance, stop him from setting his feet, then stepping to left or right, shuffling in quickly, striking in flurries with axe and seax, matching Brák's speed, both of them blocking, countering, block, strike, strike, block, counter-strike, another flurry and they both stepped away, both breathing heavily. Varg felt a red line of pain pulse across his lower leg, another across his cheek. Brák was panting, a cut across one side of his neck, but he was moving back in, swirling around Varg, sword grating across Varg's shoulder, *brynja* rings spraying, another line of fire across Varg's hand and he dropped his axe, Brák disappearing and Varg was falling to his knee, something wrong with his left leg. He looked up and saw Brák standing over him, his sword pointing at Varg's throat. Brák smiled and lunged.

Now, Varg told his wolf, and fresh strength and speed flooded him. He swayed to his left, the sword grazing his neck, stabbed with his seax and punched it through Brák's foot, felt the blade grate between bone and on, out the other side and into the ground. Heard Brák scream as Varg let go of the seax and launched himself from the ground, using his right leg, his empty hand grabbing Brák's knife hand at the wrist, a savage wrench and he felt bones crack, Brák dropping the knife, Varg's other hand wrapping around Brák's waist, pulling him close, his jaws opening, teeth growing, bit down around Brák's cheek and jaw. Blood spurted into his mouth, Brák screeching, flailing, trying to stab Varg with his sword but Varg was too close, Brák cracking the pommel into Varg's head, but the red rage was on him, and he hardly felt the blow, biting and ripping and tearing. He opened his mouth, releasing Brák, pushed him away, grabbed the hilt of Brák's sword as he did and ripped it from his grip. Spat out a lump of flesh and blood as Brák stumbled back, fell to his knees, hands clutching at his jaw and cheek, blood pulsing between his fingers. Varg strode after him and grabbed his necklace of troll tusks, hauled him half standing and dragged him across the ground, Varg limping towards the treeline. He heard Røkia, Svik and the others following.

He reached the trees and slammed Brák against the first trunk, knocking the wind from him.

"For Frøya," he snarled in Brák's face and stabbed Brák's sword into his belly, felt it punch through skin and muscle, felt it slide across the spine and on, out the other side, pierced deep into the trunk of the tree. He stepped back.

Brák screamed and writhed, one hand going to the sword, but he could not reach the hilt, sliced his hand on the blade.

Røkia put two fingers to her lips and whistled.

The rustle and crackle of footsteps on snow, and figures emerged from the shadows, five, eight, ten, more of them. Children. Seaxes glinted in their hands.

Refna Strong-Hands stepped out of the shadows and looked at Røkia.

Røkia looked at Varg. "You are not the only one who is owed vengeance."

Varg nodded.

"Do it," she said, and Refna turned towards Brák, who was whining with pain, taking short, gasping breaths.

"For Einar," Refna said, stepped forwards and she buried her seax to the hilt in Brák's waist. He screamed, high and loud.

The next child stepped forwards, slashed at Brák, then the next, and the next, and Varg watched. He felt Røkia's and Svik's presence.

"Well fought," Svik said to him.

"They are avenged," Røkia said.

Varg dropped to his knees and wept.

CHAPTER EIGHTY-FIVE

GUĐVARR

Guðvarr stared at Lif the fisherman, who was standing a dozen paces away, blocking his escape into the trees and gloom and safety. Behind him the battle was raging, Guðvarr hearing the roars and snarls of Lik-Rifa and Ulfrir, the ground shaking with their combat. He turned and looked at it, could see dragon-born running to defend their queen, locked in combat with Ulfrir's *Úlfhéðnar*, some of the dragon-born shouting out their Seiðr-magic. Rotta scampered squealing through the veil of snow, a stone wolf leaping onto his back and biting.

The sound of snow crunching as Lif took a step towards him dragged Guðvarr's attention back.

"You should walk away," he said to Lif, raising a hand and cuffing a dripping ball of snot from his nose. "You are a fisherman, not a warrior. I am a trained *drengr*. You should choose to live, take my offer of kindness and mercy before I change my mind." He looked hard at Lif, tried to give him a fierce, fjord-cold stare.

"You lost in a *holmganga* to my father but allowed an *Úlfhéðnar* to slaughter him. You stabbed my brother in the belly while he had frost-spider venom in his veins and was chained to a wall," Lif said, striding slowly towards him. "To my thinking, you are not much of a *drengr*. You are a *coward*. I have been trained by Orka Skullsplitter. Fought with the Bloodsworn, learned my craft in the forge-fire of battle. Let us *see* who has the greater weapons craft."

Orka Skullsplitter. The Bloodsworn. Forge-fire of battle. Guðvarr did not like the sound of that. He took a tentative step backwards.

"Perhaps we can talk about this?" Guðvarr suggested. "Come to some agreement?"

In response, Lif lunged with his spear, stabbing straight at Guðvarr. He swung his shield to block it, swept Lif's spear aside and hacked with his sword at his head, but Lif was already stepping in, his shield shrugging the sword-blow aside, stabbing again with his spear, this time over the top of Guðvarr's shield rim, angled down, and the blade struck Guðvarr in the chest, hit him like a punch, Guðvarr stumbling back, taking the power out of Lif's blow. He glanced down, saw that some of the rings of his *brynja* had split. Frowned. Looked back to Lif and saw the swift movement of shadows in the treeline behind him, frost-spiders scuttling out of the trees, scurrying to join the battle. He hefted his shield and strode quickly forwards, stabbed at Lif, hacked and sliced, each blow blocked by Lif's shield work, but he forced Lif backwards, first one step, then two, until he was retreating steadily before Guðvarr's assault.

A frost-spider leaped upon Lif's back, slamming the fisherman to the ground. Guðvarr smiled and strode casually past them both as they rolled, striding towards the trees and the safety of darkness, the sounds of battle behind him fading.

The thud and crunch of feet on snow behind him and he started to turn, felt an impact across the back of his legs and stumbled, fell to his knees.

"Get up," a voice said, and he staggered to his feet, turned to see Lif before him, covered in dark, blue-tinged slime and fragments of spider shell. He no longer had his spear, was holding a bearded axe in his fist, and Guðvarr looked down to see it was Lif's spear that had hit the back of his legs and tripped him.

He killed the frost-spider then, he realised. *Not a comforting thought.*

Lif strode towards him, shield held high, axe-blade hovering just above the top rim.

I am going to have to kill him.

He stepped forwards to meet Lif, stabbed high in a feint, then low, at Lif's shins, expecting Lif to jerk his shield up. But Lif slammed his shield down, pinning Guðvarr's sword, at the same time stepping forwards and chopping with his axe, splintering the top of Guðvarr's shield, the beard of the blade hooking inside the shield rim. Lif dragged Guðvarr forwards, off balance, and punched the top of the axe into Guðvarr's mouth. An explosion of excruciating pain, blood in his mouth, and something hard, a tooth, he realised, and a red-hot pain arcing from his mouth across his cheek. He cried out and stumbled back, lost his grip on his sword, tripped over something and fell onto his arse with a thud. Put a hand to his face and felt blood, probed a long gash from mouth to ear. Spat out his tooth and a mouthful of blood as Lif stood over him.

"All right, all right, you win," Guðvarr pleaded, lifting a hand. "You win. I forfeit. *Holmganga* rules. What do you want? My *brynja*, my sword? Have them both."

He looked up to see Lif looming over him, saw him snarl and raise his axe.

"No, I'll give you anything you want," Guðvarr squeaked.

"I want my father and brother back," Lif snarled, and brought the axe down.

CHAPTER EIGHTY-SIX

ORKA

Orka ran at Drekr, a silent thrown spear through the battle that raged about her, just the drum of her feet and rasp of her breathing in her head. Drekr was standing over Orlyg's corpse, ripping his long-axe out of the jarl's shattered skull. Beyond him Orka saw the scuttling movement of frost-spiders in the treeline, a swarm of them surging onto the battlefield from the forest.

Were they scattered after Snaka's destruction of the hall? Only just finding their way back here? Orka thought. Wherever they were from, there were many of them.

Dagrun, Orlyg's son, staggered to his feet, spitting blood from his split lip, where Drekr had smashed his axe-haft into his mouth. He swayed, saw his father on the ground and cried out, hefted his sword and shield and moved towards Drekr. All about them Raven-Feeders were slaughtering the last of Orlyg's *drengrs*, just a handful of them still fighting, most of those Tainted who had sworn their oaths to Orlyg after Elvar had set them free.

Drekr saw Dagrun coming at him and hefted his long-axe.

Orka spun past Dagrun, slashing her hand-axe at Drekr's face. He saw her and took a step back, grunted as he blocked Orka's blow on the haft of his axe, splinters flying, and Orka was running past him, skidding, burying her seax into the belly of a Raven-Feeder who was chopping at her with a hand-axe, grabbing onto him and turning with him, ripped her seax free as she pushed him into Drekr, who was raising his axe to strike at Orka. The impact knocked Drekr stumbling back. He righted himself, cast the dying Raven-Feeder aside and stalked towards Orka. Behind him the Bloodsworn with Orka hit the Raven-Feeders, Gunnar, Halja and Sæunn. Steel clashed and warriors screamed.

"This is your end," Drekr growled at Orka.

"If you cannot bite, you should not show your teeth," Orka snarled back at him, raised her axe high and held the seax low.

He swung his axe and Orka moved, stepping inside his swing, chopped with her hand-axe at his neck, Drekr twisting so that the blow hacked into his shoulder, burst rings apart and Drekr grunted. She stabbed with the seax, the blade grating on Drekr's *brynja*, but the mail held. Drekr let one hand drop from his axe and he grabbed a fistful of Orka's *brynja*, dragged her towards him, his eyes flickering red, teeth growing long and sharp, and she realised he intended to rip her flesh. She went with it, smashed the nasal bar of her helm into his face, mashed his upper lip and mouth to pulp and he grunted again, stumbled back, spitting blood, swung his axe, a weak blow merely intended to push her away, give him a moment to recover.

Orka twisted away from the axe swing and stepped after him, swung her hand-axe as Drekr unsteadily shuffled back, hefted the haft of his long-axe two-handed and hooked the beard of her blade, heaved his axe back and ripped her blade from her hands, sent it spinning through the air. Orka came at him, slashing with the seax, a strike across his chest, backswing across his arm and she stepped in, punched the hilt into his face, sent him stumbling back again. She looked at him, nodded to herself, and stepped away, then slowly drew the second seax from its scabbard at her belt.

"I have travelled a *long* way to return these to you," she said.

"Your husband kept them warm for me," he told her, blood flecking his lips, dripping into his black beard.

"My Thorkel was a better man than you could ever hope to be. And I know you did not fight him fair, had help." She looked into his eyes, saw that her suspicion was true. "Even then, he gave you those scars to remember him by," Orka said. "You should not have come to my steading. If you had not, you would still have your two sisters, and your own life, which I am about to take." He opened his mouth to answer her, but she was already stepping forwards, stabbing and slashing, Drekr holding his axe two-handed, blocking and striking with blade and haft, a flurry of blows given and taken. Orka ducked a swing of Drekr's blade and stepped in close, wrapped her arms around him, hooked a leg behind his and pushed, sending Drekr crashing to the ground. She went with him, sat upon his chest, one seax pressed to his throat, the other blade tip hovering over his eye. Drekr froze, blinked. A flick of Orka's wrist and then she was rising, stepping agilely away.

Drekr rose slowly, scowling at her, and frowning, confused. He spat blood on the snow. A trickle of blood ran down his cheek, a cut under his eye. He stepped towards Orka, and she took a step back. He frowned at her and took another step towards her, and she took another step back.

"What are you doing?" he said.

"Waiting," Orka replied.

"For w . . . w . . . what?" he stuttered.

"For the poison to work," she said.

Drekr took another step towards her and staggered, his legs heavy, his movements slow, ponderous. He took another step and swayed. His axe dropped from his fists. Orka saw his muscles twitching, but it was all he could do to remain standing.

"Breca," Orka called, and Breca stepped forwards with Sæunn at his shoulder.

"Here," Orka said, holding out one of the seaxes to him.

"What have you done?" he asked her.

"There was frost-spider venom on the blade I used to cut his cheek," Orka said. "Do you remember the serpents on the *Sea-Wolf*. The mother serpent and her young?"

"Aye, Mama, I do," Breca said.

"You remember how she taught them to hunt, to kill?"

"Yes."

"I will teach you now." She led Breca behind Drekr, who was trembling, using all his strength and will to stay standing. As they came close to him his fingers twitched, a muscle in his arm. "At the back of the leg, above the knee, there is muscle. If you slice that a person will drop like a puppet with their strings cut. Here," she said, touching the back of Drekr's leg. "You do it."

Breca stepped forwards and slashed the seax across Drekr's hamstring. He grunted and collapsed.

"Good," Orka said. "If you had an axe, the quickest kill is a blow to the head. But with a sharp blade there are three places. You must strike here," she touched the pulse at her throat, "here", a finger to her heart, "or here", and she pressed on the artery in her groin. "Drekr is wearing mail, so the heart is protected. The artery in the groin is harder to find, so we shall choose the throat." She hefted the seax in her fist, squatted down before Drekr and touched the point to his neck. "And you," she said, and Breca raised the seax and touched it to Drekr's throat, alongside hers. Drekr was staring at them, his body shivering, lips moving, eyes glaring.

"For Thorkel," Orka breathed, holding Drekr's gaze, and pushed the blade into his neck, blood pulsing out, sluggish with venom.

"For Papa," Breca said, and pressed on the blade, watched it slide deep into Drekr's flesh.

CHAPTER EIGHTY-SEVEN

BIÓRR

Biórr and Red Fain stood with shields and weapons, the Tainted children behind them, and stared at the battle. It raged all about them, the sound of it a swirling, deafening maelstrom, Ulfrir howling, Lik-Rifa roaring, tearing at each other and the land about them, Rotta squealing, warriors screaming, dying, trolls bellowing, frost-spiders hissing, night-hags shrieking, and all of it appearing in fractured glimpses through the sheeting snow. God was fighting god, *drengrs* fighting *drengrs*, Tainted fighting Tainted, only the vaesen fighting together against Ulfrir and his horde.

Before them a knot of *Úlfhéðnar* and *Berserkir* fought against Tainted who had come to Lik-Rifa's call, growling, snarling, stabbing, ripping, moving in and out of sight.

"How can it be like this?" Red Fain breathed. "We are supposed to stand together, against the tyrants who have enslaved us. Not fight against each other."

I have set the tainted free, Biórr heard Elvar's voice.

"Lik-Rifa said she would set the Tainted free," Fain said.

Biórr remembered Orka's words to him.

The gods did not care for the lives of anyone then, Tainted or not, I do not think they care now.

Dawn was seeping into the world, a pale light clawing over the horizon, shadows separating around them. They saw a knot of frost-spiders swarm upon a *Berserkir*, dragging her down by their weight. Riders thundered out of the snow, hacking and slashing with their curved swords, and a troll lumbered at them, swung her club and smashed a rider from the saddle. It was impossible to tell, but to Biórr it seemed that the numbers of the vaesen were beginning to turn the tide against Ulfrir and his followers.

"How can it be that only the vaesen have loyalty," Fain grunted.

A howl from Ulfrir rang out, long and ululating, and Biórr saw Skuld swirl out of the snow, climb higher and hover in the air, her red wings beating slowly, and she raised a horn to her lips, blew it, the sound echoing Ulfrir's howl.

There was a shift in the air around Biórr, and a sound rising up from the forest at their backs. Biórr and Fain turned, heard a strange sound ebbing and flowing, high-pitched, a shrieking wail, growing louder, like an approaching storm. And then shadowed shapes were appearing, small figures emerging from the treeline, looking like wood carvings, their hair spiked leaves, hands like twisted thorns. They were running, mouths twisted in snarls, shrieking.

"Faunir," Biórr gasped.

"The children," Fain said desperately, and he turned, started shouting orders and the Tainted children ran to one of the wagons, scrambled beneath it, as Fain and Biórr stood before them, shields raised.

The faunir came shrieking out of the snow, washing across the battlefield, hurling fistfuls of thorns and splintered wood as they ran, throwing themselves at frost-spiders, swarming over trolls, and then they were at the wagon. The horses whinnied and reared, wild-eyed, but the faunir swept past them. A handful skidded to a halt and glared at Biórr and Fain, who stood there with their shields raised, but they made no move to strike at the faunir. One of the small creatures crouched to peer beneath the wagon. Its head twisted to one side, looking at the children, and it spoke in a chittering, snap and crackle voice to the others. It stood and they were running, leaving Fain and Biórr alone as they swept on into the camp. The din of war rose higher, shafts rang on shields, faunir leaping, gouging, shrieking, and blood stained the snow.

Biórr looked at Fain.

"We should leave," he said.

"What?" Red Fain said.

"These gods, they are not worth fighting for. Not worth dying for."

"But our freedom," Fain said.

"We are already free. Whoever wins, the dragon or the wolf, the Tainted will not be thralled."

"And our vengeance," Fain said, a twist of his lips. "My sons, your Myrk . . ."

"I have had my taste of vengeance, and it is bitter, like ash in the mouth," Biórr said. "It does not bring the dead back to us. I am done with it. Let us do something . . . good. Let us take these children from here. Far from here. Take them from war and a red-robed death."

Fain looked at him, then at the children huddled beneath the wagon. Many of them had spoken of war, of living in a skáld-song, of their name being sung of in the hero's sagas, but looking at them now, they just looked terrified.

"Aye," Fain said. "Lads, lasses, into the wagon," he said, and they scrambled out and clambered into the wagon, Harek climbing onto the driver's bench, where he always sat beside Fain.

HELP ME, Rotta's voice screamed in Biórr's head.

Fain hauled himself up and offered his hand to help Biórr, and Biórr hesitated.

"You get along, and I'll follow after," Biórr said, "there is one thing that I must do first." He looked among the children and saw him.

"Bjarn, you come with me," he said.

"Why?" Bjarn asked.

"I am going to take you back to your mother."

"I shall wait for you," Fain said.

"No, get them away from here, while you can."

Fain looked at the swirling battle and nodded. "Then we shall wait in the woods for you, where it is safer."

Biórr nodded, sheathing his sword. Fain clicked his lips, snapped his reins and the horses jolted into movement, the wagon rumbling away and disappearing behind the veil of snow.

Biórr watched them go, turned, putting a hand on Bjarn's shoulder and guided him into the battle. They weaved around heaped piles of the dead, the roar of war washing over them. Two warriors came staggering out of the snow and Biórr slammed them away with his shield, moved on. He reached down to his belt, drew out the axe he had taken from Elvar and offered it to Bjarn.

"Just in case," Biórr said and Bjarn nodded, took the weapon.

They moved deeper into the battle, towards the heart of the storm, and then Biórr saw them. Lik-Rifa and Ulfrir, jaws biting, claws ripping, and around them the dragon-born and *Úlfhéðnar* fought, and the Seiðr-witches. Runes bloomed and flared, fire and ice crackling as they fought for their gods, fought against one another, and Biórr saw Uspa. She was standing with another Seiðr-witch, as dark as Uspa was fair. Berak was with her, too. Huge and hulking in his mail, shoulders hunched, a bearded axe in each fist. A pile of the dead ringed him.

Biórr ran, then, crouched, gripping Bjarn's wrist. Berak glimpsed their movement and turned, snarling, axes raised. Paused, axes hovering, his expression shifting from feral rage to confusion, to surprise, and then he was lowering the twin blades, a smile splitting the braided weave of his beard.

"Uspa," he said, and she turned. Mouth opening wide, and she was running, eyes bright with tears, and Bjarn was running, too, threw himself into her arms, Uspa lifting him up, laughing and kissing his cheeks. Berak reached them and swept them both up in his big arms, squeezed them tight, spun them in a circle.

Biórr smiled and turned away, began threading his way back through the battle.

BIÓRR, HELP ME, Rotta screamed in Biórr's head.

No, Biórr snarled back at him.

A sound behind him, footsteps.

"Turn around," a voice snarled at him.

Biórr froze, a ripple of fear in his gut, let the rat flood him. Turned swiftly, reaching for his sword, saw the Bloodsworn warrior he had fought before. The man's green eyes blazed as he lunged forwards, chopping with an axe. Biórr raised his shield, but the axe snaked over the top rim, crunched into Biórr's temple, sent him reeling, the ground rising up to meet him. The wind knocked from him as he hit the snow. Tried to move, lift his shield, draw his sword, but his body was not responding, a pain in his head pulsing through him. His stomach lurched and he vomited.

A weight on his chest, the green-eyed man putting one boot on him.

"I am Gunnar Prow of the Bloodsworn, and I am your *end*," he snarled, raised his axe.

"No," Biórr whispered.

"For Revna," Gunnar Prow said, and the axe came down.

CHAPTER EIGHTY-EIGHT

ORKA

Orka bent and picked up her hand-axe, slipped it back into her belt. She saw Drekr's long-axe on the ground and swept that up, too. Heard footsteps and turned to see Lif appearing through the snow. His face was grim, the blade of his axe blooded. He looked to Drekr's corpse on the ground, at the two seaxes still buried in his flesh and gave Orka a nod.

"Is it done?" Orka asked him.

"Aye," Lif said, a ripple of emotions chasing across his face.

"Good," Orka grunted, and looked at the battlefield, Breca's presence at Orka's side. Day was bleeding into the land, the snow slowing. Faunir were everywhere, swirling around clusters of frost-spiders and crawling up the legs of trolls. Shield walls still fought on in knots, and Orka saw a handful of mounted warriors riding around a troll, stabbing with spears, hacking with their curved sabres, the clash of battle rising and falling. At the heart of it all the dragon and the wolf still fought. Orka could see the survivors of Lik-Rifa's host making for her, frost-spiders and night-hags, skraeling, trolls, dragon-cultists and Raven-Feeders and oathsworn *drengrs*, a handful of mercenary bands still clinging to the hope of victory and silver beyond their imaginings.

Without a word shared, Orka and the others followed them, a river of flesh and bone and steel, claw and tooth and fang flowing towards the wolf and dragon.

Ulfrir's voice rang out in Orka's skull.

Now is the time, he said. *My strength is failing, it must be done now.*

Heya, Orka answered the wolf.

Footsteps drummed and Gunnar joined them.

"The rat-blood is dead," he said to Halja's questioning look.

The roar and snarl and thunder of gods at war led them through the snow, and soon Orka saw the crackle and sizzle of Seiðr-runes and Galdur-magic. Vol and Uspa appeared, pitted against a cluster of dragon-born, Orka glimpsing Glornir, Berak and a handful of others fighting on their flanks, defending the Seiðr-witches from dragon-cultists and the last of the dragon-born and Raven-Feeders. And beyond them were Ulfrir and Lik-Rifa pacing before each other. Ulfrir was limping, blood matting his fur, red rents in his flesh. Lik-Rifa stood before Ulfrir, one wing hanging limp, the muscle at the shoulder torn and shredded, red wounds scattered across her thick-scaled hide. She watched Ulfrir with one red-glowing eye, the other a blackened wound, saliva dripping from her teeth.

Warriors and vaesen flowed to them, *Úlfhéðnar*, Tainted, ready to defend their god.

Orka broke into a run, the others a heartbeat behind her, and they sped across the field, swerving around great ruts and rents in the ground, around smashed wagons and supplies, and then they were crashing into the flank of dragon-cultists that were assaulting Glornir and his handful of Bloodsworn. They carved through them, blood spurting in great arcs, men and women screaming, turning to rally against Orka and her handful of warriors, but it was like trying to stop the tide from rising. In a dozen heartbeats they were down or fleeing, retreating to the swell of warriors and vaesen gathering before Lik-Rifa.

Glornir touched Orka's arm.

"Is he dead?" Glornir asked her.

"He is," Orka grunted.

"Good, Thorkel is avenged then."

Behind Glornir the dragon roared, all of them turning to see the wolf and dragon separate, standing, blood-drenched, red wounds leaking, scales hanging, fur matted.

Skuld swept down out of the snow-white sky and hovered over Ulfrir, raised a horn to her lips and blew it.

"It is time then," Glornir said.

"Aye," Orka nodded.

"Let's finish this, then," he said.

Ulfrir bunched his legs and leaped at Lik-Rifa.

CHAPTER EIGHTY-NINE

VARG

Varg limped away from Brák's corpse, still pinned against the tree, his body slumped upon the nail of his sword.

It is done, Frøya. You are avenged. He did not feel the joy he had expected, no rush of euphoria, just a marrow-deep exhaustion, even the wolf in his blood quiet. Røkia and Svik walked with him, Edel and her hound, Æsa and Taras limping alongside them, Iva holding his hand.

A horn blast rang out across the battlefield and they all stopped.

But this battle is not done yet.

A few shared words, gripping hands with Iva and Taras, and then the Seiðr-witch and bull-man were walking away, towards the forest.

The remainder of the Bloodsworn looked at each other, no words, just held gazes, touched hands, then they were moving across the field, following the flow of warriors and vaesen that were gravitating towards Lik-Rifa and Ulfrir. The roaring maelstrom of the gods fighting, behind it the din of battle, steel clashing, battle cries and screams, and abruptly the snow was parting and it was raging before them. Seiðr-runes crackled, frost-spiders seethed and scuttled, Sulich led his riders, knots of shield walls clashed, trolls roared, tennúr whirred above them, dropping and tearing flesh from faces, and in front of Varg a wagon exploded into splinters, Rotta smashing into it as he rolled, squealing and thrashing, the jaws of the last stone wolf latched onto his shoulder. Rotta was lashing at the wolf with half a tail, and Skuld was swooping down, slashing at Rotta with a bright-gleaming sword.

Two trolls lumbered out of the sheeting snow, one much larger than the other, huge, yellowed tusks protruding from his lower jaw, and both hefted iron-studded clubs and smashed them down onto the stone wolf.

Æsa broke into a run, her shield slung across her back, the others following, Varg and Taras both limping from the wounds Brák had given them. Æsa hurled her spear as she ran, drew her hand-axe and seax without breaking stride, Varg watching her spear punch into the shoulder of the smaller troll, saw it bellow and twist around, snatching at the spear, and then Æsa was upon it, leaping, hacking with her hand-axe, stabbing with her seax, using each blade to climb the troll's thick hide until she was standing on its shoulders. She chopped her hand-axe into the meat of its neck, and stabbed her seax deep into its ear, up to the hilt. The troll roared, spittle spraying as it spasmed and jerked, staggered a few steps and it dropped, Æsa jumping free, rolling and coming back to her feet. She looked at Varg and the others, lifted her hands and grinned, and then the other troll's club smashed down upon her. She disappeared like a squashed tick, an explosion of blood misting in the air.

Svik shouted, Edel roared as her hound charged at the vaesen, Røkia reaching the troll first, sword and hand-axe in her fists. She chopped and slashed at its calf as she ran past it, the troll roaring and swinging his club, then Edel was there, plunging her spear into the troll's thigh, leaving it buried there, ducked the club and drew her sword, slashed at the troll's ankle, while her hound harried at its legs and danced away. Svik and Varg reached the troll, Varg drawing his cleaver and hand-axe, and they spread about the creature, darting in and stabbing, slashing, darting back out.

"Heðin will squash you all to gruel," the troll roared as it spun and stamped at them and swung its club.

Varg chopped at the troll's foot with his cleaver, severed a toe, Heðin roaring, twisting, and swiping with a huge fist, Varg leaping out of the way, Heðin smashing a table to kindling. Varg regained his feet, glimpsed movement from the corner of his eye and saw a handful of frost-spiders scuttling towards him. One reared and leaped at him and he crunched his cleaver into its clustered eyes, the spider dropping, Varg ripping the cleaver free, blue ichor spurting into his face. A pain in his arm and he twisted, saw a frost-spider had snared his mail with its thick-barbed foreleg, was dragging him towards its flexing fangs, glistening with venom. A small creature leaped onto the spider's back, a faunir, its face twisted in a feral snarl, raking its claws into the spider, punching and stabbing hard-nailed fingers into its back. Dark fluid spurted and Varg wrenched himself free. Stumbled back to see a horde of faunir sweeping into the battle, Ulfrir's new-found allies.

What did Ulfrir promise them?

Whatever it was, the faunir were turning the tide of battle. They only attacked Lik-Rifa's vaesen, the frost-spiders, skraeling and trolls, leaving the Tainted, the *drengrs* and mercenaries and dragon-cultists alone.

A roar behind Varg and he turned, saw Edel slice her sword across the back of the troll's knee, Heðin's mouth wide and bellowing with pain.

Røkia ripped Æsa's spear from the troll Æsa had slain, hefting it and she cast it, the spear punching up into Heðin's open mouth. The huge troll staggered back, Varg, Svik, Røkia and Edel all darting in. Edel's hound leaped forwards again, savaging Heðin's ankle, and the troll toppled to the ground, an explosion of snow, Varg and the others chopping and slicing, blood flowing from a dozen wounds. The troll groaned, whimpered, and died.

A squealing snarl growing abruptly louder and Rotta crashed among them, slammed into the body of the dead troll as the stone wolf flew from his back. Rotta came to his feet, turning to face Varg and the others, bared his yellow incisors at them, took a step towards them, Varg seeing the rat's claws had talons long and curved like Sulich's sabre.

He and the others spread in a half-circle before Rotta.

There was a blast of air from above and two black shapes were dropping from the sky, black wings beating, Grok and Kló's talons outstretched, and in a blur of wings and turbulence they seized Rotta.

"Rotta kill Father-Snaka," the ravens squawked as they lifted him from the ground, their talons cutting into him. Rotta squealed, twisting and writhing in their grip, snapping with his long yellow teeth, but they held onto him and climbed higher, disappearing into the snow.

Varg and the others just stood there, staring up at the sky.

Then a shape came hurtling out of the sky, Rotta falling, spinning, shrieking. He crashed into a cluster of wagons, wood splintering, exploding, and Varg and the others leaped away, threw themselves to the ground, timber spraying above them like hurled spears. Varg climbed to his feet, saw Rotta lying amidst the ruin, still, unmoving, a cloud of scattered snow settling upon him.

CHAPTER NINETY

ORKA

Orka ran snarling, swinging the long-axe two-handed in her fists. Flesh cleaved, blood spurting, bones breaking, screaming faces swirling in, falling away, all a blood-soaked haze. She glimpsed Glornir one side of her, shield punching, sword stabbing, others around her, Gunnar Prow and Halja, Lif and Sæunn, Breca growling and stabbing with his spear, Vol shrieking rune-words and her serpent whip cracking, ripping flesh from faces.

A current of faunir swept around Orka, swarming over frost-spiders and skraeling, speeding them away in a river of blood, and then Ulfrir and Lik-Rifa were before Orka, both of them biting, ripping, rending, one of Lik-Rifa's wings dragging, leaving trails of blood in the snow, her tail whipping into Ulfrir and sending him crashing to the ground, great gouts of snow and earth exploding. He scrambled back to his feet, bunched his muscles, and leaped, jaws crunching around Lik-Rifa's serpentine neck, twisting and slamming her down. She roared and thrashed, Ulfrir heaved into the air, but he did not let go.

Shouts behind them and Orka twisted, saw a wedge of people appearing, carving a path through Lik-Rifa's followers. Grend, Gytha and her *drengrs*, Sighvat and the Battle-Grim, Frek and his *Úlfhéðnar*, Taras and Iva. Taras was dragging a hand cart, Hrung's head in it. Iva ran to Uspa.

Movement beside Orka, and Glornir was moving forwards, dropping his shield, breaking into a run, just his long sword in one fist. Orka smashed a dragon-cultist to the ground with the butt of her long-axe and she was running, too, catching Glornir up and matching her pace with his. He glanced at her, grinned.

"We shall earn our place in a skáld-song with this," he growled, eyes flickering green, his body juddering and twitching, muscles hunching his back, curved claws growing. Orka grinned back at him, let the wolf loose in her blood, colours brighter, sounds sharper, felt its strength and speed, its endurance and ferocity, and they were both leaping, crashing onto Lik-Rifa's damaged wing, Glornir stumbling and righting himself, Orka landing and running, scrambling up the wing towards Lik-Rifa's back and neck.

The dragon was bucking and heaving in Ulfrir's grip, desperately trying to break free, Ulfrir keeping her pinned to the ground. Orka and Glornir were thrown from their feet, both of them digging their claws into dragon-scale, sliding and halting their fall, using axe and sword and claws to drag themselves up Lik-Rifa's thick-muscled neck. Dimly Orka was aware of voices, of Seiðr-words. The crackle and wash of rune heat and ropes of fire and ice were arcing over Lik-Rifa, draping across her like jarl-rings of silver and gold. More spell-work from Vol, Uspa and Iva and the threads were pulling tight, dragging Lik-Rifa's head to the ground.

Tennúr whirred at Orka and Glornir, long fingers lunging, tearing at their flesh. Orka dug her claws deep into Lik-Rifa and swung her axe, Glornir doing the same, swinging his sword, and the little creatures fell away in a rain of blood. They climbed on, and then they were at Lik-Rifa's head, scrambling over thick, barbed spines and horn, Orka sliding past the blood-filled eye that Skuld had ruined and almost sliding from Lik-Rifa's jaws. Snaring her axe head around a long tooth, hauling herself up until she stood on Lik-Rifa's jaw, Glornir alongside her. Together they set their feet, and together they swung their weapons.

Axe and sword chopped into the skin and meat where Lik-Rifa's jaws met. They ripped their blades free in a spray of dragon blood. Lik-Rifa roared, writhed, the ground shaking, but the Seiðr-ropes and Ulfrir held her, and Orka and Glornir swung again, and again, and again, flesh hanging in great rents, tendon sliced, until one side of Lik-Rifa's jaw was severed.

Lik-Rifa let out a deafening cry, shook hard enough to split the earth, tore herself free of Ulfrir's grip. Orka and Glornir were weightless, spinning through the air, Lik-Rifa rising, the Seiðr-ropes fraying, tearing and exploding in fountains and showers of ice and fire.

Orka hit the ground, her bones rattling, and she rolled, crunched into the body of a dead troll and just lay there, pain jolting in her chest with every breath, knew that ribs were shattered, and she stared up at Lik-Rifa as she rose above Orka, snapped her one good wing out, blotting out the sky. Her jaw hung open where Orka and Glornir had severed ligaments and tendon, saliva dripping from her mouth.

With a grunt Orka heaved herself over, a fresh pain spiking in her leg, pushed herself onto all fours, almost collapsed, saw a spear and used it to drag herself to her feet, stood there swaying, pain pulsing in her leg and chest. All around her people were shouting, Hrung's voice rising over them all.

"NOW," he was screaming, "NOW."

Lik-Rifa glowered down at Orka with her red baleful eye, roared and swiped a huge taloned claw at her, Orka standing there, pain transfixing her, giving Lik-Rifa the defiance of her wolf-toothed smile. Saw the claw coming at her, snarled up at Lik-Rifa. An impact in her side, a fresh burst of pain and she was thrown through the air, hit the ground, saw that Glornir had crashed into her. He stood there, made to leap after her and Lik-Rifa's claw hissed over Orka's head, slammed into Glornir and sent him flying, a misting of blood hanging in the air where he had stood.

Orka screamed, heaved herself over, up onto one knee, and Lik-Rifa's open jaw was coming down at her. She saw Taras, Berak and Sighvat carrying Hrung's head in his sailcloth sheet, saw Taras grip the sheet and turn with it, his body growing, muscles expanding, bulging, tendons straining, faster, once, twice, and then he was bellowing like a bull and hurling Hrung into the air, straight into Lik-Rifa's open jaws. A long wailing cry and Hrung disappeared into the dragon's maw, Lik-Rifa jolting back, unsure what had just happened. Orka saw the reflex ripple of muscle in her neck as she swallowed, then Lik-Rifa was rearing up again and Ulfrir was padding before her, limping, flesh hanging from him in sheets, huge rents and gouges, one ear a tattered mess, blood pulsing from his wounds.

"You have fought well, sister," Ulfrir growled.

"I am going to tear the flesh from your bones, one strip at a time," Lik-Rifa snarled.

"No, this is done," Ulfrir sighed.

"What, you yield to me?" Lik-Rifa said. She smiled, her jaw hanging lopsided where Glornir and Orka had hacked at her. "Oh no, you do not escape death that easily. There will be no mercy shown here. I must kill you."

"You misunderstand me," Ulfrir said. "You are done. You are already dead, though you do not know it. Slain by the same hand as Snaka, by the same poison."

"Enough of your foolish tal—" Lik-Rifa began, then coughed, a spasm tremoring through her neck. She twisted her head, one way, then the other. "What have you *done*?" she rasped.

"Not me, it was ancient Hrung. Serpent slayer. Now dragon slayer," Ulfrir said.

Lik-Rifa coughed again, another spasm passing through her, more violent, and Orka saw the veins in her belly become more prominent, slowly turning black, as if ink were running through them, not blood. Her breath rasped in her throat, and she took a ponderous step forward, then another, her whole body spasming now, huge tremors wracking her, choking and gasping. Black froth bubbled from her mouth, dripped from her lips, hissing as it hit the snow and with a rasping roar she toppled, fell with a crash that shook the battlefield and trees around it, throwing Orka and those around her from their feet.

Another spasm, a slow, rattling breath, froth bubbling on her lips and then Lik-Rifa was still, the light in her one red eye fading, dimming, and gone.

A silence, just the soughing of wind, and Ulfrir raised his head and howled.

Orka clambered to her knee, pain spiking in her chest with every breath, in her leg with every movement, used a spear to haul herself up and limped forwards, using the spear like a staff, people all around her cheering, shouting victory cries, what little vaesen were left fleeing for the forest.

She looked wildly around for Glornir, saw him a crumpled heap on the ground, blood staining the snow. She struggled to him, fell to her knees, hissing with the pain, and gripped one of his bear-like hands.

"My brother," she breathed.

He grunted, turned his head to look at her.

"We have made a song, and no denying," he murmured, coughed. Blood flecked his lips. His mail coat was torn to ragged shreds, his chest a red wound, Orka seeing the glint of bone and the soft tissue of a lung, blood bubbling.

Orka nodded, the words turning to ash and clay in her mouth, tears blurring her eyes.

A small voice shouting, the drum of feet and Breca was there, sliding to his knees, grabbing Glornir's hand. He looked at the wounds in Glornir's chest.

"No," he breathed. "Uncle," he half sobbed, lifting Glornir's big hand to his face.

"I am glad to have met you, Breca Thorkelsson," Glornir wheezed, "and glad to have seen you again, Skullsplitter, fought beside you," he told her in short, half-whispered words.

"Heya," Orka managed to say, and she squeezed his hand.

"Breca, look after your mother," Glornir whispered.

"Don't leave us, uncle, not like papa," Breca said through his tears.

Feet drummed behind Orka, and she heard Vol's voice calling his name. Screaming it.

"This will go hard on her," Glornir breathed, bubbles of blood frothing on his lips. "Look after her," he said, and between one heartbeat and the next he was gone.

Vol threw herself down beside Glornir, grabbing his hand, shaking him. She fell across him, weeping as the Bloodsworn gathered around them, heads bowed.

Hands helped Orka to rise, Sæunn and Lif. Breca staggered to his feet and fell into her, hugging her tight, sobbing. Orka wrapped a bloodied arm around his shoulder and looked around her.

The dead were everywhere, great piles of them, warriors, shattered shields, trolls heaped in mounds, frost-spiders curled in death, and Lik-Rifa, the dragon, sprawled across the field, wings draped like tattered sails. Ulfrir stood before her, back in his human form now, leaning on Skuld, one arm draped across her shoulder. The faunir stood in their hundreds, huddled together like a small wood, all staring up at Lik-Rifa. Warriors were hugging one another, others on their knees, weeping.

Orka saw Uspa and Berak hugging their son, and Sighvat there, too, tousling the boy's hair, a great grin splitting his red beard, tears staining lines through the blood and grime on his cheeks as he held up his arm and dragged the sleeve down, grinning at the white scar in his flesh and dancing a jig.

A sound filtered around them, creeping incrementally into Orka's head, like the tide. She looked around, frowning. It was a voice, muffled, as if coming from a great distance, but growing louder. Orka saw others looking, too. Grend and Taras, Gytha, Frek. Sighvat walked towards Lik-Rifa's corpse and put his ear to her belly. Then jerked straight and looked back at them all.

"It's Hrung," he said.

Grend heaved a sigh. "Can we leave him in there?"

CHAPTER NINETY-ONE

ORKA

Orka led them up a winding path, threading ever higher between trees and moss-covered boulders, the scent of pine thick in the air, stepping over a stream that gurgled, cold and clear. Her leg was aching, and at the end of each breath she felt a pinching from her healing ribs. She glanced over her shoulder, saw Breca behind her, with Lif and Sæunn either side of him, the rest of the Bloodsworn following. Varg and Røkia, Svik and Edel, Gunnar Prow, Halja Flat-Nose, a dozen others. A wagon with a horse harnessed, Vol sitting on the bench with Iva, Taras walking along beside them, a dozen children sitting in the back and Refna Strong-Hands running alongside the wagon. Sulich and his riders followed at the rear.

Vesli whirred out of the canopy.

"Almost there, almost there," she squeaked excitedly.

"I know," Orka grunted and Vesli flew over to the wagon, alighting upon an oak chest bound with iron chains that sat amidst stacked sacks. She sat upon the chest, stroking the timber and leaned forwards, undid one of the sacks with her long, dexterous fingers and pulled out a handful of teeth. Popped one of them into her mouth and began grinding.

Vol looked back over her shoulder at Vesli and the tennúr gave her a wide-mouthed grin.

Orka led them on, the ground levelling, soft underfoot, thick and spongy with pine needles. A clearing opened up before her, the remnants of a timber wall, most of it rotted and collapsed, reclaimed by the pinewoods, what was left of it still standing overgrown now with creeping vine, a wide gate, the wood splintered, one of the gates smashed from its hinges. She paused, her breath snatched from her chest for a moment, a rush of memories in her thought-cage, a fist clenching around her heart. She reached out and rested a hand on Breca's shoulder, knew that he must be feeling the same.

"Home," Breca breathed.

"No, *you* are my home," Orka said to him, and he smiled up at her.

She walked on, pushed the one gate that was still hanging open, hinges creaking and on into a courtyard of hard-packed earth, a stream running through it. The remnants of a hall still stood, wide timber steps leading up to it, not much more left than the posts and frame, and most of that was charred and blackened, wrapped with vine. What was left of the roof after the burning had fallen in, collapsed and choked by weeds. Most of the outbuildings were in better condition, the barn, forge, woodshed, and charcoal kiln still stood, though they needed scraping of ivy and some of the boards were rotted, needed replacing. The herb and vegetable patch was overgrown, but bees still buzzed around the beehive.

Orka walked across the courtyard and stopped before a mound of stones as the Bloodsworn entered through the gates. The creak of the wagon, thud of horses' hooves. She looked down on a barrow piled with rocks, flowers, weeds and vines growing in the cracks. Felt Breca's presence beside her and Vesli snapped her wings out and leaped from the chest she had been sitting upon, flew in a circle above them and alighted upon Breca's shoulder. Slowly, silently, the Bloodsworn spread around the barrow.

Orka opened her mouth to say something, found that she could not speak, words not able to creep past the knot that constricted her throat.

"I am back, Papa," Breca said, a tremor in his voice. "Mama saved me. She has brought me back home." His voice cracked and he dipped his head. Raised it again, a fierce twist to his lips. "And we avenged you, Papa."

Ah, my Thorkel, Orka thought, and his image filled her head, his smile splitting his beard, dark, shining eyes, deep creases around them. She could almost feel the touch of his calloused hand upon hers, the brush of his lips against her cheek, the sound of his whispered words in her ear.

"How I miss you," she breathed, tears welling from her eyes and spilling down her cheeks.

A grunt and footsteps behind her, Taras walking around next to Thorkel's barrow and setting a barrel on the ground, Spert's body, saved from the wreckage of Jarl Orlyg's ship. Varg, Svik, Røkia, Edel, Vol and Sulich walked around the other side of the barrow, carrying a linen-wrapped body upon their shoulders. They lowered Glornir's corpse gently to the ground.

"Thorkel, we have brought your brother here, to rest beside you," Vol said. Ulfrir had offered for Glornir to be buried alongside the heroes who had fallen in the battle for Vigrið. He had given Glornir the place of honour beside Elvar Chainbreaker, who had been laid to rest in the hull of her beloved *Wave-Jarl*, but Vol had declined the offer.

Vol looked around the old homestead, sunlight through sifting branches dappling the ground, birdsong in the air, in the distance the sound of the river, then back down to Thorkel's barrow.

"This is where you should be, my beloved," she whispered. "With your kin."

Spades were unloaded from the back of the wagon, one handed to Orka, and they began to dig.

CHAPTER NINETY-TWO

VARG

Varg set a stone from the stream upon Glornir's barrow and stood back, Vol stepping forwards to put the last one in place. The Bloodsworn stood around the three barrows laid over Thorkel, Glornir and Spert all of them silent, lost in their own thoughts, their own memories. Slowly people walked away, Varg hearing the sound of a fire pit being scraped, brush and deadwood gathered, a fire kindled.

He was thinking about the first time he had seen Glornir, standing in the courtyard of Jarl Logur's hall as he was about to fight a duel with Einar Half-Troll. That was when Røkia had named him No-Sense.

Much has changed since then. The world has changed since then.

"Come, No-Sense," Røkia said to him.

Not everything, though, he smiled. *Røkia is still telling me what to do.* He remembered his first sparring session with her, how she had beaten him bruised and bloody.

"What?" she said to his smile.

"Just remembering how I hated you," he said. "For the pain you gave me on my first day with the Bloodsworn."

She grinned, as big a smile as he had ever seen on her face.

"Ah, but I enjoyed that," she said.

"No-Sense," Svik called out, "some ale and cheese?"

Varg walked to the fire pit and sat beside Svik, took the offered cheese and cup of ale. They were all spread around the courtyard, eating, drinking, talking. Orka was sitting on the steps to her old hall, and Breca was showing Refna Strong-Hands the beehive.

"Strange," Vol said, looking at the new buds and leaves in the woodland beyond the steading's walls, "how so much has changed. So much loss, so much grief. Gods have fallen, and yet the world goes on the same."

"Aye," Edel said. "But for us the world *has* changed. We no longer have to hide what we are, no longer have to live in fear of the iron thrall-collar." She blew out a long breath. "I still can hardly believe it."

"To Elvar Chainbreaker," Svik said, raising a horn of mead.

"Elvar Chainbreaker," they all said, and drank in her honour.

"What now, then?" Halja Flat-Nose said.

"There are things to be done, to be sure," Gunnar said. "Rurik and the survivors of his fleet are still riding around Vigrið, for one."

"And there is Rotta to hunt, the *niðing* whore-son," Edel said, sitting with her hound and feeding it chunks of salted cod. Varg had thought the rat-god was dead for sure, after being dropped from the sky by Grok and Kló, but after Lik-Rifa's death Ulfrir had gone in search of his body and found that it was gone.

"We could do with building a new *drakkar* and earning some silver," Røkia said.

"Ulfrir will pay us the silver Elvar promised," Vol said.

"I know that, but . . ." Røkia said.

"She likes the raiding," Svik said.

Røkia shrugged, not disagreeing.

"The Bloodsworn need a chief," Sulich said. He looked to Vol.

"I know," she said, heaving a sigh.

"You?" Sulich said to her.

"Me! No," Vol said. "My heart and soul are bruised and battered. You are all closer than kin, but my head, it is a fog. I am not strong enough up here to be chief." She tapped her forehead, and then she looked to Orka.

"No," Orka said. Then smiled, something Varg had not seen touch her face before. "I tried that once," Orka said. "It did not work out so well."

"How about Svik?" another of the Bloodsworn said. "He is a fine warrior, and he is fox-cunning."

"Svik!" Røkia laughed. "Every job we took on would be paid for with *cheese*."

Svik gave a mock-offended twist of his face, then smiled.

"Probably true, to be fair," he said.

Varg cleared his throat. "I have been thinking," he said.

"Oh no," a chorus of voices rang out, chuckles rippling around the Bloodsworn.

"I have been thinking,"Varg repeated with a smile, "that as much as we need a chief, we also need a home."

"A home?" Gunnar Prow said. "Our *drakkar* is our home."

"Aye, well, it was,"Varg agreed. "But I have been thinking about why Orka and Thorkel left. No offence, Skullsplitter," he said to Orka's flat look.

"None taken," Orka said.

"They left to raise a child. To live in peace. That will come to us all, most likely, if we live that long."

"Do you hear that, Røkia," Svik said, others chuckling. "He is making plans for you already."

"I make the plans," she said, looked at Varg. "You want a wolf-cub child?" she asked him.

He stuttered a few half-words. "One day," he managed to get out.

Røkia shrugged. "As do I," she said.

"And I have been thinking about Einar and how he wanted to look after half the Tainted children in Vigrið," Varg continued quickly. "Breca is part of us, and Refna and the others", he waved a hand at them. "Growing up on a *drakkar* is a hard life. And what about when we are old and slow and stiff, and would prefer to sit around the hearth-fire and listen to skáld-songs rather than be in them?" He looked around at them all, saw they were thinking about his words. "I think we need a steading of our own. Where we can live our lives, those who wish to go raiding can, those who wish to raise their children in peace, can."

"Peace," Taras echoed. "Peace sounds good to Taras."

Iva patted his knee.

"To me, too," she said.

"Yes, peace for those too old, too joint-stiff or battle-weary to live the raiding life. If we had a home they would have a warm fire and young arms to protect them," Varg said. "This is Vigrið, after all."

There were heyas and hooms of agreement.

"I agree," Vol said.

"This is a rare day indeed," Svik said, "a sensible idea from No-Sense." More laughter rippled around the courtyard. They talked about the idea some more, passing it around them like a jug of mead, tasting it. In the end, all agreed.

"Where, then?" Halja said.

"How about here?" Vol said, eyes drawn to the new barrow raised over Glornir's body. She looked around the rest of the steading. "It is a good spot. Much of the land has been cleared, and foundations are here. We are high, have a view for miles. It would be hard for any enemy to take this steading by surprise. There is timber to build with, and to craft a new *drakkar*, and there is a fjord at the bottom of the hill for us to sail the whale road."

"And meadows for horses not too far from here," Sulich said.

"And a stream for Gand to swim in," Vol said, patting the serpent whip at her hip. She looked to Orka. "How would you feel about that, Orka Skullsplitter? Would it be too painful for you to stay here?"

Orka looked from Vol to Thorkel's barrow, to Breca sitting with Refna by the stream where Spert had lived.

"I think it is a gold-browed idea," she said.

ACKNOWLEDGEMENTS

Writing this book has been like no other. I finished writing *The Hunger of the Gods* in April 2021, and then in September 2021 my beautiful daughter Harriett died.

The last three years have been indescribably awful. The death of Harriett has hit me, my wife and my children like an avalanche. But grief is more than a short, sharp shock. It is an ocean that surrounds you, with no shore in sight. We have had to learn to swim through it, its presence constant, ever-felt. That is our life, now, learning to live without our Harriett, learning to live with grief. Learning to brace yourself against the pain and trying look to the good things worth living for. My wife, my children, my grandchildren. My friends.

Because I've managed to write this book doesn't mean that I have "come through" the grief, or "moved on". It doesn't work like that; at least, not for me. It's more like an ever-present pain that you learn to live with, to walk alongside. And slowly the pain moves from a constant, overwhelming barrage to an ebb and flow, though with no discernible rhythm. Some days are filled with dark clouds, some days the storm comes and other days, or moments, you can see the sun.

Writing this book has been a marathon. There were many times I feared I would not be able to finish it. Without the love, support and help of many people I am sure that I would have faltered. I'd like to say a thank you here to those who have helped me.

My family. My wife, Caroline, and my children, James, Ed and Will. They have been the reason to rise each day.

My dear friends, who have been there during this terrible time.

A huge thank-you to my wonderful agent and friend, Julie Crisp, and to James Long and all at my fabulous publishers, Orbit UK and US, who have put zero pressure on me to write and finish this book. Their patience has been unfathomable, their kindness deeply appreciated.

And of course I must say a massive thank you to you, my readers, for your patience and understanding, your kindness and thoughtful messages.

The messages and support I have received from you all has meant more to me than words can express.

You have all been amazing.

Thank you, and I hope that you enjoy this book, hope you enjoy stepping back into the world of the Bloodsworn once more, hope that it has been worth the wait.

And I will always give my thanks to Harriett, just for being her, and for all that she did to gift my life with joy and make me the person I am.

extras

meet the author

Caroline Gwynne

John Gwynne studied and lectured at Brighton University. He has played double bass in a rock 'n' roll band and traveled the United States and Canada. He is married with four children and lives in Eastbourne, where he is part of a Viking reenactment group. When not writing, he can often be found standing in a shield wall with his three sons about him. His dogs think he is their slave.

Find out more about John Gwynne and other Orbit authors by registering for the free monthly newsletter at orbitbooks.net.

if you enjoyed
THE FURY OF THE GODS
look out for
MALICE
The Faithful and the Fallen: Book One
by
John Gwynne

The world is broken... and it can never be made whole again.

Corban wants nothing more than to be a warrior under King Brenin's rule—to protect and serve. But that day will come all too soon. And the price he pays will be in blood.

Evnis has sacrificed—too much it seems. But what he wants—the power to rule—will soon be in his grasp. And nothing will stop him once he has started on his path.

Veradis is the newest member of the warband for the High Prince, Nathair. He is one of the most skilled swordsmen to come out of his homeland, yet he is always under the shadow of his older brother.

Nathair has ideas—and a lot of plans. Many of them don't involve his father, the High King Aquilus. Nor does he agree with his father's idea to summon his fellow kings to council.

The Banished Lands has a violent past where armies of men and giants clashed in battle, but now giants stir anew, stones weep blood, and there are sightings of giant wyrms. Those who can still read the signs see a threat far greater than the ancient wars. For if the Black Sun gains ascendancy, mankind's hopes and dreams will fall to dust....

PROLOGUE

EVNIS

The Year 1122 of the Age of Exiles, Wolf Moon

Forest litter crunched under Evnis' feet, his breath misting as he whispered a curse. He swallowed, his mouth dry.

He was scared, he had to admit, but who would not be? What he was doing this night would make him traitor to his king. And worse.

He paused and looked back. Beyond the forest's edge he could still see the stone circle, behind it the walls of Badun, his home, its outline silvered in the moonlight. It would be so easy to turn back, to go home and choose another path for his life. He felt a moment of vertigo, as if standing on the edge of a great chasm, and the world seemed to slow, waiting on the outcome of his decision. *I have come this far, I will see it through.* He looked up at the forest, a wall of impenetrable shadow; he pulled his cloak tighter and walked into the darkness.

He followed the giantsway for a while, the stone-flagged road that connected the kingdoms of Ardan and Narvon. It was long neglected, the giant clan that built it vanquished over a thousand years ago, great clumps of moss and mushroom growing between crumbling flagstone.

Even in the darkness he felt too vulnerable on this wide road, and soon slithered down its steep bank and slipped amongst the trees. Branches scratched overhead, wind hissing in the canopy above as he sweated his way up and down slope and dell. He knew where he was going, had walked the path many times before, though never at night. Nineteen summers old, yet he knew this part of the Darkwood as well as any woodsman twice his age.

Soon he saw a flicker amongst the trees: firelight. He crept closer, stopping before the light touched him, scared to leave the anonymity of the shadows. *Turn around, go home, a voice whispered in his head. You are nothing, will never equal your brother.* His mother's words, cold and sharp as the day she had died. He ground his teeth and stepped into the firelight.

An iron cauldron hung on a spit over a fire, water bubbling. Beside it a figure, cloaked and hooded.

'Greetings.' A female voice. She pushed the hood back, firelight making the silver in her hair glow copper.

'My lady,' Evnis said to Rhin, Queen of Cambren. Her beauty made him catch his breath.

She smiled at him, wrinkles creasing around her eyes and held out her hand.

Evnis stepped forward hesitantly and kissed the ring on her finger, the stone cold on his lips. She smelled sweet, heady, like overripe fruit.

'It is not too late, you may still turn back,' she said, tilting his head with a finger under his chin. They stood so close he could feel her breath. Warm, laced with wine.

He sucked in a breath. 'No. There is nothing for me if I turn back. This is my chance to . . .'

His brother's face filled his mind, smiling, controlling, *ruling* him. Then his mother, her lips twisted, judging, *discounting*.

'. . . matter. Gethin has arranged a marriage for me, to the daughter of the poorest baron in Ardan, I think.'

'Is she pretty?' Rhin said, still smiling, but with an edge in her voice.

'I have only met her once. No, I cannot even remember what she looks like.' He looked at the cauldron on its spit. 'I must do this. Please.'

'And in return, what would you give me?'

'The whole realm of Ardan. I shall govern it, and bow to you, my High Queen.'

She smiled, teeth glinting. 'I like the sound of that. But there is more to this than Ardan. So much more. This is about the God-War. About Asroth made flesh.'

'I know,' he whispered, the fear of it almost a solid thing, dripping from his tongue, choking him. But exciting him, too.

'Are you scared?' Rhin said, her eyes holding him.

'Yes. But I will see it through. I have counted the cost.'

'Good. Come then.' She raised a hand and clicked her fingers.

A hulking shadow emerged from the trees and stepped into the firelight. A giant. He stood a man-and-a-half tall, his face pale, all sharp angles and ridged bone, small black eyes glittering under a thick-boned brow. A long black moustache hung to his chest, knotted with leather. Tattoos swirled up one arm, a creeping, thorn-thick vine disappearing under a chainmail sleeve, the rest of him wrapped in leather and fur. He carried a man in his arms, bound at wrist and ankle, as effortlessly as if it were a child.

'This is Uthas of the Benothi,' Rhin said with a wave of her hand, 'he shares our allegiances, has helped me in the past.'

The giant drew near to the cauldron and dropped the man in his arms to the ground, a groan rising from the figure as it writhed feebly on the forest floor.

'Help him stand, Uthas.'

The giant bent over, grabbed a handful of the man's hair and heaved him from the ground. The captive's face was bruised and swollen, dried blood crusting his cheeks and lips. His clothes were ragged and torn, but Evnis could still make out the wolf crest of Ardan on his battered leather cuirass.

The man tried to say something through broken lips, spittle dribbling from one corner of his mouth. Rhin said nothing, drew a knife from her belt and cut the captive's throat. Dark blood spurted and the man sagged in his captor's grip. The giant held him forward, angling him so that his blood poured into the cauldron.

Evnis fought the urge to step back, to turn and run. Rhin was muttering, a low, guttural chanting, then a wisp of steam curled up from the cauldron. Evnis leaned forward, staring. A great gust of wind swept the glade. A figure took form in the vapour, twisting, turning. The smell of things long dead, rotting, hit the back of Evnis' throat. He gagged, but could not tear his eyes away from where two pinpricks glowed: eyes, a worn, ancient face forming about them. It appeared noble, wise, sad, then lined, proud, stern. Evnis blinked and for a moment the face became reptilian, the eddying steam giving the appearance of wings unfurling, stretched, leathery. He shivered.

'Asroth,' whispered Rhin, falling to her knees.

'What do you desire?' a sibilant voice asked.

Evnis swallowed, his mouth dry *.I must take what is owed me, step out from my brother' shadow. See it through.*

'Power,' he rasped. Then, louder, taking a deep breath. 'Power. I would rule. My brother, all of Ardan.'

Laughter, low at first, but growing until it filled the glade. Then silence, thick and heavy as the cobwebs that draped the trees.

'It shall be yours,' the figure said.

Evnis felt a trickle of sweat slide down his forehead. 'What do you want in return? What is your price?'

'My price is you,' the swirling figure said, eyes pinning him. 'I want you.' The lips of the ancient face in the steam twitched, a glimmer of a smile.

'So be it,' said Evnis.

'Seal it in blood,' the ancient face snarled.

Rhin held her knife out.

See it through, see it through, see it through, Evnis repeated silently, like a mantra. He clenched his teeth tightly together, gripped the knife, his palm clammy with sweat and drew it quickly across his other hand. Curling his fingers into a fist, he stepped forward, thrusting it into the steam above the iron pot. Blood dripped from his hand into the cauldron, where it immediately began to bubble. A force like a physical blow slammed into his chest, seemed to pass through him. He gasped and sank to his knees, gulping in great, ragged breaths.

The voice exploded in his head, pain shooting through his body.

He screamed.

'It is done,' the voice said.

EXCERPT

The Writings of Halvor

Discovered in 1138 of the Age of Exiles, beneath the ruined fortress of Drassil. Over two thousand years after it was written

The world is broken.

The God-War has changed all things, Asroth's scheming, Ely on's wrath, corrupted and destroyed so much. Mankind has vanished, annihilated or fled these shores, and we are so few, now. We giants, Sundered, the one clan split beyond all reconciliation.

A thousand years I, Halvor, have lived, Voice of the King. Now great Skald is dead, his kin scattered. I shall not live a thousand more. I lament the past, I remember and weep.

I am still the Voice, though I do not know who will listen. But if I do not speak, do not write, then there will be nothing for those who follow. All that has happened would be forgotten. And so I shall write a record…

When the starstone fell we should have listened to mankind and turned our faces from it, but its power sang to us, called us. Just as Asroth planned.

Asroth was first-created, Elyon's beloved, captain of the Ben-Elim, the Sons of the Mighty. But that was not enough for him, the great deceiver. He spread his deep malice and his lies amongst the Ben-Elim, until a host grew about him. The Kadoshim they became: the Separate Ones.

Elyon saw, but could not bear to raise his fist against his beloved, and so war raged between the Kadoshim and the Ben-Elim, there in the Otherworld, the place of Spirit. Asroth was defeated and banished to a solitary portion of the Otherworld.

Then Elyon continued his plan of creation, making the worlds of flesh, of which earth was first. Giants and men were created as lords of this earth, immortal overseers of all else that roamed or grew, and they lived in harmony with their creator and all that he had created.

And Asroth hated us.

Asroth's starstone fell to earth, vast and filled with power. Somehow it carved a link between the world of flesh and spirit, between the earth and the Otherworld. Men were fearful of this strange object, but the giants forged from it, made items of wonder and power, great Treasures. First was the cauldron, its power used to heal. Then a torc, given to Skald, the giant's king, and a necklace for Nemain, his queen.

Asroth used the starstone to spread his influence on earth, whispering, corrupting. Skald was slain, the first murder, his torc stolen, and death entered the world, immortality stripped from all things as Elyon's punishment and warning. Then came the Sundering. War erupted, giant fighting against giant, and the one clan became many. More Treasures were carved from the starstone, this time things of war: spear, axe, dagger. And finally a cup, said to bring strength and long life to all who drank from it.

The mantle of death fell upon the world as war spread. Mankind was caught in it, giving their oaths to the giant clans in the hope of capturing the Treasures and restoring their immortality. Blood was spilt in rivers, and Asroth rejoiced.

Finally, Elyon's wrath was stirred. He visited his judgment upon the earth, which we named the Scourging. The Ben-Elim were let loose, spreading his judgement in fire and water and blood. Seas boiled, mountains spewed fire and the earth was broken as Elyon set about destroying all that he had created.

When his judgement was almost complete Elyon heard something, echoing in the Otherworld. The laughter of Asroth.

Elyon realized the extent of his foe's deception, saw that all had been done to bring him to this point. In horror he ceased the Scourging, leaving a remnant alive. Elyon' grief was beyond all comprehension. He turned from us, from all creation, and retreated to a place of mourning, cut off from all things. He is there still.

The Ben-Elim and Kadoshim abide in the Otherworld, their war eternal. Asroth and his fallen angels seeking to destroy us, the Ben-Elim striving to protect us, a token of their abiding love for Elyon.

And here in the world of flesh the breath of life goes on. Some strive to rebuild what was lost in this place of ash and decay. As for me, I look upon the world and mourn, here in Drassil, once-great city, heart of the world. Now broken, failing, like all else. Even my kin are leaving: Forn is too wild, too dangerous, now, they say, and we are too few. North they are going, abandoning all. Abandoning me. I shall not leave.

I dream now, and in those dreams are glimpses, perhaps, of what may come to be, a voice whispering. Of Asroth's return, the deceiver made flesh, of the Ben-Elim's last great stand, and of the avatars waging the God-War once more…

I shall stay and tell my tale, hope that it may serve some purpose, that eyes shall see it and learn, that the future will not repeat the mistakes of the past. That is my prayer, but what use is prayer to a god that has abandoned all things…

Follow us:

/orbitbooksUS

/orbitbooks

/orbitbooks

Join our mailing list
to receive alerts on our
latest releases and deals.

orbitbooks.net

Enter our monthly
giveaway for the chance
to win some epic prizes.

orbitloot.com